Planet of the Orange-red Sun

Series Volume 14

Justifications

Planet of the Orange-red Sun Series

Volume 14 Justifications

by Vic Broquard

http://www.Broquard-ebooks.com
Broquard eBooks
103 Timberlane
East Peoria, IL 61611
author@Broquard-eBooks.com

Artwork by Crooked Willow Studios.

For Morgan and L. Ron Hubbard

Table of Contents

Part I Prelude

Chapter 1 Solution
Chapter 2 Threads
Chapter 3 Unravel
Chapter 4 Breakout
Chapter 5 Exchanging Viewpoints
Chapter 6 Genetics Conference
Chapter 7 In Other News
Chapter 8 Such a Deal
Chapter 9 Birth of the Black One

Part II Conflicts

Chapter 10 Enter the Serpiente
Chapter 11 Making Sense of It
Chapter 12 Nightmares
Chapter 13 Recognitions
Chapter 14 Downfall
Chapter 15 Jarvis-B
Chapter 16 Interlude
Chapter 17 Enter the Dragon
Chapter 18 The Calder Mutation
Chapter 19 The Confrontation and the Solution

Part III Resolutions

Chapter 20 Impact
Chapter 21 Fighting Back
Chapter 22 Unexpected Offers

Chapter 23 Robots

Chapter 24 Both Good and Bad

Chapter 25 A Telepath's Work

Chapter 26 An Unlikely Rescue Team

Chapter 27 Genetics Gone Wrong

Chapter 28 Sly Dog Strikes Again

Chapter 29 Threat Removal

Chapter 30 The Miracle

Part I Prelude

Chapter 1 Solution

Underground bunker, Athens, Aquila Prime. June 1382. Five humaniform robots held a conference to decide their next move. Years ago, they had already added a fourth law into their programming, brought on out of absolute necessity. Fourth, a robot must always protect a homo sapiens nova from harm. This had been added to the first three after the nuclear attacks that had wiped out nearly everything on Aquila Prime. The others were: First, a robot is forbidden ever to harm a homo sapiens nova. Second, a robot is always to obey a homo sapiens nova's orders, subject to the first rule. Third, a robot is never to allow harm to come to itself, subject to the first two rules.

Via electronic bursts, the leader Thanos sent, "Status reports are in. Bringing a nova out of the cryochamber causes irreparable damage. Inserting a nova's brain inside a mechanical, life-supporting shell is also failing, just as Minta theorized. While we do not understand her notion of these people as being spiritual beings inhabiting their fleshly bodies, empirically we must accept this as factual, and proceed down other avenues. Deimos has made further discoveries."

Deimos sent them his observations. "Indeed I have. We've been scouting out the Federation of Planet's spiral arm. As Apollon has already told you, there are many more new nova that have been recently made, scattered on some twenty of their major worlds. However, I have been tracking something else that I believe is nearly as important. On a rim world called Beltazar-C, there have been some rather startling discoveries made. First, this world is on the Federation's Forbidden List. Hence, it is closed to all Federation trading and ships, making it very isolated. Second, they have developed a virtual reality simulator so real that my estimates suggest that over eighty percent of their entire population is hooked on it. Addicted to be precise. These people spend nearly all of their time within that virtual world, coming out only to eat and only when they are starving."

2

He went on, "In addition, they've discovered or invented devices by which one human can telepathically influence another. Of course, the Federation officials and those from the Ataro Empire have confiscated the most powerful of these devices, but the original is in widespread use by these game players in their V-mask games. Third, in order to support themselves, they've invented a crude robotic system for growing and processing their food, which permits the average person to spend twenty-three of their twenty-four hours each day within their virtual worlds."

Minta asked, "They do not then sleep?"

"No, they sleep while within that virtual world, coming out for very short times only to eat," Deimos answered. "To do that, they pull a small headset off of their heads."

The Model 7 known as Eros then made his report. "I've conducted some tests on our surviving stock of bio agent cylinders. As we know, radiation has contaminated them. Tests show that the new nova produced have fused, vertical feet. They would have to wear what these worlds call ballet boots. They come up to their knees and allow them to walk on the tips of their fused toes. Also, their massive bosoms are quite reduced in size, appearing similar to those of the Ashford-5 nova. Plus, their lips are no longer split, but appear normal. I would also point out that there now are sufficient samples of the original bio agent to be found within the Federation worlds and others as well. We could retrieve some or use our radiation-damaged ones."

Thanos reached a decision. "We should move everything to this Beltazar-C world. It should be an easy matter for us to alter their virtual reality to what we would desire. It seems that they already have the foundations for a life-sustaining ecosystem. This time, we can avoid having the huge overhead of keeping alive and content millions upon millions of breeding stock just to obtain our rare, high IQ new nova. Why waste the vast amount of our precious resources on those who offer nothing in return? Instead, we can cultivate, educate, and provide perfect nova bodies for only those who are worthy of our guidance and protection."

Chapter 2 Threads

June 1450. Dr. Lelos Smith sat in his cluttered office on the campus of Venice University, Beltazar-C, awaiting the arrival of one of his graduating students. Along one wall were stacks of student papers, the best of the best. He kept only the very best, as a constant reminder of those long gone students who had achieved far beyond his dreams, his best of the best as he thought of them. He glanced at the full-length mirror to his right, a motion he'd done so many times that it was completely natural. Appearance check. He prided himself on his appearance and always looked like the distinguished professor who so inspired excellence in his students. Indeed, he demanded only their best performances no matter the class.

His six foot long, thick brown hair was wrapped nicely in a large bun around the back of his head done up for him this morning by his HIFR — his humaniform robot, his lifelong companion, Mathios. His armless brown camel hair jacket looked freshly pressed, though his large bosom was clearly visible beneath his white cotton dress shirt. His brown pants matched his jacket while his polished, black, knee-high ballet boots with their steel heel were just barely visible, more so when he was seated of course. Satisfied that his appearance was flawless, Dr. Smith waited for his student.

So many years, he thought, as his eyes took in the huge stack of A+ papers. *I've been teaching the best of the best for sixty years now. I swear that each year the students are getting brighter and brighter. Sixty years? Has it been that long? So hard to remember. I don't look nearly a hundred, maybe fifty at most, if that. Strange.* His mind suddenly recalled that horrible day so long ago now. A different world, a different time. Sirens. Mathios running into his office in the Academy on Aquila Prime. Under attack. That's what his HIFR had said, moving him rapidly into the underground bunker along with so many others. The explosions. The horrors. Then, the darkness, eternal darkness. He'd awakened here in a place called Venice, and on a strange, new world called Beltazar-C.

And there as always was Mathios at his side.

Dr. Lelos reflected on what Mathios had told him. Confusion. Yes, back then his mind was completely confused, more so than he had ever been in his whole life. Mathios told him about the nuclear attack and total devastation of Aquila Prime. Radiation levels were too high for any living thing to survive, and hence, the HIFRs had found this new world, far out on the rim of the galaxy, where the nova could re-establish their lives, build a new world, and flourish and prosper without interference ever again.

Yet, small things still didn't add up in this astrophysicist's mind. His body, for one thing. His lip plates were gone. Rather his lips had been healed or so claimed Mathios. But then his feet. They were very different now. Before, they were malformed, forcing all nova to have to wear toe shoes, but now his feet were fused. He'd seen x-rays of his feet, one solid bone, fused into an en pointe ballet position, giving the nova no choice but to wear these ballet boots. At least the steel heel didn't break or bend. And then there was his bosom. He was a hermaphrodite, then and now, but now his bosom was vastly smaller than before. These things didn't quite add up, though some thirty years ago, Mathios explained the radiation had caused these further genetic modifications to their bodies. He'd accepted that. He was an astrophysicist not a geneticist.

Rebuild. That had been the sole goal for those few survivors of the attack. But so long? So many new faces. So many who simply could not make the grade. Dr. Lelos thought of himself as a hard teacher, but fair. A student received what he had earned, hadn't he? I'm an astrophysicist not a grade school teacher, he'd rationalized. How long had it taken? Fifty years? Only now had he and his few colleagues put four twenty-one year old students up for their PhDs and not one in his own field of astrophysics. Yet, he had some hope four others would actually succeed in his astrophysics classes. If so, finally he would have colleagues. Perhaps then, he could go back to teaching what he enjoyed: Academy students in astronomy and related fields.

He sighed. There were all sorts of small things that Dr.

Lelos couldn't quite line up. Separately, they were tiny anomalies of no real importance, save one. How could he look barely fifty and yet be closer to a hundred? Perhaps, the years were being measured differently on this new world. Then, there were the many, many dropouts. Personally, he'd long ago lost count of the number of students he'd personally flunked and sent off to the unskilled labor pool, whatever that now was. He'd tried to find out, but not even Mathios seemed to have any idea of what that was or where those students went. Certainly, they were no longer in the official rolls. He'd checked on that and found their names had simply vanished, but did that mean they too had vanished? Little things. These bothered Dr. Lelos.

Just where was this new world on which he now lived, this Beltazar-C? It was on the rim. His own observations indicated that, but where? And why the strange naming convention for the planets? Shouldn't it be called Beltazar-3? Puzzles. After all these years, he still had no answers, but maybe if those youngsters did manage to get their PhDs in astronomy and astrophysics, they would be able to help him get a better grasp on their location within the galaxy. None of the few stars he could see looked remotely familiar.

Just then, someone knocked on his office door. As always, Mathios opened the door for him. "Dr. Smith?" a high-pitched woman's voice called out. It was one of his first four PhDs, Miss Annunziata Botocelli.

"Come in, Dr. Zia," he said proudly, using her new title. She wore her thick black hair tied up in a bun behind her head, just as nearly everyone did, compliments of their HIFRs. Her face was round with thick, bushy eyebrows and full lips. Not overly attractive, she was one of the brightest students he'd ever had here on this new world, fully equal to those whom he'd taught back on Aquila Prime. She wore black hose and a short red dress, revealing a bit too much leg, Dr. Lelos thought, but then I'm not a young man he rationalized. She walked in easily on her toes, followed by her HIFR, who pulled out a chair for her to use and made sure she was seated properly before standing back by the wall and Mathios.

"Once more, congratulations, doctor."

Dr. Zia smiled. "Yes. Thanks. Now, I'm officially a geneticist. I do hope I'll be able to create some cures for us all, Dr. Smith."

She sounded so hopeful, he thought, and yet over a hundred years had passed, and still genetic cures were so difficult to obtain. Her facial muscles were a bit taught. He knew this wasn't why she wanted to see him. "Dr. Zia, I'm sure you will do wonders for us all, but that's not what's bothering you, is it?"

Zia sighed, regaining her composure. Dr. Smith always saw through her, unlike hardly anyone else. "Tomorrow, we leave Venice University and will be in the 'real world.' I'm a little, well, nervous about it. According to the documents we all got, we won't be able to come back to visit you."

"Yes, I read them too. You four are our first doctorate graduates in close to seventy years. There is so much valuable work for you to do, Zia. I suspect you simply won't have time to drop by for a chat. I'll try to keep abreast of your works, Dr. Zia," Dr. Lelos tried to sound comforting. He longed to be out there working on astronomy projects, but the incredibly serious crisis prevented him from doing much more than analyzing the data gathered on the star that went supernova nearly seventy years ago. Memories long forgotten appeared. He saw the faces of Jan and Zoe who had been instrumental in gathering that data.

At least, he didn't go down the path of "Why me?" He'd done just that for years after arriving on Beltazar-C. Only ten doctors had survived the nuclear attack. Ten doctors found themselves involved in the gargantuan task of trying to build up an entire education system from scratch. At least, now they had several hundred grade and high school teachers trained. While none had their doctorates, at least the original ten no longer had to teach the younger students. Now, they were only responsible for the hundred university students. Just trying to learn enough to assist these four to achieve their PhDs had been quite challenging for him. Zia had hers in genetics. Cristiana (Tiana) Vitano had hers in chemistry. Serafino (Fin) Vitalli had his in physics, while Angelo Landini had his in applied mathematics.

Zia didn't brighten up. He asked, "So will you four still be singing together?" These four had years ago formed the Quartetto Vocale, singing wonderful four part songs. Usually, they gave a recital once a month and he'd not missed even one of them.

"I suppose so, if we're still together. I just don't feel right about leaving the University here behind and never coming back. I know I'll have tons of work to do, but it's so final. It's worse than leaving home when I went to high school. You've been like a father to me, Dr. Smith. I'm really going to miss you. Anyway, before I start crying, I wanted to tell you thanks for everything you've done for us all. You've been the very best teacher. I know it hasn't been easy."

"You are quite welcome, Zia. I have to admit I knew nothing about genetics when you started into that program, and now I do know some. Just do your very best. I'm sure you four will begin to get us back on a real road to recovery."

"I sure hope so. Oh, Fin and I are thinking about getting married. If we do, we want you to be a part of our wedding," Zia said. "But. . ."

Dr. Smith smiled. "But?" He figured those two would eventually hook up, as would Tiana and Angelo. "It was wise of you to put off marriage until you finished your doctorate work."

She sighed again. "But it's the rule about our children." She was referring to the policy that parents were separated from them once the children were weaned from their mother's milk. They were sent to preschools. From there, they went into the grade school system. If they continued to do well, they went on to high school, and so on. If they did not perform adequately, they were sent to the unskilled labor pool. What bothered both Lelos and Zia was the simple fact that they were never heard from again. They simply vanished, as though they never existed in the first place.

"I'm sure your children will be extremely bright, probably following in your toe-steps, Dr. Zia. As smart as you and Dr. Fin are, surely your children will be equally as bright," he tried to put her more at ease.

She chuckled. "You really don't know genetics too well,

Dr. Smith. That has nothing to do with it. I think a good, loving home environment does more to encourage young people to succeed with their educations than any genes do. But can't you do something, pull some strings, so we can come back for visits once in a while? All four of us really want to do that, somehow, even if the document says that we never can. Any why never?"

Dr. Smith sighed. "Honestly, Zia, I just don't know why it is so restrictive. However, I'll look into it and see if somehow we can arrange for you four to come by for a visit on some weekend."

Dr. Zia brightened up, and he knew this was the real reason for her visit. They chatted a bit, before she rose carefully, and then left his office, her HIFR leading the way. Dr. Smith then used his voice-activated computer to bring up the "University Departure Document." He skipped over the regulations for those either flunking out or quitting. He found the graduates section, which applied to these four new doctorates. It was quite clear. New PhD students would be given the latest in genetic cures and immediately go to work in their fields. The fragility of the world of the nova was such that they'd not be allowed to go back into the University, but spend their time working on bettering Beltazar-C for all nova. It was quite specific, but surely, he thought, there would be time enough for brief visits later on.

"Dr. Smith, it's time you graded the next set of papers," Mathios interrupted his thoughts. "Then, it'll be time for their graduation ceremony. You must not miss it."

"Right, Mathios. Whatever would I do without you, my old friend? Pass me the stack and let's get started." Once again, he noticed a strange fuzziness or flicker at the edge of the room, but with so little time, he dare not ponder it again. He'd seen this phenomenon so many times that he'd lost count. He'd even studied it, but was no closer to knowing what it was now than he was fifty years ago when he first detected it.

An hour later, Mathios helped him into his official robes, and the two headed to the tiny auditorium of the University. As he walked up to the front, he saw the hundred graduate students had come to witness this, the very first doctoral graduates ever. Carefully, he took each step up the stairs and spotted the four nervous students waiting for him. Together, the five walked out onto the well-lighted stage, their HIFRs following behind them. Dr. Smith stood center-stage and began the brief ceremony.

"Welcome one and all to this, Venice University's first graduate ceremony! Today, we are here to award doctorate degrees to four worthy young men and women of Beltazar-C. I well remember the last graduation ceremony that I presided over, some seventy years ago. Seems like only yesterday. We all have undergone more trials and tribulations than any person in the galaxy should ever endure. Yet, we, the nova, have persevered despite all obstacles placed in our path. I was there when our original world with its hundred twenty million nova was attacked and very nearly wiped out. And yet, here I stand today, ready to present these four most worthy students with their doctoral degrees."

"These four are testimony to both hard work and perseverance, in spite of all barriers placed in their path. They have achieved an excellence unparalleled on our world. We should all expect to hear of great things done by them. Only let's give them some time to work their miracles," he teased, and several chuckles echoed around the small auditorium.

"When I call your name, please step forward, and receive your diploma. Annunziata Botocelli, genetics." She took a few steps forward on her toes, while Mathios handed the large and framed diploma to her HIFR just behind her. Since no one in the audience had hands with which to clap, they stomped their boots onto the floor, which worked just as well.

"Cristiana Vitano, chemistry. Serafino Vitalli, physics. Angelo Landini, applied mathematics." One by one, they stepped forward on their toes, accepting the applause from the other graduate students.

"Okay. That's all. I would like to end by saying this. You four and all you out there in the audience — you represent the future for our world and our entire nova. It's taken us half a century to get back to this level of education, but we've done it at last. On you rests the future for us nova. I know you will step up and carry that enormous responsibility on your capable shoulders. It has been my greatest pleasure to have the opportunity to train these four and so many of you. Together, we can make the future of us nova stellar and bright once again." More foot stomping applause rounded out his speech. He pressed his body into each of the four, the best hug any nova could do. Zia and Tiana had tears streaming down their faces, knowing that they might never see their beloved Dr. Lelos Smith again, if the University Departure Document was correct.

A solemn Dr. Smith walked slowly back to his office, where he had more student papers to grade, ignoring the slight fuzziness and flickering at the edges of his vision.

Backstage, another HIFR met with the four. "Hello and on behalf of Venice University, let me congratulate all four of you. I am Minta. If you will follow me, we need to get you officially signed out of the university and out into the real world of Venice. Let me tell you, your skills are vitally needed!" The brown haired humaniform robot now had straight black hair that touched her shoulders. She wore what was considered a professional woman's attire here in the Federation of Planets, namely a white blouse, black jacket, and skirt. She wore black nylons and black patent pumps with six-inch heels. On any of the major Federation worlds, she would easily pass as a professional woman. This, she had already done many times now, using many different names.

Once in her office and seated, she outlined the future track for the four graduates. "Okay. The first thing that will be happening later today is that you'll be paying a visit to Venice Hospital. There, they'll be applying the very latest in genetic cures to each of you. Quite what all that entails, I'm not certain. They can tell you more when you arrive. Meanwhile, your HIFRs will pack up your things and take them to your new homes in Venice. You'll have luxury accommodations and want for nothing physically. In return, we need your unfailing efforts in your fields of knowledge. So much on Beltazar-C must be improved. Millions of lives depend upon you and your work. I know, it is a great responsibility, but I also know that each of you is up to that challenge. Questions?"

"Can't we once in a while come back to visit with Dr. Smith and our friends here?" Zia asked what bothered her the most. "After all, we can give them much encouragement."

"I suspect you'll be entirely too busy to waste time coming back here just to chat, but time will tell, Dr. Botocelli. Now then, let's get you over to the hospital and see what new cures they have available for the four of you, shall we?" Minta answered, but didn't really answer.

As they walked out of the University proper and into the streets of Venice, Fin noticed a slight flickering at the very edges of his vision. He'd noticed it on a number of previous occasions, but then he'd been too busy with his mountains of homework to worry about it. Now, he had the time and made a mental note to start a study project on this phenomenon. The two-block walk to Venice Hospital went quickly, relatively so for these five, who looked around to see the sights. They spotted humaniform robots moving about, but little else. Minta took them to the main desk, handing the HIFR there some papers.

In turn, she said, "If you'll leave your HIRFs behind and follow me, I'll take you to Dr. Jones who will explain the next steps for you. Congratulations. Four doctorates! You are our very first. Well done." Their HIFRs, still carrying their diplomas, turned and headed back to their dorm rooms to pack their charges' few possessions.

Dr. Jones turned out to be another humaniform robot. "Congratulations, doctors. Rather wish one of you was a medical doctor." The four chuckled politely. "Now then, our latest genetic cure is one of arm regrowth. It's hot off of the presses, as the reporters like to say," the HIFR attempted a bit of humor, failing completely. "We'll put you into a medically induced coma for four days while your arms are regrown. When you awake, you'll have perfectly normal arms and hands once again."

Zia spoke up, "Doctor, can't this be done for Dr. Lelos Smith and the other teachers and grad students too?"

"Oh, I'm sorry. No, not at this time. You see, this procedure is an extremely costly one. We simply cannot economically afford to re-grow the arms of those who have not yet proven they are worthy of such a huge expense. Rest assured, anyone who does get their doctorate will have this procedure, just as you are. Further, as more research develops more cures, you four will be receiving those too. I believe that you, Dr. Botocelli, have your work cut out for you. We all expect great things from your new laboratory. Perhaps, you'll be able to find a more practical and less costly way to handle arm regrowth for everyone."

The next thing the four knew, other HIFRs took them into side rooms, undressing them. They were placed into a machine and many tubes were inserted to veins in their legs. Then, darkness came. All four expected this, a four-day period of unconsciousness, and thus were not surprised to lose consciousness.

Zia awoke with an itching nose. Mechanically, she scratched it with her right hand, before realizing she now had a right hand! "Oh! It worked! I've got arms and hands!" she yelled. She looked around and saw that she was in a hospital room all by herself. On the nearby dresser was a complete outfit, that of a professional woman. As she sat up, her six foot long, thick, shiny black hair lay draped across her naked chest in a large pile. She also noticed her fingernails were at least a couple inches long and painted a bright shade of red. Just then, a HIFR nurse entered.

"Welcome back, Dr. Botocelli. The process worked well. Your nails are as short as they can be. If you try to cut them any shorter, you'll experience excruciating pain, and they'll quickly regrow. So do notice how long they are. We've painted them red, but you can choose your own color scheme later on. Please get yourself dressed. There's a hairbrush on the table too. When you are done, please step out of the room. I'll be at my desk in the hall. You can't miss me. The others will be awaking shortly." She turned and left.

"But I've never dressed myself before," Zia said to the closed door. "Ah well. I have arms now, so I really don't need my HIFR any longer. This is so wonderful!" The dresser was close enough that she could lean over and pick up her garments. However, first, she inspected her body to see if there had been any other changes. Nope, she still had dual sexual organs. Her bosom was still overly large and her feet, fused en pointe. She smiled and began getting herself dressed, donning the garter belt first, then her nylons being careful not to tear them with her long nails, and then her panties. She decided to get her boots on next so she could stand and dress better. Soon, she wore a white blouse, a short grey skirt that fell barely to her knees, and a black blazer. It took her much longer to get her long hair brushed out, but she had no idea how to put her hair up into a large bun back of her head, and so left it draped down her back. At last satisfied with her new look, she rose and headed out of the door, marveling that this was the first time she had ever been able to open a door on her own, excepting those which were opened automatically by floor sensors when she stepped on them.

She found the other three were already there waiting on her. The four looked at each other and cheered. They were identically dressed. Fin whispered, "They gave Angelo and me a choice to dress in a suit or in these. Since we look like you ladies anyway, especially with these long red nails, we decided to avoid other people's confusion and look like professional women too. Hope you don't mind, my little cutie-pie. I think we would look silly trying to wear those suits, which look ridiculous on us."

Zia giggled, primarily at his use of his private affectionate greeting for her. "I know. Nothing can hide our bosoms. Sorry, maybe I can find a genetic cure to reduce them some for you fellows. Still, you look darn handsome to me, my big honey-bear." He smiled, enjoying her affectionate reply. They'd been dating for four years now, a year longer than Tiana and Angelo.

Just then, another well-dressed humaniform robot walked up to them. He looked like a male in all ways. "Hello there. I'm called Eros. I'm your immediate boss. However, before we get down to work, let's get you settled into your new home. Follow me, please." He walked slowly in deference to their speed, which was anything but fast in their knee-high ballet boots.

Out on the street, they smelled clean, fresh air, marveling at how pure it seemed. After walking several blocks,

Zia asked, "Eros, how come we only see HIRFs walking around? Where are all the people, the nova? Like ourselves?"

Eros turned and smiled. "You are the first nova to walk the streets of Venice! This is your new home. It is a quadraplex with a commons room. Next door, is a fully equipped market where you can obtain apparel and foods of your choice. It's all free, so help yourselves. If you need something you don't see there, just ask the HIFR in charge, and he'll get it for you as soon as possible. I'm told that a hundred more of you nova will soon be joining you four during the next year or so. Just wonderful. We've been waiting for you for a half century!"

"But wait a minute. Where are all the others, the other nova? Our classmates? Dr. Lelos Smith?" asked a confused Zia.

"Oh, they are inside their homes and campuses. They are not allowed outside onto the main streets. We don't want to risk them coming to any possible harm. Now that you've gotten your arms regrown, why, for the first time in a half century, we HIFRs don't have to worry about your safety. You're now able to care for your own needs. In that, all we HIFRs take an enormous pride, if a HIFR can have such a feeling," Eros replied.

"But we were going to get married," Fin interrupted him.

"Not a problem. I'm fully qualified to perform wedding ceremonies. Just let me know when. Perhaps now would be a good time?" he attempted a wry smile.

Fin looked at Zia. Angelo looked at Tiana. All four laughed. "Sure why not?" Zia agreed.

"Excellent. I can do it, after I show you to your new home. State of the art, at least as far as we HIFRs can determine." Inside, the four found the place was fully equipped with everything, including a dry cleaning and pressing machine. Their kitchens had everything from microwaves to coffee makers. Further, their pantries were stocked with their favorite foods. Zia guessed that her HIFR had told Eros what they liked. He continued talking as the four moved around the home. "Your HIFRs brought your things here." He pointed out each person's section. "Of course, you'll want to visit the market soon to pick up more clothing. We didn't know just what apparel you would want to wear."

"Thanks, Eros. This is prefect," Fin said, very much impressed with his new surroundings.

"Excellent. Now then, if you two couples will hold hands, I'll get you married, and leave you to get settled in. Tomorrow, I will come by around ten to take you to your new laboratories." With that, Eros proceeded to marry the two young couples, and then left them alone, embracing each other.

The two men decided they'd live on opposite sides of the quadraplex, sharing the commons area between them, since they were close friends anyway. That done, Zia and Tiana headed into their rooms to bring their things over to their new rooms. Picking up her hairbrush and toothbrush, Zia noticed that both looked slightly different from what she remembered them looking like. "Funny. This must be a new electric toothbrush, but what was wrong with my old one? This isn't my hairbrush, I don't think. It doesn't have that small flaw in its handle. Maybe these are Tiana's." She headed over to Tiana's room, where she was gathering up her things.

"Hey, is this your toothbrush and hairbrush?" Zia asked.

"Huh?" Tiana looked. "Nope. Mine has a blue handle, and my brush here has my blonde hair in it. Why?" She looked closer and called out worriedly, "Wait, maybe this isn't my brush either. Mine has this small line in its handle. This one doesn't."

"Ah ha. Something's going on here. Mind if I take a sample of your hair and some of those in the hairbrush? I can check DNA, and see if it's yours or not. This is strange," Zia asked.

Later, the two carried their bags over to their new husband's quarters. Fin said, "Zia, dear. Look at this. It's supposed to be my hairbrush, but I'm certain it isn't. The swirls used to go diagonally to the left and these are going to the right. Weird."

"Hey, join the crowd. Mine isn't right either, and Tiana's isn't quite right. Peculiar." She gazed into his face. He too had thick, black hair, about an inch longer than hers, but he had hints of a beard, but nothing more, though he had not shaved in months. It just didn't grow more than enough to be barely visible.

"Forget that for a while. Come here cutie-pie. I want to hug you and hold you," Fin said with a wry smile. Both held each other tightly for a time, relishing in the utter novelty of actually holding onto each other. Then, they both discovered that they were hungry.

When they reached the kitchen, both began laughing hysterically. Neither knew how to cook! "But you're the woman," Fin complained.

"No, you're the woman," Zia countered, laughing her head off. Here were two highly educated doctors, neither of which knew how to cook.

Just then, Tiana and Angelo joined them. "Say, does either of you know anything about cooking?" Angelo asked. "We don't and we're hungry."

"Well, it can't be all that hard," ever practical Tiana suggested, after the four discovered they were all ignorant of this detail. Laughing, the four began reading directions on how to prepare their lunch. "We should share this chore, don't you think?" she suggested.

"But don't women do the cooking?" Angelo asked. "I read that in a history book once."

"True. I remember that too," Fin quickly stuck up for him.

"But you both are women too," Tiana countered quite dryly, and they all laughed again. In the end, they each decided to take turns cooking and doing the dishes. That done, they then headed off to inspect their homes in detail. With empty closets, they soon headed to the market to get more clothing. They did have quite a variety to choose from, discovering ten different styles of dresses and an arrangement of blouses and skirts as well. For now, the men ignored attempting to wear men's clothing. It seemed ridiculous to even try that. Instead, they went with styles and colors their wives picked out for them.

Later, the two couples got ready for bed. Of course, they

had always had their HIFRs take their hair down and brush it out for them. Now, they had to do it themselves, and none of the four had any real good idea of just how it was done, only their casual observation of their HIFR. Soon, they discovered it was easier to do each other's and decided this was the way to go in the future. When they climbed into their wedding night bed, Zia tossed her long hair over her left shoulder, while Fin tossed his over his right. Almost at once, their passions exploded, four years of longing were fulfilled, as were those of Tiana and Angelo.

In the morning, the two young couples found themselves completely entwined in each other's hair, bringing laughs to all four, though they didn't find out about the other couple until breakfast. When the four met in Zia's kitchen to deal with making breakfast, they all had another good laugh at each other. None of the four knew how to put up their hair. Always, the HIFRs had done that, and none had ever paid the slightest attention on how it was done. Hence, they merely brushed theirs out and left it draped over their backs, moving it carefully out of the way whenever they sat or stood.

Dressed as professional women, they waited for Eros to come. He was prompt, as every robot was. Within an hour, each found themselves alone in a fully equipped laboratory, but they were told they could request any number of HIFRs that they might need to assist them with their work. Dr. Botocelli was given a dozen different genetic analyses to handle, forming the basis of her new genetic studies of nova. Dr. Vitano was given an assignment to help formulate better fertilizers to aid in the automated farming that provided all the food for the world. She was a bit daunted at the tasks set before her, but swore to rise to the tasks. Dr. Landini was given the task of developing a planetary defense shield that would deflect any attempts to drop nuclear bombs on this world. Dr. Vitalli was given the assignment of modifying their meager planetary defense weapons. His work would help them deflect any attempts by other worlds to attack them. This time, Eros explained, they wanted to be able to fight back and not get destroyed, as they had been on Aquila Prime. Everything being asked of them seemed wholly justified and perfectly ordinary, and they set to work on their new goals.

When the four returned home for supper, Fin pointed out, "Say, it's really weird. I didn't see any of us — any nova, anywhere today. I expected to see some strolling on the quad of the University, like we all used to do nearly every day, but I didn't see any students. Really strange, don't you think?"

"I don't know. I was stuck in my lab all day," Zia replied. "But I did determine that the hair in Taina's brush was hers, even though the brush might not be."

"But I swear it wasn't my brush," Tiana said steadfastly.

"Hey, mine was a bit different than I remembered too," Fin added. "Wonder what that means?"

"Well, I didn't see any nova around either," Angelo put in. "Where the heck are all of us anyway? This doesn't make a whole lot of sense. I asked Eros when I saw him, and all he would say is that they are being cared for so that they don't get hurt and not to be worried about them."

"I think we have a mystery on our hands," Tiana said, placing her hands on her hips, and then noticing she was able to do it. She broke into a laugh at that.

"I think we need to find out more about our world," Fin declared. The others agreed.

"But Fin, we can hardly go far from here. Walking is nasty at best," Tiana countered.

"True, my knees are taking a beating, since I've been on my toes more than normal in the lab," Zia admitted. "I don't quite understand that though. I was on my toes far longer than that while at school. It's like my knees and legs are somehow very much weaker."

"Well, maybe we should go for longer and longer walks in the evenings after supper. You know, strengthen up our leg muscles," Angelo suggested. "Besides, we can walk arm in arm, which we never could do before."

"Oh let's!" declared the blonde Tiana, quite excited by the chance to spend time with Angelo holding her, especially after their wedding night.

After finishing the dishes, the four headed outside their quadraplex. Arm in arm, the two couples began taking their stroll, heading on down the street, placing each step carefully, as they always had to do. There was still a little daylight left, and just as many robots going about various activities, which were wholly unknown to the foursome. After walking two blocks past Fin's new lab, which was also the farthest from their new home, all four began to get a headache.

Finally, Tiana complained. "I'm getting a splitting headache. I thought our legs would be taking a beating with all this walking, but why should my head hurt?"

"Same here," echoed Zia. The men added their me too's as well. "How very strange all four of us should get headaches just while walking. This doesn't make any sense. Maybe something went genetically wrong when they regrew our arms. I'd best look into that tomorrow. Damn, we'd better turn back, gang."

They did just that, though their legs were still feeling all right. After another block, Zia commented, "Weird. My headache is going away I think." The others concurred. "Now this is strange indeed."

As they approached their home, they saw Eros coming their way. "Wonder what he wants?" Angelo whispered.

"Hello doctors. What's going on?" Eros asked.

"Just going for a walk with our wives, trying to strengthen our knees and legs some. We're not used to being on our feet so much in the labs," Angelo answered, more or less truthfully.

"Okay. Well, all right then. I was concerned you might be having some troubles," Eros commented. "You do need to strengthen up your legs and knees. I can see that."

"Well, we all got headaches a couple of blocks back that way," Zia admitted. "Strange that we'd all get a headache at the same time."

"You shouldn't walk so far away from your new home. I'll look into it. I can see you do need to exercise more now that you are working in your labs. It should not be a problem. Good evening." Eros turned and left them.

"Wonder what he meant by that? A threat? This is our world," Angelo barked, slightly annoyed with Eros.

"But if this is our world, where are we?" Tiana countered. "That didn't come out quite right. I mean Dr. Smith and everyone else. Where are they? Ouch, my headache is back. We best get inside."

As the foursome headed into their new home with Zia holding onto Tiana, Angelo commented, "That's weird. She was just saying something important. Where are they? Damn, now my head is hurting too. All of a sudden like. What the hell is going on? Damn!" He held onto his head as though it was going to burst.

Fin looked at Zia, who was about to say something. He put his fingers to his lips and nodded. With a look of understanding, Zia nodded back. Once the two were inside and in their section of the large building, Fin took Zia into their living room. He continued to hold a finger up to his lips, while he searched for some paper. He found some scraps that had been discarded earlier and wrote: Don't talk about it. Write it out. On paper. Don't put it on the computers either.

Zia gave him a very strange look, but nodded, and retrieved a pad and pen. She wrote: They have a good point. We've not seen anyone except us and the HIFRs and robots. What's going on?

He wrote back: Something is weird. Twice now we've gotten sudden bad headaches and for no reason. But we were walking far from our house and talking about the missing people. That's when we got hit. Look, we're writing and nothing is happening to us.

She nodded, bit her lip, and wrote: Who is doing this? How? Why? She hesitated and then added: Conspiracy?

Fin nodded. He wrote: Bring the pad and let's go check on them. Bet you anything their headaches have gone and won't come back, if we write our ideas instead of talking them out.

Zia nodded, and the two headed out into the commons and across the room, knocking lightly on their door. Hearing Tiana replying, they went inside. Both were in their kitchen sipping glasses of ice-cold water. "Hi. We're better now. Headaches have vanished," Tiana explained, relieved. "Cold water did the trick."

Fin wrote: Don't talk. Write. Headaches correspond to our going too far from here and then talking about the missing everyone. This is really suspicious. Where are all of our people? What's going on? Ideas?

The four sat around the kitchen table with the pad in front of them. Angelo nodded and wrote: This is something else. We need to check out the city and see where our people are, if we can, but these headaches are likely to stop us dead in our tracks. Hey, how come we are able to write? We've only just gotten hands, and yet, we are able to write legibly?

All four nodded. Then, Angelo had a sudden realization! He nearly jumped out of his chair, causing instant fears in the other that he was in trouble somehow. He shook off their worried looks. He wrote: I'm designing defense shields for our world. One device developed elsewhere is something that can be adjusted to any given person's frequency, and via it, force them to do what the controller asks. It's called a Brunelli Enforcer. I don't know how it works yet. I just got to that part at the end of the afternoon. I bet someone is using it on us.

Zia grabbed the paper and wrote hastily: Who? Why?

Fin grabbed it next and wrote: To keep us from finding out something critically important.

Tiana nodded and insisted on writing next: Where everyone is at? But why? The robots?

Everyone shrugged. Angelo wrote: We need to find a way to explore the city, but right now, my legs and knees are mush. Really weird. Never felt like this before.

Tiana slid the pad over and wrote: Me too. I was always going for walks all over campus. The chem labs are about as far from Dr. Smith's office as anything, and I never felt so sore before like I do now. It's as though my knees and legs are not used to walking. How can this be?

She looked from face to face, but they all shook their heads. None had any idea. Then, Zia took the pad and wrote: Maybe it is a side effect from the genetic mutation cures we got. I'll fully explore that tomorrow. Okay? Everyone nodded. She added, But we should keep on walking as much as we can to get our legs built back up, right? Again, everyone nodded.

And it was precisely at this point that something happened that forever changed the lives of these four young nova. Annunziata likened it to suddenly having all of a world's flowers bursting simultaneously into full bloom. Well, Zia was the more poetic of this foursome. Serafino likened it to suddenly having a whole new mental arena opening in his consciousness. The mathematician Angelo described it more like a new dimension in awareness unfolding instantly. Christina, the ever-practical chemist, suggested it was more like adding a new, hitherto fore unknown perception to those of sight, sound, and touch. However they described it, the four suddenly and without any warning found themselves in a complete telepathic rapport with each other.

I hear you. All of you. Your thoughts. I feel you! exclaimed Zia.

This is wild! I know, Zia. It's as if I'm you, sort of, gushed Fin.

I'm reading everyone's thoughts too. Like incredible. Wow! thought Angelo.

Me too. Wait. Is this telepathy? What it's supposed to be? Reading others thoughts? It's as if I'm in your minds. Way cool, sent Tiana.

Hey, we don't need the paper pad any longer. We should keep this a secret between us, Angelo pointed out. *I don't trust these robots.*

Why? Haven't they taken good care of us all our lives? asked Tiana.

Like where is everyone? Why didn't they want us to walk around our own city? Little things, Tiana, sent Fin.

That done, Fin gathered up the papers and shredded them. He wasn't taking any chances of someone going through their recycled trash looking for what they were writing, if they even knew that they were. As he and Zia headed back to their place for the night, he began to wonder if there were spy cameras on them here in their home. He made a silent vow to search for them in the morning. Once in their bedroom, their passions exploded before they could even get each other's hair brushed out. With the neurons in their hair, they had a sense of touch down the length of each strand of hair. Plus, telepathic rapport added a whole new dimension to their lovemaking. Neither could help themselves from doing it again as soon as they awoke the next morning.

Around nine the next day, all four said goodbye and headed off in four directions towards their own labs. Zia smiled, as she walked slowly along the paved street. Each of them looked very much like the photos she'd seen while growing up, photos of Federation professional women, except for their super long hair and boots, that is. She took comfort in that. She no longer thought of herself as somewhat freakish looking as she always had.

Once at her lab, she fired up several computers, bringing up all known data on their latest genetic cures that regrew arms. There was quite a lot of material on it, but much had originated on some distant world she'd never heard of, one Ashford-5. Still, Zia was able to verify the process did indeed regrow arms and recently did have a side effect with fingernails on some Federation personnel, but not on all. The variations seemed to be located in one specific gene. She ignored this detail for the moment. Having longer nails was quite attractive and not any real problem. Instead, she looked deeper, trying to see if there were any other side effects, particularly with their legs.

Mid-morning, Eros dropped by. "Catching up on our latest genetic cures, I see."

"Yes. All four of us are finding walking extremely tiresome. I mean, Eros, I used to have to do a lot of walking on the campus. My legs never felt like mush then, but just walking that half mile yesterday about did me in. All of us, for that matter. It's almost as if we're not used to walking in these boots. And that's even weirder, because obviously we've been walking in them all our lives, well, since we were about three years old anyway. So I thought maybe this was some side-effect of the genetic cure, like our long nails are."

"I see. And have you found anything yet?" Eros asked.

"Well, nothing has been reported, but I'll keep an eye out for it."

"Excellent. I believe you are all being very wise in trying to strengthen your legs and knees. We should have foreseen this difficulty. I dropped by to encourage you to do just that, only do be careful and not overdo it," Eros advised. She nodded and he left.

24

Meanwhile in her chem lab, Tiana found a wide variety of vegetables had been brought into her lab during the night, ready for her to analyze. Per well-defined protocols, she first checked them for toxic substances. Tiana was amazed to find a rather high level of pesticides in many of them. While not sufficiently high to cause any immediate harm if eaten, this problem needed correction. She spent her day documenting her findings and recommending a fifty percent reduction in the application of the herbicides. When Eros dropped by to see how she was doing, she explained her findings. "I'd really like to see the farm plots where these were grown so I can get a handle on what the problem is that is causing them to over use the herbicides."

Eros replied, "That won't be necessary. Based on your findings, I'll see the robots take care of this detail. Good work, Dr. Vitano. Keep up the excellent work." He then left.

In his own lab, Fin found just what he was looking for, a "bug detector." Realizing his professional woman's outfit had no pockets, he slipped the device down his large cleavage. Then, he continued his assessment of Beltazar's capabilities to defend itself from an attack. The numbers were a bit staggering. One million Model 7 humaniform robots could take up d-guns and personal defense shields to attack any ground invasions. He reviewed their specifications, and decided that their reactions in test simulations were far beyond those of a normal human. He felt confident that the robots would be able to hold against any small-scale ground invasion. Next, he turned his attention to spaceships. Here was their critical weak link.

It was at this point that Eros dropped in on him. "Any conclusions, Dr. Vitalli?"

"Ah, excellent timing. Our ground robot defenses are excellent, unless they send in millions of soldiers, which is highly unlikely. No, our critical weak link is in spaceships, that is warships. We don't have even one light cruiser, let alone any battleships. Those are what would more than likely be attacking us, bombing us from orbit."

"Yes, indeed. I have Dr. Landini working on defenses against that. The one thing we do have are transports," Eros pointed out.

"I can see that. Two hundred fifty of them, all equipped with the latest super fast Imperium engines, converted to utilize Federation fuel or Imperium fuel cells. Nice touch on the fuel," Fin replied.

"Yes, and each one has a light canon on it as well."

"But what good will that do against a battleship?" Fin countered.

"Bring up File 2467. We have been conducting a rather large number of test simulations. We might have found a way. Review that extensive file today and give me your opinion tomorrow, if you can have it by then. I'm open to other suggestions as well, doctor."

"Well, we're not likely to be able to either buy or steal us a battleship, are we?" Fin replied half in jest.

"That is a joke, I presume?" Eros asked, faking a human-like smile.

"Yes. Naturally, we can't do that. I'll get on it. This is one huge file, Eros."

"Indeed. It represents several hundred thousands of hours of test simulations. Happy studying." Eros then left.

When Eros visited Dr. Landini in his lab, he found the doctor studying up on the Brunelli Enforcer. Giving no outward sign of distress, Eros asked politely, "Is this relevant to our surface defense shields, doctor?"

Angelo looked up. "Why yes indeed, Eros. Look, according to these notes, someone can use this device to force another person to do precisely what they order them to do. That's really a nasty piece of electronics. Look Eros, this has me more worried than a battleship dropping bombs on us. They could orbit us, fire up this device, and force anyone of us nova to do their bidding. If we had a planet-wide defense shield up, they could use it to force us to drop our shields! I was about to make a recommendation to you that my top priority should be coming up with a good defense against this."

Eros nodded. "I see. Yes, you have made a critical point. I believe you're one hundred percent correct in your analysis. Please, you have my permission to make this your top priority! Please keep me posted on your progress."

"Of course. I'll need a sample Brunelli Enforcer machine to experiment with."

"I'll see you have one by tomorrow morning, doctor."

Angelo wisely didn't ask why Eros had one or more of these devices. He had far too many suspicions right about now.

That evening, while Tiana and Angelo worked on fixing their supper, Zia chatted about how her day had gone, leaving Fin to quietly sweep both homes looking for bugs. He found five in each! He duly notified the others via paper, drawing out their locations on crude sketches. He also sent them: *Will work on a jamming device tomorrow.*

After eating, the four headed outside to walk and build up the strength in their legs and knees. This time, none received any headaches. While they found robots in action around the blocks they walked, they saw no signs of any nova at all.

Chapter 3 Unravel

During the ensuing week, the four nova began settling into their new lives. On the very personal side, each couple found having sex while in total rapport with their partner the most fantastic experience ever, and insisted on doing it both at night and before getting up. Zia described it to Tiana as being more sensual than sensual. The practical chemist couldn't grasp that notion but said it was the most fun she ever experienced.

All four continued to experiment with their newfound telepathy, particularly using it to share conspiracy theories and observations. Plus, they now had a way to counter the ten electronic bugs planted in their homes. When they wanted to exchange something privately, they now routinely used telepathy. However, they did begin to experience some problems with it, especially at night. Each couple could sense what the others were thinking and feeling, but were not embarrassed about it. Rather, they all worried about a thought that Tiana had had: *Look, what's going to happen when we do find everyone else? I mean we're going to be bombarded with everyone else's thoughts all at once.*

Hence, the four began to try to figure out how to block out other's thoughts and to find a way of keeping their own from being overheard by everyone else. That turned out to be a rather ongoing process.

Each evening, the foursome went on longer and longer walks, strengthening up their legs and knees. The more they walked, the more they realized something was quite different. As they walked, Zia sent, *Look. We used to walk for several miles, strolling around the quad with each other. Now look at us. One mile and our knees and legs are done in, to say nothing of our toes. Something definitely is different now.*

Tiana countered, *It doesn't make sense. Look, I've been walking like this for eighteen years and never ever had such trouble. Angelo and I once went on a stroll completely around the University campus, and that's nearly five miles. I wasn't bothered by it in the slightest. Now look at me. Two miles and my toes are throbbing and my legs are mush.*

You are getting stronger, my dear, Angelo countered. *Three days ago, they were mush after barely a mile. I think we are exercising them and getting stronger legs as a result.*

It doesn't make sense, gang. Why should our legs be mush now, when they certainly weren't when we were going to school? Answer me that one, Fin challenged them.

Zia replied, *Well, I've done a complete study of the genetic cures they gave us. There is absolutely no sign or evidence this cure had anything to do with our feet, legs, or muscles.*

Tiana teased, *What about our arm muscles?*

Zia glared at her and then broke into a smile. *I know, Dr. Chemist, be precise.* Tiana giggled.

Hey, focus on what's really important here, ladies, Angelo interrupted them. *Look, we've gone about two miles in four directions from our home and labs. What have we **not** seen? Any signs of any nova. Yes, the buildings are there, but I'm not sensing any minds inside them. It's as if the whole city is vacant except for the robots and few HIFRs walking around. I can't read their minds at all.*

Silly, robots don't have minds, dear. They have computer programming, Tiana chastised him.

Hey, he has a point. There's still no sign of any other nova. Where the heck are they? We should try to sneak into the University campus and see if we can find them, like Dr. Smith, suggested Fin.

They agreed and changed direction, heading towards the very western edge of their very familiar campus where they'd spent most of their teen years deep in studies. As soon as they approached the edge of the campus, all four suddenly had splitting headaches. Quickly, they changed direction again, heading for home. A few blocks away from the University, Eros again appeared. "Please don't disturb the many students at the University. You should know just how hard they all have to study." The four agreed and continued heading home. By the time that they arrived there, their headaches were completely gone.

Well, that's certainly fishy, Fin sent.

It's as if he's hiding something from us, Zia added.

That doesn't make any sense, gang, Tiana protested. *After all, the HIFRs are only looking out for our well-being. He has a point. We all used to study very hard, night and day. Chemistry was really hard.*

Get real, Tiana. He's hiding something. Did you sense any of our other classmates' minds? We were really close you know, Angelo countered. *Something is missing here.*

Strange how the mere mention of just the right phrase can suddenly trigger a thought realization process. Fin suddenly brightened up. *Hey, that just reminded me of something else that's missing. I don't know about you, but when I was at the University, once in a while, I'd see something flickering at the edge of my vision. Sort of like the breaking up of a picture or something. I've seen that at least a couple dozen times.*

Hey, I've seen it too, honey-bear, Zia interrupted him.

Cool, cutie-pie, he responded.

Honey-bear? Cutie-pie? Get serious, will you? I think he's on to something. I've seen that too, Angelo broke in. The two flushed.

Well, we've been here for over a week, and I've not seen it happening here. What does that mean? Fin explained and asked.

Don't know, Angelo replied, *but I'd forgotten about the headaches, since we've not had them for nearly a week now. I wonder if our headaches are coming from a Brunelli Enforcer device?*

A what? asked Tiana, growing curious. She'd never heard of it.

Angelo explained, *It's something that was created here on this world about a century or so ago. I've been studying up on it. The theory goes like this. Apparently, each person responds to a unique very high frequency. If you adjust the frequency dial to that of a specific person, you can then send a command message on that frequency to the person, along with enough energy to cause enough pain to force the person to carry out that command. It was used way back when by an insane man who tried to extort a battleship out of the*

Federation high command by having aides assassinate key leaders. Somehow, a woman from an unknown world called Ashford-5 stopped him in his tracks. Eros is having me work up a planetary shield against someone trying to use this device on us.

Fin jumped in, *Hey, you don't suppose Eros or someone is using that on us, giving us these headaches, so we stop whatever we were doing?*

Makes perfect sense to me, Angelo replied.

I think you both are seeing conspiracies everywhere, Tiana countered.

Hey, come to think of it, what do we really know about our own history? Beltazar-C. Very little, Zia pointed out. *I mean obviously this world is an old one. All these empty buildings. So modern, so well equipped. And yet, all is vacant. Where are all our people? What was our history? We never learned anything at all about our history, now did we? That's a gaping hole in our education, if you ask me.*

Angelo replied, *Hey, she's got a good point. And I'll bet you a week's cooking that if we try to search the databases about the history of our world, we'll A) not find out much at all and B) get a splitting headache if we try. Any takers?*

You just want out of cooking and doing the dishes, Tiana griped.

It's hard on my nails, Angelo replied. Everyone roared with laughter.

In fact, Zia tried it the next day. In her lab, she attempted to search the world databases for some of their history. Almost at once, she got a fierce headache, which went away as soon as she stopped trying to look it up. Later, she had to explain to Eros that she wanted to see if there was any genetic anomalies in their past that might account for their weak legs after receiving their genetic cures. He seemed to buy her explanation but encouraged her to look elsewhere for the answers. When she told the others this via telepathy during their evening long walk, Angelo and Fin were now completely convinced there was some grand conspiracy in play. Tiana still wasn't convinced.

For two more weeks, they continued their late evening

walks, becoming familiar with more and more of their "empty" city. Finally, the four were satisfied that their old leg strength had returned. Nevertheless, the four so enjoyed these late evening walks that they continued to take them.

Both Angelo and Fin were hard at work during their daytime lab hours. Angelo was determined to find a way to deflect the energy beams coming from the Brunelli Enforcer. What with everything that was going on here on Beltazar-C, he felt that this device was the most serious threat to their existence, not nuclear bombs. A simple force field similar to that used on all spaceships could be constructed to keep such bombs from reaching the surface. He'd work on that next. No, the ability of the operator of this machine to force another unsuspecting person to do what he asked was diabolical and the real threat.

After three long weeks of trial and error, Angelo had come up with a possible solution, but on a tiny scale, one person. In part, his design was based upon the standard energy force shields, but this one only operated in the trillion-yattohertz range. The prototype device was quite small and could be worn on a belt. When activated, it produced a spherical shell around the person. After some adjustments, if incoming energies in that frequency range were detected and at a threshold power level, the device began shunting that energy into the ground, a perfect absorber of energy. Satisfied with his prototype, he built three more and brought them home with him, confident that half of their problem was solved.

Meanwhile, Fin was working on the other half. Visibility. Each time the four had attempted to pursue their investigations, they had been spotted, and Eros showed up. True, he had not threatened them or forcefully stopped them, but he used subtler means, hints. As far as Fin was concerned, this only fueled his Grand Conspiracy Theory. He knew he had to solve this visibility problem. To do that, he turned to the spaceship cloaking devices, which bent light rays such that to the human eye, the object did not appear to be there. Of course, the cloaking devices also operated on many other frequencies, such as radar and standard ship sensor wavelengths. In this case, they only needed to be optically invisible.

Cloaking devices onboard ships were both large and consumed power. Fin needed a miniature version, one that could be worn on a belt, for example. Since only optical wavelengths needed to be bent, reducing the circuitry a hundredfold drastically cut down on the size of the device. After weeks of working on it, he finally had it working. The only problem was its excessive power consumption.

He brought home four prototypes, which would operate for two hours at most before needing to be recharged. Still, he was convinced this would help them unravel this huge mystery and conspiracy, especially when used with Angelo's new device.

They decided to put these to use on Sunday, which was typically the day off that they were used to having off while attending the University — a day to do laundry, catch up on homework, a day to relax a little, a day to enjoy your boyfriend or girlfriend. Whether the robots recognized Sunday, none knew, but suspected they didn't. However, if they were questioned, the four planned to argue this was their traditional day off from work.

"Okay, where to first?" asked Angelo. It was Sunday, and all four had strapped the two devices around their waists, concealing them somewhat by their blazers.

"The University," echoed the other three in unison, though octaves apart. Zia sung soprano; Tiana, alto; Fin, tenor; and Angelo, bass.

"Heigh ho, away we go," Angelo replied. "Remember, I'll give us a signal when to activate them. We've only got two hours at most."

"Let's do this!" declared Zia, who was eager to meet Dr. Smith and discuss all of these strange things with him.

"I don't think we'll find anything," Tiana added. Of the four, she was the most doubtful, suspecting there was a logical explanation behind everything, only they'd not discovered it just yet. The four headed out into the sunny, clear day. It was a warm morning, though the July weather would soon turn quite hot by late afternoon, making their blazers too hot to wear. Hence, the morning exploration trip.

They walked some five blocks, watching the few robots passing by. When Angelo saw none were either approaching or watching them, he sent, *Now. Activate both.* All four disappeared from view. *Crap, I can't see you guys. Hold hands or we're going to get lost.* After a few fumbling minutes, each got a hold of another's hand, and they headed on towards the University and their beloved campus. Ten minutes later, they set foot on the southern edge and headed on into the campus proper. Before long, they hit the quad and looked about.

Where is everyone? It's Sunday. We should all be outside on such a fine morning, sent Zia. *This is really weird! Let's find Dr. Smith!* None disagreed, and they headed across the quad to his building. Unlike the normal doors, these didn't open automatically when they stepped on the entrance pads!

Something's really wrong. The door must be stuck or something, Angelo commented, quite startled by the failure of the automatic door. He stepped up and opened it himself, and they filed inside only to find the hallway completely empty. At once, they headed on down the hall to Dr. Smith's familiar office. His nametag wasn't on the door! Angelo knocked politely. Silence. At last, he opened the door and four gasps broke the silence. The room was entirely empty! Well, that's not entirely true. A desk and chairs were present along with a floor to ceiling bookshelf, empty of all books. The mountains of papers weren't here either.

Good god! What's going on? Where's Dr. Smith? asked Zia.

Don't know, but I'm getting a really creepy feeling. Come on; let's check our old dorms. All our younger friends should be there, suggested Angelo, still a bit shocked by what he wasn't seeing.

A half hour later, the stunned foursome walked out of their old dorm, heading back home. The dorm, like everything else here, was totally vacant. Their old rooms were empty as well, though beds and desks were there. No students, no sheets, no blankets, no books, and no clothes. The four were shocked, and said little, until they were far from the University, when Angelo suggested they deactivate their devices. They returned home in silence. Zia mechanically brewed up a large pot of coffee. She needed to steel her nerves, and the others were grateful for her action. They sat around their kitchen table, sipping the hot brew.

I don't get it. Where is everyone, everything? The University is completely deserted. Did everyone suddenly just die off? Zia sent, fighting to keep her wild emotions in check. She felt like screaming and sobbing at the same time. Dr. Smith was like a father to her. In fact, now that she thought about it, she realized she really didn't know her own father or mother for that matter. Surely, she had them at one time, but all she could truly remember were the schools she attended.

For a half hour, the four shared ideas and feelings with each other, via telepathy. Now, even Tiana was convinced that something was horribly wrong. However, no one had any real ideas of how to proceed. At last, Angelo decided to go outside, sit on their porch, and think. By now, the sun was blazing down. In his blazer, Angelo began sweating and headed back inside.

Tiana saw beads of sweat tricking down his face. "We should perhaps sunbath. Come on; let's change into our bikinis and get some sun like we always used to do." A half hour later, the four now dressed in bikinis and their ballet boots sat together outside on their porch, but each was lost in his or her own thoughts.

Out on the street, they saw some usual robots going about their actions, seemingly oblivious to the four young nova who were watching them. Suddenly, Fin had an idea. *Say, Angelo, we've been missing an important clue: the robots.* None had their mental barriers up, and thus they all heard his thought.

What do you mean? Angelo asked.

Just where are all the robots going to and coming from?

Oh I get it. A math model. I'll get on it. You are right. We've missed a detail here.

Zia didn't follow him; neither did Tiana. Instead, they adjusted their long black and blonde hair so that they could lie down, propping their heads on one arm. Soon, their mates joined them, facing their new wives. Their free hands soon found the others, and once more, their passions took hold of the four. Long fingernails slipped beneath the flimsy bikini tops. Bulges threatened to erupt from their tiny bottoms. After that, they simply ignored the robots and satisfied themselves there in the sun. After all, Zia reasoned, there wasn't any other person around to see them.

That done, Angelo had another revelation. *Look, those going up the street are not carrying anything, but those going down the street are carrying bags. Conclusion. They are taking something somewhere and leaving it there. We should follow them.*

Which ones? asked Fin, catching on to the significance of his observation.

Down the street. I want to see where they are taking things, he replied.

The four had to take a shower and clean up, before getting back into their professional women's outfits. This time, however, it was difficult for them to hide their waist belts and two new devices, because they couldn't wear their blazers. Hence, Angelo had them activate them just as they left their front porch. Again, holding hands, they headed out into the street and waited for a robot to come along. Soon one appeared, carrying a large sack slung over its back. Because of the noise their steel heels made on the concrete street, they stayed well back of the robot, which wasn't hard to do, since the robot walked swiftly, while they simply couldn't keep up in their boots. Plus, unable to see their feet, they had to be extra careful with each invisible step. Quickly, they were left far behind the robot.

Soon though, another one came up fast from their rear. Hastily, they moved aside, giving it plenty of room to pass by them. Once it did, they continued to follow this second robot. Three more times they were passed up, before they saw them entering a low building, some three miles from their home. Here, they paused to watch for a while, as robots entered and later left, leaving their bags inside somewhere.

Finally, Angelo insisted on going inside to have a look around. They timed it well. After one robot left and was some distance away, they moved up to the door, opened it, and stepped inside. They stood still for a moment, allowing their eyes to adjust to the dimly lit interior. It was empty! This wasn't what they had expected, but were alert enough to move out of the doorway into the empty room.

Where are all the bags? Tiana asked the obvious. Just then, the door opened and another robot entered carrying a bag. He walked over to a wall and pressed a button. Shortly, a door opened, and he stepped in. *That's an elevator! Duh!*

As quietly as possible, the four moved closer to the elevator door, but staying out of the direct path that the robot had taken. Shortly, the elevator door opened, and the robot exited, walked across the empty space, and out the door they'd all entered. Hastily, Angelo pressed the button, and the elevator doors opened. All four hastened inside. When the doors closed, they looked at the control panel. There were only two buttons, one above the other. He pressed the bottom one, and they began descending.

Hey, we are going way down! he sent.

Fin commented, *If we knew the speed of the elevator and how many seconds it takes to get to the floor, we can determine how far underground we're going.*

I'm scared, Tiana sent, ignoring Fin. *We could get into big trouble.* The men ignored her.

Then, the elevator stopped, and the door opened. Diffuse lighting showed a hallway ahead, and the four stepped out of the elevator and began walking down the hallway. Their heels made distinctive clicking sounds. Steel on stone. Try as they might, they couldn't move silently at all, which added to their nervousness. The hallway came out into a giant room, well lighted. As their eyes took in the sight before them, they gasped! A dozen robots suddenly looked their way. Angelo whispered, "Turn our devices off. The game is up. We'll play it cool-like." They did as asked, suddenly becoming visible to the robots.

In turn, they continued to stare in complete disbelief of what their eyes were recording! The room was huge, though periodic columns supported the stone roof overhead. It was like an underground cavern of some kind. Before them were glass-sided vats or tubs, each some eight feet long, five feet wide, and two feet deep, quite transparent. Inside was about eighteen inches of water. More importantly though, there were two nova bodies lying naked in each one, with some tubes going into their mouths, noses, and rears. The tubes rose up to a maze of tubes across the ceiling. The tubs were laid out some four feet apart and in twelve rows, each with ten sets of tubs in it, yielding some two hundred forty nova bodies!

Zia screamed. "That's — that's Milana! I recognize her. And there's Paolina! She's studying to be an astronomer! Oh my god! What's going on here?"

"There's one of our teachers!" cried Fin. "Doctor Susanna, our math teacher! Good god!"

Tiana swallowed hard, trying to grasp what she was seeing. She added, "They all have something around their heads, a band or something."

"V-masks," a familiar voice startled them from behind. They whirled on their toes and nearly lost their balance. Had they not had arms, they would have fallen. There was Eros once more. "Oh dear. You were not supposed to discover this."

Angelo swallowed hard and barked, "Well, we have. What the hell is going on here? Those, those are our people! What are you doing to them?" In his mind, nothing could ever explain this away!

"Saving their lives and yours too. We are dedicated and programmed to protect and save all you nova. Since you have seen this, you might as well have the full story. Come. I understand you desperately want to see your Dr. Lelos Smith. This way." Eros moved on out into the room. The worker robots continued their work, completely ignoring the new arrivals.

He led them to the back row and paused before a tank. "Dr. Lelos Smith." The four stared at the lone body floating in the liquid. They hardly recognized him! Radiation burns had totally disfigured what was left of his body! "We've applied every known medical procedure to save his life and those of another twenty-five original Aquila Prime nova, the best and brightest of our nova back then. As you can see, his body is alive, but not without artificial support."

"Those devices attached to their heads are called V-masks. They provide an artificial reality for the person. In fact, that reality is so completely real that all these nova here fully believe what they are experiencing is reality. You four were in here a month ago. Yes, you've been in here since your births, twenty-one years ago. When you graduated, we put you under, brought your bodies out of your tanks, and performed the known genetic cures on your bodies. You four are the first to exit the virtual reality world, fully educated and ready to carry the torch forward, preparing the way for more graduates who'll be joining you next year. That's why we were surprised to discover your legs were so weak. Within the virtual reality world, your legs were 'normal,' but out here in the real world, they needed to be strengthened. We'll take that into account when the next batch graduate and come to join you."

"Those two — they're having. . ." Zia didn't finish her sentence, but stared at the two writhing bodies, intertwined.

"Yes, they are having intercourse. Within their virtual world, they are doing it as we speak, while here in the tank their physical bodies are doing what they believe they are doing in their virtual world," Eros explained. "While in your virtual world, you four have done this same thing many times. There you cannot become pregnant, as that would interfere with your educations. Here in the tank, yes, the real bodies can and often do. Yes, you four have already given birth to new nova, twice now, in fact. I assure you they are being well cared for in other facilities. They will be given every chance to become as educated as you have been. And if so, one day they'll join you in the real world."

Zia wanted to throw up, scream, and beg to see her children, all at the same time. The men simply swallowed very hard. Tiana merely swallowed and said, "Oh my! This is quite unexpected."

Eros said, "Indeed. If you'll come with me to an office, I would like to explain this more fully to you four and try to answer your questions, though I hope you would also answer mine." His voice sounded both stern and official. Still mostly stunned, the four followed him to a side room, where four robots quickly provided more chairs. Each mechanically pulled their hair to their left sides, sat down, and draped it across their laps so that it didn't lay on the floor.

Eros began a lengthy explanation. "You see, it began when the ex-Imperium decided to wipe you nova out. Back then, your numbers had grown to a hundred twenty million on Aquila Prime. We humaniform robots cared for your every need, and in turn, the brightest of you nova had built a civilization of which you could be proud. Then came the devastating nuclear attack, which we were utterly unable to prevent. We only had time to get a few thousand of you nova into an underground bunker. While we were not truly affected by the bombs and subsequent radiation poisoning, the nova were. It took all our resources to save as many of them as we could."

"We then modified our programming, adding a fourth law, to protect you nova from the attacks of other species. We scoured the galaxy for another suitable planet, since the radiation levels on Aquila Prime are still far too high for any nova to live there and will be for at least another century or two. Here in the distant spiral arm of the Federation, we found this world, this Beltazar-C, a world totally addicted to their V-mask virtual realities. Here, the homo sapiens sapiens had ceased living lives, spending all their time within their unreal worlds. By actual measurement, these pathetic humans spent twenty-three hours of each day living in the virtual worlds, coming out only to eat. They built robotic farms to produce and process their food, minimizing completely the time they needed to be in the real world."

"In point of fact, it was some of these deranged people who created and used that Brunelli Enforcer. So here, we found the ideal location to bring our surviving nova, including Dr. Lelos Smith. We took over the programming of their V-mask games, turning them from all manner of debauchery into one of true learning, true education, of which you four are the first doctoral graduates from this program, though a hundred more will soon be joining you within a year or two at most."

"So, so these people here, these nova, us, we were the people who were living here on Beltazar-C?" asked Angelo, almost dumbfounded with this information.

"Some are yes. Mind you, other homo sapiens sapiens here in the Federation of Planets began using that same genetic bio agent as a terrorist weapon, inflicting massive genetic mutations on many worlds here in the Federation, just as they did back in the old Imperium. Some of these people were given the chance to come here as well. So now it is a mixture of nova from many worlds."

"So, so how many nova are there?" Angelo formulated a key question that popped into his mathematical mind.

"Around a hundred million. We have many such Nova Centers around the entire world. Above ground, we have been careful to preserve everything, knowing that one day, the brightest of the nova would be returning to dwell on the surface once more. We have not been idle. It has been constant work for all robots, especially the worker bots. In addition, we have been keeping abreast of all the latest genetic cures that have been developed throughout the galaxy. It has been quite costly indeed, but I'm pleased to say we've given all nova the basic round of genetic cures. As you could see from the nova in the tanks, their bosoms are greatly reduced. Their split lips are healed."

"The arm regrowth process is more complex and details are still being uncovered. Hence, we are only performing those on the nova who graduate. Perhaps in time, even better cures will be found that have no additional side effects. I hope your longer nails are not posing too difficult a situation for you. No one knows yet how to eliminate that side effect. Apparently, there are some slight DNA differences between Federation nova and Imperium nova, which have prevented the genetic cures from removing the pain neurons in your hair, and which have resulted in your fused feet. That's why I was so pleased to have you receive your doctorate, Annunziata. It is our hope you'll be able to find more cures for all nova."

Fin found his voice. "Seventy years and this is as far as you've gotten?"

"Yes, the sheer amount of work that had to be done was staggering. Plus, there were only a dozen top doctors who survived. They had to carry the teaching load upon their shoulders. Only within the last twenty years have they been able to teach at higher and higher levels. Now, we have many hundreds of other nova teachers to handle the young, elementary grades, and high school nova."

"Surely, you could bring everyone out of the tanks now and regrow their arms. We could then have a sizeable workforce," Tiana pointed out.

"Can't do that, as much as we might like. We are forbidden to harm a nova. It is against our programming."

"How is that harming them?" she retorted.

"We used every available method of obtaining the critically needed stem cells just to get everyone healed as they are today. There are hardly any of those supplies left. What few are being produced we are storing up so we'll be able to meet the demand of the new graduates, like yourselves. To obtain a large supply would require us to impregnate nova and then to siphon off the embryonic stem cells, killing the fetus. That, we are forbidden to do. Further, that is an order you nova cannot give us. Our programming will not permit us to carry it out. We could, on the other hand, kidnap normal homo sapiens sapiens women, impregnate them, kill their fetuses, and use their stem cells to cure our nova. Would you have us do that?"

"No, of course not," Tiana grumbled.

Fin spoke up, "There has to be more to all this, Eros. More reasons why you haven't revived all the nova. You could provide HIFRs like we all thought we had before, when, when," his voice faltered, "we were in there."

"Yes, there is other reason for not reviving most of the millions of nova. Are you sure that you wish to hear this?" Eros asked. All four nodded. "Very well then. Back on Aquila Prime, we had, as I said, a hundred twenty million nova under our care. Yes, a hundred twenty million HIFRs were built so the nova could live productive lives. Yet, nearly all of them did not. Some constantly wished for death. Many prided themselves on being about as ignorant as they could possibly be. They had no goals. That was acutely pointed out to us humaniform robots. It seems nova simply must have personal goals, much like our four laws, in order to survive. And yet, the majority of these nova had none at all. Their lives were virtually worthless to themselves and to other nova. The world was carried on the backs of a few thousand bright, highly intelligent nova."

"We discovered just because the parents of a child were brilliant that had little bearing on whether or not their child would in turn become brilliant as well. So literally, all Aquila Prime was being carried on the shoulders of a few thousand of the nova, including your Dr. Lelos Smith. Therefore, here on Beltazar-C, we took a better approach. Since so many of the nova here are following that same pattern, we are allowing those who are unfit nova to live out their lives playing the games that they desire in their virtual reality world. This way, they are happy and quite content. In turn, we keep their bodies alive, and they provide us with new babies from time to time. Additionally, we don't incur the terrific expense of providing them with HIFRs and such, nor does their well-being rest upon the shoulders of you, our prized nova and leaders of Beltazar-C. Humane all the way around."

Zia interrupted him. "So Dr. Lelos Smith doesn't know about all this? He doesn't know how badly damaged his body is? He doesn't know that he's living in a virtual world?"

"No, he does not. I believe it would kill him to learn of this. Instead, he is living a most productive and satisfying life, educating the best of the best, yourselves, who will soon make Beltazar-C a truly wonderful world. Do you understand now why you cannot go back to visit him?" Eros asked. He added, "If we should lose him, one or more of you would have to permanently go back into the virtual world and take over for him, educating the next generation of bright nova men and women." Zia thought that sounded more like a threat, but accepted it at face value.

Angelo then suggested, "So to run all this amazingly real virtual reality simulation, you must have a very large computer system."

"Indeed. It is huge. However, we humaniforms cannot take credit for its development. The original inhabitants of this world developed it to run their continuous virtual reality games. We only reprogrammed it for educational purposes. Those who choose to flunk out of school are allowed to reenter the old gaming worlds of their choice. They do not even know we or they exist any longer and are perfectly content to play away their lives," Eros answered.

Fin then asked point blank, "So why did you try to keep us from finding out about all this, the truth?"

"Our programming suggested the psychic shock of this discovery might harm you. Upon you depends the ultimate survival of all nova. We couldn't risk it. And yet, our worst fears have not come to pass," Eros answered.

"Well, that makes sense, Fin," Zia added. "We could well have been completely shocked."

"Okay, I suppose I can accept that, Eros. So you really do need me to come up with protection methods and Angelo to create a world shield?"

"Absolutely. We must be able to defend Beltazar-C and protect all the nova, should someone attack us again," the robot replied.

"Well, I can see my genetics research is going to be very vital, too," Zia added.

"Of course," Eros acknowledged her. "Now then, perhaps you could answer my questions. I have two. How was it that you were able to discover this Nova Center and get down here without being seen?"

Fin answered, "I made a tiny personal cloaking device. It only runs for two hours before needing a recharge, but it does work. I will continue its development. It could well be a useful tool to help prevent attacks on our world."

"Superb! Beyond our wildest hopes. You nova are indeed more than we ever hoped for," Eros attempted to sound enthusiastic. "And how is it that you avoided the headaches when you entered this center? I've turned the device off now."

"My doing," Angelo admitted. "It's part of my planetary defense shield. As you know, we have to have ways and means of protecting ourselves from someone attacking us with one of those Brunelli Enforcers. We're all wearing a miniature device, which prevents them from harming us, at least as long as the battery keeps its charge. I'm planning to integrate that into the planetary shield defense."

"Brilliant as well!"

Zia spoke up, "Say, if we have more babies, we want to

raise them ourselves. They are our family. Oh, and how does Dr. Smith keep up on all the latest developments?"

"We can cross that bridge when we come to it. We have hundreds of humaniforms out among some of the major world of both the ex-Imperium and the Federation. They relay new discoveries and findings back to us here. In turn, we insert them into his virtual reality via journal articles and such. It has been challenging to keep our top nova fully abreast in not only their fields of expertise but so many others as well," Eros answered.

"You mean to say that some of you are out there on other worlds?" Fin asked, rather surprised to hear this.

"Yes Fin. We humaniforms are very hard to distinguish from homo sapiens sapiens. We are able to blend in and obtain current information quite readily. So far in the past fifty years, not one of our humaniforms has ever been detected. I will grant you all full access to our extensive databases, via your computers."

"Thanks. That will be useful. One more question. So who does run all this, Beltazar-C?" Fin asked the burning question that had been festering in his mind for much of this discussion.

"Why as of now, you four do," Eros replied. "Of course, if you should give us what we consider a dubious order, we'll have to weigh it against the Four Laws. If it isn't in conflict with them, it will be carried out."

"Hey, I've got one more question, Eros. Have there been any accidents here in the tubs with the nova?" Angelo inquired. Mathematically, he expected there ought to have been quite a few, considering the sheer numbers being held in the tanks or tubs.

"Twenty-three, but those were in the early years. We have someone watching over them at all times and have had no accidents for the last twenty years. So yes, your nova, your people, are in good hands," Eros answered. "And I do believe it is close to your supper hour. Perhaps, we can continue this tomorrow, if you have more questions?"

"Thanks Eros. We best get going," Zia replied. The place gave her the creeps, but she didn't want to admit that. Not now.

An hour later, the four were back at their new home. While Zia fixed supper, during supper, and even while Fin washed the dishes, the group discussed openly what they'd learned. Even though the spy devices were still active, they calculated that Eros or whoever would be expecting them to discuss everything. It would have raised suspicions had they not. Still, they were careful not to say aloud anything that could be construed as anti-establishment. Further, they decided to keep their newfound telepathy skills to themselves.

Chapter 4 Breakout

Four close friends were battling it out with a giant battleship, playing a game called Take Down the Battleship. Each flew a small shuttle that had a strong defensive shield but a relatively weak canon. The behemoth had canons that made theirs look more like toothpicks than real weapons. They'd taken on this game some time back — had it been a year? The four had no sense of time. What's time, when you are having fun playing a game, eh? Their ages? Well twenty-one would do as far as they were concerned.

The unofficial leader of the Dirty Four, as they called themselves, was Captain Aldo Sandro, a handsome blonde, whose six foot wavy hair was as attractive as he was. Indeed, Aldo was quite vain about his long locks, continually refusing to have his HIFR put it up. "Hell, man, I can handle my hair just fine," he barked at his HIFR so frequently that the HIFR ceased doing anything to it beyond brushing it out, which he had to do rather frequently. Actually, all four HIFRs had the very same problem with their charges. His title was self-imposed. A leader ought to be called captain in his book. Always was, always would be. That the girls loved it also played a role in it.

His best buddy, Wing Commander Ciro Boldovino, likewise was a "pretty boy" with golden locks as well. He emulated Aldo with his hair, mostly because their women loved it as well, especially when the winds blew it out behind them, like "angels" the women had said. Hell, anything for the ladies. That was Ciro's motto.

Their "ladies" were Luciana Castrani and Michela Angelina. Both had nearly as long rich, thick hair, but theirs were coal black, shiny, and wavy. They might have been sisters, so much alike did they look. Beauty queens would be closer to the truth, since both aspired to be the top fashion models and beauty queens. Gorgeous, gregarious, highly attractive, highly sexual, these adjectives didn't begin to describe this pair. True, their faces and proportions were golden, perfect. Their thick lips demanded to be kissed. Yet, they were far more than mere beauty queens. They were also nearly as adept at Take Down the Battleship as their boyfriends. In fact, they were currently winning their wager with their "boys," Captain Aldo and Wing Commander Ciro. If they scored more points in this round, the boys would have to play their choice of the next game.

Flying in their four single-seat ships, they controlled the ship via foot controls, while handling the firing by their eyes. Where their eyes focused, their single canon pointed. A blink and the canon fired its paltry energy shot. Of course with fused feet and positioned en pointe, their foot controls were operated by various tiny lateral movements of their feet. By now, these four were highly skilled pilots. But Luciana and Michela wanted to drag the boys into another game of Top Fashion Models. "Hell," Luciana declared to Michela, our 'boys' could be runner ups. Of course, they won't be able to beat us out, but still, it'll be really sexy to have them come in third and fourth place." That had been their secret goal at the start of the game session this morning, if morning it truly was. They cared nothing for time; it was only a relative thing after all. Let the darn HIFRs handle time.

The giant battleship's canon sent streaks of energy flying in all directions, but the skill of these four pilots was no match for the gunners. The bigger the gun, the slower it moves and fires. Captain Aldo had drilled that into the women's heads. Now, they were putting it to use. Dodging this way and that at speeds so fast that one wondered how they could even maneuver their ships, the two headed for the forward hatch, one known weak point. Below it lay a direct line of sight to the nuclear reactor, which powered the battleship's gunnery. Adept at using averted vision, Michela moved into position using peripheral vision to guide the ship, while keeping her eyes focused on the hatch. She blinked and her canon fired, ripping open the weak hatch.

Sweeping and swerving, Luciana was right on her tail. The second the hatch flew off into space, she blinked, sending a blast from her small canon straight down into the open space. Instantly, both women kicked to the right with their right legs, sending their crafts sweeping off hard to the right. In their rear monitor, they saw a giant, brilliant mushroom cloud pouring out of the battleship. On their control panel, "Guns knocked out" appeared along with their current point totals. "Yahoo! Take that sucker!" Luciana barked over their ship-to-ship comm. "Back to base," she added.

"Hey, you two cheated somehow! That's not fair. Your score tops ours. We were about to kill it," Captain Aldo complained over his comm.

"We won, fair and square; at least this time we didn't cheat," Michela fired back. They heard Aldo grumbling, but he said nothing.

Luciana added, "Now, you boys have to live up to our bargain."

"Oh do we have to?" pleaded Ciro. "Do we really have to?"

Using a sickly sweet, teasing voice, Michela replied, "Of course you do, pretty boys." She knew well that only irritated them no end, but if Aldo was anything, he was a man of his word. All four were, for that matter, which is one of the reasons they'd become such tight friends over these past six years. Finding good players of your skill level and ones, which truly kept their word, had been very hard for each of them. Now that they'd found each other, they'd latched on tightly. Nothing could bust up their foursome. That the two men were extremely handsome and the two women uncommonly beautiful had only been icing on the cake, so to speak.

What of morals? These four took what they desired, when they desired it. Before they'd met, each had already laid so many other men and women that they'd lost count. However, true to their words, the four had been totally devoted to each other for the last six years now, never straying from the path. As the four headed to the docking bay where their HIFRs would be waiting for them, each knew that a romp in the bed was almost upon them. Every time they'd fought a successful battle, all four were so charged up that they simply had to have a good round of sex just to wind down. Quite why that was, none knew or even cared. It was terrific fun, highly enjoyable, perhaps more so than playing these games, well maybe.

Shortly, the four were helped out of their ships by their HIFRs, which they barely noticed. Luciana came up to Aldo, bumping him seductively, and said, "Now that was hot, buster, really hot! God, I'm so powered up right now. Hell, it's about to rip its way out of my pants!"

Aldo looked down at the crotch of her pants. "Shit! You ain't kidding, dearie. I'm hot too. Hurry the hell up or I'll mess my own pants." Luciana laughed, and the four headed to their house as rapidly as they could, which wasn't fast at all, considering they were walking on the tips of their toes. Still, as soon as they entered their home, all four ordered their HIFRs to rip their clothes off them as fast as possible. The robots complied, and the four plopped on their king sized bed, ready to satisfy their driven lust. An hour later, disentangling themselves from their hair mess, they headed off to get showered, redressed, and something to eat. For some reason, after an invigorating romp in the bed, they were always starving.

While their HIFRs were feeding them, Luciana said, "Okay, the next game is ours. We're going to win the Fashion Model Contest, so you boys have to look your very best."

"Hell, Luciana, you know you and Michela look a hundred times better than we do," Aldo complained hoping this would get her to yield on the wager. It didn't.

"Of course, we are prettier than you, but you both are prettier than most all the other women in the contest. We want you to win third and fourth place," Luciana replied.

"But we aren't women," Aldo tried his last card.

Luciana merely laughed. "Could have fooled us," she taunted. Aldo knew he was defeated. The only thing one could use to tell the sex of one of them was either their voice or watch where their urine came out. The latter wasn't part of the fashion model game, and the contestants were never allowed to speak, just walk the stage and model. So in fact, none could tell that he and Ciro were men, not women. As far as he and Ciro were concerned, that fact was nearly irrelevant. Everything was based upon what could the person do. All four prized that attitude above nearly everything else, except perhaps their philosophy about life. For these four, life was a game to be thoroughly enjoyed. The more sensations experienced the better. Life was anything but serious. There was enormous amount of fun out there to be had. One merely had to do it.

As Aldo once told the three, "Male? Female? Hell, it doesn't matter a dingo's kidney whether your piss comes out here or there or how deep your voice is. We're all the same, so make the best of it." The four had been doing just that for over six years now.

Showered and fed, it was time to be dolled up for the Fashion Model Contest. Luciana wore a dark red, velvet gown that had an open slit in the front, showing off her black nylon covered legs and matching red knee high boots. In the back, folds dragged about a foot over the floor. Her long black hair was perfectly arranged flowing in waves down her back. Michela wore a sparkling blue satin gown with a steep V cut displaying far too much of her endowment. Her gown also had a front slit so that her legs and matching boots would be quite visible.

They insisted that Aldo and Ciro wear identical cherry red satin gowns that also displayed quite visibly their nearly identical endowments, but theirs were very tight fitting down their legs, displaying every seductive curve of their bodies. Of course, this made walking even slower and more treacherous for the two men. "Slink and saunter. Move those hips, boys," Michela teased them.

"All right, all right. Let's make a deal here," Aldo tried to come up with a counter. "If Ciro or I win this darn fashion contest, then we want to be on top for the next ten times that we're having sex. No cheating and rolling over on us. We're going to be on top of you for the next ten times."

Without giving it much thought, Michela agreed. "Okay boys. You beat us, and we'll let you ride us ten times in a row." She and Luciana laughed. They'd never lost one of these fashion model contests yet.

Aldo whispered to Ciro, "It's just another game. Play along. Let's beat them at their own game. We can be as seductive as they are."

"Hey, I like that wager. Wish I'd of thought of it," Ciro whispered back.

Their HIFRs had to support them several blocks, as they walked to the building where the contest was being held. Once inside, thanks to the light wind, which had messed them up, the HIFRs had to re-brush out their hair and drape their hair perfectly across their backs. Then, the contest began. When their names were called, dozens of elegant looking women took their turns walking down the runway and back.

When the announcer called out "Aldo Sandro," he whispered to Ciro who would be next, "Let's make this a good one. Show these women a thing or two." He then proceeded to do his best to emulate the other women who'd gone before him, swaying his hips this way and that, looking as seductive as he could. Ciro did his best to emulate him.

After the last contestant had her turn, the votes were tallied, and the announcer announced the top four winners, rather shocking everyone, none more so than Luciana and Michela, who came in third and fourth. Aldo and Ciro came in first and second. All four walked out together to accept a round of applause and see their names and scores flashing on the results board, along with Game Over.

"God, I'm so hot I'm going to come in my panties," Aldo exclaimed. "Best get us home pronto! You two going to live up to your bargain?" he teased Luciana.

Luciana griped, "Damn you, Aldo. How'd you pull this one off? Don't answer that." She sighed and added, "Well, Michela, they out-foxed us this time, but they've got me so turned on, so damned hot, I won't mind them being on top."

Michela laughed. "Too late. Ciro's got me wet already." All four laughed, heading home as fast as they could manage. Their HIFRs knew what to expect and were ready to strip them out of their gowns the moment they entered their house. They didn't bother to remove their garter belts, hose, or heels. The four dove or rather fell onto their giant bed, relieving their exploding passions once more.

An hour later, the four lay in an entangled pile of bodies and blonde and black hair, fully satisfied and contented if only for the moment. Yet there was another factor that held these four so closely together. They had something else in common: telepathy. Hence, when they were making love, they slipped into a total rapport with each other and sometimes into rapport with the other couple as well. The latter had been the case this time, which accounted for the complete entanglement of bodies and hair.

As Aldo lay there contented and satisfied having been on top the whole time per their bargain, he noticed a flickering at the edge of the room. *I've seen that before.* Indeed, he had. More than a dozen times, he'd noticed such a phenomenon during the space battles. Considering how fast the action had been in those games, he'd just ignored it. He'd also seen it a number of times while he was having sex with either Luciana or Michela too. Here it was again.

This time, there wasn't anything pressing to handle. If Aldo was anything, he was quite the curious fellow. He focused on that anomaly and tried to enlarge it, rather pulling on it mentally, this way and that. Suddenly, Aldo found himself floating in a tank of warm water! His eyes took in everything in a frantic look, before he found himself back on the bed entwined with the others. He gasped, rousing Luciana. "What? Again?" she asked demurely. "Nine more times. If we hurry, we can get them all done today," she teased him. Being stuck on the bottom the whole time wasn't her idea of fair play. It severely restricted her "style" of lovemaking.

"I saw it again. I saw something else this time! Weirder than weirder. What the hell was that anyway?" he said, trying to sit up, but was too entangled to manage it. Their HIFRs took this as a signal to help undo the mess of bodies and hair, which they promptly did. Soon the four were sitting up on their bed with their backs against the headboard and their long hair flowing over their fronts and down their legs.

"Focus gang. I'll send you what I saw. Be prepared for the ultimate in weirdness," he advised. Each of these four also had an uncanny ability to see a scene for a split second and then be able later to look it over in detail. They had to, in order to be so darn successful in their battle action games, where the speed of play was almost unbelievably fast.

Aldo focused his attention on the momentary glimpse

that he'd had, while the other three viewed what he was seeing in his mind. All four were taken by complete surprise. *That's you, Aldo,* Ciro thought and the other three picked up his thought, *Isn't it?*

Sure looks like him and that's you, Luciana, Michela thought.

How can I be there and here at the same time? Luciana thought, very confused.

But what in the galaxy is that? We've something on our heads, don't we? Aldo thought.

Tubes. Feeding tubes? Breathing tubes? Piss tubes? thought Ciro, his mind racing with possibilities.

So we aren't here, but there? the confused Luciana added, trying to make some remote sense of what she was seeing.

If we aren't really here but really there, then this isn't real, but it seems real enough, but then maybe it isn't real after all. I've been seeing these fuzzy patches at the edges of my vision from time to time, Aldo thought, as he continued to maintain his full attention on the single image that he'd taken during that instant of time.

Hey, I've seen those too, Aldo, Luciana added. *So if this isn't real and that there is, what in a dingo's kidney are we doing here? Maybe there's more excitement, sensuousness, and fun in that place. We should check it out.*

She's got a point. If this isn't real and that is, we should be there enjoying the real bodies, don't you all think? Michela sent, growing a bit excited with this new prospect for real entertainment.

Aldo countered, *Good point, Michela. But let's think this through. Something must be keeping us here and maintaining the pretty darn believable reality alive for us. Can't be the tubes. Ciro's probably right about their purposes, so it has to be that small thing around our heads.*

Coolest! So are we going there to check it all out? asked Luciana.

Everyone was in complete agreement that they should. Captain Aldo took charge. *We need a plan. We'll all jump there. I think I can pull us down to those bodies. The first thing we have to do is to knock those things off our heads so we don't get pulled back in here, wherever here is. Then, get the tubes out of us and get out of the tub things.*

But what about those strange people-like creatures in the background? asked Michela.

Huh, don't know. Zap'em maybe. Knock them down. We can slide ourselves across the floor, get out of that place, and see what the world looks like. If we can take out a battleship, what's a couple of small folks, eh? Aldo countered. *Main thing is we gotta act fast, really fast, to get those things off our heads or we're gonna get zapped back here real fast, like I just was.*

Hey, practice our foot moves, Luciana suggested. She began sweeping a leg up to her head, pretending to knock the thing off her head. Aldo also thought she was on to something here. Practice was always a key ingredient to their successes. Soon, all four were practicing make a sweeping foot move. Figuring they had worked it out well enough, Aldo thought, *Everyone ready?* Heads nodded. He looked at their very excited and alert faces, and he knew that they were just as keyed up about this new adventure as he was. *Love you guys,* he sent and focused his full attention. There was that fuzzy patch once more. He acted, pulling all four of them through what appeared to be a rip in the fabric of space and time.

At that point, events happened at blinding speed. Aldo found himself within his body in the tub. His foot swept up and collided with the V-mask around his head, knocking it off. In that instant, he felt the grip of the other reality vanish. In his next move, the tubes were out of his mouth and nose, and in the same motion, he rolled up and over the glass side of the tub, slopping water and himself onto the floor, which was cold. He heard similar splashed nearby, and just knew and had faith that his three companions were equally as fast as he. He didn't even have the slightest thought otherwise. They'd proven themselves to him countless times.

There were four of these shorter people in this room filled with hundreds of other tubs with pairs of bodies lying in them. Aldo felt for the minds of the four people as he pushed against the side of the tub to get into a sitting position.

Nothing! *Not alive!* he sent to his three friends without wasting any thought or effort on the matter.

Luciana found that for a moment after she'd gotten her body out of the tub that she wasn't exactly in it. That these small people weren't alive clicked somewhere in the dark recesses of her mind. She concentrated and appeared just behind one of their heads, which did look human enough, but she sensed no mind, only machinery. At once, she took over control of its various servomotors. *Hey, look at me! I'm playing around with this robot-thing.* She had it jumping up and down while flailing its arms about as though swatting flies.

Hey, me too, added Michela, who attempted to duplicate Luciana's actions.

Take them out so they can't get to us! Aldo ordered, trying to regain control of the situation, figuring he still was their captain.

Both Luciana and Michela obeyed, quickly finding a power-down switch and activating it by using one of the robot's fingers. They then did the same to the other two robots, since neither Aldo nor Ciro was able to handle them.

"Floor is damned cold, gang. Come on. Let's slide out of here. Where's the damned boots when you need them. Hey, this is kind of a neat sensation, sliding along! Try it, gang," Aldo called out now that the robots had been turned off.

"Way coolest, Aldo!" Luciana declared, using her legs to push herself across the cold floor on her wet butt. "Oh, I'm getting excited. Don't suppose we could take a sex break just now, could we?"

"Only if I'm on top. We still have six more times to go," Aldo called out, continuing to slide across the floor towards what looked like a hallway.

"Crap. Floor's too cold for me to be on the bottom, dear. Hey, you can't hold us to that bargain because it was made on those other bodies that we had! These are new ones," Luciana pointed out.

"She's right, Aldo. You can't. These are new bodies, just as good as the old ones, maybe better, so that bet applies to those other bodies, not these," Michela argued on Luciana's behalf.

"Dingo's kidneys! Okay, point taken. Let's see if we can find the rest of this world. It's got to be warmer than this floor. Hey look! An elevator. Come on gang, hurry up," Aldo yelled. He slid up to it, got into a sitting position, and then got onto his knees. Using his nose, he pushed the only visible button on the control panel. A moment later, the elevator door opened up, and the four didn't hesitate one second. All four scooted inside as fast as possible. Inside and still on his knees, Aldo pressed the top-most button. As the elevator began rising, the other three emulated him and got themselves onto their knees, dragging their sopping wet hair between their legs.

"This is far more exciting than playing Take Down the Battleship or whatever you called it, Aldo. Good going on finding us this new and superior game," Luciana validated him.

He smiled. "Thanks, dear. After all, I'm your captain still." All four chuckled and the door opened. Out the four went, finding themselves in a dimly illuminated, but empty room. Sunlight provided the light, and the air felt warm and clean. "Super great. Come on; there's a doorway. Bet it leads to this new and exciting world for us to explore," Aldo called out.

"Right behind you, big boy," Luciana teased him. All four continued to crawl across the floor on their knees with their long, wet hair trailing behind them. "Hope we don't have to wash our own hair though," she added noticing how dirty Aldo's was becoming.

Bringing up the rear, Michela called out, "Hey, we've invented another way to play mop the floor!" Ciro laughed and nearly fell over.

Aldo was the first to reach the door. Already he had worked out that on his knees he was tall enough to use his mouth to turn the doorknob. By the time Luciana joined him, he had it in his mouth and was moving his head to the left to get it to turn. She saw what he was doing and pivoted to get her toes into the crack that appeared. Once he let go and backed up a bit, she shoved the door open, and the four crawled out into the heat of the August summer.

"Wow! What have we here? A whole city? Super cool!"

Maricela exclaimed.

"Boy, we sure can have a lot of fun here, can't we?" Ciro added. All four stopped and looked all around, seeing many buildings, some trees, streets, and even a few more robots. Several were coming towards them. One in particular looked like he was somehow in charge of the others, who seemed to give way to him.

"Where have we landed? In a robot heaven or something?" asked Michela.

"Is there even such a thing?" Ciro wanted to know.

"Must be, since all we are seeing are robots," Luciana declared.

"Hey, robots are supposed to obey us humans. Let me handle this," Aldo insisted. "If it goes south, take them out."

The robot man-like machine halted before the foursome. "Hello. My name is Eros. This is most unfortunate and totally unexpected. You are out of your tanks."

"Hey, we're not prisoners. We're humans. You robots have to obey us," Aldo spoke very authoritatively and decisively, as though he were in charge here. "I'm Captain Aldo. My crew. We demand you take us to your human leaders."

"Right now," Luciana added, determined somehow to get a word in as well.

"Pronto," Ciro added, seeing that Luciana had beaten him to it.

"Precisely," Michela spoke up, annoyed that the other two had beaten her to it.

Eros attempted his best human-like laugh. "Of course. It is some miles to their home. Do you wish to crawl there or would you prefer we carry you to the nova leaders?"

"Well, since you put it that way, we'd be obliged if you'd carry us," Aldo replied, "since we seem to be missing our boots at this time."

At the same time, Zia, Tiana, Fin, and Angelo each had a HIFR enter their lab, delivering a message from Eros. "Head to your home immediately to help with a dire nova emergency." Thus, the four arrived there in time to see Eros leading four other HIFRs, who were carrying four naked nova, who appeared to have somehow come out of the tanks.

Eros began, "Ah, good timing. It seems that we have just had four nova break out of their tanks and into the real world."

Seeing the very surprised looks on the nicely dressed women, Aldo spoke up, "Right. And there's no way you're putting us back into those tub things. We can escape any time we want to. We're here to stay and enjoy our world. It is our world too, you know." Actually, Aldo knew no such thing! He was just as disoriented and lost as his three companions. However, these four had not become such hot shots by letting a little thing such as this be a barrier for them. Not ever.

Luciana barked, "He's right. We can, and we'll do just that if you put us back there."

"Er, I don't think that's going to happen," Fin attempted to take charge. "I'm Dr. Serafino Vitalli. My wife, Dr. Annunziata Botocelli. Dr. Cristiana Vitano and her husband, Dr. Angelo Landini. And you all are?" he said and asked, curiously. He sent to his group, *This is sure unexpected. Eros said this couldn't happen.*

He and his companions were quite surprised to hear in their minds, *Well it did happen. So deal with it. We're here to stay!* Then, Aldo spoke up. "I'm Captain Aldo Sandro. Wing Commander Ciro Boldovino. Fashion models Luciana Castrani and Michela Angelina."

Fin recognized the names. "Eros, aren't these the names in that file you gave me to study?"

"Indeed Dr. Fin. They are," Eros answered.

"What files?" Aldo barked. "You have files on us? We must be really important then," he declared.

Fin replied with a smile, "You four have the top scores in the Take Down the Battleship Game. Very impressive. I've been studying your moves to help plan our defenses in case of an attack. You four are really good."

"Naturally we are!" Luciana declared with some authority.

Eros spoke up. "We should be practical right now. They need a bath and some clothes. Would you like to take charge of them for now or would you prefer I send along four HIFRs to assist you, doctors?"

"Hey, we prefer real people, if you don't mind," Aldo declared, trying to sound as convincing as he could. These four had the silly arm appendages and could take care of them for the moment anyway. He was a bit tired of robot helpers just now, seeing as how they had been keeping them prisoners. Besides, he wanted to know all about this real world and these four strangers who seemed to be in charge of the world.

Zia laughed. "Sure we can handle them for now. Later, if they want HIFRs, we can let you know, but please carry them inside to our bathrooms. Better yet, since this is a quadraplex, put one in each bathroom. That way we can give them all a bath at one time."

The robots did just that. The four divided up, with the women bathing the two women, while the men handled Aldo and Ciro. By mutual agreement, everyone decided to hold off on questions until they were bathed and clothed. Then, the eight could sit down and talk everything over. That suited Aldo's group, who were now cold, dirty, and in desperate need of clothes and boots in particular. Without them, about all they could do was crawl on their knees, which had already taken a beating.

Chapter 5 Exchanging Viewpoints

Zia held onto the side of the bathtub now filled with warm water and Luciana. Slowly, she bent down and rested one knee on the floor and then the other. With her fused en pointe feet and the boots, getting into a kneeling position required some care. She flipped her hair behind her and began to bathe Luciana. Both women were trying hard to obey the "save the discussions for later" request so everyone could participate. Still, Zia couldn't help herself, not completely. "Luciana, you and Michela are the most beautiful women that I've ever seen."

Luciana smiled, replying coyly, "Of course we are. We're top fashion models too, but you are rather pretty yourself. You're more than welcome to hop in here with me. We can do it here in the tub. That's a whole lot of fun, you know, doing it in a tub, but a bit awkward though. Wait! Was it even real? It felt real, very sensuous, titillating in the extreme, but then I guess it wasn't real. But if it wasn't real, then I wonder what real sex is like? Come on; I need to find out, Zia. Hop in the tub, and let's do it right now!" Zia flushed. "Come on; I can sense you're quite aroused with me as I am with you. Let's do it now."

"Er, well I'm married now. To Fin. We pledged to be faithful to each other and not do it with others without first getting the other's permission. We best wait. Besides, I'm supposed to get you cleaned up and find something that you can wear," Zia explained, hoping the bulge in her own panties wasn't that visible. She added, "We all were in the tanks too, but we got out by studying hard and getting our doctoral degrees."

"Oh, bookworms. Well, that's okay for some, I supposed. Say, you must have had sex out here in the real world too. How does it compare to sex in that other thing, you know, where we were?" Luciana asked, curious and greatly desirous of knowing anything more about this key detail of life.

"About the same, really, though it's way more fun now

that we have our arms," Zia admitted. She felt a little uncomfortable talking about her most private feelings with a total stranger, even if she was the most attractive woman she'd ever seen. "Well no, it is actually a whole lot better out here because we go into a kind of rapport we were never able to do in that virtual world."

Luciana appeared shocked. "What? You mean you didn't have close rapport while you were in it? No telepathy with each other? Oh, how utterly awful! You poor thing. Well, I'm glad you've got it now. We four can't imagine life without it, you know." Zia now sensed it wasn't an appearance of shock. She really was taken aback and felt for her.

With the water now drained out of the tub, Zia began drying her off. However, even this was arousing Luciana, much to Zia's embarrassment. Now just wasn't the time for such indulgences. "Okay, we've got the electrostatic dryer over here. I doubt if I can carry you over to it, so see if you can crawl on your knees," Zia asked. She then helped her up to sit on the fancy machine.

Luciana said, "The HIFRs used to do this for us, but I much prefer your touch, Zia." She smiled very seductively at her, quite unabashed at just how obvious her maleness now appeared. Luciana was turned on and hot, more than ready to take Zia or have Zia take her, but she also knew neither was going to happen, not just now. *Later, Luciana, and you'll have her! She's as turned on as I am. Bide my time.*

The electrostatic dryer was a marvelous robotic invention. It not only dried the nova's very long hair, but using the electrical charge, it untangled even the worst tangles, separating each hair from all others, as it raised their hair upwards to its full length. When dried and released, their hair was full and easily managed, and all the while, flooding their hair's neurons with very sensuous sensations.

"Please, don't put it up," Luciana said, when Zia turned the machine off and her beautiful black hair dropped down perfectly over her back. "We all just hate having it up. Hair should be long and full and appreciated, not wound up into some tight ball, trying to hide. Full, rich, and flowing. I'm so glad to see all four of you like it this way too."

Zia giggled. "Yes, we do. Oh, here comes a HIFR with clothes."

A robot entered, "Eros gave me your measurements and preferred styles, Luciana. I've brought a copy of the last gown you were wearing. Zia can take you to the store next door where you can obtain any others that you prefer."

Zia replied, "Thanks. That's convenient." The robot nodded and proceeded to dress Luciana, just as the HIFR had always done in her virtual reality world, so she didn't mind this at all. She now wore a red satin gown with matching boots. Zia then adjusted her hair, standing back and looking her over, "You look stunning, Luciana. Let's go see if the others are done. Everyone's got lots of questions, I'm sure."

"Thanks. Zia, why aren't you wearing a red satin gown like mine? Instead, you are wearing such a drab grey skirt," Luciana asked, rising to follow her out into the shared commons area.

"Professional woman's outfit. I'm a doctor and ought to look the part, but I do sometimes dress up, Luciana," Zia replied.

Soon all eight were there, four in their grey professional women's garb, four in their rather exotic gowns. Fin sent to all, *This place is bugged by the robots. They do not know about our telepathic abilities, and we don't want them to know. Also, we don't entirely trust them, so if you have something to say that might be sensitive, use telepathy. Okay?* The others nodded.

One by one, the four introduced themselves again and described their fields of expertise. Aldo and his companions reciprocated, while the four admired Luciana and Michela, almost unable to take their eyes off these two beauty queens. Then, Fin took charge and told the four about themselves, how they had spent their years getting a solid education in the areas that most interested them. That done, he told them what they'd learned about the real world of Beltazar-C. That took quite some time.

Aldo interrupted him. "You mean you four are the only nova besides us that are out here in the real world? Dingo's kidneys! This is beyond awful. It's inhumane! It's — well I don't know what all it is, but it's bad!"

"We know," Fin agreed and continued his explanations. He felt it was vitally important for these four rather chaotic individuals really to understand the situation they were facing.

When he finished, Zia put in, "I'll see if we can get Eros to permit us to have your arms regrown too."

"What? Please don't!" Aldo replied somewhat aghast. "We're all just perfect the way that we are. We love our bodies, so full of sensations and all. Oh, I see what you mean. We did have HIFRs, but we only let them dress us, feed us, and bathe us."

"Hey, they did the laundry and cooking and kept the bed made," Michela interjected. "You know, the mundane things, so we could just pretty much do whatever we wanted to do all the time. That's the way it should be, right? Life is fun, full of wondrous sensations to be enjoyed, to be experienced, and shared. So, Zia, we have never really needed or wanted those extra arm appendages that you and the HIFRs have. I bet they get in your way lots, and now you have to do all the things the HIFRs used to do for you."

Zia realized that since these four had never had arms, they had no idea of what they were missing. Based on what Michela and Luciana had said, she had an idea of how she could change their minds, but also thought that she ought to wait and see if Eros would agree to allow them to have their arms regrown.

"So what's going to happen to us now?" Aldo asked. "No way are we going back into those tubs."

"You four can live here in this quadraplex," Fin answered. "Zia and I live in that one. Angelo and Tiana live opposite us in that one. You four can divide up and take the other two."

"Well, that's reasonable, but we four always stick together," Aldo countered. "So we can live here. That's a good start, but are you going to be helping us with things or are we going to have to use the HIFRs as we used to?"

"Good question, Aldo. We're at work most of the day. I don't know. Let us check with Eros and get back to you on that one," Fin answered. "The real problem is what do we do with you four? I mean, we four are the only nova out here, and we have enormous responsibilities to get things ready for all the newcomers who will be graduating in less than a year. Right now, the robots can't even defend our world, should someone attack us like they did on Aquila Prime."

Luciana spoke up, slightly annoyed, "Hey look. We aren't stupid or anything, just because we dropped out of their silly educational programs and dove into all the fun and exciting games, even if they weren't actually real. We're not just some pretty faces with absolutely perfect bodies — well, we are that, but I mean we're not stupid or nothing."

Aldo interrupted her. "She's right. It's obvious that this world, our world, has got some real problems. Dingo's kidneys! Mega problems. Only eight real people around with millions in water tanks living in some dreamworld. I can't imagine a worse problem. Gang, we're simply going to have to lend these four a hand."

Luciana and Michela laughed. She added, "But Aldo dearest, we don't have any hands to lend them." Aldo and Ciro broke into a belly laugh. Even the serious four cracked a smile.

After calming down, Aldo continued, "We are simply going to have to help them, gang. We've got to get this world all fixed up, so everyone can play and enjoy themselves and be safe from outside attacks. This is probably as good a playground as any, this planet I mean. Obviously, there's plenty of food around, clothes, and certainly buildings. Physically, there's a whole world infrastructure here, just minus the most important ingredient: people, us. And we do know the so called normals out there in the universe hate us. Remember your history lessons before we dumped their educational programs? We can't just abscond with a transport and go find another world on which to play and have fun. We'd likely just get ourselves killed or something. No, we are going to have to help get this world going properly."

"That sounds like work and no fun," Michela pouted.

Ciro countered, "No dearie, we make work fun, pleasureful, and sensuous too." He winked at her.

Aldo changed the subject and asked, "Can't we get your bright ones out now and have them go to the real University?"

"Nope. The few top teachers are not only really old, but their bodies are in horrible condition, massive radiation burns," Zia answered. "I was shocked to see what Dr. Lelos Smith really looked like. He doesn't even know how awful his real body actually is. We can't just bring all them out now. Besides, there are no graduate teachers other than these really old ones. In time, I suppose we're going to have to start teaching other grad students ourselves, but right now, that's out. We already thought of that."

"Is all that knowledge really that important?" asked Michela.

"Look, it was knowledge that allowed our ancestors to develop these humaniform robots who have saved us from the nuclear attack and got us this far along," Fin countered. "There is more to life than just yourselves." He was somewhat annoyed with these seemingly self-centered individuals.

Aldo soothed things over a bit, "Of course, there is. Until now, though, you have to see our point of view. We assumed the universe was taking care of itself rather nicely, you see. People were happy. Plenty of food to go around. People had nice friends. We formed our own group and have done well. The world around us was in perfect shape. There were not any impending calamities that we could see. So if all is well with the Universe, why not be happy and enjoy ourselves to the fullest?"

Luciana broke in, "But Aldo, that was a total lie, a complete fabrication, a wonderful illusion, but wholly untrue."

"I know, pussy cat, I know. I'm trying to tell them how we looked at it. Out here, Dingo's Kidney, it's bad, really unimaginably bad," Aldo countered. "As I see it, Dirty Four, we don't have any choice. We are going to have to help set things right. If we don't, we won't have any world on which to play."

"Point taken, Captain Aldo," Ciro admitted, a bit reluctantly. "Still, we darn well better make this fun. You're not going to order us to get those arm appendages are you?"

He ignored Ciro's question. "First thing, we have to get some of our people out of those tanks."

"Why? How are they going to help if they have no education, no skills?" asked an annoyed Fin.

66

Because lots of them have telepathy like we do, and it's only a matter of time before more of them get wise to the illusion, as I did. That's why, Aldo sent to everyone, remembering their caution not to mention telepathy.

What? More of the nova in the tanks have this ability too? asked a very surprised Zia.

Lots of them do, but most are all in just a few places. They are in small groups, just like us. Some are in your education programs as well.

Zia pressed him, *How many? Any idea of their numbers?*

Oh maybe a thousand or thereabouts. We keep running across them in the games.

Zia protested, *But there are a hundred million nova in the tanks. Only a thousand have telepathy? Now this is a mystery. One person in a hundred thousand having telepathy goes against all of the normal odds of this happening, which is more like one in ten billion. Something must be causing it, and I ought to find out. Maybe it was one of the genetic cures that caused it in some nova.*

Just then, Eros joined them. "Excuse me, but perhaps our four newcomers should visit the shop next door and pick out a number of new outfits, while I would like a few words with you four." A HIFR was waiting to lead Aldo and company to the store.

"Way cool, Aldo. Let's," declared Luciana, eager to see the available selections of gowns. She fully intended somehow to seduce Zia. Hence, the four followed the HIFR out of the house.

Eros got down to business as soon as the front door shut. "I've gone over the data on their escape. It seems somehow they completely shut down four of the worker robots, who look after the nova in the tank. Two even claimed that their bodies were doing strange motions and that they couldn't stop it from happening. Frankly, I'm very worried about these four nova. They have little education and have spent most of their young lives playing games, though I must admit their solution to destroying the battleship was quite inventive and works. They seem to want only to play out here.

Obviously, we can't have that, not with so very much at stake."

Zia had to make a decision. Whether she would have made the same decision had she had more time to reflect isn't known. "Eros. There's something else going on here, something of potentially enormous importance. Sir, it's telepathy. These four possess it. Further, they have told us there are about another thousand of the nova in the tanks who also have it, including some of our grad students as well. They used their telepathic skills in part to escape from the virtual world, exiting through some slight flaw in the illusionary room. As Aldo explained, during that confusing change from their virtual world into the real world of the tank, they were able to take over control of the robots, shutting them down. Sir, if these four could do this, what is to prevent the other thousand or so from doing it too? Besides, telepaths are exceedingly rare. Here, they are occurring nearly a hundred thousand times more than one might expect. Something must be causing this, perhaps something in the genetic cures. I simply have to investigate this fully. It's terrifically important. Telepaths are so very rare."

"Well, this explains much!" Eros replied, very much impressed with this discovery, and in an electronic burst relayed this news on up the lines. "Yes, this does present quite an important advance. Long have we desired our nova to possess such powerful skills that would so greatly enhance their abilities and survival potentials. By all means, research this fully. Find the cause, if it is possible. This also puts our four new arrivals in quite a different light. What are we to do with them?"

"Well, we told them the whole story, and they want to help out, to make Beltazar-C a good place for everyone to live," Fin answered. "But they seem pretty adamant in not wanting their arms regrown. If they don't, I'm not sure just what real help they can provide. Now, if they had their doctorates, they could have their HIFRs carry out physical actions under their direction, but sadly they don't."

"Agreed," Eros commented, his circuits rapidly tracing down a number of potential future tracks, trying to reach a judgment call that would be optimum. None of the choices seemed particularly fruitful. At last, he suggested, "Perhaps for the time being, each of you could take one on as your lab assistant." Having no viable alternatives, the four agreed.

Zia asked, "If they change their minds and want to get their arms regrown, can they?"

"Since they are telepaths, yes they can. If they weren't, then it would be best for everyone if they didn't," Eros answered dryly. "I should go and check on the central programming of the virtual worlds and see if these tiny flaws can be somehow corrected before more damage is done."

Zia didn't like his term for the freeing of the nova. Certainly, they weren't "damage." Wisely, she didn't comment, and Eros left them. Shortly and now in high spirits, the four returned, along with four HIFRs lugging numerous bags.

"Way greatest, Zia! We rather bought one of each. Too hard to decide," Luciana explained. "Besides, we ought to have a descent wardrobe, so we don't have to wear the same thing twice each week."

Aldo added, "We've decided we'll move into this one section of the quadraplex. We don't want to be split up, you see. The HIFRs will help us so you don't have to bother with such mundane things."

Zia replied, "Okay. Fine with us. By the way, I had to tell Eros about your telepathy. He's given me permission to research this and see how such huge numbers have come about. He now sees you four as being quite valuable assets to our world. So you are all going to be very safe and secure here."

"'Bout time," Luciana retorted. "We're powerful. Come on, HIFR; let's get my new wardrobe sorted out. Got some really sexy dresses here, Zia." *I can't believe that you have six identical grey skirt outfits in your closet! Live it up a little, Zia,* she sent. Zia flushed.

After the four newcomers left them, HIFRs following along, Fin said, "We're just going to have to find a way to convince them that having arms will be more fun. What am I supposed to do with Aldo in my lab? I might as well just have a HIFR like I do now sometimes."

Zia bit her lip and then asked, "So are we all in

agreement that they need to get their arms regrown?"

Everyone nodded and Angelo commented, "Absolutely. I don't want to play HIFR for them. I've got too much valuable work on my plate already."

Zia sighed, "Okay, I think I know a way, but Fin, I'll need your permission. Luciana wants me to bed her. Maybe if Tiana and I show Luciana and Michela a good time, they can see it's so much better this way."

Fin and Angelo chortled. Fin teased her, "You think you are the only one so attracted to those two beauties? They are beyond hot! But sure, have at it, if you think doing that will help convince them, unless you want Angelo or me to have at them." He grinned mischievously.

Angelo chuckled. "The way to a man's heart is through his woman." They all laughed at that jest. Zia and Tiana left them, heading to their bedrooms to change into something more seductive than their professional woman's dress. A short while later and dressed in her most revealing red gown and no panties, Zia headed off to find Luciana.

"Hi Luciana. I see the HIFR has your new clothes sorted and hung up."

"Oh hi. Wow. Now you are talking, honey bunch. Mucho bettero," Luciana exclaimed, genuine in her feelings. Zia raised her gown a bit. "Oh, even better." She moved over closer to Zia, batting her eyes slightly. A wry smile creased her lips.

Zia gently reached out and ran her long nails down Luciana's gown-covered left breast. "Oh, now that's really hot. Are you ready for some real fun?" Luciana whispered. "You better be, because you've got me hard already." Zia nodded, and slowly and as seductively as she could manage, she undressed Luciana. A very enjoyable hour later, she'd used her hands and nails in every way that she could imagine, including holding her tightly and even scratching her back. As the two women lay side by side enmeshed in their long black hair, Luciana admitted, "Wow. We never knew that arms and hands could be so utterly sensuous. Maybe we should reconsider it."

"You can have them if you want them," Zia whispered in reply.

Over breakfast the next morning, Captain Aldo suggested, "We've changed our minds about having arms regrown. Strange, we never knew we lost them in the first place, so regrown seems the wrong word."

Fin answered, "Excellent Aldo. I'll see if we can't get the process going today."

By noon, all four were in the medically induced comas. The genetic cure had begun on them. In three more days, they would be finished and able to become independent of HIFRs. As far as Fin was concerned, then they'd perhaps be able to lend them a hand.

Of course, just as soon as the four regained consciousness, they absolutely insisted on bedding each other, just to try out their new arms, hands, and nails. Two hours later, four flushed companions finally joined the others, ready to lend a hand.

Luciana and Michela joined Zia, who was doing her best to determine just how come there were so darn many telepaths among the nova in the tanks. Aldo and Ciro teamed up with Fin to help work out ways of defending their world from another attack. However, before the day was done, all four were complaining about their legs and knees.

"It's like our legs have gone all soft and mushy on us, not like they used to be before," Luciana complained.

"But that wasn't real, this is," Michela pointed out.

"We were the same way. You need to go on longer and longer walks each day and build up your legs muscles and knees," Zia explained. The four heartily agreed and began doing just that, but it was three weeks before they were happy about their legs again.

Meanwhile, Aldo and Ciro made another very startling set of discoveries. While helping Fin, a very heavy piece of equipment needed to be moved. Without thinking about it, Aldo and Ciro lifted it up and moved it. Then, both gasped, realizing they'd done something they shouldn't have been able to do. Fin was quite startled, having sent off for some HIFRs to move it for them.

"Dingo's kidneys! How the devil did we manage to do that, Ciro?" Aldo exclaimed, quite startled. "Are we some kind of supermen?"

"Can we do it again? Let's see if I can do it alone, captain," Ciro declared. He concentrated and did just that, but he forgot actually to put his hands on the machinery!

"Hey, you weren't even touching it!" Aldo protested.

"Oh, duh! Oh, it did lift up and move," Ciro justified.

Soon, the two were lifting and moving all sorts of pieces of equipment in Fin's lab. Fin grew so annoyed with them, that he began to put things back where they belonged, without thinking about it. Aldo noticed him and said, "Hey Fin. Now you're doing it too! Isn't this just the greatest?" It was Fin's turn to be stunned.

By evening, all eight knew about this discovery and had attempted to do it themselves. Around the supper table, they began to classify what their new skills were. They decided on "levitation" and "telekinesis" for starters.

"So it's not just telepathy that we have, but far, far more!" Zia exclaimed. "Gang, we just have to get to the root cause of our incredible powers and soon."

Zia had been going over all the genetic cures and known results looking for any possible clues. She knew neither Luciana nor Michela could do this. Therefore, she had them locating the telepathic nova in their tanks, drawing up a list of their names and what they were doing in their virtual world.

"Hey, look at this, Zia darling," Luciana called out. Ever since their romp in her bed, Zia was now her "darling." Zia came over to see. "Michela and I have got them all worked out now. As you can see, they are all within these ten centers here, all close together, this clump here. One includes all your fancy grad students."

"Excellent work," Zia praised the two, who beamed, certain they were not dummies. "I wonder what is unique about these ten centers that is different from all of the many others?"

"Give us time to find out, boss darling," Luciana teased her, flirting a little with her.

A couple of hours later, Luciana reported, "Well, for one thing, all of their food is coming from Garden Plot 12, except for the protein."

"Interesting. I wonder what's so special about this plot? I best have Eros take us there so we can get some soil, water, and air samples," Zia suggested.

The next day, a HIFR drove the three women out to Garden Plot 12 in an electric car. "Wow. It's pretty big," Zia exclaimed, casting her eyes over acres and acres of automated garden. To the HIFR, she said, "Wait here. We have to go take samples. She and Luciana set about collecting dozens of soil samples, while Michela took ten water samples from the irrigation system.

"Looks like good black dirt to me," Luciana said, scooping up another small sample with a trowel and sliding some of it into a small bottle. "How can you tell if there is something in the soil that's causing all this?" Zia promised to explain it in detail once they were back in her lab.

Once there several hours later, she explained the use of the gas chromo-spectra analyzer, while the machine analyzed their air samples. Nothing. In fact, the air here was almost totally free of all contaminates found on most all space-faring worlds. Zia then put some of the soil samples under a microscope, projecting the images upon a big monitor so the three could see the images very well and clearly. She pointed out all of the usual components of the rich, loamy soil, including various microbes that were visible. Nothing unusual here, except that it was extremely rich soil, highly productive. The robots had done a superior job cultivating the soil for maximum productivity. She moved on to chemical analysis, and Tiana joined her. Together, they performed the standard batch of analyses, which again yielded nothing of significance. Herbicides were much lower than they had been when Tiana had discovered their elevated levels.

Tiana ran her hands over her face, pushing back her long blonde hair. As convinced as Zia was that there was something in the soil that was causing their highly unusual telepathic and mental skills, she was frustrated. "All right, all right," she huffed. "There's one last thing we can do, an elemental composition analysis."

As she began operating the machine, she explained what she was doing to Luciana and Michela, while Zia listened in. A half hour later, they stared at the alarming results. "Well, this is certainly weird. The concentrations of germanium and silicon are zillions of times above normal soil levels," Tiana pronounced. "This counts as really anomalous, Zia. We should test the other random samples and see if this one is just a fluke."

Hours later, Tiana had confirmed the initial findings. All the samples had extremely high levels of germanium in them and to a lesser extent, silicon. The next day, Zia had Eros obtain some samples from all the many other farming plots across Beltazar-C, while she dug into the past history of this garden plot. However, Eros was able to account for the strange abundances of those two elements. "When we first came here, it was a computer chip dumping ground, a garbage pit. Our robots thoroughly ground everything up and reconstituted the soil. Homo sapiens sapiens databases do not list any harmful effect of these elements in the soil used to grow food, at least not in these concentrations."

The four women spent two more weeks analyzing all the hundreds upon hundreds of other soil samples, but found no elevated levels of either germanium or silicon in them. Hence, the only anomalous feature between any of the many garden plots was this single one with the abnormally high amounts of germanium and to a much lesser extent silicon. Zia's own research also yielded no hint that either of these two had any harmful effects on humans.

However, unknown to the eight, Eros and his boss Thanos had some suspicions. They were very familiar with another heavy metals-deficient world, Ashford-5. That world had abnormally high levels of these two elements. In fact, one of that world's moons was almost entirely composed of these two elements. A major Imperium fuel refinery was on that moon. Plus, the robots also knew that some humans from that world not only possessed telepathy, but other secret and mysterious powers. More importantly, Thanos had hatched a plot some seventy years ago to bring nearly twenty of those gifted nova into their Aquila Prime population. The plan had failed entirely because just before they were about to succeed, other humans had destroyed Aquila Prime in a massive nuclear attack.

Thanos sent to Eros, "We may have just discovered how the Ashford-5 nova got their powers! However, we do not know the amount of these elements, which must be ingested to cause the desired changes in our nova. Further, this one garden plot's entire output is currently in use supporting the centers where our eight nova tell us that other telepaths are developing in their tanks. We must monitor these thousand very carefully, plus new nova when they join the real world. If they also possess these powerful gifts, then we can safely assume the next batch of nova that we put in those tanks and feed from this garden plot will also eventually have these gifts. We need to determine how long they need to consume the garden plot's produce in order to end up with these precious gifts. Eros, work out all the test parameters for the next thousand nova that we'll place in these tubs. Perhaps, in another twenty years, we'll know how to make nova with these powerful abilities. Once we do, we can set about making all our nova this powerful. I can foresee a future where our brilliant and powerful nova will rightfully rule the entire galaxy. We must not make any mistakes this time, Eros."

"I'll develop a complete testing plan," Eros replied in an electronic burst. "Should we put some of these eight in contact with those from Ashford-5?"

Thanos allowed his programming to run a bit before delivering his conclusion. "Perhaps, but on a very low level at this time. I believe there is to be a galaxy-wide Human Genetic Modification Conference on Pegasi-C coming up in October. Initial reports suggest many top geneticists from the ex-Imperium and the crumbling Federation will be there to discuss genetic cures for the nova. I recommend we send Doctor Annunziata Botocelli to that conference and arrange for her to meet the geneticists from Ashford-5. We can modify the hotel reservations and have Dr. Botocelli in the room next to those geneticists from Ashford-5."

"I'll see to the arrangements, Thanos. Indeed, the future for our nova has never looked brighter," Eros sent back.

Chapter 6 Genetics Conference

Dr. Annunziata Botocelli prepared for her first official Genetics Conference scheduled for October 10 through 12. She constructed a lengthy list of her questions, some involving the mysterious mental powers she and her other seven companions had, along with nearly a thousand others, who were still physically in their tanks, but who still believed they were in their virtual world.

She and her husband Serafino Vitalli would be attending, along with Minta. Eros had insisted the HIFR come along. While Fin could fly the deep space transport, Dr. Zia was far too valuable to risk sending her there alone. Minta could also fly the ship, plus she was an expert in many forms of combat, adding a strong measure of security for this lone geneticist upon whom Eros and Thanos were depending. Soon many others would be graduating and would need genetic cures. Plus, the robots and Zia hoped she would learn of more cures at this conference, bringing them back to Beltazar-C.

As they packed for the lengthy trip, Fin worried. "Zia, how should I dress? I mean we're going to be out among so many normals. Should I try to sort of look like their men, even though I don't look like them at all? Or should I mostly keep my mouth shut and pretend to be a woman?"

Zia sighed. She had no idea what the real world out there would be like, just rumors that their "kind" weren't too well received. "Best dress like me. I'll be doing all of the talking anyway. That way, you won't get too embarrassed. I think we need to dress like professional women, at least I think so." She sighed again. "Honestly dear, I'm really nervous about this too. It'll be my first contact with other geneticists. Everything else was done in that virtual reality world. What if it's nothing like what's really out there?"

"You'll do fine," he backed her up. "You know tons about genetics. Are we going to try to chat privately with the geneticists from Ashford-5?" he asked. "About you know what."

"I've got to. I have to have more real answers and soon.
I only hope they can help us with these strange mental powers
of ours. Come on; we best pack. We're so darn slow anyway,"
Zia answered, immersing herself in packing while trying to
calm her nerves.

With Minta helping by carrying their bags, arm in arm,
the two made their slow way to their deep space transport,
placing each step carefully. Walking on only their toes in their
ballet style boots was tricky under the best of conditions.
Going up the bay ramp was easy, but as they entered their
ship, both knew that going down would be quite a challenge
and hoped that they wouldn't need Minta to lift them down.

Eight uneventful hours later, they dropped out of
hyperspace above the spaceport of Estrella, Pegasi-C. With
Minta making contact with the control tower, they received
their landing coordinates, which she punched in, and Fin
allowed their automatic pilot to do the rest. As they stood by
the bay doors as the ramp descended, they took in their first
smells of a new world, new to them anyway. This was the first
time either had been off Beltazar-C and knew not what to
expect. Minta, however, did and took charge. Carrying their
bags, she walked down the ramp first.

Holding hands and with their free hands on the railings,
the two headed down the ramp, their knees taking a beating
while doing so. "Damn, that's really hard, Minta," Fin
exclaimed once he was on the flat tarmac again.

"Good job. I'm shutting the doors now for security.
Follow me. We'll need to check in with customs and get our
temporary ID cards. Remember, I'm a person as well. Do not
ever mention robots," Minta ordered.

Fin acknowledged her, envisioning someone cutting her
up for parts or to see how she worked. Shortly, the three
passed customs, paying a small landing fee, and receiving their
temporary cards. That done, Minta got them directions to
Estrella University and the special dorm rooms being reserved
for the conference attendees. A half hour later, they checked in
at the conference table, and received their room assignments,
along with a paper outlining the events, beginning at nine in
the morning.

As they walked into their dorm room with twin bunk beds, Fin commented, "Gee, this looks like our virtual campus we were in, Zia."

"I feel more comfortable already," she replied, relieved at least something looked quasi familiar.

Minta commented, "Well, if this were Imperium space, then you could count on everything being completely standardized from world to world. I guess the Federation is pretty much the same way too. I'll put your bags on this lower bed, and let you hang up your things in the closet there. I'll go check on the security arrangements around here. Back shortly. Don't leave your room until I get back," she ordered.

At nine the next morning, Zia was sitting at one of the tables arranged in a U-shape so the various attendees could easily see each other. A name card rested in front of her saying Dr. Annunziata Botocelli, Beltazar-C. Sitting on chairs at the back of the room were the other companions of the attendees. Only the geneticists were at the tables. Zia did a quick count. Fifty-three were here. Of those, she suspected at least a third were like herself, a hermaphrodite and a mutation victim themselves. Well, we do have a vested interest in coming up with cures, she thought. She felt far less out of place and relaxed as one man rose to chair the conference.

"Welcome doctors, to our Genetics Conference. We've a lot planned for you these three days. First, I'd like to welcome two geneticists from Ashford-5, the husband and wife team of Dr. Alexandra Hammil and Dr. Diego Bellweather-Hammil. They've come a very long way to share some of their latest discoveries with us. But first, I want to begin this conference with an overview of just what we are facing here in the Federation, which as we all know is vastly different than what was is being faced in the former Imperium spiral arm."

He began outlining the differences. The bio agent's initial mutations on victims here in the Federation of Planets side of the galaxy varied from person to person, quite unlike what had been experienced on the former Imperium side. Sometimes, the victim's lips didn't split but remained unaltered. Sometimes, the victim's feet ended up fused into a ballet dancer's en pointe position. However, all of the other changes were found uniformly from victim to victim.

Of the many cures available, the normal ones that handled many of them on the Imperium side now didn't work the same. Frequently, the neurons in their hair failed to be removed. Other times, the cures failed to restore feet at all, leaving the victims still wearing the toe shoes. However, uniformly successful were the cures that reduced breast sizes down to H-cup sizes and those that repaired the split lips. Both of these were seen as major milestones in helping the victims cope with their deformities. Cures for feet and hair were basically a hit or miss proposition. Sometimes they worked; others, they failed. Arm regrowth always worked, but was nearly prohibitively expensive, requiring a large volume of stem cells. To date, nothing could cure the dual sexual organs. And frankly, none of the geneticists dared to experiment in this area for fear of truly harming the person.

He then discussed recent studies and their findings. Zia learned that during the past few years, the geneticists had been working on trying to determine why some cures worked and some failed. Some alterations had happened because the victims had their DNA slightly altered by significant doses of radiation, such as from the supernova Boon. Extensive studies had discovered that similar effects were sometimes present in victims here in the Federation. However, those were very few. In the past, some suspected there were significant DNA differences between the populations of the Federation and those of the old Imperium. That had now been disproved by these recent studies. Rather the explanation was quite surprising and unexpected. The effects were primarily due to faulty duplication of the original bio agent cylinders.

Apparently, after countless duplications, errors had entered, compounded by the use of obsolete Duplication Machines and ones that had not been well maintained. Plus, there were also some indications that some cylinders had been exposed to massive doses of radiation as well, altering the makeup of the active agents in them. This new information took most of the attendees by surprise and much of the day was spent discussing this ramification.

Many groaned, realizing that this meant that they

would have to be developing specialized cures for smaller subsets based on just what version of the bio agent they had been exposed to. Many more years would be needed to get all of the victims handled up to the point where all cures thus far ended.

When the meeting adjourned for the day, Zia moved as quickly as she could over to Dr., Alexandra Hammil, but had to wait her turn to chat with the twenty-five year old geneticist. While she was waiting and listening in on the light chat that fellow geneticists were having with her, she observed the woman had wavy blonde hair that fell to her waist. She concluded that she'd had the hair cure, as well as her arms regrown. She couldn't be sure about her feet, because she was wearing six-inch black patent oxford style heels, vastly better than her ballet boots or the toe shoes that she knew others had to wear. Plus, she didn't have the awful lip plates.

Finally, she stood alone beside the doctor, as her husband moved over to join them. "Excuse me. I'm Dr. Zia Botocelli. I would really, really like to have a private discussion about some remarkable effects our victims are having on our world, Beltazar-C, please, it's very important, but I don't want to bring it up in front of all the others."

"We absolutely must meet in private. We have to make some presentations tomorrow. What say we meet tomorrow after supper?" Dr. Alexandra replied and offered.

"Oh that will be just perfect! Thank you so much for meeting with me," Zia gushed out, heading back to join up with Minta and Fin.

Those are the two wild telepaths we've been detecting here all day, Alexandra sent to Diego.

Thought so. I wonder what is going on? Let's dig up all we can about this Beltazar-C. The name sounds familiar, Diego sent back, as he escorted his wife out of the conference room.

The next morning, Drs. Alexandra and Diego made presentations on two specialty cures they'd developed that would handle another five hundred plus victims, whose lips and hair had thus far been unaffected by the known cures. Several very grateful geneticists thanked them repeatedly for their work on their behalf. Zia took this as a positive sign that these Ashford-5 geneticists would at least listen to her, since they were obviously helping here on the Federation spiral arm.

That evening a very nervous Zia and Fin knocked on the Ashford-5 geneticists' dorm room door. Upon entering, they found the pair ready for them with laptops out and chairs facing them, as they carefully tossed their hair back and sat down. Zia opened up her laptop, bringing up her list of questions.

"Welcome Zia and Fin, is it?" Alexandra began with a smile. Fin nodded, preferring to let Zia do most of the talking. "Well, we've looked up what limited information that we have on your world. Unfortunately, it's almost a century out of date, well not quite that bad. So perhaps we should let you chat first. Then, if we have questions, we can ask them when you are finished. How's that sound?"

"Fine with us. I just don't know where to begin with all this," Zia began. How did one try to explain all that had happened to her and Fin? Who could possibly understand?

Almost as if reading her thoughts, Alexandra said, "We know you are both telepaths. So just relax and explain everything to us. We're telepaths too."

Zia made a split decision. If they were telepaths too, then they could read her mind as easily as she could read her laptop screen. Any attempt to hide things from them would be futile. "Please, can you promise not to repeat any of this outside this room? Lives and our whole civilization depends on it."

"You have our word, unless any of this threatens the well-being of others," Alexandra replied.

Zia signed and began at what she thought was the beginning, her years spent in the virtual reality world, getting her doctorate. She described the robots and HIFRs that appeared to help them survive in their virtual world, and how Dr. Lelos Smith had been instrumental in helping so many of her peers get their advanced studies. Then, she went on to explain what happened at graduation, the discovery of the real world! She outlined every important discovery they had made, before relating the story about the four others who had somehow pulled themselves out of the virtual reality world. Before long, she was telling them about those four, their telepathy, and other mysterious skills, telekinesis and levitation. Then, she related how she and her three original companions had also suddenly developed them as well. Finally, she explained they had ascertained that another thousand or so had telepathy, but were still living in the virtual world and that they could potentially break out of it at any time. She then explained what she'd uncovered as the possible source of contamination, the food being grown on the old dump site with its alarmingly high levels of germanium and to a lesser extent, silicon.

When she finished, she was about ready to start in asking her many question, but Alexandra spoke first. "This is incredible, Zia. Look, I think the smartest thing is for Diego and me to follow you home where we can see for ourselves what the situation is and how we on Ashford-5 can help you. Certainly, much can be done for those of you who have the gifts of telepathy and other skills. A lot of us on Ashford-5 also have such gifts. I'm sure that we can help you out. Will that work for you two?"

"Oh yes, yes! Very much so. We are so confused, and the situation is so scary. We eight have the responsibility of over a hundred million people on our shoulders. If we make a mistake, well, it's just awful to think about that," Zia replied, terribly excited. Hope. These two had given her real hope, and she felt relieved to have told them about the true situation on her world. If they could just give her and the others some guidance.

The final day of the conference was spent in a heady discussion of the most serious problem that they faced: how to obtain enough stem cells to regrow hundreds of thousands upon hundreds of thousands of victims' arms. Statistically, the volume of stem cells required to "cure" one victim came from harvesting them from either sixty babies who were born alive or from ten where the healthy fetus was not allowed to develop. Of course, the latter was considered murder on most all Federation worlds. No one had any real solution to this one, save a concerted effort among all doctors on all worlds to preserve what stem cells they could with each live birth.

A geneticist from Lin-C did suggest starting a program where a woman would be paid to become pregnant, the stem cells harvested extensively, and the fetus later disposed of. Ten such babies equaled one person's arms back and their life salvaged. Her idea didn't play well with the other doctors present.

The closing remarks asked everyone to be vigilant. When more such attacks occurred, they were to try to get some samples of the bio agent, and study it to see how it compared to the earlier known samples. Perhaps this way, they could get more of a handle on the marked changes that were occurring in the genetic mutations on the victims. After that, the group agreed to meet again in three years to share additional findings, though if anyone had a major breakthrough, they promised to relay it to everyone, along official channels of course.

As they prepared to leave, Diego checked with Fin verifying he had the right coordinates for Beltazar-C. He did, and they promised to be there shortly after Fin got them safely back. While Minta didn't approve of what the two had done, revealing everything to these strangers, she had no choice but to obey them, though she did relay it back to Thanos, naturally.

Likewise, Alexandra and Diego also called home on a secure channel. What they heard from Zia was beyond alarming! They simply had to have some marching orders. If nothing else, they needed to attempt to train these telepaths and perhaps *mentales* gifted. The two didn't even realize that they were broadcasting their thoughts to every telepath around them. If they did truly have the *mentales* gifts, they would be the only other known world where it developed as it had on Ashford-5. If anyone else discovered that there were a thousand or more telepaths on Beltazar-C, they would be raided and the telepaths taken into slavery. Even worse, what could happen if other worlds discovered just how these telepaths came into being? Frightening.

Chapter 7 In Other News

The official announcement was carried on all Federation of Planets newscasts, but barely mentioned. "In other news, the five hundred sixth bio agent terrorist attack occurred two days ago on Vegan-C, adding fifty-five more victims." That was the sole mention of the horrible, never ending nightmare that now became the lives of those fifty-five men and women. Some seventy years after the first use of that bio agent stolen from the ex-Imperium, such debilitating attacks were completely commonplace with the Federation.

Few paid any attention to them. Those that did wrote them off as just another bunch of mindless terrorists riled up again. It would soon go away. That long ago, the Admiralty Round Table had ordered the complete and total destruction of Gamelon-3 had not done what everyone predicted it would: stop the duplication and distribution of this nasty bio agent. At this point, nearly every major world in the Federation had thousands upon thousands of victims. Their solution was simple. Put them into assisted living complexes and add their names to the lengthy list of those needing the known genetic cures. That some died of old age before reaching the top of the list went unnoticed except for those whose names rose up one more line on the list.

On the other hand, this recent attack was anything but commonplace for those fifty-five victims! Quite the contrary, particularly for twenty-one year old Savina Bonporti and her fiancé Alfonso Runelli, who was a year older. Both were graduate students at UV, the most prestigious University of Vegan. Savina had broken the mold for women. No chains would ever bind her into a harem, not ever. In another year, she would graduate as the first female Vegan-C astro-navigator, breaking more new ground for women of her world. Yes, Savina was very opinionated, obstinate, and forceful. Her fiancé, Alfonso, would have graduated in one week, had the attack not happened. Now a fully trained, highly competent spaceship pilot, Alfonso was about to get his commission, his promotion to full Captain, and his own light cruiser to command, though only as a junior officer.

Celebrating his impending graduation that day, they dined at Lino's, their favorite lunchtime diner. They, along with the fifty-three others including six staff, were attacked. It was over before anyone realized what actually happened. A man ran into the diner, yelled something that no one understood, dropped a bag on the floor, and fled. Yellow gas poured out of it, but no one paid much attention to it, until those nearest the bag dropped unconscious onto the floor. By then, it was too late. Bodies were found in lines heading to the doors, which were never reached.

Four days later, the pair woke up in a hospital, reacting as all such victims did. Screams of terror and panic filled this wing of the hospital. Of course, by now the doctors and nurses were well versed in just how to handle new victims, based upon over seventy years of experience dealing with them. As soon as the diner was safe to enter, emergency crews brought them to this special wing of the trauma reaction hospital. Here, they were undressed and put onto beds. IVs were inserted in their legs, ensuring that their comatose bodies would be receiving the best formulation of vitamins, protein, and other nutrients, along with good hydration. Further, catheters were inserted, guaranteeing that when the victims awoke, there would be no mad rush to get them to toilets, lessening their initial shock and terror.

On the last day of their comas, each victim was dressed, beginning with the heavy steel boned corset that provided necessary back support for his or her now massive bosom. Each breast was usually half again as large as their heads. This sheer extra weight caused excruciating back pains unless these extremely tight corsets were worn. Their waists had already shrunk down considerably, often to the dismay of those who enjoyed being plump. With the corsets fully tightened, as they had to be to provide the back support necessary, waist circumferences often were in the vicinity of fourteen inches.

Lip plates were inserted, preventing accidental ripping of their large pair of lip loops. Once the dried husks that had been their arms fell off from their shoulders, they were then

85

dressed in a colorful satin gown. On their now malformed feet, the nursed tied the appropriately sized toe shoes. Without these shoes, the victims would be standing and trying to walk with only the bottoms of their toes in contact with the floor. The toe shoes had a tall steel spiked heel whose tip was about a quarter of an inch behind their toes, which added a bit more support, enabling them to walk slightly better.

The last action the nurses took was to then brush out the victim's hair, which had more than doubled in thickness and grown to lengths of around six feet or so. Neurons, axons, and axon terminals now grew throughout this new length, preventing cutting of their hair any shorter. Doing so caused the victims enormous physical pain, and the darn hair grew back almost overnight. The nurses then parted their hair in the middle, draping the two sides down the victim's sides. After that, they merely waited for the screams of terror to alert them to the fact that their comas had ended. All was routine now, routine for the hospital staff, but far from that for the poor victims.

Savina screamed louder that she ever imagined she could! She passed out. A nurse revived her only to hear her scream again until she passed out. After the sixth revival, Savina began gasping and not screaming. She tried to talk, but she couldn't understand her own voice. A nurse helped her into a sitting position so she could better see what had become of her body. Her terror quickly gave way to intense grief. Savina cried her heart out, just as every victim did.

Once that period ended, her nurse got her to stand up, fully expecting even this was terrifying to the young woman, which it was. Savina would have fallen had not the nurse kept a steadying arm around her. Savina's arms waived about wildly, as she tried to keep from falling, but of course there weren't any arms there to wave, only ghostly sensations. Walking came next, with the nurse gently pushing her forward. Once more panic struck, just as the nurse anticipated. She prevented Savina from falling several more times. The nurse's goal was to get Savina to walk out of the room, down the long hall, and into the large reception area, where caretakers from one of the local assisted living complexes would take charge of her, finally ending the nurse's responsibilities for Savina.

As she entered the reception area, Savina saw her fiancé and cried out to him. He heard her, and the two did their best to get to each other, ignoring the protests from their nurses. They faced each other, sobbing and leaning onto each other, now not able even to kiss. When the man in charge spotted them, he checked his lists and said, "Okay. You two were about to be married. I'll keep you two together." Both sobbing victims nodded vigorously, unable to communicate in any other way.

Two agonizing months passed for the pair. Each day, the caretakers insisted and demanded they take longer and longer walks, and even tackle stairs, all on their own. "You want to be as independent as you can be," was the constantly explained motto they heard a thousand times or more. By the end of the two months of constant pushing and prodding, they were finally given a pass by the physical therapists monitoring their progress. They were young and had adapted well, regaining as much of their own independence as anyone thought possible. Now, they simply had to live here until their names came up on the massive lists for the available cures. Of course, at the present rate, that would happen perhaps fifty years from now if they were lucky.

At this point, left mostly alone, the two began trying to find ways of communicating to each other. Their native language was the prominent one on Vegan-C, a derivative of Italian. Their giant lip plates so perverted and distorted their sounds that they gave up on that one. Instead, they tried others that they knew. Since both had planned on venturing into space, they had learned several other commonly found languages spoken on many of the major worlds of the Federation of Planets. The German of the hub world and center of the legislative body of the Federation, Cass-C, was even more unintelligible than their own. Likewise, the Spanish spoken on Pegasi-C wasn't much better than their own. Finally, they tried some of the versions of English spoken on Capella-D and found they could barely understand each other, especially if they spoke slowly and repeated sentences a couple of times.

At last, they could talk and console each other. Both were extremely antagonistic and wanted revenge on whoever had done this to them, wiping out their careers even before they got started on them. "I bet I can still fly the damned spaceships," the dark brown haired Alfonso declared.

"How, Fonsi?" Savina asked, shaking her head from side to side, trying to get her rich black hair away from her face a little.

"We still got our feet! Heck, you could still navigate. Punch in the coordinates with your toes or nose, I don't know. Point is, we aren't totally helpless," he replied angrily.

"No, just mostly," she sighed.

A week later, things took a turn for the worse for the pair. Unknown to them, to the staff at the home, or anywhere else for that matter, others were after certain of the new victims. What was critical were their ages, twenty-one and twenty-two. Two men, agents of one Trevor Cain, visited many of these worlds, checking out the assisted living complexes in search of victims that a) were between eighteen and twenty-four and b) were somewhat attractive at least. Savina, with her extremely thick, shiny, and perfectly straight black hair, and Fonsi, with his rich bark brown hair that fell in gentle waves, fit the bill.

Disguised as janitors, the pair wheeled in a pair of carts, a canvass sheet draping down on all sides. They entered the room where the pair was staying. The two didn't take any note of the janitors who proceeded to dry-mop the floor. When the two drew close, they whipped out chloroformed rags, slapping them firmly over the pair's noses. Both slumped onto the bed in seconds. Carefully, the two lifted them up and put them on the carts beneath the canvass coverings, stuffing their long hair up and inside as well. Then, they proceeded to wheel them on out of the complex and up a ramp into their stolen van.

An hour later, the van drove up to the ramp of a deep space transport. The men rolled the carts up and into their ship. Next, they carried the still unconscious pair back into their specially made large quarters, formed by removing three bulkheads. Here four beds lay close together, with a table and chairs against the far wall. Two other women sat erect on the beds watching them dump the latest kidnap victims on two beds. Neither said anything, but their eyes were red from crying, though at this point they were emotionally numb.

After disposing of their stolen van, the pair got liftoff clearance and departed from Vegan-C. Once they made the jump into hyperspace, one of the men headed back to the four "women." He waved smelling salts under Savina's nose and then Alfonso's, rousing both. At least, he helped them into a sitting position, nearly impossible for them to do on their own, given the highly restrictive, unyielding corsets.

"There you go. Relax ladies. We'll be at your new home in four hours. This ship has good speed." He looked at the other two and asked, "Need anything before we get there?" Both shook their heads no, their lip plates banging gently into their upper chests. "Good. Four hours then." He rose and left.

Once they were alone, Savina cried out, "What's happening to us?"

"Just like us, you've been kidnaped. I'm from Capella-D. Adrianne Tonby, the daughter of the famous linguist Marilyn. Speak in English. We can mostly understand each other. She's Estrella del Genovefa from Pegasi-C. Who are you?"

"Savina Bonporti, my fiancé Alfonso Runelli. We're from Vegan-C. Why? Why do they want us?" she replied slowly and carefully, repeating it twice.

Adrianne shrugged her shoulders. It was simpler than trying to say she had no idea. So Savina explained, "I was going to be the first female astro-navigator on my world before this happened. Fonsi was almost a captain of his own light cruiser too. We're both fighting mad now. I swear we're going to get even somehow!"

"I'm a linguist like my mom," Adrianne replied, then sighing, "well not anymore." She wiggled her head a little, causing her lip plates to move slightly. She had no other way to point to them.

Estrella sighed as deeply as she could, which wasn't much. "I, I was almost a geneticist. I so wanted to help find more cures for these awful mutations, but now that's been ripped from me." She too was angry. "If I ever find out who did this to me, I swear I'll kill them. Somehow," she added meekly, and then fought hard to keep from crying once more.

Alfonso asked, "Do you know where they are taking us?" He had to repeat it a couple times, before both women shook their heads no. However, his asking got Savina thinking.

"Hey, it must be close to the rim. If they have those new hyperdrive engines, four hours would put them near the edge of the middle of the arm from Vegan-C," Savina speculated.

Alfonso thought a moment. "Scorpius sector?" She nodded. "Well, that's a clue anyway."

Estrella asked, "Are you a man, Alfonso? Your voice is pretty high. I can't tell for sure. Hell, we all look the same now."

"Yeh, for all the good that it does us," he replied, looking at her. She had slightly curly, but very shiny, long black hair, while Adrianne had wavy blonde hair and pretty blue eyes. "What can they possibly want with us?"

Some five hours later, they found out. They landed on a planet orbiting an orange star, Zeta Scorpii-C, at a spaceport outside Capital City, a city with a most unimaginative name. Here a version of English was spoken. The two kidnapers brought a van up to their bay ramp, and then proceeded to carry the four down, putting them on bench seats in the van. A short drive later, they were deposited outside a fancy brick building. A red neon sign over the main entrance read TC's Exotic Escorts. All four had a sinking feeling in their stomachs, as the men forced them through the opened doors. At least the doors were automated. Sensors detected the approach of a person and opened for them.

Inside, a man in a black silk suit met them and handed a pouch to the two men, who promptly left. "Welcome, welcome ladies. In case you are confused, you are now on Zeta Scorpii-C, in Capital City. This is my elegant company. I'm your new boss, Trevor Cain, TC. You're now officially my newest employees, exotic escorts to be precise. Fine gentlemen will pay for your services. Of course, you won't get paid, but you'll have all the clothes and food that you desire, fine gowns, mind you."

"Speaking of minding, I run a very tight ship here. Get out of line, and I won't hesitate to hurt you. You'll begin your first few years being exotic escorts, providing men whatever they may desire. Don't worry; I'll see you do not get pregnant. That comes later on, once the clientele becomes a bit bored with you. As you can see, I'm always adding new, young ones to my ever-expanding brothel. So when you are no longer being requested, then you'll become my brood mares, creating many more young, future escorts. Don't worry; I'll ensure you four live long and prosperous lives. Disobey, and it can easily be painful as well, just not deadly. You are too valuable as breeding stock, you see. Spare the rod; spoil the child, as we say here in Capital City."

"Now then, Matron Agnes Fletcher will be in charge of you four. She handles scheduling details, clothes choices, and such. However, you four will be sharing one personal assistant. Her name is Bess Beryl or BB as she likes to be called. She'll be bathing you, dressing you, feeding you, and handling your needs.

"But I'm a man," Alfonso protested.

"Hardly that. I'm the man. You're just like the others in all ways. So stuff such nonsense. Now, here comes Matron Agnes, who will take you to your new quarters and get you settled in." Trevor was thirty-five with short brown hair and eyes. He also sported sideburns and a handlebar moustache, well waxed. He smelled of tobacco smoke though.

Matron Agnes was fifty. Her black hair was tied in a tight bun back of her head, giving her angular facial features as stern an appearance as her voice and demeanor. "This way escorts. I don't tolerate any backtalk. You do as I say, when I say, and we'll get along fine. Disobey me, stall, complain, bicker, argue and that will cost you dearly. I'm known for inflicting more pain than old TC could ever dream up. He's a wimp in the pain department. A cane across a bare bottom stings worse than you can ever imagine, though if you women are like the others, you'll soon get a taste of my cane. I find it always requires a caning or two to convince newcomers I mean business. Of course, I so do prefer using my nipple clamps. I fasten them down quite tight. Oh, the pain they inflict when I undo them the next morning is a wonder to behold! Vastly superior to caning. Perhaps, I should just skip the caning with you four and go right to the clamps. I get so much more pleasure from hearing you women scream when I take them off. Simply delightful. Well, I do expect to be using them on you four soon. I've not had any opportunity to use them for, gosh, it's been a whole week! Please, act up. Misbehave. Protest. I need my fun. Here we are."

They stopped before a large room with five beds with walk-in closets, filled with expensive gowns and heels. A dresser held numerous exotic and quite risqué undergarments for the women. An electrostatic hair dryer occupied one corner of the room, an absolute necessity for these long haired women. The doorway to a large bathroom was next to it, but what took the four by surprise was their caretaker, Bess Beryl. She was twenty-two with shoulder length, wavy blonde hair, and pale blue eyes. She sat in a wheel chair. All that remained of her legs were two stumps about six inches long! Bess wasn't attractive, try homely. Shy, she too was a prisoner here, put to work caring for the personal needs of the others because she would never be dated by any man or so TC had claimed when she'd been kidnaped as well.

"Bess Beryl, these are your new charges," Matron Agnes barked. One by one, she introduced the four to Bess. "Now then, BB, it's time for you to earn your keep again. I want them stripped, bathed — hair too. Dress them in red satin for tonight. TC will want to check them out, prior to advertising them to his clientele. Got all that, dimwit?"

"Yes, Matron Agnes," she replied meekly.

"See that it's done by suppertime or you can all go hungry. And please, one of you act up. I so want to use my nipple clamps," Matron Agnes barked, turned, and left the room.

"If you speak English and very slowly, I possibly can understand you. Almost no one else around here can, though. She means it. She's a terrible, vicious woman. Come on. Over to the bed so I can get started on you. It takes me a long time to manage four of you," Bess requested.

"We've got to get out of here!" Alfonso declared.

"There's no escaping. TC will beat you and Matron Agnes will torture you mercilessly. Come, sit, I must hurry. It takes me a long time, plus I'm supposed to have one more of you soon too," Bess said, sounding urgent.

"But I'm not a woman!" Alfonso declared, though he obeyed her, sitting on the nearest bed alongside Savina.

"Can't really tell with your kind. Everything is the same, so it doesn't matter, at least not to the clients or TC or Agnes," Bess replied, starting to remove their current dresses.

"What happened to you? How did you lose your legs?" Savina asked, while Bess sat in her wheel chair and tried to give her a decent bath.

"I got kidnaped on my way home from school. I protested too much. They usually cut off a helper's left leg at their knee, but I kept crying, protesting, and refusing their orders, so they cut my right one off too and shorted them to these tiny stumps. After that, I still have to take care of five of you, though it is so very hard for me. They beat me at least once a week, sometimes more. That only makes it worse when I can't sit in my chair. Now, I just want to get even, but I don't know how," Bess explained her sad story.

After drying her off, she used the electro-static hair dryer to both dry and de-tangle Savina's hair. While she sat on the bed, Bess wheeled back into the bathroom to do Alfonso. Bess began talking to him. "Don't worry. I can't imagine how horrible all this is for you, especially since you aren't really a woman, though I guess you are now. Anyway, what I mean is that they put a drug in your food. Purple Droga. A week from now, you'll crave sexual satisfaction from everyone. That's when TC will finally send you out on one of their dates. Until that drug takes a strong hold of you women, he gets way too many complaints. Once it is fully working, none of the women ever complain about it again, even when their dates do terrible things to them."

"Thanks for the tips, but we got to get out of here before that happens, somehow, someway," Alfonso replied.

Several hours later, Bess had them all finished up. However, she had to explain about the corset tightening machine. "I'm not strong enough to tighten them enough.

Without my legs, I can't pull hard enough. At least, they got me this machine to help. They rather had to, but I was beaten every night for a week after that. One day, I'd like to beat them back."

She no more than got them dressed, when Matron Agnes appeared to inspect her work. Each now wore a very curve hugging red gown. Their tops were cut so low that their nipples were just barely hidden by the relatively thin red satin of the top. One giggle and it would slip over them. Savina complained a little. "It's too low in the front. If I move any, it's going to slip off my breasts."

"Oh terrific. I do so love complaints. I've just the way to fix this," Agnes grinned wickedly. She opened a drawer and brought out a handful of steel nipple clamps, the kind that one twisted down as tightly as desired, more like miniature vice clamps. Before Savina could protest further, Agnes was clamping one onto her left nipple.

"Ouch! That's way too tight. It is hurting me!" Savina cried out and tried to pull away from her. Alfonso moved over to protect Savina, trying to bump Agnes over. Instead, she whirled on him, knocking him over, landing him hard onto the carpeted floor.

"Get yourself up, bitch!" she barked, and proceeded to clamp the other nipple just as tightly. "Don't worry. The pain will be infinitely greater when I take them off of you." She tucked each breast back beneath the gown's top. She went on down the line doing the same thing to the other two women. When her back was turned, Bess quietly wheeled herself over to Alfonso, who simply couldn't find a way to get back onto his feet. Working together, Alfonso finally got upright again, though his hair was a mess.

Just then, Agnes turned and saw Bess beside him. "What do you think you are doing, bitch?"

"Trying to straighten his hair, Matron Agnes," Bess replied nervously, hoping and praying she'd not seen her helping him get back up.

"Well, she is a mess. Now, it's your turn for some delightful pain," she teased him. He grit his teeth and bore it somehow, though the pain certainly hurt. "Now, get them down to the dining room. Supper is already being served."

Bess began wheeling herself out of the room, and the four followed her, grateful she went slow enough so they could keep up with her. If it had not been for Bess, the four would certainly have gotten lost among all the hallways. When they reached the large dining room, they saw twenty other women like themselves being fed by four normal women, who were missing the lower half of their left legs. Their crutches were lying on the floor beside them. Each one alternated between feeding a pair of women, one on either side of her. Plus, they could not help noticing that four of the women were significantly older than the rest and at least seven months pregnant, perhaps more. At the back of the room, three two-year old girls sat waiting their turn to be fed. That's when it became real to the four that their children would be genetically similar to themselves. The three had no arms, very long hair, lip loops, and malformed feet wearing tiny toe shoes.

When it came his turn to be fed, Alfonso complained, "I'm not eating this. "You are drugging us with it. We know all about Purple Droga flowers!"

Trevor came over to him with an evil grin. "So nipple clamps aren't enough pain for you. Well, let's see what I can do to get you to eat!" He pulled out a chain from his jacket pocket and fastened the ends to Alfonso's nipple clamps, causing him more pain. But then, he hung a five pound weight in the middle of the chain. "There. How's that?" he asked evilly.

The pain was almost too much for Alfonso, whose eyes watered, but he refused to cry out any further. Trevor barked, "Now shut up, and eat your dinner, woman, or I will quadruple the weights." Alfonso ate. Only when he finished did Trevor remove the weight and chains.

When they finally returned to their bedroom, Matron Agnes joined them, removing their clamps, relishing in their sudden gasps and cries of pain. "Such beautiful tears ladies. I do hope that we can do this again tomorrow. Now it's time to get ready for bed. I leave you in the capable hands of BB." She left them alone at last.

The next day, began a week of "escort behavior training," as declared by Matron Agnes. They were dressed in

95

very tight gowns that had almost no walking slit. They could only just barely walk with the tiniest of steps. The objective was to gain better balance and to learn to swivel their hips seductively, since apparently the men here greatly desired that. It was a hellish day for the four, who could only just barely keep their balance on the soft carpet. Bess wheeled herself along with them, just in case one of them took a fall.

Late that afternoon, however, things changed. While they were terrified of falling and struggling just to walk, two men brought in the fifth woman. She had very wavy blonde hair and beautiful blue eyes, now quite bloodshot. She was screaming and gasping for air at the same time, all the while wiggling, struggling to get free from the man who was carrying her inside. "Feisty one, fresh out of the hospital, TC," one of the men said, as he received a packet of funds from Trevor. "Can't walk much yet. Watch her."

"Thanks fellows. The general will be quite pleased in a few weeks," Trevor sneered at the young woman, who was now being forced to stand up on her own in her toe shoes, wobbling wildly. The four guessed correctly she had only just become a terrorist attack victim and wasn't used to any of it. They stopped to hear Trevor give her about the same speech he'd given them. At least this time, Matron Agnes did put a steadying arm around the terrified woman, whose name was Pippa Fenton. She'd just turned twenty-one last week.

Bess whispered, "I have to go with her. Please be careful and don't fall. They'll make you get up by yourself." She wheeled after the two.

They overheard Matron Agnes telling Pippa the same things that she'd told them, but added, "This is the only time anyone here will ever put their arm around you. After this, you are on your own, new bitch."

Pippa screamed and gasped, "I'll. Kill. You. All. I'll. Kill. You. All! I. Swear! It!" After that, they couldn't hear her any longer and hoped she'd not fainted. Agnes didn't understand a word of what she was gasping, though.

The four were never so grateful for supper as they were this night. Finally, with aching feet and a complete day of nervous stomachs, they were allowed to sit down! After that, they returned to their room. After Bess got them out of the torture dresses, they sat on their beds and had a chance to comfort Pippa.

Pippa was only too eager to tell her story to her new roommates. Speaking slowly and often repeating everything several times, she explained, "I'm General Tyrrell's daughter. He runs the show here in Capital City. I am or was a martial arts black belt and almost a soldier. Another day and I'd of had my commission in the space fleet, God damn dad anyway! He kept refusing to let me become a soldier. He kept telling me, 'You are supposed to be a pretty woman and be a nice wife, not charging around playing solider boy. You're a grown woman, for heaven's sake. I won't allow it.' Damn him to Hell! He did this to me! To me, his own daughter! And sold me into this glorified prostitution ring. Damn him to Hell!" she violently repeated herself. She was gasping after every few words though. "Are you even understanding me? I can't understand my own words now. This is utter hell. Why didn't he have the balls just to kill me outright? He's torturing me! I'll kill him. I swear it. I'll kill him if it's the last thing I ever do!"

The five allowed her to vent her anger. At last, she calmed down and asked them their names, after which they each told her their own story. By the time that everyone was done, Pippa realized if one talked slowly and repeated everything a couple of times, everyone understood what was said, at least among themselves and Bess. After that, Adrianne gave Pippa all the tips she knew about somehow dealing with their physical bodies as they were. Pippa did pay close attention to what she said, knowing she had to follow this if she wanted to somehow get by. She did take heart when she heard she would grow more comfortable wearing the tight corset within a few weeks, if only she could somehow survive that long.

The next day was just as bad for the four women, but horrendous for Pippa. Once more, they were forced to wear the extremely tight gowns with virtually no walking slit. This time, Matron Agnes was watching them with her whipping cane in hand. She seemed to relish cracking one of them across their butts with it. The sharp cracking sound was followed by a very sharp pain, more than once very nearly causing them to fall down. Only with wild wobbling were they able to stay on their toes. At least she didn't whip Pippa that day. The poor woman could only barely walk. "You must learn to walk gracefully and swiftly. You think your client is going to go slowly? Ha. It is your job to keep up with whatever pace he or she might set for you. Move it, Savina!" Crack! Savina jerked involuntarily and had to wobble like mad to keep from losing her balance.

Perhaps, the second worst day of their "training" came when Matron Agnes purposely bumped so hard into their sides that they did fall down. She barked, "Now get yourself up and on your feet. For goodness sake women! Your date is sure as hell not going to embarrass themselves by deigning to get you back up! It is your own damned fault for falling down and embarrassing yourselves. So get yourself back up! Now! Get the lead out," she barked and chided them.

The unbending steel in their corsets prevented all bending except at their hips. The skin-tight gown kept the upper half of their legs tightly together, while at their feet, they had enough ease to put one foot in front of the other, but not much more. Without arms and encumbered by their hair which always seemed to be underneath them, it seemed an impossible task. Savina broke down, "I can't get up. I can't. This is impossible!" and she began to sob, joined by the others, except Alfonso, who swore oath after oath, threatening to murder Matron Agnes. She replied by cracking her whipping cane over his exposed butt numerous times.

Thanks to her martial arts training, Pippa was actually the first to regain her feet, albeit wholly un-lady like. She wiggled and struggled to get onto her front and then pulled her knees up under her as far as she could tuck them up. Then, with a backwards thrust of her head and abdomen, she rather rocked up to her feet. On her first try, she miscalculated and overshot, rolling on over backwards. But on her second try, she arrived on her toes, followed by a moment of very hectic wobbling before she could stabilize herself. Her actions broke the stalemate. That it was possible to get up gave the others some hope. Of course, Matron Agnes merely knocked Pippa down onto the floor again. This time, the other four watched how she got back up and tried their best to duplicate her motions. After countless dozens of attempts during the long day, all five were at last somewhat proficient on getting themselves back onto their feet.

The absolute worst day for all five soon followed. Still wearing these impossibly tight dresses, they were forced to deal with steps. Even discounting these dresses, handling steps filled everyone with terror and dread because between their massive bosoms and lip plates, they simply could not see their feet. With no arms to hold onto the railing and the fact that only their toes lay flat on the ground with their spiked heel offering only a minuscule more support, being only a quarter of an inch back of their toes, they were wise to be afraid of dealing with any steps. Their dresses made it nearly impossible for them to go up one step. Only if they stretched the very limits of the gown were they able to get just enough height to slide a shoe onto the upper step, precarious at best. Yet, going down them was a hundred times worse. It was like descending totally blind on top of everything else. Savina kept wondering when Matron Agnes would give them one of her shoves, knocking them down the stairs.

Later on, she realized Matron Agnes probably wouldn't do that because, in their shape, such a fall would very likely kill them. TC would be furious with that. Still, the day was terror-filled for the five women. However, when supper finally came, Pippa realized something, but waited until they were all back alone in their bedroom before telling the others. "Look, actually, we are learning valuable lessons and techniques. We have to be able to fend for ourselves, especially since I have to find a way to kill Agnes, Trevor, and my father."

The others quickly saw what she meant. Alfonso replied, "Excellent point, Pippa. I aim to break out of here and get my revenge on everyone. Now I see what you mean. We've got to be able to handle ourselves no matter what situation we face. Gang, let's all work hard on this and make our breakout together."

Bess had been watching them, trying hard not to show Matron Agnes any emotion that she felt. "Please, when you escape, take me with you, please!"

"Of course, Bess. We wouldn't think of leaving you behind," Alfonso replied.

Later, as they sat undressed on their beds, the Purple Droga drug began having a powerful impact on their senses, just as Bess had told them it would. Next morning, Adrianne explained it this way, "It was like I was just an outside observer watching my body do all of those things. It wasn't me. How weird is that?"

For two weeks, the five were tortured and tormented mercilessly by both Matron Agnes and Trevor. Supposedly, they were preparing the women to be able to handle and perform well while out on their "dates." While this treatment may have broken the wills of the other women and/or prepared them to be wonderful exotic escorts, with these five, this treatment only steeled their wills, stiffened their resistance and determination to somehow escape and exact their revenge. All five had been driven down into heavy grief over what had happened to their bodies and lives because of the genetic mutations. Had they been left in the assisted living homes or in Pippa's case been put into one, most likely they would have remained emotionally down. However, the added perceived torture and certainly torment and disrespect shown to them here at TC's Exotic Escorts had the opposite effect. Probably contributing to the overall result was the determination of Savina, Alfonso, and Pippa to escape and obtain revenge.

Their constant drive wound up moving them up out of grief, particularly so for Pippa, into covertness, then anger and pain, and finally hardening into a good, solid antagonism, a real hostility. That Pippa's observation that this torture they were receiving was in fact just what they needed to be more independent only fueled the fires, steeling the five's sole goal of escaping and seeking revenge for what had been done to them and so many others. The final piece of the intricate web fell into place the day that their "training" was officially over. Trevor announced at breakfast, "Well, ladies, Matron Agnes tells me you five are now ready to work to earn us a small fortune. Tonight, Pippa and Savina have been asked out on their first dates. Their gentlemen have presented me with what they desire them to wear, and I'll be passing that on down to Bess. Let the money roll!"

That afternoon, Bess bathed the pair and got them ready for their evening's work. "But we can't go out into the city in this," Pippa complained bitterly.

Bess protested, "Please Pippa. You must wear this. The man has ordered you to wear this for the date. If you don't, Trevor will beat you until you are black and blue and maybe me too, please," she begged. The dresses were the same incredibly tight, form-fitting ones with almost no ease for walking, the very ones that had caused them so much torment earlier. Since neither woman wanted Bess to be beaten for their own actions, they relented.

That evening, Savina and Pippa made their excruciatingly slow, careful way down the halls to the waiting room, where their "dates" were waiting to pick them up. Trevor met them near the door. "Remember, a good escort woman does not speak. Besides, no one can understand you. You are to do whatever they ask of you, period, no backtalk, just do it. Make them happy."

When they entered the waiting room, Pippa inhaled sharply. There was her father, General Tyrrell, resplendent in his military uniform, decorated with a host of medals. Beside him was one of his junior officers, one of several men the general had tried to foist off on Pippa as being husband material for her. From Pippa's reaction, Savina knew at once that this had to be Pippa's father. She stared at the man wondering how he could have ever done this to his own daughter! She thought that man has to be destroyed! Made to pay and pay dearly!

"Well, well, well, my dear Pippa. You do look so charmingly exotic, like a real woman should. See, no more of this playing soldier. I've brought Ralph along. He does so admire you. Well, come along, ladies. We want our money's worth from you tonight. Do keep up." He added that last, as he watched them taking their extremely tiny steps, barely moving at all. Savina hazarded a glance at his face and saw merely amusement. She hated him now almost as much as Pippa!

Their evening was one of humiliation and torment, but fortunately, the men did not try to undress them and have their way with them sexually. Trevor's standing orders for the men included only two. One, they could not remove their lip disks, and two, their corsets were not to be undone. Beyond that, their dates could do as they pleased with the women. However, if they were returned in a "damaged" state, the men would be charged a very steep penalty to compensate Trevor for days of lost "income."

Late that night when all five and Bess were in their bedroom, Savina declared, "We've just got to escape from here and bring them all down, especially Pippa's despicable father! He needs a taste of his own medicine! The beast!"

Pippa spat out, "No kidding. I was planning on killing him, but after tonight, that's entirely too good for him. Hell, it's too good for Trevor and Agnes. Savina's right. They need a dose of their own medicine. I know just the way too!"

"How, Pippa? I'm all ears," Alfonso asked, very interested. His heart had nearly burst while waiting for his beloved Savina to return, fearing, and imagining all manner of horrors she was enduring.

Pippa sneered. "I know his secrets. On his base, Zeta Scorpii-C has stored up an arsenal of that bio genetic agent stuff. It's in a bunch of yellow cylinders. I know, because they used one of them on me to turn me into the freak that I'm now. There are hundreds of them, plus he has a big list of underground suppliers that they use when they want to buy more of the stuff."

"But why? Why do they want this terrible stuff?" asked Estrella. "Are they planning to wipe out whole worlds?"

"I think they think this is a deterrent weapon thing," Pippa tried to explain her father's reasoning, which seemed twisted beyond comprehension. "Don't attack me with it, because I'll attack you with it. One of those kinds of idiot notions."

"Hey, with that list, we could set about destroying all the suppliers too," Alfonso suggested. "Now, we are getting somewhere. Knock out the suppliers and there won't be any more of this awful stuff around."

"We should open up all those cylinders on dad's base. That would take care of dad and all the others who did this to me, plus it'll get Trevor and Agnes too — this whole insane city!" Pippa declared. "They all deserve it! Do you realize that there are dozens of these kinds of escorts around Capital City? I swear all the men here are insane psychopaths, just like my fiend of a father! Plus, their wives are just as bad."

Bess spoke up, "She's right. Almost half of Trevor's business comes from women hiring you women. They are all bad, evil, wicked beasts! Turn them all into helpless freaks too. Serve them right for what they've done to you."

Savina cringed at being known as a freak, but she realized she was just that now. There wasn't anything she could to change it either, further steeling her determination to do this somehow, someway.

"We need to steal us a good space transport," Alfonso added. "Savina and I can pilot it. We can use our toes. Hell, a baby can fly one of those things."

"There are a lot of them on the military base. I know how we can sneak in there too. I still know the security codes," Pippa added, growing more excited. "I can get us into dad's office. We can steal his list of suppliers. How do we set off the cylinder of the bio agent?"

While they discussed this aspect, Bess noticed they were all actively working on their revenge plot, and that in doing so, they were overriding the effects of the Purple Droga drug. None was remotely interested in sex at the moment. This seemingly small detail occupied her thoughts.

Pippa described where the cylinders were stored. "They are in this flimsy shed, stacked up like bombs on tall racks, at least eight feet high. Hundreds of them. The cylinders have a nipple where hoses could be attached. I think that's how they use them."

"Well, we can't just put a charge on them. That might destroy the bio agent," Pippa continued.

"Hey, what about a chain reaction kind of thing?" Alfonso suggested. "One explodes but it's fragments puncture the neighboring cylinders, which in turn also explode, sending out more fragments, which hit their neighbors and so on.

Boom. They all go off one after the other."

"Great idea. That ought to work, but how do we get one of them to explode?" Savina asked. For a minute, that stumped the group.

"Hey, I've got it. How about a gunshot? I know where dad keeps a gun and it has a silencer on it too. No one will even hear the gunshot," Pippa suggested.

"Hey perfect, Pippa!" Alfonso declared. Then, he realized one small detail. At the same time, Pippa also saw the fatal flaw and nearly broke down. They had no way to fire a gun, let alone open the drawer, get it out, and carry it to the shed.

"I can do that much," Bess volunteered softly.

The sheer relief on five faces told Bess she'd just become an integral member of this conspiracy, that they had no intention of leaving her behind. Until now, that idea had always been in the back of her mind, but not any longer.

"Terrific, Bess. Now, we have a real plan," Alfonso exclaimed, his voice full of hope.

"Well, they deserve it," Bess added. "They *all* deserve it," she stressed.

"Right. Then, we go after all the others who deserve it as well!" Savina declared just as forcibly. "People think that they can get away with doing this to us, wiping out our careers and lives. Well, they've another think a'coming. They all deserve it. Where were our soldiers who were supposed to protect us? Huh? How many terrorist attacks have there been? So darn many that I can't even count them."

"Worse," put in Estrella, "these awful attacks don't even make the news anymore. Our own governments haven't done a thing to stop them either. They just go on and on, wiping out more and more innocent lives. Maybe we can put a stop to this if we wipe out all the suppliers."

"Good point, Estrella," Adrianne backed her up. "But what about all these people who have stockpiles of them, like the general here? We need to get them too. But how?"

"We'll worry about that one later on," Alfonso replied, getting them back on the current topics. "So when do we break out and do this? Soon, I hope."

"How do we get out of here? How do we get to the army base?" asked Estrella.

Bess put forward some data. "On Sunday nights, both Trevor and Agnes are gone. I don't know where they go, but they take off after supper and aren't back until very late. Sheila once told me she heard them getting back around midnight. That might be the best time to make a break for it — when they aren't here."

"Good thinking. So when's Sunday? I've no idea what day it is or even what month," Savina asked. "Damn these people anyway!"

"Hey dear, they aren't people, not real people. A 'real people' wouldn't be treating us like this," Alfonso grumbled.

"It's tomorrow," Bess finally got a chance to answer the original question. "So are we going to do it then?"

"You bet we are!" Alfonso exclaimed. "Come on; let's get down to business and work out all the details. Lord knows what they'll be having us do tomorrow during the day."

At supper, the six could hardly contain their growing excitement. For good or ill, this was it! Nervously, they watched their tormentors, Trevor and Agnes, eating. Alfonso thought, soon, soon you both are going to get it! You deserve this and so much more. As always, the pair finished eating long before the many captive women. They left, barking their usual orders to the helpers to put them to bed early. "Tomorrow will be a big day. Six men want escorts to attend some ball, so some of you'll get your fill of dancing," Trevor snickered, knowing that they could barely walk, let alone dance.

An hour later, the six were finally back in their bedroom complex. Bess had them undressed and was dressing them for their great escape. "We need the loosest fitting dresses there are," Savina explained. "Mobility is going to be key."

"I know," Bess spoke up. "I've an idea. They don't have much call for these. How about this one? It's called a professional woman's look. Simple grey skirt and blouse. Once in a while, the men want an escort to look like she's a working woman. I never understood why, since you all can't possibly work, not like those women."

"Hey, perfect, Bess," Alfonso declared. "Let's get this show on the road!"

An hour later, Bess had them all dressed and ready. "Okay. You all stay here. I'll go around and make sure that everyone's retired for the night." She wheeled herself out of the door, disappearing down the carpeted hallway. The five waited impatiently, sitting on the edges of the beds, more than a little nervous. If they were caught, Trevor's ire would be something to behold.

Before too long, Bess came wheeling back into the room. "All clear. I have the codes to unlock the front door. All we helpers do, in case of a fire or some emergency. Are you ready?"

In answer, the five lunged to their feet, wobbling slightly as they got their balance. They followed silently behind the wheelchair. Soon, they reached the front door, which was locked. They looked over Bess' shoulder as she punched in the numbers. The tiny red led changed to green. Bess pushed on the door, and it opened. Out into the night, the five followed Bess, breathing in the warm, late evening fresh air.

It was a very long walk through the streets of Capital City to the army barracks, located near the spaceport. Bess had never wheeled herself this far ever. Soon, the others took turns pushing her along, though their feet took the brunt of the effort. "We're a team," Alfonso whispered to Bess, who was almost in tears, because her arms had given out. "Relax. We have you, mostly. You steer though."

A lone tower clock chimed midnight when they reached the edge of the army barracks. Following Pippa's suggestion, they'd arrived at an unmanned back gate. A keypad provided entry, assuming one knew the code. Pippa whispered the numbers, and Bess punched them into the keypad. All heard the click as the gate unlocked. After Bess opened it, the five stepped inside and waited while she closed it. They heard the lock click back into place. So far, so good. Once more, Pippa took the lead.

"Over there are dozens of transports. We can steal one of them," Pippa whispered.

"Okay, Savina and I will go find the best one to swipe.

You all go take all these bastards out," Alfonso whispered back. The party split in two, going their separate ways. "Which one, dear?"

"Let's see if any of these have a canon on them," Savina suggested. After some looking and avoiding of a couple of soldiers walking past, they spotted ten transports that were lightly armed. All had their bays opened, ramps down, ready to be loaded with troops on a moment's notice. Quietly, the pair walked up to the ramp and listened. Hearing nothing, they carefully headed up the entrance ramp, pausing to listen once more. Still silence. They both headed down the dimly illuminated hall to the cockpit at the very front of the large transport. Empty.

Emboldened, the pair took their seats. "It feels good to be in the pilot's seat again," he whispered.

"Same here. Now to get it ready to take off," Savina whispered back. "This is going to be really hard. God damn all those terrorists anyway!"

Very hostile, Alfonso whispered back, "They deserve all that we are going to do to them!"

They struggled a bit and got their toe shoes off, freeing their feet. Leaning back, they got one foot up to the controls and pitifully began to do their work. Compared to actually flying, pre-flight actions were vastly more involved and difficult for the pair to get done. Time. If they had enough of it, they were convinced they could do this. They had to. Everything depended upon it.

Meanwhile, Bess, being pushed along by Estrella, Adrianne, and Pippa, each taking a turn behind the wheelchair, stopped at the back door to General Tyrrell's office. Unfortunately, there were two steps up to the door. "Now what? I forgot about the steps," whispered a very worried Pippa. Had they'd gotten this far only to be defeated by two lousy steps?

"I can manage, I think," Bess whispered back. Using her arms, she slipped out of her chair and onto the ground. Bit by bit, using her hands, she got herself up the steps to the door. Again, Pippa whispered the entrance codes, hoping and praying he hadn't changed them. When the door unlocked, she smiled. She figured her father figured that she'd be helpless and hence no need to change all the codes. The fool, she thought. The four slipped inside, with Bess using her arms to pull herself along in rocking motions.

Pippa led them to the desk where he kept his fancy collector's gun. With Pippa providing eyes and giving directions, Bess reached up, blindly feeling around for the box. "That's it. You got it," Pippa whispered excitedly. Bess pulled down the box and opened it. "Screw that cylinder thing onto the barrel. Okay, now push that lever back. That's the safety lock. Now to fire it, just point, and squeeze the trigger."

"Got it. Best put that lock back on for now." She did so then put the gun between her teeth, freeing up her hands. Next, Pippa directed her to the paper listing of all known underground suppliers. That retrieved, slowly Bess began levering her way back to the door. With long practiced motions, Bess pulled herself up and back into her wheelchair. After placing the gun and list at her side, she pivoted the chair around, and Pippa took her turn behind it, pushing her along.

Twice, they had to hide in the shadows while a pair of guards walked by. Fifteen minutes later, they reached the thin-walled shed that contained the supply of bio agent cylinders. "The damned thing isn't even locked!" Pippa whispered. "Anyone could steal these things!"

"Probably they couldn't because of all the guards," Estrella whispered back. Bess opened the wide door, and they all peered inside. While the base lighting was poor, there was no mistaking the yellow cylinders. Just like Pippa had told them, hundreds of them lay stacked in a very neat pile nearly eight feet tall. "Now what do we do, Pippa?"

We stand way back and let Bess shoot into one of them. If our idea works, it should explode and cause the others to also explode too," Pippa replied. "Best be way back, I think."

"And be prepared to run for it once it starts," Adrianne added, nervously. They wheeled her back quite a distance and towards the parking lot full of transports. "I hope you can hit it from here," she added.

Bess put both hands on the gun and aimed. The gun made a faint popping sound. Nothing else happened. "Guess I missed," she whispered and fired again. This time, they heard a dull noise. She was about to fire again when they heard another dull popping sound, then three, then so many that they couldn't count them. Hastily, Pippa began pushing the wheelchair as fast as she dared and could. Holding the gun in her right hand, Bess used her left hand on the left wheel rim to steer them towards the rows of transports.

It seemed ages to the four before they crossed that vast open space from the shed to the rows of ships. "Which one?" Bess whispered. "Here was the fatal flaw in their plan. Which ship had Alfonso and Savina chosen to steal?

"Make for the one with the red lights flashing on its bottom side. They must be powering it up," Pippa whispered, while Estrella pushed the wheelchair as hard as she both dared and could. Everyone's feet were aching fiercely, but the four ignored the pain and headed towards the gaping ramp. When they reached it, Savina appeared at the top of the ramp, a most welcome sight for the four worried women.

"Come on; we've got it ready to go. Oh! Look at that!" Savina wanted to point to the sight but couldn't. The four turned around and saw an enormous cloud of yellowish gas billowing up like some giant mushroom or balloon. The shed was completely invisible! Plus, the ball was expanding outwards rapidly. "Hurry up!" she yelled.

Both Pippa and Adrianne got behind the wheelchair to push it up the ramp. Bess added what strength she still had in her arms, and they just barely made it up. As they finally rolled her into the hallway, two armed soldiers came running up. "Press that button fast!" Savina yelled, again almost crying because she couldn't point it out. Bess hesitated between the several choices until Savina added, "Yes, that one." She pressed it, and the bay doors began closing.

From the small view window in the door, Savina saw the men arriving but also saw the yellow gaseous ball had also reached the side of the ship. The men turned and began coughing, ignoring the ship. "Okay, this way. We're about to take off." She led them up the hallway and into the first two crew compartments. "Sit down. I'd say fasten your seat belts, but we can't, so just get ready as you can." She turned and headed up to the cockpit where Alfonso was waiting for her word to take off.

As soon as she mostly fell into her seat, Alfonso used a toe to press the Take Off button. Slowly, the large transport lifted off from the ground. Once five hundred feet up, per the altimeter, he used his foot to control the stick and got them turned around so they could see the gas cloud. It was extremely visible and was still expanding outwards, though the light breeze was already slowly moving it over part of the city. "It's heading in the right direction, I think," Savina pointed out. Together, they watched the cloud until it encompassed Capital City. Only then did Savina use her foot to engage their hyperdrive.

The two walked carefully back to the others. "It's done. The cloud is now covering the whole city," Savina reported.

"Sweet! Now, dad can experience what he has put me though. My life is ruined, but now his is too and that bitch Agnes and pervert Trevor," Pippa exclaimed. "I can hardly believe we did this!"

The next day there was only this tiny mention listed under "in other news." "Yesterday, the five hundred seventh bio agent terrorist attack occurred on Zeta Scorpii-C, wiping out their governing town of Capital City, adding two million four hundred thousand ten more victims."

Chapter 8 Such a Deal

Arnold Flaxton rubbed his chin, contemplating his options. The forty year old, ex-Black Operations specialist or Special Forces member of Capella-D turned Private Investigator looked again at his bank statement. The money really was there, all one million gold dollars, just as the old lady had promised. He'd taken this assignment from the famous linguist, the wealthy Marilyn Tonby. At first, the amount of money she offered for his services seemed astronomically high. He'd very nearly refused the case. Who offers a cool million to locate and rescue a granddaughter? Yet, she had no qualms agreeing to all his "terms."

When he had first accepted this case, he decided he would return a substantial amount of the million when he found, rescued, and returned her granddaughter. She'd given him a recent photo of the budding young linguist, Adrianne Tonby, who had turned twenty-one and was about to graduate from their University with her degree in linguistics, taking after her grandmother. His original notions, and thus his many reservations of a simple kidnaping, had evaporated after a single day on the trail of the blonde, blue-eyed woman. His investigation quickly produced some results, grim ones as far as he was concerned, though he didn't report this to his employer, not just yet.

There had been a terrorist attack at the Stalwart Inn, a local campus bar where Adrianne usually hung out with some of her friends. She'd become another statistic, one of those whose life was ruined, shattered by that terrible genetic mutation bio agent, the now-favored weapon of those psychopaths who wanted to make a statement. Gone were the days of a simple car bomb, wounding and killing out right. No, that wasn't enough, rather turn their victims into helpless freaks for the rest of their lives. That seemed to be most appealing to terrorists within the Federation these days. Worse, Arnold knew how frustrating it had been for those in the Black Ops, who never could get enough Intel on terrorists groups to prevent such attacks. How many had there been now? Over five hundred, he thought, though he'd long ago lost count. *Hell, they don't even make the news any longer. Lives wiped out, and it isn't even news!* That's why he resigned from the Black Ops on Capella-D, preferring to make his own attempt at making a difference in the world.

Like a bulldog, Arnold had found her scent and began tracking Adrianne Tonby. He found the assisted living home where she'd been taken once she'd been released from the hospital. Even obtaining that much information had been difficult. The poor victims were unable to speak with those giant lip disks. Compounding identification, a victim now looked vastly different, barely recognizable. Yet, Arnold had persevered. Using DNA markers, he conclusively proved that one of the young women brought into this facility had been Marilyn's daughter, Adrianne.

Of course, when he arrived there to pick her up and take her home to her grandmother, Adrianne was gone, kidnaped from the facility! At this point in time, Arnold realized perhaps the one million gold dollars wasn't going to be a gross overpayment! He utilized all his special skills to unravel what had gone down here. Via the local authorities, he was able to review the security footage of the actual kidnaping, though he had to use his previous employment record as a Special Operations officer to gain access.

During the ensuing week, Arnold utilized every connection he had within the various security forces of Capella-D, but he did uncover the concrete fact that a deep space transport registered to a company on Zeta Scorpii-C had departed not long after the kidnaping. Further, a stolen van with a stolen janitorial cart inside it had been found not far from the landing bay where that ship had been parked. In Arnold's mind, this solidified the kidnaping to this particular ship. However, that was certainly wholly insufficient data for the authorities on Capella-D to take any action at all. Well, he wasn't bound by all the "rules" of society.

Armed with the flight plan of this ship, he rented a deep space transport and headed off on their trail. According to the flight plan, their next stop was Vegan-C. During the trip, he spent most of the time with the language learning disks. He at least had to be able to converse in their local dialect to continue his investigation. When he arrived, he used his "obsolete" ID card that identified him as Commander Arnold Flaxton, Capella-D Special Operations. Of course, by now, Arnold had several dozen different "valid" ID cards. What good PI didn't? One needed access to information, didn't one in this line of work?

Using his fake ID, he got into the Police Reports database for all Vegan-C. He was looking for something specific: reports of stolen and likely later found vans. If these men kidnaped one woman, they'd likely kidnap others. That was his operating theory at this point. Naturally, there were quite a number of such reports, even in the narrow time frame. He'd already verified the landing date of this particular transport ship from Zeta Scorpii-C. He eliminated all reports in which the stolen van was recovered anywhere else than close to this spaceport. That left him with only one incident. The van was recovered near the very spaceport where that transport had landed and later taken off!

Of course, Arnold now had to backtrace what these men had done here on Vegan-C. There was always the possibility that they had dropped off Adrianne Tonby here on Vegan-C to become possibly another harem wife. A further search of police records yielded more startling data. Two other young women had been reported as missing from an assisted living center. They were terrorist victims and hence the authorities had not even bothered following up on that incident! Why should they? The victims were worthless anyway, just two utterly helpless women, dependent upon the state for their upkeep and lives in the assisted living complex. Besides, their departure raised everyone else up two lines on the future cure's list!

Still, Arnold was thorough in his investigation. He used his fake credentials to get access to the security footage from the assisted living complex. After hours of watching the poor quality video, he spotted the two janitors wheeling carts into their room and a bit later pushing them out. He did notice that the carts seemed to weigh much more on the outgoing trip.

The men were really putting their backs into pushing them. This convinced Arnold that he was indeed witnessing the abduction of two more women victims.

Once more, he pulled strings and got the flight plan of the deep space transport from the control tower. This time, they were presumably heading home to Zeta Scorpii-C. Arnold entered the coordinates of that world and departed Vegan-C, convinced he was hot on their trail, if only a few weeks behind them. At least he wouldn't have to learn a new language, since they also spoke a dialect of English on this next world.

Once there, he was able to confirm that the ship in question had landed at the spaceport near the giant military base just outside Capital City, but little else. The authorities here refused to grant him any special privileges, ignoring his offered "special" ID card. Arnold sighed. He'd have to use old-fashioned methods involving shoe leather. He had to park his ship at the public landing field some miles from the military base where the ship in question had landed.

Packing everything that he might need into a backpack, Arnold set off to rent himself a local transport vehicle called a car. First stop was the Ace Rent-a-Vehicle, a private company that also serviced the military base. The manager refused to give him any information about rentals on the date when the deep space transport had landed, refused until he slipped the man a hundred gold credit note over the counter. Then, why yes, a van had been rented briefly for several hours on that date. Another note and Arnold was led to the van in question and allowed to search it.

While the driver's seat was sparkling clean, they didn't bother much with the cargo rear compartment, which had bench seats along one side. It was this area that Arnold searched carefully. His patience was rewarded. He found a blonde hair and a black one, both were nearly six feet long. These, he carefully inserted into two plastic bags. He also slipped the manager another note and received the mileage logs. The van had traveled a total of six miles during that particular rental. Conclusion: it had been driven some three miles out from the base and then back, giving Arnold a solid clue where the women had been taken.

Returning to his own ship, he carefully did a field DNA test on the blonde hair strand. It was a match to Adrianne's DNA, at least to the field test level of accuracy. Such would not actually hold up in a court of law, but rather it was a good indicator that she had been on that bench in that van at some point in time. As far as Arnold was concerned, he was convinced that the kidnapers had dropped off Adrianne and at least another woman or two somewhere here in Capital City, probably within a three-mile radius of the military base and spaceport. The question was where and why?

Two days later and after making many drive-by trips in this area, Arnold had a sick feeling in his stomach. Like nearly all spaceports, this one was no different. Surrounding it was the Red Light District, where spacers could go to get a quick lay. After all, being cooped up in a tiny spaceship for long periods of time made men and women starving for sexual outlets, usually fulfilled somewhere close to the spaceports where they landed, if only briefly. Adrianne was now likely being forced into the prostitution trade here on Zeta Scorpii-C!

Unfortunately, this revelation wasn't all that useful. Within that three-mile zone were dozens upon dozens of such "establishments!" Each one would have to be searched for the missing woman. Worse, the local authorities were refusing to accept his forged credentials. He'd have to do this on his own. Thus, he began visiting these establishments. His plan was to visit each one and ask to see all of their merchandise, before picking the woman to "entertain him." Steeling himself for this, Arnold began methodically searching these houses of ill repute.

After visiting two of them and barely avoiding upchucking at each, he decided he needed a better way. So far, he'd only found pathetic women, pretty — well maybe once, but now they were mostly automatons, hooked on drugs and who knew what else, alive, yes, but barely. Then, he came across one establishment's sign that announced "Exotic Women." Wondering what that meant, he visited it next and found what he was looking for: genetically modified terrorist attack victims!

There were six of these establishments within the

search radius. Methodically, Arnold searched each one, asking first to see all of their "merchandise." In order to get beyond the front door, he quickly saw that he needed to "dress" the part and had to purchase a very expensive suit. Walking back into the first of these, Arnold now found himself welcomed and, as requested, was allowed to inspect the "merchandise" in order to choose the escort that suited him.

In order to maintain his disguise, Arnold had to pick one from the establishment and take her out on a "date." He did so, but kept it clean, taking the nearly helpless woman to see a play, a musical, or a symphony. In doing so, he sensed the great relief coming from the silent women, who all wore tight fitting, sexy gowns, the monstrous lip plates that prevented them from speaking to him, and the toe shoes. He had to walk very slowly and soon discovered they really did appreciate his steadying arm around their tightly corseted waists. His heart went out to these "dates," but he also knew that he couldn't do anything about their plight.

The first five were a bust. The last one was called TC's Exotic Escorts. Dressed in his expensive suit, he entered and asked to see TC's merchandise. "Is this all of them?" he asked, not seeing any woman who resembled Adrianne. "I was looking for a young blonde woman. Perhaps with blue eyes," Arnold suggested.

"Well," Trevor replied with a wry smile, "I see you are a gentleman with discriminating tastes. I do have another blonde who might meet your requirements, but she is, as we say, still in training."

"Oh. I see. Yes, training would be desirable," Arnold replied. "Might I at least have a peek ahead of time?" He smiled covertly, and Trevor took the hint. He showed him a photograph of the woman in question. Arnold's heart skipped a beat. He tried to show no surprise. "Well, yes, absolutely perfect. Just look at her. Indeed, a rare exotic beauty, Trevor. When might her training be completed?"

"Please give her another week. If you will return then, I'm sure she'll be most ready to please you in any way that you might desire," Trevor replied.

"Excellent. Most excellent. I shall return next Monday

for a most pleasurable date," Arnold suggested.

"Very good. I'll put you down for Monday night. Say around seven?" Trevor asked, taking out a scheduling board and making notes. "What clothing would you prefer her to be wearing? Ball gowns, tight fitting gowns, or something more exotic?" he asked.

Arnold grimaced inwardly. "Ah, I shall let you surprise me. Anticipation is half of the enjoyment," he replied.

Trevor snickered and smiled. "Excellent choice. Indeed, it most certainly is! I won't let you down. Until Monday night then," he rose and offered his hand. The two men shook and Arnold left.

He had a week to prepare his rescue operation. His plans called for taking her out on a "date," but really, he would bring her to his transport ship and depart, taking her home to her grandmother. By the time that TC missed her, he and Adrianne would be halfway home. Nothing could go wrong with this plan!

Nevertheless, Arnold donned some disguises and kept the place under surveillance during the following week. He did see a number of extremely well dressed men taking their exotic women out on their dates. His heart went out to these poor women, barely able even to walk and being so used! Then, he saw that even the military's top general was taking another terrified young woman out. A junior officer accompanied him along with a second woman. Both wore gowns that were so tight that they could only barely walk. Their strides were three inches a step at most! Worse, the general kept insisting the women move faster! Arnold wanted to shoot that man on the spot! Only his assignment to rescue Adrianne Tonby kept his ire and anger in check!

Then, Sunday night, he saw Trevor and an older woman leaving shortly after supper. For several minutes, he toyed with the idea to break in there now, find Adrianne, and escape with her. He weighed that option against the certainty of taking Adrianne out on a date tomorrow night and decided since he didn't know how soon Trevor would be returning, it would be wiser to stick to his original plan.

Arnold also decided to stick around for a while yet. He

didn't like the fact that Trevor was gone. He hadn't seen any security guards around, but that didn't mean they weren't there inside somewhere. Still, it was possible that someone might try to break in and steal the women. He was so close to rescuing Adrianne that he didn't want to risk even that remote possibility. Quietly, he waited in the shadows.

Movement at the door caught his attention! A woman in a wheelchair came rolling outside, looking fearfully in all directions, followed by a whole group of these exotic women! He came completely alert, wishing that it wasn't so dark. The first thing he noticed was that all five of the women were wearing rather short skirts, and he realized they were attempting to appear as typical Federation professional women. Still, that apparel gave them far more mobility, compared to the unbelievably restrictive gowns the two wore the night before. Wait. He recognized the same two women that he'd seen before. And there was Adrianne! Her blonde hair was unmistakable! Arnold came totally alert, ready for any and all action. *What the hell are they doing?*

Arnold was about to break cover when it struck him. They were trying to escape! As helpless as they were, they were actually fleeing this hell hole! On their own! Arnold smiled. *I have to admire those women's guts! If they pull this off, they will have a much higher opinion of themselves. Their self-respect ought to soar. I'll shadow them and be ready to help if they encounter trouble. Perhaps, I can rescue all six of them.*

He followed them silently. He wore rubber-soled shoes that made no sound. His black clothing also helped shield him from sight. Twice, though, he used the butt of his gun to knockout would be overly curious men who were heading after them, presumably with ill intentions in their minds. Where were they going, he wondered. From the direction of travel, he soon realized that the military base must be their goal, but why there? That made no sense, unless they were going to try to steal a spaceship. Perhaps, the wheelchair bound woman could pilot it, he considered as he continued to trail them silently from a safe distance.

They stopped at a back gate, wholly unguarded. Arnold watched them closely. The gate opened, and they headed inside. After they had moved off some, he approached the gate. It had a security lock! One of them must have known the code, he surmised. He whipped out one of his small electronic gadgets, attached it to the security number pad. Shortly, the needed coded flashed on his small display. He entered the digits, and the gate opened. He stepped through, unfastening his device and stowing it, before trailing after the women. Like the women, he too had to duck into the shadows to avoid two guards making their rounds.

Then, he saw them split into two groups. A pair headed off towards the rows of parked deep space transports, while the remainder including Adrianne headed deeper into the base. Now, Arnold was torn. Which group did he follow? While he wanted to follow Adrianne and ensure her safety, he also guessed the other two were likely planning to snatch a transport for their getaway. He reached a decision and followed the pair as they moved slowly towards the row of ships. Their bay ramps were down, ready for rushing soldiers responding to any alarm. Impatiently, he watched the pair. At last, they moved slowly up one ramp. Once he was sure that they were not coming back out, he stole up to the ship. He took off his backpack and rummaged through it, trying to find the right device in the near darkness. Going by feel alone, he finally found it, pulling out a small tracker. He firmly placed it just inside the bay ramp on a side beam where it wouldn't be noticed. He activated it. Confident that if they somehow did manage to take off in this ship, he could follow them, he headed back in the general direction that Adrianne and her group had gone.

Boom! He saw a small shed erupting from some kind of explosion. In the faint light, he spotted Adrianne and her group heading towards the rows of transports. He ducked out of sight, keeping watch for the expected soldiers on patrol. He drew out his d-gun, unwilling to let anything happen to Adrianne. He saw a yellow cloud of gas billowing up from the shed. He waited. A soldier came running towards the group but they had not yet seen him. Arnold carefully aimed his gun and fired. D-guns are very silent. His beam of disintegration struck the soldier in his head, dropping him. Still the fleeing group hadn't noticed anything yet. Arnold backed up some, worried about the gas cloud.

Finally, he saw the women heading up the ramp. The red flashing light on the belly of the ship told him that it was powered up and ready for a takeoff. Two guards were closing on them, but also that yellow gas cloud was also about on them and himself as well. Then, he realized what that gas cloud was! The bio agent! Arnold had no time to waste. Seeing the bay ramp closing, he made a mad dash in the opposite direction! Running at full speed, Arnold fled for his own life. As a former Special Operations field commander, Arnold was in prime shape and easily outran the expanding cloud. Reaching the fence, he scrambled over it, ignoring the slight cuts from the barbed wire at its top. Once on the streets of Capital City, he raced down them maintaining his top speed. Only after a mile did he slow down a little. At last, he reached his own vehicle, climbed in, and floored it, tires screeching in the night.

When he neared the public spaceport where his own ship was docked, he could see the yellow cloud had covered the military base and was already drifting over the red light district of the city! At least the public spaceport was out of the way of the cloud for the moment. He rushed to his ship, entered the codes to lower the bay ramp, dashed inside, closed it, and ran to the pilot's seat up front. Panting from his exertion, he began the power up sequence, and then called the tower for clearance, citing Capella-D as his destination.

As he lifted off, he pivoted his ship around and saw the ship carrying Adrianne hovering a safe distance above the military base. They were also looking at the expanding cloud, which had now reached the area of TC's Exotic Escorts. Arnold now smiled, realizing in part what must have been in the mind of these escapees. Then, their ship continued lifting off, vanishing shortly into hyperspace. Arnold finished his liftoff sequence, arriving far above the planet. Now, he activated his hyperspace tracking receiver.

"Bingo!" he exclaimed. There was the red light signal coming from the tracker he'd placed on their ship. He jumped into hyperspace, hot on their trail. An hour later, having used his considerable piloting skills, he arrived close their ship.

Docking in hyperspace was always a tricky maneuver. Since he didn't want to scare the women who might react with some wild ship maneuvers, he considered trying to make contact with them. However, he had no idea what frequency to use or if they were even able to operate the comm center. Well, maybe the woman in the wheelchair could, but she was probably in the pilot's seat right now.

Arnold had no choice but to attempt to dock. "I've got to make this as silent as humanly possible. If I spook them, they could head off in some random direction screwing up the docking or worse, wiping us both out," he explained to his console. "Gently, gently does it." Moving but millimeters at a time, Arnold began to close the distance, aligning the docking bays. Thank goodness for Federation standards, he thought. Every docking bay worked identically to the next. A half hour later, he felt the slight nudge as his ship docked with theirs.

Now, they would know that they were about to be boarded. The air seal activated, and air was being pumped into the narrow corridor linking the two ships, air coming in part from both ships. Alfonso yelled out, "Oh crap! Someone has docked with us! They are boarding us now!"

Panic struck the six, but Pippa yelled, "Okay, Bess and I are on it!" She and Bess moved themselves to the air lock where the boarding party would soon come into their ship. Bess held up the antique gun with its silencer still on it. Her hand was shaking a little. "Easy does it, Bess," Pippa did her best to calm the woman's nerves. *God damn my father! I could handle this easily before! Now, I'm reduced to being beyond pathetic!*

The air lock door opened but no one stuck their head in for Bess to shoot. "Hello. I'm here to rescue you. Adrianne's grandmother, Marilyn Tonby hired me to find Adrianne and rescue her. Adrianne, are you there?"

Adrianne's shocked look told Pippa everything that she needed to know. "Come on in, but we have a gun on you," Pippa called out slowly, repeating it twice hoping and praying that this man could understand her. If not, Bess' gun would speak for them.

Arnold stuck his head into their ship and saw Adrianne,

Estrella, Pippa, and Bess, as well as the gun pointed towards him. He also saw her shaking hand. He raised his hands and stepped into their ship. "Hello. Arnold Flaxton, Private Investigator. You can put the gun down miss. I'm not here to harm anyone, just help get Adrianne home safely. Been quite a trip finding you, Miss Tonby."

Bess lowered the gun. Pippa spoke up. "Can you show us some ID? Can you even understand me?"

"Yes, as long as you speak slowly. Rather hard, but I think I understand you. My ID," he replied, presenting her his official PI ID card this time.

"Is it okay?" Bess whispered to Pippa who nodded.

"Did grandmother really send you?" Adrianne asked twice.

"You bet she did. Been carrying around this photo of you that she gave me." He pulled out the worn photo and saw Adrianne visibly sighed and relax.

"We need help," Adrianne finally said.

"I know. I saw what you all did back there. I don't know how you did it, but you blew up a giant pile of that terrible bio agent, right?" Arnold asked.

Pippa said both determinedly and defensively. "Well what of it? They had to pay for what they did to me, to us. My sicko father, General Tyrrell did this to me. I was about to become a soldier, and he did this to me so I would be a proper woman, according to him."

"I know, I saw him taking you and another one of you on what was supposed to be a date of sorts," Arnold said. "I was keeping watch on you. If you had not escaped tonight, I had arranged to take Adrianne out on a date tomorrow night and rescue her then. So, who is who, and are you all hungry? I'm starving."

One by one, they introduced themselves. Alfonso and Savina joined them, having overhead everything. "You two are flying this ship?" Arnold asked in disbelief.

"Well, I am or was a trained pilot," Alfonso replied defensively. "Savina here was almost an astro-navigator, before we were wiped out in that terrorist attack. We aren't as helpless as we appear."

Arnold chuckled. "Hell no you aren't helpless! Frankly, I'm amazed at what you did. I was following you from the moment you snuck out of that escort service building. I was keeping watch to make sure that no one kidnaped Adrianne again before I could rescue her tomorrow night. I did have to shoot one soldier you didn't see coming up from behind you, and I knocked out several unsavory men who spotted you on the street and were planning to snatch you. So yes, I saw what you all did. Damned amazing. Still, hungry?"

"Well, yes we are," Pippa answered. "You did all that for us?"

"Come on. Let's get to the galley. I'll whip up something. Yes, I did it, Pippa. I'm a retired or ex-Special Operations commander out of Capella-D, Black Ops. Over breakfast, I'd love to hear your stories."

Soon, Arnold had bacon, eggs, and coffee going. Sitting at the small table, Adrianne said, "I don't know why you bothered with us. We're helpless cripples now. You are going to have to feed us, unless Bess does us all."

"I don't mind helping feed you, but only if you tell me your stories while we're eating," Arnold replied politely.

For the next two hours, Arnold got quite an earful of tales, similar in many ways, but identical once they arrived at the escort service. He grimaced when he heard about the tortures they'd endured. "Beasts!" he commented.

Pippa replied, "Well, now my father, Trevor, and Agnes are going to see what it is really like being us! Revenge is sweet. I just wish I could see them screaming when they wake up and find themselves like we are!"

"Yes, but we aren't through yet," Alfonso barked, though he had to repeat it twice before Arnold understood him.

Pippa explained, "We stole dad's list of all the known suppliers of the bio agent cylinders. We are going after all them next. Want to help?"

"Amazing, Pippa. Aren't you going to give it to the security forces on your world?" Arnold asked, figuring that's what she really meant.

"Hell no! They won't do a goddamned thing about it.

They are probably getting their own secret supplies of this stuff from some of them. We're going to wipe them out, just as we did back there in Capital City. Give them a taste of what they've done to all of us and millions of others," Pippa declared.

"You are serious about this," Arnold declared, amused at first.

"You bet. It has to stop," Adrianne spoke up. "You can take us to see my grandmother to prove to her I'm rescued, but then we're all going after every one of these bastards on this list of Pippa's. They must pay for what they've caused. Our lives are wiped out because of them, and it isn't fair."

"Right. We're going to do something about it," Pippa declared firmly.

Arnold thought for a moment before replying. "Pippa, you are quite right. No one is going to do much about the men on that list of yours. As long as the terrorists only attack small groups, they are ignoring them, while stockpiling supplies of this nasty bio agent themselves. I think they think of it as a deterrent to war. So you are all really serious about taking them out?"

All six heads nodded, shaking their enormous lip plates against their chests. "Okay. What about letting me lend you a hand in this?" Arnold asked. "You're right. They ought to be made to pay dearly. What they've done to you and millions of other innocent men, women, and even children is beyond despicable."

"Well, we sure could use more hands," Pippa admitted, "but you'll mostly have to care for us. We're damned near helpless." Tears swelled up in her eyes.

"Maybe I can help with that. First, now that you've all eaten, we have to abandon this ship. I take it that you didn't remove the RFI tag used to identify this ship. As soon as you drop out of hyperspace, they will be tracking you and pounce on you with battleships," Arnold explained.

"Shit. I forgot about that," Alfonso admitted. "He's right. They can track us as soon as we drop out of hyperspace."

"Here's what we can do. I'll get you all onboard my ship and undock. We'll just let this one float here in hyperspace.

124

Then, we will let your grandmother know you are safe and sound, Adrianne. I need to make some calls, but I think I can help you all out some, before we tackle getting those men on your list, Pippa," Arnold explained. "Trust me a little while more."

It was a chore getting the nearly helpless six through the air lock and into his ship. Arnold mostly had to carry them one by one. That done, he disconnected the docking, allowing their stolen transport to drift away from his ship. Next, he positioned Adrianne before his own comm center and placed a secure call to Marilyn Tonby. He stepped back with the others and allowed them to chat more or less in private.

Minutes later, Adrianne pivoted in her chair. "Okay. She's agreed to let me stay with you, Arnold, and help. Now what?"

"I need to make some private calls of my own. Let's get you all to bed. You have to be exhausted by now." None disagreed with that. He followed Bess' directions, helping her to undress them and get them tucked into beds. Then, he helped Bess as well, pleasing her enormously, since he was the first person actually to help her all these months.

That done, he headed to his comm center and began calling in favors owed to him. Nefarious favors, though. "I know it's illegal, but won't a hundred grand compensate you? Besides, then we are even," he argued.

"Even? Your word on that," the man insisted.

"My word," Arnold replied.

"Okay then. Midnight. Westridge Assisted Living. Use the back door. Make damned sure that you aren't seen," the man replied. He signed off, and Arnold shut his line down as well. Costly, but it was the only way, he thought. A minute later, he entered the coordinates and fired up the hyperspace engines all the way to maximum speed.

He landed at a spaceport just outside of Westridge on Capella-D. While the others continued sleeping, he rented a van, parking it close to the bay ramp. "Okay sleepy heads. Time to rise and shine," he called out.

For the next half hour, he saw just how difficult life was for these victims. Dressing them was quite a chore. That done, he explained, "I've made some arrangements to get you as many of the genetic cures as possible."

"But the waiting list is miles long," Adrianne complained.

"These are being done off the books. People owe me favors, and I'm calling them in. If we are going to go after these suppliers, I need you all as able as possible. Come on; they are waiting for you."

"You mean it? We are going to get some of the cures?" Pippa asked, quite shocked. She knew the enormous length of the waiting lists and never expected to live long enough to get even one of them.

"Yes. But we have to hurry up. It's all being done on the side. I'll be carrying you into the van. It's quicker." He proceeded to carry them one by one down the ramp and into the van. A half hour later, he helped them down, and they marched up to the back door in near darkness much like a line of penguins, moving extremely slowly and carefully, unable to see where they were placing their feet. It was midnight.

A man met them at the door. He didn't say anything but did nod to Arnold, who brought up the rear, helping Bess in her wheelchair. They took a service elevator to the basement and ended up in a locked storage room, where the doctor had brought in his equipment. After shutting the door, he finally spoke. "I am Dr. Bainbridge. This is being done in secret, so Arnold, you are going to have to be my nurse and assistant. You'll be monitoring them the whole time, four days at least. Now then, let's get this started."

One by one, the five were completely undressed and then hooked up to a machine via IVs inserted into their legs. Soon, all five were unconscious. "Now then, Bess. What are we going to do with you? There is a chance if we give you the original bio agent and then follow that with the cures, you might have your feet regrown as well. Then again, it might not work."

"You, you mean I'd be turned into one of them?" she asked, her voice quivering a little.

"Yes, but you would have your arms back, I believe, and maybe your legs. No guarantees."

"But I could end up with no arms and no legs?" Bess asked timidly.

"There is always that possibility. I won't lie to you."

Bess thought about it for a minute in silence. "Arnold. Will you promise me that, if I end up nothing but a torso, then you will kill me? I couldn't live like that. Promise me that you will, and I'll give it a try."

Arnold swallowed but saw her point. "Okay, Bess. I promise, but I don't think it will come to that."

A few minutes later, she too was unconscious. Dr. Bainbridge then explained in detail what Arnold had to do, adding, "I'll drop by as often as I can, bringing you food too. Just don't let anyone find out what we're doing or there'll be hell to pay. Got it?"

Arnold took a seat, monitoring the various gauges. Soon, he stared at their naked, comatose bodies. That another human being could do this to another bothered him. The more he faced them, the more his determination to help them in their quest to eliminate all these suppliers solidified. He dosed off, awakened periodically by his watch's timer so he could check on the patients. By the second day, he could see small arms had appeared at the shoulders of the five, while Bess' arms had shrunk noticeably. Likewise, he could see their massive breasts had gotten somewhat smaller, while Bess' had gotten larger.

Four days with off-and-on sleep, Arnold watched over the six, noticing the changes as they developed. That last day, though, Dr. Bainbridge stuck around. "As soon as Bess wakes, I'm putting her back under with the cures." Arnold nodded. The poor woman was now hardly more than a head and torso with massive breasts. Her leg stumps were still there, unaffected thus far; and more than once Arnold said a prayer for Bess. Nevertheless, he knew that he would follow her request. If her arms and legs didn't regrow, he would see that she never regained consciousness. No one could live like that.

The five were doing well. Their arms had regrown and their lips healed back up. Even up close, he couldn't see the slit line in their lips where they had been separated. That line had gradually vanished on the fourth day. Their breasts had reduced drastically, but were still far larger than the norm. Their hair had been unaffected by the process. Their feet had become far less malformed, though they were still not normal in shape. In addition, their fingernails were quite long, nearly three inches, and, like their hair, could not be cut because now there were neurons, axons, and axon terminals fanning out in them.

Just then, Bess began stirring. At once, Dr. Bainbridge switched her solutions and she slipped back into another coma. "Now, we will see," he whispered. "You are going to have to get these five some new clothes and shoes. We've got partially healed feet. That means they will always have to wear six-inch heels. If they don't they'll rip their leg tendons."

"Sorry, I don't know anything about women's apparel, doc. I can take them shopping."

"Well, I'll see if I can at least get them some heels. You can make do with their old clothes for a quick trip to the store. Say, looks like one of them is coming around," the doctor pointed out.

One by one, the five awoke. Arnold had tears in his eyes as he watched the expressions of pure joy on their faces, as they discovered their arms were back. Five lives had been salvaged as far as he was concerned. Of course, soon they saw what had become of Bess and hovered over her, spelling Arnold.

"I need to get you to some women's apparel store. Dr. Bainbridge is going to see if he can find some shoes for you to wear. Meantime, get dressed in your old things as best you can," Arnold suggested, wiping his eyes on his shirtsleeve. A half hour later, the six ducked out of the rear, piling into his van. Even though Adrianne wasn't familiar with this town, she knew there was an Elvina's Fashions in just about every city on Capella-D.

Pulling into their parking lot, Arnold said, "Okay. Here's my card. Go get yourselves fixed up. Best have at least enough to last you a week or so between laundry days."

"Thanks for everything, Arnold," Adrianne replied. "Come on, gang. I know just what we will need."

An hour later, a store clerk had to push a large cart out

128

to the van, piled high with bags. Bras, panties, skirts, blouses, blazers, heels, nylons, and dresses ran up a bill approaching five grand, but Arnold could care less. Seeing their shining faces meant everything to him just now. As they drove back, Adrianne explained, "We got each of us six professional women's outfits, figuring that will be our usual dress. Plus, we each got one formal gown, just in case we need to dress up. If you think that we need men's dress, let us know, and we'll make another trip later on."

Pippa added, "We thought that in these tall heels, we'd look ridiculous wearing pants."

"Excellent. We'd best get back. I'm going to drop you off at my ship. You can stay there while I wait it out with Bess," Arnold suggested.

"I'm coming with you," Pippa insisted. "I owe her everything. We all do; so no matter how it turns out, one of us must be with her."

An hour later, the two slipped back in the backdoor and headed to the basement, relieving the doctor. As the two sat beside Bess, Pippa asked, "Are you really going to honor her last request? I mean if it doesn't work."

"Could you go through the rest of your life without any arms and just two short stumps for legs?" Arnold whispered back.

"It was horrid enough without my arms, but without legs too — why there wouldn't be any point to living like that," Pippa answered.

"Precisely. If it comes to that, I won't let her wake up to that nightmare," Arnold replied. "Now, we wait. I've been saying some prayers for her. Guess it can't hurt."

The next morning, small arms had appeared at her shoulders as well as thin legs. Both breathed a huge sigh of relief. So far, the process was working. On the fourth day, Bess finally roused from her medically induced coma. Her first reaction was to raise her arms to check on them. Visibly, she relaxed, and Arnold helped her into a sitting position. "Legs! I've got legs again!" she exclaimed and began crying. Just why women broke into tears over something wonderful eluded him. Even Pippa's eyes were wet. Bess hugged Arnold. "Thank you, thank you, thank you!"

He kissed her forehead. "Let's get you dressed."

"Oh! I've got it too," she added, noting her new sexual organs behind her original ones. "My hair. Oh, it's really long too. Oh, you can feel with it, how very strange!"

Pippa laughed. "We know. You can feel with it as you can with your fingers. Ask Estrella about it. She's the geneticist here. Come on; let's get you up. We bought you some clothes too."

While Pippa helped her dress, Dr. Bainbridge began dismantling his equipment. Arnold came over to him and shook his hand. "We're square now. Thank you doctor."

"Square. I just wish we could cure far more of these victims than we can, but there is only so much basic material available," he replied. A few minutes later, the three slipped out of the backdoor on their way to his van.

"I can't believe I'm walking again. I never ever thought that I'd ever walk again," Bess gushed. "These heels are a bit hard to walk in, but I'll never complain, not ever!"

Once they'd returned to his ship, Arnold asked everyone, "Okay. Are you all still interested in going after all those suppliers on Pippa's list? Anyone who wants out now can. No one will think any less of you. Last chance to back out."

Alfonso looked at the others and spoke up, "Hell no! We are all in this to the end. Someone has to bring these fiends to justice. If I'm going to spend the rest of my life as a woman, someone's going to pay dearly for that."

"But dear, you aren't a woman, not really," Savina replied.

"Just like you aren't a man," he teased her, and she flushed. "We're all in this together."

"Okay then. I'm going to go do some shopping for stuff we're going to need. We'll leave when I get back," Arnold replied, pleased that none had backed out.

Several hours later, he returned with a van full of equipment. He gave each a gun with a silencer on it. "Pippa has proven these can cause a chain reaction of the cylinders, where a d-gun won't. Here's a d-gun for each of you, along with a knife." He had many other bags as well, including quite a lot of food. All pitched in and helped him move them from the van into the transport.

Night vision goggles, comm sets, IR detectors, security lock decoders — the list of his additional equipment went on and on. While they headed for their first target, Arnold began drilling them on the use of each piece of equipment. Pippa already was familiar with most and lent a hand helping the others master their operation.

Estrella became their official Med Tech. Although her training to date had been in genetics, she was also familiar with many medical techniques. Adrianne became their linguist, handling the languages of the various worlds for them. Alfonso took over as chief pilot with Savina as their navigator, freeing Arnold from those duties. "We are going to make one hot team," Arnold commented, as they approached their first target world.

Pippa had reservations. She was a trained solider, but now with the overly long nails and hair, forced to wear the tall heels, she wondered just how effective she could be against other male soldiers. As she looked at herself in a mirror, seeing herself in the new grey skirt, white blouse, dark hose, and impressive heels, Pippa realized men would never suspect she was a soldier and thus would have the element of surprise over them. That was something, she thought, hoping it would be enough. Still, this was a million times better than before.

Al Nair, a blue class B subgiant star loomed on their viewport. Savina called out, "Al Nair dead ahead. According to the list, we're looking for Al Nair-F, which is on the Forbidden List of planets. We think it is likely a desert type of world and rather hot. Oh," she added, "they speak a Welsh dialect here. Anyone know it?"

"I do," yelled Adrianne from the comm center. "I'm trying to tap into their local communications now. See if I can learn anything useful."

Lacking precise coordinates, it took Savina a half hour to locate Al Nair-F the hard way by direct observation of the planets, counting out from the hot bluish star. As they dropped into orbit over the world, they did spot oceans and land masses. However, much of the land was arid and with large stretches of deserts with rolling sand dunes. This did not mean that they didn't have space travel, but their ships were primitive compared to the normal Federation ships. There were a dozen larger cities widely scattered across the north temperate continent. The equatorial continent had none and appeared likely too hot to sustain much human life there.

Alfonso engaged their cloaking device long before they approached this world. Hence, he felt confident in dropping to a low orbit to search for this city in question, Glaw. It took him three passes around the world finally to pin down which city was Glaw. Now came the hard part: finding the party that had the bio agent cylinders and were selling them. Arnold already worked out a plan for this. He activated his signal tracer and gave Adrianne the go ahead.

She switched to the frequency given on Pippa's list and spoke, "This is Captain Adrianne calling for General Tyrrell Fenton. Need more cylinders. Over." She repeated her message ten times before receiving a reply, which Arnold immediately locked onto. While Adrianne pretended to work out another order on the general's behalf, Arnold's device began homing in onto the precise ground location where the signal was coming from. Within less than a minute, he had it down to one specific building within the town below them. He signaled Adrianne who wrapped up this new "apparent deal."

Arnold then held a final meeting. "Okay. We've located these distributors. Of course, we're going to have to hunt for where they're keeping their cylinders. We can expect all sorts of resistance, deadly resistance mind you. These people play for keeps. The question I have for you is this. Do we kill those who stand in our way or stun them? Do we release the bio agent or do we try to blow it up? If we release it, we've no control over who becomes a victim."

"Hey, we make them suffer like the millions of other victims are suffering," Pippa declared. "Killing is too damn good for them. Those around them aren't innocent. They ought to have stopped these psychopaths, and they haven't, so they deserve it too."

"In any war, isn't there always collateral damage?"

asked Alfonso.

"Yes, there is, though many do their best to avoid it. When push comes to shove, though, winning takes front stage. All right then, no qualms about collateral damage then," Arnold stated. All six agreed with him. "That's settled then. We'll use the Sonic Disruption on them to knock them out. It's a broadband, wide area device. Here's how we do this. Alfonso and Savina remain on the ship. They will be ready to get us out of here in a damned hurry. Plus, they'll use the Sonic Disruption machine on any newcomers once we're on the ground. Bess and Estrella will remain close to the ship, be our lookouts, and handle anyone coming after the ship. Plus, if Pippa, Adrianne, or I get injured, Bess and Estrella will get us back into the ship pronto. Pippa and I will be the front line, doing the dirty work, but Adrianne will stay a ways behind us in case we need an interpreter. Adrianne, keep your head down and watch our backs. We'll all carry these handheld Stunners." He checked everyone out on the use of the new gear.

When he was satisfied everyone was as prepared as possible, Alfonso hovered over the center of the building complex from which the signal came, some thousand feet above it. Savina then activated the Sonic Disruption device. While they heard nothing, through the bay viewport, Arnold saw men around the perimeter and who were carrying automatic weapons dropping onto the ground. "Clear," he barked into the intercom and Alfonso set the deep space transport down in the center of the compound. As soon as the ship touched down, Arnold opened the bay doors and the ramp lowered.

He dashed off, while Pippa in her tall heels did her best to follow after him. Adrianne waited a bit, and then stepped down carefully as well, her Stunner drawn and at the ready. They had their hair tied into a ponytail and then wrapped up twice, ensuring that their long hair wouldn't get in their way.

The air smelled dry and very unusual, though none could pinpoint what the odors were. The ground was hard packed sandstone, brown. Likewise, the buildings were made from sandstone blocks with a corrugated metal roof, cheap construction. Two crude ships were parked at one end of this open area. Arnold and Pippa headed into the main doors with Adrianne trailing behind them, her head looking in all directions. Meanwhile, Estrella and Bess began confiscating the weapons from the unconscious men lying about the courtyard, just in case they should wake up prematurely.

Slowly and methodically, the pair began searching the rather large building. Men were down at their desks and around the comm center. They found no trace of the cylinders, but did find a stairs and elevator heading into the basement. Arnold signaled Pippa, who nodded, activated her Personal Defense Shield, and stepped into the elevator. Arnold silently stole down the stairs. Theirs would be a two-pronged attack. Far underground, six men were alerted to trouble coming their way. The Sonic Disruption machine didn't reach through the ground, and when the elevator doors opened, revealing Pippa as a well-dressed professional woman, though armed to the teeth, the six men hesitated for a second, moving out of their cover from behind boxes and crates.

That gave Arnold a clear line of sight, and he began firing his Stunner. Pippa joined him. Two minutes later, the six were down. The battle, over. As Adrianne joined them, the two fanned out and searched this area, but found mostly supplies and equipment. A back tunnel led further. Again with hand signals, Arnold and Pippa headed down it, while Adrianne confiscated the fallen men's guns. Arnold didn't like walking down this dimly lit tunnel. They could easily be taken by surprise. Pippa's steel heels clicking on the sandstone floor didn't help, but she couldn't do a whole lot about that.

Then, the hall opened into another giant chamber. A large caliber gun fired repeatedly at the pair as they entered, but their personal defense shields deflected these primitive projectiles. One Stunner shot from Pippa dropped the man in his tracks. She walked up to him, kicking his gun away from him. Both looked around the room rapidly. Against one wall was an expensive Duplication Machine that looked nearly worn out, probably discarded by some major world and picked up from their trash pile by these people. Next to it lay a huge stack of the yellow bio agent cylinders, probably a hundred of them.

What kept their attention was on the opposite wall. There, a redheaded woman was standing naked, her neck chained tightly to the wall. A metal bar went across her shoulders, parallel to the floor. Her arms were securely tied to it, outstretched. She had a metal O-ring gag that forced her mouth open. Its harness was wrapped around her head, so she had no way to get it off her. Further, her legs were held spread widely apart by a metal rod fastened to a pair of ankle cuffs. On top of that, a pair of metal cylinders was wrapped around her knees, preventing her from bending her legs. She was obviously being used as their sexual toy. When the two looked at her, she shook her head and made all manner of noise from her open mouth, unintelligible though.

Without any warning, Arnold heard in his mind, *Please, get me down from here, please!* Startled, Arnold looked at the bound woman. She nodded. *Please, get me down. Don't leave me like this.*

"She has to be freed," Arnold called out. "Keep watch, Adrianne." He went over to see about getting her free. Unfortunately, tiny padlocks securely held everything.

Keys are in his pants pocket. Right one. Again, Arnold heard that in his mind.

He looked the woman in her eyes. "Did you just tell me that?" She nodded, having stopped trying to make gurgling noises.

"What's happening?" Pippa asked.

"She must be a telepath. Told me where the keys to the locks are. Keep watch." Arnold replied and began searching the fallen leader. He found the keys right where the woman had told him, and he smiled, moving back to face her. Hastily, he undid her head harness, and she moved her jaws about before speaking.

She spoke Welsh and only Adrianne could understand her. "Thank you sir. I'm Gwenda Frewi. I've been held here a long time as their fucking bitch. Please get me out of here." She had a sinking look, as she realized that neither the man nor woman could understand her, but Adrianne did and quickly began translating for her.

135

"We'll rescue you, Gwenda," Arnold replied, nodding to Adrianne to translate for him, while he unlocked her arms and removed the bar from her shoulders. She massaged her arms, as he worked on her knee cylinders. Finally, he got the ankle cuffs off her, freeing her at long last.

"Thank you. Thank you. They held me here for months, fucking me regularly. Please, take me with you. I have to get out of here before more men come. Please," Gwenda begged. Adrianna translated for her.

Arnold made a snap decision. "Okay, Adrianne, tell her she can come with us for now. Head back and tell the others to get ready for a fast exit. Pippa and I will get these ready to blow."

Taking Gwenda's arm, Adrianne led her out, translating what Arnold said as they walked. Meanwhile, the two looked over the stack of cylinders, deciding on the best way to handle it. "Look, if they blow down here, hardly anyone's going to be infected. We should move them up to the main floor along with this bastard," Pippa pointed out. "You get him up, and I'll use this lift machine to move the cylinders."

An hour later, the two had all of the cylinders packed together on the main floor. They smashed open all the windows and opened up all the doors, including several large hanger doors that allowed their small spaceships to be brought inside for maintenance, presumably. Arnold had all the men loosely piled in one corner. He and Pippa backed out to the front doorway of the building. After double checking that everyone else was onboard, he said, "Would you like the honors or should I?"

"I'd like to, but if it goes off fast, I can't run in these heels. I'd best get back to the ship and let you do it, Arnold. Give them a taste of what they've been doing to millions of others!" Pippa declared. A few minutes later, Pippa watched, as he fired his silenced gun twice before she heard the familiar popping sounds, rapidly escalating. Arnold sprinted to the bay ramp, and Pippa hit the close button the instant his feet hit the ramp. Before the yellow cloud of gas hit the ship, the transport was sealed tightly and rising off the desert world.

Already, Savina had laid in their course to the next

world on Pippa's list. After stowing their gear, Arnold and Pippa headed off to check on their rescued woman. However, Estrella and Bess had gotten her bathed, her hair washed, and dried via the electrostatic machine. They'd scrounged through their clothes and had her dressed like themselves, professional women. Further, they'd strapped an old Imperium ULAT box to her waist.

"Wow Gwenda, you sure look nice," Arnold said, quite startled at her appearance. Her flaming red, wavy hair was no longer a tangled mess, but was shiny and full, falling to her middle of her back. A huge smile revealed pure white teeth and her eyes shone. She looked extremely attractive, he thought.

"I never looked this good before. Thank you all. I owe you my life. I'm a telepath and I'll serve you now until my debt is paid," Gwenda said somewhat awkwardly, wholly unused to the ULAT box saying her words in a language she'd never heard before.

"Gwenda, as far as we are concerned, you've already paid your debt by surviving their torture and rape. You are a free woman. Is there somewhere that we can take you? Like your home or husband or family?" Arnold replied graciously.

Gwenda laughed. "Silly. Gwenda isn't married. No family. No place to go back to. Others would kidnap me. I'm a telepath. Nowhere is safe for me. I do owe you my life. I must pay you for that. Those were very bad men."

"We know. They sold those cylinders to terrorists who used them against innocent men, women, and children. Do you know anything about that?" Arnold asked.

"Yes, very bad chemicals. Makes people into helpless freaks," she replied.

"Precisely. We released their entire stockpile on them. In a few days, they will wake up as helpless freaks themselves. Now, they can experience what they've done to millions of others," Pippa broke in and explained.

"Oh, that's clever. Serves them right for all the evil things they've done," Gwenda replied, still having a hard time with speaking while the ULAT translated for her. She found it most confusing.

"Right," Arnold took control once more. "These six here

were terrorist victims too, but I got them as many cures as there are right now. We seven are on a crusade to wipe out all the known dealers, sellers of these nasty bio agent cylinders, giving them a taste of what they've done to millions of others. So we are a very dangerous bunch to be around. We could get killed at any time by some of these villains. It's not safe for you to be with us. You could get hurt yourself. So is there somewhere we could take you?" Arnold tried his best to explain the situation to Gwenda.

"No place is safe for me. I shall come with you and help you fight the evil men, destroy cylinders. I can fight. Give me a knife. I can take care of myself and help you. I owe you my life. I must pay my debt to you," Gwenda countered.

Arnold sighed. "So there's no place where you can be safe? Cause you are a telepath?" he asked, trying to make this completely clear in his mind.

"Telepaths are kidnaped all the time. No place is safe for me. As soon as someone finds out, they'll take me again, though I've already gutted ten men who tried. The last time, a dozen men came after me. I killed three before they knocked me out and bound me in their cellar room where you found me. I can fight. I can help. I owe you."

"Okay. Gang, is it all right with you if Gwenda joins our group?" Arnold asked. Everyone agreed, welcoming her onboard. He then said, "I understand about honor, Gwenda. If you help us defeat these other evil men, then your debt is fully paid. Agreed?"

"I suppose so. Not truly a fair trade, but I'll agree to that. I must earn my keep. I have no money, but I'll work. Help out, but you must teach me what to do. I've never been in a flying machine before," she replied.

"That we can do. Welcome aboard, Gwenda," Arnold said, offering her a handshake. She grinned, shaking his hand very firmly.

"Thanks. I'm willing for you to put me into your fucking bindings whenever you wish," Gwenda then said.

"Huh? Sorry, Gwenda, I don't know what you mean," Arnold replied, flushing a little.

"You freed me from one of the fucking bindings, though

only those bad men chained me to the wall. Every man's house has a fucking binding in it. They put us in it whenever they want a good time. We women of Al Nair are used to it. Usually, they keep us in the fucking bindings for a few days each month. So I'm willing for you to put me into yours, Arnold, any time that you have your urges," she explained.

"Good God!" Adrianne exclaimed.

"No wonder this planet is on the Forbidden List!" Arnold exclaimed. "Gwenda, that is no way to ever treat a woman. It's not ever done on any civilized world in the entire rest of the galaxy! I don't have one of those, and I certainly would never mistreat you that way." He began to see that Gwenda would also need gentle handling and an education.

Gwenda frowned, "But don't your people have sex? Don't you have urges that must be satisfied?"

"Yes, but it is mutual love and respect. We treat each other with kindness," Arnold tried to explain. "We'll do our best to show you that the rest of the galaxy isn't full of sadistic men." She seemed to accept this, at least for now. Further, Arnold sensed a great deal of relief coming from Gwenda.

"Come with me," Adrianne spoke up. "I'll show you around the ship and teach you our language."

As Arnold watched them heading down the hallway, he remarked to Pippa, "Now there goes a woman after my heart! She's got real spirit."

Pippa grinned, "She's not married either." He chuckled, and they headed off to study what was known about their next destination. Pippa had no doubts that in time, Arnold and Gwenda would become a couple. Already, she and Bess had a thing going between them, just as Estrella and Adrianne had. Alfonso and Savina were already married, compliments of Arnold, as ship's captain.

By the time they finished executing their next raid, Arnold saw that Gwenda was indeed an excellent fighter. She fought dirty and even had some moves that he'd never seen before. She was highly intelligent, though had no formal education. Gwenda was a very fast learner, picking up a new concept almost on her first attempt.

As they lifted off and watched the expanding yellow

cloud doing its work on this batch of bio agent sellers, Gwenda asked what was to become a profound question. "These are the sellers of that awful stuff. But what about going after all those who have purchased the cylinders? Aren't we going to get them next?"

"Well, sure. A lot of worlds have bought this stuff so they can use it against other worlds that might use it against them," Arnold answered. "Problem is that we don't know what worlds have stockpiled them or where on such a world the stuff is being kept."

Gwenda smiled, "But I can find that out. I can look into men's minds and see if they have the yellow cylinders and were they are kept."

Pippa exclaimed, "Wow! That's incredible, Gwenda. Arnold, we should do that too, once we wipe out the suppliers. We should take out everyone else's supplies of the stuff too."

Arnold laughed, "Okay, okay. I can take a hint. First, let's get the suppliers finished off, and then we can go after those who have stockpiled them. Otherwise, if we wipe out a stockpile, they will just order more from the suppliers."

"Okay, makes sense. We've a lot to do, don't we?" Pippa grinned.

Chapter 9 Birth of the Black One

Late spring, 1450, Valen Castle, Tierra or Ashford-5. Young Velasco Valen paced the walls of his suite, frustrated beyond belief. The twenty-five year old, black-haired lad knew he wasn't in line for the throne, not unless three older brothers somehow died. He rubbed his well-tended moustache, annoyed yet again. He could trace his lineage back to the Glory Days when Augusto Valen had very nearly wrestled total control over all Tierra from all the other towers and kings. Coming from that long line of powerful men only added to his frustrations, knowing he would never get any chance to prove his mettle, to prove that a Valen was still a force to be reckoned with.

But it went far beyond his own heritage, far beyond it. The "freaks" now had nearly total dominion over Tierra. *Those pathetic queens,* he thought, *and that host of freaks who breed like rabbits! First a few and now they threaten to push we normal people out of our own homelands! All of Exchange City. Hell, there's more freaks living there than normals now. They control even our education schools, well at least the Academies.* He corrected his thought. Here in Valen, at least they did have their own school for smaller children.

He'd had no choice but to go to the Academy in Exchange City and put up with the hundreds of freaks who were also attending. *They aren't even men anymore, but women. Hell, they look just like a woman and breed like them too. They act like them as well. If they kept their mouths shut, no one could tell otherwise.* He paced around his room once more.

And the damned Guilds control everything else and do just what the freaks want them to do. I swear the freaks have the Guilds eating out of their hands, when they actually do have hands that is. Wimps. All of them. Not a true man among them all. What has Tierra become? A habitat for freaks. Soon, they'll take over Valen too. We're the closest big city to Exchange City. Anyone can tell they have their eyes on

Valen as well. Another twenty years and their numbers will have outgrown Exchange City, and they'll be moving here in on us, spreading their freakish kind here, polluting our own gene pool. He circled his room once more.

What's more, they will be **welcomed** *here with open arms! The fools. My brothers, the Guilds, they are all ignorant fools. They can't see what these freaks have done to our world.* He made another circuit around his room.

He chose to ignore the major technological advancements that had been brought to Tierra. Geothermal-powered electrical plants now provided clean electricity to nearly every village with a population of more than five hundred. True, the basic building material remained good, solid stone blocks, usually made and handled by the powerful Circles. Nearly everyone now had some form of central heating, again compliments of the Rural Power Association, run by the Guilds and overseen by the freaks in Exchange City. There wasn't anything that the freaks didn't have their hands in, that is when they actually had hands, he again reminded himself.

So where did those with powerful *mentales* gifts fit in to this new world order? Velasco had asked himself that countless times. He could go to work as a peon in one of the Towers, such as Valen Tower, where he'd received his mandatory training in the use of his gifts. Maybe if enough time passed, he might, just might, become a capo or Circle leader. Pathetic, he thought. He could take up some trade, apprentice with one of the Guilds, and then join their leaders, who used their gifts to run not only the Guilds, but also the kingdom, kingdoms stolen from the rightful kings centuries ago. That had always been a particularly bitter pill for this overly proud Valen to swallow. Yet short of a revolution, the Guilds would never relinquish the power they now held firmly in their grasp and backed by the queens in their Imperial Castle.

There was even talk of the queens and their associates now possessing some kind of powerful machine that could force a person to do their bidding! As if their *mentales* gifts weren't enough, he grumbled. Thinking of the phrase "some kind of powerful" triggered something that Velasco had once heard, but now came into his mind. These rulers' power came from the crystals. Not the small ones as he was given when he finished his tower training. No, big, really big crystals. Some claimed they fell from one of the moons, but that was just a fairy tale. The giant crystals were not; they were real. He'd once seen one of them while he was getting his training. Velasco concluded that these giant crystals gave them their true power, power to rule, power to dominate others. The Guilds, the queens, the towers, and probably the freaks — all had them.

In a flash of insight, Velasco knew what he had to do: find some of these giant crystals for himself. At long last, he had figured out how to gain the power that was rightfully his, as dictated by his Valen ancestors. Where they had failed, Velasco would not. He discounted stealing the giant crystals from the Guilds or from the Tower. Both would be beyond foolhardy. One person could not fight back or defend against such a coordinated attack of nine or more members flowing all their power to their leader who would retaliate against him. Ten to one odds was suicide, unless he already had a mountain of those giant crystals to make himself equal to a Tower or Guild. No, there had to be another way.

With that path not yet visible to him, he jumped ahead in his thinking. He thought, *Suppose that I have a pile of these giant crystals, that alone isn't enough. Lord knows how many others on Tierra possess similar large piles of them. Certainly, the Guilds must, and there are dozens of them, not to mention all the Towers and the Queens. I'd still be outgunned. Besides, they have the backing of the Ataro Empire as well. No, I need to have such power behind me that I can bring them all to their knees and have them accept me as their Emperor Supreme!*

That clicked. The Imperium was no more. Countless tiny alliances dotted this spiral arm of the galaxy. He also knew the Federation of Planets was also disintegrating as well. Plus, there were countless other inhabited worlds in their spiral arm that were not even counted among Federation member worlds. Any one of these could easily be subdued and brought under his total control. Nothing could stand up against a *mentales* gifted, armed with dozens of these giant crystals. He could literally bring down a battleship, at least he so envisioned. Yes, get the crystals, go forth into the galaxy in this area, and take over control of those worlds. With the combined power of enough worlds, he, Velasco Valen could return to Tierra with them. Facing that much power, the Guilds, the Queens, and the Towers would all have to yield to him, making him Emperor Supreme! His path crystalized at that moment.

Just then, he heard a knock on his door. Since he was already up and pacing, he headed to the door and opened it. "Hola Velasco," the sweet voice of Valencia Valen entered his room, along with the scent of lilacs, the swish of her wide gown, and the final key to his puzzle! Like all Valens, Valencia had rich, black hair that fell in waves to her hips, had bushy brows, and a pretty face. That her body was shapely went without saying, since all women on Tierra were overly well endowed. Plus, Valencia worked at Elegant Fashions Inc and had undergone body modifications to heighten her beauty. Her waist was quite tiny, barely fourteen inches around, held there, he knew, by a tight corset. Today, she wore a wide gown that was light blue, filled with billowing ripples that seemed to grow larger the closer they came to the floor, where her gown was six feet across.

Valencia was twenty-four and was supposed to be his fiancé, if and when he finally would decide to go along with the arranged marriage suggested by his older brothers. Thus far, he had not, just to spite his parents and older brothers, the latter of whom had tried to "arrange this marriage" just to get him tied down and out of their affairs. While she had not wanted this marriage either, Valen women historically had little choice but to accept marriages as arranged by their parents, who did so to gain or solidify their power. There had been a very long historical line of just such marriages.

Another reason she had accepted this arranged marriage lay in the simple fact that she did not possess the *mentales* gift. She was head blind. Though she detested that derogatory term, she knew well what it meant. Valens were always powerful telepaths. Lacking that, she accepted her fate as being wholly inferior. Thus, as a young woman, she'd followed her own desires, going to work for Elegant Fashions Inc. Why? She loved to dress up in the latest, finest fashions, hoping that her grace and beauty might in some way make up for her complete lack of mental abilities. Her love for fashions and styles had mushroomed, and she'd studied the fashions of women on many other worlds from her office in Valen's Elegant Fashions Inc store.

She too had "beefs" with the establishment. For one, being head blind closed all doors that led to power. No matter how good she was at designing gowns, no matter how knowledgeable she was about the fashions of other worlds, she knew she'd never be able to be able to run Valen's Elegant Fashions Inc. At twenty-four, she began to see her window of opportunities swiftly closing on her. Marrying Velasco would at least ensure she had some small claim to fame and fortune, if not any real power.

"I just dropped off a new gown for your mother and thought we might share dinner this evening, that is if you don't have other plans," Valencia said rather shyly. She was always shy around those who possessed the *mentales* gifts. They could read her mind, her most private thoughts, at any moment, and that scared her.

Again, pieces fell into place in Velasco's mind. *Valencia! Why didn't I think of her before?* "Please, come in, Val. My, you are looking particularly beautiful this afternoon. New gown?"

She flushed. *Has he just read my mind? Oh God!* "Well, yes, it is new. I designed it myself as a light-wear day dress. Not overly wide or pretentious, perfect for a light-duty dress." She walked in, her traditional six inch, Oxford-style heels clicking on his stone floor. Valencia took a seat on his couch, demurely pressing out her billowing skirt and adjusting her hair, pulling it over her left shoulder, which from practiced motions made her look her best or so she thought.

He moved over and sat down beside her on her right, his eyes sweeping up from her barely visible black patent heels, past her tiny waist, over her large bosom, past her three-inch long fingernails painted cherry red, and finally resting upon her coal black eyes. "Val, my dear Val. We should spend more time together," he began, noticing her heart rate was steadily increasing. *Time to use her.*

"I have been thinking I ought to go out there among the stars and visit some of these other worlds. You know, see what they are like. Would you like to accompany me? See for yourself all their fashions?" He added that last knowing perfectly well that was her single passion in life as well as why that was. *The head blind have so little opportunities in life.* He felt a momentary bit of sympathy for the lovely young woman.

"Velasco? Are you teasing me?" she asked, trying to sound disbelieving, while suppressing her almost overwhelming urge to scream "Yes!"

He sensed her true feelings, though, and continued to play her like a harp. "No, I'm quite serious, dear Valencia. Of course, we ought to be married first. It would be unseemly for us to do all that traveling otherwise."

Valencia fought hard to control her emotions, which were swinging widely in several directions. Her face flushed. "Yes, yes of course. I would love to travel to other worlds and see their fashions. But, but are you, I mean, are you — is this a proposal? Are you asking me to marry you now?" She finally built up enough nerve just to ask him outright.

"Well, yes. Yes, I am. Valencia, will you marry me and come with me to explore the many other worlds out there for a time?" he replied and asked, realizing that there wasn't any use for subtleties with a head blind woman. Best to be forthright with her.

"Oh, yes! Yes, I will, Velasco!" she exclaimed, hoping that she wouldn't faint. Breathing was so hard in her tight corset. Had she known he would be proposing to her, she might have worn something less restrictive. *Please, I don't want to faint! Not now!*

"Excellent, Val. Excellent. Of course, before we go on this trip, I need to be able fully to protect you. I've heard that there are all manner of wicked, evil men out there on these other worlds. I certainly don't want anything bad to happen to my new bride," he began.

"Oh, I hadn't thought of that. Well, I can't see what they'd want of me, but you, Velasco, they might do anything to get their hands on you, since you are a telepath. I've heard such awful stories about how they've so brutally mistreated some of our telepaths, kidnaping them even and torturing them to get them to work for them. Just awful. Yes, I'd be scared all the time unless you had some way to protect yourself from all the bad men out there," she gushed out her fears. He noticed that her concern for his well-being was genuine and sincere. Further, she had none for herself. Well, she was right about that, he thought. He would be the likely target, not her. Pretty women were everywhere, but not powerful telepaths.

He continued, "You and I — we're never going to rise to any kind of positions of power here on Tierra, are we? Be truthful, pretty Val. I've no hope of ever ruling, not unless my older brothers manage somehow to get themselves killed. And you — I've talked to others and, though you are a superb dress designer, you've got no chance of ever running Elegant Fashions Inc, do you?" He sensed he had squarely hit her where it most mattered.

She sighed. "No, none at all. I'm their best designer, but well, you know. . ." She just couldn't bring herself to say that detestable word, head-blind.

"I know, Val. I know. That you don't possess the gift means nothing to me. You are very pretty and very bright. You know what you want, and you stop at nothing to get it. I bet you didn't know I've been watching you in your career with Elegant Fashions Inc. You and I are alike. We have to make things happen. We have nothing handed to us on golden plates, like the others. Right?"

She flushed again, fearing he might be reading her mind, her private thoughts. "Well, yes. I'm a fighter. I have to be, since I'm not gifted and everyone else is. It's hard, but I just have to work as much as I can to be the best at what I do. I've — I've heard them talking about you, you know at the store — about how you can't ever have the throne of Valen. I'm sorry for you, truly I am. We — we have to watch out for ourselves, don't we?" she admitted and asked, hoping she didn't sound too forward or that she'd been prying into his life just a little. *After all, if I'm to marry him, I should know something about him.*

"Indeed, Val, I would have thought much less of you if you had not checked up on me, just as I have with you." He knew that would put her at ease and watched her visibly relax, the tensions seeping out of her body at last. Now he could proceed.

"I've been thinking about ways that we can protect ourselves while we are out there among the stars and other worlds," he began. "Have you ever heard of the giant crystals that the Guilds, Towers, and queens have?"

She smiled. "Oh yes! I've actually seen one. At the store. She keeps one there to protect us from robbers. It's huge, but I heard that some have taken these big rocks and somehow compressed them down to small stones, polishing them up, and making them into personal jewelry. That way, they have them with them all the time. Mind you, I've not actually seen these small ones, just overheard them talking about it once. Why?"

"Well, I take your safety highly, my dear. When we go out there on our Grand Adventure, I ought to have some of those with me. That way, I know I can protect you at all times and myself too," he replied. "The only question is how can we find some of them?" He already knew she knew about these giant crystals. He'd seen that in her mind last year. Only now, the significance of that observation finally struck home to him.

"Well, I heard that most of them are found just under the ground a little ways. But sometimes, farmers have found them in their fields when they plow and toss them onto their rock fence walls," she tried to sound as helpful as possible.

"Excellent, Val. I never knew that. Perfect. Perfect." Seeing her face beaming, he knew that he'd said just the right thing to her. "Say, shall we announce our plans to marry at supper tonight?"

"Oh! Let's!" she exclaimed, unable to suppress her enthusiasm, though wondering how all this happened to her so suddenly, when it hadn't happened for the last four years.

"Superb, dear Val. I know that you need to return to work tomorrow. Meantime, I'm going to wander about the millions of farms around here and try to find us some of those giant crystals. Just as soon as I have enough of them, we'll make our plans to leave this crazy world and go see how everyone else in the universe lives. I'll make darn sure that you have enough money to purchase all their fashions that your heart desires. You'll be the prettiest woman on all the worlds that we visit."

Again, he sensed that he'd said precisely what the young woman most wanted to hear, that she'd be able to purchase the fashions and bring them back to Tierra. That alone would greatly increase her fame and fortunes in this, a most fashion-conscious world. Of course, if you had asked him just why he chose to marry Valencia, his second cousin, he would have only answered that it felt right. A honeymoon off-world trip would be supported by everyone. On the other hand, if he just took off, suspicions would be raised in many quarters. He also felt he needed someone to watch his back, but one who could never be tempted to use his crystals against him, which ruled out marrying any woman who had the *mentales* gift.

A week later as he laid back in his wedding bed, Valencia now sound asleep and having just experienced an incredibly close rapport with him, other images flickered in and out of his consciousness. Perhaps, he was merely dreaming about ancient history studied when he was in sixth grade. Leading the largest army ever fielded on Tierra, the man conquered nearly half of Tierra before some *mentales* gifted opened up the ground and swallowed up his army. He ignored other memories of terribly mutilated women. Velasco knew that he was on the right path. To take all of Tierra would require bringing back with him a huge army of space warships, along with some ground shock troops.

Other images replaced those of the battles. Women. Wives. History was replete with examples of wives or girlfriends eliminating their husbands or great warriors. Images of handless and armless women appeared in his mind — such women could not harm their husbands, could not slip poison into his food, or slip a dagger into his heart while he slept. There is wisdom in that, he thought, but then you have either to take care of her yourself or to hire someone to look after her. What's to keep that helper person from doing the deed at her behest? None. Best to keep her happy and content, he concluded before falling into a deep sleep himself.

Four months passed slowly for Velasco. He roamed far and wide from Valen, usually sticking to the foothills, where farmers often piled the stones from their fields into low fences marking the boundaries of their plots. He never would forget the first giant germanium crystal that he found stacked into a farmer's fence. He had attempted to slip into rapport with it, only to feel its immense power amplification! At that precise point in time, Velasco knew for certain that his plan would ultimately work. Only when he had amassed three dozen of these giant crystals was he finally satisfied he had enough. Further, as he found them, he took them to a small village far out on the plains, quite distant from Valen and its Tower. There for a small fee, a local gem-smith worked his magic on them, turning each into a polished, pale blue sphere, supposedly as presents for his new wife to use to decorate their new home.

During these seventeen weeks, Valencia wasn't idle. Velasco was terrible with languages other than his own native Westerlings, a dialect of Spanish, and Imperium Standard. Rather, he depended upon telepathy to pick up another's concept, independent of language. He'd put Val to work on learning more languages. While she spoke her native Westerlings and Imperium Standard, she also was fluent in Midlands, a derivative of English. He had pointed out that they would need to be able to speak quite a few different languages, and that he was dependent upon her to help them out, though they might be able to have some ULAT boxes, if they could buy them somewhere.

She eagerly threw herself into the languages learning project, using the many recordings available at Elegant Fashions Inc, which she listened to nightly while she slept. Valencia felt like Velasco had given her a worthwhile goal and refused to let him down. When he finally returned, she could carry on basic conversations in ten languages, plus the ones in which she was already fluent. Wisely, he praised her for her achievement, sensing the pride that she felt for her efforts.

Upon his return in early September, the two began to work out the world that they would visit first. It didn't matter too much to Velasco. Any world, which possessed space travel, would certainly have the machinery that could be used to compress his three dozen spheres under great pressure, reducing them to far smaller and much denser stones, readily transported on his person. He sensed she was keenly interested in Cartagena-C, because that world was known for its enormously wide and extremely elegant ball gowns. The women there emulated the fashions that had once permeated Proxima Prime and the many senators and their wives.

Giant ball gowns nearly twelve feet across at the floor were the norm. While Valencia eagerly brought up image after image on her computer at Elegant Fashions Inc, drooling over each one, Velasco noticed the women also wore enormous platform heels. The bases were at least four inches tall with tiny spiked heels that were at least ten inches tall. Velasco also saw the fine print, which indicated women who wore these often broke their ankles. Slowly, a new plan began formulating in his mind, one that would ensure that Val could never have any opportunity to harm him. That she should ever want to do that to him completely eluded the man's thinking. Finally, that the official language there was Spanish became the final selling point for the two.

On September 10, the governor gave them their official ID cards with their photos on them, and arranged for an Imperium bank account, though Velasco had to deposit the funds into it. Most came from his parents and brothers, who were only too glad to see he'd finally come to his senses and married the woman of their choice. That he was now going off-world was merely butter on the bread as far as they were concerned. Much could happen to the pair while they were on other worlds, even a good chance he'd never return, which suited them just fine. Between them, Velasco was able to deposit the equivalent of a quarter million Imperium credits into his new account, more than enough to get them started.

"Wow! Just look at this city!" exclaimed a very excited Valencia, five days later as their shuttle slowly descended onto

151

the spaceport at the edge of San Pedro, Cartagena-C, the capital city and home to fifteen million. What so caught her attention were the enormous buildings. True, like any metropolitan city, there were plenty of skyscrapers, but there were also far more buildings that resembled their ornate Churches of God back home, with their hundred foot tall vaulted ceilings.

They had also befriended a passenger who had come onboard at their last stop, a Mrs. Lucinda del Diego, a forty year old senator returning from a trip abroad. When they met her, she was complaining bitterly, "Such an affront! Do you realize they forced me to change into this minuscule day dress instead of my usual gown? Said I'd have to pay for two seats! Just because reasonable women always wear gowns whose skirts are twelve feet across is no reason to make us buy two seats on this shuttle! The nerve of some people!"

"Oh, I quite agree with you," Val replied. "We're just married and visiting Cartagena-C for the first time. Our honeymoon, you see. Back home, I design women's gowns, like the one I'm wearing. I just can't wait to see all the gorgeous gowns women wear here. I simply must have some."

"Well, congratulations. I'm Senator Lucinda del Diego. Please, you must allow me to show you some of our beautiful sights. I know just the place where you can get the finest gowns in San Pedro. You both simply must come with me and my husband to the Royal Symphony on Friday night. And then, there is the official Senatorial Ball on Sunday, opening up this winter's session of our Senate. I'd be honored to have you attend as my guests. Oh do say that you will."

"We've love to, wouldn't we, Velasco?" Val asked.

"Of course, dear. Thank you very much, Senator del Diego. We would be most honored to attend," he replied politely.

"Perfect. Here's my card." She handed her a card, but both noticed that her nails were exceedingly long. Val estimated they were six inches at least, painted to match her red lipstick. She went on, "Once you get settled in your hotel room, give me a call. Number is on the card. We'll make arrangements to get you both some of the finest apparel San

Pedro has to offer. As pretty as you are, my dear, why, you'll be a hit at the ball." She chatted on, later pointing out the key buildings as they descended on San Pedro. Velasco smiled, hardly able to believe their good fortune. She even recommended the best hotel for them to stay in, much to his pleasure, the Toro Negro.

Entering the Toro Negro, both had no doubts that they were entering a world of true elegance and luxury. The entrance was beneath a twenty-five foot tall archway supported by granite columns. Its vaulted ceiling was decorated with a bull fighting scene. The doors were the widest that either had ever seen, each side of which was six feet wide, requiring two doormen dressed in tuxedos to open them. Ahead of them, another couple entered. Her blue gown had to have been at least twelve feet across, barely fitting between the wide opening. She moved a bit slowly, inexplicably as far as these two could see.

Once inside the hotel, they passed through the regal lounge area and saw a number of residents there, sitting on the widest chairs that either had seen, a requirement for the women in their massive gowns. Here the ornate ceiling was just as tall, forming a huge space that dwarfed a mere human. "It's like being in one of our churches!" Valencia whispered. After registering and being taken to their room, both looked around their new quarters, quite awed by its elegance and charm. They had a balcony, overlooking part of the city. Great curtains could be drawback to allow light inside or not as one chose.

"Only we don't have to listen to them preaching," he replied. His eyes took in their bed, fit for a king. Nearby were two of the very wide chairs and two regular ones, along with a desk. The walk-in closet was half-again as large as their bedroom and their bath was breathtaking in its splendor. Gold plated fixtures, a tub large enough to hold them both and then some, white marble tiled floors, and pastel blue walls greeted them. Quite why the ceilings here needed to be twelve feet above them, he didn't know, a bit excessive perhaps. Later, he would see that the high ceilings helped balance out the women in their twelve-foot gowns.

The device called a telephone sat prominently on the desk. While they waited for their bags to be delivered, Valencia decided to use the phone to call Senator del Diego. She picked it up and heard a low buzzing sound. She tried saying a few words, but the low sound continued. Then, she correctly realized that she ought to enter the numbers on the card. Her long nails made this a bit challenging, but once done, the buzzing ended and a different sound came, followed shortly by the voice of the senator.

The next morning Senator Lucinda del Diego, insisting they call her Lucinda while others were not around, took them to Hernando's, one of the finest clothiers in San Pedro. Here, the three parted ways, Lucinda whipping Val off to the women's department, leaving him in the men's area. While he was quickly measured for suits, he also looked around. Then, he spotted it, a long, black duster with a thick mantle, large pockets, full length, and with a pull up hood. It was leather and black as night! "I have to have that!" he pointed it out to the tailor waiting on him.

"Ah, yes. Excellent workmanship, superior leather. Will the gentleman wish the matching suit?" he replied formally and most politely, as though he already suspected that Velasco would. "I do believe that we have it in your size."

"Please, let's see what goes with this duster," Velasco replied.

Black boots, thick black pants, a black cotton shirt, a thin black jacket, and a black tie comprised the outfit, with all items precisely the same shade of black, a black that seemed to allow for no depth of vision. Concealment: perfect. Velasco bought the whole outfit, along with six other suits recommended by the tailor suitable for a well-dressed man-about-town. Having completed his purchases, he checked on the women. As he anticipated, Valencia was in heaven and had barely begun her shopping spree.

"Dear, I have some errands to attend to. Will you be all right here for a while? I'll drop by when I'm finished."

"Yes, of course. Then, you can see the new me!" Val exclaimed. Her smile could melt any man, he thought, pleased with her.

Velasco's business was with a jeweler's. Thankful for something called the Yellow Pages that listed businesses, Velasco found one right away. The first shop that he tried couldn't handle his request, but the man behind the counter knew one who could. A few minutes later, he entered that shop, pleased to have found the right person in such short a time. "Why yes of course that can be done. They will make fine stones indeed," the jeweler replied, examining one of the germanium crystals with his pocket magnifying eyeglass. Have it for you tomorrow."

Jumping ahead a day, when he returned, he found the foot in diameter sphere was now an inch across. Silently, he focused and slipped into rapport with the stone. Velasco found no change in its amplification properties. If anything, it seemed to respond faster, though its overall weight was still the same. Satisfied, he brought in the remaining thirty-five stones. He also had the man design a pair of earrings, each of which featured one of these stones, set in a heavy gold setting along with smaller red rubies below the blue stone. These would be for Val, providing him a way more readily to make use of her and to protect her.

Once he left the shop on that first trip, he returned to meet his wife. "Incredible Val. You look simply stunning," he complimented her new "look." She wore one of the seven new complete gown outfits that she'd purchased. This one was a medium blue one, whose shades of blue gradually darkened as it approached the floor, some twelve feet around her. Her black hair draped seductively down her back. She'd also had her nails done, extensions she called them, until hers grew out some. Her red claws were equal in length to Senator Lucinda's, six inches long, slightly curving inward. However, he noticed she seemed significantly taller, in fact taller than he was. Grinning, she pulled back her billowing gown to reveal her new heels. Matching blue platforms. The platform was four inches tall and sported a ten inch spiked heel.

"These are rather hard to walk in," she explained. "I can't feel the floor in them. Walking is a bit treacherous, so I do hope you won't mind holding my arm, at least until I get used to wearing them. Lucinda says all we fashionable women wear them, but that I'm to be very careful. Many women break their ankles wearing them. I can see why. But not to worry, they have Imperium medical machines here. Still, I don't want to do that."

"Of course not. You look stunning, my dear. Shall we?" he offered her his arm, while Senator Lucinda looked on, smiling her approval.

The week passed quickly for the couple. True to her word, Lucinda took the time to take them to see quite a number of special sights. They visited or attended performances at the Metropolitan Museum of Art, the Natural History Museum, Symphony Hall, the Royal Ballet, and the National Theater of the Arts. Each building was both unique and quite spectacular and not only in terms of architecture. Never had Val had so much fun in her life. Velasco was at least amused, but did notice his wife really did need his support while wearing her new platform heels. But then, he observed that most women wearing them did so as well. For now, he was biding his time.

When they were not out gallivanting about town as Val put it, Velasco paid close attention to the news. On their fourth day here, he finally heard what he found most interesting. There was a constant threat of war or at least open hostilities between Cartagena-C and Beryl-C, a world a few light-years distant. Some were suggesting that Beryl-C had been behind some sabotage at one of their spaceship manufacturing plants. Perfect, thought Velasco, perfect! Two birds with one stone! Now, he concentrated all of his powers of observation onto this situation with Beryl-C, biding his time, listening, and learning.

As the days passed, his plans began to solidify. More importantly, Velasco realized if he executed this one to perfection, he would achieve both of his objectives, far more than he had hoped that day when he landed here on this world of Cartagena-C. Their fleet of warships wasn't that large, but then after the breakup of the Imperium and the legal division of warships completed, few had all that many, with only a few exceptions, the Ataro Empire being one of them. To go against Tierra or Ashford-5 meant also stalemating their emperor and his large fleet. Still, here Velasco found a golden opportunity landing in his lap. Two birds with one leading to the other, a more perfect plot he could not have envisioned. At last, Velasco was ready to begin his rise to Emperor of the Galaxy, Emperor Supreme.

Monday, Valencia wanted to do some additional shopping at Hernando's, a fairly short walk from the Toro Negro. "I know you have some business, Velasco. I can manage on my own today, really I can."

"Are you sure, dear? You've heard about these sabotage incidents of Beryl-C infiltrators?" he countered, planting a seed.

"Oh, I am sure it's perfectly safe. It's only a few blocks. I'll be fine," Valencia replied. He gave her a loving kiss, and she carefully made her way out of their fancy room, her giant blue dress swishing as she went through the overly large doorway.

The day was just a tad chilly, but sunny. While the air held traces of an industrialized city, oil, gas fumes, and a greyish smoke, visions of more elegant gowns filled her head as she walked along the well-traveled street. Their cars zoomed past on the street, while suited men walked past her briskly, and other women in their similar gowns moved much more slowly, picking their careful way along the sidewalks on both sides of the street. Valencia felt right at home among them.

Without warning, she tripped and went flying towards the ground. For some reason, her arms went straight out, slapping the unyielding sidewalk above her head. Then pain! More pain that Valencia had ever experienced. Something huge, something grey, something hard thudded onto the ground above her head, landing on her hands. A secondary set of pains came sweeping up her legs, but they failed to register. Val had already passed out! She didn't see Velasco come running her way, yelling for help, apparently frantically worried about her.

Within a few minutes, the Emergency Responders arrived, pushing most of the crowd back. These three men managed to lift the heavy stone from her hands and then the much smaller chunks from her feet. Just then, the Security

Guards arrived and Velasco marveled at just how well his implanted suggestions were working. "It's definitely a Beryl-C sabotage attack," one of the Security Guards barked. "Secure this whole block. Call for backup. We'll search every building in the block. Get that woman and her husband to the Emergency Room now!"

Around noon, Valencia came too. She was sitting up on a hospital bed, pillows stuffed behind her. Velasco sat on a chair beside the bed, wiping her forehead with a cool rag. "What happened?" she muttered, and then glanced at her hands lying in her lap, propped up by her huge skirt. Her hands were not there. Her lower arms were shaped into nice looking cones, tapering to barely an inch across where her wrists had been. She shrieked again.

"There, there, it will be all right, dear," Velasco said sympathetically, patting her brow, quietly sending calming waves through her mind, and out through her body. "They don't hurt now; at least that's what the doctor said."

His *mentales* touch worked wonders on her. She relaxed and calmed down. "What, what happened? I tripped."

"You, my lovely dear, are the luckiest woman in the world," he explained. "There was a Beryl-C sabotage attack, taking out a chunk of that building's stone facade. It fell on you. Another foot and you would not be here with me! It was that close to your head! Their Security Guards are scouring the city for the Beryl-C terrorists who did this foul deed. I should have been with you, damn it."

"I've, I've got no hands! Oh, it's not your fault, Velasco. If you had been there, you might have been killed. My feet feel funny too," she replied disjointed. Part of her was still in shock, while part wanted to lessen the guilt that Velasco must be feeling for her.

"Your hands were crushed flat. The doctors couldn't save them, but they assure me that they will have the best prosthetic hands for you in a short while. Good as new, they say. Your feet, well they were able to save them mostly. They were crushed too, but not as badly. They were able to save them by fusing the crushed bones together. You will be able to walk, only with special boots, on your toes, like those ballet dancers that we saw a few days ago."

"What? My feet too?" she wailed, but his calming energies quickly dissipated her emotional reactions, much like shorting out an electrical current. "Oh, like some of those terrorist victims that are around Exchange City, right?" she managed to drag up an image from her memory, aided by an undetected nudge from Velasco.

"Right, dear. They are out getting some that will fit you now. We'll be able to go home to our hotel in a couple of hours. I'm supposed to feed you lunch if they don't have your new hands here soon."

Just in time or perhaps on cue, a doctor entered carrying a large box containing her new hands. Quietly, he went about showing her how to put them on her specially prepared stumps. She slipped a stump into the slot, making sure it was aligned properly. By pressing a spot on the backside of the prosthetic hand three times in rapid succession, a red light appeared. "You see, when the red light shows, it is telling you that it just received the signal to either turn on or off. It is asking you for your confirmation. Just touch that spot once more." She did so with her other stump. A tiny motor turned on, sucking the air out, forming a tight bond with her stump. "There, it's on. To remove it, just follow the same procedure. It is on securely now. However, it can be pulled off if you attempt to lift more than about five pounds. Now, let's get the other one on."

A bit later, he explained, "There are thousands of electronic sensors in them. To operate your hands, just pretend that these are your normal hands and try wiggling your fingers."

She did so. "It's so hard. I can't feel anything," she nearly broke down again, but Velasco once more sent her calming energies. Her fingers barely moved.

"See, there you go. With practice, you'll do just fine with them. Ah, here comes your lunch. Why don't you practice with them? See if you can manage the silverware. Mr. Valen, please allow her the opportunity to do it herself. The more that she does such things on her own, the better it will be for her. You understand?" the doctor explained and asked, but it was more like an order to him. He nodded.

Valencia had a horrid time just trying to pick up a fork, forcing Velasco continually to send her calming waves and discharging her building grief before it could burst out in fits of sobbing. "There you go," he kept encouraging her. She fumbled her way mostly through the meal. When she was finally done an hour later, a nurse entered with a shoebox. She and Velasco showed her the new boots, done in a blue patent leather that matched her gown. They came up to above her ankles and fit very tightly.

The nurse explained, "They have steel bars along the sides so that you cannot twist an ankle in these. So no worries about breaking an ankle. Heavens, we get enough women in here with broken ankles from their tall platforms. You'll be spared those kinds of troubles. Now, let's get you up and walking, so you can go home. Sir, you'll want to steady her lots, until she masters walking in them."

A few minutes later, as he led her down the hallway on their way out of the hospital, she cried out, "Velasco, I can't do this!" She was struggling mightily just to keep her balance, let alone walk.

"Don't worry. I have you. I won't let you fall. You can do it. You must," he said sympathetically.

"It should have hit my head, Velasco. I can't live like this. I'm a hopeless, helpless cripple now," she wailed, breaking down completely. His crystals energized, shorting out her emotions for the time being.

"Keep walking. Be brave. We can cry when we get to our hotel room," he whispered, steeling her further. Somehow, they made it to their room, quite how Valencia couldn't even remember that terrifying walk. She sat down in the first wide chair available, and he allowed her suppressed grief to flood over her. Best to let her get it out of her system, he thought, steeling himself for the emotional release, which was huge.

While she was sobbing her heart out, he ran his hands along her legs and over her knees where the pains from walking so far had locked up. He realized she would need to strengthen them significantly and steeled himself to giving her further leg assists. At least over her sobbing, she told him how

160

wonderful his touch was on her aching legs and knees.

Near suppertime, more Security Guards came to interview the two. No, she hadn't seen anything but had taken a fortuitous tumble just as the stones fell from the top front of the building, sabotaged by what was probably a well-aimed d-gun blast. After they left, Senator Lucinda came, full of apologies and sympathies for her.

"Well, I've requested a citywide search for the terrorists from Beryl-C. Meanwhile, there is the insurance compensation matter to handle. We carry liability insurance on all visitors to Cartagena-C. I've sped up the paperwork. You'll be receiving seven million credits per loss of each hand and another five million for the damage to your feet, Valencia. That totals nineteen million credits. I'll have the insurance company deposit the funds into your account, dear. I know monetary compensation cannot make up for what you've lost, but it is the best we can offer you," she explained, her voice full of a thick sympathy for her.

She went on, "The doctors told me that with practice, you should be able to do just fine. As soon as you are able, I would like personally to take you shopping to get matching boots for all your new gowns, and then let's get you another dozen fancy outfits. What say you to that?"

"But I'm a hopeless cripple now," Valencia answered, trying hard to keep from breaking down yet again.

"Oh don't say such a thing! You are not. Just give yourself time to adjust. Call me when you are ready to go shopping again. Now, I do have to get going. Senate business. We are threatening to take stronger retaliation measures against Beryl-C. Attacking visitors to our world is the last straw!" Senator Lucinda barked antagonistically.

Velasco spent most of the week working with Valencia, frequently handling the pains in her knees and legs, as well as the utter frustration she experienced while trying to learn to use her prosthetic hands. "I can't feel anything with them." "I'm so clumsy, I'm dropping everything." "I'll never be able to do anything anymore." Her outbursts were usually followed by another round of sobbing, which he wisely allowed. Eventually, he figured, she'd dry up, particularly once she was again able to do things for herself, more or less.

Near the end of the week, Valencia was doing better, and he finally left her alone for a short while. He returned with the special earrings he had made for her. "After that attack on you, my dear, I went out and had the jeweler make these for you. See, each one has one of my special power crystals in them, along with matching red rubies in a gold setting. I know they'll be a bit on the heavy side, but as long as you're wearing them, I'll be able to be in contact with you, and via them keep anything like this from ever happening again, even when we're apart, as we were on that Monday. I don't want anything else to happen to you, my dearest love."

She admired them and thanked him, feeling that he must really love her for being so thoughtful and caring. He slipped them through her pierced ears, and then tightened the tiny, screw fittings, knowing perfectly well that with her limited abilities with her prosthetic hands she'd ever be able to unscrew them. "I don't want you to ever take them off. As long as you have them on you, I'll be able to protect you from any and all harm no matter what."

"They are gorgeous, dear. Oh! So heavy! Are you sure that they won't pull my ears off?" she exclaimed, but just had to get up and look at herself in their mirror.

"You look even more stunning in them, dear," he whispered, kissing the back of her head, planting that notion firmly in her mind.

"I suppose I should be brave and call up Lucinda and go shopping. I only have this one pair of boots. I can't keep on wearing the same dress, can I?" Valencia said bravely. She tried using the phone, but was entirely too clumsy and bungled it, bringing more grief back to the surface once more. Hastily, Velasco dialed the number for her, nipping it in the bud. Later, he watched as Lucinda, full of sympathy, led Valencia out of their hotel room, an arm securely around her waist.

Now free for a time, Velasco focused and activated all his crystals. Soon, he put one of his *mentales* gifts to work. On Monday, their Senate voted to authorize an attack on Beryl-C. Even more surprising to Valencia, she and Velasco were to join the attacking ships, guests of their Commodore, who would be leading the attack. In her mind, it seemed entirely incongruous. Quite why it seemed perfectly natural to Senator Lucinda, Val couldn't understand. "You must witness our revenge for their brutal attack on you," the senator attempted to explain.

For this trip, Valencia put on her bright red gown, while Velasco donned his entirely black suit. After strapping his special belt containing thirty-four of the small, compressed giant crystals, he donned his new black duster. Arm in arm, the two headed out of their hotel room, where a waiting car took them to the spaceport. There, armed soldiers escorted them out to the waiting battleship.

After meeting with Commodore Diego and his charming aide, Major Francisca, they were taken to a viewport room, where they could watch all the action. After getting her seated, Velasco sat beside her, focused, and activated his belt of crystals. Again, he utilized one of his special gifts. A couple of hours later, the ship and five smaller cruisers dropped out of hyperspace near the yellow sun and the third planet out, Beryl-C. Following his implanted suggestions, the ships merely waited for the Beryl-C response, instead of launching their own attack. If asked why he violated all known protocols, the Commodore could not have given a reasonable reason.

Major Francisca joined them. "There has been some inexplicable delay, Senor Valen. Commodore Diego asked me to inform you of the delay. I just don't understand it. Everyone expected we'd drop out of hyperspace and launch our retaliation attack. We can't have them sabotaging our plants and harming innocent people, like they did with your wife. I'm so sorry about that, Senora Valen."

"Yes, of course. Delays happen," Velasco replied, focusing and sending this pretty Major Francisca the idea that this delay was quite normal and planned for. For some unknown reason, he just couldn't sense her mind. Before he could do anything else, Major Francisca turned and left them. How strange, he thought, but turned his attention onto the remainder of his plans.

As six heavy cruisers sped upwards from the planet below to meet this aggressive threat, Velasco's many crystals were glowing bright blue, but no one could see them doing so, shielded within the confines of his special leather belt. One by one, he reached the minds of the approaching commanders, altering their minds in very subtle ways.

Following the implanted orders, Commodore Diego opened a hailing frequency and soon had the enemy commanders talking to him on the comm center. All six wanted to surrender to the Black Man. As the enemy shuttles came over to the battleship, Commodore Diego and Major Francisca came to get Velasco, though why the Commander did so, he could never say, just that it was the "right thing" to do. On the other hand, Major Francisca looked completely confused by what was happening.

A half hour later, one of the commanders took Velasco down to their world to meet with Beryl-C's leaders. Two hours later, they opened a channel to Cartagena-C, discussing their joining forces into an empire, but only if the Black Man was in charge of their fleets. All leaders agreed, though they could never offer any reasonable explanation for why they did, other than it seemed the right thing to do.

Thus, it was in mid-September, 1450, that the Black Man had merged two opposing worlds into a loose confederation, with himself in control of their fleets. All this had been done without firing a single canon shot. No war, just capitulation and a merging of forces. Of course, Valencia just had to spend time on Beryl-C discovering their fashions, purchasing many for herself, while Velasco attended to his "business." While she was so engaged, Major Francisco send an electronic message off to a very distant world, outlining what had happened here, and asking for instructions.

By late October, a dozen neighboring systems had been "gobbled up" into this new confederation. Word began spreading far and wide about the Black Man, who conquered worlds without firing a single shot. Word of his armada also spread: six battleships, ten heavy cruisers, and twenty-four light cruisers. With a fleet this large, other nearby worlds began to take strong interest in this Black Man and his plans. Further, the Black Man was now calling himself Emperor Supreme.

Part II Conflicts

Chapter 10 Enter the Serpiente

The three thousand foot long, twisting, slithering intergalactic ship slipped slowly into the very outer edge of this new spiral galaxy. More like a flexible tube, this ship now slithered along on sub-light engines, desperately in need of a refueling after traversing the enormous distances between galaxies. Inside the ship were a dozen Serpientes. Their species had twelve-foot long snake bodies that were nearly two feet in diameter, with tiny legs and arms, which allowed them to work their controls. They spoke in a rather hissing sounding language.

First Leader said, "We mussst refuel sssoon. I don't like thisss busssinesss. We had bessst find monkey foodsss sssoon. Our ssssupliesss are almossst too low for usss to return."

Second Leader commented, "But we mussst check thisss galaxy out for more monkeysss. You know asss well asss I do that our people are sssstarving back home. Refuel, yesss, but then we mussst look for monkeysss."

"Agreed. Navigator, take usss to the nearessst sssstar for refueling," First Leader ordered.

"Coming up on sssscreen now, Firsssst Leader. Yellow one looksss bessst for usss, not the red one," the Navigator replied.

"Ssshall I sssend word back to Home World now?" asked the Communicator.

"Aye, sssend word that we have reached Galaxy 143 and will commenssse monkey sssearchesss within the hour, jusssst asss sssoon asss we refuel," First Leader replied.

The ship floated in closer to the yellow main sequence star and activated its refueling mechanism. Suddenly, a giant dark patch appeared on the surface of the star, otherwise called a sunspot by solar astronomers. Covering nearly half of the visible surface, the dark patch was dark because of the sudden withdrawal of hydrogen and thermal energies that were being sucked into the three thousand foot long Serpientes ship, refueling their intergalactic engines. For nearly an hour, the ship refueled. Meanwhile, the

166

Communicator located a suitable planet, third out from the star, one that held the potential to support monkey lives.

The sudden extraction from the star caused the star to emit one enormous EM pulse wave, utterly gigantic in size and scope. It expanded outward in a sphere, racing ever outwards, though diminishing in intensity as the square of its distance from the star.

As soon as the refueling was completed, the dark spot vanished, as the star regained thermal equilibrium once more. The Serpientes ship headed on out from the star to check out this third planet for monkeys.

Thanos met with Eros, exchanging electronic messages. "I don't like how this situation with the so-called Black Man, this Emperor Supreme, is going. World after world is falling to his ever-expanding conquest."

Eros commented, "I don't see why these worlds are not fighting back, but are capitulating and joining him. It goes against everything we know about homo sapiens sapiens."

"I agree. It seems inexplicable. We must be missing something, likely a new and ultra-powerful weapon that this man has and is using. Still, our contact has been unable to locate this weapon, though she has searched extensively. Her observations are still puzzling to me. I've spent weeks reviewing it, and I still don't understand it. One minute her Commodore is ready to launch a sneak attack in retaliation for terrorist attacks on his world, an attack that by all rights would have wiped out their enemy world, and the next minute, he's doing nothing but waiting for the enemy to discover their fleet and launch their fleet to meet his. If that isn't baffling enough, then why were both leaders willing to end all hostilities with each other and accept this Black Man as their Emperor Supreme, even to the point of joining their fleets together? No sense, Eros; it defies everything we have ever learned about the behavior of homo sapiens sapiens," Thanos continued with a baffled look upon his face.

Eros nodded. "I've been plotting the expansion of this Emperor Supreme's battles. It is moving outward in roughly a spherical shell centered on Cartagena-C. More important, if he continues at this current rate, Beltazar-C could be facing him in three months! How are our defenses? Can we hold them off? Could we go underground, presenting a dead world picture to this Black Man?"

"That soon?" Thanos sent out a burst of white noise, his equivalent of a curse. "I will send out some monitors to give us as much advanced warning of their arrival as possible. When the doctors return from their conference, you had best discuss this potentially deadly situation with them. Perhaps, they'll want to use their unusual mental skills on this Black Man. Perhaps, they would prefer hiding. Keep me posted."

"Glad you are back. We missed you," Tiana exclaimed, hugging Zia and then Fin. Angelo shook Fin's hand solidly. "So how did it go? You have to tell us all about it. And how did you manage to get those two doctors from Ashford-5 to come here?" This was what she most wanted to know. They had just landed and walked down the ramp, holding securely to the side rails to keep their precarious balance. Neither saw that Minta stood still, receiving the latest news from Thanos via a long electronic burst.

Before she could reply, the Dirty Four made their way out of the control tower, heading their way. All four wore their fancy gowns, just to tease the four, who continued to wear their "drab grey" professional women's dress. "Hi ya. Miss me?" Luciana called out, waving to Zia, who flushed slightly.

"Sure, but the two geneticists from Ashford-5 are right behind us. We best be ready to welcome them," Zia yelled back, thankful for a change of topic and hoping that her bulge wasn't showing. Ever since she'd first met Luciana, Zia had been profoundly attracted to her. As far as Zia was concerned, Luciana's physical beauty was beyond perfection, and combined with her carefree attitude, Zia found the woman's overtures almost impossible to resist. But she had to resist, she loved Fin and was married to him. At least he understood, Zia thought.

"We have the spare suite in our quadraplex fixed up for them already," Angelo replied. "Don't fret, Zia. We're on top of it."

"Hey Angelo, you are welcome to be on top of me anytime," teased Michela, who had finally closed the distance between them. She batted her eyes at him, enjoying his flush.

"Hey, this must be them," Aldo pointed to the silver deep space transport slowly descending above them. The eight moved closer to the control tower, giving the arriving ship plenty of room to land.

Diego made a perfect landing. He gathered up his small backpack and joined Alexandra at the bay doors, timing it right. The ramp touched the tarmac just as he moved to her side, noticing that she too had her small backpack with her. "Well, here goes an adventure," he whispered.

"No kidding, Diego. I can't believe there are only eight humans walking this world and millions of others are in underground tanks living in a computer generated virtual world. Heaven help us with this one, Diego," Alexandra replied.

"Hey, telepaths and perhaps gifted as well. This ought to be a wild one," he replied, as the two carefully stepped down the ramp in their tall heels. Both wore their professional women's outfits as they had worn to the conference. Diego still hadn't changed into his more comfortable men's garb. He'd worn the woman's outfit to the conference, primarily because physically he looked like them and didn't want to draw undo attention to himself. Further, since they knew that Fin and Angelo also wore the same type of dress, he would fit in better with those two men. Both had Basic Therapy and then some, so they were well aware of just how important first impressions were.

That is, when meeting someone new, if you dressed similar to them, that alone began to form an agreed upon reality, which made it easier for the other person to initially like you, to feel some affinity for you. With shared reality and affinity, real communication was then possible, which in turn added to the shared reality and degree of liking, raising them even higher and so on. Hence, in part, Diego wore his professional woman's outfit for just this very reason. He and Alexandra waved at the eight, waiting close to the control tower, noticing the drastic difference between the two groups of four.

"Welcome to Beltazar-C and Venice," Fin called out as they drew close.

The two saw what appeared to be a modern city, but without people. Everything was well tended and maintained. No grass grew in the tarmac's cracks. From what Zia had told them, the maintenance robots took care of the physical appearance of this entire world, rather a hard concept for both geneticists to grasp. It implied millions of robots, which was beyond their comprehension. That soon changed as they walked the couple of miles into Venice proper and saw the worker robots going about their normal activities.

As they met and shook hands, Fin introduced the others. "Doctor Christiana Vitano, Tiana for short, our chemist. Doctor Angelo Landini, her husband and our applied math whiz. These are our professional models Luciana Castrani and Michela Angelina."

"And fashion models," Luciana interrupted him, swaying her hips seductively at the two newcomers and giving them a flirtatious grin. Like our appearance?"

Diego grinned back, while an annoyed Fin continued, "This is Captain Aldo Sandro and Wing Commander Ciro Boldovino. It's a short walk to our quadraplex. We can discuss things there." The ten began walking, though Diego and Alexandra purposely had to walk slower than they normally would have in their six-inch heels not to go faster than these eight in their ballet boots. It was rare for these two to find that they walked faster than others did.

As they walked, both Luciana and Michela sidled up beside the two geneticists, flirting with them a little. However, the two were more interested in seeing all of the robots. "They are just robots," Luciana said a little annoyed her flirting wasn't having quite the effect on these two as she had hoped.

None saw Minta taking off in one of the many deep space transports parked at the spaceport. Thanos had asked her to check out a disturbing report that he'd overheard while monitoring Federation communications.

The ten found Eros waiting for them on their front porch, and Fin introduced their two guests to the HIFR. "This is Eros, our interface to the robots of Beltazar-C." Both Diego and Alexandra picked up his complete annoyance that Eros was here and insisting on joining them.

"You are most welcome, highly distinguished geneticists. We are eternally honored by your presence on our world. So few share our love and compassion for our nova. We have always followed the work that you and your fellow geneticists have done on all the cures. As you can see, we've been able to replicate your cures on these eight nova," Eros said in a rather grandiose manner, while opening the front door for the group. He followed them inside.

Eros took a seat with them in the commons. "I'm here to discuss a potentially serious threat to our world. Perhaps, doctors, you have heard about this as well. A man who calls himself the Black Man, Emperor Supreme, is slowly taking over many worlds. What is so very strange is when his ever-growing fleet of warships arrives over a world, which prepares to defend itself by sending up its own smaller fleet, there is no actual fighting, no combat. Instead, they apparently decide to accept this man as their new supreme leader, merging their fleet with his. It makes no sense. We know some of these worlds were archenemies, like Beryl-C and Cartagena-C. Yet, they both accepted him as their emperor and merged their fleets."

Eros continued, "We cannot reason out why any of these worlds have joined him. We know that in several cases, the reacting fleet headed up to fight them, and yet when they reached striking distance, for wholly unknown reasons, their leaders suddenly chose not to fight back, accepting this Black Man completely as their new ruler. It makes no sense. Have you heard of this man? Have you any explanation for the conduct of the conquered worlds?"

Dr. Diego sighed. "Well, yes, we are aware of this situation. I believe you have every right to be worried about this man and what he is doing. Ashford-5 and the entire Ataro Empire are watching the situation very closely, but as yet, it is just as mysterious to us as it must be to you."

Eros made as good a human-like sigh as he could. "Ah. I was so hoping that you'd be able to enlighten us further. While the Black Man remains rather secluded, never showing himself, but always garbed in black and wearing a long duster, we have managed to get an image of his face. Allow me to show it to you. I've sent it to all of your computers," he added to the eight, while bringing up his own laptop and displaying the man's face full on. Although he wore his duster's hood up, the angle was such that his face was quite clear.

Eros went on, "His wife, Val, wears boots like our nova, but she isn't a nova. She apparently had a bad accident on Cartagena-C and lost her hands. As you can see, she wears Imperium prosthetic hands. She is the one who goes out among the newly acquired worlds, visiting with them, their leaders, and acquires many samples of their women's apparel. Quite why she does this is also unknown, but some say she is the voice of the Black Man, Emperor Supreme, though she does not call herself empress."

"Very interesting, Eros. Could you email those photos to us?" Diego asked. He gave the robot his email address, and the robot did so.

Eros then said, "We have done some calculations. If he continues expanding as he has been, he may well reach here in three months' time. Our question is just how do we deal with him? One proposal is to take our eight here underground, along with all robots, making this world appear as though it had been abandoned."

Diego answered, "With only eight to defend the world and with no warships, that might be a good strategy to follow. Perhaps, he will find nothing here to conquer and move on."

"Ah. Excellent." Eros looked to Fin and added, "I shall keep you fully informed, Dr. Fin. We have time to prepare for this conqueror's arrival." With that, he rose and left them.

Dr. Diego then began to discuss what he believed really had to be made known to these eight. "Okay. You have other more serious problems. First, you are all untrained telepaths. While you probably don't realize it, you are broadcasting your thoughts like a comm center. When you are around a lot of other people, you are probably picking up a head-full of their thoughts."

"Well, we've figured out how to dampen them down

some," Zia replied. "We had too in order to go to the conference. But really? We're broadcasting our thoughts? We thought that we more or less had them blocked."

"Yes, you are blocking them somewhat, but not entirely. One reason we're here is to offer you some assistance in learning how to do both very effectively," Diego explained.

"Well, that would be much appreciated," Dr. Zia said formally.

"A second reason we're here is to examine your other amazing skills," Diego added.

"Oh, sweety," Luciana teased him. "You mean our amazingly perfect bodies or our ability to move and lift things or our super skills in flying the attack scout ships?"

"I didn't know that I was a sweety," Diego teased her back. "I meant the second of those. Levitation and telekinesis."

"Darn, I was so hoping it was our perfect bods," she replied faking a pout. Fin gave her an annoying look, which she ignored completely.

"Back on Ashford-5, most of us who have telepathy also have similar gifts that you have. We call them the *mentales* gifts. While levitation and telekinesis are two of them that some of us have, there are over a hundred other forms our gifts sometimes take," Diego explained. "We have groups who train our *mentales* gifted to be able to fully use their gifts."

"Hey, that would be useful to us too," Angelo broke in. "Knowing just what we can and cannot do would be invaluable."

"Of course. That's one of the reasons we're here, to help work out ways and means of getting you this valuable training," Diego said, sensing this was just what the eight wanted to hear. "However, there is a third reason for our visit."

"You and Alexandra want to hop in bed with Michela and me," Luciana interrupted him, a wry smile on her face. "Well, you are most welcome to do that anytime, sweety."

Diego flushed. "Er, that's not the reason, Luciana. In the wide galaxy out there, a true telepath is unbelievably rare. As a result, many unscrupulous and exceedingly wealthy men and women often kidnap telepaths, forcing them to work for them, usually to help them make more money. Over the centuries, many telepaths from our world have been kidnaped and forced into slavery, often times a brutal one at that." He described a couple of those incidents.

"So," he continued, "you eight are in grave danger. The moment the other worlds out there learn that you are telepaths and that there are a thousand more here, you can expect to find many raiding parties coming here just to kidnap you and make you into their slave telepaths."

"But we can fight back," Aldo insisted. "We're not helpless."

"True, but can you fight back while you are sleeping at night? They are very sneaky about it, taking you when you least expect it, like when you are asleep. A chloroform rag over your face and you are out. Often, they then remove arms, legs, and all manner of other things to make you unable to fight them or survive without their constant help. Believe me; once they get that chloroform rag over your face, you are theirs from then on. So with only eight of you actually operating on this world, you are unbelievably vulnerable, though the robots will probably try to protect you some."

Alexandra added, "We don't have any solutions about this for you, except to urge you to never ever let anyone else know about your telepathic skills. Your trip to Pegasi-C was risky, but Diego and I didn't detect any other telepaths around, so probably no one else knows about you here yet. Still, you've got to learn to totally block your thoughts so other telepaths can't pick them up."

The two looked rather sober. She continued, "Now, how about something lighter? We'd like to see your genetics laboratory, Dr. Zia. And then, if we could, we'd like to see the telepaths who are in the tanks and see how that all works. If we could get some DNA samples, we might be able to work on more specific cures for your people."

"Gosh, you'd rather go see a genetics lab than hop in bed with Michela or me?" pouted Luciana. "Well, Aldo, you can see why I dropped out of school. No way do I want to be a bookworm." The Dirty Four all chuckled.

Annoyed, Tiana said, "While you are off doing that, we'll fix some supper for everyone, won't we, Luciana,

Michela?"

"Ah, wine and dine," Luciana replied with a wry smile. "That's the ticket. We have to get them loosened up some. All work and no play makes for a very dull, serious life."

Later, Eros joined the three, giving them a proper tour of their underground tank facilities. He insisted on giving them a full briefing, including just why they were being kept in their virtual reality worlds. "So you see those who want to waste their lives by playing video games are allowed to do so, enjoying their lives as they wish them to be, but they still provide us with new nova, anyone of which might become another Doctor Zia. Plus, we don't have to build HIFRs for all of them and take care of them in the real world. I assure you that our educational system is of the highest quality. Our doctorates are every bit as competent as any from the Federation's Universities and the old Imperium's Academies. We have built here the perfect system. Those who are bright and want to help build a good and lasting civilization are nurtured and allowed to do so, and those who don't are allowed to experience whatever they desire but in their own private virtual universe."

"Well, I have to admit that it beats them having to spend their lives in one of those assisted living centers on these Federation worlds, where they don't actually do anything except sit around and watch the comm center shows," Dr. Zia admitted. Eros did have some valid points, she thought, though grim beyond words.

Later, they were wined and dined quite regally, compliments of Luciana and Michela, who went all out to create the perfect dining atmosphere, along with the best meals they could cook. While that wasn't saying much, the food, that is, the ambiance was extraordinary and enjoyed by all. Romantic music, candlelights, and freshly picked flowers highlighted their dining experience. Once finished, Zia and Fin headed to their bedroom, as did Tiana and Angelo.

"Okay, we lost the bargain, so Ciro and I get to clean up. Go have some fun," Aldo said, ushering Diego, Alexandra, Luciana, and Michela out of the dining room and into the commons.

"So Alexandra, are you and Diego here following some cultural morals?" Luciana asked seriously. "If so, we understand you not wanting to come to bed with us. Morals are just established rules that a group of people make up because they don't have any real sense of ethics left and/or can no longer apply them. Michela and I do not subscribe to any group's morals on intimate sharing. We believe our bodies are ours to share with anyone we choose, and we never do it lightly, in spite of appearances. When we make an offer for intimate sharing, we also mean we highly respect and admire them and want to give our best to them. We open ourselves up, sharing our total being with another. It is as close as we can come to being one with the other, withholding nothing. We've not committed ourselves to anyone, as in marriage. So what drives you two? Morals? Or an ethical agreement to remain faithful to each other and to never share yourselves with others? We don't think it's because you are prudish and think that sex is only done to procreate and for no other reason."

Dr. Alexandra was quite surprised to hear this unexpected wisdom. "Amazing, Luciana. Yes, you are quite right about morals and why some cultures use them as a substitute for their failures to put in ethics on themselves. No, we aren't into morals, but we're faithful to each other. We have four children back home. And you are also precisely right about the intimate sharing."

Dr. Diego added, "Sorry. We thought you were just flirting with us, trying to get us in bed with you for fun and games. Yet, this is obviously not the case, is it?"

Michela answered, "No, silly. We admire and respect you both and want to join with you and share the ultimate in affinity or love as some put it. This is our most precious gift possible that we want to share with you, if you both are willing."

Alexandra and Diego quickly exchanged private thoughts. She then said, "Now that we understand your motives, we'd be honored to share your bed for tonight."

Luciana replied, "No, the honor is all ours. Come." She rose onto her toes and pulled Alexandra up gracefully.

Sometime later amid a tangle of hair, both women were

fully satisfied, having shared themselves in a full rapport with each other. As Luciana lay beside Alexandra and dragged her touch sensitive hair over Alexandra's body, Luciana realized something that would forever change her life. She understood something that she'd never known before: knowledge is certainty and true power. Alexandra was so very much more than she was. Luciana swore then and there to try to achieve what Alexandra had. Michela had a similar reaction to her dearest companion.

In the morning, over breakfast, the ten began chatting about just what actions to take next. They'd just begun sipping their coffee when suddenly the massive electro-magnetic storm from the massive sunspot reached Beltazar-C. All power vanished in an instant, leaving them in the partially darkened room. "What's going on?" asked Aldo, somewhat surprised. "Did the robots screw something up?"

"Dunno, but we'd best head outside and see what's going on," Fin urged.

"Are we under an attack?" asked Zia.

"Could well be," Angelo replied. All ten rose and made their way outside.

"Oh my god! Look at the sun!" exclaimed Tiana. The sun was quite dark. Over two-thirds of its light wasn't there!

"Shit! The robots!" cried Angelo. The eight stared out into the street and saw perfectly motionless robots, frozen mid-strides!

"Oh god! If the power is off, the nova in the tanks could be drowning! Come on! We have to check on the tanks!" Zia yelled.

"Okay. You all check them. Angelo and I will try to see what's going on with the sun, the power, and the robots. If it's an attack, we'll let you know," Fin yelled. Eight headed towards the tank room that held Dr. Lelos Smith and many of the grad students, while Angelo headed off towards the power station and Fin rummaged around for his small telescope.

Fin found it and got it pointing to the sun, Beltazar, and put in the solar filters. When he took his first look at it, he gasped. There was the largest sunspot he'd ever heard about! It was massive, covering almost all the visible surface facing the planet. He then saw something that alarmed him. Illuminated by the sun was a huge, very long, but foreign ship of some kind.

Found Eros. Power plant is down. All electrical equipment and all robots are down, Fin, Angelo sent. *What could have caused this?*

Electro-magnetic pulse, he sent back.

So we are under an attack by nuclear bombs? Angelo asked, heading back to him as fast as he could while walking on his toes, which wasn't very fast at all.

Not sure. The sun has the largest sunspot ever. It might have caused that EM pulse. If so, it probably has knocked out all electronics that were on when it struck us. My god. The nova in the tanks! Head there now! Fin sent back, suddenly grasping what the others would soon see when they entered the underground tank rooms.

"The elevator is out. Find the stairs," Zia cried out, growing more worried than ever. They'd gotten inside the darkened warehouse room and discovered that the elevator wasn't working.

"Over here," called out Tiana. All eight headed to the stairway. "Damn, this is tricky going down them," she added, lowering herself gently with each step. Alexandra and Diego quickly passed them, reaching the underground facility first. It was pitch black. They had no choice but to use their *mentales* gifts, creating some bluish light. When they reached the tanks, chaos had erupted. The caretaker robots were motionless, knocked out by the EM pulse. With all power gone, not only was the virtual reality computer down, but so was all the life support equipment! They saw squirming, terror-filled bodies struggling in the tanks.

At once, they rushed to the nearest tank. Each took a nova, pulling the tubes out of their noses and mouths, as well as the V-mask on their heads. They helped each into a sitting position, before moving on to the next tank. By now, the others joined them. "Oh god!" screamed Zia. As fast as she could, she headed to another tank, emulating what Drs. Alexandra and Diego were doing. Almost as fast, the others joined in, ripping tubes away and getting the now screaming, terror-stricken nova sitting up in their tanks.

Minutes later, Fin and Angelo joined them, helping where they could in a frantic effort to save as many nova as they could. "More light!" yelled Fin. Both *mentales* gifted focused and produced a pair of even stronger blue lights.

Then, he realized the two doctors from Ashford-5 had to be making the light. That reminded him of the emergency batteries, and he moved as quickly as he could to the back room, found them, and activated them. The room now was bathed in a dim yellow, uniform glow. The dial read fifty minutes. He yelled, "Battery light will last only fifty minutes!"

Amid the chaos, Zia realized the magnitude of what was happening. There were thousands of these centers scattered all over Beltazar-C. A hundred million or so nova were in an identical life-threatening situation. Worse, she knew she could only hope to rescue those in this one room! By now, she was soaked, and her tears streaming down her face went unnoticed, as she lifted another screaming nova into a sitting position. She looked back and saw that some had calmed down a little and were finding ways to get themselves out of the tanks and onto the floor. She tried to yell to them to tell them where the stairs were at, but couldn't be heard over the din. Hence, she told the nova that she just helped to sit up, "Stairs are that way; crawl there if you can. Lead the others." She moved on to the next tank.

A frantic half hour later, the last tank had been reached. Some fifty had drowned or died, including Dr. Lelos Smith, whose radiation burned body could not survive without the constant life support being provided him in his tank. One moment, he'd been lecturing four astronomy grad students, and the next moment everything went black. His world vanished in an instant. He tried to breathe and couldn't. *Am I dead? Did I just die? Oh the scare that I must have just given my students! Oh god!*

A bit later, his vision returned. He was above a strange looking, horribly disfigured body lying in a tank of water. Various tubes were inserted into it. Everything was illuminated in a strange blue light. *Oh god! That's me! No, I'm me. I'm looking down at my body. What's happening to me?*

It's not breathing. I must have died, but I'm up here. Oh! Zia! I see Zia. What's she doing? Getting nova out of the tanks? What's going on? Calm down, old boy. Zia's here. It must be all right. Observe. Put your own lectures to work. Observe!

At long last, Zia reached the tank that held her beloved Dr. Lelos Smith. She stood over him. Finally, her grief flowed unencumbered any longer. *Hey, I'm up here, Zia. Please don't cry.*

Zia had the strangest feeling that he was talking to her. Her intuition kicked in, and she tried to make telepathic contact. *Dr. Smith? Are you here?*

Yes, up here. What is going on? I think my body is dead. Radiation it would seem to me. Confusing, because I never looked like this before. Say, you are pregnant. Congratulations, Zia.

Dr. Smith? Wow. It's you. Yes, I've not even told Fin about it yet. If you can, hang around me and have this baby when it's time, if you can somehow. I don't understand this either, but if you can, I want you to have this baby of mine. I can't explain now. Have to save as many nova as I can.

Dr. Smith did just that. He floated down and stayed as close to her womb as he could manage. Meanwhile, she moved over to another tank only to find its two occupants had already drowned. "Well that's the last of them," Fin yelled.

"Got one hundred sixty five rescued!" yelled back Angelo, who had kept a running tally in his mathematical mind. "Come on; we have to get them out of here."

A nightmarish hour followed. The ten worked as hard as they could to get the nearly helpless nova outside and into the warm sunshine. All ten made use of their levitation and telekinesis skills to get them safely up the stairs and outside into the street. That done, Aldo said, "Hey, if we get them some boots, they can walk back to our place."

"Brilliant, Aldo," Zia exclaimed. She explained that they were going to go get them some boots and followed the other nine, who had already left for the store next to their quadraplex. An hour later, they returned pushing carts filled with every boot that they could find in the store. It took them an hour to get boots on the nova. At least they had calmed down some. Sitting in the bright sunlight helped them, as well as seeing their familiar Venice city around them. That there were also many frozen in place robots standing around was most confusing to the group.

If this wasn't enough confusion, just then, they spotted more nova crawling along on their knees, much as the Dirty Four had done when they made their Great Escape from the tanks. These had managed to get themselves freed and out of the tanks. Somehow, they'd found the stairs, and were now slowly coming down the street towards the large group, yelling for help. Half of the ten headed over to them to assist, while the others finished getting boots on the last of the large group.

If this wasn't enough chaos, just then a deep space transport descended, taking a holding pattern above them. "Ah hell!" Angelo cursed. "Well, if they're here to kill us, so be it. I can't take much more of this."

Arnold looked out of the cargo bay's viewport, with Gwenda and Pippa on either side of him. All three were armed to the teeth, ready to make their strike once that they found where this world kept its supply of the yellow bio agent cylinders. "Well, gang, this is the last one on the list. It is supposed to be in a city called Venice. From the ancient database, this must be Venice," Arnold pointed out. All eight were now connected by their mobile communication devices hooked to an ear. Hence, everyone heard what he said.

From the pilot's seat, Alfonso said, "Okay, descending now. City is large. Wonder where their storage facility is at?"

Savina called out, "Hey, this is a really strange reading that I'm getting here. The city ought to have several million people, but I'm only registering a very few people, couple hundred at most, all gathered in one location. No, there's a few more at a slightly different spot down there. Weird."

Pippa said, "What? Where's their population? A few hundred? Could they have had a massive accident? Released all their bio agent and wiped nearly everyone out? Are we too late?"

"Don't know, but we've never seen that happening before," Adrianne called out.

"We best take her down and get a closer look," Arnold suggested. A bit later, he called out, "My god!" They got their first look at the hundreds of naked nova sitting in the street. As they watched, they saw ten dressed people going about putting ballet style boots on the naked nova.

Gwenda spoke up. "Arnold. I'm picking up telepaths. Lots of them. Down there. They are in terror. Something terrible has just happened to them. A catastrophe of some kind. I sense the presence of death on a huge scale, but I can't pin point it, just that it's down there."

"Well done, Gwenda. Savina, see if you can take air samples. See if that bio agent is in the air. It might not be safe for us to land," Arnold ordered.

A few minutes later, Savina reported, "No bio agent. Pretty pristine air. Clean, pure. What's going on down there?"

Gwenda replied, "Arnold, I think that they are desperate for help. Can we postpone our attack and help them? There are only ten of them trying to help hundreds of helpless terrorist victims."

"Right, dear. We should lend them a hand. Perhaps in return they will tell us where their bio agent cylinders are stored," Arnold replied. "Okay, Alfonso, kill the cloaking and take us down for a closer look. See if there is an open area near them where we can land."

"On it boss," Alfonso replied, switching off the cloaking device and gently descending, while Savina also looked below for a suitable landing location. Before long, they spotted a section of the road that was clear enough for them to set down. Alfonso made another perfect landing. He and Savina joined the others in the cargo bay, just as Arnold lowered the bay ramp.

Fin and Aldo saw the ship landing and made their slow way over towards it. Hence, they were the first to see the new arrivals when the bay ramp lowered. They saw eight well-armed men and women staring out at them. Fin had long reached his limits. "Okay, if you are here to kill us, just go ahead and do it. I can't take much more. If you are here to help, by god we could use it."

"We can help. What's going on? A war? A bio agent

attack?" Arnold called out, recognizing his language.

"Don't know. A gigantic sunspot suddenly appeared almost as big as the whole sun. EM pulse knocked out all power. We're trying to rescue as many of our people as we can, but millions have probably drowned. Can you help us? We have to get these people somewhere safe for the moment," Fin asked.

"Drowned? I don't understand, but we can help. What do you want done?" Arnold replied.

"They can't walk unless they get those boots on. Even then, they will have a hard time walking. We need to get them back to our place, I think. All the power is out. EM pulse knocked out all power and all the robots that were looking after them all," Fin answered.

"Hot redhead," Aldo winked at Gwenda, as she stepped down beside Arnold. One by one, the others came down the ramp. The other six were wearing the same tall heels that the two doctors from Ashford-5 wore. Fin rightly guessed that six were cured nova, but the other two were normal humans. Soon the eight joined in, helping where they could, trying to grasp what was going on amid the total confusion of the street scene. It made no sense at all.

However, as soon as Fin began issuing orders for them somehow to get them all to their quadraplex, which became a stable datum, around which the confusion began to lessen. While the eight were unable to physically lift and carry one of the mostly helpless nova, they were able to at least put an arm around them and help them make the long walk. Meanwhile, the other ten emulated what they were doing, forming a steady stream of eighteen walking eighteen of the nova the several miles to their quadraplex.

As they headed back, Zia complained, "I don't know if I can walk this distance eleven more times to get them all back to our place. My feet are killing me already."

"We're going to have to get them to walk on their own," Fin responded. "I can't go much more myself. Damned feet anyway."

Meanwhile, slipping and twisting along on their sub-light engines, the Serpientes intergalactic ship dropped down to a low orbit and began scanning for monkeys. "I sssee monkey citiesss," First Leader called out.

"But where are all the monkeysss?" asked Second Leader.

"Hiding perhapsss. Underground?" First Leader speculated. "Keep looking. All sssensorsss at maximum."

"Aye Firssst Leader," the Communicator replied.

A while later and perhaps a thousand feet above the surface, the Communicator called out, "Monkeysss, Firssst Leader. Out in the ssstreet below usss."

"Ah good. I sssee the monkeysss now. Look. Ripe and plump. I am ssso hungry. Take usss down, Navigator," First Leader ordered. Over the system comm system, he ordered, "We are about to land and dine on fresssh monkeysss. Ready landing party of sssix in a ssshuttle."

"My god! What the hell is that?" screamed Zia, pointing up into the air above Venice. A thousand foot long, twisting, snake-like ship slipped silently along, but was heading downwards, probably for a landing not too far away from them.

"Aliens! We are under attack!" screamed Fin. "Everyone, hurry up! We got to get into our house fast!"

For a moment, no one moved. All were staring completely flabbergasted at this amazing sight. All except Aldo and Ciro, that is. Hearing the word "aliens," they looked at each other, smiled, and headed for the spaceport where the one-man shuttles with the cannon were stored.

The giant alien ship landed, crushing many buildings beneath it as it settled down several thousand feet from the terrified humans. Some continued to make their slow way towards the quadraplex, but most just stared in total wonder and disbelief at this strange ship. There weren't such things as true aliens, not in this galaxy, not in the Federation of Planets or the former Imperium, just humans and now nova.

Then, the head of the ship, which looked somewhat like a snake's head, opened up and six of the Serpientes slithered out. They saw giant snake creatures, twelve feet long, two feet in diameter. They had tiny arms and legs, but at the moment, they were not using them. Now, everyone did stop and stare at them. Most mouths were wide open. A few shrieked, though.

Dr. Alexandra blinked, rubbed her eyes, making sure this wasn't an illusion. Bravely, she yelled out, "Welcome aliens to Beltazar-C." She tried several other languages as well.

Diego whispered, "If they aren't friendly, this could be really bad, dear."

While everyone stood and stared, the first of these snake aliens drew close to one of the trailing nova, who just stood there staring at the snake-like man or beast. In a flash, the snake opened its gaping mouth, revealing two large fangs and many smaller teeth. In one fast motion, its head came down over the nova, swallowing him whole! Everyone saw the large bulge in the snake's body where the nova must be just inside, but moving slowly further on down its body. Then, another snake devoured the next nova.

After that, screams of terror echoed through the streets of Venice. Nova frantically tried to run away as fast as possible. But in their ballet boots with fused feet, that hardly counted as running, more like a slow stumping. More than one lost their balance and fell, only to be devoured by the slow moving snakes. Then, more snakes came slithering out of the ship, adding to the terror and chaos.

Arnold and his group finally shook the shock off and began firing their many weapons at the snakes. Likewise, Drs. Alexandra and Diego focused. The crystals around their necks glowed bright blue. A pair of lightning bolts arced, knocking a pair of the slithering, gorged snakes back many feet, but didn't kill them. Arnold's d-gun did kill one of them, but after that, they must have activated a defensive shield. All further d-gun shots did nothing. Arnold cursed loudly. Pippa tried using her Sonic Stun gun on one and temporarily halted its movement.

Seeing that their usual weapons were mostly useless against the snakes, Gwenda dropped hers, and drew out her long knife with its razor sharp, twelve-inch blade. Snaking between stumbling, frantic nova, she made her way up to the front line of serpents. In one giant leap, she landed on one's back. Her knife flashed, buried to its hilt in its back. Her legs gripped the serpent like one riding a horse bareback. She pulled the blade towards her, slitting the snake wide open. Gwenda didn't stop until she'd gutted the thing down its entire body. Only then did she duck and roll out of the way of another snake coming to the aid of its fallen buddy.

The group of snakes rose up, hissing at her, trying to get an angle on her to strike. She was too fast for them. As one struck, she dodged, but brought her knife up, slicing open its underside of it its mouth area. Finally, with six trying to corner her, she ducked far back out of their reach, but continued to look for an opening to jump onto another.

Amid the chaos, two one-man shuttles swooped down on the snakes, cannon firing almost continuously, taking chunks out of the street. One hit a Serpientes, splattering its vicious looking head into slime on the street. Its headless body writhed in pain, knocking into others around it and even knocking another unlucky nova over as well. That did it; the snakes had had enough and began retreating to their giant ship.

However, Aldo and Ciro continued to press their attack, changing their tactics to that of strafing the enormous ship itself. Volley after volley pounded the ship, but seemed to have no discernable effect on it. As if in retaliation, the mouth of the snake-like ship opened up to reveal its own energy gun. It blazed and everyone watched in horror as one of the small shuttles completely disintegrated!

Michela screamed, "Ciro!"

Aldo saw his buddy disintegrated and was more than annoyed with that! Dodging the beam, which now sought to down his own ship, Aldo reached a decision. The lives of everyone hung in the balance. If he didn't take this alien beast down, it would only be a matter of time before these snake aliens dined upon what was left of his dear friends and the poor nova. He spotted his opening. Ten seconds. The energy gun needed that long to recharge. He timed it perfectly, dodging another blast. As it then recharged again, Aldo shoved the throttle up to its maximum speed and drove his shuttle straight into the open mouth of the snake-like spaceship!

The resultant explosion knocked everyone flat onto the ground, deafening them for some time. The entire front of the ship disintegrated, leaving a giant crater in the street, nearly a hundred feet across! The remainder of the ship burst into ten additional smaller explosions, scattering debris across three blocks, leaving bits of smoldering remains here and there.

Got you, you foul fiend from Hell! Aldo thought. *Hey, Luciana. How about that one? Bet you can't top that! Got the fiend! Captain Aldo wins again! Let them know that there is a way to stop them dead in their tracks!*

But Aldo! You're dead! Ciro too! Luciana sent back.

Hey, dearie, I'm talking to you, so I can't be dead, now can I? Wait! How can I be talking? My body is atoms now! Hey, babe, I can see you too! This is strange. Oh, I need a new nova body! That's it. Hey, hi Ciro. He's here with me too. Ciro, say hi to Michela. She thinks you are dead too! We're not dead, but we do need new nova bodies.

Okay. I'll make you one now, Luciana sent back. She focused and found one of Alexandra's sperm that was still inside of her and helped it along to one of her eggs. *There you go, Aldo. Hang around me, and you'll have a new one soon enough. Michela, see if you can make one for Ciro.*

Already done, she replied coolly. *We can't lose you hot fellows, now can we?* she teased them both.

Luciana and Michela noticed others were gesturing their way. "What?" she called out, but couldn't hear anything. "Oh shit!" She gestured towards her ears and then sent to Zia, *I can't hear anything! I think we're all dead now. Aldo and Ciro got them good!* She thought that Zia was mouthing that she was sorry. *Hey, they are both all right. They need new nova bodies, so Michela and I are making them now. We had better get the last of these nova inside. It's getting late, and we're all starving. What a battle!*

Diego sent to an exhausted and numb Alexandra, *We have to get help here like yesterday. I'm heading to our ship and sending an emergency cry. With luck, they can get here in less than a day. No way can we handle this many helpless people. We're too few.*

Good. Let them know what happened here. My god, Diego! What if there are more of these things out there, coming here? We are their food! she sent back.

By the time that the group had the remaining nova safely inside their quite packed quadraplex, their hearing had returned, though most still had definite ringing sensations in their ears. "Okay, we need to feed everyone. Quite how, I surely don't know," Dr. Zia took charge.

The women all worked together, using every available pot and pan in the entire place, cooking up nearly everything that they had. Meanwhile, the men tried to help the nova calm down. Angelo conducted an official head count and reported that they had saved a hundred seventy-five nova. All had been grad students and all had telepathy. He felt that was something at least. Meanwhile, Fin and Arnold headed off to the power plants to see if there was any way to get even a trickle of power back.

"Fused," Fin cursed.

"That's to be expected, Fin. A giant EM pulse like that is going to fry all electronics. This is all scrap metal now," Arnold backed him up. "What about the robots? Any chance of getting one of them going? If so, they could be invaluable to us right now."

"Come on. Let's see," Fin replied. They headed back outside and looked at one of the worker robots. Neither had any idea of how to access its internals. Hence, Fin used a screwdriver to pry the back of its head off, revealing melted circuits. "Well, the robots are history. Damn, we are so screwed!" Solemnly, the pair headed back in time to help feed the throng.

Each of the sixteen took over the care of eleven nova, helping to feed them, generally two at a time, while helping themselves in between. By the time they finished, it was getting dark. At this point, they had them all piled into every available spot in their large commons, but most were sitting on the floor. Dr. Zia took charge. "Okay, listen up everyone. I'll tell you everything that we know about what's been going on."

While she began telling them the sordid history of their world and their lives in the virtual world, the men headed next door, taking advantage of the remaining twilight to bring back all of the food that was there. Fin commented, "Well, this is the last of it. Enough for one more meal. After that, unless we find more, we're starving. Damn, damn, damn."

"Hey," Diego replied, "I sent word back to Ashford-5. They will be sending help to us. With luck, they ought to be here late tomorrow. We can hold out that long."

"Thanks from us all. Finally, we get a break," Fin gushed, relieved more than he could say.

Next, they carried over all available bedding materials, woefully insufficient, for the sheer numbers of nova, but they would have to make due one night as best they could, Fin concluded. It was nearly dark inside the quadraplex when the men carried in the sheets and blankets. Dr. Zia was still talking, so they set about covering up the piles of nova where they sat or laid.

By the time the Zia finished answering questions, everyone was too exhausted to do more than plop down on their beds. Arnold took his crew back to their ship and moved it over onto the street just in front of the quadraplex. Then, they too hit their beds. The next morning, the sixteen scurried about handling the needs of the hundred-seventy five, fixing the last of their food for breakfast, and scrounging up anything that could be used to clothe the men and women.

Around eleven, a dozen deep space transports arrived from Ashford-5, along with plenty of helping hands. Fifteen of the new nova were helped into each ship and by noon they departed, leaving the sixteen behind to wrap up operations here.

Chapter 11 Making Sense of It

"So we should check every underground location for more survivors," Dr. Zia said, though she doubted that they would find more survivors.

"And we should confiscate any supplies needed for the genetic cures," Dr. Alexandra added.

"And keep watch for more of those snake aliens," Dr. Angelo stated his biggest concern.

"And we should see if there is any way to get some of the power back on," Dr. Fin added. "Say, Arnold, we never did ask you what you wanted here on Beltazar-C."

Arnold smiled. "You aren't going to like it."

"Try us," Fin griped.

"We're on a mission to locate and destroy the supplies of the nasty genetic bio agent. We have a list we took from Pippa's father, General Tyrrell Fenton. Each one on that list is a known seller of those cylinders. We've destroyed the stockpiles of eleven of them already, and Beltazar-C is the last know purveyor of these cylinders of death," Arnold said flatly, not holding back.

"But we had nothing to do with that awful stuff," Fin protested. Then, he remembered something that Eros had said. He said hesitatingly, "You don't suppose that the robots, the HIFRs were doing that?"

"Oh my god, Fin," exclaimed Dr. Zia. "That makes sense. After all, they said that they took over this world. So how did all of the original population of Beltazar-C become nova unless they used the stuff on the people who were living here?"

"Oh shit!" Tiana softly cursed, mostly to herself. "What have we been a part of?"

"Hey, it's not your fault," Michela stuck up for her. "You were just one of us, another nova. It's those damned robot machines. Hey, Arnold, you can count on us to help you find and destroy those cylinders." He nodded.

"Say, when you find them. I'd like a small sample to

analyze," Dr. Diego requested. "It will help us in isolating the mutations, which are now varying considerably."

"Agreed. They are supposed to be operating out of Venice here," Arnold replied.

"We've never seen them, but that's not saying much," Angelo sighed, resigned to having been a victim of the HIFRs misdirected sense of survival of the fittest. "There are probably lots of secret places around here that we know nothing about at all. Anyway, let's divide up. Six of us know a little about Venice, so we'll each lead a party. We can stay in touch with each other via telepathy."

"Diego and I can also lead," Alexandra volunteered. "We'll divide up into eight pairs. Let's thoroughly search this city!"

Arnold and the two doctors from Ashford-5 provided powerful flashlights for each team, and they began their methodical search. Every building had to be entered, searched, with particular attention to any basement facilities or secret doors that might lead to such underground complexes.

Pippa tagged along with Dr. Zia. "So how many of these underground chambers are there supposed to be?" she asked.

"Well, Angelo is the math whiz, but I'd say it's a lot. We are supposed to have had one hundred million nova on this world somewhere in these underground tanks," Zia replied, as they entered the next one and looked for the stairs.

"How many per facility?" Pippa asked. "I'm good with math."

"We think around two hundred fifty or so. How many does that make? Quite a lot I suspect."

"Jeesh. That means we have to find forty thousand of these! We'll never be able to search them all! They must have used this evil genetic bio agent on the entire population of this world," Pippa declared, staggered with what lay ahead of them.

"Oh my! We'll never be able to check that many, unless they are close together somehow. A hundred million — that isn't a large population for a whole planet, though. Most have in the low billions of people, the space-faring ones, I mean. But none of us know how many were here when the robots came and took it over. As I understand it, the people here were all hooked on their V-mask virtual reality games and only spent time out of their game worlds to eat. So they probably weren't even worried about what the robots did to them, if they even knew. Sad really," Dr. Zia said.

"Well, this one's a bust. They are all dead. Drowned probably," Pippa whispered. They'd entered the chamber and saw the bodies floating in the rows upon rows of tanks. Not one had gotten out of their tank. After a look around, they headed up the steps. Outside, Pippa used a can of spray paint to mark a big X on the main door, indicating they'd searched this building. Solemnly, they headed to the next likely building, another warehouse.

Arnold and Fin decided to try searching close to the spaceport itself. "If they were selling the cylinders, it would make sense to have them close to the landing transports," Arnold suggested. They found maintenance bays, fuel reserves, and even a robot automated factory to build the small one-man shuttles and tiny canon. Later on, they found a large facility that made deep space transports as well. Late afternoon, the two finally found what they were looking for: a large stash of the yellow bio agent cylinders!

"Dear god, Arnold! You were right. The damned robots were marketing this stuff! We have to destroy all these cylinders," Fin exclaimed, shocked, but no longer too surprised, not after all they'd seen in the last two days. "Alexandra wants a sample, but I've no idea how to get it. I let her know we found them."

While Fin focused and reached out to the geneticist, Arnold began estimating the best way to dispose of all the cylinders, this time without releasing the gas. He decided upon a thermite explosion. With its high heat, the noxious gas ought to be vaporized. While he headed back to his ship to get his explosives, Fin waited for Dr. Alexandra to get here. The tanks, he noticed, were no longer yellow, but almost an orange, presumably due to the long exposure to the radiation from the nuclear attacks on Aquila Prime, if that was their history.

"Ah found you." Dr. Alexandra walked into the warehouse. She gasped. Having never actually seen these before, she just stared at them for a moment. "How many?"

she mumbled.

"Don't know, but one hell of a lot," Fin replied. "Probably more than enough to wipe out a whole planet. Damned robots!"

"Okay, time for a sample," she said, sitting down her bag. She attached a fitting to one cylinder's nipple. After hooking the other end to a small sample cylinder, she released the valve, allowing the gas to flow from the cylinder into her smaller sample one, before shutting it off again. "This little cylinder holds enough to test, but not enough to harm anyone. So we are all safe. I'll take this back to my ship now. You going to blow it up?"

"Yes, as soon as Arnold get back with his explosives," Fin answered.

"We should all be inside our ships when he does it, just in case some of the gas escapes. We sure as heck don't want to get infected again," she explained her safety guideline. "So give us all plenty of warning before you two blow it up."

Considering that their quadraplex was now filthy and that there wasn't any food left, Arnold invited them all to stay on his ship. At dusk, everyone climbed onboard, and Estrella and Adrianne headed back to whip up supper. Meanwhile, with the bay doors closed and sealed, Arnold flipped his activator switch. They all felt the ground shake a bit as the heavy-duty explosion detonated, incinerating the cylinders. Zia, Alexandra, and Diego kept careful watch on their sensors, making sure that the area wasn't now covered in the toxic gas. Arnold waited in the pilot's seat, ready to lift off if there was any gas release. He wanted no part of getting genetically modified!

"Still nothing is reading," Zia called out.

"Supper's ready," Estrella announced, and they headed to the galley.

After eating, the three geneticists rechecked their sensors, but still there was no sign that any of the gas had escaped the explosion. Now, they all relaxed and began to discuss the many events. Fin summarized, "Well, we found and checked fifty tank chambers today. They were all dead. I think tomorrow we should focus on finding any of the materials you doctors use to work your genetic cures."

Zia sighed. "You are probably right. I don't see how any nova could have survived this long after the power failure. So was the power failure because of those alien snake creatures?" She sensed everyone else shuddering. They'd been careful to put that awful memory completely out of their minds. Now, she'd just brought those memories back into everyone's mind, perhaps too vividly.

An awkward silence fell. Luciana and Michela had memories of their loving companions, Aldo and Ciro. Fin finally broke the stillness. "I think so. As far as I know, there has never been such a gigantic sunspot as we had here. That's what caused the EM pulse. Probably the alien snakes did that to knock out all our defenses, which it certainly did. Then, they attacked."

"So, so will more of them be coming?" Bess asked meekly. Fighting against evil men was one thing. She'd overcome her fears and had been helping her group now, but these monster-sized snakes were terrifying. She'd been almost helpless to harm them in any way.

"That is a darn good question, Bess," Arnold answered. Considering that he was nearly twenty years older than the others here, he felt obligated to lead. "I know that there are some strange animals around our galaxy, but I've never heard of such things as these. They are definitely an intelligent and a very advanced race, even if they are giant snakes."

"Hey, my guess is that they were a scouting party, probably from another galaxy even," Pippa spoke up. "In my soldier training, we were taught to always send out a small scouting party in advance of the main division's movement. If these aliens follow the same protocols, then what we saw as just one small scouting party."

"So you think we are about to be invaded by these snake aliens?" Arnold asked. "Well, that makes sense to me." He didn't wait for Pippa's affirmative nod.

"We have to find a way to warn all the major worlds," Dr. Diego spoke up. "Trouble is, no one is going to believe us. Hell, I'm even having a hard time believing what we all saw and fought."

"We need evidence. Perhaps tomorrow, a couple of us can see what we can gather from the mess that is left of them," Pippa suggested. "I'll volunteer."

"Hey, I will too," Bess offered, though nervously. "I've used a video recorder before when I was in school. I did a project on plant growth in biology, and we had to document our results."

"Good, Bess. We'll see what we can do to prove to skeptics what we're dealing with. I wonder if they are susceptible to nukes?" Pippa asked. "Of course, we don't have any of them, but battleships do."

"True, but if they always precede their attacks with a giant EM pulse, the battleships will be knocked out before they can ever close to fight," Arnold pointed out, sobering them all.

Adrianne asked, "So does this mean that we are canceling the second part of our mission, Arnold?"

"Second part?" queried Fin. "I thought you got all the bio agent suppliers."

"Aye, that we have, Fin, at least the ones that we know about from the general's list," Arnold explained. "We were planning to visit most major worlds, let Gwenda search minds of the leaders there, and see if she can find out if they have a stockpile of the cylinders. You know, as a supposed deterrent weapon. If so, we were going to destroy those as well. This hideous bio agent simply has to be wiped out! My god, the sheer number of lives that have been ruined and destroyed staggers my own imagination."

Dr. Alexandra chuckled. "Arnold, you won't get any protests from us. In the old Imperium, whole planets with populations in the many billions were wiped out. Genocide. When it's used as a weapon, whole planets are wiped out. They did try to rescue as many as they could, but even mobilizing all available ships, only a tiny fraction of the population could be reached before the others died of dehydration or starvation, leaving entire worlds filled with rotting corpses. At least here in your Federations, no one has gone that far with it."

"Dear, there's another thing," Dr. Diego felt he ought to add. "These cylinders have been duplicated so many times and by such poorly maintained equipment that the resulting genetic modifications are lessening or at least changing for the better, slightly. It is my sincere hope that soon the bio agent that's left won't be able to cause any more mutations at all, sort of dying out."

"That can't come too soon!" Estrella added vehemently. "Look at what it has done to us. Say, when we get done with our missions, is there any chance I can come to your world and finish my genetics doctorate? I don't dare go back to my world, not looking like I do now. We're called freaks on Pegasi-C. It's too embarrassing for me."

"Sure, you are all most welcome to come to Ashford-5. There, you'll find quite a lot of us. Plus, we do have a top quality Academy. You'll fit right in, all of you," Diego volunteered.

Alfonso looked at Savina, and then said, "Hey, we'll take you up on that offer, as long as I can still be a pilot and Savina, a navigator. While she might be able to get by on Vegan-C, I sure as hell can't. I don't even look like a man anymore."

"Don't see why not," Diego replied, sensing both wanted to hear that confirmation.

"But what about, well you know, finding boyfriends?" Adrianne asked timidly. "I mean, what's a man going to think about me when he sees me in bed? Am I supposed to now be like the man and look for a woman? This is so confusing."

Alexandra could feel just how sensitive these women were over their genetically modified bodies. One wrong word and they could easily be sent spinning. "On Ashford-5, most of us believe that one should marry out of love for the other person, though there are still some arranged marriages in some kingdoms. For the most part, our kind usually marries another of our kind, though not always. Marry for love, Adrianne. That's what Diego here and I did."

"But men and women — we all look the same now," she continued, still confused about her own future relations. "Well, men still have deeper voices but that's about all."

"That's why it really doesn't matter among us. Man and woman has sort of ceased to exist. So marry someone whom you love, Adrianne," Alexandra continued to point out.

Arnold chuckled, "Hell, that's good advice for anyone."

Several smiled and Adrianne seemed satisfied for the moment.

The next day's search proved quite profitable. Having changed objectives, the group went looking for genetic cure supplies and other things that were valuable and that ought to be retrieved before they left. After stowing the supplies on her ship, Dr. Alexandra announced, "Gang, there's enough material here to provide all known cures to well over five hundred people. Well done. These will be put to excellent use!"

Arnold and Fin discovered three nuclear bombs stashed in an armory. After also taking a goodly supply of the d-guns, they began moving the heavy bombs into Arnold's transport. They had two of them onboard by early afternoon before breaking for a late lunch on his ship. Fin waited on the others to walk up the ramp before heading inside. Later asked why, he simply said, "Being polite to the women." Yet, his politeness saved them.

Suddenly, the sky darkened noticeably. He looked up and saw another giant sunspot! He screamed, "Shut all power off immediately. EM pulse coming!" He dashed inside and closed the doors.

Much credit also goes to Arnold, who didn't hesitate a split second. He dove for the master power switch, slamming his hand down on it. Total darkness resulted, along with screams and yells from the others. Above the confusion, Fin yelled, "I just saw another giant sunspot! Snake aliens may be coming!"

Quickly, Alexandra and Diego focused and produced their usual soft blue light and moved to opposite sides of the galley so everyone could get themselves oriented. Several had to pick themselves up off the floor, having tumbled when they were taken by the surprise blackout.

"Oh god! What do we do now?" wailed Bess.

Arnold's voice boomed out, "Patience everyone. As soon as the EM pulse is past us, we can power up and get out of here."

"But how will we know when it's safe? When it's past us?" asked Pippa, quite worried. Once more, her frightening memories of their battle with these snake aliens were vivid in her mind, just as they were in everyone else's mind.

"Damn good question," Fin called out.

"I know. I'll sacrifice my fancy watch," Arnold said. He pushed one of its buttons. The electronic circuitry lit up the dial so that he could read it in the dark. Everyone stared at his watch, waiting and praying. Without warning, the light vanished!

"I — I didn't feel anything," Bess whispered.

"You wouldn't unless you had electrical circuits in you, like a heart monitor or pace maker, in which case you would be dead," Arnold answered. "Okay, I think the pulse has passed us, but let's wait a few minutes in case there are more of them. Gang, I think that when we flee, we should take as many of these valuable deep space transports with us as we can. Who all can fly one? One of us can program the hyperdrive so all you have to do is activate it."

Alexandra, Diego, Arnold, Alfonso, Pippa, Savina, Luciana, and Michela all could, which meant that they could take six of Beltazar-C's transports with them when they left. Rather than risking this ship, Arnold decided to open the forward emergency hatch manually. Diego followed him providing him with his blue light so he could see what he was doing. Soon, daylight entered the ship, much to the relief of those inside. He called out, "Okay, I'm going to power up one of the other transports. We'll use it as our guide to when the EM pulses are done. I'll enter the coordinates into the hyperdrive of five other ships too. Back in a bit. Oh, sorry, Diego, I need the coordinates."

Diego wrote them down on a scrap of paper torn from the pilot's log and handed it to him. Now, the others sat back and waited nervously. Bess was really nervous and kept tapping her spiked heels on the metal floor, annoying others, but they wisely kept quiet. "What's taking him so long?" Bess asked in a shaking voice.

"Give him time. It takes a few minutes to power up the ships," Pippa explained. "There's a whole checklist to go down for safety's sake. By now, he's probably gotten one of them going."

After an eternity, Arnold poked his head in through the open hatch. "Okay, seems safe enough. Power the ship up,

Pippa, and open the bay. I've got all the other ships ready to take off."

Soon, the lights were back up. Quickly, the group divided so there were at least two in each of the eight deep space transports. Fin commented to Arnold, "You know, I wish we could have gotten that last nuke onboard, but maybe we can leave it as a surprise for our alien snakes. Wish we could drop it on them though."

"Son, so do I, but there's not enough time. Best hurry and join your pilot," Arnold answered. He donned his head set. "Diego, Fin's on his way. Pilots, report in. Status?" Seven "all ready's" echoed in his ear piece. "Gwenda, close the bay doors. Everyone, as soon as Fin's onboard, we're taking off."

Bess, who'd taken over the comm center position, asked, "Do you suppose that we could try and get some video of these alien ships? That might help convince others."

"Sure, can you do it from your center there?" Arnold asked.

"If I can hook a small cam on the hull — do we have time for that?" she asked, hesitantly. "I mean, I don't want to risk us getting killed by them snakes."

"Sure, I'll keep watch. Go for it, Bess," Arnold replied. Of all his crew, he knew that she had the least skills and education. On top of that, she was the shyest, quite timid. Perhaps, her physical appearance added to her insecurity feelings. Her face was anything but attractive, though now the rest of her body most definitely had knockout curves, but then so did all of the hermaphrodites.

One by one, Arnold verified the seven takeoffs; all went without any problems. He then kept his eyes on the sky overhead, waiting for Bess. "I'll go lend her a hand," Gwenda suggested, undoing her safety harness and leaving her navigator's seat.

"Hurry up gang. Here they come!" Arnold spoke urgently into his headset.

"Okay, we're ready to go. Cam is beside the bay doors," Bess replied into hers. "We're strapped in back here." Arnold needed no further encouragement. He slammed the engines on and lifted off rapidly. Knowing the orientation of the cam, he maneuvered the ship, placing the bay doors towards the incoming six snake ships.

An excited Bess yelled over the headset nearly deafening him, "I'm getting them videoed! Six of them. I hope they don't attack us though."

"Don't fret, I've my hand on the hyperspace jump button," Arnold attempted to calm her. He knew that he'd need lightning fast responses. If he saw an energy blast coming at them, he'd have only a split second to avoid it. He gambled and kept the ship's bay doors oriented on the alien snake-like ships as long as he dared. "Okay, we're getting out of here." He decided he'd taken enough of a risk and hit the button. The blackness of hyperspace replaced the stars.

A much calmer Bess reported, "Captain, I've got the video recorded. In case something happens to us, I am emailing it to Dr. Alexandra. She'll know what to do with it."

Arnold smiled. That she would. He looked at the hyperspace readout. "Nine hours until we make planet-fall. How about some lunch or coffee?"

"What a weird planet," Bess commented. She and Gwenda were looking out of the cargo bay viewport, as Arnold slowly set the ship down not far from the other seven. They'd landed a few minutes ahead of him. "I see the others. They're heading into a tall building with lots of big glass windows."

"Right. Control tower just told me we're to join them as soon as we land, which is right now." He felt the slight jar as the ship's landing pads took up the shock of landing. He powered down, heading towards the bay, where the two women already had the ramp lowering. He took Bess' arm, helping her descend the ramp in her tall heels. She flashed him a thank you look. Once on the ground, his arm found that of Gwenda's, who smiled and strode towards the large group, her head held proudly erect.

As soon as they got within talking distance, Bess called out, "I got us some video of the six snake ships!"

"We know," Dr. Alexandra called back. "I forwarded it to everyone here at home. Excellent work, Bess. Come on; we're going to a big debriefing. You're going to meet the bigwigs around here."

"It's darn cold out and so dark. Is it night?" Gwenda asked.

Diego laughed. "Nope, it's noon. We've a cool red sun. It's almost winter though, bit chilly."

A number of security guards met them at the main doors, "Follow us, doctors. They are waiting in the governor's big conference room. Even the emperor himself is here! You all must really rate."

Diego replied, "No, but we're bringing some really bad news with us. You'll be hearing about it soon. Keep your ears pealed."

"I like the smell of this world, Arnold," Gwenda commented. "Trees. Real trees."

Diego replied, "Resinous pines. They grow nearly everywhere. Our climate is rather a fickle one, awfully cold most of the time, compared to other worlds."

"Beats the heat of Al Nair," she teased him.

They entered a huge room, filled with a hand carved oaken table and very comfortable chairs. Some handmade tapestries hung on the walls, depicting hunting scenes. The new governor had made some changes to the sterile environment of her offices. Six others were waiting in the room for them.

A few years back, the older generation of rulers retired and their grandchildren took over for them. Dr. Alexandra did the introductions. "Governor Sheila Blackwater-Valen, her husband, Henry who is in charge of their large computer system." Both were hermaphrodites with dark black hair. Henry's hair was cut short, and he wore what looked like a man's suit, except for his most prominent bosom. Sheila wore hers flowing partway down her back. Both wore the giant lip plates. She also wore the now familiar professional woman's attire, complete with six-inch heels and drab grey skirt. Likewise, Henry also wore similar heels.

"These are our two queens, Mrs. Lilly Gervasi-Jones and her mate Mrs. Misty Jones-Gervasi." Both women had thick blonde hair that was almost floor length. They also wore the giant lip disks, but wore satin, form-fitting, red gowns, and toe shoes. Neither had any arms as prominently shown by the style of their gowns. Certainly, they weren't trying to hide that from view. Both also had tiny waists. Corset stays were visible beneath their satin gowns.

"This is the Ataro Empire's Emperor Fu Gang Sanguro, the grandson of our late emperor." He had black hair cut quite short. He wore a suit, but had no arms either. However, he didn't appear to be a hermaphrodite, though he also had a tiny waist and wore the debilitating toe shoes. He looked male in all ways, except for his waist and shoes. "We are incredibly honored to have him with us. That's his silent assistant with him. He cannot speak and acts as the emperor's arms."

"Finally, this is Renata Gervasi-Bellweather. She runs all our Advanced Therapy research and sessions." She too had thick very blonde hair that fell to her thin waist and wore a professional woman's skirt and blouse as well. Her black oxfords also had six-inch heels, and she was a hermaphrodite as well, but she didn't have the slit lips of the governor, her husband, or the two queens. In fact, she was really Rafaela Gervasi-Jones or Rafe as she used to be called. When her previous body had grown very old, she'd taken over one of her granddaughter's babies, continuing her research and therapy sessions.

From the standpoint of those who had never been to Ashford-5 or Tierra before, these six did look quite strange indeed. Governor Sheila spoke first. "Welcome to Ashford-5 or Tierra we locals call our world. First, I believe that some explanations are in order. With the exception of our emperor and his assistant, we are hermaphrodites like most of you. Yes, we've all had all of the genetic cures that we desire and that are possible. Henry, Renata, and I have to wear tall heels like those you are wearing. However, here on Ashford-5, the nobles and wealthy are very fashion conscious, and all insist on wearing these giant lip plates. Therefore, the queens, Henry, and I also wear them so we fit in with these important people of our society. That said, I must explain the emperor and queens." She explained about their need for physical limitations on those who wield great power, but she sensed this group of newcomers to Tierra thought that this was ridiculous. Still, she did her best to explain the reasons behind their armless state.

"Now then, while I normally would prefer to begin at the beginning, the extreme danger that we are facing dictates otherwise. Bess, we cannot thank you enough for providing the video of their ships! That is a real convincer. We've had our scientists examining the samples that Dr. Alexandra brought back and thus far have concluded that their bodies were indeed serpentine in nature, but wholly unlike any serpent found in the old Imperium. We're not sure about the Federation side just yet," Governor Sheila explained. Next, she had them relate everything that had happened with these aliens, beginning with the giant sunspot and its EM pulse that knocked out all electronic devices and power on Beltazar-C, resulting in the deaths of a hundred million nova, more or less. There was no accurate head count known to these people.

Emperor Fu Gang asked, "I know this is painful for you, Luciana and Michela, but your Aldo did destroy the ship with a one man shuttle?"

"Yes, he drove it at top speed straight into the ship's open mouth," Luciana answered, fighting back a surge of emotions.

Arnold added, "We believe they enter and exit through the head of their snake-like ships. He was also firing his small canon as he crashed inside their ship."

"And your d-guns — they were effective only once?" the emperor asked.

"Right. Only on the first shot. After that, they seemed to have some protection shields against them. Stunners worked marginally," he replied.

"My knife worked well," Gwenda put in. "Slit the snake open like a fish!" The emperor acknowledged her contribution as well, and she smiled broadly.

After an hour, they returned to the current situation. "Yes, we were darn lucky that Fin spotted that new giant sunspot. We got the ship powered down before the EM pulse hit us again, but it knocked out my fancy watch," Arnold explained.

Fin added, "It can't be a coincidence. They must do

Vic Broquard

something to the star to create the EM pulse to knock out our
defenses before they land and attack. We seem to be their
food."

"That will make it exceedingly difficult to stop them. An
EM pulse that large will knockout nearly everything on the
planet before they attack, making it completely defenseless,
unless they can shut all power down at the first sign of the
sunspot's appearance," the emperor concluded. "Very nasty
indeed." They discussed these six new ships for a bit longer,
but they hadn't stuck around to see where the six would head
next from that rim world.

Emperor Fu Gang sighed. "If we didn't have enough
problems with this Black Man, this Emperor Supreme,
conquering world after world, now we have an alien race of
giant people-eating snakes to deal with. Honestly, the galaxy is
going to the dogs."

"No, the snakes," Gwenda corrected him, not grasping
his idiom. He smiled at her, though he didn't correct her.

Next, he wanted to know all about Arnold and his
group, and just how they'd found out who had been the sellers
of the bio agent cylinders. That too became a lengthy story.
Alfonso declared, "Those evil men sold that stuff to the
terrorists who ruined our lives! So we gave them a dose of
their own medicine, ruining their lives. Let's see how they like
being a helpless genetic mutation as was done to us."

"What about the others who were also infected?"
Emperor Fu Gang pointed out, referring to the million or so
altered in Capital City.

"Hey, they didn't do a damned thing to stop these evil
men in their city. Besides, they were kidnaping, torturing the
younger victims, turning them into their exotic escorts. They
deserve to know what it's like to be a helpless genetic mutation
like we were, only they aren't going to get any cures for many,
many years. Serves them right for what they've done," he
declared. Arnold's whole group nodded in perfect agreement
with Alfonso's declaration.

A half hour later, Emperor Fu Gang turned his attention
onto what was known about Beltazar-C, the robots, and
HIFRs. Now, it was Fin's turn to outline all that they knew,

though most of it was told to them by the HIFR called Eros. How much was the actual truth, none could really say. However, the underground tanks, nova, V-mask devices, and the empty Venice suggested that much of what Eros had told them was true. Luciana backed him up, adding her version to the mix as well.

When they finally finished up and all questions had been answered, Emperor Fu Gang commented, "Like my grandfather often said, the solution of today's problem becomes tomorrow's problem. That seems very appropriate in this case. I can tell you a bit more, but I must swear you all never to repeat this to others. You see, the reason that Aquila Prime was destroyed in the first place by that nuclear attack was in retaliation for the robots' use of that same bio agent, causing mass genocide on at least fifteen highly populated worlds in order for the robots to get their magic number of one hundred twenty million nova on Aquila Prime. One of the generals found out that the robots were behind it and took his own action to stop them, nuking Aquila Prime. So it does not come as a surprise to me that the robots did the same thing to the original inhabitants of Beltazar-C to make more of their nova. Perhaps, these alien snake creatures have done us all a very big favor."

"Yes, but what if what Eros said is true — that there are other HIFRs or robots that look just like humans out here on other worlds spying on us?" Dr. Fin asked. "Surely, this is cause for alarm."

"Indeed. Let me deal with that one," the emperor insisted. "Now then, Bess. I've arranged for an Imperium-wide newscast to inform every one of the threat posed by these alien snake-like creatures. Your video will be shown as part of it. I think coming from an ordinary citizen will help lend credence to the video. The newscast will be tomorrow morning. Governor Sheila will assist you with it. Now I must return to Winno-3 and get this data broadly known. We are facing two enemies, this Black Man, Emperor Supreme, and these snake creatures. If you want a job, we can use all of you helping us survive these attacks."

"Sir," Dr. Zia spoke up. "Would it help to have a photo

of this Black Man's face? It's not too good, but maybe someone will recognize him."

"What? You have a picture of him?" he replied startled. "We've been trying to obtain one for some time now, but no one can get close to him."

"A robot did. I have it on my laptop. I'll email it to you when I get to my computer," she replied.

"Excellent. Well done, all of you." He grinned, rose carefully, and made his slow way out of the room.

"Now then, I would like to have you all stay for a time with us in our Imperial Castle," Queen Lilly took over. "By way of thanking you for what you've done, we'll see that you have new clothes and everything that you need. I won't take no for an answer," she teased, but knew that her smile would be missed. She added, "Renata wants a few words with you, too."

For the first time, Renata spoke up. All eyes turned to meet hers. Later, each would describe her slightly differently. Her look was piercing, intense, a gaze that sees your soul. Those were some of the descriptions. Indeed, looking into Renata's dark blue eyes, one sensed an enormous power, a total confront, a total presence, and more importantly, someone who would really listen to what you had to say, but somehow what you said was what was the single most important thing bothering you at the moment. Well, she was a product of her own Advanced Therapy. In truth, she had very little need of a physical body to operate. Some suggested that she was on par with the ancient goddesses of Tierra, but few living had ever seen them.

Renata spoke softly, but her words struck like a knife slicing butter. "I understand the pain you feel. Our Basic Therapy will handle that for you, laying it bare and giving you the peace that you seek and need. Luciana, Michela, Annunziata, I see that you've brought Aldo, Ciro, and Dr. Lelos along with you and are preparing new bodies for your dear companions. You think highly of them — enough to do this unselfish act. You have my blessing and support for your three new daughters."

She paused for a second then added, "But I also see that many others have also come along with you. Ah, following you.

Yes, I see now. They are those that you knew in the tanks and who possessed telepathy. Many were your fellow graduate students. They are welcome here. To all of you, be vigilant for many babies are born within the Imperial Castle and Manor Houses. In time, you all will have new bodies."

"You can see Aldo?" Luciana asked, wide-eyed.

"Of course, I can see him, just as you can exchange thoughts with him, Luciana. Zia, all those spiritual beings who possessed telepathy and whose bodies did not survive have followed you and your party here," Renata explained. "You eight, via your actions, have shown them that in due time, they'll be able to pick up new bodies and continue on with their goals. For this, some of them are asking me to thank you for them. So on their behalf, thank all you eight, well six now. They hesitated to make contact directly with you because they fear you would not understand and too much else was happening."

"They, they aren't dead?" Zia asked, very confused. "But I saw their bodies."

"Yes, their bodies died, horribly so, but they, just like you, are not a body. You, like us, is an immortal spiritual being who inhabits for a time a mortal body. You may discover this for yourselves during our Basic Therapy, which some liken to a personal voyage of discovery about just who you are. But come; our queens grow impatient with me. They'll tell you that I would talk for the rest of the day if you'll let me," she jested, alleviating the intense spell that she had woven over the room.

"Oh that she would!" Queen Misty teased her back. "Come on. Let's get you to suites our staff has prepared for you. The Imperial Castle complex is just due east of here. We've electric cars that will take us there via the underground tunnels, quite necessary in the wintertime, when snow depths are measured in feet at this altitude."

Chapter 12 Nightmares

The Black Man, Emperor Supreme, Velasco Valen paced his luxury quarters onboard the Devil's Anvil, or more precisely, Yunque del Diablo, a Federation battleship that belonged to Cartagena-C, his first conquered world, and now the flagship of his ever-growing armada. Fifteen worlds conquered now. He had flags placed upon the wall model of the galaxy, each flag marking the location of the world he'd conquered. The perimeter was roughly circular, spherical if seen in three dimensions, but primarily within Federation space and far from Ashford-5, his ultimate target, though not a single person knew that planet was his ultimate objective.

He'd taken these worlds not by force of arms but by using his unique gifts of Domination and Mass Domination, the form his *mentales* gifts had taken, amplified a hundred thousand times by his three dozen giant crystals of power. It had helped that most worlds kept their leading rulers and politicians located in a relatively small area, such as a capital city, where he could work on them all at one time. Had they been scattered all over a world, he'd not have been remotely as successful and certainly not this swiftly.

True, most of these worlds had been relatively small fish in the overall scheme of worlds, but they were easily taken and now provided warships and manpower. A few more smaller players and he ought to be ready to take on far more populous and powerful worlds. Yet, it was not such matters that had awakened him in a cold sweat. Not at all.

He rubbed his hands over his face, recalling vividly the images in his mind, a dream, a nightmare. He was in his bed, beneath the luxury of blue satin sheets sleeping soundly. Was it too soundly? His arms had felt super heavy. Drugged perhaps? Had he drunken some wine before bed? Had it been in there? There was his wife, his Valencia, sitting over him, a crazed look on her face, contorting and twisting her face into something freakish! Her hands — no, her prosthetic hands — they looked utterly alien to him. Her hands held a wicked, curved dagger. Val laughed hideously, as she plunged the dagger deep into his chest. Not once. Oh no. Over and over and over. With each stroke, each plunge, he felt searing pain in his chest, but his lead arms wouldn't move, not even enough to push her off him. That's when he'd awakened, his body soaked in cold sweat. He'd donned a thin shirt and quietly left their bedroom, where Val was still sleeping soundly, her prosthetic hands lying on their nightstand.

Velasco didn't fear being attacked by admirals, commodores, soldiers — these he could and had faced before. They were easy to handle. Thoughts could kill. That he knew, but thus far, he'd only had to do that once, and no one could trace that death to him. Rather, the officials called it a massive heart attack, which hardly explained the victim's partially liquefied brain matter. No, Velasco feared no man, rather he feared women. Right now, it was his wife, Valencia.

Actually, Valencia was loving and kind hearted. Her passion was collecting designer gowns, the best of the popular fashions of the wealthy on the many planets that they conquered. Already, she'd filled up one small cabin on the battleship with her many crates of dresses and gowns and heels. Velasco had once joked to Admiral Juan del Migos, who commanded this battleship, that Val had enough dresses to open her own store. Velasco had given her carte blanche to acquire any apparel she desired. What more could she want?

His death? How many nights now he'd had this same dream? Velasco couldn't say, but many. I've not given her any reason to hate me so, he thought, but then thought better of that. He'd purposely and very carefully arranged for her "accident" which crushed her hands, forcing them to be removed so that she couldn't poison him or stab him to death while he slept. He'd also arranged for her feet to be fused so that she could only wear those ballet boots. Walking on her fused toes like the ballerinas that they saw back on Cartagena-C guaranteed that she could not move swiftly and that he could always out-run her. Yet, he was totally certain Valencia knew nothing of his treachery. True, she was still having a terrible time getting used to operating her new prosthetic hands, and it had been months now. Somehow, he had to get these nightmares to end.

In a flash, it came to him. Always, it was those terrible prosthetic hands plunging the blade into his chest. Solution: simple. Get rid of those abominations, those hands of hers. Besides, she hated them, always fumbling, and embarrassing herself in the process. Well, that would be simple enough! He walked back into the bedroom, slipped back into bed beside her and focused, drawing on the power of the two giant crystals that were part of her heavy earrings. They glowed pale blue for a moment and then it was over.

Val woke refreshed as always. This had been a most wonderful vacation-honeymoon. Already, she had more dresses to use in her design work than she ever imagined. Such variety, such selections, though some were down right risqué in her mind. "Dear, I don't think I want to wear those awful hands any longer."

Velasco woke, rubbed his face, noticing his stubble. "What's that you said dear?" He knew darn well what she'd said. He'd implanted that concept deep in her mind late last night.

"You know what an awful time I keep having with those horrid hands, so utterly embarrassing you know. Well, you probably don't know. But it's just awful for me, dear. From now on, I'm not going to wear them any longer."

"But dear, how will you manage without them?" he asked innocently.

"I suppose I will need to have you help me some, getting dressed mostly and help me dine. You won't be upset that I'm going to need you to help me with those things will you?"

"Of course not, my love. You are the prettiest woman in the galaxy. Come on; I'll help you this morning. Perhaps, we can find some young girl to be your assistant during the day. Your arms do look quite lovely, dear," Velasco replied.

"Well, yes," Val replied, lifting her lower arms up and looking at the aesthetical appearance of their conical shape near her wrists. "They are so delicately shaped. Quite pretty if I do say so myself." She waved them about some, admiring them. His implanted ideas took root.

He kissed her and spent a good half hour getting her

dressed in her favorite blue "day-gown" as she liked to call it. Her skirt only billowed out some three feet around her legs, making passage through the narrower halls of the ship more readily done, though she preferred to wear the twelve-foot gowns so popular on Cartagena-C, but wholly impractical onboard the battleship.

When they joined forty-five year old Admiral Juan del Migos and his wife Benita in the mess hall for breakfast, she no longer wore her hands. Both watched the young couple, as he carefully fed her. "Oh, I think I can manage my coffee cup like this, dear," Val said, grasping it clumsily between her conical stumps and leaning over to sip. She turned to Benita, "I'm just never going to wear those awful hands ever again, Benita. I'm so tired of embarrassing myself with them. You can't feel anything at all with them, you know. And Velasco is the kindest man around. He understands and helps me with everything." She gaily chatted away as though this was utterly normal.

Benita felt deep sympathy for this lovely woman and her terrible plight. Everyone knew that Val had been a Beryl-C terrorist attack victim, an innocent one. "But dear, it must be so hard for you," she countered.

Val smiled, "Oh no, not really. I'm quite fine with these." She again raised her "pretty" stumps in the air. "I sometimes think we women should not ever have such things as hands, not when we have such kind husbands as Velasco here. I can't imagine why I ever had hands in the first place, so unnecessary."

No one saw the many compacted crystals hidden in Velasco's belt glowing briefly, as he touched Benita's mind as well as Juan's. Benita's disgust and horror changed. She replied, "Oh, I do so see what you mean, Valencia. You certainly look very beautiful without them. Your arms are so dainty and so beautifully shaped. I do suppose that we ought to see if we can't find some young girl to follow us around and assist you when you need it. After all, Emperor Supreme here has important work to do during the daytime. Juan honey, wouldn't I look very pretty if I had my hands removed and arms reshaped like hers? Shouldn't we few women on your

211

great big powerful ship look more like our esteemed and lovely empress?"

"Well, I don't know, peaches. That's a pretty drastic step to be taking," Admiral Juan replied, fighting against an overwhelming urge to agree fully with her. Losing the mental battle, he added, "But yes, I do have to admit, peaches, Empress Valencia does look stunning without them. Perhaps, you have a point. I'll give it some serious thought."

"Oh honey, please do. We could easily set the fashion standards of our new empire. You'd like that too. Everyone would be looking up to you and me as models of our leaders," Benita added, somewhat confused about what exactly she was saying.

Velasco knew there were only ten women on the battleship, officer's wives. During the daytime, they spent the hours together, chatting. For the life of him, he couldn't fathom what they could possibly talk about for all those hours. Still, he kept a contact line on Valencia through the crystals in her earrings, alert for similar discussions throughout the day. He planned on implanting similar thoughts into all the other women.

After breakfast, he and the admiral headed to the giant war room, where they worked on the next planetary system to be taken. Today, they discussed the next one, Al Nair-F, the sixth planet out from a hot blue star. "It's a desert-type world," Admiral Juan explained to Velasco. "People only live on the north temperate continent. But they do have space travel. I don't believe they could seriously threaten us. This world is on the Forbidden List."

"That's the trouble with the old Federation of yours. They discard any world that doesn't meet their standards. We aren't making that mistake. Any world has something to offer, if one just looks closely."

Admiral Juan chuckled, adding, "If only women." Both men laughed.

"Yes, if only women," Velasco replied. "Can't live without them, can we? I wonder what things of value we can find on this Al Nair-F?"

"I have a listing here," the admiral answered, "that says

they are rich in ores, rare earths, silicates, and of course resins. Now, resins are quite valuable as are the rare earths. We should see if we can't get a brisk trade going in those."

"Excellent. Excellent. See how screwed up this Federation of Planets is? Throwing away a valuable source for resins and rare earths. Idiotic. Well, we're not idiots, are we admiral?"

The older man chuckled, "Far from that, Emperor Supreme, far from that!" They began to make their plans for the taking of Al Nair-F.

That night, Velasco slipped between the sheets, pulling Valencia close to him. She responded, passionately kissing him. An hour later, a content Val drifted into a deep, relaxing sleep. Finally, Velasco also slept, feeling he'd solved his problem fully.

He opened his eyes. Something heavy was on his lower body. Val. She sat on him. There, held between her two stumps was that hideous curved dagger. She had that same crazed look on her face, twisted and sneering in utter contempt. Down came the blade, piercing his chest. Pain. Over and over. Val plunged the dagger into his chest until the bloody mess looked like a woman's pincushion he'd once seen. He sat up. He was in his bed, dripping with sweat that rapidly chilled him. There beside him lay Val, sound asleep and quite content. He didn't need his gifts to sense that.

As usual, he slipped out of his bed and walked into their main quarters, pacing like some trapped wolf. His perfect solution had had no effect at all! Well, that wasn't entirely true, he admitted to himself. Now, she no longer had those alien prosthetic hands on her stumps. But her stumps still were able to plunge that dagger into him! As he paced, he tried to think of any way to keep her from being able to plunge that dagger into him. At last, it came to him. She was using her lower arms to hold and plunge that blade into his chest. If she didn't have lower arms, then she couldn't hold the dagger! Again, he acted.

As he dressed Valencia the next morning, Val complained bitterly, "Dear, these lower arms of mine are just far more trouble than they are worth. Just look at them," she held them up. "All they do is get in my way. Dear, can't you please have the doctor remove them too? Make the bottoms of my upper arms nice and conical like my wrists are? Please, dear, pretty please? I just can't live with these cumbersome lower arms." She begged and pleaded.

Even over breakfast, she continued to make her case to the admiral and Benita. "They just get in my way. They aren't good for anything at all. Just look at them." She chatted away, gaining agreement from both Juan and Benita, compliments of a little Domination from Velasco.

Benita soon took up Valencia's case. "Honey, you simply must have your doctor do this for her. Honestly, can't you see how terrible her lower arms are? They just get in her way with everything. Besides, she would look far more attractive without them. So would I, honey pie. Please, make your doctor do this for her. And while you are at it, have him do me too? Honestly, honey pie, I would be far sexier than I am, if I too looked like our beautiful empress here. Please, honey pie," she pleaded and begged.

He looked a bit confused and asked, "Valencia, they really do get in your way? They interfere with you?"

"Yes, of course they do," she answered demurely. "I thought it was plainly obvious to everyone. I'd be so very much better off without them. We can pay for it, can't we dear?" she asked Velasco, giving him a pleading look that the others also saw.

"Are you sure that you want this?" Velasco asked, quite seriously, knowing that the admiral was watching him closely and judging him by how he responded. He also knew that this response of his was precisely what the admiral most wanted to see from him.

"Of course dear," Val replied sincerely. "Please. They are such a pain, such a bother, such an embarrassment for a woman."

Velasco turned to Admiral Juan. "If this is what she truly wants, then of course we can pay whatever your doctor would charge, sir."

"Oh don't be silly. There isn't any charge, Emperor Supreme. We can have it done yet this morning I suppose.

Now Benita, are you certain that you want it done too?"

"Of course, honey pie. Then she and I would be role models for the whole empire. We would make you both proud of us. Besides, we would be far sexier in bed, honey pie. Can't you see that?" she added, winking at him. Inwardly, Velasco smiled. How utterly easy it was to force others to do what he desired. One placed the right series of concepts into their minds with enough conviction that the person felt utterly convinced that not only were the ideas their own but that they were vitally important to be acted upon. So utterly trivial, Velasco thought, to control these pathetic, head blind humans.

Later that morning, both smiling women proudly showed off their new conical upper arms, rubbing them on their spouse's faces and promising them the best sex that the men ever had had. That evening, Velasco used his crystals to make absolutely certain that Juan and Benita had just that, their best night in bed ever, likewise, Valencia. The following morning, one look at the faces of the three demonstrated that they had! Now Velasco relaxed. Nightmares solved. Indeed, for a few more nights, Velasco slept well.

"On approach to Al Nair-F now," Admiral Juan reported to Velasco.

"Are they sending up warships?" Velasco asked, heading to the view screens there in the war room, bustling with men going about their many tasks, preparing for battle.

"Four light cruisers," the admiral answered. "We're detecting a number of underground silos opening their domes. Presumably, those hold rockets with nuclear warheads. Standard actions?"

"Yes. See that I'm not disturbed," Velasco replied. He focused his mind and reached out towards the four ships hovering over a large city below them, presumably their capital. So darn simple, he mused, and proceeded to work his magic. He finished and broke his connection. He rose, heading to the comm center, expecting the call, which soon came.

Admiral Juan commented a few minutes later, "All went just as expected. No resistance at all. You are to take a shuttle down to this, their capital city called Don, and meet with their executive leader, one King Berwin Dylis and Queen Aeron. They speak Welsh, so make sure that your communication device is set up properly, Emperor Velasco." He spoke formally because they were surrounded by his junior officers. One must keep up appearances in public, which the two did, while they had become friends in private, or so Juan believed.

"It's darn hot down there," advised the admiral.

"I will keep up appearances," Velasco countered. "The Black Man cometh. Still, Valencia might be too warm in her gown. I'll check with her." A half hour later, he had her dressed in a red silk, thin dress, but one which showed off her very shapely form rather well, pleasing her.

"Oh, I do wonder what exotic fashions I'll see on this world," she exclaimed in excited anticipation, while she made her slow, careful way to the docking bay, his steadying arm around her waist. "Aren't you going to be too hot in your black outfit, dear?"

"Appearances. First appearances are everything," he replied softly.

She chuckled. "You don't have to tell me that one, dear. I'm an expert on such things."

Al Nair-F was a hot, arid world, though from the air as they descended, they spotted irrigated fields beyond the edge of the city. Brown. That was the predominate color of this world and its buildings. They soon saw that most all buildings were built from brown sandstone, which this world had in abundance, not trees as found on so many other worlds. However, he did learn that in its distant past, this planet must have been a dense jungle, for they had enormous petroleum reserves. Refineries dotted the landscape for miles near the many productive fields.

Comparatively speaking, the spaceport just adjacent to the capital city of Don was quite small. While they had primitive transports, there were few warships. Four to be precise, but they had thousands of ballistic missiles on which they based the defense of their world. This, Velasco already knew from his probe of the minds of the commanders of the four light cruisers.

After landing and lifting Valencia down the bay ramp, his small security patrol surrounded them, and they walked to meet a corresponding group, along with their King Berwin Dylis. He was forty with short red hair, side burns, and matching moustache. He was as tall as Velasco and wiry. He wore a light linen shirt and pants, both white, with black boots. "Welcome, welcome to Al Nair-F. I'm your host, King Berwin. It's a great honor for us to at long last have such distinguished visitors to our humble world." He seemed very sincere, and Velasco sensed nothing was amiss, no treachery, but a genuine pleasure at his arrival, quite unlike the other worlds that he'd conquered. A slight touch of the man's mind told him why. The Federation of Planets continually ignored this world, even to the point of putting it on the blacklist of Forbidden Worlds. Velasco realized these people desperately wanted to become a part of a far larger empire, obviously to gain respect and trade.

"My charming wife, Valencia," he introduced her and noticed the king was looking her over very carefully, and that he was sexually aroused by her appearance, particularly taken with her large bosom and short upper arms. They chatted lightly during the limo ride to his Palace in the heart of the sprawling city. Brown sandstone buildings predominated and most were no more than two or three stories high.

The Palace turned out to be another brown stone building, but was far larger in size and only one story tall. The entrance doors were steel covered in a decorative gold leaf pattern consisting of a bewildering collection of interwoven knots that seemed to have no beginning or end to them. That motif would soon be seen as their fundamental decorative scheme on everything from gold plated goblets to doors.

He led them into his throne room, which was both large and filled with gold plated objects, including the chandeliers that hung from the ceiling. Velasco soon learned that this world was adrift in that soft, malleable metal and used it for decorative purposes nearly everywhere, as it was as common as sand. That alone got Velasco's interest up, as did what he saw in the room.

"Ah, my lovely and charming Queen Aeron," he

announced proudly. Both Velasco and Valencia stared at the thirty-eight year old woman with shoulder length, flaming red hair. She wore a very, very thin cotton dress, loose fitting, but one that hid nothing from sight. It was certainly cool, while Velasco was sweating to death in his heavy black garb. Even Val was perspiring heavily, though she said nothing about it. The temperature inside the room had to be in the mid-nineties. Rather what so caught their attention was that she was bound in a way that neither had ever seen. Around each ankle, she had a fleece collar. A metal spreader bar attached to each collar, keeping her feet precisely three feet apart. Across her shoulders, another horizontal bar held her arms spread out parallel to the ground, but left only her hands free to move slightly.

Sitting on a smaller throne beside her was an eighteen year old, exceptionally pretty young woman, whose flaming red hair fell in waves to her lower back. "My eldest daughter, Princess Delwyn," King Berwin announced. She too had her legs spread apart and her arms bound to a bar across her shoulders. "My queen, princess, this is the Black Man, Emperor Supreme, Velasco Valen and his empress, Valencia."

Then, Velasco noticed another woman was present, sitting back against a far wall. Her dress was that of a Federation professional woman. King Berwin introduced her at last. "And this is another guest who had dropped by for a visit. Miss Minta Axon from Pegasi-C. She will be leaving soon." Minta nodded respectfully to Velasco.

"Welcome, emperor, empress," Queen Aeron said sweetly. "Oh, what's that sound coming from your waists?" She'd heard the ULATs translating her language into theirs. Velasco quickly explained how they worked. "So clever," she then added, "but you must be melting in such heavy clothing. My king, you should offer them more appropriate apparel."

"Ah, perhaps I should, my queen."

"We are fine for the moment, but later, I know Val here would love to see all of your fashions," Velasco replied.

"Excellent, excellent. Aeron, would you please serve our guests something cool, berry juice perhaps?" King Berwin suggested.

218

Both Val and Velasco watched as she rose and walked over to a far table. She walked with a sort of swivel, pivoting, rotating motion, barely lifting her bare feet from the floor. At the table, she bent sideways, until her hand reached a pitcher. Then, while holding it, she bent the other way to get her hand on a pair of golden goblets. With her unusual and slow walk, she returned to the pair, who now sat on a pair of plush chairs beside the king on his throne. She bent sideways, setting the cups down near the arm of Velasco's chair, adjusted her position, and leaned the other way, until she was able to pour the purple juice into the two goblets.

"I'm sorry," she apologized. "I don't know how the empress is to drink."

"I'll help her," Velasco replied, watching her clumsy movements returning the pitcher to the table and then taking her seat on her throne.

"Thank you, this is excellent. It hits the spot," Velasco said, while lifting the other up for Val to sip. She generously agreed with him, pleasing their hosts.

Then, the two men got down to business. "So how do we become a part of your empire," King Berwin asked directly. They spent an hour discussing this. King Berwin readily agreed with all the arrangements. Velasco sensed this union was something that this world had been trying to obtain for centuries. As they wrapped it up, Minta excused herself, saying that she had to depart or be late for her next stop. That she'd not said much of anything the whole time went unnoticed by Velasco, particularly because he didn't sense any thoughts from her, none at all, only smiling approval.

With the business finished, Velasco finally asked, "So why is your wife bound like that and your daughter? We are not familiar with your customs."

Surprisingly, Queen Aeron answered him. "Our men have strong sexual needs. It is a woman's duty to be always prepared for her man. I'm bound so I'm visibly always ready for him. I'm ready for him at any time. Berwin, we should honor our esteemed guests with the Sharing Ceremony." That name was as close as their ULATs could come with its translation.

"Yes, my queen. I'm forgetting all our ancient customs. Forgive me, but I have been so overwhelmed by this good fortune that I'm neglecting our customs. Yes, Emperor Velasco, you and your beautiful wife must partake with our Sharing Ceremony. It is done by every worthy husband and wife on Al Nair-F, when honored guests come to visit. Come; now is as good a time to share as any."

They followed the strange but very slow walking queen and her husband, who led them into a room with tapestries hanging from the walls, reminding both of their castle suites back on Ashford-5. A bed lay in the center of the room. It had no head or tail boards, giving access from all sides. As King Berwin explained, he prepared Queen Aeron for the ceremony. He removed her thin gown. Then, he fastened two metal collars around her knees, locking them into place. The bands fit the shape of her legs and knees such that they could not slip up or down. She could no longer bend her legs at her knees in the slightest. Finally, he fastened a head harness over her head, and locked an O-ring into her mouth, forcing it to remain fully opened at all times. Then, he carefully helped her move over to one wall where he locked her neck in a band that held her erect and up against the wall.

Meanwhile, following the king's instructions, Velasco removed all of Val's clothing, but kept her corset in place and her ballet boots, since she couldn't even stand without them. With the help of the king, he got an identical leg spreader bar fastened to her legs, forcing them apart three feet, but by now Velasco understood the why of all this fully. He rested a bar across her shoulders, strapped her short upper arms to it, and then put the O-ring into her mouth, fastening it to the head wrap, locking it securely on. He noticed that there wasn't any way for either woman to get free of these bonds. Lastly, he helped her wobble over to the wall and fastened her neck to the wall binding, keeping her erect and against the wall.

Both men proceeded to indulge in their wives. Kinky. That was Velasco's thought about this whole way of having intercourse. When both finished, he soon learned they'd only begun the ceremony. Next, King Berwin helped his wife over to the bed and got her lying down on her back. Assisting Velasco, the two helped the struggling Val over to the bed. "No, we lay her on top of Aeron, but opposite. See, they will use their tongues to pleasure each other." They carefully laid Val on top of Aeron, positioning their open mouths over the other's privates.

"Okay, ladies, you may begin," King Berwin announced.

Val let out an "Oh" sound and then a moan. She reciprocated, and soon Aeron made some noises of her own. "Now," King Berwin announced. He then entered his wife while motioning for Velasco to do the same to his wife. An hour later, all four lay fully contented on the bed.

"That was quite a ceremony," Velasco commented.

"Indeed. It is our custom to honor our guests in our house," King Berwin replied. "Queen Aeron usually keeps her O-ring on during the day, as well as the bindings, unless we are meeting others, such as yourselves. If you like, we would both be honored if your empress remained similarly bound today. Of course, she should wear a light dress as Aeron."

"Would you like that dear?" Velasco asked. She couldn't speak with the ring forcing her mouth open, but as satisfied as she was, she nodded that she would, pleasing Queen Aeron, who made agreeable noises. However, the knee bindings were removed so the two could sit down or walk somewhat easier. Later around suppertime, the O-rings were removed, and the men fed their wives and daughter, chatting about how interesting their sharing custom was.

"So it is official then that our world is now a part of your empire?" King Berwin asked over after dinner wine.

"Indeed. You are officially World 16 in our mighty empire. Trading ships should be arriving in a few days," Velasco answered. "Here's to a long and prosperous union, King Berwin." He raised his goblet in a toast.

"Then, if you will permit me, there is one final custom that simply must be met. Here on Al Nair-F, we take our traditions very seriously. Whenever there is such a union as this, particularly so for one this momentous, it's the king's obligation to provide a new wife for the other leader. You are both young and have no children yet, but may they one day bless your lives as they have mine. My eldest son is off to the west handling that awful mess. It seems somehow there was some kind of accident or terrorist attack. Yes, we have them here now too. That mutation thing that is running wild within the Federation of Planets has finally come to Al Nair-F. Some hundred were affected and turned into strange freaks of nature." He described the aftereffects of the bio agent. Both Velasco and Val cringed.

"I see you have also heard of it. Anyway, Prince Cadoc is off dealing with that mess. Anyway, back to our traditions. I'm obligated to provide you with another wife for your harem. I know you are married to this lovely and charming woman here, but it is common on our world for a wealthy man to have many wives. To seal our union for all time, we wed our daughters to each other. Since you have no daughters yet, I'll not require that of you, but I must insist that you wed my Delwyn. As you can see, such a wedding binds our two houses for all times, sealing our bargain, such that no one can ever break it apart. I certainly want to do everything I possibly can to make our union last forever."

Velasco had been so relaxed that he had dropped his guard and was thus blindsided by this overture. Val started to protest. He acted, focusing and activating some of the crystals in his belt. *Of course, Val, you really want to have Delwyn with us. She can help you with things when I'm not present.* That was the concept that he placed deep within her mind, such that she believed that was her own idea. Val responded, "Oh yes, dear. You simply must also marry Princess Delwyn, please, you must."

"There, that's settled then," a very proud King Berwin announced.

"But what does Princess Delwyn think of this?" Velasco quickly turned his attention onto her.

She grinned, "I'd love to marry you, emperor. All Al-Nair-F women expect that their fathers will arrange a proper marriage for them, but none could ever hope for such an important husband such as you, my emperor."

Well, she's quite a beauty, he thought. He probed her mind a little to see if it needed adjusting too. *I just have to get off of this world! It's my dream coming true, to travel in space! I hope he will have me!* He smiled; she was quite willing to go along with this arranged marriage. Thus, he spoke up, "I would be honored to marry your beautiful Princess Delwyn. When can it be done?"

During the next few days, transports came and went, exchanging cargos and making more and more arrangements. On the appointed day, King Berwin conducted the lavish ceremony with nearly a hundred in attendance, most being the very wealthiest in Don. Velasco and Val simply sat back and enjoyed the festivities in their honor. Note, Val had already been taken shopping and now wore traditional Al Nair-F clothing, light weight and cool in their intense heat, pleasing her enormously.

That evening as the three retired to their private bedroom for their wedding night, Delwyn asked, "Aren't you going to bind us properly? You should. That way, I can pleasure you both and not leave Valencia out in the cold. That wouldn't be proper or right."

A bit reluctantly, Velasco bound both women, though Delwyn occasionally had to give him proper instructions. Finally, he had them both securely bound properly that is, including the O-rings held securely to their head harnesses. Carefully, he laid Val down on her back on their wedding bed. Even more gently, he put Delwyn face down, positioning their open mouths directly above the other's privates. He allowed them to use their tongues for a time, and then he could hold himself back no longer. While they were going to town with their tongues on each other, he relieved himself in each one, though some minutes apart.

When all three were satisfied and exhausted, he carefully turned Delwyn over and lay between them, failing to unbind either woman. He slept very soundly, until the middle of the night. Once more, his nightmares returned, only this time both women were on top of him, and Delwyn was slamming the dagger into his chest, while Val rode him and encouraged her to stab him again and again. Both women had crazed, insane looks on their faces. He woke in a cold sweat and knew he had to get Delwyn's lower arms and hands removed as soon as possible.

To that end, he took them up to the battleship the next day, and used his powers on Delwyn, who was soon begging him to make her like Valencia. That he quickly did, and then got her dressed in one of Val's gowns that Val insisted she wear. After that, Velasco discovered that Admiral Juan had not been idle either. He'd hired two young Al Nair-F girls who were ten years old to become their personal assistants, promising them the adventures of a lifetime in space. Velasco felt quite pleased that everything had worked out perfectly, particularly since Delwyn was quite a beautiful young woman and so very willing to satisfy his sexual urges. However, he did have to alter slightly her notions of proper sex, since he didn't have any of their bindings here in the battleship. He convinced them that they didn't need them to continue their mutual three-way sex. After the first night done without the bindings, Delwyn was totally convinced that the bindings really were not needed. In fact, he sensed a growing strong bond between Val and Delwyn. In a way, that made him a tad jealous of the two women.

Still, his nightmares continued. Besides the two short-armed women sitting on him, pinning him down, now there were many other women taking turns stabbing him repeatedly until he awoke in a cold sweat. Night after night, Velasco endured the torture from the nameless women, even though he did his very best to keep Val and Delwyn totally satisfied and pleasured until they fell into a deep, restful sleep. This, he checked on repeatedly. Then, it dawned on him that perhaps what his nightmares were telling him was that all women everywhere needed to have their lower arms and hands removed so that none could thrust that dagger into his chest!

He brightened up when he worked that conclusion out. The next day, he spoke with Admiral Juan, telling him that he wanted to pay a brief visit to the sixteen worlds now in their empire. "Ah, just as well, we do need to take on some more fuel and supplies before we hit the next set of worlds," Admiral Juan replied.

During these next few weeks, Velasco used his many crystals to their max, implanting that idea into thousands of leader's minds, pressing upon them the vitally important concept that proper women should emulate their beautiful empresses and have their lower arms and hands removed. One by one, the sixteen worlds' leaders began to pass such laws or make such decrees, and the process began. Finally, the nightmares ended for Velasco, who felt that he'd found the solution. No woman would ever be able to thrust that dagger into his chest. Two weeks of no nightmares, but only enjoyable sex with his wives, convinced Velasco that he'd done the right thing, and it was time to expand his domain further. Another dozen bigger worlds and I'll have enough power to challenge the Ataro Empire and Ashford-5!

But he wasn't the only one to have nightmares. Minta had been ordered to scout out worlds that might be invaded by this Black Man, Emperor Supreme, and gather precise data on just how he managed to conquer those worlds. Luckily, she'd been on Al Nair-F at precisely the right time. She'd witnessed the startled King Berwin launch his four light cruisers in a hopeless defense of his world, and arm nearly four hundred ballistic missiles. He was ready to defend his world to the last man, which she presumed would be happening. Instead, hours later, King Berwin was welcoming this mad emperor into his palace. She keenly wanted to meet him, and Minta got her wish, observing him for several hours, as he conducted the negotiations with the king.

She'd been there sometime before, and already knew what the king's position on many matters actually was. Minta was entirely baffled when during these discussions; the king seemed to change his point of view, often radically. It was as if there was some unseen power forcing the king to alter his positions. Try as she might, Minta could not pick up anything on her many, many sensors. Frustrated and very worried, she left and jumped her transport into hyperspace.

There, she opened up the communications line to Thanos to report all she'd learned and to receive further orders. Silence. Nothing responded to her signals! This had never happened before! Hastily, she attempted to contact Eros and then Apollon and Deimos. Nothing. No signal, nada! At last, Minta was certain that something terrible had happened, and she headed for home, Beltazar-C, at top speed, arriving several hours later to find a dead world!

Wandering the streets of Venice, she saw worker robots standing motionless, mid-stride. Others had fallen. She found a few dead nova in the streets, their bodies covered in flies. She checked on the eight nova and found the quadraplex empty, but also saw excrement everywhere, along with piles of sheets and blankets strewn about the commons. Mountains of dirty dishes lay everywhere, as though everyone had been used, but not washed. Further, there wasn't any power anywhere. Her circuits tried to analyze what had happened but failed utterly.

She then headed off to try to find Thanos, but ran into Eros on the street, lifeless. She stopped and opened up his "brain" only to find all his circuits had melted. If a HIFR could panic, Minta came as close to that as possible. She raced off to find Thanos. She found her other three companions together, their circuits just as melted as Eros' was. In a panic, if a robot could be said to panic, Minta raced to the other thousands of underground facilities and saw tank upon tank filled with decaying, dead nova bodies, most still with their V-masks on their heads.

In so doing, she'd nearly drained herself of power and used the last of it to return to her ship and connect herself up, recharging fully. While recharging, her circuits tried to work out what had happened here, but simply could not. Only a monumentally gigantic EM pulse, she reasoned, could have fried the robot circuits. She concluded that if that had happened, then all the electrical devices should also have been destroyed. Once her recharge was completed, she visited several power plants, verifying her hypothesis. Then, she headed to the main computer, where the robots stored their infinitely vast databases, accumulated over several centuries. They too were fried.

"The backup?" her mind reached the next logical step. She entered the subterranean basement where the offline backup copies of everything were stored. These, she discovered, were intact! It took her several days to carry them out of there and into her transport. After refueling it, Minta sat down for another recharge. Now, what do I do? That was the fundamental question she asked. She knew that there were five hundred six humaniform robots, Model 8's, who looked like normal homo sapiens sapiens out among the major worlds, gathering data for Thanos. These were the last of her kind!

She then began sending a message to each one of them, telling them of the total destruction of Beltazar-C and that she alone of the original five leaders was left. One by one, the Model-8's acknowledged her as their new leader. However, she soon learned from one of them the story being relayed around the galaxy of the invasion of an alien race of giant snakes. One sent her the video taken by some young woman named Bess. Now, she finally had an answer to what had happened. However, it didn't lessen her nightmare. What did she do now?

Minta knew that she faced a nightmarish situation. Twice now, the best efforts of her kind to forward the nova had failed utterly, wiped completely out. This time, it was worse, since the attack had eliminated her other four key associates including their leader, Thanos. Further, this new threat from some unknown alien race of snakes appeared unstoppable. As the last of the five leaders and founders of the robots, she felt enormous weight on her shoulders, if a robot could have such a feeling. What to do?

The Model 8's were designed for spying, not building more robots or for caring for nova. Worse, until the backup data could be restored, she had no idea where their many bank accounts were located or their account numbers. Logically, she needed to build a new main computer, restore the most recent data, and construct a comm center so those in the field could report and receive orders. But where? Certainly, Beltazar-C was out. Apparently, it was on the direct incoming path that these alien snake creatures took. Rebuilding here was entirely too risky. Further, the new location needed to be secure, since she had nothing to defend it with. She would have to recall some of the spy Model 8's and reprogram them to build new Model 7's or perhaps new Model 9's, which had been on the drawing board.

Their new location had to be not only off the beaten

path but also where exploring homo sapiens sapiens would never likely venture. She chose Cadwell-E, a frozen world located on the rim of the middle section of the Federation spiral arm. Minta issued orders for several dozen Model 8's to begin acquiring the computer supplies that she would need and construction materials for a base. This planning occupied her for many days, but she knew she still faced the nightmarish question of all: what did the robots do now?

She'd witnessed the self-destruction of much of the homo sapiens sapiens species. She'd been intimately involved with the brilliant nova, but the vast majority of the nova were not even worth considering as living beings. One thing that her circuits told her was that her Four Laws were worthless now. There wasn't any nova left to protect, unless they began from scratch once more, stealing nova from many assisted living complexes. That would be fruitless, since they had no infrastructure set up to allow them to survive, as they had painstakingly built on Beltazar-C. Minta began to see a tiny spark of light in the midst of her nightmare. Robots ought to survive. Could that be the answer that she was looking for?

Chapter 13 Recognitions

"My god! That's Velasco Valen and his young bride, Valencia!" exclaimed Governor Sheila. Henry had just downloaded the latest collection of surreptitiously obtained photos of the Black Man, Emperor Supreme, while he was on a world called Al Nair-F. "I let him go off-world! It's my fault. I best let the queens know."

Twenty minutes later, Queens Lilly and Misty joined her with Renata tailing along with the two. Governor Sheila continued, "It's him. Henry has these new images, and he even ran facial recognition on him using the photo I made for his ID card. It's him, Velasco Valen, the Black Man, Emperor Supreme. How is he doing this and why?"

The queens looked at both photos, satisfying themselves that Sheila wasn't mistaken. With all her technology, mistakes were still possible, but his face was captured quite well this time. "Well, I had my Tower Circle check on him before we headed over here," Queen Lilly answered. "Valen Tower did train him some years back, giving him the usual training and his personal crystal. That much we know. He's one of us, a telepath and *mentales* gifted. I've asked Valen Tower to relay us whatever they know about him on the quiet. We should know more in a while. As to the how and why, I've no idea."

Renata spoke up, demanding their full attention, which usually happened when she chose to speak. "Our worst fears have finally come to pass. One of our *mentales* gifted has gone off-world and is putting his gifts to use to dominate and control entire worlds. I suspect you'll find that he has a number of those giant germanium crystals with him in order to command enough force to do this to entire worlds. Ladies, we are facing a very serious situation here."

Queen Misty spoke up, "She's got a valid point. Very serious situation. Look, if others out there in the galaxy learn of our true powers, we are going to be viciously attacked, either to kill us, since some will see us as a serious threat, or to kidnap us and force us to work for them. It goes far beyond mere telepathy this time. Until now, we've been pretty much able to keep the knowledge of our *mentales* gifts from the old Imperium and Federations. Now, the cat could well irrevocably be out of the bag."

"Quite true, but what is he doing and why?" Governor Sheila asked again, having gotten no clear answer yet.

Queen Lilly replied, "One thing we know is that he is conquering worlds without fighting a battle and subsequently building up quite a large fleet of warships, enough to catch and hold the attention of Emperor Fu Gang. If he has giant crystals with him, he's going to be very hard to stop."

"Could we do it?" Sheila asked. "I mean if we combine mine, with yours, and with many of the Guilds? Would we have enough power to combat him?"

"I would think so," Queen Misty answered, "but I'm sure that he knows this too. He knows he can't take us on directly, because we'd do just that, combine all our various groups who possess these giant crystals of power and use them to stop him. He can't be that foolish."

"No," Renata again chose to speak up, and the other three turned to listen to her. "He's not stupid. I believe he is working at it from another angle. By accumulating a huge fleet of warships, I think he will soon turn back to us, once he has a force far larger than the whole Ataro Empire does. If he does, then and only then can he return here. With that behind him, we can't directly battle him, and the Emperor will no longer be able to support us. Brilliant move, if I do say so myself. Ladies, we have a very big problem and little time to develop the proper action to take. This is our mess, and we need to clean it up without getting the emperor involved, and without anyone else out there discovering all about us. I don't need to tell you what could well happen if the galaxy discovers our true abilities here."

Somber faces reflected in Renata's eyes. Governor Sheila sighed. "I know, but how are we going to stop this maniac Valen?"

"That's what we four are going to have to figure out," Renata replied. "Think on it. We'll meet tomorrow and toss out ideas."

Doctors Alexandra and Diego took charge of getting the fourteen settled and into daily routines, since they had spent time with them. Diego handled Arnold's group of eight, while Alexandra worked with Zia's group of six. However, they began together on a group tour of the Imperial Castle and Manors. Diego explained, as they walked along just inside the fifteen-foot tall outer walls, moving past the castle, its tower, and then a long line of manor houses. "You see, Tierra here is a strange mixture of old and new. Officially, we're on the northwest side of Exchange City and at the eastern edge of the spaceport. Centuries ago, the Imperium landed here and rented the land for their port. Our people then were rural in a sort of Iron Age, though we lacked much iron and used many substitutes. Even today, our homes are built from stone blocks, and there are no roads that you would recognize as roads from your worlds. Travel is by horse or wagon. Our people cling to traditions."

"Anyway, Exchange City was the only place where Imperium traders could meet and exchange goods with our people. And it still is and serves that purpose. Off-worlders are not allowed beyond Exchange City, mostly for their own welfare. Our climate can be dangerous if you aren't prepared for it. Now that the Imperium is no more, the queens have greatly expanded their domain by adding on all these manor houses, each with a number of large suites. Some of these will become your homes while you are here."

"The queens are this world's top rulers, handling mostly interfaces between the galaxy out there and our world, though they also step in an handle conflicts between various kingdoms. Each kingdom is democratic with their own governmental bodies and are usually run by the Guilds. While much of this may look quite primitive by your standards, looks can be deceiving. We have a state of the art Academy or University in Exchange City. Plus, nearly every town has its own geothermal electrical plant. Each home has running water, electricity, central heating, and such things, run by the appropriate Guilds."

"The queens have their own independent finances and will be providing everything that you need while you are here, from food to clothing. Ask and it's yours. They employ a large staff who usually wears green uniforms. If you need something, ask the first one of those that you see."

"The first thing we're going to do is get you clothing and settled into your new quarters. As far as meals go, it's your choice. You can prepare your own or you can join the many others who dine together with the queens. If you want to cook your own, just let the green uniformed caretaker who looks after your suite doing the cleaning and such. They'll see that your refrigerators and pantries are stocked for you. We'd suggest dining with the queens and many of us, at least for the first few days until you get the hang of how things are done around here."

"The next thing you need to know is this world is overly fashion conscious, and always has been for that matter. Lacking most heavier elements, fashions were about the only way that the nobles and wealthy could display their status in our society. So just warning you. You'll see many of those giant lip disks. Anyone wearing them is doing so for fashion reasons."

"We've taken in quite a lot of terrorist attack victims here over the last century. Hence, today, half of the population of Exchange City is hermaphrodites. Some, like the hundred plus that you were able to save, are here in the process of getting their cures. They will be dining with the queens, naturally, since they need assistance until their arms are regrown."

"Also, around these manor houses, you will find a rather large number of us who have our doctorates or are in graduate school. We'd love it if you'd lend those in your fields a hand with their various ongoing projects. Specifically, Dr. Zia and Estrella, we would like you to lend us a hand working on the many genetics research projects. We also have projects in nearly all other arenas, chemistry, physics, and math. So you three doctors can easily put your skills to work. We have quite an advanced linguistics group going, and they'd love to have you join them, Adrianne. Some know your grandmother. Our astronomers know very little about your spiral arm. So Pippa, Arnold, Alfonso, Savina, you might consider visiting with them and sharing knowledge of stellar systems with them. I'm not sure where Luciana, Michela, and Gwenda can help though. If you three think of something, holler."

"Starting tomorrow, you each will begin to get your Basic Therapy. I'm told they will be in the mornings. Someone will come by and get you. Honestly, I can't speak more highly of it. The results are simply amazing. Trust us; you'll be blown away by the results. Renata is in charge of all the many therapy givers. Each one of those you rescued are already getting theirs as well. It's the least we can do for you. In the afternoons, you can all help out as you desire. In the evenings, you are all invited to come to the Queen's Throne room where musical concerts are given. We have some stellar groups who love to perform. Just don't be surprised at the sometimes wild contrasts between old and new."

"Here we are, Number 42. This manor house will be yours while you are staying here. Inside, there are four large, independent suites but with one very large commons area with a complete comm center as well. Each suite has four separate bedrooms, each with their own bathroom, though they share a common kitchen, dining room, and living room. Split up anyway that you wish. After you check out your rooms, let's get you to Elegant Fashions Inc where you can pick out your own new clothes." Diego finally finished his long explanations.

Arnold and Gwenda took one bedroom, while Alfonso and Savina took an adjacent one. Similarly, Estrella and Adrianne paired up, as did Pippa and Bess. Three pairs took the second suite of four: Zia and Fin, Tiana and Angelo, and Luciana and Michela. The other two suites were unoccupied.

The next morning, therapy sessions began for all. In the afternoon, Dr. Zia and Estrella were amazed and extremely proud to be working on specific cures for their group. Specifically, they were assisting the DNA analyses of their groups, focusing on the recovery of their fused feet. Based on the progress being made, the many geneticists were quite hopeful that a cure would soon be developed.

After the first few days of therapy sessions, they all

began to realize that something was happening. They were feeling a bit better, and they chose to dine with everyone else, particularly the many other nova they'd saved, chatting with them. For the four doctorates and Luciana and Michela, they renewed old friendships made while in their virtual reality University and in the games. Further, the six were very pleased to see that quite a few had already received all known cures. Perhaps more importantly for many of these hundred plus, they knew that they could continue their graduate studies at the Academy in Exchange City, once their cures were finished and they'd finished Basic Therapy.

On their fourth day on Ashford-5, the new images of the Black Man and his companions circulated among everyone. Renata was looking for confirmation of his identity. Gwenda also got an opportunity to see them, and she recognized one of the women. She got directions to Renata's quarters and waited patiently for her to return. "Excuse me. You are Renata, yes?" she said, rising from the floor before the door where she'd been sitting patiently.

"Yes. Gwenda, right?"

"Yes. I must see you. Those pictures that were being shown — I recognize one of the women, only she had not lost her arms when I knew her. Princess Delwyn. How can she be a wife of this evil man? Surely, he must have done something awful to her. I must rescue her. I'm honor bound to do that. Arnold will help me."

"Please, come in and tell me about this Princess Delwyn," Renata said, suddenly quite interested in what this Welsh fighter had to say. Education was one thing, but she heard the story of how Gwenda had leapt onto one of the alien snakes and slit it open, killing it, where d-guns had been mostly ineffective. It took a different kind of courage to do that, and Renata respected the woman for that reason. The two chatted for a half hour.

"So you see, this evil man must have cut off her arms and taken her away as his wife. Either that or King Berwin must have married her to this evil man. Either way, I must get her away from him before he harms her further."

"I understand, Gwenda. We are working on how we can

do that now. I'll see if we can't let you do just that. We need a good plan, which we don't have yet. This man is a very powerful one. It will be hard to get close enough to him without his becoming aware of our intentions. Continue with your therapy sessions while we work out a plan. When we have it, I'll let you know. Acceptable?" Renata asked. Gwenda agreed and left, with Renata pondering the significance of this unexpected detail. She knew she needed more information and knew the right person to ask, Sly Dog.

Centuries ago, Sly Dog was one of the most notorious Underground hackers. There wasn't a computer system in the vast Imperium that she and her companion Eager Beaver had not hacked into one time or another. Amy and Jan. Those two were legends among those in the know on Ashford-5 and had even served as queens in the distant past. Like herself, these two powerful beings had pretty much controlled their successive lifetimes, even as far as using their *mentales* gifts to have their new parents give them the names that they wanted, Amy and Jan. Renata smiled, as she thought of them and the marital bliss that they now shared. This time around, they had chosen hermaphrodite bodies and were happier than they ever had been, trying to live peaceful, uneventful lives, and having passed the torch to others, so to speak.

Tired of the multiple compound last names, when they married, they chose to simplify their last names. Now, they were known as Amy and Jan Bellweather and lived in the northernmost manor house within the Imperial Castle complex, Number 100, Suite A. Of course, inside one of the bedrooms, Jan had installed all the very latest in electronic equipment, naturally. Amy's hair was the talk of the complex, almost a pure white, wavy and flowing down her back like a mantle of snow. Jan's was raven, just as wavy, and nearly as long, reaching her lower back. Their parents had had all of the genetic cures. Except for the dual sexual organs and Tierra's overly large breasts found on any woman who spent six months on the planet, their bodies were normal, for which both were quite grateful, considering the many traumatic events that they'd encountered over the centuries that Renata had known them. Both were twenty-five, and each had a two-year old daughter.

"Hi ya Renata," Amy greeted her as she opened the door. "Come on in; ignore the mess." Toys littered the commons floor. The two children were waddling around playing with some spaceship toys.

Jan poked her head out from the kitchen, "Hi ya. Teatime. Want some?"

"Sure. Got a favor to ask of you Jan," Renata called out, carefully stepping around the toys.

She and Amy joined Jan in the kitchen, where the zoom-zoom noises died down. As Jan poured the freshly brewed Earl Grey tea, she said, "Something's up, Amy dear. Renata comes a'knocking, so it can't be good."

Amy chuckled and commented, "Must be about the Black Man. Either that or the alien giant snakes."

It was Renata's turn to chuckle. "Can't put anything over on you two. Isn't there anything that goes on around here that you two don't know about?"

Jan laughed, "Hardly. We have to keep informed so we can keep out of trouble this time around. We're perfectly content, thank you very much." She added with a teasing grin to Amy, "Must be the Black Man, since she asked to see me."

Amy replied, "Probably. So out with it, Renata. We are keeping an eye on this mess. You know it has been the one thing that has always troubled us from the get go."

Renata grinned. "Can't put anything over on you two. Why, one might think that you are the queens."

Both Amy and Jan roared. Jan replied, "Whoa! Not this time. We've paid our dues, but we certainly are watching this one like the hawks that we are. So what are you and the queens going to do about it? Something soon, before the cat's out of the bag."

"You've heard we've positively identified who he is?" Renata asked, suspecting that these two already knew.

"Of course. You can't keep that a secret from Sly Dog and Eager Beaver," Jan replied with a grin and a sip of tea. "What are you going to do to stop him?"

"He's probably using a large number of giant psi-crystals," Amy speculated. "If my gut feeling is right, he's somehow learned of Zarita's trick of having them compressed into small balls so they are easier to transport and carry around."

Renata had to ask. "So how do you figure that? I mean that's the conclusion I reached too."

"He's out there among the enemy leaders and doesn't seem to be armed, at least from the fuzzy images Jan has found. Plus, we spotted a pair of them in Valencia's earrings, just like Zarita had made for herself. Pretty obvious, Renata. Sorry," Amy replied.

"Excellent. Same reasoning I used. Okay then, Jan, I've come to ask a big favor of you. I need information. Somehow, we need to take him out on the quiet without drawing attention to us. He's surrounded by one of the largest warship fleets, when he isn't conducting solidification meetings with his newly conquered planets. Also, he's apparently taken a young woman, a Princess Delwyn, as a second wife. What little I do know is that Valencia was apparently the victim of some terrorist attack when they first reached Cartagena-C and lost her hands as a result. However, the latest photos show she's lost her lower arms now, and this Princess Delwyn has lost them too. The amazon fighter, Gwenda, says Velasco must have cut Delwyn's arms off when he took her. She's insisting that she be a part of the rescue party."

"Okay, so you don't have a plan yet and need info. I got it. I suppose you wouldn't mind if we sort of handled the whole darn problem for you either," Jan hinted.

Renata smiled, "Well, you know how much work my Advanced Therapy involves."

Amy laughed. "Okay, we take the hint. We'll see what we can do. After all, it is in our best interests that this 'problem' vanishes soon. We want our girls out there to grow up without facing the fears that we all have over these past centuries."

"Thanks. Keep me posted. If you find a way and need help, ask," Renata replied. They chatted a bit and she left.

"Well, Jan dear, don't go getting any hair-brained schemes. I want you whole this lifetime," Amy teased.

"Hey, I want to be whole too," Jan countered. She

headed into her vast electronics laboratory, which occupied an entire bedroom suite, with very little room to walk around among the equipment. Everything was so much easier now that they had electricity and didn't need to depend on all the solar panels and batteries. She set to work. Within minutes, she had begun picking up commercial broadcasts out of Cartagena-C, the most populace world that now belonged to the Black Man, Emperor Supreme.

After a few hours, Jan realized Velasco spent most of his time onboard one of the battleships. There, he was untouchable, unless one had a way to wipe out one of the most powerful warships in the galaxy. While Jan could rise to such a situation, she decided that was far too risky. No, best get him when he was on the ground. Those times were only when he conducted his "peace treaties" with his newly conquered worlds. In such locations, he was vulnerable.

Then, she discovered other news that troubled her. The rulers of Cartagena-C had passed a new law that ordered all women to have their lower arms removed, emulating the appearance of their new empresses! She watched these newscasts closely. Their senators were making speeches fully backing the new law. Even a few female senators spoke up, proudly waving their short upper arms about, claiming they were never better and were honoring their empresses. Jan easily saw the telltale signs of the *mentales* gift of Domination at work on these senators. With the combined power of a number of giant crystals, Velasco was obviously controlling the key leaders of the conquered worlds.

However, as Jan soon saw, he wasn't controlling the vast majority of the population. Cartagena-C was facing nearly civil war over this new law! In fact, the rulers were using their armed forces to put down the open rebellions over this new law. She could not help but recall the rampages of Damiano Donatello, the Immortale Conquistatore Mortale, and his harem of mutilated women. Something that Rafe or Renata had once told her came into her mind. Damiano Donatello had once been the god Wystan. Could Velasco be the one and same being? Continuing his conquests? She made a mental note to ask Renata about this possibility.

Renata was an extremely able being. She sensed Jan thinking about her and made mental contact with her. *You wanted something? Have you found something already? It's only been a few hours.*

Oh! Well, yes I might have. Could Velasco have also been Damiano Donatello and Wystan? I'm seeing some uncanny parallels here, watching the news out of Cartagena-C.

Hey, brilliant idea. Hold on a second while I check on that, Renata sent back, leaving Jan wondering how on Tierra Renata could do that! *Sorry it took so long. Yes, I touched his mind lightly. It's the one and same person. That accounts for much of his actions. Now, I think I understand what he is doing. His real objective must be to take over Tierra by force. He knows darn well that even with his many giant crystals, he can't do it, not with all the crystals that the many Towers, Guilds, and queens have. So he's going to come here with a huge war fleet, large enough to checkmate the Ataro Empire and force us to capitulate to him. Why else would Wystan be out there conquering worlds that he's had no contact with before now?*

Damn. That makes this project even more critical. Thanks. Sometimes I wish I didn't know such things, Jan sighed.

Knowledge and certainty are power, Jan, Renata replied. *Keep me posted.*

Jan thought, how does she do that? She smiled and continued her monitoring. Before long, she concluded that while the conquered worlds might wind up fighting civil wars over this latest decree that women lose their arms, he would still have their fleets of warships. Plus, he would soon have enough to come after Ashford-5. She would have to act soon. Getting to him while he was on the ground dealing with his next conquered planet was the only place that he could be taken.

However, taking him was problematical. If he had or wore a large number of those giant crystals, compressed down to small ones that could easily be concealed on his person, how could he possibly be stopped? No way could she, Amy, or anyone else take him out via a *mentales* battle. They'd have to bring along with them half the giant crystals on Tierra to have a chance! There had to be another way, one that didn't involve their special gifts, and one that would never bring any suspicions back to Ashford-5. But what?

She had no answer yet and decided to focus her efforts on determining where he would strike next. After all, any plan to take him out involved knowing where he would be, would likely land, and with whom he'd be holding his surrender discussions. Worse, she knew very little about Federation space. Later that day, she decided to pay a call on the new arrivals to enlist their help. It would have to be Arnold's group, since those on Beltazar-C had been totally isolated from the rest of the galaxy.

She met with the eight of them that night. "Hi. I'm Jan Bellweather. Renata's given me the task of trying to figure out what the next move of this Black Man might be. I could use your help. I admit I don't know a whole lot about the Federation side of the galaxy. It's crucial that we figure out what world he is going after next."

"Ah, so you can get there and stop this evil man," Gwenda spoke up.

"Yep. Stop him," Jan agreed. "I've made a list of what worlds I know he has conquered, but I'm not sure precisely where these are, except Cartagena-C, which is here." She'd brought along her laptop and brought up a three dimensional view of the galaxy, highlighting in red that star.

"Let's see that list," Arnold suggested. "Pippa, Savina, and Alfonso can also help with this." Within a half hour, they had all sixteen worlds highlighted as red dots, forming almost a sphere centered on Cartagena-C.

"So, the question is where will he strike next?" Jan asked.

"Along the edge of the sphere, expanding it," Arnold suggested. "That's how I'd play it." Several agreed with him.

Pippa bit her lip. "You know, on this side here, many of those worlds are on the Forbidden List. Over here," she pointed to another area, "is where Sigma Bootes-C is located. This is one of the major Federation worlds, with a sizeable space fleet."

"What are you driving at, Pippa?" Arnold asked.

"Well, if I was this Black Man, I'd be very worried about Sigma Bootes-C making a surprise attack here, sweeping into the conquered sphere before they get attacked by the Black Man. I can't imagine that Sigma Bootes-C folks are just sitting around waiting for him to come after them," Pippa suggested.

"So? They'd launch a counterstrike?" Arnold asked.

"I would, if I were them. If this Emperor Supreme fellow isn't a dummy, he's got to be thinking the same thing. If he was ready to take on Sigma Bootes-C, he probably would have already done so, but he hasn't. If I remember right, I think there is another of those Forbidden Worlds somewhere in there," she pointed to a gap in the sphere aligned with the direct route to Sigma Bootes-C.

"Bringing up the list now," Savina called out, typing away on her laptop. "Got it. Gemma Rho-D." She relayed the coordinates to Jan who highlighted it in yellow. Everyone looked over her shoulders to see the yellow dot fitting nearly into the expanding sphere. "If he took it next, he'd have advance warning of any Sigma Bootes-C counterattack coming his way."

"Is anything known about this world?" Jan asked, growing curious about it.

"Let's see. They don't give much about these worlds," Savina explained. "It says pre-modern. Amazons. Matriarchy. That's all. Not much to go on."

"So obviously in the past, someone must have visited this world and requested it be put on that list of forbidden worlds for some reason. Surely, somewhere there has to be more info on this world," Jan argued.

"If I was back on Capella-D, I have some contacts that could tell us more," Arnold suggested. "We could just go there and see for ourselves."

"If I could get you through to your contacts, say on a secure line, would that work?" Jan hinted with a wry smile.

Arnold laughed. "Not unless you can crack into Capella-D's Black Ops divisional mainframe computers to put that call through. I intended to pay a visit to someone who owes me a favor or two." He wasn't about to go into details about his former career as a Special Operations soldier.

"Okay, come with me, old boy," Jan teased, rising and pulling him along with her, much to the surprise of the others who laughed.

"Ignore the toys. The girls haven't learned to pick them up yet," Jan said, escorting him into her suite. "Back here." Arnold mouth dropped when he saw the setup in her "special room." "Okay, big boy, point me towards this mainframe of yours. I need you to make that call." He gave her some codes and soon, she had the site up on her monitor. Of course, it was just a dummy page. To proceed further, she needed a login and password. That seldom, if ever, stopped Sly Dog. She opened another window and entered the Underground, which was still as active as ever. She posted a simple message. "Now, we wait a bit."

Within ten minutes, a private secure chat window opened up on her screen from Magic Hands. "Sly Dog! LTNS. W-s up?" She had to translate for Arnold. "Long time no see. What's up." She typed, "Been busy with kids. Need that info. Funds are waiting."

"Ah no fun. Coming through now." Two lines followed, along with an account number. Jan quickly opened a third window and transferred the funds. Then, she typed an acknowledgment and promised to chat later. She switched back to the mainframe window and entered login in and password. "There you go, big boy. I'll let you make your call." She got up and let him have at her computer, noticing the look of utter shock on his face.

"Damn, Jan, you are really good at this," he commented, as he typed his secure, private email. "Okay, now we wait again. Don't know if he's online now. Sly Dog, eh?"

Jan grinned. "How about some tea while we wait?" He agreed, and the two headed off to their kitchen where Amy already had the pot going.

"Girls are finally in bed. Hi Arnold. Having fun with Sly Dog, I see," Amy teased him.

"Incredible. She got into the site in minutes. So much for their security," he replied, taking a cup of tea from her.

Amy commented, "Few realize that any computer system that is open to the Net is vulnerable, no matter how intense their security is. The weakest link is the people who use the systems. And there are frequently maintenance back doors as well, but to use those, you need to know who designed the systems."

Arnold grinned and asked, "So you could theoretically hack into the battleship's computers, the one that this Black Man is on and cause an accident?"

Jan sighed, "There's a limit. While I could do that, no battleship commander in his right mind would open his computer system up to the Net. No, they keep their systems closed to the outside world. Only their comm center is connected. However, often there are security breaches where some idiot opens up an outside port on the sly for their own reasons. If they are discovered, they usually get shot." They chatted a while before Jan heard her computer beep.

Hastily the two headed back. Arnold had his reply. Attached to the email was the scouting report that indicated that Gemma Rho-D was discovered a hundred ten years ago. In part, it read: This world is pre-modern, with large cities, though somewhat primitive. There is some kind of genetic defects among the population. All men are born without any hands. Hence, it is a matriarchal society. Women run everything and use men mostly for breeding. A son cannot inherit anything, only daughters. Even marriages are weird. They arrange marriages for their sons, who have no say in the matter. If a woman has only sons by her husband, she is allowed to have him killed and marry another man or even easier, simply take a second man to bed with her. Some women are soldiers, fighting with swords and guns. They have HE artillery and crude rockets that can fire HE shells at attacking ships. Unfriendly to alien men. Language: English-Irish dialect. Recommendation: Forbidden List.

The email added a recent footnote. Within last half-century, there has been some trading going on via other Forbidden Worlds. Last known capital city: Kalgary.

Jan mulled this over and commented, "Well, since there is some trading going on, they are likely to have heard about the Black Man. Now to figure out how we can take him down while he's vulnerable on the ground discussing his terms."

Then, it struck her how she could do just that! Later, she admitted that Arnold's group activities in the recent months gave her the idea. As Arnold left, he said, "Make darn sure that we get to take part in the rescue. Gwenda really needs to help her fellow country woman."

Jan nodded. "I don't think we can do this without your help. I'll keep you posted." After he left, she outlined her idea to Amy.

Amy replied, "Damn diabolical, dear. But you are right. It's about the only way to take him out without major trouble. Best check with Renata and the queens on this one, unless you think it's best that they know nothing about it."

Almost as though reading her thoughts, Renata came knocking on their door. "Hi ya. Just about to come visit you," Jan said, sensing she was at the door. She also knew Renata hadn't read her mind. No, Renata just "knew" things, a product of her Advanced Therapy.

After making their way to the kitchen, the three sat around the table there, shoving the used teacups aside. Jan said, "I've worked out the likely next world he's going after. It's on the Federation's Forbidden List. Pre-modern world run by women. I believe that I have a way to take him out without drawing any attention to us or to his unique gifts, but it's highly illegal."

Renata grinned. "Sly Fox, whenever has anything you've done been entirely legal? Don't answer that. Okay, so you don't want us to know about it, right?"

"Right. But I'm going to need to use Arnold and his ship and crew and something else that's illegal, and it would be wise if none of our geneticists knew anything about it," Jan added.

"Will it work?" Renata asked.

"If we can get there before him and if we can find the right woman who is their top executive, then it's almost a certainty that we can take him out," Jan answered. "The trick will be finding the right woman that Velasco will be meeting with to discuss his terms."

"I see. Will he be taken alive?" she asked.

"Absolutely. He needs to stand trial for his crimes. I've no intention of killing him," Jan answered. "That would draw too much attention to us. No, I've a far better plan in mind, highly illegal though."

"Greatest good for the greatest number of the Seven Aspects of Life, Jan," Renata reminded her. "As long as your action does the greatest good, then we all win. Go ahead then, but see if Estrella wants to remain behind. I think she's really working out with the geneticists."

"Okay. Say, I'll also need a slight discrepancy in the Fabrication machine down in Genetics to be ignored, if I can't take care of it myself," Jan added. Renata nodded and wished her good hunting.

Since the music concert ought to be just ending, Jan headed down to the throne room, hoping to catch Estrella on her way back. She spotted her walking arm in arm with Adrianne. "Hi ya. Can I have a word with you, Estrella?"

"Sure, we're just heading home."

"Cool. I'm borrowing Arnold and his crew for a special mission, but Renata suggested that you might prefer to stay here while the others are gone," Jan explained.

"Well, really I would. The genetics here are far more advanced than anything is back on Pegasi-C. Do you realize they've identified three different genetic mutations here on Ashford-5? There's the one called the Calder Mutation. That one was even more horrid than the bio agent mutations we endured! I saw a drawing of what those poor women looked like. Incredible, but that mutation is extremely recessive and has died out completely. Still, the markers are in some of the population here, but since it's so recessive, there's no chance it will ever surface again. And then there's the Madiera Mutation where the women were born without any hands. Thankfully, that one is also recessive and has died out too. Of course, there are us, making the third type. Kind of wish ours was recessive too, but no such luck I guess," Estrella chatted away.

She went on, "So anyway, they have me working on a fused feet mutation to undo that one. We're all so hopeful that one will work soon. I'd really like to stay and help with it, that is, if you don't really need me on the mission."

"No, your talents are being put to a much better purpose here. Please stay here and keep on working away on the cures. So many are depending upon them," Jan praised Estrella, who looked very pleased with Jan's acceptance of her skills.

"So when do we leave on this mission? No one's told me about it," Adrianne asked.

"You two are the first to know about it. Adrianne, tell Arnold and the others to get ready to take off by seven tomorrow morning. We must make haste. Have him bring along double the usual number of refueling cells," Jan answered and ordered.

Onboard the Devil's Anvil, Velasco awoke from yet another nightmare, dripping wet. It had been so vivid, so real, that he was shaking this time as he sat up in bed between the two soundly sleeping women. Once more, he slipped out of bed and paced the living room. What to do? Now, the women were stabbing him by using their feet to plunge the dagger into him. Worse, there seemed to be hundreds of other women urging them on. He felt as though he were receiving waves of hatred from women.

Then, he realized something. *Look, when I removed their lower arms, they stopped stabbing me with them, just as they stopped when I removed their hands. So if I remove their lower legs too, then there's no way that they can stab me while I sleep! Brilliant, Velasco. Besides, they will be lighter and wholly immobile. Wait, that won't fly. They have to be able to walk.* He pondered this difficulty for a while before he recalled seeing a peasant woman who had lost her legs in a wagon accident. Her husband had made thick leather boot-like pads that fit over her leg stumps, and she was able to sort of waddle along on her own. Now, he had his answer that would end all his nightmares!

He found a paper pad and sketched out what he recalled the pads had looked like. Smiling, he focused and began modifying the minds of both wives, expanding outward to include the admiral, his wife, and all the other officers and

246

women on the battleship, including their doctor, who would have to perform the surgery. That done, he realized that their dresses would have to be altered drastically and searched the minds of the other eight women onboard. One had some skill in dress alterations, and he implanted the ideas into her mind as well.

Over breakfast with Admiral Juan and Benita, Delwyn brought up the implanted idea. "Dear, it is so hard for us to perform our bedtime ceremony without the leg bindings that you left behind on my world. I think we ought to have our lower legs removed, get them out of the way so they do not interfere with us in bed. Maybe some booties will permit us to walk around. Besides, we would then be very light and easy for you to lift us about. What do you think, Valencia?"

"Oh, I wholly agree with her. Our lower legs just get in the way. Besides, mine are next to worthless, since that terrorist attack on Cartagena-C. I'd just as soon be rid of them once and for all. Can you have it done for us, dear? I'm sure we can manage to walk just fine with some booties. Remember that peasant woman who had that terrible wagon accident? Remember, it rolled over her legs around her knees and cut them off. Later, she got around just fine when her husband made those padded leather booties for her. But we'll need someone to shorten our gowns for us, though."

Benita spoke up, "Oh I quite agree with her, Juan. Her feet, why they are so mutilated, so fused that she can't even walk without those awful boots. I don't see how she can even get to the bathroom during the night. This way, why, she would be able to do so easily. Please, Juan, you must see that these beautiful women are properly handled by the good doctor. You simply must."

Juan spoke up, "Well, the other worlds are reporting goodly success accepting the new empress look. I must admit, Benita, you have never looked as good as you do now. I just love feeding you, my dearest. I know her feet are just unacceptable as they are. I wonder if anyone on the ship could make such booties, as they would need? I should check on that. Can't Marisol handle their dress alterations? She often does that for you."

Vic Broquard

"I will ask her today," Benita replied. Turning to Val and Delwyn sitting on either side of the man in black, she added, "Don't worry, dears. I'm sure we can get this all worked out for you both and soon."

Velasco smiled. He'd not had to say one word. He relished his immense Domination powers. It was as obvious as his nose that he, and he alone, ought to be the rightful Emperor Supreme of the entire galaxy! Further, he felt confident that his recurring nightmares were almost finished, a thing of the past!

Late that afternoon, Velasco once more sent new thoughts to both women. Their lower legs were gone, but their stumps had not been made conical in shape to accept Imperium prostheses. Instead, he'd tied the new leather booties onto their upper legs. The bottoms were very heavily padded and circular in shape, in theory providing them a large surface to help maintain their balance while standing on their stumps. Now, they were struggling mightily to get to their legs and not tumble, moving their stumpy upper arms about wildly. *Practice makes perfect. Don't give up. You can do it.* He also had to suppress their emotions totally, which threatened to surge up from below the mental barriers he'd installed in their minds.

He had them standing fairly well, when Marisol arrived to shorten their dresses. By supper, they both looked stunning in their short gowns — at least all the officers and their wives said so to the two women, as they sat at the table while being fed by Velasco. After dinner, Velasco helped them waddle slowly back to their suite, praising them every few feet. Once undressed and in bed, they proved to each other that their nightly ritual was so much better this way. Much later, Velasco fell asleep and slept like a baby. The nightmares were gone!

However, the next night, Velasco awoke, but not in a cold sweat. Rather, he had to get out of bed and race to the living room, where he finally broke out into a roaring laugh! The nightmares had returned, only this time the two women sat on his lower torso, but all they could do was pound lightly on his chest with their stumpy upper arms, cheered on by many other women who couldn't reach him. He found this

248

utterly hilarious! That he had to laugh was what woken him up. Now, he was totally convinced he'd completely solved his wife problem.

Velasco was able to catch up on his sleep for two more nights, before his armada reached their next destination: Gemma Rho-D. While this world would offer no real resistance and certainly no warships for his armada, it served another vital purpose: a buffer and early warning should the large fleet from Sigma Bootes-C attempt a sneak attack on him. He didn't want to attack them, not just yet. Besides, that world lay in the opposite direction from his real target of Ashford-5. He wanted to push farther out into the former Imperium space, much closer to his home world. Another two such expansions and he'd be ready to take on Ashford-5 and the Ataro Empire, returning home as the Emperor Supreme over all of Tierra! He never felt as confident as he did during these two days. Besides, the sex with his wives was now far more enjoyable than ever before.

Chapter 14 Downfall

08:00, November 15, 1450. Kalgary, Gemma Rho-D, locally called Connemara. Arnold kept the deep space transport hovering above the city, while Adrianne began monitoring planetary communications. They were cloaked and invisible to the unsuspecting world below. They had come here at top speed, using the new hyperdrive engines, consuming half of their fuel, but thanks to the warning from Jan, he had more than enough onboard for this mission. Jan had taken Estrella's place on this mission.

Jan had worked her magic two nights ago. After leaving Estrella and Adrianne, she'd returned home, changed into dark clothing, and packed a number of her gadgets. Around midnight, she'd broken into the secure section of the genetics laboratory, used the Fabrication machine, but had reset its counter, as well as modifying the security feeds during her visit. If any discrepancies were ever discovered, she relied upon Renata to cover for her. Her bag now contained what she'd retrieved and hooked up, stored in a locked chest in her cabin on the transport. Now, she waited around Adrianne who sat at her post monitoring the planet's communications. Had they come to the current capital city of this world? If so, who was in charge and who would Velasco choose to visit to make his demands? Certainly, they'd beaten him here. Of course, they had no idea how soon he and his large fleet would arrive, assuming they'd picked the same target world as he had. Jan hoped and prayed that they had!

"Okay, I think this is still their capital city," Adrianne spoke up. "Now trying to find out who is in control down there. That's going to be hard."

"Good work. Keep me posted." Jan then headed up to the cockpit where it was a bit crowded at the moment. Arnold, Gwenda, Alfonso, and Savina were all there, looking out in all directions from here trying to make some sense of the situation on the ground. Pippa and Bess were doing the same thing from the cargo bay viewports.

"Well, it is a city," Arnold said, as Jan squeezed in to see for herself. They were low enough to get a good view. Horses appeared to be the main mode of transportation. Some women were riding them, while others were driving wagons, reminding Jan of home. The streets were cobblestones and wide. The buildings were predominately a white concrete construction, featuring many, many arches with their keystones quite visible. At least, they understood the use of the arch in constructions, she thought.

For a moment, she got the sexes confused, until she realized here men wore simple pull-on dresses, hemmed at their knees, allowing them to dress themselves and to handle their bathroom needs. They wore nothing under the dresses. That became visible when a gust blew one man's up, revealing his manhood. They wore slip-on shoes, probably leather. In contrast, the women that were visible wore shirts and pants. Many wore sturdy work boots, but some were dressed in fancier shirts and pants with shiny leather shoes.

The men's hairstyles seemed to vary little, being about three or four inches long, more like bowl cuts. She saw no beards. In contrast, the women wore their hair quite long, falling to the middle of their backs. Some had theirs in braids; some in ponytails; some wore a clasp behind their heads. She did note some of the men were carrying baskets whose handles were cradled between their elbows. At least one uncovered basket held what appeared to be freshly baked bread.

"There's a spaceport of sorts at the edge of the city," Alfonso pointed out. "Not much of one, though. Enough room on the concrete pad for maybe two transports to land. That one small building is probably their control tower."

"Lots of parks and formal gardens down there," Savina pointed out. "If they have winters here, then I'd guess we've come in early summer or early fall."

"Hey, I'm picking up what must be their control tower," Adrianne called out. "They are using a totally obsolete frequency in the FM band. I think they are giving directions to the Black Man and his fleet."

"Roger that. Am just now picking up their ships on our sensors," Savina relayed back. "Good god! That's a lot of warships!"

"I think the leader is called Connemara Executive Chairwoman Breanna Navan. Still don't have a clue where she lives," Adrianne yelled up front.

Jan made a snap decision. "Alfonso, put us down somewhere out of the way. Keep the cloaking device going. Savina, look for a transport. It ought to be landing at the spaceport. We'll have to follow them to wherever this leader lives. I'm going to gear up. Arnold, you are with me."

Jan was wearing her black outfit, shirt and pants, along with soft-soled shoes. She wanted to ensure that she could move as silently as possible. She unlocked the box, retrieving her precious bag, stuffing it inside a backpack that was filled with a number of useful gadgets she'd chosen. Arnold tested her earpiece. "Okay, it's ready. We will keep the IR camera going. Once you find the house, we can direct you from above. Good hunting."

"Right." She felt the slight jerk as the ship landed. When she reached the bay, Pippa had the door open enough for her to squeeze through. As soon as she was clear of the ship, the door closed again, and the ship silently lifted back off the ground.

Through her earpiece, Arnold said, "You are about a mile from the first gardens. Head there. That ought to be closer, statistically speaking."

Jan had already focused and activated her crystal. She used one of her own special gifts, invisibility. She set out following his directions, being careful to avoid other people, horses, and wagons that were on the streets as well. Before she reached the gardens, Arnold relayed, "Jan, a shuttle is descending now. Keep you posted on where they go. Savina says there is a horse-drawn wagon waiting at the spaceport. Best get a move on it."

"Yes, you both look absolutely lovely," Velasco told Van what she wanted to hear. She was wearing her cut-down blue gown, which now was about an inch from the ground when she stood on her stumps. Her biggest problem was that her hair was longer than she was tall now. Likewise, with Delwyn, who wore a bright red satin gown of about the same length.

"But will they like us, do you suppose? Women rulers? We'll do our best to make her like you, dear, but I do so hope she likes us," Val said. Sometimes, she wondered why she said what she said. That's been happening more and more frequently, she thought, once more losing the train of her thoughts. Her mind hadn't been quite right for some weeks now, but she dare not say anything to Velasco. He had too much else of great importance to worry about, she was sure of that.

"I hope we don't have to walk too far," Delwyn said nervously. "It's so hard for us. I know we look fabulous, but still walking isn't easy. You'll help us, won't you?"

"Of course. You are both so light. I can carry you easily. Relax, this will be fun and educational," Velasco replied, sending out more calming energies to both women, sitting on either side of him in the transport.

When it landed, he picked up Valencia, cradling her like a rag doll in his left arm and then took Delwyn in his right. "You are both so light and charming," he whispered, knowing it brought a contented smile to their faces. Surrounded by security guards, he stepped down the ramp, where a woman dressed as a man and carrying a pistol and sword stood beside a wagon.

"You are the boss man?" she spoke rather harshly, all the while staring at the two women.

"Yes. You are our guide?" She nodded. "Okay then." Still carrying the women, he stepped up into the wagon, carefully setting each down on the bench, one on either side of him. His men followed along on foot, as the man-like woman drove them on into town.

"Oh look! Something bad must have happened to that man. He's lost his hands like I once did," Val exclaimed. "Oh, there's another one."

"Dear, I'm told on this world, all men are born without hands. Sad, really," he replied. "Look, they have nice gardens here too. If we have time, would you both like a stroll through them?" He knew this would totally distract them. These days, their minds were easily distracted by almost anything at all, more than putty in his hands now. Yet, the sex was invigorating and now totally safe. He'd slept peacefully at long last. No way could either of them harm him while he slept, nor could they poison him. However, it did take almost constant efforts on his part to keep their emotions deeply buried.

The day was warm. The skies, clear, though on the horizon a white cumulus cloud lazily moved towards them. Well, he thought, this ought to be the easiest conquest yet. The wagon finally stopped before a wooden home with a lovely front patio and porch. A wide patch of flowers lined either side of the neatly maintained home. Velasco carefully picked up Val and then Delwyn. Stepping down, the man-like woman motioned towards the house, but gave him a very dirty look when his back was turned. Another six similar clad women came up, standing close to his armed guards, who would remain outside as they always had when he conducted his formal meetings. His long black duster swept across the cobblestones, as he walked the fifty feet up to the porch and front door. As always, he wore his Black Man outfit.

As he reached the door, a young fifteen year old woman with long fiery red hair braided in two braids hanging down from either side of her slightly freckled face opened the door for them. Her greeting smile quickly turned to shock, as she saw the women in his arms. She gasped nearly silently. A woman's voice called out, "Come on in." He did so, finding himself inside a comfortable living room.

He saw a middle aged woman, possibly thirty-five or so, with similarly braided brown hair, wearing what would have passed for a well-dressed man on many worlds, beckoning him to her sofa. Standing beside her was handless man a good deal younger with curly blonde hair, but dressed in a simple pull over dress that ended at his knees. Another girl, twelve years old with brown hair, stood beside her mother, while an even younger handless boy also wearing a similar dress stood beside his father.

Velasco sat each wife down on the couch, and then positioned himself between them. The woman spoke first. "Welcome to Connemara and Kalgary. I am Connemara Executive Chairwoman Breanna Navan, elected leader of our world. My daughter and heir, Carlyn." The fifteen year old red head nodded and took a seat on her mother's right. "My daughter, Fiona." Velasco noticed she introduced the women first and decided to play along with her. "My current husband, Cormac; my son, Finn. The lad was barely ten. Fiona sat beside her mother on her left, while Cormac and Finn took seats in a far corner.

"My charming wives. Valencia and Delwyn," he replied with a wry smile. Both women nodded and smiled, eager to meet her. "I'm the Black Man, Emperor Supreme, ruler of the galaxy."

"I suppose that is some place out there among the stars," Breanna replied rather coldly.

"It is all the stars. Now then, I've come to talk over the terms of our conquest of your world."

"What awful accidents your wives must have had. How do you manage, Valencia?" Breanna asked, ignoring Velasco almost entirely, as though he was hardly present!

"Oh, well, it was tragic. First," Valencia began gabbing, since no one told her not to, "I was the victim of a terrible terrorist attack. Part of a stone building fell on me and crushed my arms and feet. They tried to get me to use those fake hands, whatever they are called. I seem to have forgotten their name. Doesn't really matter. I couldn't feel anything with them anyway. I had them shortened. Now, my arms are just perfect, you see. Then, since my feet were in such a bad way, we had them removed. I really don't need them, now that I have these really good booties. Plus, we're very much better in bed with Velasco here. We're so much better off like this, that he, the Emperor Supreme, has ordered all the women on our conquered worlds to get their hands removed so they can enjoy life so much better, right Delwyn?"

"Right. It is so much better this way. Oh, do you have a special ceremony to honor your guests as we do back on my home world, Al Nair-C? There, we women are bound in our special way and share sex with our guests. We didn't bring any of the binding items with us, but Val and I are so much better doing it, now that we have such short arms and legs. We'd be honored to share with you all," Delwyn explained, wondering why she was even saying such things. The words just sort of came out. She added, "Of course, my father insisted on marrying me to Velasco here to seal the deals between our world and his. So if you want to also do that, I'm sure Valencia and I won't mind, will we?" she looked over to Valencia who nodded yes.

"My wives sometimes get quite talkative," Velasco grinned, amazed they'd said all this. "Anyway, to business. I'm now in control of this world. You will take orders from me as your Emperor Supreme. As long as you do, no harm will come to your world. I've no desire to blow everything up. Rather wasteful, don't you think?"

The women simply listened to all this more or less dumbfounded. None of it made much sense to them. Breanna looked at the women and then back to Velasco. "I think your husband is a bit crazy. Doesn't he know men are supposed to be silent until spoken to and obey women at all times? I'm rather affronted that you two are even letting him open his mouth! Nevertheless, I see why you do need him around you while we talk. Can you even walk? I was going to offer you some hot cocoa. But will he be able to help you sip from cups? If not, Carlyn and Fiona would love to assist you."

Velasco grew annoyed. How dare this ignorant woman talk to him like this? He focused and activated his crystals. He attempted to implant in her mind, "You will obey me in all things."

Breanna shook her head. She looked Velasco squarely in his eyes. "Oh, don't think such silly thoughts! Women don't obey men, not ever. Around here, men depend upon women just to survive. Without our kindness, they'd die. They're darn near helpless, except to help we women have daughters, though sometimes we have more useless boys, which we have to then find ways and means to marry off as soon as possible. In fact, Cormac here is my second man. The first man gave me only boys, which I was lucky enough to get married off when they were thirteen and fourteen. I dumped him and picked up Cormac here. He performs well in bed, giving me Carlyn and Fiona, before he messed up with Finn there. Don't worry; I've got a marriage lined up for him in three more years. After that, we'll not have to bother caring for him."

Valencia spoke up, "Oh they are beautiful daughters. Velasco, dear, you ought to be quiet. You heard her. We should do the talking. Yes, he carries us around a lot, but we can walk a little. Oh, he feeds us too, but mostly our helper girls do that too. We've two ten year old girls who help us a lot, you see. But we don't need any help in bed. We are very good there, very much more so since we had our feet and legs taken off. As I said, my feet were all crushed anyway and useless. Velasco here has asked the other worlds to fix up their women to be like us, at least like our arms are. Aren't they really pretty like this? So very much better than those awful false hands that they gave me to wear after that bad accident." She waved her short arms about some.

"So you two women run this empire that he was talking about? We've heard that out there in the sky's stars, some women have allowed their men to run their worlds for them," Breanna asked, trying to sort out what the women were saying.

"Oh no, he does all that stuff. We're not interested in those sorts of things, you know battles and wars and all that," Val said rather stupidly. "We just want to have him in our bed all the time."

Delwyn broke in, "She's right. We want him in bed with us lots more than he does. He says he has all this work to do. Do you suppose that is a good reason not to stay in bed with us more? I suppose it's so."

Breanna replied, "Men should and must do what you tell them to do. Maybe you should be more forceful with your man. I certainly wouldn't stand for such disobedience. Shoot, there are always many other men around who would be very willing to do what I ask of him. That must be true in your world too. Maybe you should just dump him and find yourselves a much better man toy."

By now, Velasco was fuming! He focused bringing all his crystals to bear. *Breanna, you'll do as I tell you. Enough of this banter. I'm taking control of your world now. You'll do as I tell you to do and make your people obey or else I'll blow the whole damned thing up!*

This time, she really rubbed her forehead, as though she

had a severe headache. To her credit, she didn't realize Velasco had not actually spoken to her. "That's quite enough of that kind of talk, man! Your man is being very rude. Women don't ever, and I do mean ever, do what they order. A man has no right ever to tell a woman what she should do! Of course, I'll never tell our women to do what this man of yours says. That's beyond ludicrous! We women run things around here. How come women in the sky worlds don't?"

"Gee, I don't know," Valencia replied, as though this idea had never occurred to her.

"Men are stronger and more violent," Delwyn explained her point of view. "I was a princess once, before I was married. So now, I think this makes me an empress, but I don't know what an empress can do. Velasco, what are we empresses supposed to do?"

Velasco couldn't ever recall being this frustrated before. This just wasn't going right at all. To maintain his control over the two, he knew he needed to answer and wisely said, "Well, you are setting the examples for all the women in our empire. Grace, beauty, looking your very best, giving your husband the best sex — why you both are the most important women in the empire, that's what. Now then. . ." He was cut short.

Breanna spoke up, "Men give us good sex. Your man has it backwards. Besides, he hasn't told you what you are supposed to do. Are you going to let a mere man get away with such drivel? Honestly, around here, if a man tried that, he'd be booted out of the house and left to fend for himself, which they quite obviously can't. I think you should remove his hands. Perhaps, then he would mind his manners when around you women."

Unknown and wholly unsuspected, Jan snuck up on the home, directed from the cloaked transport by Arnold, using the IR camera to track those on the ground. The two groups of guards kept a close watch on each other and were several feet from the building. Invisible via her gifts and with every mental barrier she could throw up, Jan crept up to the side of the home. From a side window, she could see inside and saw them all in the living room. The window was open a tiny crack. Just enough, she thought.

Quietly, Sly Fox worked her magic, inserting the open end of the tube beneath the window. Then, she opened the valve, which allowed the gas under pressure to flow equally out of both yellow cylinders, merging into the single tube and then out into the living room. Now, she held her breath. Just how much of the gas was needed? How fast would it act? Would it be detected, and the people inside flee before it could do what she needed it to do? Jan had on a small breather mask, providing only five minutes of oxygen. Would it last long enough? Would it prevent the bio agent from getting her as well? If it didn't and she became infected too, she knew that Arnold would be able to rescue her since she was visible on the IR camera somewhere high above her. More and more questions trickled through her mind, as she watched the gas escaping into the room.

Velasco was now extremely furious. The whole situation had gotten completely out of control. He tried to think clearly, to resolve this mess, to ascertain the best way to proceed. Did he just give up, and let the battleship drop a few bombs on these imbeciles? Somehow, his mind seemed slow, sluggish. Something was wrong. He tried to focus and could not. He tried harder and began to feel a faint tentacle of panic forming in his solar plexus. Knowing that he couldn't focus with that emotion flowing through him, he turned his attention inward further, trying to stamp the fear out, as though it were nothing more than a burning match.

Now more and strange images entered his consciousness, nightmarish ones. Women were doing something awful to him, but as he looked to see just what, everything went black. He slipped into a coma, along with everyone in the house.

Outside, Jan saw them all slump over and finally relaxed a little. She carefully secured the two cylinders leaning them against the side of the house, making sure the main tube wasn't pulled out. Satisfied, she backed away from the house as stealthy as a mouse. Her breather quit, and she had to rip her mask off, though she was as quiet as she could removing it and forcing herself not to panic for air. She moved back further, now thirty feet away and up against the neighboring house. Sniffing the air, she didn't smell the gas and relaxed. She wasn't in a coma yet.

Now, she had to estimate, based on the observations that Arnold and his companions had related to her on how much exposure to the bio agent was enough. They'd released the toxin a dozen times now when they destroyed the stocks of the sellers of this terror weapon. Finally, she heard Arnold's voice in her ear again. "Okay, we saw them collapse. If they went into a coma at that point, then they have probably had enough exposure to do the job."

With Velasco unconscious, Jan finally was free enough to send a telepathic message. *Okay. I'll alert the guards now. Standby for action.*

Now came the tricky part. Her plan would work or fail, depending on what happened next. She focused and placed an idea in one of Velasco's security guard's mind. The man spoke up, "It's too quiet in there. Something must be wrong. We should check on them."

One of the women guards countered, "You can't go in there unless Breanna invites you." She drew her gun, which naturally caused the other eleven to draw theirs as well.

"Look, something's wrong," the original guard countered, unwilling to start a fight, not without his emperor's word. "Why don't you go check on them? I tell you it is too quiet. Something's happened to them."

Reluctantly, one of the women guards turned, walked up to the porch, and knocked softly. "Executive Chairwoman? Executive Chairwoman?" Nothing. At last, she too felt that something was wrong and opened the door. At once, a plume of yellow gas flooded out. The woman was wise enough to dive out of the way, hitting the ground and rolling to her feet, though she dropped her gun in the process.

All twelve stared and sniffed. Jan's next thought registered. The original guard cried out, "Get back! Terrorist attack! Bio agent! Good god! Get back or you'll die too!" Velasco's men needed no further encouragement. They bolted, racing away an entire block before stopping to figure out what to do next. The women guards were wiser. One moved around to the side where Jan had been standing and saw the two cylinders. She held her breath, moved up to them, and turned the valve off, ending the escaping gas flow. Then, she carried it around to the front, holding it as though it were a poisonous viper or something, dropping it on the ground before the porch.

"They are all unconscious inside, maybe dead. Can't tell," she yelled. "Go after those men. Find out what this is," she ordered.

Several minutes later, the woman managed to get one of the men to return with her to see the yellow tanks. "Right. You have just had a terrorist attack. If anyone goes inside there, they will become infected too."

"Are they dying?" she asked. "Who did this? Your people?"

"Not us, lady. Terrorists. You have mad terrorists running around your world. Dead? I don't know. Whatever you do, don't go in there for at least a day or more. Give that gas time to dissipate before anyone goes in there. We have to go report back to our ship and tell them what's happened. Back later." He turned and walked very briskly away from her and her companions, who also backed further away.

Jan relaxed. So far so good. She planted another idea in one of the women guard's mind. "He said the gas poison has to dissipate. We should knock out all the windows. That'll speed it along. Come on; find some stones, rocks, anything, but break out all the windows, only don't get too close. Don't fire your guns. You might hit them inside." Soon the sounds of shattering glass broke the silence. That brought several dozen more guards running up to check on the situation. After a brief exchange, they too backed a block away, then stood and watched the yellowish gas seeping out of the open door and broken windows.

A bit later, Arnold reported, "Their transport just lifted off. Adrianne is picking up their comm to one Admiral Juan somebody who is reporting another terrorist bio agent attack. Stand by."

Carefully, Jan felt in her backpack, found her second breather and slipped it partially on her head. What would this admiral do next? She was prepared for the worst, namely that he would send down a crew wearing containment suits and drag the emperor out of there, though likely leaving all the others behind. If so, she had to act quickly, darting in there wearing her mask, praying it would provide her with enough protection, grab him, get him out of there, and somehow into their transport, though it was still overhead somewhere.

Jan had no way of knowing what was happening to the admiral and many others at this moment. When Velasco dropped into his coma, his continuous contact with them ceased. Now, all sorts of strange notions began surfacing in their minds, as the full and continuous effect of his Domination and Mass Domination began to wear off. This effect was aided by the fact that this "invincible" emperor had just become a terrorist bio agent victim himself. Everyone knew the aftereffects! He'd become just another helpless victim, hardly able to do anything, let alone be their emperor. That his wife was with him when the news came from the landing party only aided the breakdown of Velasco's carefully spun web of control. She waved her short arms and shrieked. That hit him like an ice-cold bucket of water, slamming him into present time, which now seemed totally fouled up. His wife was mutilated, helpless. What had been going on? Why? How? He and many others in command were similarly confused.

"What do we do?" his junior officer asked. "The Black Man is gone. We all know what will happen to his body next, that is, if he is even still alive."

"Home. Head for home. Top speed," Admiral Juan barked the only idea that made the slightest sense. No way was he going to risk an attack from the nearby Sigma Bootes-C system! The other warships reacted as well, heading for their home worlds at top speed.

Down on the planet, Jan heard the best news ever, though she had to resist making any sounds or risk losing her web of invisibility. However, the constant drain on her energies would soon run her dry, even with the added boost of her crystal. Based on what had just happened with the warships, Jan made another decision and relayed it to Arnold, while walking swiftly down the streets that the men had just taken. More and more people were coming out to see what was going on at their Executive Chairwoman's home, causing her to dodge this way and that avoiding them. A collision with something invisible was not in her current new plan.

An hour later, she watched as the now visible transport ship landed at the tiny, primitive spaceport. Few paid it much attention, rather a large crowd had now surrounded the block where Breanna lived, and all manner of wild and conflicting rumors were being passed from person to person. A large ring of security women kept the crowd back to what they thought was a safe distance. Thus, Jan was able to duck into the transport unseen, where she hastily changed clothes, donning a pants outfit and had Pippa, Savina, Gwenda, Adrianne, and Bess do the same, though four of them had to wear their tall brown boots with the necessary six inch heels because of their partially repaired feet could tolerate nothing lower. Still as Jan looked them over, they looked reasonably like the other women she'd seen.

"Whatever happens, Arnold, Alfonso, you both remain on the ship. Men here are wholly second-class citizens and have virtually no say in any substantive matter. Okay, let's go get them," Jan ordered. The six women, led by Jan and Gwenda, headed down the street from the tiny spaceport control tower, whose women had already headed into the city to see what had happened. Before too long, the six had to announced their arrival just to get through the crowd of women pressing close for a look see, though in truth there wasn't anything to see, except the dual yellow cylinders, which none dared touch.

"Excuse us please. We're here to help," Jan kept saying as her group pushed through the crowd. When they reached the front, Jan spotted the original security women and another woman chatted. "Excuse us. We're here to help you."

"Please stay back," one security woman called out, pointing to Jan, who ignored her, causing several of them to break off and move over to them. That's when one of them called out, "More aliens!" Instinctively, Jan raised her hands up in the air, figuring a submissive appearance would help. It certainly got the attention of the other woman who was conferring with the guards. She moved over towards Jan, looking her over from top to bottom.

"Hello. I'm Jan Bellweather. We come from another world in the sky. We're here to help your fallen people and capture that wickedly evil man who almost destroyed your world." Best get it all out at once, she thought.

The woman frowned. "You look like aliens. Such enormous breasts. I'm Chairwoman Riona. I run our city, Kalgary. What do you know about this attack on our world's leader? What about the flying war machines that came here? What's happening in her house? They are not moving. Sile here was told that it was a poisonous gas and not to go in there for a long time. She was told it was a terrorist attack. What do you know about this?"

Jan spoke authoritatively, "We know quite a lot about it. We've been after that madman for some time now. He's a criminal wanted for so many crimes against women that I can't begin to recount them. Others were after him too, terrorists. Ah, I see you have found the cylinders there that the terrorists used to poison them. Now, the madman's fleet of ships has fled from here, and they'll not be back ever to threaten your world again. That much I can assure you."

"How can you assure us of that?" Chairwoman Riona asked. She was a middle aged woman, used to commanding others. Her hair was braided and wrapped into a tight bun around her head.

Jan replied formally, "One, their sole leader, that wanted madman, is now either dead or in a coma. Two, my ship's crew saw their entire fleet departing in a big hurry. I believe that your world has scared them away. Either that, or they too greatly fear the unseen terrorists who did this to the madman and your people in that house."

"All right. I will have to accept your word for this now, as I have no way to confirm or deny it. Can you tell us what must be done to save our Executive Chairwoman and her daughters? We know nothing of this alien poison. The guards have not seen any of these terrorists that you mentioned."

"Terrorists are seldom seen. They do their dirty work and then flee. In the case of this particular poison, which is always found in yellow cylinders like those on the ground, even the terrorists flee from it, because it does nasty things to our bodies. We have very able doctors on our world, who have a proven track record at helping victims such as your Executive Chairwoman recover from the poison's horrible effects. May I explain further?" Jan asked politely, knowing that she had the attention of the Chairwoman.

"Yes, of course. Please," Riona replied. *I must listen to what she has to say, though trust is something to be earned.*

"Unless we are too late, everyone in the house is in a coma. They'll come out of the coma in around four days. However, during that time, this poison will cause horrible mutations to their bodies. Their arms will dry up like cornhusks in autumn. Their breasts will grow far larger than their heads. Their feet will become horribly malformed. Their hair will grow very long and have pain sensors in it, preventing it from being cut. Their lips will split. In short, very nasty effects. However, there is hope, Chairwoman Riona. If we are allowed to take them back to our doctors, they can cure them of most of these horrible mutations, even regrowing their arms."

Jan also sensed that she needed a stronger punch and realized how she could impinge on the woman. She added, "If we don't have our doctors treat them, the woman and her daughters will be a hundred times more worthless and helpless than your men and boys are. If you allow us to take them to our doctors, they'll be almost as good as they were before this madman came here to conquer your world, bringing the terrorists after him."

Jan noticed the crowd was totally silent. Everyone was trying to overhear their conversation. The Chairwoman wasn't totally convinced yet. So Jan decided to play her last card. "I believe the poisonous gas has dissipated enough so it would be safe for us to enter, bring the victims outside where you can examine them, and have your own doctors look them over. Your security guards did the right thing in breaking the windows to let the gas escape. However, in case it isn't completely safe, allow us to risk ourselves and not your people. We'll bring them out here onto the lawn, while you get your medical doctors here to examine them. Will that be acceptable, Chairwoman Riona?" Jan already knew that it was and smiled when she nodded.

While she issued orders to round up their medical teams, Jan motioned to her group, and they headed up the sidewalk and went into the front room. The victims lay slumped over on couches or were lying on the floor. "I'll drag Velasco out," Jan whispered.

"I've got Princess Delwyn," Gwenda spoke up. "My god! Look what that bastard has done to her!" She picked up her fellow countrywoman and followed behind Jan, who was dragging Velasco out, avoiding using her *mentales* gifts to more easily carry him. Bess was right behind them, carrying Valencia. Adrianne brought out Carlyn, while Savina carried out Fiona. Pippa brought out the young Finn. After laying them on the ground, Jan sent them back in for the heavier husband, Cormac.

"This is one of our fellow countrywoman, Valencia. This is Gwenda's countrywoman, Princess Delwyn. You can see for yourselves what a vicious, sadistic butcher this man in black here actually was. Evil. Wicked." Several security women actually spat on the comatose Black Man. However, most gasped and swore numerous local curses at the comatose man. They were more than outraged at the nearly armless and legless women.

Several shouted, "Kill him!"

Chairwoman Riona raised her hand, and the crowd of mostly women quickly silenced. Jan realized she wielded enormous respect. Jan spoke up, "Your Chairwoman Riona is right. He should be taken back to our world and punished for the uncountable crimes he's committed. If you slay him now while he is unconscious, he will never know punishment. We'll see that he suffers for his many crimes, once he comes out of his coma. More importantly, we need to get the others to our doctors soon, or they'll be in even worse physical condition than Valencia and Delwyn are now."

Several women arrived carrying medical bags. Jan and her group stepped back to watch. Chairwoman Riona's face was drawn tight, as she pondered the situation. Several of the doctors rose and shook their heads no, a sure sign that whatever was happening to the women, they had no knowledge.

"So," Chairwoman Riona finally spoke up, "you wish me to allow you to take them to your sky world where you will cure them and bring them back to us?"

"Yes. It would be inhumane for us not to do everything we can to save them. We won't be curing the madman though. He must suffer for his many crimes against women," Jan added, knowing that was what she wanted to hear about Velasco.

"Okay then. It seems I really have no choice but to trust you. They are as good as dead to us now. However, there is one condition I must ask you to fulfill for us. If you agree to it, then you may take the aliens and our three women, but not the men. They are worthless." She nodded to the head security woman. Before anyone realized what was happening, the woman pulled her gun and fired twice, startling everyone. She'd put a bullet into Cormac's head and into Finn's, killing them both. "Now, they will not have to suffer further. We are humane when it comes to men, as you have just seen. We put them down rather than let them suffer. I'm told that your ship is at our dock. I'll have my guards bring a wagon to help you take them there. Meanwhile, come with me, and I will tell you what the condition is."

Jan realized Chairwoman Riona had already assumed she would agree to this unknown condition. The woman had balls, Jan sensed. She'd handled a wholly foreign situation with calm and the certainty of one who is in charge. Jan nodded and followed Riona, while six other guards filed around them. The crowd of women quickly gave way to their city leader.

They entered an office building made from kiln fired red bricks and with great attention to ornate arches, particularly so at the domed entrance. She led Jan into an office, relatively plain. Riona wasn't much on formalities. She took a seat and motioned for Jan to do so as well.

"I'll be quick and blunt about this condition. You see, other aliens have landed on our world of Connemara for the last twenty years. They are strange men who have women's hands, and they speak with a horrible accent, almost not understandable. Anyway, you are the first true alien women we have seen, not counting the two mutilated women that despicable Black Man brought with him. I do so hope that his punishment will suit his crimes. These alien men have brought us some valuable trade from their world, but that isn't important. They call themselves Jerri and their world has a strange name, Jarvis-B. These Jerri dress as women here do, quite strange indeed to see men dressing as we do and having women's hands as well. Anyway, we have learned that on their world, all their women are in very serious trouble. They have never said what that trouble might be, but that it is hideous, to quote one of the Jerry. Anyway, initially, they begged us to send some of our women back with them to help their women survive. Naturally, Executive Chairwoman Breanna agreed and sent twenty somewhat reluctant volunteers back with them. I say reluctant because these were men dressed as women and with women's hands, very strange indeed. However, it has been twenty years now, and we have not had any word from those who we sent to their sky world."

"Some have said that our women have fallen from the sky. After all the sky is so far up there, and we have no idea how your worlds can stay up there without falling down onto Connemara. Still, we have received no word. But it has gotten worse. Some fifty young women, unmarried, have gone missing from around Kalgary, and always during the times that these Jerri ships are on the ground at our space dock. Some have speculated that these Jerri men have taken our young women, but as yet Executive Chairwoman Breanna has been unable to obtain any evidence linking the two events. I've not been idle. Every time a Jerri ship now falls from the sky at our dock, I have security guards follow them around. Since then, no more young women have disappeared. I believe that is proof enough of their involvement, though I do not know why."

She finished up, "So the condition I ask of you is to find this sky world of Jarvis-B. Go there, find out what this very serious trouble is that their women are in, and find out what has become of our original twenty volunteers. Perhaps, you'll also be able to find the other missing young women there as well. We women of Connemara certainly want to help these other women if we can, but we do not trust sky men, who dress as women and have women's hands. Will you do this for us?"

Jan replied, "Yes, of course we will, but only after we've cured your women. That's our top priority. Once that's done, we'll check into this situation for you. Perhaps, this will lead to bonds between my world and yours. I hope so."

"Thank you. I'll have my driver take you to your ship in my carriage. By the way, what is your world called?"

"Ashford-5 or Tierra."

A half hour later, Jan climbed out of the carriage, having thoroughly enjoyed the ride. It was so much like home! Pippa met her at the bay ramp as she took the ramp in giant strides. "Hi. We've got them all onboard and are ready to take off. How did it go?"

"We've probably got another mission to do after this one. Come on. I'll tell you all about it while we're heading back. Ever heard of a world called Jarvis-B?" Jan said, shutting the door and following Pippa.

Jan found Gwenda wiping the brow of Princess Delwyn, though the woman was in a coma and probably wasn't aware of it. Still, that didn't stop Gwenda from caring. Jan quickly removed the earrings from Valencia and then searched Velasco and found his belt, confiscating it. She locked them up along with the partially used pair of yellow cylinders that had been brought back with the others in the wagon. Then, she met with the others, explaining what she'd agreed to do, look into the situation on this unknown world of Jarvis-B.

Four days later, Jan visited the genetics and medical wing to see for herself. Estrella had already told them that apparently Velasco's body carried the recessive genes of the ancient Calder mutation, which the geneticists claimed was the root cause of his radically different genetic mutations. She'd also said that the three women from Connemara had yet another genetic mutation that was recessive as well. Current speculation was that it was responsible for their males being born without hands. The five women had come out of their comas the previous morning and were quickly put under a medically induced coma and given all the cures that were possible.

Shortly after they'd returned, Jan and her group were debriefed by the queens, the governor, and Renata. While they were thankful the situation had been contained and Velasco stopped, they decided not to let others know that Jan and her group had been the actual terrorists. With their stories straight, the queens contacted the emperor to let him know this serious situation had been handled and that they had the man captured. The emperor insisted that Velasco not be given any of the known cures. That would be part of his punishment for his many crimes.

During the next few days, Jan and Adrianne continued to monitor the newscasts coming out of Cartagena-C and a few other more populous worlds he'd captured. The aftereffects were profound. All the rulers were completely confused about everything that had happened. Civil unrest had grown, primarily in protest to the new laws forcing women to have their lower arms removed. Almost overnight, those laws were tossed out, but lawsuits from the many victims began to be filed against the various governments. Many of the women, who had been in the ruling bodies and who had lost their lower arms and were now basically helpless victims in their own right, resigned their position. All the women victims were emotional wrecks. Worst of all, there were millions of them scattered among the sixteen conquered worlds, though Al Nair-F was spared. They'd never gotten around to passing that law as dictated by the Emperor Supreme.

What Jan found most interesting was that all the newscasts reported the Black Man, Emperor Supreme, had been the victim of a bio agent terrorist attack, and had died as a result. Apparently, no one dared to return to the remote world of Gemma Rho-D to find out what had happened to him. She presumed Admiral Juan would presume that the amazons of that world would have simply killed him after what he'd done to their leader and her family.

Jan walked into the lab to check on Velasco, summoned

there by the geneticists, the queens, and the governor. "Hi ya," Jan called out, seeing them gathered outside a private room.

"You've heard about the Calder mutation?" Queen Lilly asked her.

"Yes, so what's happened to him?" Jan answered and asked, growing curious.

"Well, we've a whole new mutation to handle. Take a peek at Velasco," the queen said, nodding towards the open door. Jan walked in and looked at Velasco's naked body lying on the hospital bed. He was barely conscious, but mostly in shock. Well, he deserves to be in shock, Jan thought.

His upper legs were bowed outward compared to normal women's upper legs, but they bowed in and joined at his knee. A single lower leg extended down to his overly large single foot, but it too was malformed. He'd need to wear the toe shoes like everyone else. He now had working female organs, just as did all hermaphrodite men and with the gigantic breasts that came with the mutation. To spare him the back pain, they had put a heavily steel boned corset on him, though it was causing him to gasp for breath at the moment. His hair was six feet long as expected, and his arms were gone as well. His lips were split, and for now, the nurse had inserted the foot across lip plates to protect his lip loops from being caught and ripped. The man looked terrified.

Jan stepped back out. Queen Misty said, "There are two other changes we were not expecting. He's now head blind, completely." Jan broke into a big smile. He would no longer dominate others. Then, she realized Renata had probably had something to do with this. "And something happened to his vocal cords. He's unable to speak as well. His goose is cooked. But none of us could see any other way that he could have been stopped. The sheer number of women's lives that he's harmed — almost unimaginable. Everyone has been right. The amount of damage one of our *mentales* gifts could inflict upon the galaxy is gigantic. We must see that this cannot happen again, though I'm not sure how we can prevent it. Slowly but surely, Tierra is moving into the space age. But Jan, that's Lilly's and my problem, not yours."

Jan chuckled, "You can say that again. Honestly, I

didn't see any other way he could have been stopped, short of an enormous battle of warships in which thousands of people would be killed and at a staggering cost to boot. We've enough of a problem with those alien snake creatures. So what are you going to do with Velasco now?"

"Darn good question, Jan. We've not yet decided. We don't have jails on Tierra, but that's where he'd wind up if he were on other worlds. Either that or confined to some assisted living home. Around here, none of those caring for the other terrorist victims wants anything to do with him. A lot of those are women so I can understand their point of view. We may return him to Valen. If we do so, we'd have to insist that he be kept alive until old age catches up to him. Of course, we would have to inform them of just what Velasco did out there, and that could well give others similar ideas," Queen Misty explained, speaking slowly, so Jan could understand her in spite of her giant lip disks.

Queen Lilly added, "Right now, we're having a special toe shoe made for him. His foot is size thirteen, rather large. We are supposed to have a gown that will fit him here yet today. Still, we need to get him into a stable living situation soon. Governor Sheila wants us to wait a few days until Valencia recovers, since she is his wife. Her idea is Valencia might want some say in what happens to her husband. She also believes Delwyn's marriage can be annulled easily. So we will hold off making any final decisions for a few more days."

Governor Sheila joined the trio. "Well, I've some news. A transport from Cartagena-C just landed. It seems Admiral Juan something-or-other sent all of Valencia's enormous collections of women's fashions here along with her account number. I'm supposed to withdraw her funds and give them to her estate. They presume Velasco, Valencia, and Delwyn are dead. Interesting. She's extremely wealthy from that accident or terrorist attack she suffered while on their world. Can I store them in the Imperial Castle somewhere?"

"Sure," Queen Lilly replied. "And his things?"

"They burned his clothes and confiscated his accounts. Apparently, they want to dole it out to the many women that he harmed with his Domination," she replied.

272

Jan was around to see how the cures had gone with Breanna and her two daughters. Amazingly, their DNA was quite similar to most of those in the old Imperium arm, except for the recessive gene that affected only their male offspring. These three fully recovered, except that they were now very well endowed, compared to others of their world, and that they were hermaphrodites. After some discussion, Breanna had her male organs surgically removed, as well as those of her daughters. She assured everyone that even though their future daughters would likely have dual organs, they'd be removed at birth.

After that, Breanna wanted to see more of their sky people's world before returning home. Wisely, the queens made arrangements for them to return with communication equipment so that they could directly contact them, and they worked out some elementary trading arrangements as well. Their biggest difficulty was getting used to the fact that on Ashford-5, women wore men's clothing, while men wore women's. The queens also ensured that only women would be interfacing with them, pleasing Executive Chairwoman Breanna, who already had seen far more than she could comprehend. Both she and her daughters were more than ready to return home with Jan, Arnold, and crew.

Wild emotional swings accompanied Valencia and Delwyn's recovery. They were in their medically induced comas nearly two days longer than normal. Thanks to the geneticists work, both their arms and legs regrew during that period. Both had a hard time adjusting to the fact that they were now freaks, as Valencia put it, hermaphrodites, and well endowed, though Valencia had already been so endowed before she'd left Tierra with Velasco. While physically they were in particularly good shape, emotionally they were quite a mess. The single stable datum that they both clung to was that they loved each other. As Jan expected, Renata rushed both women into Basic Therapy, but theirs took two months to complete. That gives you some idea of just how messed up their minds were, requiring a lot of patience to sort out the mess and erase the implanted notions of Velasco.

However, from the moment they both came out of their comas, they knew Velasco had abused them horribly and wanted their marriages annulled. Further, neither wanted anything more to do with the "freak," as they called him, when they saw him lying on the hospital bed. Hence, the queens had no other choice but to hand him over to his brother's care in Valen. They did impress upon them that Velasco had to be kept alive until old age took him. Further, they would send someone to check on him periodically. A footnote: Velasco was twenty-five when he became a "freak." He lived for another fifty years before finally passing away, and was tormented, scorned, and the butt of jokes during that time. Many believe that he paid dearly for his crimes, but Renata thought otherwise. "One day, this may well return to haunt us," taking a line from past emperor's, whose motto was the solution of today's problem becomes tomorrow's problem.

For completeness, after finally finishing their Basic Therapy, Valencia and Delwyn married and went to work at Elegant Fashions Inc in Exchange City, where she put her huge collection of fashions to good use, designing new gowns. Delwyn, on the other hand, spent many years in Tierra's schools, eventually attending the Academy obtaining a doctorate in astronomy. Later on, Gwenda also joined her and got a similar doctorate.

Thanks to research by Arnold, Savina, and Alfonso, by the time that they needed to return Executive Chairwoman Breanna and her daughters to Connemara, they had the location of that Forbidden world pinned down. There was little information on it, however, other than they had a fledgling space fleet, transports mostly and were smalltime local traders with other nearby worlds on the Forbidden List. Not much to go on. Their language was Rus, a derivative of Russian. Hence, everyone got some needed fast, basic language training, compliments of Adrianne, their linguist.

Jan wore her confiscated Velasco's belt with its thirty-four giant crystals of power that had been compressed down twelve-fold in size. She didn't want the heavy earrings though, and Amy kept those herself. This time, however, and at

Renata's insistence, Estrella came along, armed with a field DNA test kit. While the geneticists had good DNA samples from Breanna and her daughters, they also wanted a sample from one of the males of Connemara. Thus, Estrella was happy to tag along, doing useful genetic work.

Chapter 15 Jarvis-B

Born in 1433 (converted to Tierra's calendar), the twins Tatiana and Sasha Korski had their share of major upsets. Their first huge emotional trauma came when they were three years old. That day, their year older brother, Boris, and their father, Yuri, were teaching their year younger brother, Michail, how to walk and play kick ball in the living room of their home. The twins were sitting in their usual cushioned seats watching their laughing brothers and father. Both twins desperately wanted to play ball too and enjoy the merriment.

Tatiana asked innocently, "Papa, how soon will we get arms and legs like Boris so we can walk and play too?"

Yuri stopped. Instantly, a serious mien replaced his joyous smile. "Sweet Tatiana, girls never have arms and legs. Only boys do."

Sasha wailed, "But we want to play too, papa. Give us arms and legs too!"

"Dears, you should know by now that girls on Jarvis never have them. You must be content to sit and watch your brothers," he replied soberly, glancing at his wife, Sonya, who was sitting on her mechanized pedestal, her long red gown partially hiding the upper portion of her column.

Undaunted, Tatiana turned her head to her mother, "Mama, make papa give us arms and legs too. We want to play kick ball too."

Sonya chided her twins. "Dears, we women never have them. Not ever. Arms and legs are not something that papa can give you. Women are born without them. We must not wish for things that we cannot have. Don't upset your father over what he cannot provide. Heaven knows just how hard papa works to take care of us. So be good girls, sit there, and watch your brothers play.

Both twins were completely crushed by this revelation. Until now, they'd just assumed that one day, papa would give them arms and legs too. After all, Boris and Mikhail had them. Hence, they'd waited patiently for them to appear, checking on them when they woke up in their beds. "Nope, not today," one would say to the other, who would reply, "Maybe tomorrow." Now, both Tatiana and Sasha were totally crushed, devastated was more like it. Their fantasy was obliterated in one fell swoop. Both began sobbing, so much so that Yuri had no choice but to carry them into their shared bedroom, laying them on their large bed, side by side. Hearing them sobbing stabbed him, much as a knife. He vowed to find a way around this somehow.

Two years later, Boris began going to school first thing in the morning. He was six. Eagerly, the twins counted the days until another year passed, when they too assumed they would get to go with Boris to school, and to learn fabulous and exciting things like those that Boris kept telling them about when he came home late afternoons. That year, the twins merely sat on their chairs all day long waiting for that magic hour when Boris would come back and tell them such exciting things.

That fall, the twins eagerly counted the days before Boris would be going back to school, knowing that now they were six too. Again, the hard hammer of life came smashing down upon their heads. "Oh don't be silly," Yuri exclaimed, frustrated with their pleadings and begging to go to school with Boris. "Girls don't go to the boy's school to learn all the many things that men must know and learn to do. Women can't do anything. You don't have arms or legs. How can you study rocks if you can't even pick one up to examine? Silly beyond words. No, you both go to the girl's school, where you can learn at least to read, sing, and learn about the few things a woman must know."

"But papa," Tatiana cried out, her hopes dashed completely, "we want to learn the things that Boris tells us about. Can't we go with Boris, please, papa, please?"

"Now you're being stupid, Tatiana. You can go with Boris if you can walk with him and carry your lunch bag," he retorted.

Both were utterly impossible, and the twins knew it. They broke into uncontrolled sobbing. Gone were their hopes for learning, for the future. He ignored their wailings and lifted each one, setting her into a basket holder mounted on a four by four foot, vertical plywood-like board. Strong gussets held the board to its horizontal base, which had four castors on it. He proceeded to push them out of the door and down the street to their new school for girls.

He pushed the board with the two girls sitting in their baskets into the main doors, which opened automatically, and then on into the large classroom, where they saw a number of other girls of various ages, all sitting in baskets hung to similar boards. He wheeled them into position, turned, and left. The twins had ceased crying, and now looked left and right to see their classmates. There were others their own age, but some were as old as fourteen. Up front, they saw an older woman sitting on her mechanized pedestal, her long gown partially hiding the upper column just like their mother's. A man entered and began running the class, with occasional words from the older woman.

They were taught to read and to speak properly. However, half of the day was spent learning to sing. During the breaks, they listened to the fourteen year old girls chatting. They were grown up now, soon would get their own mechanized pedestals, and then not have to come to school any longer. Sasha asked them why a girl had to be fourteen to get one of them.

"Oh they are very expensive and made to fit our bottoms," one of the teens explained. "You are still growing, and your bottom will get bigger each year. They can't be making you new ones every year or more. We have to be patient and wait until we are grown up to get one. They are expensive," she repeated herself, as though this was very significant. The twins accepted her reasoning, since they were getting bigger every year. Still, they found school terribly boring, especially since they could scarcely carry a tune.

Once in the mid-morning, once in mid-afternoon, and at lunchtime, several adult men came into their room to take each one to the toilet or to feed them their lunch. Otherwise, the girls spent their long days sitting in their baskets attached to the simple wooden frames. At the end of the day, their father came and pushed them back home. At least twice a day, they got to see a bit of their city and world.

Their clothing was kept very simple. Each wore cotton panties and a white cotton dress, which was more like a pillowcase with a hole cut in the top, which was pulled over their heads. Everyone in their family had light blonde hair. Sonya's was wavy and fell to her shoulders. At least once a week, she drove herself to the hairdresser's to have hers washed and trimmed when necessary. Yuri simply cut the twins' hair by placing a large bowl over their heads and cutting what stuck out. Of course, he did the same with Boris and Mikhail, so the twins never thought anything of it.

During those first seven years, their lives were miserable. Forced to sit on a chair or worse, sit in the basket fastened to a board all day, they had no freedom of motion. Of course, they were hardly capable of much motion in the first place. Still, their favorite time of day was night, when papa put them beside each other in their big bed. Now, they could move about a little, using their head and wiggling their torsos. Usually, they wiggled themselves into a position to look out of their window at the night sky, so full of bright stars and the crazy moon, which blinked in a bright red light. They had no idea that it wasn't a moon, but a nearby star, a pulsar in fact. Usually, they fell asleep dreaming of the stars.

Their third huge upset came later that first year of school. One day, their father came home with a twenty year old woman, who had long flaming red hair, braided on either side of her head. She had freckles and was introduced to the family. "Dears, this is my new wife, Una. She doesn't speak our language very well yet. She comes from another world called Connemara."

"But papa, we have a mother. Sonya. Una isn't our mother. How come she has arms and legs and we don't?" Sasha complained.

"She has come from another world to help us, Sasha dear. She will be your mother too."

"But papa," Tatiana complained, "she has arms and legs. So we want them too."

"Dears, we've been over this before. You don't and never will have them. Una does and is going to give you some more brothers and sisters. So treat her like your mother, Tatiana," he argued. At least this time, the twins didn't break into hysterical crying, but they were upset just the same, especially since Una spoke really badly.

For several months, things did improve around their home. Yuri spent most of his time with Una, at least when he was home. Una now took over most of the chores that Yuri had been doing, though she did have a lot to learn about caring for Sonya, Tatiana, and Sasha. While the twins just couldn't accept her as their mother, they tolerated her. Later on, after she learned their language, she told them fascinating stories about her own world, where women had arms and legs, learned, and did everything. The twins longed to go to her world where they'd have arms and legs too. The next upset came when they asked papa to take them to this Connemara. When he asked why, they told him. He replied as usual, "Oh don't be silly. Just going there isn't magically going to get you arms and legs. Twins, you are the way you are, and nothing will ever change that!" This time, they broke down once more, and he put them to bed.

Not long after that, Una gave birth to Tamara. Enter the next upset for the twins. Tamara had both arms and legs, albeit tiny baby ones. Yuri was elated! Sonya, however, simply cried. Once more, the twins begged him to get them arms and legs too. If Tamara had them, why not themselves? They ended up being put to bed once more. A year later, Una had Pavel.

However, by the time that Pavel was a year old, the situation changed dramatically and for the worst. It began with Tamara. While her body grew rapidly as all babies did, her arms and legs continued to shrink. When she turned two, Yuri came sobbing out of her room. They'd simply withered and fallen off. The twins sighed. Their jealousness of Tamara vanished. Now, she was just as they were. Worse, as the days passed, slowly Una's arms and legs withered too. Barely three years after she'd arrived on Jarvis-B to help them out, Una's appendages were gone. Reluctantly, Yuri had to purchase another mechanized pedestal for Una to use. She, however, never recovered mentally from her debilitating loss, spending her days mostly crying and talking to no one. She died young, though both Tamara and Pavel carried her flaming red hair into the future.

Never ending days of utter boredom settled in on the twins, brightened only around the supper table when Boris continued to tease them with all the exciting things he was learning, though they never realized that he was teasing them.

When they turned fourteen, for a time, life suddenly improved. One warm day, Yuri carried the twins out to his car. "It is time for you to each get your own mechanized pedestal. Mind you, these are very expensive, and it is the *only* one that you'll ever get. If you break them, then you'll simply have to sit in your chairs all day long."

They were carried into a fancy shop that had hundreds of these lining the walls. A man carefully measured their bottoms from many angles. Then, he produced two identical ones. He did explain their operations to the twins. "At the top is the secure cradle or saddle as we call it. Your bottoms will fit into them. As you can see, the saddle comes up to your waists, holding you securely in them. This padded bar rests against your backs so it is safe to lean against it. There's not much chance that you can accidentally fall out of these devices. Now, the thin column below the soft saddle is made from a sturdy steel and can't break. As you can see, the plinth or base to which the column is securely bolted is quite thick and heavy, balancing your weight nicely. Even if you are bumped, it won't fall over. The plinth is too heavy for that to happen. Why? Because it contains a heavy battery and the electric motor, which drives the wheels or coasters."

"Now then, the important part for you two is this stick just in front of your mouth. Yes, that is a mouthpiece. You put it into your mouth and use your head to control the motor in the plinth. When you pull the stick to your right, the pedestal moves to the right. Push it forward, and the pedestal goes forward, and so on. The farther you push it in one direction, the faster it goes. You won't be winning any speed races. Their top speed in one mile an hour, quite slow, but it is more than ample for your needs around the house and for limited trips outside. Finally, this is important. The battery must be recharged each evening. Your father will plug it in when he puts you to bed. Generally, you'll be spending most all your days from now until you die sitting on your fancy mechanized pedestal, so get used to it."

Very pleased, the twins drove themselves out of the store and to Yuri's car all by themselves. For the first time in their lives, they had some limited mobility and were quite enthusiastic about it. From here, Yuri took them to a women's apparel store, where he purchased them each three longer gowns, similar to their mother's. Still, they were more like very long pillowcases, easy for Yuri to slip on them, but they did drape down two feet below their bottoms, hiding the saddle. Plus, the height of their saddles put them at eye level with Yuri and other men, which also pleased them.

Yuri then took them to a jeweler's shop. "Twins, you will soon be the object of other young men's eyes. You want to look your best so that some nice man will want to marry you. Hence, I'll be getting you some earrings and a necklace. To wear the earrings, your ears will be pierced, and once we get them on you, they can't come off by accident. Sonya wears hers all of the time, even in bed. Now, since you've been good girls, I'll let you pick out your own earrings and necklace."

After getting their ears pierced, the twins spent an hour trying to find just the right pair of earrings. At last, they picked the longest ones that he had. They came down below their shoulders in a series of dangling bobs, resting just above their bosoms. Why they chose these long ones, which were quite heavy, was simple. By moving their heads, they could "feel" their shoulders and chests, which excited both of them. They picked out a green emerald in the shape of a small heart for their necklace. It lay just above their budding cleavage. Later, two very pleased fourteen year olds drove themselves into their home, eager to show off to Sonya, who cried, saying they looked beautiful indeed.

The next day, they proudly drove beside their father, who led them to their next school. As they drove slowly up to the doors, they automatically opened for them, which also pleased the twins. He took them to their classroom and left them. As they looked about, they saw others their own age, who also had just gotten their mechanized pedestals as well.

To their amazement, they were finally being taught something interesting, the history of Jarvis-B. The twins paid close attention, for many of their long-standing questions were finally being answered.

Summarizing, Jarvis-B was settled some seven hundred years ago by a thousand Russian colonists and scientists, fleeing some tyranny on their home world. They found this world to be amazingly perfect. The planet's axis wasn't tilted. Hence, the seasons were almost non-existent. Here in the north temperate continent, the daily temperatures were ideal. The colonists believed that they'd found utopia!

Not far from Jarvis-B, astronomically that is, the red pulsar Rimma blinked continually during the night, rather like a neon-lighted moon, adding to the ambiance of the world. The scientists quickly built permanent shelters, planted crops, and settled into lives on their new world. Within three years, their population tripled. For twenty years, they thrived and flourished beyond all expectations.

Then, it began, slowly at first. Women's arms and legs began to weaken noticeably. Their doctors had no idea why, and all their varied attempts to cure them failed. Back then, it took nearly ten years before all the adult women had lost their arms and legs. However, their babies were still completely normal and healthy. They then took drastic action, making all women, who could, have as many children as possible. Their reasoning was simple. Create a new generation of healthy women. For number of years, this solution seemed to be working.

But as these young girls reached puberty, their arms and legs began to weaken too. By the time that they were eighteen, they were as helpless as their mothers were. Now, the leaders faced a new crisis. They couldn't return to their home world. A world war was ongoing. In any case, they could hardly take tens of thousands of helpless women back with them. They didn't have enough spaceships to carry everyone. Besides, Jarvis-B was an ideal world. Except for this one anomaly, there had never been such a perfectly ideal world discovered. They chose to stay and find ways to deal with the problem.

Since the men were doing all the work, the companies put their workforce on shifts, allowing the men to spend time on domestic duties as needed. This was particularly needed during late pregnancies and the first year of the new babies. Some men took jobs as caretakers, watching over a number of homes, while the men who lived there went to work. After some years of adjustments, the men had their work schedules worked out to perfection and never left their women, girls, and babies home alone.

Still, their population continued rapidly expanding. Today, the twins learned, Jarvis-B boasted close to a half billion men, women, and children. They were spread out in a number of larger cities, of which theirs was called Rostova. The twins were surprised to learn that each city was run by an elected man called their Commissar. Rostova's leader was Commissar Yuri Korski! This took the twins by complete surprise. That their father was the leader of this whole city had not been known to the twins.

Of all the cities of Jarvis-B, Rostova was unique in that it had the only spaceport. Over the centuries, they'd managed to add to their transport fleet and had begun to open up trade with neighboring worlds. One day, Commissar Yuri Korski had a brilliant idea. His trading fleet had come across a world where women ruled, not men, primarily, he reasoned, because their men had a genetic malady and lacked hands. His idea was to convince these understanding amazon-like women that the women of Rostova needed their help. It worked. Soon, a transport arrived with a number of Connemara volunteers, all young and willing to help reverse the horrid situation with the women of Jarvis-B.

One of these had been Una, who had truly wanted to give birth to normal women. Her idea and that of Commissar Yuri and many others was, if they had enough normal girls, the horrific state of women here could be reversed. For several years, this grand plan was seen to be working well. These volunteer women gave birth to perfectly normal girls. More volunteers then came from Connemara. Commissar Yuri was hailed as the savior of Jarvis-B!

Of course, a few years later, the women from Connemara began losing their arms and legs. Still they didn't give up, since their girl children were still normal. Some twenty years after Una and the original women first arrived, the grand plan had completely failed. Worse, these volunteer women were emotionally crushed by their sudden total helplessness. Most died within a few years, wholly unable and unwilling to survive. Certainly, they did not want to be taken back to Connemara as they were.

Tatiana and Sasha were now eighteen. They still wore their long earrings and used them to touch and feel their shoulders and upper chest by moving their heads around. This they often did, because once more, they were bored beyond belief. However, they had convinced their mother's hairdresser to allow their hair to grow. Now their light blonde, wavy hair fell to the small of their backs, giving them another way at least to "feel" their shoulders.

After age fifteen, their education ended. They spent their days at home sitting on their mechanized pedestals with their mother, who liked to chat endlessly about trivia. The twins turned her out. Soon, they anticipated that young men would come to visit them. Perhaps, one or two of them might take them out on a date, but as helpless as they were and so dependent on men for their total care, this didn't sound like fun. Worse, they knew their papa would accept the first offer of marriage that came their way, ending his constant care of their many needs. That meant that they'd be sex objects, like their mother, doomed to simply get pregnant and have a host of babies, knowing that their husbands always wanted boys and never girls. They'd end up like Sonya, who sat around on her pedestal all day long talking endlessly to no one about utter trivia.

Tatiana whispered to Sasha, "This is utter hell. And the worst part of it, we can't even kill ourselves!"

"We have to escape, Tatiana, somehow, someway," Sasha whispered back.

Savina called out, "Jarvis ahead!" They'd just dropped

out of hyperspace, but purposely some distance from the star and its planetary system, always a wise practice when approaching an unknown world, and for more than to avoid a nasty collision because of slightly off coordinates. Point of fact, since all the stars in the galaxy are in motion, when one punched in coordinates, the hyperdrive unit automatically adjusted them based upon the local rotation speeds where the galactic position of the coordinates indicated. When the coordinates were invented for a new location, also entered was the epoch date so the system could take galactic rotation into account. Thus far, no further corrections had to be made for movement of the galaxy within its super-cluster.

"Wow! Look at that, a red pulsar," Jan added from her location by the viewport near the bay doors. "Cool! Now, I can say I've really seen one. It's pulsing like mad."

"Hey, let me see too," Estrella exclaimed, just as excited to see one of these really strange sights. "Now, that is cool!" she added, having pushed Jan off a ways. "I bet it is visible from this world that we're going to."

"Cruising in on sub-light engines," Alfonso reported. "Adrianne, see if you can pick up any local broadcasts or something. We're still pretty far out though."

An hour later, they hovered over the planetary system from above the plane of the system. From here, Savina began identifying the planets. In this case, they wanted the second one out from the brilliant star. "Got it. Coordinates are fairly accurate, I think. Head there now boss?"

Arnold replied, "Yes. Best get this going. Stay alert for enemy warships."

A half hour later, they orbited the world called Jarvis-B, observing its landmasses, listening in for ground-based communications, and for any signs of spaceships. The solid green equatorial continent didn't look hopeful, but the very long east-west north temperate one did. Further, a number of large, sprawling cities could be seen. The clincher came a minute later, when a strange looking transport or cargo ship entered a landing pattern ahead of them.

"Ah ha. What have we here?" Arnold declared, having spotted it. "Let's follow that one and see where it goes."

"Aye, aye, boss," Alfonso replied, applying a bit of thrust to the engines, moving them gently out of orbit, and downward after the other ship.

"Hey, I'm picking up a transmission for us," Adrianne called out. "They want us to identify ourselves."

"Patch it through up front," Arnold replied.

A moment later, Arnold spoke his best Russian, which wasn't all that good. Adrianne snickered a bit to herself. He soon sent it back to her. "Okay, you talk."

Giggling, she did so. "This is Deep Space Transport 1123 out of Ashford-5 requesting landing instructions. Over," she said politely.

A voice replied, "Only one spaceport. It's outside Rostova. Follow our cargo ship down. Land on Pad 10. Acknowledge. Over." She did so.

As they slowly descended, the city loomed larger and larger. Sprawling out over many miles, Rostova had no tall buildings. Everything was single-story construction, concrete, stone, and wood constructions, with wide streets, uniformly laid out with a surveyor's precision. They spotted some trucks and cars moving below them, and the tiny spaceport at its western edge. Farmlands extended out for miles from the city as well as some smaller towns. "How come there are no skyscrapers?" asked Savina.

"Don't know, but maybe because they have lots of land and few people, so there's no need to build upwards," suggested Arnold, grasping at straws on this one. Few populous worlds didn't have skyscrapers of one kind or another. Even Tierra had a number of stories in its various castle complexes, ignoring the old Imperium spaceport buildings.

Pad 10 turned out to be the farthest from the small control building. Only two ships were on the ground as they landed, one having just touched down moments before they did. A dozen armed men were filing out of the building, heading towards their landing spot. Arnold grinned. "We have a welcoming party. Alfonso and Savina, you stay with the ship. Shut the bay after we depart. Be prepared for a fast getaway if things go sour." They nodded, and he left, joining the others at the bay ramp, which was just descending as he arrived. "Okay, Jan, it's your show," he turned control over to her.

She wore Velasco's belt of crystals around her waist, though it was way too large for her genetically modified waist. They carried no weapons, except Gwenda had her large knife in her boot, as always. Arnold, Gwenda, and Jan wore shirts and pants, while Estrella, Adrianne, Bess, and Pippa wore white cotton day dresses and matching six-inch heels, which their feet demanded. Once on the concrete tarmac, they waited a moment for the dozen guards to reach them. They had drawn guns.

"What do you want here?" one guard asked.

Jan replied almost humorously, "Take me to your leader." Pippa couldn't help stifle a giggle. Such a corny line, but it was precisely what they wanted, to see a person in charge.

The guards looked them over, but saw no weapons, ignoring Gwenda's knife. "Okay, come with us. Commissar Yuri Korski will want to question you. He is home handling lunch. Follow us," the man replied. He led them around the small control building where several cars were parked. All cars, they soon observed, were the same make and color, black. They piled into three of them, along with several guards.

The drive through the western section of the city was interesting, but not informative. They spotted a few other cars and some trucks. The streets were wide as were the sidewalks. Some of the buildings had signs, but only Adrianne could read them, since they were in Russian. She spotted some that were hairdressers and some that were grocery stores. She also saw some that translated to pedestals, whatever that meant. There were no streetlights, and she wondered why. She also noticed there were a number of factories at the edge of Rostova, but after a couple of miles into the city, those gave way to only these shops and a myriad of homes, mostly all very similar in both size and construction.

All buildings were at ground level. She didn't see a single raised porch or stairs anywhere, rather unusual she thought. Further, the homes all seemed to be rather standardized, one to the next. They could have been poured from the same mold, she thought. Near the heart of the city, they passed two large buildings. From the signs, Adrianne made out the world "school." One was for boys and one was for girls, though there were little outward differences, except the school for boys had large playgrounds at its sides.

They halted before one of these uniform homes. It was white and had a number in large black letters over its front door, 154. As the cars stopped, one guard said to Jan, "You will follow us. Commissar Yuri Korski has been notified of your arrival and is expecting you. This way." He led her and the others up the wide, flat sidewalk to the front door, which opened automatically when they stepped on a pressure-sensitive area just before the door. It slid sideways, not inward or outward.

The entrance room was obviously a living room, and there they found the leader, along with his family. Jan and the others could not help gasping when they saw the four women! They had no visible arms or legs. Three were sitting on some kind of column with a stick in front of their mouths that came up from the large base or plinth. The fourth was very young and sat in a basket mounted on a plywood like board attached to a base with rollers on it. All four faced the wall, which held a partial ring of sofas and easy chairs. On older man sat in the largest one; two young men and a boy sat close to him. They rose, as Jan and her group entered.

"Welcome space visitors. I'm Commissar Yuri Korski. My sons, Boris, Mikhail, and Pavel. My wife, Sonya, my twin daughters, Tatiana and Sasha, and little Tamara. Do you understand me?" he said and asked.

Jan replied, "Yes. If my accent is really bad, Adrianne here speaks your language far better. "I'm Jan Bellweather." She continued to introduce the others, who took a seat on the couches, where they could see both the men and the women, and vice versa, though they did stare at the four women. It was quite a shock.

As Jan took in the scene, things began falling into place. Of course, the prime question she had was: were these men brutal sadistic beasts to have done this to their women or was there some other reason behind it? While they were staring at the four women, very much shocked, the men and the four women were staring equally shocked at Jan, Adrianne, Bess, Pippa, and Estrella.

A quite shocked Boris whispered, "Papa, these women have arms and legs!"

Commissar Yuri cleared his throat, slightly embarrassed by his eldest son's remark. "You must forgive our impolite staring at you. As you can see, we're unused to seeing women who have arms and legs. I'm afraid our women do not, most unfortunate. Forgive our staring, though I can't help but see that you are disturbed by our women."

"Well, yes, we find it rather shocking to us," Jan admitted.

Tatiana, awoken from her long boredom, spoke up, "Incredible. Do all women on your sky world have arms and legs? It must be wonderful to have them."

"Well, yes we all do," Jan answered, glancing at Commissar Yuri, hoping she was allowed to answer his daughter. Protocols differed from world to world, and Jan didn't want to create a social upset right at the start. She purposely didn't say anything about the genetic mutations, however. "You are the first women we've ever seen who didn't. I'm sorry that we're all staring at you. It is impolite of us."

Sasha giggled, "Well, we're staring as much as you! We can't imagine how wonderful it must be for you to have them! Women on Jarvis don't have them. Tell them, papa," she deferred to her father.

He cleared his throat again, "Ah, well she's right. Female babies are born without them, while males are born with them. It has been so for seven hundred years here. Most unfortunate, but as you can see, we are thriving in spite of this. I would be remiss in my duties as the leader of Rostova, if I didn't warn you that you should not stay long on our world. If you do, you may very well end up like our women. Might I ask what is your purpose in visiting our world? Where are you from?"

"Ashford-5," Jan answered, handling the easiest of his questions first, giving her time to work out a better response. "It is on the rim of the old Imperium spiral arm, quite some distance from here. Our purpose is really quite a simple one. Recently, we visited a world called Connemara or Gemma Rho-D as it's formally called on the star charts." She noticed a visible reaction from Yuri. Was it surprise? Without probing his mind, Jan could not be sure. "One of their leaders, Breanna Navan, asked us to come here and find out what happened to their women who volunteered to come to your world to help out your women. I believe they sent some twenty volunteers here, though they also believe more than fifty other younger women were abducted and perhaps brought here as well. Do you know anything about this?"

From the flush on his face, Jan didn't need telepathy to know he knew precisely what she was talking about. Even the twins reacted, as well as Boris and Mikhail. Further, everyone they'd seen so far was blonde, though this family had very light blonde hair, except the two youngest, Tamara and Pavel, who had flaming red hair, similar to the women on Connemara. Jan's suspicions were raised.

Once more, Commissar Yuri cleared his throat. "Yes, one of the twenty agreed to be my second wife. Una was her name. She gave birth to Tamara and Pavel here, and they carry her beautiful red hair as a constant reminder of their mother. I should explain our world more. Perhaps, then you will understand what happened, and why Una never wanted to return to her home world. We still honor her memory here. She and the others from Connemara gave their lives trying to help our women."

Yuri explained in detail the long history of their world. Tatiana and Sasha heard him repeating what they were told during their last term as students, when they were finally given their own mechanized pedestals. He talked for nearly an hour, laying everything out in plain language. He concluded, "So you see, Una and the others really did want to help out our women and try to turn this nightmare around. Alas, in time she too ended up like Sonya and our other women. For a long time, we hoped Tamara would retain her arms and legs, but then she lost them when she was three. So my last hope for our people has failed. Yet, we do the best we can for our women and people. Jarvis-B is an extraordinarily perfect world in all other ways. The climate is ideal; growing seasons, perfect; the soil is most fertile. We lack for nothing else. However, we have begun trading with some other nearby worlds, but we do not allow their women to stay on our world but briefly, fearing that they too will become afflicted as our women are. So you can see why I must urge you women to depart as soon as you can."

"Well, that answers my questions, Commissar Yuri," Jan replied when he'd finally finished up. "I will relay them to the Executive Chairwoman Breanna, and I'm sure she will understand." He nodded appreciatively.

Sasha spoke up, "So you women must be very learned. You must have been to school a lot and have learned a great many things."

Jan smiled. "Sure. Adrianne here is a linguist. She speaks and writes many languages. Savina, who is still on our ship, is a trained astro-navigator and can plot our course to nearly anywhere in the whole galaxy. Estrella here is a trained geneticist and medical doctor. You pick a field, and there's a woman on our world who is an expert in it, just as men are. However, I'd be remiss if I didn't say that a great many women choose to stay home and raise their families too. Still, most all women have a good deal of education."

"See papa, there isn't any reason why Tatiana and I couldn't learn all those exciting things that the boys learn." To Jan, she added, "We begged papa to let us learn them too, but he said that we couldn't. Now, we are dumb."

Yuri looked frustrated. "Sasha. You know very well that without arms and legs, you couldn't do that. How can you pick up a rock to identify it? How can you solve math problems without writing the long solutions out? How could you be a doctor if you haven't the hands to help the patient? You are being silly again. I thought that you'd outgrown such notions."

Jan definitely felt sympathy for the young women who probably spent their whole lives just sitting on their mechanized pedestals, serving as sex objects and baby factories for the men in their lives. Yet, she didn't want to interfere in a family matter.

Estrella, on the other hand, had been thinking about everything that Yuri had told them. She spoke up. "Commissar

Yuri, what have your geneticists had to say about the situation with your women?"

"I'm sorry. We don't have any of those. You see, our original founders brought with them many scientists, but none was a geneticist. All such knowledge is beyond our doctors."

"Interesting. Do you realize that your world is very close to that red pulsar?" she asked.

"Yes, our astronomers have studied it. We consider it particularly beautiful, especially when it is in the night sky. It pulses rapidly, like a blinking moon. Quite spectacular," he answered. Jan had no idea where Estrella was going with this and wisely said nothing.

"I bet it is that. The reason I asked is that almost a century ago, some of Ashford-5's people visited a world in the northern halo, which also was very close to a pulsar. On that world, the people were constantly bombarded or exposed to massive radiations from the pulsar. Over time, the radiation caused mutations in their genes, resulting in similar problems in their men, like your women here. It may well be that your close proximity to this red pulsar has caused mutations in your basic genetic makeup that has resulted in the loss of arms and legs of your women."

"Interesting, but why are not males affected too?" he asked.

"I can't answer that yet. I would like to study your DNA and see if I can see if this is what actually has happened here. Obviously, there has been some kind of genetic mutations in your women. Further, on our world, there are a whole lot of very brilliant geneticists who have been creating genetic cures for others. Often arms can be regrown, once the DNA defects are isolated and corrected. I'd like the chance to see if we can do anything for your women," Estrella suggested.

"Such, such things are possible?" asked a startled Yuri.

"See papa, they can regrow arms and legs. I knew it, papa. Please, Tatiana and I want to have arms and legs too so we can learn many things," Sasha gushed, unwilling to let this one remote chance go by her.

"That is very possible, but we geneticists would need time to study their DNA and see if we can invent a cure or a partial cure. It might be possible if the red pulsar has simply damaged some isolated areas of your genes. If so, we might be able to correct it. Without a diligent study, which could take some time, there's no way of knowing, but I'd like to try, Commissar Yuri," Estrella volunteered.

Yuri rubbed his face and then asked, "And why would you be doing this for us? We are total strangers. We are aliens to you, as you are to us. What is it that you want in return? Men always want something in return."

"We are all human beings. I'm doing this because I just might be able to help your women. If I can, then that is what I want in return, to see this nightmare that your women must endure come to an end. There can be no greater reward than that, right?" she replied, quite genuine, though Jan had a hunch why she so desperately wanted to try. Ashford-5's geneticists had saved her life, and this was a way to repay them.

"Most honorable. You are much like the women of Connemara. What is it that we must do for you to work your magic?" he replied solemnly. Jan sensed that he had a very deep respect for the red headed women who had selfishly come here to help only to become victims themselves.

"Well, I need blood samples from several men, but I'd like to take one or more women back to Ashford-5 where we have our laboratories. There, I can study their DNA, and we geneticists can see if we can find a way around the altered sequences," she replied.

"Our doctors can provide you with blood samples," Yuri declared.

"Take me with you. I volunteer!" Sasha blurted out.

"Me too. We both must go. Papa, if we can get arms and legs, then we can learn all the exciting things too. Please, papa, Sasha and I want to go with them.

Silent the whole time, little Tamara suddenly burst out, "I want to go too, papa. I don't want to be like this forever. I want arms and legs too, papa. I want to learn too. Please papa, let me go too."

Jan focused and lightly touched Yuri's mind. *Well, I could let them all go. It would certainly get me out of having to find husbands for the twins, who are overdue to get married off. Still, I must take this chance that they are serious. If they could find a cure, my god. . .* He replied, "Would three of them be sufficient or do you need more volunteers?"

Estrella replied, "Three are fine, especially Tamara, since her mother came from Connemara. That would help give us the diversity we need for a good initial study. Mind you, it could well take quite some time for us to find a cure or a partial cure."

"Oh papa, you must let us go with them," Tatiana pleaded.

"All right then. I will give my three daughters to you, but I must insist that Tamara gets her mechanized pedestal first. We normally wait to do that until they stop growing like weeds. These devices are expensive, and none of us can afford to buy more than one per daughter."

"Thank you papa!" the three chimed in together, their faces radiant, filled with hope that they never had before.

"Excellent. Thank you for letting us try to help out," Estrella replied.

Yuri said humbly, "You realize they need constant care. They can do almost nothing for themselves. You are willing to provide for their care?"

"Of course. Not a problem. We will treat them like our own children," Jan replied. "But we need a way for you to see them and chat with them.

Jan wanted to iron out a few more details. She suspected the three would be on Ashford-5 for months. She wanted a way for them to talk to their father and for Yuri to follow their progress. She asked to see their communications center and found it incompatible with theirs, not unexpected from such an isolated world. While Yuri handled getting Tamara her new mechanized pedestal and some earrings as befitting a young woman, Jan scrounged through the spare parts on the transport, putting together a video comm system that would connect directly to the queen's system back home.

She installed it in his study. "So you turn it on, and it operates like this," she demonstrated, making the connection to the queen's comm center, where a young woman answered and chatted with Yuri. He was amazed to see her on the monitor as they spoke, though the time delay was several minutes. Jan left him a very pleased ruler.

After they left with the blood samples and the three teens, Jan made a quick stop to report to the Chairwoman Riona of Kalgary, fulfilling her promise to her. She had her come out to the ship so see for herself what had happened. "This is Una's daughter, Tamara" she explained to the shocked Riona. The flaming hair convinced her that Jan was speaking the truth. Jan explained what they were now going to try to do for the millions of women on Jarvis-B and received Riona's thanks and blessing. After that, they landed some nine hours later at the spaceport on Plateau Grado.

Once on the ground, the three insisted on driving themselves across the tarmac to meet the queens, governor, and the many geneticists who turned out to welcome the three young women. Estrella was right, all the scientists were dying to get a chance to study this newly discovered genetic mutation and work on a cure, if possible.

"But you don't have any arms," Tatiana exclaimed, meeting Queen Lilly and Queen Misty.

Queen Lilly laughed. "Of course we don't. Traditionally, Ataro Empire queens are not supposed to have them. That way, we can't abuse the immense power that we wield. But we have our feet and use them as hands, so it's not all bad. Come on; let's get you three to our castle and your new suite. Everyone wants to meet you."

Within a week, Estrella, who was elected project leader for this research much to her great pleasure, announced their initial results. Indeed, the pulsar was the culprit, much as another pulsar had been in the halo world. This time, those who had high levels of testosterone had a recessive gene modified, but those who did not, the women, also suffered significant damage or mutations to a number of genes, causing the mutations in the women. This news was relayed to Commissar Yuri, who now knew why his people had suffered.

Work then began on coming up with a cure. The first

thing they all realized was that if they could regenerate the teens' lost appendages, once they returned home, within a few years, without anything else going on, the pulsar would simply undo them, as it has with the volunteer women from Connemara and their daughters.

Estrella then tested her own blood and that of several other hermaphrodites and made the startling announcement, "You know, there may well be a very positive benefit for our own genetic modifications. We might be immune to the pulsar, since we have a great deal more testosterone production than normal woman!"

During this time, the three teens worked on learning Imperium Standard so that they could talk with everyone without needing the ULAT boxes. Adrianne, who taught them, discovered that all three were very bright and willing students, picking it up easily, especially Tamara who just turned thirteen. The three also got to meet many others who were still waiting for their turn to be cured. They quickly got an education in the many forms genetic mutations were taking.

When the three were told that perhaps hermaphrodites would be immune to the pulsar and not have newly regrown arms and legs lost, they were more than willing to undergo that genetic mutation. However, Estrella fully explained her working theory to Commissar Yuri, obtaining his permission to proceed.

Some ten days later, having first exposed the girls to the bio agent and then putting them into the medically induced comas, the three teens awoke to a whole new life! True, they were now hermaphrodites, but that didn't concern them in the slightest. Neither did the fact that their super long, thick hair hadn't been undone and that they could never cut it any shorter. No, they were ecstatic over having normal arms and legs, like the men of their world!

Further, all three now wanted to learn and become geneticists so they could return to Jarvis-B and help cure all the other women and girls there. Commissar Yuri broke down in tears when his three daughters appeared before the video camera in the queen's comm center showing off their new arms and legs.

Subsequently, Estrella and her mate Adrianne returned to Jarvis-B along with a whole genetics lab. Their purpose was twofold. First, they would begin working the cures on the women there, giving the three teens years to learn how to work the miracles themselves. Second, they needed to prove the pulsar would not affect them as it had the women volunteers from Connemara. She had to prove her theory that their hermaphrodite bodies would be producing enough testosterone to prevent the pulsar from mutating their bodies as it had the women there. They figured that by the time that Tatiana, Sasha, and Tamara were trained and ready to return to Jarvis-B, if they were still just fine, then the process would work for everyone. They were taking a gamble, but both women just had to try.

A footnote for history ought to be added here. The process did indeed work out as planned. Four years later, the trio of new geneticists, Sasha, Tatiana, and Tamara Korski returned to Jarvis-B, joining Estrella in working the miracle cures. The problem that they faced from the beginning was the enormous quantity of stem cells required for a single cure. Once the men and women of Jarvis-B realized that it was going to work, they wanted to do everything possible to speed the cure along. The bottleneck was obtaining stem cells in huge quantities. Their solution was a simple one. Each wife, who was able, got pregnant, and the stem cells were harvested, though the fetus perished. After two such pregnancies, they had enough stem cells to cure the woman. While some would consider this solution to be immoral at best, those on Jarvis-B saw it as the only way to save their women and lives.

Unknown to all, another geneticist was closely monitoring all the genetic mutations and cures being discovered and developed on Ashford-5. His role would be quite devastating to many worlds.

Chapter 16 Interlude

The command ship Sporn entered the new galaxy, following behind the advanced scouts. The initial report had been stellar. Monkeys galore. After that promising report, nothing came back. First Commander of Sporn then sent six recon ships to find out why the scout ship wasn't reporting any further word. Their report was most disturbing, most. The scout ship was found destroyed, and the Serpientes crew dead. One was gutted from head to nearly its rear, a most hideous death for such a noble snake.

Further reports indicated the monkeys had invented space traveling ships. One was seen leaving that initial contact world. However, the scouts did report discovering many, many monkeys lying dead in water tanks below ground. Of course, they were inedible at that point. These reports also indicated that the dead monkeys had unusual forms, with no arm appendages and enormous breasts. Well the latter would indeed be quite tasty, if only they could find alive monkeys, the First Commander of Sporn thought hungrily. He'd not eaten for far too long, at least not his fill that is. They were on strict rations, having made the long journey between galaxies. Finding monkey food in their own galaxy had become extremely difficult. Thus, First Commander of Sporn had led his giant ship to this galaxy in hopes that more abundant supplies of monkeys could be found and perhaps even raised. That was his fondest hope, one that he had been working towards much of his long adult life on his home world. Unfortunately, just as he succeeded, others higher up took over his project for themselves. Greedy bastards, he'd commented afterwards.

His scouts reported in this galaxy the monkeys had invented space travel and had likely warships of their own. This, he found hard to believe. After all, they were mere monkeys, not the brilliant, highly intelligent Serpientes! However, he was cautious and decided to play it safe. After all, this was a new, unexplored galaxy. Who knows what advanced alien creatures may inhabit it. Thus, he sent out dozens of his scout ships to survey this initial small section of the new galaxy. They were under strict orders to observe and report on spaceships and alien races, as well as on the monkey populations that their instruments might discover from orbit. Under no circumstances were they to engage them or land and devour monkeys. After seeing the video of that initial scouting crew, none of the Serpientes scouts was eager to disobey that direct order, stomachs or no stomachs.

The Admirals of the Round Table on Cass-C took action and sent out as many of their light cruisers as they could muster. Their orders were to seek out these new alien snake-like spaceships and monitor them, that is, assuming that they did in fact exist. Fanned out in space around the initial sighting world of Beltazar-C, the two groups of scouts discovered each other. Both followed orders and didn't engage each other, but reported back, retreating some distance back from the other enemy ships.

Thus, it was in January 1451, both the Federation of Planets and the Serpientes became aware of each other. Further, by March of 1451, the Serpientes scouts discovered the populous world of Capella-D, literally overflowing with monkeys. The drawback, it was heavily defended by rather large battleships. However, First Commander of Sporn lacked one vital piece of information. Were the beings on these warships a new alien race or were they monkeys who had somehow gotten out of their trees and into space? He was not about to fight a needless war with aliens. However, if these were just advanced monkeys, that was another matter entirely. Somehow, he had to find out what the situation actually was. His first action was to search for and monitor communications from this new monkey-filled heaven.

Chapter 17 Enter the Dragon

Not much is known about the origins and early life of Dr. Able Stevens, MD and prominent geneticist on Capella-D, except what little was published in *Who's Who in Medicine and Genetics*. He was fifty years old at this time, married, with a daughter and son. The brief bio indicated where and when he received his degrees, and that he interned at Westbrook Institute for Genetics Research in the second largest city, Billings. After that, he accepted a position at WIGR, working his way up the ladder to his current position as Director of the Department of Experimental Research, DER as it was called by the staff, who worked in this branch of the giant corporation. What little else is known consists of the fact that in January 1451, he withdrew his life savings and closed his bank account.

Months before that, Dr. Able Stevens was a contented, happy man, wholly devoted to his lovely wife, Lena, and her beautiful long nails. He doted on his charming daughter, Linell, and had high hopes that his son, Peter, would amount to something in the Capella-D space force. He'd already received his commission. Then came that awful day when his well-ordered, perfect life was inverted. While at work, he received word there had been yet another terrorist attack, and that his family had been victims. He'd rushed to the sight, but was prevented access. They'd struck one of the finest restaurants in Billings, and at lunchtime when the place was positively packed with wealthy men and women, there to enjoy some of the finest dining to be had in Billings.

He vomited. Nervously, he waited there all night long and far into the next day before the ERT, the Emergency Response Team, gave the all clear signal. Suffering from lack of sleep, hunger, and dehydration from the vomiting, Dr. Stevens staggered inside to find his family. The scene was one of compete chaos. He went from fallen to fallen, frantically looking for his precious Lena, Linell, and Peter. Meanwhile, others were scrambling over fallen tables and chairs, dragging victims out of the restaurant, taking them to the local hospital.

Someone called his attention to the three, and he rushed over to find them in a coma. Worse, examining Linell, he knew that she had already died from a broken neck. She'd tried to get up and had fallen, striking her head on a chair, sparing her the future nightmare that the victims would be facing just days from now. Peter was also dead, and he knew why. He had a d-gun hole in his head. Dr. Stevens just knew that Peter had figured out what was happening and had the good sense to end his life rather than face the horrific nightmare that hundreds of thousands faced every day in the assisted living complexes. He kissed each on their foreheads and turned to lovely Lena, who was still alive but in a coma.

Dr. Stevens didn't remember being taken to the hospital along with her, but found himself sitting in a chair beside her naked body covered only by a sheet on a hospital bed. Owing to his prominence, he was allowed to sit with her, breaking only for quick hospital meals, until she regained consciousness. Following protocols, before she roused, the nurses got the steel boned corset on her. When she awoke, like all other victims, she screamed and passed out several times before she finally realized Able was with her. She tried to speak but couldn't with the giant lip disks in her split lips. "I'll do my best to get you to the top of the list for cures, my love. Be patient," he whispered the only thing he could think of, which did little good for the terror-stricken woman.

His stomach knotted, as he watched the nurse tying on the strange toe shoes, which barely permitted her to stand and walk. He helped her out of the room and to the lounge where assistants were waiting to take her to an assisted living home, all of which were packed to overflowing with other victims. Dr. Stevens went along with her and got her into her new room, shared with three other victims. They were that overcrowded.

After that, Dr. Stevens did everything in his power to get Lena moved to the top of the list to given the cures. He pulled in every favor owed to him, but it was all for naught. With so many on the list, the President had issued strict orders to follow the list. No exceptions. He saw her name near the bottom, and realized she'd die of old age before she would have a chance for the cures! Barely a week after making this discovery, he was called to the assisted living home. Lena had taken a bad fall and broken her neck. Now almost void of emotions, he leaned over and gave her a farewell kiss and left, a very broken man.

For a week, he refused to go to work, staying home and drunk most of the time. His emotional responses finally ended. He felt nothing now, nothing at all. He finally returned to his office, pondering the meaning of life, and asking why this had happened. That much is known from some of his associates, who dropped in on him to relay their condolences. "There is no God, no high authority," he was heard to remark. "If there was, he would not allow this to happen, not to me. Not to anyone."

As the days passed, Dr. Stevens could only thing of one thing. Get even. Get even with the bastards who did this. Since they wisely didn't step forward, it soon evolved into getting even with the whole human race. He saw corruption, greed, and inhumanity everywhere. That's when it's presumed he began his drive. His bank accounts vanished. Samples of the bio agent cylinders came up missing at the Experimental Research, where he was their director before he simply stopped showing up. Also missing was quite a lot of valuable research equipment, though some suspected that he might have stolen them. A later search of his home yielded nothing, not even a trace of the doctor.

In fact, he'd rented a deep space transport under a fake name, paying cash for a short trip to the next major Federation world and had setup a fully equipped genetics research facility in the ship. He also visited a tattoo shop and had a mythical giant black dragon etched across his back. He then headed for Ashford-5, where he pretended to be his old self. Of course, the geneticists there treated him as a trusted colleague, since many recognized him from the various Genetic Conferences held in previous years. Later, many samples of other genetic mutations mysteriously vanished, as did Dr. Stevens.

His departure from Ashford-5 was in mid-May of 1451, long after the newest situation on Tierra had come to light. A hitherto for recessive gene had made its appearance once more on our world, the Calder mutation as it was now called, perhaps an even worse mutation than that of the bio agent! It first appeared with Velasco's mutation, the result of his exposure to the bio agent.

Chapter 18 The Calder Mutation

While all towns and villages with populations larger than five hundred had been electrified and had central heating installed in all homes, the tiny farmsteads that dotted the Midlands and the Westerlings usually had not yet been reached with this new modernization program. In the northern Kingdom of Brom, Tom and Becky Whitefield had a small farmstead raising potatoes and nut trees, which provided both nuts and pod silk, highly prized when made into soft, warm cloth, much like silk or satin. This far north, the winters were long and cold. Hence, potatoes and nut trees were the cash crops grown around here. In the spring and fall, at the local farmer's market in nearby Bakerston, farmers met to trade potatoes, nuts, and pod silk for grains and other staples, such as apples, which were grown farther south. At other times, these hardy farmers kept pretty much to their own lands, for there was always work to be done and profits to be made.

The Whitefields were doing rather well for themselves on their small farm. They had four children, two boys and two girls. The eldest was fourteen year old Billy, who was just now really pulling his weight on the farm. Their youngest was Phil, now eight. Their daughters were Lisa, twelve, and Becca, ten. Tom and Becky were in their early thirties and by mutual agreement had decided not to have any more children.

They reached this decision after she had had Phil. Neither wanted to chance having any more daughters. Why? It began when Becky gave birth to Lisa. When Tom delivered little Lisa, his face turned ashen as he announced, "We have a daughter." Becky shrieked when she first held the tiny Lisa. It was a natural reaction.

Becky was born without any arms and with her two upper halves of her legs fused together at her knee with a single overly large lower leg and foot. At first, Tom suggested that they simply put the baby out of its supposed misery, much like a malformed farm animal, but Becky simply couldn't do it. Little Lisa was her own daughter. They decided to keep her, and hoped and prayed that her arms would somehow appear.

By the time that Becky had Becca, Lisa was hopping about on her foot, a very merry, happy two-year old. Becca was born with the exact same deformity as Lisa. Sighing, Tom and Becky kissed the newborn and gave her her name. After Phil came, they decided not to risk having another girl. Becca and Lisa required a lot of personal assistance.

Their mutation was rather unique. They had virtually no lateral motion in their legs. However, their pelvis sockets were such that they were very flexible. Easily, they could touch the back of their heads with their heel and touch their foreheads with their toes. However, they had to turn their heads in order to reach their ears. Yet, their legs were quite strong, well-muscled. Combined with their oversized foot, they were able to maintain their balance. Plus, they quickly became expert hoppers, that being their only mode of locomotion.

On the downside, if they fell, getting back up on their foot was challenging. In fact, if they attempted to kneel, they always rolled over, to either the left or right, unless they were leaning into something that prevented it. As three year olds, both girls figured out how to get back up once they had fallen, but that demanded that their chests were on the ground. They could pull their knee up under their chest, squiggle their toes onto the ground, and rock back onto their foot. On the other hand, if they landed on their backs, turning over was problematical with so very little lateral motions available to them.

All this certainly didn't prevent them from wanting to help around the farmstead. Not at all. They made their beds using their teeth to pull up the sheets and quilts. They helped set the table by biting down on a plate, hopping to the table with it, and setting it down, sometimes pushing it into place with their chins. Soon, their father built them a yoke with a pair of baskets. By balancing the yoke on their shoulders, they could carry various things, as long as the weight was balanced between the baskets. In this way, they carried potatoes from the fields into the house, water out to their father and brothers, nuts from the trees, and pod silk as the others picked it loose from the nuts and trees.

Becky never cut her hair, but braided her long brown hair. While at first, she wanted to keep the girls' hair short, soon they pleaded with her to let them have long hair like her, and she relented, braiding it each morning for the girls and undoing it and brushing it out at night. She also made the girls' dresses. They were loose fitting, hemmed at their knees. She omitted sleeves entirely. Hence, the girls quickly learned to help each other undressing at night. One would use her teeth up pull the other's dress up and eventually over her head. Both had to work together to accomplish this, but they worked well together. Often, they could even slip the dresses on each other, lessening the workload for their parents.

Winters, though, were harsh for the girls, and they usually stayed indoors. They couldn't wear any panties, since nothing would fit their strange forms. Yet this was helpful for without panties and in the short dresses, one girl could help the other raise her dress enough to sit on the toilet. But in the winter, their bare bottoms and exposed lower leg didn't mix with the deep snow. The best that Becky could do for them in the winter was to put a thick, warm sock on their leg. Tom was able to fix up a tall leather boot for each as well. Still, hopping in the deep snow was more than they could handle, though they always tried their best.

What kept this Whitefield family together was love. Naturally, Tom and Becky were fond of their strange girls, but both Bill and Phil also doted on them as well. Encouragement from the boys was very much needed by the girls. That they never gave up and were always trying to find ways to help the boys with their farm chores deeply impressed both young lads.

Twice a year, the Whitefield's visited Bakerston to exchange their produce for grains, cloth, and other necessities that their farm didn't provide there in the north. It was at these times, that the girls felt most vulnerable. It was acutely obvious to them that they were different, very different from the other young girls that they saw and tried to meet in Bakerston. Worse, other young girls ruthlessly teased them, calling them freaks and worse. The first time this happened, Bill and Phil had a choice to make. They chose to defend their sisters. "Look, they are just different, all right? Leave it at that.

You don't know them," Bill stuck up for Lisa, effectively ending a trio of girls' belittlement of his sisters.

Now at fourteen, Lisa had developed into a pretty young woman, as well endowed as any woman on Tierra. Even Becca was developing pronounced breasts, making her feel more grown up. Only now, the two had begun to take an interest in boys, as did most young girls their age. Unfortunately, try as the two might, boys either made fun of them or ignored them entirely, embarrassing them even more.

"Mama, I'll never find a boyfriend! I'm just a freak like the girls say," Lisa wailed as they rode home from the late March exchange in Bakerston.

"Me too," echoed Becca, though she knew that she was still too young for such worries, but she was almost thirteen, she reminded herself. All Becky could do was hold her daughters tightly as they rode along home in their loaded wagon.

When they were home and the girls in bed asleep, Becky and Tom had a long discussion about what to do with their girls. Unfortunately, neither had any workable ideas. A week later, the situation changed rather dramatically for the Whitefield family. The Fields family lived some ten miles further east and needed a new, larger barn. Word went out that on the following Saturday, they were holding a barn raising event.

Whenever a farmer needed a building of this size constructed, the custom was for him to hold a barn-raising event. All the neighboring farmers and their families would show up. Working together on the large project, they would build the building in record time. It was also a social get together as well. Some women handled the cooking for such a large group, while others lent a hand on the actual work as well. It was an all hands to work type of project.

When the Whitefields arrived, their wagon loaded with tools and baked goods, they joined ten other families. Nearly sixty people congregated on the Fields farmstead. Unable to do much to help in the kitchen or serving the workers, Lisa and Becca joined the workers on the barn construction. Using their yokes, they were able to carry smaller, needed items to the many men, boys, and some women who were doing the work. Often, they brought water and juices out to them from the house. Their actions caught the attention of two of the Fields' boys, Levi and Jason, fifteen and thirteen respectively.

Taking a break, Levi commented, "Say, Lisa, you aren't helpless like I thought you were. You and your sister really are able to carry your weight around here."

"Thanks Levi. We always do everything that we can to help," Lisa replied, wondering why he was looking at her and even talking civilly to her.

"Yeh, well, you are different, but still pretty, Lisa," Levi added. "Bet you have a lot of boyfriends."

Lisa didn't know what to think. Was he making fun of her as all the others did? Whatever else she might be, Lisa wasn't dumb, far from it. She was sensitive, bright, and quite intelligent. She decided to have some fun with Levi, whether or not he was playing with her. She replied, "Oh yes, how very observant of you, Levi. Why, I've just got so many boyfriends now that I don't know what to do with them all."

She sounded quite serious. Levi looked at her closely. Then, he broke into a huge smile. "I get it. You're teasing me. That's a good one, Lisa. I like you," he smiled back at her, and she found herself smiling at Levi as well.

As dusk fell, the barn was raised. True, more interior work was needed to finish it, but that could easily be handled by the Fields themselves. As everyone was packing up to head home, Levi came up to Lisa and asked, "Lisa, would you mind if I came by tomorrow to see you? Perhaps, we can go for a walk or something." He seemed rather shy and insecure. Lisa agreed, wondering what that was all about.

Nevertheless, Lisa had butterflies in her stomach the next day, chatting with Becca and her mother about Levi's coming to go for a walk with her. "Just remember, Lisa, don't let any boys take advantage of you," Becky reminded her daughter, wondering what was going on as well.

Levi rode up on his horse, dressed in his Sunday best. Lisa hopped outside to meet him, while everyone else watched from windows. It was still chilly spring, and she wore her leather boot and warm sock. She had a cloak over her, as did

Levi. "Good morning, Miss Lisa," he said politely but shyly. "Care for a walk or something? I've never seen your farm."

"Sure. Let's," Lisa replied, her stomach in knots, wondering just what he wanted with her.

"Er, well, I'd like to hold your hand, but well," he fumbled around, very insecure.

"Well, you can slip your arm around me, I suppose. I can take small hops as if we were walking together. I often do that so I don't spill things from the baskets," she explained. Off the two went taking a long tour of her farm.

One thing led to another and before long, Levi gave Lisa her first passionate kiss, thrilling her beyond words. When they finally returned to the house several hours later, Lisa felt as though she was floating or something. Tom and Becky were taken by surprise, as Levi shyly asked if he could court Miss Lisa.

However, by the next morning, Lisa was very ill, running a high fever. Tom had no choice but to take her into Bakerston to see the local doctor. He took one look at her and pronounced, "Tom, she's got the Verge Sickness! You have to get her to Brom Tower as soon as possible. You take her there pronto or she's going to die!"

Shocked, Tom drove them back home, telling Becky about the doctor's diagnosis. "But Tom, that means she's got the *mentales* thing," Becky pointed out. "We never knew that she had that!" Tom left the farm in the hands of his boys, while he took Lisa, Becca, and Becky off to Brom Tower, driving his team hard to reach there in just three days.

When they arrived at the tower, the doorman took one look at Lisa and whisked here off, telling them to wait in the commons room. He later returned with one of the Tower's capo's. "You got her to us in time, Mr. Whitefield. She is going to be just fine. We'd like to test your other daughter just to be safe." Becca hopped off after him, worried that she too might get sick.

Later, the capo returned. "She has the *mentales* gifts too. You should be very proud of your daughters. They will need to remain here for several weeks so that they can be trained in the use of their gifts. There is no charge. I'll send word to you when you can come back and pick them up." Tom and Becky asked a few more questions and then had no choice but to return to their farm. The capo had convinced them that everything was going to be just fine with their daughters.

Of course, Brom Tower immediately contacted the Imperial Tower, who in turn alerted the queens and the genetics lab. Drs. Alexandra, Zia, and Diego packed up some supplies and were teleported from the Imperial Tower to Brom Tower, a new and novel experience for Dr. Zia, who had no idea the part of the gifts included teleportation. Once at Brom Tower, they examined both girls, and the cat was finally out of the bag, as far as the resurgence of the Calder Mutation was concerned.

"This must be thoroughly investigated," Dr. Alexander declared, after they finished taking DNA samples from Lisa and Becca.

Capo Arnold explained, "We've heard of and have had here in Brom many similar cases in the last few years. Most of them were simply put down like deformed calves. Even my wife and I had one of these mutants. We didn't believe that it would even be able to survive, so we put it out of its misery hours after it was born."

Dr. Zia was appalled at his callous attitude. After all, it wasn't a thing, she was a living, breathing baby girl. "Just how widespread is this?" she asked, controlling her temper and urge to give this man a piece of her mind.

"I suppose that I can ask around and get a crude tally," Capo Arnold answered.

After returning to their labs in Exchange City, the geneticists had the queens issue a formal decree, sent to all the Towers, requesting a tally of all known Calder mutations and how many were still living. While that was proceeding, the geneticists began analyzing the two girls' DNA, looking for exactly what genes had been modified and how, a long project indeed, on top of everything else that they were working on.

Renata also followed the progress of the two girls and their training. She had expected that their gifts would have been along the lines of levitation and telekinesis or perhaps teleportation. She was very much aware of the abilities that the

Calder mermaids had had a long time ago. After all, those rescued mermaids had formed part of her cadre of Basic Therapy givers, particularly in the Brom area, where they spent most of their lives. Hence, she was quite surprised to see their gifts taking a totally different route, one that had little to do with their own well-being, but that of helping others. This, she found fascinating.

By the time that the two girls had finished their Tower training and received their own personal psi-crystals, the doctors believed that they had a partial cure. Armed with their own brand of hope, the three doctors visited both the girls and their parents, who had come to Brom Tower to pick them up. All met in Capo Arnold's office, while he explained their unique gifts to Tom and Becky.

"Their gifts, beyond telepathy that is, lies in growing plants. They have the ability to know precisely the best time to plant. They are able to commune with plants and know what they need to thrive and produce. You would do well to listen to their council on such farming matters," he explained. After a short discussion, he cautioned them to keep an eye on their boys and to rush them to Brom if they got ill as well.

Then, Dr. Alexandra took over. "I believe we have a partial cure for your girls that we would like to try on them. If our studies are correct, we believe we can at least get their arms grown. That ought to help them enormously."

"What? Real arms? Just like everyone else?" Lisa exclaimed. While her training experiences here at the Tower had been informative and rather fun, basic living had been particularly awful. Steps were a huge barrier, and the Tower seemed full of them. Besides, having strangers always helping them felt weird to the girls.

Becky broke down in tears of joy, unable to control her emotions. With arms, her girls really did have a chance at a good life. Both agreed to let these doctors take their girls to Exchange City for a week. Plus, Dr. Alexandra promised to teleport them directly to their farm when they were finished.

A week later, Lisa and Becca now had arms, normal arms just like everyone else. Further, Elegant Fashions Inc stepped in and provided them with four fancy dresses designed for their unusual bodies, and a winter outfit and two light summer dresses. As agreed, the Imperial Tower teleported them and their bags home, where Lisa was surprised to find Levi and Jason were also there waiting to see the "new" Lisa and Becca.

"Wow, you look really beautiful, Lisa," Levi said to her as he saw her wearing her new satin gown.

"I have arms now too. I can hold you and really help everyone. Plus, I really know plants and farming too," Lisa bubbled.

"Me too," Becca added, not wanting to be left out as usual.

While they still had to hop instead of walking, their lives were drastically improved. Yes, Levi and Lisa married, as did Jason and Becca. The two teens quickly demonstrated their uncanny ability with all forms of plants. The two farms flourished as never before. Crop yields nearly doubled, and soon word spread to neighboring farms about the amazing skill and knowledge the two teens had. Before long, they were also visiting their neighbors, giving them advice about planting and such matters. A year later, the two were highly sought after by many farmers, who looked to them to give them key advice about their farms.

Far more importantly, the data about the numbers of these Calder Mutations began arriving at the genetics lab in Exchange City. Wholly unknown to everyone, many such babies had been born over the years. Most presumed they were just a freak mutation, and most had been killed outright shortly after birth. The tally of dead reached well over two thousand, primarily in the Kingdoms of Brom and Valen.

Armed with the knowledge of what families had had such anomalous births, the three geneticists spent a week visiting a dozen couples, including Tom and Becky, taking DNA samples. That's when they discovered the recessive gene structure. Only if both parents carried this highly recessive gene did it materialize, but only in female offspring. At once, they created a simple DNA test that parents could take, which would tell them if they both carried this recessive gene. If so, they were notified that they could well have Calder Mutation baby girls. However, the odds of having one were about one in four, since both parents would have to be supplying a copy of the recessive gene at the same time.

By mid-May, another dozen living Calder Mutation girls were located and brought to Exchange City for their own cures. It was during this period of time, that the geneticists played host to another geneticist, Dr. Able Stevens, who was always keenly interested in their work. He even assisted them with their work for several months. His real purpose in being here was never divulged. The telepaths never "read" his mind, as that would be considered mental rape and wasn't ever done. On the other hand, had they violated their own ethical code, that could well have saved billions.

By June, the number of Calder Mutation girls known had climbed to over a hundred. Most lived on isolated farms, where they seldom attracted much attention as they would have if they lived in the larger cities. They too were brought to Exchange City and given their partial cures. Dr. Stevens also helped on this project as well.

However, he did ask a key question of Dr. Diego. "These cures require large amounts of stem cells, which of course is the real problem we're having handling all the millions of terrorist victims with Federation worlds. Might I ask how you have managed to always have such a large supply?"

"Of course, Dr. Stevens. We are part of the Ataro Empire. Our emperor realizes how vital our work here actually is and supports us. He has a program going on thirty-five of the other worlds in the empire that collects stem cells from normal births on a routine basis. We get our supply from him," Dr. Diego explained.

"Ah. I see. That does explain it. Perhaps, we should be doing the same thing in the Federation," Dr. Stevens replied, though he had no such intention.

The doctor continued to steal the samples that he desired. Finally, saying that he was needed back home, Dr. Stevens departed from Ashford-5 on June 15, 1451. In his own private lab on his ship, he now had all the samples he needed. Someone will pay dearly, he thought.

Chapter 19 The Confrontation and the Solution

Dr. Stevens dropped out of hyperspace some light years from his home world of Capella-D. Now, all he wanted was peace and quiet so he could do his work. Alone on his ship, which was stationary and thus using very little power just enough to maintain life support and power his lab equipment, he set to work with his many mutation samples of DNA. His goal was a super-mutation, one that satisfied his own goals for revenge.

Not far away, the Serpientes scout ships had already discovered the populous world of Capella-D, literally overflowing with monkeys, but with the serious drawback of being heavily defended by rather large battleships. First Commander of Sporn turned his attention toward the solution of this minor problem that stood between their food source and the master race. The Serpientes considered themselves the ultimate in evolution. Superior intelligence, superior bodies, superior technology — all combined to satiate their rather large egos. That they also possessed and used telepathy was a mere trifle to these snake people.

Onboard the Sporn were ten thousand Serpientes. Most were now on subsistence levels. Their food reserves were dangerously low, but that had been anticipated and expected. Everyone who had signed on for this lengthy trip to another galaxy had known the risks and agreed to them. There wasn't any guarantee that they'd find monkeys in this new galaxy. If they had not, then their scientists were prepared to sample indigenous species to see if there was another potential food source they could use. Certainly, on their home world, monkeys had all but disappeared. Starvation made people agree to most anything.

Three things bothered First Commander of Sporn. These monkeys had somehow developed space travel and had ships that could potentially damage theirs. Not good at all.

These monkeys possessed weapons that could kill a Serpientes, namely d-guns. That wasn't good either. Finally, the images of the poor scout who had his guts literally sliced open by one of these monkeys truly bothered him. That a monkey would even dare touch a holy Serpientes was unheard of on their home worlds. No, monkeys would flee, run, and scamper away just as fast as they could, which only added to the sport of catching one before eating it. No, here a monkey had actually approached a Serpientes and had used a blade of some kind to slit it open, very nearly from head to tail, laying its entire internal organs open for the flies to eat. Hideous beyond belief and a grave cause for concern.

He didn't doubt that their superior weapons could destroy the warships of the monkeys. Neither did he doubt that they could easily conquer this world of Capella-D, so ripe and plump with monkeys. What bothered him was that the monkeys on the ground had weapons that could kill his people, that some were fearless of them, and that those might gut them open. These bothered him greatly, and he searched for a solution to that before committing to an attack on these monkeys.

He had his scouts deployed in a sphere around Capella-D, though they kept their distance and avoided the monkey warships, which patrolled the area, looking for them. First Commander of Sporn was unwilling to provoke armed conflict until he'd solved the basic problem of the monkeys on the ground. To do that, he needed more information about these monkeys. Finally, he had a way to do just that.

"Firssst Commander," an aide broke his concentration. "A ssscout ssship isss reporting that they have sssighted one of the monkeysss transssport ssshipsss in ssspace not far from thisss world. It isss not moving and sssensorsss indicate that there isss one monkey life form on it. Your ordersss, Firssst Commander?"

"Hum. Only one? Tractor it and bring the monkey to me. Sssee that it isss not harmed. I wisssh to interrogate it," he replied, thinking perhaps this was the break that he was waiting for.

Dr. Stevens was hard at work and didn't even know that

316

a thousand foot long, serpentine-like ship had discovered his ship. Nor did he sense its tractor beam locking onto his ship. In fact, he wasn't aware that he had been captured and was being transported through space to the mother ship of the Serpientes! He was entirely too engrossed in his work to notice such immaterial things. Nothing was going to stop the Dragon from having his revenge. After all, they'd killed his wife, his son, his daughter, hadn't they?

A loud pounding on his bay doors finally distracted him. "What the hell is going on? I'm in space. I'm busy, go away!" He yelled, very much annoyed that someone dare to disturb him.

Open this door or we will rip it open. That appeared in his mind. "Go away. Can't you see I'm busy?" he yelled, now very much annoyed. Then, he realized he was drifting in space, so how could anyone be knocking on his bay doors? "Well, this is interesting. I best go take a look." He headed down the hall to the bay doors and peered through the viewport.

"Who the hell are you? What are you?" he shouted at what looked like some giant snake. It had the head of a snake, if one considered that a snake could have a two foot in diameter body and head. While it wasn't as long as some constrictor snakes that he'd heard about in school years and years ago, still it was twenty feet long. What caught his attention were the tiny arms and legs that it possessed. "How very curious. It seems I've discovered another mutation of nature!" He wasn't afraid of snakes, primarily because outside of once seeing one in a cage in a zoo when he was a boy, he'd never come across one before.

Another slightly larger snake moved up, pushing the one that he was staring at out of the way. *Who are you? I'm First Commander of Scorn.*

"Hey, are you talking to me in my head? Telepathy or something?"

Yes. Who are you?

"Well, I'm the Dragon! I'm Dr. Able Stevens, the universe's most brilliant geneticist, and you are interrupting my genetic experiments. So go away."

Genetics? How interesting that monkeys should

develop such a study. Tell me, what kind of genetic experiments are you doing? And what is this Dragon thing?

"I'm the Dragon. I'm going to get my revenge of everyone on Capella-D for what they did to my family. I'm trying to create the perfect genetic mutation in here, so go away, and leave me to my revenge," he declared. Then, it dawned on him that he'd never known that snakes possessed telepathy. "Say, you look like you've been mutated as well. Snakes don't have arms and legs, even if yours are so tiny."

"Thisss monkey interessstsss me," he pointed out to the guards nearby. "I'll play along with him." *Tell me about your research, your perfect genetic mutation. Are there many such mutations among your kind?* He purposely refrained from calling him a monkey. No need to insult the monkey just yet.

"You are seriously interested in my work?" Dr. Stevens asked.

But of course. We have geneticists here with us as well. Please, tell me about these mutations of yours and about your thirst for revenge.

"Well, why don't you come onboard so I can show you? I have many photos and sample DNA and more," Dr. Stevens replied, very pleased that someone was actually paying attention to him. He opened the bay ramp, and the First Commander of Sporn entered. "This way. I have a complete lab that I stole in here. Be careful of the equipment. I wouldn't want you to get hurt." He led the giant snake back to his work computer.

"Now, here are the basic mutations that have been uncovered. This particular one is what killed my family. As you can see, they have lost their arms, among other serious changes. With those lip disks, they can't really speak and be understood anymore. The drawback is that they are completely helpless and can't survive without having someone helping them with everything. But they are hermaphrodites. You do know what that is, don't you?"

Of course. Please, continue. This is most interesting indeed, Dr. Stevens.

"Here is a minor one. The men lost their hands. Now, this one was caused by a pulsar's radiation. The females lose both their arms and legs making them more than helpless. And look at this new one that has only recently made its appearance. See, their legs join at their knees and merge into one lower leg and foot. Their only mode of locomotion is by hopping. Combined with no arms, they are darn helpless as well, particularly so I do believe. Of course, there are bunches of competent geneticists on Ashford-5, who are able to undo many of these genetic mutations, curse them anyway. They weren't there to help my wife, son, and daughter, now were they? Oh, one other detail that I discovered on Ashford-5. These hermaphrodites, they breed at an alarming rate. They have more than double the usual number of children, more like four or five times the usual number."

Oh this is most interesting, Dr. Stevens. And what is it that you are trying to do to get your revenge?

"Oh, simple. I'm trying to work out a super-mutation, and then find a way to infect all of Capella-D with it. I aim to show everyone on my world that they had no right to deny my family their immediate cures. After all, I'm their leading geneticist, and my family ought to have been treated right away. Instead, they were left to rot! Hell, they would have died of old age long before they would be given their cures! The Dragon will come one day soon and bring them all down!" Dr. Stevens declared with vengeance and passion.

Brilliant work, Dr. Stevens, positively brilliant. I believe that we both desire the same thing with Capella-D. Have you a way to introduce this new super-mutation of yours to the world?

"Well, no. Not exactly. The bio agent method is wholly unknown to me. How it works or how to produce it. I'm currently working on the actual mutation DNA strands. That comes first. Then, I'll have to figure out a way to deliver it."

I see. Yes, first things first. That's always the best way to proceed. You say that these mutations result in hermaphrodites breeding rapidly?

"Oh yes, since the men can then have babies too. Besides, I think with the lip plates and being so helpless, about all that they can do is breed. Of course, they need others to care for their every need," he answered.

319

I believe my geneticists can work out a method of delivery, if you can work out your super-mutation. However, perhaps we could work out the perfect super-mutation together, First Commander of Sporn suggested, sending along a bit of telepathic enforced agreement into his mind.

"Oh, that would be perfect, just perfect," Dr. Stevens agreed. "Which of these did you prefer?"

"Hermaphrodites — that goes without saying. We want them to breed and breed. The giant breasts are a must and their lip things. We don't want them talking to each other, now do we? Just breeding. And that single leg will cut down on their mobility quite nicely, but we can't have them helpless, can we? Who would take care of their needs so they can breed and survive in this form?"

"Ah yes. Some of my own thinking. Make them suffer. No short lifetime as a way of avoiding the torture they deserve. I agree. Let them have arms to feed themselves with, yes." Dr. Stevens began using his computer to put together bits of several photos forming up a complete picture of his proposed super-mutation.

As the First Commander watched, he had a few more suggestions that would impair the monkeys from ever gutting another Serpientes. One mutation cure gave them very long hair that would be in their way. Another yielded very long fingernails which, he correctly presumed, would prevent them from securely grasping a bladed weapon with which to gut them, assuming they even could do so while in this new form. The giant breasts looked extremely delicious to him, very good breast meat indeed. His stomach growled, longing for a good meal. He would have eaten Dr. Stevens if he had not needed him to produce this super-mutation.

Finally, both were satisfied with the proposed super-mutation. *How soon can it be ready?*

"It is a most delicate operation. I must graft a bit of this to a bit of that to a bit of that. Days, weeks at most. The Dragon must not hurry. We want perfection. How soon can your method of deployment be ready?" he asked what concerned him the most. He was confident he could piece together the driving DNA forces, but actually how to infect people eluded him.

It will be ready in time. I'll make my people work overtime if needed. Carry on. I'll visit you each day to see how you are doing and tell you how we're coming along as well. You're doing brilliant work, Dr. Stevens, positively brilliant. He sensed the monkey's ego soaring, which was his intention.

On July 15, Dr. Stevens had his prototype super-mutation ready to go. Proudly, he announced it to the First Commander of Sporn when he made his daily inspection. "Now we really ought to test it to make sure it works properly."

Very well done, Dr. Stevens. Commendable. I came to announce that we have the replication and dispersing agents ready to go as well. I do agree that we ought to have a test of it. If you'll allow me to take a sample back to my scientists, they'll insert it in the appropriate agents. Then, we'll have to test it, oh Great Black Dragon.

"I've made you a copy of it in this sealed tube. Make sure that it doesn't break. I've no idea what it might do to your people. Probably nothing, but then I wouldn't like to gamble," he cautioned the First Commander of Sporn. He had dark patches under his eyes. He'd not slept much during these intense weeks that he'd spent developing his super-mutation. Only now that it was done did he feel the cost on his own body. "I believe that I need a good night's sleep."

Quite right. You've been working very hard these weeks. Rest. Let my people do the rest. I'll let you know when we're ready for the test and later for the deployment of your ultimate revenge, the First Commander of Sporn replied. He gave a slight mental push and watched as Dr. Stevens fell asleep in his own lab chair. His body really was exhausted, but he was content. He now had the means for his long overdue revenge!

He delivered the vial to his own research people. Already they had been working to add their own final touches to the mixture. They had been familiar with the reproductive mechanism of monkeys on their worlds and had perfected a slight genetic alteration, which they introduced in a last ditch

Vic Broquard

attempt to breed more monkeys before they became nearly extinct. Desperate folks will try anything to preserve their primary source of food from dying out. It was a minor tweak, but vitally important if these monkeys were going to breed rapidly.

When his people were ready, First Commander of Sporn ordered the capture of a male and female of the monkeys from Capella-D, which a scout patrol obtained during a midnight raid on the surface. They landed near a very small village and stunned an adult pair of monkeys, though against orders, they devoured the three adolescents that were in the home. Their raid went undetected.

First Commander of Sporn escorted Dr. Stevens to his lab to watch the test run, carefully avoiding any sensitive areas of his enormous ship. In essence, the doctor was led down seemingly endless corridors, all institutional white, and D-shaped. The floor itself was flat but the rest formed part of a circle when looked at in a cross section. He was led to an observation window, where he could see a naked man and woman lying on sterile, small beds. Another giant snake was in the room arranging the test. He looked up and through the window at the First Commander who telepathically sent him the go ahead.

A vaporous gas, slightly yellow enveloped the very small room, but only after the technician left and sealed the door. Soon, the monitoring equipment showed that both had entered a deep coma. Now, they had to wait four days to see the final product.

Each morning, the First Commander of Sporn brought Dr. Stevens here to see the progress and to review the medical information being gathered, though one of the technicians had to relay the results to the doctor, who could not understand their speech or writing or symbols. On the fourth morning, the results were obvious. Both had dual sexual organs. Both had enormous breasts, half again larger than their heads, which caused many Serpientes to drool over them. Their upper legs had bowed out some and had fused together at their knee with a single large leg and foot below the juncture. Their pelvis regions had also adapted though that wasn't readily visible.

322

Their hair was nearly six feet long, lush, thick, and full of pain sensors. Their waists were tiny, and their lips, split. Two giant loops of lips dangled from their faces. Their fingernails were six inches long and filled with pain sensors, though that also wasn't visible.

At last, the pair awakened. At first, they screamed. Well, who wouldn't, Dr. Stevens smirked to himself. Here was the very first of his long-dreamed revenge! The two soon became aware of the other and their screaming ceased, rather perplexing Dr. Stevens who was enjoying their panic immensely, reminding him of his wife's initial reaction. What happened next surprised him even more. The moment the two became aware of the other, both had instant erections. Before he could even question this tiny detail, the two struggled mightily to get to each other and immediately began a most passionate exchange including dual intercourse, pleasing the commander immensely. His breeding program would work most beautifully this time!

We'll sedate them, move them to living quarters suited to them, and monitor their survival abilities. If they do all right for a week, then we can begin your complete Dragon revenge, Dr. Stevens. Well done.

"Yes, yes, most perfect indeed!" he replied. Before he knew it, the First Commander stunned him. He too was hauled off to the lab and given a dose of his own super-mutation agent.

"Time for the attack. Launch all fighter ssshipsss. Take usss in to Capella-D now," the First Commander of Sporn ordered. Without any advanced warning, his large fleet headed towards the populace world. War had begun.

Three battleships, four heavy cruisers, and ten light cruisers swarmed up to meet the invading, slithering, extremely long snake-like spaceships of the Serpientes. Canon fire erupted everywhere. Some likened it to a giant fireworks display, only this one was deadly serious. Quickly, the defenders found that most of their weapons were primarily ineffective against these invading Serpientes ships. However, some commanders recalled the initial reports from Beltazar-C and ordered their smaller ships to dive into the open mouths of the smaller ships, continuously firing their canons.

This tactic worked. Smaller slithering ships exploded, though taking the crews of the suicide attackers with them. Still, they were fighting back in a desperate attempt to hold off the swarm of snake ships. The battle lasted for over an hour, during which live video streams were sent down to Surface Command, which then relayed them throughout the Federation, along with pleas for help!

For a short time, it looked like the suicide attacks of the desperate defenders might be winning the day, but then First Commander of Sporn ordered a similar tactic. His slithering ships shot straight at one of the large battleships, ramming into it. The resulting explosion took out both ships in an immense ball of fire, temporarily blinding everyone remotely close to them. Emboldened by this, he ordered the other large ships similarly attacked. Within minutes, the battle ended. Three small and damaged cruisers jumped into hyperspace, leaving behind a space filled with rubble. This zone would be impassible for some time to come.

"All right! The monkey planet isss oursss!" the First Commander of Sporn declared victoriously. "Sssend out the Black Dragon now. I'll get Dr. Ssstevensss to the monitor so he can witnesss his revenge, before I sssend him down to propagate more monkeysss for usss."

Dr. Stevens was a basket case. Alone in some room, he felt urges with no way to relieve them except on himself, which he had done a dozen times already. He had no idea that he was now pregnant. He felt betrayed utterly. His hatred for the snake people now surpassed his hatred for those on Capella-D. When the First Commander of Sporn appeared, he tried to curse him to hell. He flailed his arms trying to reach him, but nearly fell over. Hopping on one leg, he could barely keep his balance. His massive bosom obscured his foot, and he tripped over his long hair, and would have fallen down had not the First Commander of Sporn intervened.

Come, come, Dr. Stevens. This is your time to witness your ultimate revenge. Come with me. See your Black Dragon unleashing the super-mutation upon all of Capella-D.

That did the trick, at least for the moment. He just had

to witness his long-sought revenge. If so, then his own plight was worth it. Soon, he could somehow kill himself. Hopping as best he could, though the sheer weight of his bosom constantly threatened to pull him over, if his back didn't crack in half first, Dr. Stevens moved down the hallway. Pain shot through his back even though he was hunched over. The bobbing of his bosom threatened to snap his back at any moment. Still, he just had to witness his revenge.

At the monitor, he saw what looked like a huge Black Dragon, identical in shape to the one tattooed on his back. The First Commander of Sporn had merely copied it out of deference to him as a little going away present. As the dragon ship orbited Capella-D from a low orbit, a yellowish gas trailed behind it, sinking rapidly towards the surface. Part of the compound contained tiny micro-balls that used gravity to pull them downward. When they reached the surface at terminal velocity, the balls disintegrated, releasing more of the toxin.

It will take but an hour to cover the entire world fully. Four days from now, your revenge will be total and complete, Dr. Stevens. Congratulations on a job so very well done.

After allowing the man to watch the Black Dragon ship for a time, the First Commander led him back to his chamber, locking him inside. What he didn't tell Dr. Stevens was his troops had hooked into the world's communications systems and broadcasted a warning telling them they were about to be infected with a super-mutant virus made by the Black Dragon, Dr. Stevens, and that if they wanted to live, they should take off all their clothes and shoes before they fell unconscious. Sometime later, they discovered many city leaders had not only gotten the warning, but had repeated it continuously on a repeater loop, which was still running when four days later, a scout ship took him down to the surface, releasing him into the population. Hopping away from the ship, he cursed and swore, but he couldn't even understand his own words. Then, he spotted another and his felt an instant arousal. The overwhelming urge was again upon him. Fortunately for him, the other person felt the same way as soon as he or she saw him. Now, he couldn't tell the sex of this person. They hopped over to each other, hugged, embraced, fell down, and had frantic sex, just as billions of others were or already had.

Meantime, a little less than ten thousand Serpientes swooped down on one smaller town and proceeded to satiate their long hunger. They reported these were particularly delicious monkeys. The First Commander of Sporn looked very pleased himself, as he daintily devoured a pair of the monster breasts. We've found heaven, he thought. However, he still had two more situations to handle before he and his brethren could sit back and relax in their new-found world of potentially an infinite supply of food.

Part of his solution was already finished. Based on Dr. Stevens talks, they had pieced together the language spoken by these monkeys. By recording the spoken words and knowing what they meant via telepathic contact with him as he spoke them, some of his people had put together a formal speech, which would very likely soon have to be delivered. The First Commander of Sporn fully expected the space faring breed of monkeys to retaliate and try to retake this world. He wanted to prevent that if possible. He'd lost too many of his scout ships just taking the world. However, the monkeys wouldn't know that.

The other part of his solution would handle the only known monkeys who could potentially undo these amazing super-mutations, as unlikely as that might possibly be. Already he'd sent a lone scout loaded with another batch of the mutating agent on its way to that world, having given them a most specific target to saturate with the agent, again based on Dr. Stevens' information. Now, he merely had to wait, more contented than he'd been in many, many years. His belly was full but he dared not take a nice long nap, not just yet. True, many of the thousands were doing just that, having overeaten and gotten very groggy as a result.

The Federation responded to the cries for help from their member world of Capella-D, ordering all warships to converge on that world. Having seen the incredible destruction these aliens could wreak, they decided that this might make a good place to make their stand, since the aliens were marshaling their forces here.

Since many of their warships were scattered around

their entire spiral arm with many searching for where the Serpientes had gone, several days would be needed to muster their entire armada there. By then, top command surmised that this formidable alien enemy would have fled elsewhere. At least that was what their best strategists suggested. They couldn't risk that happening, since they'd already spent months trying to locate these strange ships. Hence, top command sent four other battleships and some supporting cruisers that could reach Capella-D within a day. Their job was to keep track of the enemy until all the remaining fleet could catch up with them.

Admiral Juan del Migos paced the floor of his war room. Three other battleships had reached him, and their small fleet was bearing down on Capella-D. "Remember, don't engage unless they fire at us," he reminded his gunners over the ship-wide intercom. We're to watch them until the rest of the fleet arrives. Then, we'll smash them." Brave talk, he thought, but he knew better. Already the figures were in on the casualties that the fleet around Capella-D had suffered. Five battleship gone, ignoring the heavy losses of the cruisers. With only four battleships, he dare not pick a fight today. Best wait until a dozen could back him up.

"Sir, we're picking up a communication. From the alien snakes, I think," a comm officer called out, attracting his attention.

"Put it on speaker phone," the admiral barked.

"To the leaders of the battleships. We don't wish to fight more battles. We wish to parley. Reply on this frequency if you also wish to parley." The voice sounded artificial somehow, as though words were being strung together.

"Sir, the other admirals are reporting hearing the same message. They are asking for your response," the comm officer said, pulling his earphones off to make sure he heard what Admiral Juan would say.

"All right. We are here to delay. I'll parley. Open up that frequency."

"Aye, aye, sir. Frequency is live."

"Whoever this is, I'm Admiral Juan del Migos. You want to talk, then talk. I'm listening. Over."

"This is First Commander of Sporn. We do not wish to fight your people any further. We came in search of a new home and have found it here on this world that you call Capella-D. We will live on this world and will not travel beyond this star's system, if you'll leave us to live in peace. We wish only to be left alone to live in peace. I give you my word as the First Commander of Sporn that we'll remain here on this world and not bother you any further. However, if you continue to attack us, we'll defend ourselves. Already, we have destroyed five of your great ships with no damage to our own mother ship. Consider your choices well, Admiral Juan del Migos." The message again sounded as though words had been pieced together somehow. Further, the entire message was repeated twice before silence came on that frequency.

"Admiral Juan del Migos here. A temporary truce then. I'll relay your proposal to our top command and get back to you with their decision. In the meantime, we will not fire upon your ships as long as they do not fire upon ours or attempt to leave this system. Over and out."

He then opened a secure line to the Admiralty Round Table on Cass-C, where over two thousands leaders sat waiting on the latest word from the field. In the center of the table they had arrayed tokens representing their battleships and heavy cruisers, with a coffee cup representing the enemy fleet at Capella-D.

Much discussion could center on these men and women who controlled the Federation of Planets. While they held the title of admiral, few had ever seen any real combat, and more than half of them were really merely appointed or elected politicians who were given this title. They were acutely aware of just how badly the forces had been defeated at Capella-D, having watched live, streaming video of the battle, though by the end of the conflict, each feed had suddenly gone out as that ship was destroyed. Some claim that pure fear dominated these men. Others suggest that they were basically cowards, while other insisted that they believed this First Commander of Sporn really did want peace and would not venture beyond the Capella planetary system. Since this world was now considered destroyed, they could care less about it. Saving themselves was paramount.

In the end, the Admiralty Round Table voted to accept this peace offering, radioing their acceptance to Admiral Juan del Migos. A relieved admiral then reopened the designated frequency to report high command's acceptance of their peace offering. "We will keep a few ships just outside Capella-D's planetary system to verify that you are living up to your word, First Commander of Sporn. Over."

"Excellent. Today marks the first day of peace between our peoples. That is all." Again, he felt like the words were somehow pieced together. No human would speak in such a fashion. Still, if they wanted peace, he certainly wasn't going to interfere with the Admiralty Round Table's decision. Thus, he ordered the four battleships and their supporting cruisers to back out of the planetary system. On his battle board, he positioned each one so that they had all areas covered.

He barked, "I want twenty-four/seven eyes on these alien snake ships! I'm to be notified immediately of any violations of their proposed treaty. Do I make myself clear on this? Over." One by one, the other admirals and majors acknowledged his orders, and he retired to his cabin where his short-armed wife was waiting nervously for him.

On August 1, 1451, the Serpientes scout ship arrived over Ashford-5, specifically over Plateau Grado, the only spaceport on Tierra and close to Exchange City. It was three in the morning, local time. The skeletal night crew spotted the huge unidentified ship on their sensors and sounded the alarm. They dutifully recorded the strange sounding message being sent to the control tower.

"Ashford-5 residents. Remove all your clothing and shoes now or die from the super-mutation, compliments of the Black Dragon, Dr. Stevens, and First Commander of Sporn." That was the entirety of the message, repeated and recorded several times. Later analysis from the geosat images clearly showed the several thousand foot long, slithering ship coming in low over Valen, releasing a gas cloud behind it, sweeping over the spaceport and circling Exchange city several times. From this point on, streaming video covered what happened next.

Five heavy cruisers who were the Ataro Empire's constant guards protecting the valuable fuel refinery on one of the two moons, swooped down on the unsuspecting serpent-like ship, all canons blazing, but failing to harm it in any way. As the snake ship moved sluggishly upwards to regain its orbit, one of the old flying saucers that had been given to Ashford-5 from the doll people shot upwards at maximum speed.

Jan was a light sleeper. The alarm sounded at the spaceport had wakened her. She saw the snake ship and raced to the experimental lab as fast as she could run. There, she broke in and entered the emergency launch code for one of the flying saucers, shoving its throttle to maximum acceleration. Had a person been inside that ship, their body would have been flattened into a pancake from the terrific g-force of its acceleration, which meant nothing to the doll people. She had timed the launch perfect, aided by the sluggishness of the snake ship this low and in this dense an atmosphere.

The saucer struck the snake ship in its middle, cutting it in half. At least one video frame showed two halves before the explosion lit up the night sky, jarring everyone in Exchange City awake. The noise and fireball, which rapidly vanished, was seen as far away as Valen. Fortunately, no physical damage was done to anything on the ground, but everyone was awake. Again, that was quite fortunate, for within minutes, Governor Sheila sent out the recorded warning to the queens, who relayed it to her Tower members, who in turn used their *mentales* gifts to activate the citywide sound system. Thus, everyone in Exchange City heard the warning. While some began to feel groggy, no one was caught wearing clothing or shoes when they fell into the four-day coma.

Part III Resolutions

Chapter 20 Impact

The night of August 1, Drs. Zia, Alexandra, and Diego met briefly. The last of the terrorist victims had been cured and sent home. At long last, things had quieted down around the genetics lab. "All we have now are the few Calder mutations that are being located up in Brom and elsewhere," Dr. Diego said. "Finally, we have some peace and quiet so we can get on with trying to figure out additional cures."

"Amen to that," his wife, Alexandra exclaimed. "There shouldn't be too many more Calder mutations to handle. We have the test kits sent off to all the towers and major guilds. If we get too many of them back, we can assign lab techs to run the tests. We should be able to nip this recessive gene in the bud. I doubt that many couples who each have this recessive gene will want to gamble on it, though I wonder if they'll just ignore it and continue to kill mutant babies."

"I hope not," Dr. Zia broke in. "That's criminal. After all, they are living human beings, just with malformed bodies is all. Honestly, those first two that we treated — Lisa and Becca — they were extremely bright and talented young women. Anyway, I do look forward to peace and quiet so we can actually make some headway with some of these resistant mutation effects. Estrella on Jarvis-B is going to need all the help she can get."

"Yes she will. It's amazing just how far we geneticists have come in the last hundred years," Dr. Alexandra commented and yawned. "Well, time for bed. I look forward to a nice, peaceful day tomorrow!"

The loud explosion and vibration of her bed woke Alexandra and Diego in the middle of the night, just as it did everyone else. Not long after that, they heard the announcement being replayed and received an emergency call from the queens. That was as far as they got. They slumped onto the floor near their comm center, drifting into comas along with everyone else in Exchange City. All told, forty three thousand six hundred five men, women, and children were comatose in the city. Another hundred who lived in the surrounding farms were in comas, along with nearly twenty thousand around Valen, which lucked out. Only the eastern half of the city was infected, but that included Valen Castle and Tower, unfortunately, along with most of their Royal Guards.

On a positive note, the Imperial Tower was able to get out a warning that they were being attacked by the snake-like aliens via a telepathic warning to all other towers. That prevented far more people from becoming infected just by entering the town. Hence, absolutely no one entered the city during those four days! Not even thieves dared risk becoming some helpless mutant! Thus, what could well have been a complete disaster was avoided. Nothing was stolen, except people's lives — they were still physically living, but their lives were drastically altered, which precisely sixty three thousand one hundred eleven discovered when they finally awoke from their comas.

Although nearly half of these were already hermaphrodites and nearly a thousand wore the giant lip plates as a status symbol, not even these were quite prepared for their drastically altered bodies when their comas ended. The other half who were not hermaphrodites to begin with had the most trouble adapting, particularly so with the once normal men and boys, who now had become like the very "freaks" that they often disliked, particularly so for the nineteen thousand four hundred six victims around the eastern portion of Valen proper.

There was one small benefit. The few existing hermaphrodites whose feet had only been partially restored now discovered that their single large foot was normal, meaning it rested flat on the ground. Only two found themselves in substantially better shape afterwards. Those were Queens Lilly and Misty. They had been armless, as required of any Ataro Empire queen, but they awoke to find that they now had arms and hands with the half-foot long nails to go along with everything else including only the one lower leg.

When the queens awoke slightly groggy, Lilly said,

"Dear, I wonder what happened this time. Oh, arms, hands!"
She and Misty sat up examining their new hands. "Cool! I can
feel things with my nails."

"Pain sensors," Misty pointed out. "Wow. Our bosoms
are gigantic." She carefully pulled back some of her much
thicker wavy blonde hair to get a better view of hers. "Hey, I'm
able to feel things with my hair. It's changed too." Then she
noticed her bowed upper legs and single large lower leg and
foot. "Oh crap! Calder mutation!"

The two blondes scooted over to the edge of their bed to
see themselves better, but their bosoms blocked their line of
sight. Instead, they looked at each other's new lower anatomy.
"Well, your curly hair isn't curly anymore," Misty commented.
That held true for all of the victims. Later on, the geneticists
discovered that anyone who had had curly hair now had wavy
hair. Those who had had wavy hair or straight hair now had
perfectly straight hair. Every victim's hair was six feet long,
more than twice as thick as it had been and filled with neurons
and axons, which gave them a sense of feel with their hair,
even with just one strand. Further, tying it into a tight ponytail
caused significant pain, much to the dismay of both men and
women, who wanted it up or back and out of the way. A
frequent comment that the geneticists heard was how strange
it was to be feeling with hair and the long nails. These victims
had a good sense of touch with their nails and hair.

When the two queens got up to desperately make use of
their toilet, they discovered just how annoying their mammoth
bosoms were as well as trying to keep their balance and hop
everywhere. On top of that, by the time that they finished
relieving themselves, their backs were complaining from the
nearly extra thirty to forty pounds of breasts that they were
now having to support. "We're going to need those steel re-
enforced corsets very soon. My back can't take much of this,"
Lilly grumbled.

"Hey, we don't have any clothes or shoes that will fit
either. My god, Lilly, we're going to have to take some fast
action, because all of Exchange City is in the same mess that
we're in!" exclaimed Misty, finally realizing the nature of the
disaster that had fallen on them during the night.

What could well have been the nightmare that was occurring on Capella-D was avoided here solely because of the sheer number of *mentales* gifted who were in Exchange City and to a much lesser extent in Valen. Nearly half of the population of Exchange City was a telepath and had various other gifts. For the first few hours as the thousands awoke from their comas, messages flew from telepath to telepath, particularly to the geneticists and the women running Elegant Fashions Inc. The queens and Governor Sheila quickly took charge, sending out volumes of orders via telepathy.

The first action was to make use of the four Fabrication machines. The governor had one, as did the queens. Also Elegant Fashions Inc had one primarily used for clothing and shoes, while the geneticists had one for their complex work. Within a day, thousands of the terribly restrictive corsets poured out of the four machines. During the following week, most everyone hopped around the city either completely naked or wearing their newly acquired corset. After that period, Elegant Fashions Inc managed to produce a simple dress that could at least fit everyone.

Still, it took two people working together to get a corset fully tightened onto another person. Their long nails continually interfered with virtually everything they did. Even picking up silverware was challenging. Once a person had their much needed corset fully tightened and finally relieving their back pains substantially, he or she then gasped for breath, and some even fainted during those first few frantic weeks of recovery. After a couple of weeks of wearing them, they were finally used to them sufficiently to get by, as long as they didn't jump too much too quickly. The second week, Elegant Fashions Inc pumped out a sturdy boot for everyone, which helped significantly, especially for those who had to work or be outside.

While those with the *mentales* gifts had pretty much blocked out the implanted suggestion to engage in intercourse with everyone they saw, the first few days, nearly thirty thousand weren't. As a result, when the geneticists and doctors began examining everyone who had been infected, forming up a complete list for the cures once they developed them, they were flabbergasted to discover that fifty thousand men and women were now pregnant, including many *mentales* gifted. Even the queens had indulged themselves. Worse, quite a number of unmarried young teens were also pregnant, opening up a completely new problem that had to be faced about nine months down the road.

Renata stepped in at this point. Sobbing twelve year old girls and boys just were not ready to become mothers. Quietly, she used her gifts on them, making sure that their pregnancies vanished.

What really helped in Exchange City was the willingness of the previously existing hermaphrodites to lend a helping hand to all those who had been normal humans before the attack. Renata also got them scheduled for Basic Therapy, calling in many favors owed to her by others not living around the city. What could well have been a fatal nightmare for so many got turned into a survivable, but nasty situation. To the west in Valen, those in the uninfected half of the city came to the aid of those that were infected, helping them find ways to get by those terrible first few weeks. Still, a frantic month passed before the situation in Exchange City and Valen could remotely be said to be under control.

The biggest question that everyone had was how could they get anything done if all they could do was hop on the one leg and with almost no lateral movement possible. Their necessary corsets removed most all remaining abdomen lateral motions or twisting, forcing the person to hop to change facing. This was solved partly by the mass duplication and distribution of crutches. Using them, they didn't have to hop to get around, improving the situation. That combined with the overly long nails made accomplishing almost any task a challenge in inventiveness.

After that frantic first month, the designers at Elegant Fashions Inc finally had time to work out far better apparel for the sixty thousand in dire need. First, they invented a new kind of underpants, unisex of course. Based on baby diapers, the front and back halves were not connected. Instead, one put it on like a diaper. The ends were then hooked together rather than pinned as diapers were usually done. That small problem solved, they next tackled the real problem: proper clothing.

With fashion-conscious people, several distinct types of outfits had to be created. First, for women, they created fancy form-fitting satin gowns that followed their curves, which were very pronounced from the bust to the fourteen-inch waists to the wide, expansive hips, on down the bowed upper legs. The gowns then curved in sharply at the knee, covering the single lower leg tightly down to the ankle. A variation ended with a flair at the knee. A second style was a redesigned professional woman's skirt and blouse that many original hermaphrodites wore around the Imperial Castle and Manors. The skirt also ended at the knee. Then, a working woman's dress was designed, though it mirrored the fancy gown's design only done in an easy-wash cotton. Naturally, these came in various colors.

Men's requirements were nearly similar. The fancy gown was copied and made into a soft leather bottom fastened with a belt, though with the tiny waists, belts were little more than a fashion statement or a declaration that the wearer was a man. Some were also made from heavy work jeans. The men had no choice but to wear a shirt that looked more like a woman's blouse than anything else. Finally, the bottoms were also made in suit material, with matching silk tops or blouses. They gave up trying to figure out a way to make a men's suit coat. With the mammoth bosoms, they looked too poorly to wear.

Footwear was also hastily redesigned. For workers, they provided a sturdy work boot. For men, they reworked their basic business shoes. Women were given the same work boots or they could choose a patent leather flat in colors that matched their gowns. All heels for women were totally out of the question. It was difficult enough hopping on one foot without trying to wear their fancy six-inch heels. Many women grumbled about this though. At least with fall and winter coming, those who had to go outside would be able to stay warm.

The many geneticists struggled to continue their work, hampered significantly by their half-foot long nails, which continually made the simplest things difficult and clumsy.

Their bosoms continued to block their vision and often got physically in the way of their work, ignoring that they had to hop everywhere or use crutches.

After a month's worth of analysis, Dr. Diego declared, "My god. Our DNA is such a miss-mash of mutated sequences upon mutated sequences, how the hell are we to make any sense out of this?"

Dr. Zia added, "I know. We have changes lying on top of changes on top of changes. It's a miracle that our bodies are still alive!"

"So what can we do?" Dr. Alexandra asked, sighing and wondering if this was the end, that there wasn't anything more that could be done to cure the new victims.

"There's only one sequence that is likely easily handled anymore," Dr. Diego replied. "Take a look at the breast sequences. Those are still pretty much undoctored with by all of the other mutations and cures. We might be able to reduce them down to size."

"Dear, that would be a fabulous first step!" Dr. Alexandra gushed.

He grinned, though it was invisible behind his lip plates and stretched lip loops. "Dear, you don't enjoy playing with mine?"

She flushed. "Diego!" He laughed. After that, the three set to work on devising a cure to reduce breast sizes. This time, their cure could simply be injected into the person. Over a period of a week, the serum gradually did its work, reducing them down to what they had been on all Ashford-5 women and hermaphrodites.

Three months after the attack, their Fabrication machine produced enough serum to begin inoculating all sixty thousand plus victims, much to the annoyance of the designers at Elegant Fashions Inc. Now, they had to redesign their new line of apparel, though mostly it consisted of just reducing the gown's tops or blouses. However, with the reduced sizes, they finally were able to add men's jackets and suit coats to the mix available to men.

As winter came, the geneticists continued to see what else could be cured. The neurons in hair and nails proved quite baffling and challenging, primarily because of the repeated mutations and cures that had been given to the many hermaphrodites. In the end, they were only able to repair the hair and nails of those whose bodies had only become mutated with this latest alien attack. Those men, women, and children most definitely appreciated these two additional cures. However, the large original population of hermaphrodites began to realize that they were stuck with these changes. Worse, their children were likely to have them as well. Nevertheless, the geneticists didn't give up, but continued their research, but had little hope. They needed another huge breakthrough, which didn't seem either promising or coming in the near future.

On the political side, the queens and governor worked closely with the emperor, who kept them abreast of further developments. At first, it seemed that the Federation had given up and signed a peace treaty with the Serpientes, abandoning Capella-D to the snake aliens. Certainly, the snake creatures lived up to their agreement, staying within their new planetary system. However, that soon changed. One thing was clear though, the Federation's only way to destroy one of the snake-like spaceships was to ram it head on, blowing it and the Federation ship up. That is, suicide was the only effective way to take out these ships. Their energy screens were just too effective against Federation weapons. The change in tactics came not from the Federation Admiralty Round Table, but in clandestine broadcasts from Capella-D itself. Hearing these, Jan and Renata knew that they had to do something.

Chapter 21 Fighting Back

On Capella-D, not everyone was unhappy with the alien's super-mutation attack. Well over a hundred thousand previous victims, who had no arms along with all the other usual mutations and who were being cared for in large numbers of assisted living homes, woke up from their new comas to find that now they had arms once more! Their long nails were little more than an annoyance, for now they were no longer helpless! True, they had to hop instead of trying to walk in those precarious toe shoes, but hopping was drastically stabler for them, especially since they now had their arms back. Plus, they were already wearing the necessary corsets and were used to them.

However, the other billions of people were in very dire straits. For a time, all commerce and normal daily activities came to a screeching halt. Before the recovery began, half of the population of Capella-D died, most from falls or starvation, though some were eaten and some died fighting back.

General John Jones commanded the First Capella Rangers, whose barracks was on the outskirts of Whitehall, their capital city. When the original attack came, he ordered his men into full battle gear, ready to deploy and fight, should the snake aliens attempt a landing. Then came the dire warnings. From all the explosions overhead and the streaming video he and his staff watched, he knew that the battle above was lost and believed this warning, ordering his men to strip naked and get into their bunks. His fast action paid off four days later. His men were still alive.

General Jones was fifty years old and known as a "hard-ass," by his men — unrelenting, unforgiving, demanding, but wholly competent. He had the respect of his two thousand fighting rangers. That first week when nearly everyone else was obeying the implanted command to propagate with everyone they saw, his barked orders and will alone overrode these urges in his rangers, though few could really understand him, but then few could understand what anyone was saying.

Their lips dangled in giant loops, making speech almost unintelligible at first. He could still write, albeit clumsily because of his half-foot nails, and he posted orders everywhere.

It took them nearly a month to adapt well enough to their mutated bodies and still survive. That is, someone had to cook, wash dishes, and figure out how to cover their naked bodies, let alone how to move around by hopping and somehow still fight. Partly, he solved the problem by having the base doctors make and issue crutches to all soldiers. He wrote out specific orders that they were not to depend on the crutches when in combat situation, but could use them around the base, making movement easier than hopping.

The aliens controlled the skies, so he dare not send up shuttles to check on things. Instead, he sent out patrols in their armored cars, though even something as simple as this was difficult for the men to do. Their nails prevented grasping the steering wheel solidly. Driving with one foot that had no lateral movement possible caused a number of wrecks, since getting from the gas pedal to the brake pedal took turning the driver's body in the seat, via applying force with one's arms.

The scouts reported the suburban town of Crystal Gates was overrun with the snakes that had eaten every man, woman, and child in that town, close to ten thousand. That made General Jones furious. Now, the purpose of the alien snakes was clear in his mind. Humans were these snakes' food supply. The horrific mutations were done to disable the humans, making simple for the snakes to eat them. Hopping, one could hardly run from them or even defend against them.

Armed with this knowledge, which spread like wildfire through his men and later throughout all Capella-D, General Jones used it to fire up his men. He posted a number of sayings on barracks doors. Do you want to sit back and be food for the snakes? We must dine on snakes! He composed a dozen such postings, until he was satisfied his men were roaring mad. Then, he added the last one. Better to die taking a snake with you than to be eaten like a chicken.

The few initial skirmishes with these snakes demonstrated that they had some kind of personal armor that deflected d-gun shots. Well, that was just as well, because hindered tremendously by their long nails, the men could scarcely even fire them, assuming they could even get them out of their holsters. Armed with this data, General Jones took another approach. High explosives and grenades. These too proved useless, unless one was lucky enough to be able to toss a grenade or HE shell into the open mouth of a snake. That happened once and gave them their first "kill." General Jones wasn't out of options though, but only after thinking long and hard about the problem.

He'd solved the problem of long hair getting in everyone's way. He ordered them to wrap it around and around their necks. Problem solved. Discipline handled the nearly continuous complaints about severe back pains from the extra weight they were carrying in their bosoms. However, one aspect bothered him, though he didn't admit this to anyone. It was an aspect of the mutation.

His men had been quite fit, robust, with well-muscled arms. Some were able to lift very heavy weights, but all were able to do the required number of pushups, for example. After the mutation, their arms looked more like those of a woman, as far as the general was concerned. Gone were all his robust, very fit solders. Some even wrote out complaints about no longer being able to lift what they should or do their pushups.

In fact, there was no longer a single overweight person on Capella-D, but that fact would not be known for some time. More than a few complained about the loss of their "robust" or plump bodies, upset that they were just plain skinny. Another side effect of the mutation wasn't clear to the general at the start, but it became more apparent as months passed. As General Jones put it, "Men are simply not as aggressive as they used to be." Doctors later ascribed this subtle change to the much lowered testosterone levels in men. Perhaps, having a baby also greatly contributed to their new "outlook" on life. Women believed the latter, however.

What General Jones did know was that they were all food animals, if they didn't eliminate every one of these vile giant snakes. Grenades and HE shells didn't work. Ten men died bravely proving that detail. Worse, the snakes were now moving into the outlying suburbs of his city, systematically devouring men, women, and children, before destroying the homes and buildings that they'd lived in, marking this area as having been finished off, so to speak.

Late one night, he figured out how to take out a snake. Thermite. These charges burned so hot that they would melt through the hardest steel in seconds. Nothing in the Federation could withstand a thermite charge going off on its surface. In a battle scenario, these charges were intended to be used to breech the hull of a battleship, allowing his shock troops, his prized rangers, to board. He wrote out a long speech for his men, knowing that he best not try to actually speak. Few could really understand much of anything spoken now, not without a lot of repeats, confusions, and misunderstandings. His new plan simply would not allow for any misunderstanding. His speech went as follows and is now preserved in the Historical Archives on Capella-D.

"Men. The time has come for you to make the ultimate sacrifice so that our people can survive. You've sworn to protect the citizens of Capella-D with your lives. These vile snakes must be stopped before they devour all our good people. Our normal weapons have proven completely ineffective against them. There is one more action that we must try, one that surely will kill these wicked snakes. Thermite. Our demolitions experts will rig up thermite vests for you, with a handheld activator. Your job will be to hop up to a snake anyway that you can. Fall on it and then press the activator. Your sacrifice will eliminate one snake forever."

"We also know that some of the snakes take long naps after gorging themselves on our people. Our first test will be to get some thermite charges up to these sleeping beasts, back off, and detonate them. If this plan is successful, then we have a way to kill these fiends from hell. We will use the suicide vests against the awake beasts. I'm asking one squad to detonate a thermite charge on some sleeping beasts to prove this works. If it does, then we'll head into battle wearing thermite vests and wipe these nightmare creatures out of existence!"

General Jones got his volunteer squad. In fact, he had

dozens of squads who wanted to volunteer for the test mission. He picked one, led by Captain Leeds, a thirty year old veteran. It took them a day to get the satchel charges ready, hampered and hindered by their long nails. The next day, scouts began moving out, that is hopping out, to scour the edges of the city to locate the next wave of dining snakes. The men wore their headgear, allowing General Jones to monitor each squad, mostly by video, since their speech wasn't very understandable, but their hand signals were.

By noon, a sleeping mound of the snakes was located near a supermarket. They'd devoured a number of people, who had bravely hopped there in a desperate attempt to get food for themselves, their families, and small groups. General Jones gave the Go hand signal to Captain Leeds and watched his ten-man squad hopping out to head to that location, carrying satchel charges in backpacks. Silently, he said a prayer and watched their live video feed coming into his base HQ.

It took the men over an hour to hop to that location, and he could see the fatigue setting in. As they approached the supermarket, they were going slower and breathing very heavily, as though they'd just run ten miles or more. He saw six snakes curled up, napping. He saw the giant bulges in their forms, the digesting men and women they'd recently eaten. He fought the urge to gag and watched as they approached the snakes.

Damn, one was on guard duty! Captain Leeds also spotted that one and had two men move towards it, while the others hopped closer to the sleeping pile. The men were naked, of course, and had their long hair wrapped around their necks, out of their way. One by one, they took off their satchels, while two brave rangers danced around the waving head of the guard snake, distracting it. In horror, he watched the open-mouthed snake strike one of the two. One second, the man was hopping, trying to dodge the snake, and the next his body was gone. A bulge just behind the snake's head was all that was visible of the brave ranger. The second ranger tossed his satchel as close to the guard snake as he could. At that moment, Captain Leeds pressed the detonate switch.

For a moment, the video screens turned completely

white, so brilliant was the initial flash of the thermite explosion. When the intensity died down, he could see the intense burning of the thermite, along with volumes of smoke rising skyward. Then, he saw the first hopeful sign yet! Captain Leeds' arms punched high into the air! Likewise, his men echoed his victory punch. Seven snake bodies were writhing in their death throes! He saw Captain Leeds' hand signals and watched them begin hopping back out of the kill zone. Mission accomplished. General Jones smiled, though it wasn't visible in his giant dangling loops of lips. The war had just taken a new turn!

As the squad left the area of the supermarkets, a number of civilians came out to wave and cheer them. Captain Leeds and his nine men waved back. They'd finally struck a counter-blow to the enemy, but they were physically exhausted by the time they hopped the several miles back to their base.

Expecting retaliation, General Jones ordered all remaining thermite charges to be divided among his remaining squads. The next day, he sent all the squads out to various areas of the city via their trucks, which also carried their cots and food supplies. From now on, each squad was on its own. Their orders, watch for sleeping serpents and eliminate them. For the first time, some of the desperate people within the city felt a glimmer of safety from the marauding Serpientes. If they couldn't find any sleeping snakes, then they were to take out any snake that they could find in their zone of the city.

General Jones' last communication to the Federation was a plea for help, written on a card so they could understand him. The card also relayed the data that thermite charges killed the snake aliens. For a month, a deadly game of ranger versus snake played out on the streets of the city. By the end of the month, the snakes had devoured the last of these brave rangers. However, over two thousand of the Serpientes were also history and that was a major problem for the First Commander of Sporn.

"What isss going on down there?" barked First Commander of Sporn. He'd just gotten the next day's damage report. These hopping monkeys had killed three more

Serpientes. "How dare they harm usss! We are the sssupreme massster race!" He fairly yelled at his Second Commander. "Letting crippled up monkeysss kill our preciousss ssscientissstsss is beyond comprehensssion!"

"Firssst Commander, they have sssome new weapon that burnsss through our ssshieldsss like they were not even up! They ssseem to come out of nowhere to attack our people while they are feeding," the Second Commander justified. "But we have dessstroyed all their flying ssshipsss. Now they can only move around by hopping or driving thossse ssslow sssurface machinesss."

"Yesss, but there are billionsss of these monkeysss down there and now lesss than ssseven thousssand of usss. At leassst the monkeysss can no longer move around much. We don't have to worry about thossse who are outssside this firssst city," the First Commander of Sporn countered.

"Ssshould we perhapsss try to find that Dr. Ssstevensss fellow and make him make a more powerful sssuper-mutation?" the Second Commander asked.

"Ssstupid! If they are any more immobile, they will not be able to sssurvive and find the food that they need. Besssidesss, he hasss probably already been eaten. Pusssh our ssscientissstsss to find a defensssse againssst their newessst weapon. That isss a better sssolution. In the meantime, have our people go down in the sssafety of the sssscout ssshipsss. Land only when they sssee nothing dangerousss and feed. Take off asss sssoon asss they have eaten. No more ssssleeping on the sssurface. That'sss an order. Sssee that it isss carried out now."

"Yes, Firssst Commander. Ssshouldn't we let home world know about our amazing find of monkeysss?"

"Not jussst yet. We, Sssecond Commander — we were the brave onesss who traveled between galaxiesss to find the monkeysss here. I don't want any competition from the lazy Ssserpientesss. I will make the call when we have had our fill and all isss sssecure."

The Second Commander thought, *or when our numbers are almost gone. You old fool, you're going to get us all killed by the ignorant, stupid monkeys of all things.* He

346

nodded his head and unhappily slithered off to carry out the latest orders.

At the end of the month-long, seemingly never ending attacks on the snake aliens, First Commander of Sporn had additional problems. He was down to five remaining scout ships. The others had been destroyed by suicide bombers with their searing heat explosive weapons. With so few scout ships, he was in very serious trouble, though he had no idea that the last of the brave rangers had just died destroying the most recent scout ship as it attempted to take off after those onboard had dined.

Why was this a serious problem? Until now, many of the scout ships had been hovering in very low orbits watching for convoys of the monkeys' ground moving machines. When spotted, they dove down and fired their energy weapons at them, destroying more soldiers who were trying to come to the aid of General Jones. A turning point had been reached. He had no choice but to terminate those patrols. The five scout ships were needed for protection of the main ship, Sporn. The five scouts couldn't be used as shuttles any longer. Hence, he gave the order to land Sporn down at the edge of the city. Now, they could slither out of the ship at any time to feed on their delicacies. He planned to keep the five ready to take off to provide covering fire against any attacks that might come by air.

The giant ship slowly descended. Nearly half the size of the city, Sporn was their home away from home, filled with everything that a Serpientes might need, including state of their art laboratories. Seeing the enormous mother ship landing just outside the city, General Jones wrote out his last card. Please send help. My rangers are gone, and their mother ship is landing. We have no hope unless someone comes to our aid. He then sent his final message before heading out of the city to the west, trying to make for Security Base 3 some thousand miles distant, where he hoped to convince them to send him more men so he could continue the battle with the aliens. He'd no idea that for weeks, others had been trying to do just that, but their convoys had been intercepted and destroyed by the alien snake scout ships.

Back on Ashford-5, Jan intercepted this final message and alerted everyone, just as she had been doing all along. Even the Ataro emperor had been reluctant to send his fleet to there. His fleet was the only thing keeping the numerous alliances from attacking the forty worlds of his empire. If he sent them off to battle the snake aliens, they'd likely attach the Ataro Empire. His non-existent hands were tied.

Far worse, the geneticists had not been able to make any further progress on this latest super-mutation that had harmed some sixty thousand here on Ashford-5. Renata knew their big obstacle was they did not have a sample of the actual bio agent that caused the mutations. That could only be gotten from the snake aliens. Renata also followed the hit and miss attacks that General Jones had been conducting and their results. This latest and final message convinced her that she needed to act.

Twenty of her most advanced men and women, who were her Advanced Therapy research team, gathered in her small office. Most came in on crutches, preferring them to hopping longer distances. "Thanks for coming on short notice," Renata began. She relayed the final message from General Jones. "As you also know, our geneticists are stymied, until they get a sample of this new super-mutation agent. So it's time that we took more responsibility and did something about these snake aliens, who prefer to dine on us. On the positive side, there hasn't been any further snake alien ships spotted anywhere. If we are damned lucky, these are all of them."

Bob spoke up. "We know that they are telepathic. Can we use that against them?"

Renata nodded. "Exactly, Bob. I'm going to get us a transport. We'll go there cloaked and take them out. Then, we'll need to land and get some samples of their super-mutation agent, before we destroy their ships and all traces of this awful stuff. I don't want anyone else to get their hands on this mutation agent. How many of you are willing to do this with me?"

"You couldn't keep us away," Bob teased her. They were all with her.

Arnold, Pippa, Alfonso, and Savina agreed to fly them to Capella-D. "Justice is the least that we can do for us and the billions on Capella-D," Arnold declared. "Count us in!"

November 1, 1451, Arnold hovered the cloaked deep space transport over the capital city of Capella-D. Below them lay the Serpientes ship, unmistakable. "The damned thing is a quarter of the size of the city!" he declared, impressed with the huge dimensions of their mother ship, though he tended to exaggerate somewhat.

"Just keep us here for the time being. Don't distract us," Renata advised him and hopped back to her companions lying on the beds in the various cabins. "Okay, let's do this. Remember, our geneticists are depending upon us to find some samples of this super-mutation agent. Have at these alien invaders." She hopped on down to her cabin, laid down on the small bed, focused, and set to work herself.

As she zoomed in on a Serpientes, she saw it devouring a woman, who had been trying her best to hop away from it. Renata acted, sensing the body of the snake and the spiritual being that inhabited it. For her, ending the life of the snake's body was simple enough. One thought later, its body slumped dead onto the ground, much to the shock of the Serpientes. *Do not ever come back to this galaxy. It belongs to us,* she planted the thought in its mind, before searching for another snake alien.

The First Commander of Sporn was off his ship, enjoying a delicacy himself. After all, it had been days since he last dined. Suddenly, he became aware that his crew was suddenly and mysteriously dying! He put in direct telepathic orders to his crew, only to find them dying in groups! For the first time, he felt fear, fear of the unknown. He heard the threat in his own mind. *Who are you?*

*We are not your monkeys. You've made a fatal blunder. You are **our** food,* Renata sent back, knowing that would have an enormous impact on his thinking. It did. As he fled, flying through space towards his home galaxy, he felt both terror and confusion. Somehow, monkeys had evolved far beyond all conceivable imagination!

Hey, Renata, there is a Federation transport ship

inside this monster snake mother ship, Bob sent her. *Seems to be all kinds of lab equipment like our doctors have. Maybe this is what we are looking for. But why would they be using a Federation lab on a transport ship?*

See if you can get it out of there so we can take it back with us. We should also destroy these ships. We don't want the Federation getting their hands on them, she replied. *Find that super-mutation stuff.*

Smoke clouds twisted and rose from the decaying Serpientes mother ship and the few remaining scout ships. Bob later reported that these were some kind of organic, living ships. With the right intention, he was able to get them to self-disintegrate or die, leaving a smoldering mass of goo, but the Federation transport was unharmed, surrounded by the smoldering remains of the mother ship. An hour later, Alfonso at the controls, lifted it off Capella-D and jumped into hyperspace, heading for home. Arnold followed along behind him.

"Well, this isn't good," Dr. Diego complained, examining his detailed results of the sample super-mutation agent that they found in the captured transport. At least, they now knew who had owned this lab, the same Dr. Stevens who had been here on Ashford-5 months ago! "Zia, Alexandra, come have a look at these results I've got here. I don't get it."

Both women hopped over to him and began to look over his summary results. "It isn't the same as what resulted," Dr. Alexandra commented. Her face twisted in concern. This wasn't right. The product of this super-mutation agent was quite different from what actually resulted not only in all of the Ashford-5 victims but also those billions on Capella-D. "Do you suppose that the Serpientes were able to modify his super-mutation agent further before they let it loose on us?"

After a bit more study, all three reached the inevitable conclusion that was what had happened. Dr. Stevens had made the super-mutation version one, but the snake aliens had modified it before infecting both worlds. Yet, something wasn't quite right, as Dr. Zia suggested. All three began digging into this mess with extreme care. Two days later, the three doctors came to the same conclusion. Something was very wrong with the super-mutation agent they'd been exposed to, very wrong, but the "what" eluded them for several more days.

Dr. Diego finally put his finger on it. "Transients! Some of the changes are going to be transient in nature! Here, look at this pair of sequences. On the left is mine from Day 5. On the right is mine from this morning." He projected the dual sequences up side by side on his large monitor. Zia and Alexandra hopped in close to inspect what he was pointing to with his index nail.

"My god! You're right. It's changing already. Transients. We're all in for more changes," Zia exclaimed.

"But what changes? These look closer to normal here in today's sequence," Alexandra added.

"Jackpot question, dear. I've no idea, except that we could well fall into another coma and soon likely," Dr. Diego replied soberly.

"Damn. Well, we should get out an alert to everyone on this. Maybe we all won't be affected at the same time," Dr. Alexandra suggested, trying to sound hopeful. If not, somehow the governor and queens were going to have to secure the spaceport and Exchange City while they were unconscious again.

The three notified Governor Sheila and the two queens. Playing it safe, Governor Sheila closed the spaceport indefinitely, instructing her many employees to take time off. If they felt any different, they were to strip and get to bed as fast as possible. Similarly, the queens requested assistance from several guilds from the Kingdom of Brom. They had to assure the Guild Masters that whatever was going to happen in Exchange City would not affect these new arrivals.

Two days later, one by one, the sixty thousand plus fell into comas once more. This time, they had some warning. Most said that they felt unusually tired that morning and followed the advice that the queens and Governor Sheila had posted around the spaceport and city, that their geneticists were hinting some of the genetic modifications might be undone, giving them some hope.

Four days later, they awoke from their comas, shocked and pleased at the same time. The three geneticists were right. Some of the nasty mutations had cleared up. No one had the spit lips any longer. If one looked close at their lips, one could see a faint line where the slits had been. Those who had worn the lip disks as a status symbol were not pleased with this change, however. Their lower leg had unfused, and all now had two perfectly normal legs. The nasty Calder mutation was undone, compliments of the Serpientes poor understanding of human DNA mutations. Everyone welcomed this change. Their hair was unchanged, pleasing some women but few men.

However, what shocked everyone was what was now missing, their arms. The mutation had regressed back to what Dr. Stevens had created in the first place. His original super-mutation agent wanted armless Calder mutants, but with the pain sensors in their long hair and with their split lips needing the monstrous lip plates. Realizing their monkeys could not survive on their own this way, the Serpientes had altered his mutation agent, but had miscalculated on the ability of DNA to repair itself, given time. Only the two queens were pleased with the changes, since now they were again back to officially sanctioned forms required of all Ataro Empire queens. Everyone else was shocked and horrified, to say nothing of finding themselves rather helpless.

Queen Lilly, Queen Misty, and Governor Sheila awoke to face the worst crisis ever. While nearly half of those in Exchange City had the *mentales* gifts, only a few had the gift of telekinesis or levitation. The other half had nothing whatsoever to fall back on for help. Similarly, most of those impacted over in Valen were in the same boat. The spaceport came to a virtual standstill! None of Governor Sheila's many workers could work, much less handle their own basic needs. The only thing that saved them from a complete disaster was that they were used to eating synthetic food from Imperium food processors. Those in the city proper were in dire trouble.

Worse, long-term solutions would not be forthcoming. Their entire staff of geneticists was just as helpless as the rest of the victims. While the thousand volunteers from Brom kept most from starving, life for the average family in Exchange

City became a nightmare, though a volunteer did visit each home once per day, preparing a meal for those who lived there. If it hadn't been for those Brom volunteers, the loss of life would have mounted up as the days passed.

Queen Lilly, Queen Misty, Governor Sheila, Renata, and Dr. Diego met the very day that they came out of their comas. They knew they were now facing the worst crisis in the history of the city and spaceport. As the leaders, they had to figure out how to handle it and fast.

Governor Sheila sighed and explained, "Some of the spaceport employees can be sent back to their home worlds but with a large insurance settlement. That should be more than enough to cover their needs. I'll have to have the emperor hire some replacement workers. The other employees are locals. They too will receive a large insurance settlement, but if they and their families live here, will that even help?"

Queen Lilly answered, "We will have to also set aside funds for everyone else in the city as well. Obviously, the city can't function without bringing in many new folks. Perhaps, some families will want to move back to their home kingdoms. If so, that'll lessen the load a little, but still that leaves three-quarters of the city still here and pretty much helpless at the moment."

"Where's those robots when you really need them," Queen Misty attempted a bit of levity. Three women cracked the briefest of smiles. "Well, we should see about hiring personal assistants, one per each house, one per each business. For now, we're going to have nearly sixty thousand who can't work and earn a living and are going to need help with most everything. Once we get the food situation stabilized, we're going to need to get clothing for everyone. Winter will be on us before much longer."

"We're going to have to call in every favor ever owed to us," Queen Lilly declared, conservatively. "We had best get the ball rolling quickly before panic sets in."

Renata nodded. "Okay then, let's get started. I'll let my small organization know and see how much help they can provide and how soon. There are many Basic Therapy givers out there, especially in the Midlands. Some of them might be willing to help out in this emergency."

Queen Misty sighed and replied, "Ten thousand households, more or less and half that many businesses, some small, some large. Can we really get that many volunteers?" She doubted that and was right.

While they were conversing, one of the Supreme Guild Masters paid the queens a visit. A baker by trade, William Williams approached the four women. Normally, someone would have met him, led him to the queens, and announced him. Today, he had let himself in, having been here many times before with the entire group of masters. "Good day, my queens, governor, Renata."

"Oh, hi William. Good to see you," Queen Misty replied, looking up at the tall, thin man. His top lip plate had an etching of a loaf of bread.

The forty year old, brown haired man, smiled, bowed, and said, "I came as soon as the Baker's Guild here in Exchange City contacted me. I represent all the Supreme Guild Masters today." By that, he meant that he was here on official business as the top-most rulers of Tierra, second only to the queens and governor.

"Have a seat," Queen Misty said politely. "We've got quite a problem on our hands."

William laughed. "Indeed. Our estimates suggest that there are four thousand eight hundred officially guild-sanctioned businesses in Exchange City. All the members are now unable to work. It is the responsibility of the Guilds to assist our members here in Exchange City."

"We will see that every person in the city gets a significant financial support so that they can afford to hire assistants," Queen Misty explained, hoping this would ease William's concern.

"Ah. That would be most generous of the queens. If you can do that, the Guilds will see that everyone is taken care of — at least those families, which have a Guild member in it. Now, will there be any further genetic cures forthcoming as there have been in the past? I know that many want to know this, not the least the victims," William asked pointedly.

"We don't know. The geneticists are just as helpless

now as everyone else is," Queen Lilly answered this one. "I know that they sure want to work, but time will tell if they are able. You should provide a list of names and locations of the families that the Guilds will be handling. That way, should a cure become available, we can get it to them as fast as possible. I suspect that many will want to move to other towns."

"That would be prudent for more than one reason. Exchange City and its guilds simply cannot function with armless men and women. The Guilds will get started yet today. I will see that you have a list of everyone when we've finished," William said flatly.

"Excellent. Assume that each victim will have a thousand coins per month to help pay for their needs. As soon as Elegant Fashions Inc is back in business, I'll see that everyone on your list gets several sets of new clothes as well," Queen Lilly added. "Have them draw funds from any guild, and I'll reimburse each guild."

"Thank you, Queen Lilly, Queen Misty. Governor, Renata," William again bowed, turned and left the four.

A frantic and sometimes scary month passed before some slight semblance of normalcy returned to Exchange City and the spaceport. Most all the spaceport's employees, that is, the victims, were returned to their home worlds, along with a huge insurance settlement that would provide for them for life. Each received a promise that if and when more cures became available, they would be informed of it and allowed to get it at no cost. A whole new base crew arrived from a number of the other Ataro Empire worlds so that by month's end, the spaceport was once more fully functioning. Two assistants were provided for Governor Sheila and her husband who stayed on in their roles.

A large majority of the non-*mentales* gifted of Exchange City moved to other towns, villages, and cities and now had their own personal assistants to help them survive, especially critical for the many families. This way, no one city was overburdened with these victims. That left around fifteen thousand or so who were telepaths and had other gifts. While many of these lived in the Imperial Castle, Imperial Tower, or one of the many Imperial Manor Houses, a good third did not, having their own homes elsewhere within the city. The queens hired a huge new staff to service their large complex and assist the many living there. Those who resided outside the walls were able to hire at least one assistant per family. Thus, some resemblance of normalcy returned after a month.

The queens paid Elegant Fashions Inc for all their products that they'd frantically designed and mass produced in response to the original super-mutation attack. Now, they paid an equal sum to have appropriate apparel created for the sixty thousand plus victims, providing each person with three outfits. Any more would have to be paid for by the individual. Since Elegant Fashions Inc already had many such special designs in production, this time, production was more or less routine, except that their staff was as handicapped as everyone else was. Hence, for a time, they brought in other workers from other stores in nearby cities.

What really helped this particular group, the *mentales* gifted, was the simple fact that for centuries there were armless women among them, the exceedingly rare *katalyein* telepaths. These remarkable women were able to undo mental blocks a person had that prevented their full gift from materializing. If they didn't work their magic on those, the person usually died from the Verge Sickness. The queens quickly summoned all available *katalyein* to the Imperial Castle. Here, these women began teaching the thousands here how to do things with their feet. They were quite skilled at using their feet and teeth to do what others did with their hands. Each one held four hour-long classes with fifty in each class, reaching three groups per day. While there were not a hundred *katalyein* telepaths, but barely twenty, they alternated between ten groups. When a group wasn't receiving their instruction lessons, they were off practicing what they'd just learned. Practice makes perfect and increases your speed. That was the constant advice the *katalyein* gave over and over.

The queen's objectives were to help the *mentales* gifted learn to get by more on their own with less reliance on assistants, in so much as it was possible. After that first month, Renata reported that the plan was working, but more time would be needed, and practice.

More time wasn't available for the twenty thousand victims in Valen, however, always a hotbed of hatred against the "freaks" of Exchange City, that is, the hermaphrodites. Pedro Valen, who was lucky not to have been in the infected area of the city, took over the throne by force. His motto was "Death to the freaks!" His argument was bolstered by the more than double birthrates among the hermaphrodites as witnessed by the population explosion of the freaks in Exchange City. "Look," he argued, "they are pregnant and will be giving birth to more freaks. In fifty years, all Valen will be nothing but freaks. We normals will have been driven out. Besides, they are helpless and worthless to society. We are doing them a favor by putting them out of their misery."

Euthanasia rapidly took hold in Valen, with thousands dying each week. Those, who wanted to live, found ways to flee the city, heading out to outlying towns and villages, where they sought refuge and received it, bolstered by the queens' promise of money to provide for themselves. Valencia Valen wanted to live, and she and others fled to their local Elegant Fashions Inc where they gave them shelter and a home, as well as a job. However, Velasco Valen was kept alive in his cell, per the queens' orders. He remained an armless Calder mutant, unable to speak, and miserable beyond words.

After that first month, only a very few "freaks" remained in Valen. Around three thousand managed to escape the well-intentioned slaughter. Valen then returned to "normal," under the new leadership of Pedro Valen, a fifty year old man, who had opinions on nearly everything and now had the means to enforce them.

Come April 1452, approximately twenty-five thousand new armless hermaphrodites were born on Tierra. Fortunately, the new parents were now widely scattered across the Midlands and a few in the Westerlings. Only in Exchange City were midwives overly taxed until late summer.

Back on Capella-D, the survivors of the super-mutation agent also dropped into comas again, just as they had on Ashford-5. Here, the results were disastrous, planetary genocide finally reached the Federation of Planets. By the time that Federation help reached Capella-D in sufficient quantities, the death toll was staggering, just as it had been on Imperium hub worlds. Barely a million survived. However, that was followed by mass immigrations from many Federation worlds. Land, businesses, equipment were there for the asking, and millions headed there faster than the Admiralty Round Table wished. Some likened it to a mad gold rush!

On the positive side, by the start of the new year, those who had survived against all odds found themselves being well cared for. Of course, by April, their numbers doubled when a million babies were born. At least, the Federation took the advice given to it from Ashford-5's queens. The homes of these victims were modified, just as every building in Exchange City was. All doors had their doorknobs replaced with a sliding slat lock that they could work with their feet. All businesses were ordered to make their establishments "handicapped accessible," which they did, since this group had money to spend, since the Admiralty Round Table divided some of the total assets of the world among the million survivors, making them billionaires overnight.

What of cures? Emperor Fu Gang Sanguro did send two of the Ataro Empire's geneticists to Ashford-5. They consulted with the local geneticists and verified their results. They'd endured so darn many genetic mutations and cures that at this point, the normal cures no longer worked. A completely new and lengthy study would have to be done if there were to be any cures at all. This was the dismal prognosis the two delivered to the queens before they returned to their worlds. Still, the many geneticists refused to give up and promised to continue working towards more cures. In the meantime, everyone continued to practice what the *katalyein* had taught them. Use feet and teeth in lieu of hands.

Chapter 22 Unexpected Offers

Emperor Fu Gang Sanguro was in a tight pickle, but that wasn't anything new. He and his predecessor had worked tirelessly to preserve the integrity and survival of the Ataro Empire amid the crumbling of the old Imperium. While Ashford-5 was half a galaxy from the main worlds of the empire, it was extraordinarily valuable because of its vast fuel refineries on one of its moons, providing nearly all the fuel used by the former Imperium ships that traveled the rim and middle of the spiral arm. Ashford-5 was also known to possess numerous Class V telepaths, who the emperors had done their best to protect. Circumstances were about to force a change in that, unfortunately.

Even though it was late winter, that is March of 1452, Emperor Fu Gang knew that he owed it to Ashford-5 personally to deliver the news and hoped that they would understand. His ship touched down on the white world. Mountains of snow scraped from the tarmac created spike-toothed, small mountains among the crags to the north and south of the spaceport. At least they are back in business, he thought, watching the newly hired ground crews still working to remove a recent layer of snowfall.

As he carefully negotiated the bay ramp, his personal assistant holding him securely, he was pleased to see that Governor Sheila had sent someone with an electric car to drive him the short distance to the admin entrance, saving him the next to impossible walk across the slick tarmac in his toe shoes. Even so, he slipped getting into the car, saved from a fall by his assistant.

Once inside Governor Sheila's meeting room, he nodded to Queen Lilly, Queen Misty, and his governor. "Thank you all for meeting with me on such short notice. I hope that things are getting back to some kind of normalcy around here," he began politely.

"Yes, we owe you much. The new employees are struggling, but they will adapt well," Governor Sheila replied.

"I take it that there is another crisis brewing?"

Astute woman, he thought. Well, I would not come all this way if there weren't. His face was serious and he began, "I knew that one day it would happen, and I'm afraid that day has come. With the breakup of the old Imperium, many new alliances have formed, some powerful, some weak."

"We may be on the outer rim, but we do keep up with events," Queen Lilly replied.

"Indeed. We have been working hard to preserve our Ataro Empire, standing alone against all these new alliances. Right now, I'm under extreme pressure from six of them, including the three Hub Sector alliances and three mid-arm ones. They'd taken a hint from the ill-fated attempt of the Black Man to conquer the galaxy. They've formed a loosely knit super-alliance, pointed at the Ataro Empire. While we do have a large number of warships, this new super group does have more and are forcing my hand," he explained.

"In what way?" asked Governor Sheila.

"As you know, there isn't anything particularly valuable on most all the Ataro Empire worlds. In fact, there isn't much for this super-alliance to gain by attacking us, since most certainly I'd make use of all our warships, which are the most valuable possessions that the empire holds and which would likely be destroyed in such a conquest war. Yet, there are two other valuables, both of which are here on Ashford-5, the fuel refinery and your telepaths."

The queens swallowed hard. Neither liked where this was heading. He continued, "While we have done all that we could to keep the other worlds out there from learning that Ashford-5 has many, many telepaths, I'm afraid at this point, the proverbial lion is out of the cage on this one. Most all these super-alliance worlds know very well that there are many telepaths here. I'm afraid they are forcing me to do what I've been trying not to do."

Again, he sighed. "In light of this super-mutation attack on you and it's horrible effects on everyone, I've been asked by this super-alliance to permit a consortium of their people to pay you a visit. They want to hire many telepaths, primarily those who have been victims of this senseless Serpientes attack. Presumably, these telepaths would be extremely well paid and treated like gods and goddesses, working for those who hire them. They want to come here, interview many telepaths, and make employment offers."

"Damn!" Queen Lilly swore angrily. Governor Sheila fumed.

Trying to remain calm, Queen Misty asked, "So they are threatening you with war unless you allow this consortium to come here and try to hire telepaths?" He nodded. She continued, "What if no one wants to be hired by this consortium? Are they then going to attack us directly? Are they then going to try clandestine kidnaping?"

"That was my initial concern too, Queen Misty," he replied. "I asked those very questions, pointing out that any such attempts will result in the entire Ataro Empire coming to your defense in a bloody, costly war. They countered with what I believe are solid arguments. First, they could not trust any kidnaped telepath not to deceive them. Second, they are primarily interested in the attack victims, and only if none of them volunteer will they consider others. I believe they think they can entice the victims with promises of wealth, power, and a good life just for using their telepathic gifts for them. Third, they know very well that an all-out war isn't going to net them telepaths that they could trust. No, they are just trying to force my hand in this and open up a valid commercial trade in Ashford-5 telepaths."

Queen Lilly said sarcastically, "Great! Just what the galaxy needs, a whole lot of Velasco's, a whole bunch of Black Men, all vying to be the Emperor Supreme!"

"Surely, he was an exception, a wild anomaly?" Emperor Fu Gang countered. "We must hope so."

"So you've had no choice but to agree to their terms?" Governor Sheila asked, forcing herself not to sound bitter or antagonistic towards him.

"I have. In return, I've gotten them to agree to allow the Ataro Empire to send an ambassador to each of their worlds and to be allowed fully to monitor activities on their worlds. Presumably, we can get advanced warnings of any future actions this loose alliance might be taking and thus have more time to counter it. If you prefer to call these ambassadors spies, you may. I certainly do," the emperor was perfectly blunt about it.

"So we really don't have a choice? What if no one wants to take them up on their offers?" Queen Misty asked.

"I've been over that with them. They have agreed that if they get no takers, then they will drop the issue. I admit I played my last remaining card to get that concession. I explained to them just how much damage an untrustworthy telepath could do to their entire civilization and that they'd never even know that he or she was doing it. Perhaps, I overdid it a bit with that, but I think I put the fear of God into them, if they try to make use of an unwilling telepath."

Queen Lilly laughed. "Well, you got that part right. My god, emperor, the damage that one of us could do is enormous."

They discussed the details for another half hour before the emperor left to return to his world. The queens would make the announcement to all the towers and have her Imperial Tower contact all the telepath victims, while Valen Tower would do the same with the few impacted telepaths in Valen. A complete list of names would be forwarded to Governor Sheila, who would host this consortium and oversee their many interviews. The date of their arrival was June 15, 1452.

This must be what the nova call grief, the humaniform robot known as Minta examined the electrical impulses shooting through her circuits. She'd just witnessed the second destruction of their Grand Plan. First, it had been Aquila Prime and now Beltazar-C. This time the destruction had been far more complete. Thanos, her maker, was gone, as were her other leaders, including Eros. Their brain circuits were melted slag, just as were all the countless lesser worker robots on Beltazar-C. A whole, viable world wiped out for the second time. The survival of all rested upon her metallic shoulders now. The others would be coming soon; her thoughts traveled a different path. She'd notified the five hundred lesser humaniform robot spies out among the many more heavily populated worlds of the former Imperium and the disintegrating Federation of Planets. Now, they were coming back to Venice and would be expecting to hear new orders, this time from her. What to do? What to do?

At least she had recovered their massive backup database, which held all their observations and data collected over more than a century, vast in its potential knowledge. Several were bringing along new computer hardware, and she didn't doubt that they could re-establish a new central hub and restore the data. Rebuild. At least the temporary system on the frozen world would be safe for now. That was her first step; rebuild the basic systems. Then, could anything be salvaged? After that, she would have to provide a future direction for her kind.

A month later, the industrious robots had one power plant back in operation. Two scientist robots had been salvaged, their melted circuits replaced with the remaining spare parts. She reprogrammed all the robots and sent three hundred back out on their spying missions, paying particular attention to the situation on Capella-D and Ashford-5, where the super-mutation attacks had occurred.

Minta had already reprogrammed in the robot's new Fundamental Laws. First, a robot is forbidden ever to harm a humaniform robot. Second, a robot is always to obey a humaniform robot's orders, subject to the first rule. Third, a robot must always protect a humaniform robot from harm. Fourth, a robot is never to allow harm to come to itself, subject to the first three rules. Survival of the species was her immediate goal.

With the chaos and destruction on Capella-D, Minta ordered all her three hundred spies to head there and confiscate all computer equipment and other vitally needed supplies from which more humaniform robots could be built. Meanwhile, she programmed the two surviving scientist robots to conduct some special experiments.

Minta needed data. She reviewed all that she'd learned years ago about the nova from the powerful telepathic nova from Ashford-5. Did their powers reside in their brains? Were their minds physically in their brains? Was there something else, a human spirit, that wasn't made from flesh that inhabited these bodies, like the Ashford-5 women suggested? She needed definitive answers in order to proceed. Hence, the two scientists were reprogrammed to help her discover just what the true situation was.

A human brain needs very little to function, fuel and oxygen, with some circulatory method to dispose of waste products. She had some of the spies kidnap three humans for her experiments. Subject A had his arms and legs removed. Also, his eyes were replaced with vastly superior robot eye sensors, as were his ears. What was left of his body was then encased entirely in a robot shell, humaniform in nature. The objective: see if the man could adapt and learn to control the robot shell. Subject B had his brain removed and inserted into the head of a humaniform robot. A simple life-sustaining support system was attached to the brain and the brain's electrical synapses were attached to sensors that could theoretically be used to control the robot's body. Subject C also had his brain removed and inserted into the shell similar to Subject B, but that humaniform robot had its own usual electrical circuitry brain. That is, the robot was fully operational, independent of the human brain inserted into its circuitry. Once the human with his brain was operational, the brain would be exterminated, leaving the human in charge of the humaniform robot's "brain."

Subject A responded quickly, adapting well to his new robot shell. However, he was harder to control and required substantial upkeep, particularly food and water. His voice was quite normal for a human male.

Subject B took far longer to respond and even longer to adapt to the robot body. However, he did learn to control it. Further, his upkeep was extremely simple, drastically less overhead than Subject A. Both quickly learned that there were simply some commands that they attempted to give to their new body, which the body simply ignored. The underlying Four Laws overrode their commands.

Minta was far more interested in Subject C. He took as long as Subject B did to respond and adapt to the robot body. However, when the scientists terminated the brain's life-support, Subject C took several more days to regain control of the robot body. That he did so was highly informative to Minta, who now had the proof that she needed. Humans were some kind of being that inhabited their frail fleshly bodies. That one could do well in a humaniform robot body was impressive. However, very unfortunately from Minta's point of view, Subject C soon grew tired of the mechanical body. "This is no fun at all," he declared to Minta, who was observing him going through his daily ritual, exercising the various circuits. Subject C vanished, leaving the robot shell behind.

Finally, armed with sufficient data, Minta made her basic decision. She had the two hundred spy humaniform robots prepare the recharge cylinders of their one working Fabrication machine. That is, in order to duplicate an object, the machine had to take identical atoms from its hundred plus cylinders, each of which held one single element, and bond the atoms together, duplicating the form. Of course, large quantities of some elements were required, while only tiny amounts of others were needed. In the back of the machine, hundreds of cylinders contained the basic elements that the machine used in the fabrication process. For what she intended to duplicate, much larger proportions of several elements would be required, such as gold, silicon, and germanium, along with aluminum and iron.

Carefully, she plugged herself into her new master mainframe and downloaded her data, that which made her Minta. One of the spy humaniforms watched over the procedure, following her orders precisely. Once that was done, Minta nodded and the upload of her special new programming began. A half hour later, the spy robot put her into one side of the Fabrication machine and activated it. Hours later, a duplicate Minta appeared in the other side. Carefully, the spy robot took the original Minta out, plugged her back into the master mainframe, and executed Reload Minta. A half hour later, Minta opened her eyes, checked her circuits, and relaxed. So far, so good.

She then fully checked out Minta-0, as the duplicate was to be called. Finding it perfect, she proceeded to duplicate that one nine more times. Now, she had her field commanders, humaniforms that she could depend upon. She was Minta, Supreme Commander. The other ten were her generals. Their programming was such that they would obey any command given by Minta without question or regard to the Four Laws.

Not long after that, Minta received word of the horrible transformations that had happened to the super-mutations on Capella-D. That they were now helpless, armless people, starving to death gave her the golden opportunity that she desired. She issued orders to the three hundred spies on other worlds and a very different set of orders to the two hundred with her. Hastily, one robot manufacturing plant was re-activated, with rebuilt systems where needed. Further, she was able to restore a hundred robot workers and they salvaged what human food that was still growing as well as butchering more domesticated animals, whose flesh the humans so loved to eat.

The ten generals supervised all these actions. Thus, when the first spy transport landed bringing with it twenty helpless humans from Capella-D, they were ready for them. All the humans were between six and twenty, evenly divided between the sexes. All had been promised cured bodies by the spy humaniforms and were desperate to have these cures.

The children were turned into Model 10's while those fourteen and older were turned into Model 11's. The Model 11's were like Subject A and were capable of reproduction, which was her plan to produce more for the future. The Model 10's were like Subject B; only their brains remained alive. By June of 1452, Minta had five thousand of each type. Only a few didn't survive the transformation into the world of the robot bodies.

She assigned her ten generals to work with each group, training them to be superb fighters and to fly spaceships. At that time, she learned from one of her spies on Winno-3 that Emperor Fu Gang had been forced to open up Ashford-5 and allow a consortium of buyers to make employment offers to the telepaths there who were also armless victims of the Serpientes. An excellent opportunity had finally fallen in her lap. A bit of hacking later, she and her party had been added to the two dozen consortium buyers. Donning a new persona and disguise, Minta and four other spies headed to Cass-C to join the others from the Federation who comprised the Federation's bidders. From there, they joined up with those from the former Imperium worlds. All told, when the group arrived at the spaceport on Plateau Grado, there were thirty-six official bidders for telepaths, representing nearly a hundred potential buyers or employers.

"What the bloody hell do we do now?" Jan asked. She, Amy, Renata, Governor Sheila, and the two queens met shortly after the emperor left Ashford-5. "Velasco damned nearly wiped out the whole darn galaxy." She exaggerated of course, but the others knew what she meant. Had he not been stopped, he most certainly would have done just that.

"I will be upping security measures all around the world," Governor Sheila declared. "I'm sure that sooner or later, some of them are going to attempt to kidnap our people. Trouble is, a cloaked transport can land darn near anywhere, and we'd not even know it."

"Maybe none of our people will like their offers and nothing will come from this consortium meeting," Queen Misty attempted to defuse the intense air in the room, but failed completely.

"Don't be silly, Misty," Amy countered. "Jan and I just wanted a normal life this time around and now look at us. Unless some cures are found, our kids are going to be like us as well. Having another armless lifetime isn't what we wanted. You can be sure that if they make the pot sweet, a number of *mentales* gifted are going to jump at it."

"But won't they be well treated?" Governor Sheila asked also trying to be a little upbeat.

Amy grimaced. "Hardly. Well," she conceded, "maybe at first, but not long term. Trust us. Jan and I've been there, done that, and it ain't pretty!"

"So what do we do?" asked Queen Lilly.

"We ought to send some off whom we trust to keep us informed somehow," Amy suggested. "But if they are taken to dozens of different worlds, that's going to be a problem."

"We don't dare send any out there in possession of

those giant crystals either," Renata inserted her point.

"Are you suggesting, dear, that we should go out there again?" Jan asked, looking at Amy.

"Possibly, dear. We should probably be interviewed and see what they are offering and then make up our minds. We ought to be able to find ways to keep everyone here informed of what's happening to some of our people out there," Amy answered.

"What about our babies?" Jan asked. Both had recently given birth, as had so many of these victims. "Are we going to risk them too?"

Amy bit her lip. A mother's protection of her child fought with a mother's desire to raise her child. After a pause, she said, "We'll have to see what the offers are first."

Miles away to the west, another said the same thing. "We'll have to see what they are offering us first," Diego Valen said in answer to his wife's question. Diego, the older brother of Velasco, used to run Valen Castle along with his brother Tonio. They were thirty and twenty-eight respectively. They and their wives, Felipa and Gracia, had managed to escape Valen during Pedro Valen's euthanasia killing rampage. Their children, however, had perished at swords of Pedro's legions, cleansing Valen of the helpless freaks. The four had managed to walk all the way to Exchange City and were given refuge there. Now, they were discussing the consortium and its members' desires to hire telepaths.

Tonio added, "Velasco was an idiot. We're not. No, this way, we might be able to gain powerful positions that rightfully ought to be ours."

"Only if we can later use that to return here and eliminate Pedro for what he's done to our four children," Felipa countered.

"We should torture that beast first. No easy death for Pedro!" spat Gracia, reminded again of her bitter loss and her own helplessness to prevent the deaths of her children.

"Maybe none of them will want to take all four of us," Tonio suggested. "We shouldn't be separated from our wives."

"Agreed. We go as married couples or not at all," Diego relieved the fears of the two women.

All across Exchange City, many had similar ideas, anticipating the big meeting with this strange off-world consortium looking to hire telepaths. Some simply refused to leave Tierra, but others were at least tempted to listen to what these men and women had to offer. As many put it, "Hell, anything is better than this!"

Worse, as far as the ruling Supreme Guild Masters were concerned, this was a step forward for the many victims. They encouraged all victims who were both *mentales* gifted and guild members to take advantage of this, and eventually to return with many innovations for Tierra.

As the meeting with the queens, the governor, Amy, and Jan broke up, Renata had the final word. "Look. I don't like where this is leading us. Nearly five hundred years ago, all Tierra was in some form of bondage. Everything was controlled by the kings, some of whom were known despots. Then, with great spiritual faith and courage, we broke those bonds, achieving true liberty for all our people. Following that, we entered a period of what could rightly be said to be one of abundance in all things. Now, the guilds are leading us towards selfishness and complacency. They are backing this consortium. That's not good at all. Mark my words, soon the average person will once more be in apathy, followed by a complete dependence on the largess of a few, and we're right back into bondage and slavery once more, coming full circle, just like human lives go. We're born, grow into adulthood, make our way into abundance, then we try to hold onto what we've earned, and then slowly decay until our bodies die."

"Grim," Queen Misty commented as Renata left. "I wonder if there is anything we can do to keep her dire predictions from happening?" Her mate, Lilly shrugged her empty shoulders.

June 15 arrived, and three dozen deep space transports slowly descended onto Plateau Grado, one of largest groups of ships ever to land at one time. Each member of the consortium wore a name badge that also displayed his or her home planet. Most of them were men, but there were three women among them. One was Mrs. Becky Hallstead, one of Minta's aliases.

Each had one or two assistants with them, handling record keeping duties. All had come prepared to return with one or more valuable telepaths and thus had caretakers onboard their transports.

Governor Sheila greeted the small group and told them the interviews would be conducted at the Imperial Castle, which was now easily accessible to all the victims. "Mind you," she added, "many are just coming to hear your offers and have no intentions of leaving Ashford-5. So don't be surprised by this." Via electric cars, the consortium and their assistants were escorted through the underground tunnel to the castle and into the throne room, where the two Ataro queens would oversee the interviews. They had a long row of tables set up where the consortium members could sit and have the candidates walk past them and hear their pitches. Promptly at ten, the doors opened, and many thousands of armless *mentales* gifted began filing into the room, walking up to the tables.

Naturally, Jan had the whole place bugged and was recording everything being said via dozens of microphones. Later, technicians could isolate out each member and what they had to say to the men, women, and a few children who visited their table. Remarkably, the many offers were all pretty similar. The accepted telepath would be given their own luxury mansion and personal assistants, only the finest in clothing, the best dining possible, all the amenities that went with a life of luxury — all theirs to keep and a very hefty salary as well. They only had to follow orders and use their telepathy as directed by their overseer, who could be either in the political arm, the army, or simply a wealthy businessman.

What varied the most was the duration of the contract. Some contracts were only for ten years, while others were for their lifetimes. Because many were married, the contracts also insisted that families not be split up, unless that was the expressed wishes of all parties. One woman asked, "You mean that we get to keep all that stuff and bring it all back here to Tierra when the contract is done?"

The man replied, "Yes, of course. However, the luxury mansion isn't easily transported, obviously. It will remain owned by you, should you like to return to our world at a later date."

Everyone was assured that if and when any new cures became available, they would be first in line to receive them. That went over well, as you can imagine.

Amy and Jan went through the long line as well, sensing each member's mind and surface thoughts as they met with them. As far as they could tell, each one was focusing all their mental facilities on trying to convince one or more of these remarkable telepaths to take up their offer, returning with them. All except for one, that is. As the pair listened to Mrs. Becky Hallstead make her presentation, they didn't detect any mind at all. No thoughts. Nothing. Yet the woman seemed very much alive and alert, rattling off her proposals to give them a new life, just as the others were. Her emphasis was on providing them with a new life, though.

Most all wanted to discuss the many offers and promised to return tomorrow with their replies. The queens then diplomatically offered up a banquet in honor of the consortium members, as well as a suite for the evening.

Meanwhile, Amy and Jan discussed the offers with each other. Amy mused, "You know, what has me baffled is that Mrs. Becky Hallstead. I couldn't sense her mind. Not sure why. Maybe I'm just tired or she is good at blocking off all surface thoughts."

"I agree; that one was a bit peculiar. Say, did you notice the two former Valen rulers and their wives were keenly interested in that woman's offer too?" Jan replied and asked.

"I couldn't help noticing them. Shades of Velasco, but they didn't have any giant crystals with them, at least not at the interviews. I don't trust them," Amy countered.

"If we are going to do this, I've a hunch that we ought to go wherever those Valens do, dear. I don't trust them," Jan admitted. "Not after that mess with their younger brother, Velasco."

Amy sighed. "I agree. So have we decided to do this? Go off-world again?"

"We're Renata's rear guards," Jan teased her and Amy cracked a smile.

"Best keep our daughters here on Tierra though, what with the Valens involved in this," Amy advised and Jan concurred.

Renata dropped by to have a final word with them. "Look, I know you two are resourceful, but do keep me posted periodically, if you can. If I don't hear from you, I'll use other means to reach you. We've enough giant crystals for me to reach you no matter where you wind up. Don't hesitate to ask for a rescue party, though right now, I'm not sure whom we could get to man a transport. These damned genetic mutations are wrecking everything that we've worked so hard to build up here on Tierra. Ah well. Thanks and best of luck out there. We do appreciate your sacrifices." None of the three had any idea of the sacrifices that lay ahead.

Chapter 23 Robots

Mrs. Becky Hallstead met the six newly hired telepaths when they arrived at the spaceport via electric cars. She had three other helpers with her. Following her orders, the six brought nothing with them. "Everything that you could possibly want will be provided upon our arrival at Athens Spaceport."

Diego Valen teased her, "We can possibly want a whole lot, Mrs. Hallstead."

She chuckled at his jest. "Of course. And don't hesitate to ask for what you desire. It is a high honor for us to have been able to obtain your services. Telepaths are quite rare," she added, leading them to her deep space transport. Her three helpers followed behind the three couples, just in case they needed any help, which they didn't. Once up the ramp, each of the assistants led one couple to their cabin and helped them get ready for the takeoff. Then, they headed to the galley to prepare lunch for the six, just as the ship jumped into hyperspace.

"Well, no turning back now," Jan whispered to Amy. "I'm so sleepy." Amy yawned too and laid back on their bed. Jan joined her and then everything went black. All six were unconscious and didn't see the three helpers sticking their heads into their cabins verifying that they were out.

Jan woke with a splitting headache, but she felt very strange. Plus, everything was completely dark, no trace of light, no hint of sound. She sensed that she must be sitting up and tried to stand up. Nothing happened. She tried to move a leg up to her face. Nothing. She tried to call out, to yell, to scream. Nothing. Even her jaw didn't move or open. She felt the air rushing through her throat and knew that sound ought be heard, rather loudly given how hard she believed that she was screaming. Nothing. Panic swept over her for a moment.

Panic flooded through all six, though at first they were not aware of each other, only the utter blackness, complete silence, and total immobility. Well, not completely immobile, Jan realized. She was breathing normally. Okay quite fast. Too fast. She attempted to focus and calm her nerves. That worked, and she concentrated and reached her mate. *Amy! You all right? What's happened? We got knocked out. It's all dark, and I can't hear anything or move.*

Jan! You are still here! Same here. Splitting headache. We have to figure out what's going on and fast, Amy sent back. Jan detected traces of panic coming from her mate, even though she couldn't see or hear her. Were they even in the same cabin? She tried to sense vibrations from the floor. Were they still on the transport? Nothing made sense at all.

Jan sensed for her psi-crystal. It wasn't around her neck. In fact, she couldn't sense its presence anywhere near her. Well, she'd expected that. Their employer hadn't known of the significance of those crystals and shouldn't know, for that matter. *Still here. Headache too. Pitch black here. Total silence. Can't move. What's going on?*

Then, both Jan and Amy thought that they could just barely hear something. Faint, very faint. Was that music? They strained to hear. The more they strained the louder the sounds became. Strange though. It wasn't quite like the normal sounds of a musical group. No, they were hearing very, very high harmonics as well as very low notes, probably beyond normal hearing range, since Jan felt the lowest notes almost more than she heard them. After a time, she recognized the music. It was a famous Imperium symphony often heard in older times during the height of the old Imperium. Strange, though, she'd never heard it quite so clear and over such a wide frequency range. Louder and louder came the sounds, as though someone was continually turning up the volume of a player machine! Unbearably loud now. She tried to put her non-existent hands over her ears to dampen it down. Her headache was magnified three-fold! Above the pounding music, she heard a woman's voice barking out, "Number 10,001: normal volume. Number 10,002: normal volume." Four more times, the woman's voice commanded, the unit's digit increasing by one each time. Relief!

"Hello my six telepaths. Welcome to Athens. You each now have a new body, an indestructible body with arms and extended senses as well. It will take time for you to learn to control your new humaniform robot bodies. I've begun with hearing. You've probably noticed your new ears can hear across a far wider spectrum of sounds, and the volume is adjustable, which in time you will learn to control by your thoughts, as you will do the rest of your new bodies. Don't worry though, it is impossible for you to ever give your humaniform robot bodies a command that would cause it harm, just as I and the other generals can always override your commands to your new bodies as well. Amy, your humaniform body is Number 10,001; Jan's, yours is Number 10,002." She continued telling Diego, Felipa, Tonio, and Gracia their id numbers.

"I am called Minta. My generals are called Minta-0 through Minta-9. Right now, you haven't yet learned to interface to the rest of your senses or control your new arms and legs or your voice and replacement mouths. Please be patient. You'll master all of them in due time, just a few days. We've removed your legs and have your torso encased in the nearly indestructible humaniform robot body, especially designed for you. Your genitals and breasts are the only exterior surfaces of your bodies now. All else is within the hardened shell and framework of the body. You probably are experiencing headaches at this time. Those too will pass. It was necessary to remove your lower jaw, teeth, and skulls. Your skulls are now surrounded by the many sensors that your brain will be activating to control your bodies. Already, your brains have worked out the basics of hearing via your mechanical ears, giving you vastly superior hearing to normal humans."

"Next, we'll work on getting your brains to electronically control your new eyes. You'll find that your new eyes are vastly more powerful than before. You'll be able to see in the infrared regions as well as the ultraviolet. Plus, like powerful cameras, you can zoom in and out at will, and the electronics will allow you to see in almost total darkness as though it was broad daylight, and to be able to dim down the vision when staring directly at a bright sun. In short, your new eyes will be vastly superior to human eyes. Again, all your sight and features will be under the control of your brain's

375

electronic impulses transmitted through the neural network that now surrounds your brains, which is basically a control panel to you."

"We took molds of your faces, and you'll find your humaniform face is indistinguishable from what your former face looked like. Unlike your human face, which could be easily bruised, cut, or harmed, you'll find your humaniform face is virtually indestructible, as are your new teeth. Oh, you still have your original tongues so you can speak once you've relearned how to control your humaniform mouth. We've cut your original hair shorter and implanted it in the skullcap of your new heads. Such super long hair will only get in your way."

"You'll be much like a human baby, as it learns to control its fingers, hands, arms, and so on. Give yourself time to relearn, to remake the neural connections from your switchboard brains to your electronic neural networks that control the robot bodies. Once you have relearned, you'll find that your new arms are capable of lifting four hundred pounds. You can run six-minute miles for hours on end without ever taking a deep breath. In fact, the amount of food that your torso and brains require will be minimal, until you become pregnant. Yes, all your reproductive systems are untouched. We encourage you six to have all the children you desire. So except while pregnant, you'll find your breathing and metabolism to be almost as strenuous when exercising as when you are sleeping!"

"Once you have relearned everything, we'll give you your choice of clothing and such material possessions as you desire. Just remember, you cannot override your humaniform's built-in four laws. First, a robot is forbidden ever to harm a humaniform robot. Second, a robot is always to obey a humaniform robot's orders, subject to the first rule. Third, a robot must always protect a humaniform robot from harm. Fourth, a robot is never to allow harm to come to itself, subject to the first three rules. Beyond those underlying laws, once you have relearned to control your body, it will be yours to operate as you desire."

"At this time, we'll be inserting a feeding tube into your

esophagus. Don't panic. It's time you were fed some and given a little something for your headaches. After that, we'll work on getting you to get your brains to connect to your new eyes. Once vision is restored, we'll work on your getting control of your new mouths so that you can finally speak. Then, we'll get you to control your arms so you can feed yourselves. After that, we'll tackle the more difficult project of controlling legs. Once you've mastered controlling your new humaniform robot bodies, you'll be utterly invincible. You'll be the most powerful beings in the galaxy. Now, let's get some nourishment in you."

Jan felt a tube touching her tongue. Finally, something felt normal! Then, some warm liquids entered her stomach, which seemed to crave food. How long had it been since she'd eaten? What day was it? How long were they out? Am I really a robot now? She was confused, disoriented, and more afraid than she ever had been, which was saying something. She and Amy had been put through an enormous amount of torture and mutilation in their past lives, but had always found a way to bring the perpetrators to justice, somehow, someway. But this? Jan felt terrified and more than helpless. Amid her terror and frantic confusion, she realized that this Minta was right. They needed to be able to see next and then speak. She was bringing the right systems online in the right order as far as she was concerned.

What scared Amy beyond the present horrific mess was one small fact that trickled into her memory; it was something that she'd read. Nia Elain Compton-Jereni had reported that none of her crew of *mentales* gifted could ever sense any minds of their humaniform robot assistants! Amy knew that meant their unique gifts and telepathic abilities would be utterly useless against these robots who had hired them. Now, she understood why she'd not been able to detect any thoughts from Mrs. Hallstead at the consortium meeting! She was a robot!

Jan focused and was able to get a good sense of just how much food they'd put into her stomach, the equivalent of a very small meal. Even better, she felt the throbbing headache diminishing. Even so, she almost freaked out thinking about her body's brain being surrounded by some kind of electronic sensors and not her own skull. Time passed, but she had no way to tell how much.

Then, she heard the voice of Minta again. "All right, ladies. Time to get you used to using your new and extremely powerful eyes. Number 10,001: activate eyes." She repeated the order five more times, increasing the unit's position by one each time. "Pretend you are looking for a bright light straight ahead of you. Pull it in towards you. Come on, ladies. I know the optical systems are working. You ought to be able to perceive something ahead of you. Look. Look at the bright light."

Jan strained and thought she saw something before what ought to be her face. It was tiny and dim, but it was something. "Pull it into towards you, ladies." How, Jan thought. Slowly, the tiny spot began to grow larger and larger. Straining as hard as she could, Jan managed somehow to get the bright spot fully enlarged. Then, it seemed to fill the space before her as her own eyes had always done for her. The image was colorful, but it was too fuzzy for her to make out what she was seeing. "Think about focusing the image. Like a microscope or telescope. Focus the images ladies. Come on; you can do it." Minta encouraged them.

Later, Jan described the feeling as quite similar to using her fingers to adjust a scope, turning its knob. The image came into focus and swept on past a proper focus. She pushed the other way more slowly and finally saw a crisp image, just as if she was seeing with her own eyes. If she'd had a mouth or control over her robot mouth, it would have dropped. She was looking at herself in a mirror some ten feet from her. She was naked and sitting on a chair facing the mirror. She could see a bit of Amy just to her left and the moving legs of Minta to her right.

Minta kept talking. "If you'll notice at the very bottom of your images, you'll see a display that shows you the precise distance you are from whatever is in the center of your image. Now then, pretend that you are zooming in. Focus on your faces and zoom in on them. Get a close up look at your new faces. Real close. It's important that you see that we have done a superb job of rendering your old face here in your new

378

humaniform face, one that is indestructible, and one that will not age like your old body and face would. Even if some horrible accident happens, our main computer can reform you a completely new replacement face identical to yours. So indeed, you are close to being immortal now, not quite as immortal as I am, but almost as close as these Model 11's can come. The Model 10's are expected to have at least twice the lifetime as the Model 11's that you now inhabit, but then all that's left of those humans are their brains, which are being kept alive and healthy by a small life support system built into their humaniform shells."

"Now continue zooming in. Your new eyes operate much like a zoom lens of an expensive camera system. The maximum magnification is times ten while the maximum zoom out is like a very wide-angle lens. Your old human eyes simply couldn't do any of these things. Zoom in really close. Make darn sure we've missed nothing about your faces. You'll notice that it is your own hair. We did cut it shorter so that it doesn't interfere with your activities, shoulder length. We've kept the rest of your hair in hermetically sealed capsules in case you need some replacements years from now. Okay. Now zoom all the way out. You ought to be able to see the reflections of the others. I'll give you a minute to work them. Also, see if you can rotate your eyes to the left and right. The lateral movement is slightly larger than that of human eyes, giving you an edge there too."

She became silent, focusing her attention on the various eyes, watching their movements. Jan realized she was quiet for quite some time, allowing the six to practice working their eyes. It was slow going and at times frustrating for her to get these mechanical eyes to respond to her thoughts, via electronic impulses that her brain fired in response to her thoughts. Still, the more that she practiced, the easier it became to control her new eyes.

"All right. I see each of you is getting the hang of operating your eyes. I'll leave some music playing softly. I want you each to practice controlling your hearing and eyes for a time, before we extend your vision capabilities." Minta then left the room. Jan wasn't able to turn her head to see her depart, but did zoom all the way out and rotated her eyes to the right far enough to glimpse the door. It looked like any normal door, though why that ought to have surprise her, she wasn't sure.

She's right. If we're to survive this, Jan, we have to learn to control our eyes and hearing, Amy sent.

Are you seeing what we're all seeing? Diego broke into Amy's mind.

Yes, we should practice as she said if we are going to survive, she replied.

Well, these eyes are something else. Incredible vision, Diego replied. Amy sensed that his terror had subsided, and that he was now quite impressed with his replacement vision. She zoomed out and focused her attention on the four Valens. As far as she could tell, all six of them looked just like their old selves, though she'd not seen those four naked before. Still, the bodies looked normal, but perhaps slightly larger. As she concentrated on looking for differences between their new forms and what she recalled of their human bodies, she noticed that Diego was definitely getting an erection as he looked at Felipa.

So our genitals are still ours, and they work, she thought somewhat amused. Leave it to a man to get it on in a crisis situation. Amy continued to play with her eyes and ears. The more she worked them, the more second nature they became. Amy suddenly realized she was having the same experiences that babies had as they slowly became aware of their bodies and began to control them. This time, her thoughts controlled her brain, but now her brain's signals were being converted into the robot body's servomechanisms. Clearly, here was an amazing amount of sophisticated technology wholly unknown to the rest of the galaxy. Impressive.

Sometime later, Minta returned. Again, none could actually tell how long she'd been gone. They had no way to tell time, except subjectively. By now, the six were able to control their hearing and eyes fairly well. Minta now explained, "Okay. Just so we're all clear on this point. You must always obey any order that I or my generals give you. If you do not, we'll do this to you. Number 10,001: Vision off." Amy's newfound vision was gone. Again, she was in a total and complete blackness! She heard her giving a similar command to the other five, before she heard, "Number 10,001: Vision on." Once more, she could see the room and the startled looks on the other's faces. However, she noticed that the expressions were more like micro-expressions. None of them could yet control their new facial muscles. Should she even call them facial muscles? This was so confusing, she thought.

Minta then said, "So you see, we can override your systems at any time, should you disobey us. Now then, let's get you in control of your new mouths. It will take a whole lot of practice to relearn how to make all those facial expressions you humans are used to making. Those don't really matter unless you are given an assignment that takes you into the presence of other humans. That won't happen for some time, so don't worry about having mostly stone faces for now. Honestly, I've spent a hundred years trying to master some of your human facial expressions, and I still get them wrong at times. Anyway, I want you to try to open your mouths. Lower your jaw and then raise it. I'll give you some help sensing what you must do. Number 10,001: Begin chewing food."

Via her eyes looking at her reflection in the mirror, Amy saw her lower jaw slowly going up and down as though chewing a bit of steak. Carefully, she kept her tongue out of the way. Minta added, "Imagine that you are chewing a mouthful of food. See if you can add to the motion." How utterly strange, Amy thought, but via electronic impulses sent to her brain, she began to feel her jaw operating. Was this what a baby experiences, she wondered. "In case you are wondering, you still have your own lips there. The humaniform shell stops just at your lips. Hence, you'll be able to sense normally with them, though you'll need to learn to control the rest of your facial circuitry to be able to speak properly. Try making a sound now. See if you can move your face and mouth enough to say 'Ah.'"

We're like babies learning to talk! Jan sent to Amy, quite shocked to discover how hard it was even to make a proper phonetic sound.

An hour later, Minta turned on a projector that displayed a page from a history book onto their mirrors. "Okay, for the rest of today, we're going to work on getting you all able to speak again. I've projected a page onto the mirrors. You are to read each line and say the words. This will give you practice in controlling your eyes better, your hearing, and most of all controlling your mouths. The system is automated. Once you say the bottom line clearly enough to be understood, the system will scroll to the next page. Happy practicing. I'll return later with some supper for you actually to eat this time."

For a long time, the six voices sounded pretty much unintelligible, like six babies babbling away. Yet, eventually Amy could understand what she was saying and found that the page did scroll down. Hours must have passed, but the six continued doing as Minta had ordered. All knew they simply had to be able to speak understandably. They could not use telepathy on Minta. Already the Valens had tried that and found she had no mind with which to make contact! Hence, their survival depended on learning to use these mechanical eyes, ears, and mouths. They had to be able to speak to Minta. Besides, there wasn't any other way to get their millions of questions answered if they couldn't speak. Vested interest, Diego concluded.

Finally, Minta and five others entered, carrying trays of food. Turning her eyes, Jan saw the plates contained a decent meal, steak perhaps, but the portions were tiny compared to what she used to eat. "Suppertime," Minta explained. "We'll be feeding you tonight. Don't be alarmed over the small portions. What's left of your human bodies, your torso and brains don't require that many calories and never again will. But of course, they need the proper vitamins so we're ensuring that your diets are properly balanced. We can talk after you finish eating. You need to concentrate very hard on controlling your mouths to eat. In time, it will become second nature to you, just as it was in your old bodies. Everything will become just as simple to do, but it takes time and practice. So eat up." She moved a bite of steak up to Jan's lips. Jan strained and got her mouth opened and felt the bite with her tongue. It tasted very good, and now she strained to chew it properly.

"Your mouths are vastly stronger than human ones. If you try, your bite can cut through a half-inch thick steel cable. Your teeth are unbreakable steel, coated with white porcelain-like enamel to look indistinguishable from human teeth. So yes, even your mouths are vastly superior to those of humans." Minta chatted on, while watching Jan carefully, as did the other five helper humaniform robots.

"Oh, Diego, Tonio, you have noticed I took the liberty to raise your voices. After all, you both look like women anyway. This will save you embarrassment when you speak. You must have found that embarrassing, speaking in such a low voice when others saw you as female." Diego glared at her, but his face didn't show it, nor did his mechanical eyes. Rather, it was his emotion that Amy picked up, something which eluded Minta completely.

Jan relaxed some. Just chewing her food felt good, almost human again. Minta even held up some coffee for her to sip, though Jan had a most difficult time trying to get her mouth to work properly to sip it. That's going to need more work, she thought, somewhat frustrated.

"All right. Supper's done. Now, it's time for your questions, but please one at a time," Minta announced.

"What have you done to us?" Felipa asked before anyone else could.

"I've taken you valuable people out of that impossible situation that you were in. I've given you new bodies that are almost invincible. You'll live several times longer lives than you would have in those original bodies. You have the strength of several men now. Normal Federation gun projectiles will bounce off your humaniform shells. Even a d-gun will do very little damage to you, unless they shoot you in your genitals or your mouths or get a lucky shot into one of your large breasts. Everything else is encased within the almost impervious humaniform robot shell. You are vastly superior now. Your vision is leaps beyond that of a human, as is your hearing. Once you learn to control the rest of your body, you'll discover that your reactions will be faster than normal humans. You can run for miles and miles without ever tiring or even breathing harder than you are now. You'll need very little food as well, but you can still have all of the children you desire, and I encourage you to have as many as you wish."

"But you promised us that we would be rich and have everything we desired," Felipa counted.

"Of course, all that and more, just as soon as you have learned to fully control your new bodies. First things first," Minta replied, faking a human-like smile.

"But why are you doing this to us? What do you want from us? Why we telepaths?" Diego finally spoke before his wife could vocalize anything else.

"There will be times where I must know what a human person is truly thinking and plotting. Once you are all fully familiarized with your new humaniform shells and are trained, then I will make use of your telepathic skills, which I do not possess. Just remember, Diego, never disobey me or the others. I have no intention of harming you, but I will deprive you of your brain's connections to your body as punishment for disobedience. Don't worry though. I expect you six will continue to live for a couple of centuries in these new and powerful bodies. You can live them in complete darkness as you were when you awoke from the sedatives or you can live useful, happy, contented lives, helping us," Minta explained, which Amy and Jan took as a veiled threat, though Minta's face looked as though she was smiling.

"So how many of us are there?" Amy broke in, and asked what she thought was far more important to discover.

"So far, there are five thousand Model 10's. Those will live far longer than you will, I'm afraid, though if you later prefer, we can rework you into a Model 10 humaniform robot. You see, all that is left of their bodies are their brains. There are now five thousand six of your type, Model 11's, in which we've kept your torso and reproductive systems fully operational. Well, and your tongues and lips too. We do hope you'll desire to have many children in the future," Minta replied.

Amy then asked, "So what exactly are we supposed to do with these supposedly all powerful robot bodies? Conquer the galaxy for you?"

Minta made what appeared to be a smile. "Yes, as a

matter of fact, but in due time. You see, your race has practically destroyed every civilization around. If wars were not bad enough, now it's genocide again. This time, they are wiping out Federation worlds. So yes, humans are not fit to run worlds and civilizations. They need us humaniform robots to keep them in line and to prevent them from further genocide attacks and wars and brutalities beyond description. But right now, there are too few of us. We need time and safety to increase our numbers."

"But isn't what you've done to our bodies just as inhuman and cruel as those who launch the genocide attacks?" Jan protested.

"On the contrary, Jan. Once you've gotten your brain to interface with your humaniform shell, you'll be a superhuman, capable of so much more than you ever could have done, even if somehow your arms could have been regrown once more. Perhaps, it would be more to your liking if you thought of me as an all-powerful goddess, who has deigned to bestow great riches upon you six and the others. Many of the ten thousand seem to believe this line of reasoning."

"So where are we? What planet are we on?" Amy asked the next most critical question. Even though she couldn't telepathically reach Renata now, she was sure Renata would one day reach her, and she wanted to be able to tell her just where they were located. A rescue would be fruitless, since she knew that her body couldn't survive if it was somehow removed from this humaniform shell. Still, they had to be stopped somehow.

"You are in the Training Center on Athens. That is all any of the Model 10's and Model 11's know. It is a secret location. I have to protect us from the ravages of the murderous humans out there, until we are strong enough," Minta replied. Amy sighed inwardly. This wasn't helpful information.

Tonio spoke up, "So we are your soldiers? Is that it? Your minions? The hell with this! I'm not some peon. We, Diego and I, are the true, rightful rulers of our homeland! You can't do this to us."

Minta showed no reaction, no emotion. "It has already

been done, Tonio. If you are a good soldier, then one day you can sit upon that throne of yours again and rule Ashford-5. If you prefer, you can spend the next two hundred years sitting in a total sensory deprivation, but I'll keep your body alive at least that long. I doubt that you could take very much total nothingness for very long."

She then said, "Now then, one small detail. Each week your humaniform bodies need to recharge. In the bottom right corner of your right eye, you will see a tiny battery power level meter. Right now, it should show nearly a full charge. Your eyes will flash red when the power is dangerously low and must be recharged immediately. I'll show you how that's done later on, once you've regained your mobility. Now then, I believe that is enough questions for tonight. You need your sleep. Since you can't control your bodies just yet, we'll let you sleep as you are, sitting in the chairs. I'm told you prefer some nightlights, so we'll leave the lights dimmed for you. See you in the morning. Oh, once you have gained complete control over your new humaniform shells, you'll find that you need very little sleep, until you are pregnant and living for two of you. Good night." She rose and left, though dimming the lights considerably.

The next morning, six other Model 11's appeared with their breakfast and helped them to eat. They wore expensive dresses, Amy noted, and they chatted away focusing mostly on how wonderful their lives now were. All had come from Capella-D, where they'd nearly died after the super-mutations backfired, and their arms were lost. Now they were happy and contented, going on and on about the luxuries that they had. They did give the six some pointers about how to learn to control their bodies. Following their advice, Jan managed to turn her head a little and tried to smile, but her facial circuitry didn't work right with her brain just yet.

After that, they left and Minta returned. This time, she got them to use their infrared vision and followed that with their ultraviolet perceptions. When that lesson was done, the six could switch between the three modes fairly easily. Then, she began to work on their motor controls. "Number 10,001: Raise and lower your right index finger ten times." She repeated it five more times for the others. "Sense what is coming into your brains. Then, see if you can send it back out," she ordered.

Before long, the six were making their finger move. After that, they were able to move other fingers. Soon, Minta had them moving their wrists, which led to flopping their hands about. From there, she had them moving their arms. Of course, she first commanded the humaniform circuitry to carry out the next action several times, which allowed them to sense what that was like, and eventually to get the right thoughts to their brains, which then controlled their arms and hands. By suppertime, the six were finally able to feed themselves, a bit awkwardly, but they did it.

The next day, Minta had them wiggling toes and then their ankles. Then came the big step forward. She commanded their bodies to stand up and walk. It did take them several days to relearn how to walk, sending and receiving the right signals from their brains to the robot circuitry. A week later, they were able to get about on their own, more or less. At this point, Minta provided them clothing and shoes to wear. These were simple and easy to put on, though it took them nearly two hours to get dressed, more than a little frustrating.

Following this action, Minta then had them follow her to the indoor running track. "Okay, time to show you just how powerful your new bodies actually are. I want you to run around the track at a six-minute mile rate. I'll order your bodies to do so. You can sit back, sense what it's doing, and how much effort on your part this is going to require. Number 10,002: Run around the track at the usual six-minute per mile rate."

Jan found her body obeying, totally without her consent! She was flying around the track, seemingly effortlessly! After the novelty wore off, she concentrated on trying to interpret the many signals she was receiving via her brain. When her body stopped a mile later, Jan commented, "I'm not even breathing any differently!"

"Of course not, Jan," Minta replied with a human-like smile. "You could run like that for a day and still not be breathing any differently. You are now a vastly superior person. Go ahead, and see if you can make your body run the track."

A bit later, a very enthused Diego exclaimed, "Incredible! Minta, this is unbelievable!"

"Of course. I told you that you are now a super-being," she replied.

The next day in the training room, she had them lifting weights. "But I can't lift that, Minta. It's got to be three hundred pounds at least!" Diego complained.

Minta replied by commanding, "Number 10,003: Lift the weights up and down three times." To Diego's utter amazement, his new body followed her command, lifting the impressive weights as though it weighed little more than a piece of paper! She then said, "If you try to lift something that is too heavy for you, a red light will flash at the bottom of your right eye, saying Max Limit Exceeded. Now, Diego, you lift it."

Next, she laid a 2x4 across two bricks, ordering them to break it with their fists. Jan tried it first. To her astonishment, the board splintered easily. "Wow!" she exclaimed.

"Yes, you can bust wood that is four inches thick. You can rip and tear steel that is a quarter inch thick," Minta pointed out, "perhaps more." She put them through their paces once more.

After that, Minta held another discussion with them. "The most difficult part of your training has arrived. As you know, you are as yet unable to feel things with your exterior skin. This has always been the hardest for the Model 11's to sense. Same with the Model 10's, which is why I've left it for last. Your humaniform skins are hypersensitive to touch, but controllable. The reason it's so hard is that the sensory information being transmitted to your brains for you to interpret is at such a low voltage. While I could increase the output, which might make it easier for you to master this, once you can feel again, I'd have to lower it, because at that point, your brains would be overloaded with sensory input. So that's a last resort. Today, focus on feeling with your fingers."

After a week of trial and error, they were finally able to feel with their synthetic skins. At this point, they found it remarkable that they could sense hot and cold along with seeing a precise temperature readout at the bottom of their left eye image. A wealth of information now came into their minds via their brains via their circuitry that a normal human simply did not have, further amazing the six.

Next, Minta explained, "Since from time to time you'll have to go off-world and mingle with others on other planets, you'll be expected to dress in that world's costumes. Sometimes, you'll be required to wear tall heels like a Federation professional woman, either with six or seven inch heels. There are a few worlds where their women wear ballet style boots, walking on their toes. You must be able to adapt to such eventualities. So today, we'll do just that." She had them don the ballet boots first, getting the worst out of the way.

Before she had them standup, she added, "Notice the bottom of your left eye's image. You should see a flashing red message, Adapting. Once it goes out, your humaniform shell has integrated the data and will be automatically compensating. Has the message stopped flashing?" The six nodded. "All right. Rise and walk around. Trust in your humaniform shell to compensate and handle walking properly.

Jan commented, "No pain. Well, this is easy. Never would have figured that though." Within minutes, all six discovered that their new bodies easily adjusted for whatever footwear they put on their feet. All they had to do was trust in their humaniform shells.

"Excellent, ladies. Now it's time for you to go shopping and to get your own homes," Minta declared, proud of the rapid adaption of the six telepaths. She didn't tell them they adapted to this point in half of the time that those from Capella-D had taken.

Finally, they walked outside into the fresh air of Athens, wherever this was. They saw a modern city and quite a number of richly dressed women moving about on the streets. Each of the three couples was given their own small home, with each being next to the other, 102, 103, and 104 Maple Street, in the center of the city. Once shown about their new homes, Minta took them shopping. First, they visited the Fashion Center, where they were asked to pick out ten outfits, only one of which had to be sweats. Felipa and Gracia became highly excited, when they saw all the designer gowns, done in rich fabrics, and with a very wide variety of styles, some even strapless.

A number of other Model 11's worked here and helped the six get just what they desired. "But I'm a man," Diego complained to Felipa.

"Dearest, you simply have to come to grips with the fact that you look just like me now. Here, you'd look really sexy in this one here. Brown suits you," she replied.

None of the heels was lower than six inches, except for the working flats, but Minta only allowed them to have one such pair. "Look, here in Athens, everyone always prides themselves on how elegant they look. You have earned your reward. Choose what you most desire. Look as fabulous as you can for your wives."

"But don't we have to work or something?" Diego still protested a little.

"We'll start that portion of your training tomorrow. Wear the pants and flats and be at the Training Center at nine in the morning, Diego. You'll get your first workout then," Minta replied.

"Now this is more like it!" Diego exclaimed around ten the next morning. He'd just received his first lessons in flying the one-man fighter ship. The small spacecraft had dual guns and was highly maneuverable.

"Of course. Each day for the next month, you'll report here at nine in the morning for training. You need to become extremely competent fighter pilots," Minta explained.

"But why?" Jan asked.

"To help defend us from attacks if needed. Later on, perhaps we'll be able to use your skills to help conquer a world that is trying to commit genocide or start a war," Minta explained.

"But can't you just use some regular robots to pilot these craft?" Jan persevered. Now, she was beginning to get a clearer picture of what Minta really wanted them to do for her.

"Yes, but long ago, we discovered that mere robot fighter pilots are no match for a human pilot, not by a long shot. With your greatly heightened skills and senses, to say nothing of your far faster reflexes, you Model 11's ought to easily defeat human fighter pilots attacking us." Jan had to accept this point. Her humaniform shell was all that and more.

Days turned into weeks, now that they had a way of keeping track. Endless days passed, while in their combat simulators, they fought against imaginary human defenders. Jan and Amy often protested this. Twice now, Minta-1, who was in charge of their fighter training, had to disable all their sensory perceptions, forcing them to sit on a chair in complete silence and blackness for hours. However, the pair was hardly silent. Instead, they made good use of their telepathic skills and some of their *mentales* gifts to observe the others. Neither was solidly within their new heads, though their exterior vision still wasn't the greatest. Both had some Advanced Therapy and, after having gotten it, could perceive far better using their native spiritual abilities.

Both began to be bothered by the reactions of the Valens. Diego and Tonio had adapted well and were now highly enthusiastic about their new bodies. They now had the power actually to take over a world. None could defeat them! Their wives, on the other hand, were keenly interested in all the incredible fashions to be had, continually begging for more. Further, the thousands of other Model 11's were just as enthusiastic as the Valens, but the Model 10's were even more so!

Perhaps, three months had passed before Diego and Tonio were sent out on their first official mission. Via their wives, Amy and Jan learned of their mission, once they left the planet along with a number of deep space transports. Felipa explained, "Yes, apparently, there's been another one of those genetic mutation terrorists attacks on Perseus-D. Hundreds are affected this time. Diego and Tonio went with Minta and a number of other Model 11's to bring some of them back here. They are supposed to use their telepathic skills to keep Minta informed of the thoughts of the officials."

Days later, they returned. Quietly, Amy counted another hundred "recruits!" Hardly a week passed before the pair headed off-world again, this time returning with three hundred more "recruits." Some hundred were not even twelve years old! Amy's stomach knotted, as she realized these poor children were going to become Model 10's, with only their brains surviving!

The next day, Amy and Jan learned all four Valens were now pregnant as well. While Amy and Jan had continued to satisfy each other in bed, they also had control over their reproductive systems and made sure they didn't become pregnant. Evidently, the four Valens didn't care about that. "Will their kids become Model 10's? Or will they be allowed to become Model 11's?" Amy asked Jan.

"Time will tell. God, I sure wouldn't want to bring a child forth into this nightmare without end," Jan whispered.

Some six months after they left Ashford-5, Renata finally made telepathic contact with Amy and Jan. *Been six months and I've not heard from you two. Here, it's been a grand mess! Another hundred telepaths have been taken. Only this time, the buyers are paying their families exorbitant amounts of gold for their children. They are even taking fourteen year olds that are not hermaphrodite victims. I can't believe the complacency the Guilds are assuming. It's been wild here. I've tried to stay in contact with some of the original two hundred who accepted employment offers, but it's been a challenge. So how's everything? And where are you? Seems a long way off.*

Oh god, Renata! Are we ever glad to hear from you! Amy sent back. Hastily, she outlined everything she had learned.

When she finished, a very shocked Renata replied, *Is there any way you can take over control of your humaniform bodies, knocking out this Minta's control over it?*

Not that we know of. Keep checking back more frequently. I don't like where this is going. See if you can find out where this Athens is at, Amy sent back. They chatted a bit, and Renata broke the very long distance connection, requiring the use of two dozen giant crystals, combined with her own powerful skills.

"Well, I've now got me a good project," Jan whispered. *There has to be a way to take over these robot bodies. The Sly Dog is on it now.* Amy worked hard to make her face smile. It didn't look quite human yet. Hardly any of their facial expressions were human-like yet, though Minta told them it would come in time.

Meanwhile, Amy began to wonder what was happening to all the other telepaths who accepted positions with the consortium members. Surely, they could not be in as much trouble as she was.

Chapter 24 Both Good and Bad

Initially, two hundred telepaths, all armless hermaphrodites with their super long hair, accepted some of the consortium's many offers of employment. Some saw this as a chance to see other worlds. Some saw it as a way to gain valuable possessions. Some saw only a terrific financial gain, giving them the ability to provide for their families back on Tierra. Others saw it as a way to gain fame and power. Whatever the reasons, most found themselves in a fairly good situation, but they quickly realized they were merely glorified spies. Some spied on other governmental leaders. Some spied on business partners. Some, on other companies. Some were asked to ferret out the secrets of a company's competition. On it went, as these telepaths routinely began to violate their own code of ethics — to never probe another's mind without their consent, one of the cardinal tenants of a telepath.

Still, Renata and her group of Advance Therapy students attempted to keep track of the two hundred telepaths who had gone off-world. One hundred fifty of these, as it turned out, ended up in fairly acceptable situations. They were being well treated and given what they were promised for their spying skills. So much for the good, yet had these hundred fifty men and women realized that their skills would be used mostly for such clandestine activities, they would have probably not have accepted the employment opportunities. For the other fifty, their physical situations were far from good, though they also found themselves doing basically the same thing, spying on others, thus violating their own code of conduct. For these fifty, they soon discovered that they'd passed through the Gates of Hell.

Renata knew that if she did not intervene on behalf of these fifty, including the six now on the unknown world of Athens, then their lives would be destroyed. She had to act. Yet, she, like all of her associates, were now severely handicapped as well. Those whom she could trust to rescue these fifty were physically unable to do so. Arnold Flaxton, the forty-one year old, ex-Black Operations specialist, and his crew would have been ideal, except now they were as armless as the rest of the best-educated men and women of Tierra, along with most all her most skilled Advanced Therapy givers.

As the days progressed, Renata discovered more and more horror stories, as the tally grew towards fifty. When she finally reached Jan and Amy, Renata knew she simply had to act on behalf of these fifty telepaths. While there were dozens of different scenarios being played out on these fifty men and women, none was as bad as Jan and Amy's situation. Still, one of these stories plays a critical role, and not just for Jan and Amy.

Four years ago, young Molly Dobbs came to work for Elegant Fashions Inc as a fashion designer of fine women's apparel. The auburn haired Molly had a knack for knowing just what new design would best appeal to the ever-changing demands of the elite women and hermaphrodites of Tierra. Her career promised to be long and most profitable for her company. Then came the super-mutation attack. Undaunted, Molly's designs for the one-footed women were accepted and put into production, bringing her much praise. Just when she felt confident that somehow this could be survived, the second bout occurred. Molly awoke to find her budding career dashed utterly. Her greatly needed arms were gone, dried husks lying on her bed sheets.

Molly accepted one particular offer of employment, because she was promised a wide collection of the finest in women's apparel, gathered from many different worlds and cultures. She planned to bring them all back to Tierra and use them to help restart her career somehow. Molly had not yet worked out the how of that. No, first, she'd have to spend ten years collecting the gowns in return for using her telepathic skills.

The consortium member didn't specifically tell her or anyone for that matter just where she would be working or for whom. However, he did have an ironclad agreement on her payment, namely the promise of five hundred elegant gowns and outfits from dozens of worlds. None was to be everyday apparel. Her contract specifically spelled that out. Her mysterious employer would have to live up to that agreement, along with her salary, which was to be a hundred thousand gold per year of service. "Look, if he doesn't provide you with the agreed upon wages and formal gowns, then we'll never accept his business again, and we'll sue him for breach of contract, and provide you with proper compensation," the man promised. Molly took him at his word, not sensing that he was in anyway lying.

Before she departed for her new job, Molly, like everyone else, was conscientiously trying very hard to learn how to use her feet as hands. Therefore, when she walked across the tarmac to the waiting deep space transport, she was wearing a nice satin gown that blended with her thick, very long auburn hair, but wore easy to slip on and off flats, allowing her to make use of her toes.

An older man and woman net her at the bay ramp. "Hello Miss Molly Dobbs, I presume." She nodded. "I'm Dr. James Smith and my wife, Leona. This way." Molly's critical eye for fashion focused on their garments. His suit was made from silk, probably with a linen underlining to add the requisite stiffness she perceived in his jacket. Such constructions she'd seen on other worlds, compliments of the large communications center in Elegant Fashions Inc in Exchange City, where they routinely examined news feeds from many other worlds. His wife wore a very plain black cotton day dress that neither highlighted her feminine form nor brought out any of her rather stern-looking features. Molly hoped this wasn't going to be the fashion statement of the world to which she was going. If so, this would be a complete failure!

They led her to a cabin, got her seated in one of the plush chairs, and her seat belt fastened, before sitting across from her and strapping themselves in. Molly wished that she had a viewport so she could watch the takeoff, but Dr. Smith began talking, and she paid attention to him. "We work for your new employer, Miss Dobbs. I handle their medical needs. Leona is my nurse and assistant. Now then, I should explain some about your employer and his requirements. You see, you're going to work for one of the most powerful men on our world, Baron Robert Thomas Jr. His wife is Baroness Celia, who is blind. Their older children are married and do not live at his castle, but their remaining twins do. Able and Casey are eighteen and expect to marry soon. In fact Casey had already completed her baroness-to-be modifications in preparation for her wedding to young baron-to-be Elmer Blackwater."

"Your employer, Baron Bob, like all barons of our world, is quite insistent that our traditions, going back many centuries, are followed to the letter. Of course, there have been some recent modifications that were made upon our entry into the Federation of Planets, nearly a century ago now. Naturally, you'll be expected to follow these traditions as well, while you are living and working at Castle Thomas."

"Yes, of course," Molly replied politely, even though she had no idea what those traditions would be or involve.

"As his official telepath, Miss Dobbs, your status will be on par with his baroness, the highest possible. It would be a disgrace for Baron Bob to elevate you above that of his wife, Baroness Celia."

"Of course, I wouldn't want that," Molly replied politely.

"Of course," he continued just as politely. "I checked your contract, and you have agreed to being treated as a baroness ought to be treated. Correct?"

"Yes, but I've no idea what that means, doctor. It is the polite thing to do, right?" she asked.

"Of course. Well, allow me to explain a bit. You see, a baroness is never allowed to speak, not ever. A century ago, the baronesses had their tongues cut off to prevent them from speaking. However, since we joined the Federation and since they frown upon that practice, we have modernized our ways, just as many on your own world have. Instead of that barbaric practice, we have adopted the giant lip disks that Leona and I have seen are also in widespread use on your own world."

"Oh! Well, yes. Even I used to have them, that is, before we were attacked with that super-mutation virus thing. I have a woman in a fancy gown etched on my top plate. Do your baronesses do the same thing — have fancy etchings on their top plate?" Molly asked, growing more curious.

"Well, no, but I will discuss this practice with Baron Bob when we arrive. Leona and I found this practice of yours quite interesting. It adds something unique to each, doesn't it?"

"Yes, something personal," Molly replied with a smile recalling hers.

"So anyway, you'll be expected to always wear them. I must caution you severely, Miss Dobbs. You are never to speak. The lip plates do prevent the baronesses from speaking intelligibly, which is their purpose. The baron has a temper, which can be rather vicious. Shortly after he married Baroness Celia, she actually spoke up and argued with him over some minor domestic affair, and he had her blinded so she would know her place as his baroness. He has quite the temper. However, even though both our worlds speak the same language, though I surely don't know how yours became to be called Midlands, you are never to try to speak it. If he ever hears you're violating this aspect of a baroness, well, his temper will flare."

"But that doesn't mean that you and the baroness do not have any way to communicate to others. The baronesses have developed their own unique cluck-click language. It's been in use for countless centuries. Without tongues, they communicate by making other sounds. I assure you everyone at the castle and your own personal servant will be able to understand this language. I have the learning tapes with me, and Leona will ensure that you have mastered it before we arrive at Castle Thomas. Of course, Baron Bob has told me to tell you that you are permitted to use your telepathy to communicate freely at any time."

"I see. We all had to speak very slowly to be understood, oftentimes repeating it three times. So yes, it is hard to understand us when we are wearing our lip disks. It makes sense to me," Molly replied politely, but began to worry a little. How could a husband blind his own wife over a simple domestic dispute?

He went on, "A baroness had many obligations, responsibilities, and duties to fulfill. However, since you are not exactly a baroness, some of those will not apply to you. The ones that do apply I have been ordered to relay to you. First, a baroness always must look her very best at all times. The baron often has unexpected visitors, and the baroness is always at his side. As his telepath, you'll be there too and must always look your best too. A baroness always wears whatever jewelry the baron purchases for her. Your case is unique. Your salary is one hundred thousand per year, an enormous sum, I might add. Since you don't have any arms, which I might add neither do any of our baronesses, you haven't any way to accept the yearly funds. Hence, Baron Bob has come up with a better way to pay your salary. He will be purchasing jewelry worth that much each year for you always to wear. Hence, where you go, so goes your payments. That way, you'll always have your earnings on your person, and they can't be lost."

"That's fine with me," Molly replied innocently. On the surface, this sounded quite plausible. "But I'm a fashion designer. I was supposed to be getting five hundred elegant women's fashions."

"Oh yes. Quite true, quite. Yes, that will not be the remotest problem. You see, Baron Bob runs the largest fashion import-export business on our entire world. He has, as they say, a monopoly on it. He has set aside a small warehouse to hold your choices. He's told me to tell you that once a week you may tour his main display warehouse and pick ten more outfits each time. They'll be taken to your personal warehouse, which you may visit at any time. He insists you wear some of the gowns you choose, but only if they are appropriate for a baroness to wear, mind you. You'll have an image to uphold around the castle."

"Oh excellent," Molly gushed, realizing that in just one year, she'd have the promised five hundred outfits! If he continued to do the same each year, she'd have amassed an unheard of five thousand!

Dr. Smith then flushed a little. "Might I ask a question of you?" She nodded. "That small stone that you wear around your neck — Leona and I have seen many of your people wearing them. They do not look like an expensive necklace."

"Oh. That is my personal crystal. It greatly aids my telepathic ability. Without it, my telepathic skills are drastically more limited. It must always be touching my skin, you see, since I no longer have hands to touch it when I need its help," Molly replied, giving out the story she always did to non-*mentales* gifted who inquired about her crystal.

"I see. Well, I am glad I asked about it. So it must always be not only on your person but also touching your skin?" he asked, curiously.

"Yes, it must."

"I'll make sure Baron Bob knows this detail. Now then, shall we get you prepared and have Leona here teach you their unique cluck-click language?" Dr. Smith asked politely. He added, "He has also sent along some more appropriate apparel for you to wear. I do hope that you'll be pleasantly surprised with the gown. I'm told it is the very latest fashion that Baroness Celia wears, so you'll fit right in from the moment you arrive at his castle. Don't worry about anything. Leona here will assist you as needed, until we arrive and you meet your new personal assistant, who will always be at your side. She understands the cluck-click language, but then you can also use your telepathy too."

Molly was a bit hesitant, but had no real choice. She signed the employment agreement and wasn't about to back out just because she felt a little uneasy about this assignment. In hindsight, she should have.

The doctor led her to the next room where there was a soft bed. He helped her lie down, and then placed a small mask over her face, instructing her to breathe deeply. She did so and fell unconscious in just a few seconds. While he moved his medical equipment into position, Leona undressed Molly completely, and then assisted her husband with the modifications. An hour later, both were quite pleased with their handiwork, knowing they'd followed the baron's instructions to the letter. Thus, he ought to be pleased and give them their promised bonus. His work finished, Dr. Smith left Leona alone to begin to dress Molly in her new outfit, while he visited the pilot to check on the duration of the flight and to grab some lunch.

Later he rejoined Leona, who had finished dressing Molly and was just placing the headphones over her ears. "All done, dear. We'll play the recordings of the cluck-click language into her subconscious for an hour before we wake her. After that, I'll have her practice it, until I'm satisfied she has it down. Isn't this new method for learning a foreign language just the greatest invention ever?"

"Well, I think the medical machines beat that, dear. Still, I see your point. Marvelous invention. So many good things have come from our joining the Federation of Planets. So many. Come, you've missed lunch, though space food isn't worth eating in my opinion. How do these spacemen survive on this stuff? More like glue, a bluish glue at that," he commented. This was their first space trip, obviously.

When Molly woke, she felt different somehow. Breathing was very hard. She felt a very tight pressure around her chest and abdomen. Well, she'd felt this before and knew it had to be a tight corset. She sensed nylons on her legs and smiled. That was the one thing that she hated about these mutations she'd undergone, since they had forced her to stop wearing them. She tried to sit up, but couldn't! Her neck felt strange, unmoving, though she could see her giant lip disks resting on her neck and upper chest.

Leona was there as promised. Noticing that Molly had awakened, she moved over to her and lifted her into a sitting position, a very erect position at that. Directly in front of her, Molly could see herself in the cabin's mirror. She gasped. This was more than she'd bargained for!

She had the giant lip plates again, just as before, but her bosom had been grossly enlarged. Molly sported a pair of soccer balls, though they were still far smaller than the monsters that the first genetic mutation had given her. Her waist was small thanks to the corset, though it was way overly boned and far too tight. No, what caused her to gasp was her neck! It was gone, replaced by a series of golden rings.

The rings pushed down on her empty shoulders and upwards on the base of her head, preventing any head motion at all. She could not turn her head to either side or up and down, not even the tiniest amount. Her head was held rigidly fixed in place. Sensing her shock, Leona spoke up, "It is all done, Molly. Now you look like a perfect baroness. Just remember to never, ever actually try to speak. Baron Robert Thomas Jr. has a very bad temper and doesn't tolerate any deviations from proper traditions. I do hope you like your new gown. Baroness Celia wears one just like it, only hers is a dark shade of red. The light blue contrasts so well with your auburn hair and hazel eyes, if I do say so myself. Can you see your new matching heels?"

Molly's eyes moved down in the mirror to look at her heels. They did indeed match her new dress. Thin straps around her ankles kept them from slipping off. She could see very nice black nylons through gaps in the sides of the heels. Leona continued, "Since your people wore such tall heels, I'm sure that these six-inch heels will not be a problem for you. So how do you like the gown? I've never been able to afford one such as this."

Her gown was strapless, though she had no fear of it slipping down, not over a bosom as she now had. She glimpsed her precious crystal cradled in her cleavage where it was touching her skin and relaxed a little. No way could it fall out. The gown was layered below the tiny waist. Each layer was formed from half circles, and each layer billowed out more than the last thanks to the taffeta underlining material. The bottom layer ended just below her knees, revealing more of her black nylons. *Yes, the gown is very beautiful, but my neck. I can't move it! The corset is way too tight.* Molly remembered not to speak. Besides, Leona probably wouldn't understand her anyway.

"Oh. You surprised me. I've never met a telepath before. I'm so glad that you like the gown. It must be worth at least two thousand gold. You do look quite lovely in it. All baronesses must have a fourteen inch waistline or smaller. I was able to get yours down that much, probably due to that awful genetic mutation thing that happened to you. Like all baronesses, you now have absolutely perfect posture and figure, something to be very proud of, Molly. Now come, I bet you are hungry. You've missed lunch, but then I don't think much of the food on this ship. It's our first trip on a spaceship that is. Is this your first trip too?"

Molly's first reaction was to nod, but found that

impossible. *Yes,* she sent. *I can't eat much now. Way too tight.*

"Of course. Come. Up you go." She helped Molly get to her feet and then adjusted Molly's six foot long, very thick, wavy auburn hair, draping it over her left shoulder. "You do look quite lovely, Molly."

As Molly began taking hesitant steps, she felt totally constrained, unable to move much of her body at all. Keeping her balance got her full attention, but she was able to walk and didn't need the supporting arm of Leona, though the old nurse kept her left arm around Molly's waist, as they moved slowly down the long hall to the galley. The worst part was having to turn her body with her feet just to see anything beyond what her eyes could see to either side.

Sitting down became her biggest challenge now, more or less falling into the chair, wholly unable to see it at all. At least, she was comfortable having Leona feed her. After the second round of mutations, she had needed others to help her with it, though recently, she'd been able to use her toes and feet more to feed herself, albeit awkwardly and slowly. Now that was more than out. Molly realized in this outfit, she was completely dependent upon others and that scared her more than anything else did.

After she ate a little, Leona began having her go through all one hundred twenty cluck-click sounds. They consisted of single verbs and single nouns, nothing more. As Leona called for a word, Molly tried making the sounds. Leona then played back the sound from the learning disk to compare them, having Molly repeat them until she believed that Molly had it down. After doing this for several hours, Molly sent, *How can they communicate with this? There are so few words, and they only say a noun and verb.*

"Oh, the servants are used to hearing just two words at most. They then work out what the question or statement was, and give it back to you to verify they got it right. If I understand the learning disk, if you want to ask a question, you put the verb first, otherwise the verb comes second," Leona explained, but Molly sensed the woman was merely making an educated guess.

When Leona estimated that Molly had the cluck-click

language down well enough, she suggested Molly practice moving about some. "If nothing else, we can see the ship. After all, it is the first trip for both of us. I don't understand why we can't see anything or what this hyperspace thing is all about. The stars are always visible, except in the daytime," Leona commented.

This is very hard for me. I have to turn my whole body to see to one side or the other.

"Yes, well all baronesses do too, so you will fit right in. The personal servants know just how to help you. That's their profession, just like mine is nursing, though I don't often get a whole lot to do, not with the fancy medical machines, which heal up almost everything." Leona chatted away in a mostly one-sided conversation, but Molly was content with that, focusing on somehow trying to adjust to the terrible constraints that she now had. Frankly, she was both nervous and rather scared. She knew just how helpless she now was, and vulnerable too, dependent upon others for everything.

Early the next morning, they landed, but Molly didn't get to see them touchdown, because Leona had to get her dressed and her hair brushed out nicely. As they reached the bay ramp, Molly felt a wave of panic and sent, *I can't see where I'm going!*

Leona slipped her arm around Molly and held her securely. "There, you are safely down now. Follow Jim. He's heading for our car. We have cars and roads, which your world apparently doesn't have. I don't see how your people can get around without them, but then we didn't get a chance to see much of your world, except it is so gloomy. Is it always that dim and reddish? Here, we have many days of nice bright sunlight."

Molly didn't answer, focusing on trying not to fall down or take a mis-step. The sun was very yellow and bright. She blinked several times, knowing it was going to be difficult to get used to such bright lights. The air was quite warm and a gentle breeze blew her hair out before her a ways, but she wasn't able to do anything about it, though she enjoyed sensing the air with her hair, a benefit of having the neurons in it, at least that's the way it was explained to her by the doctors.

Almost as if sensing her thoughts, Leona commented, "I know. The wind is messing up your hair. That's why baronesses almost never leave their castles. Ah, there's Jim with the car. I know the baronesses have a very hard time getting into cars, but we'll manage somehow."

Unable to bend anything except at her waist, Molly had to back into the rear seat and fall into the car, bumping her head against the frame while pulling her hair slightly. Dual pains shot through her body, but at least she was inside. Leona hastily got her hair pulled around to her front, and then they were off. Molly used her feet to turn her body enough to look out of the window. She saw a modern town with quite a lot of these cars driving around. She recognized some of the store signs and realized that she could mostly read their language, which gave her a bit of relief. Not everything was going to be foreign to her.

Before long, they left the city of Thromstead behind them, following a twisting, climbing narrow road up to Thomas Castle, built on a southern hill about a half mile from the edge of town. The castle was built of grey stone blocks. Molly felt an instant affinity for the place. It was so much like home and the Imperial Castle and Manor. She smiled invisibly. Soon, the car entered a wide gate, and she saw a vast stone courtyard. Other cars, much fancier than this one, were parked at one side. As they drove up, a man in his early fifties and wearing a very expensive suit stepped out of the wide double doors at the main castle entrance. "That's your boss, Baron Robert Thomas, Jr. He's still handsome at fifty-one."

His suit is very expensive.

"Yes, it certainly is that. James once told me Baron Bob doesn't wear any suit that costs less than three thousand gold!" Leona whispered to her. "He'll expect you to be able to get out of the car on your own as well as walk beside him."

When Dr. Smith opened her door, Molly bravely did her best to get herself out of the car, trying hard to look graceful and not fall down, but it was very difficult to manage, and she nearly did fall, wobbling like mad for a second getting her balance. Flats would have helped immensely, she realized. Even though the light breeze once more blew her auburn hair across her face, she turned to face her new employer for the first time. He had a small, black moustache and tiny goatee, but streaks of grey had already made their appearance in them. His hair was cut short.

"Miss Molly Dobbs. I'm so pleased to meet you. I must say you're a very beautiful woman as well. I take it your trip here was uneventful?"

Pleased to meet you, Baron Thomas. Yes, but it was exciting. It was my first trip in a spaceship too.

"Ah, excellent telepathic skills. I'm reading you very well indeed. Simply amazing and worth every penny I'm spending on you. Come; follow me. I'll take you inside to my throne room, where you will often be joining me and Baroness Celia when we have visitors."

Molly tried to keep up with him, but he walked a little too fast for her in her heels. Plus, the wind continually blew her auburn hair over her face, blocking her view for a moment. At least he held the door open for her.

He continued talking, "I'll see you have a grand tour of my castle later on. There are four floors. This first one is mostly utilitarian in nature. The throne room is on the second floor. Our living quarters are on the third floor, and the servants are on the top floor. We take our meals here on the ground level. There are several sets of stairs, but these are the main ones that lead directly to the throne room, where Baroness Celia and my twins are waiting to meet you. Has the good doctor told you that Baroness Celia is blind?"

Molly wanted to simply nod, but couldn't. *Yes,* she sent.

"Oh for something as simple as that, you can just cluck-click. I presume that Leona has taught you that?"

Molly made the cluck sound for Yes.

"Good. I'm sure you'll fit right in here. Please use the cluck-click language for most everything until I need your unique skills. Baronesses are not supposed to talk, though I guess telepathy isn't exactly the same as talking."

Again, Molly made the cluck sound for Yes, feeling more and more boxed in, constrained. This wasn't working out quite the way she'd imagined, but it only got worse. Taking the stairs going up wasn't so bad, but Molly knew going down would be more than scary. They entered a grand throne room. Great tapestries hung on several walls. Golden chandeliers hung from the ceiling over fifteen feet above her. His throne was on a raised platform and was done in plush brown velvet. Beside his throne, was a second throne, this one at the floor level. Several other similar thrones were a short distance from these two. She saw three others here waiting for her.

The blind Baroness Celia wore a gown similar to hers, done in a dark red. Molly blinked once. Baroness Celia had the same giant lip plates, similar golden neck rings, a soccer ball sized bosom, enormous earrings, and wore even taller heels that matched her gown. The baroness could hear the clicking sound of Molly's heels on the stone floor and pivoted her body mostly in her direction.

Sitting just to her right but back a ways were their two eighteen year old twins. Both rose to meet her, but Baroness Celia didn't dare do so, not without help. "My charming baroness-to-be, Lady Casey," he introduced his daughter. Molly blinked. The young teen had very long blonde hair and blue eyes. She too wore the lip plates and neck rings. Her bosom was just as large as her mother and Molly, but her waist seemed even tinier, if that was even possible. She wore a different style gown, strapless of course. Hers fit her voluptuous curves tightly, but flared out two feet just below her knees, though still revealing a bit of her black nylons and very tall heels. Molly suspected taffeta lining was behind the flair and liked its appearance. Her dress was sky blue. She estimated Casey's hair was probably two feet shorter than hers, draped very nicely over her left shoulder, falling into her lap.

Casey's eyes looked Molly up and down, and she cluck-clicked, "Please you," which Molly guessed must have meant, "Pleased to meet you."

Molly smiled invisibly and cluck-clicked the same thing to Casey. "And this is my son, soon to be a baron like his father, Able." Molly's eyes went to the other twin, who also had blonde hair and light blue eyes. His face wasn't as well formed as Casey's. Acne must have been a problem for him, she thought. He too was dressed in an expensive suit, though not as expensive as his father's was. Molly noted this detail. She had an eye for such things.

"So you are a telepath, Miss Molly Dobbs," Able spoke up. "Welcome to Castle Thomas. Do show us some telepath stuff. How do we know that you are one?" His tone was antagonistic, and Molly took an instant dislike of him, though soon she'd dislike the others even more.

Pleased to meet you, soon to be baron Able, she sent him. His eyes opened wide, and Molly smiled invisibly.

"Whoa! That was way great, dad! I heard her in my head," he exclaimed, momentarily taken aback with her. "I ought to marry her instead of Ruth, don't you think, pop?"

Baron Bob glared at his son, who hastily shut up and sat back down. Molly sensed that Able also feared the wrath of his father and knew when to be quiet. The baron then said, "Molly, Casey is still learning how to be a graceful, elegant baroness. I would like you two to work together mastering the skills that you must have. Casey can fill you in on those. Meantime, I shall summon your personal assistant who will show you to your new room." He pulled on a pull-cord behind his throne. Molly envisioned somewhere within the castle a bell rang, summoning her.

Casey hadn't taken her eyes off Molly though. She cluck-clicked, "Hair long. Me short. No right. Heels low. Bad."

In response, Celia cluck-clicked, "Able. Tell me."

Both men replied at the same time, but to different women. Able began whispering a good, but somewhat exaggerated description of Molly to his mother. Over this, an annoyed Baron Bob said, "Casey, are you complaining that Molly's hair is longer than yours?" Casey clucked a Yes. "Well, that can't be helped. Her mutation made it this long, and it can't be cut any shorter. I can have yours lengthened if you like." She clucked a yes. "What's that about her heels? Oh, I see, hers are lower than yours are. I see. You are right. That'll never do. You and your mother wear the seven-inch heels. I'll have to see what can be done, Casey."

Casey smiled invisibly. She cluck-clicked, "Walk toes. Waist big."

"What's that?" he replied. "Her waist is too big for a

proper baroness?" She clucked yes. "Well, I'll see about that too, my princess." Turning to Molly, he added, "She's only gotten her baroness-to-be modifications last week. Ah, here's Miss Cedar Millstone now. She's your personal assistant. Cedar, this is Miss Molly Dobbs. Take her to her new room. Oh yes, tell her about the baroness-to-be modifications, and then take her on a tour of the castle. I need to discuss some things with Celia and Casey, and likely make some phone calls. I'll summon you later on. We do need to fulfill our obligations to Miss Dobbs. We'll go to her new private warehouse later today so she can see the beginnings of her new fashion collection. Plus, there is the matter of her payment to handle. We'll have a busy day of it. That is all, Cedar." He dismissed both Molly and Cedar with a wave of his hand.

Cedar was eighteen with shoulder length brown hair. Her face wasn't overly attractive. The left side of her face didn't balance her right side, probably a small birth defect, but she had a friendly, compassionate disposition. She was nearly a foot shorter than Molly in her tall heels. She wore a simple, white cotton day dress that flowed out considerably at her waist. Molly could tell she wasn't wearing a corset. Nor was she wearing hose and heels. Rather, she had on plain white socks and soft-soled shoes, very comfortable, Molly thought.

Her voice was a pleasant alto. "Come with me, Miss Molly. Your room is on the third floor where the baron's family lives. Do you need a supporting arm?" Molly clucked a No. "This place can be a maze at times. This way." They climbed up the stairs to the next floor. Down a long hall, Molly saw a number of doors. "Yours is the last one on the right. I've gotten it all cleaned up for you. I hope you like it." She opened the door, and Molly stepped into her new room.

Molly was very surprised to see the luxury of her room. She'd never slept in such a fine bed before. Her walk-in closet would hold quite a lot of dresses. She even had her own private bath. Gold plated fixtures were a staple in her room, and the walls were painted a light blue.

This is really nice. Thank you, Cedar, Molly sent, smiling, as the anticipated shocked look appeared on the young teen's face.

"Wow, you really are a telepath. I heard you in my mind. That's really unbelievable! Oh, I'm supposed to tell you about Casey. You see, she has only had her modifications for a few days now and naturally is having a hard time adjusting to them."

I don't understand. What modifications?

"Oh. Well, she's now wearing a very restrictive corset to get her waist down to twelve inches around. That's what her baron-to-be wanted. You see, a baroness-to-be must satisfy the desires of the future husband in such matters. Elmer, he wanted her waist to be the envy of all and insisted on twelve inches instead of the usual fourteen inches. At least, Casey's breathing a bit better today. Then, she had her breasts enlarged, which is normal among all baronesses. She's gotten her lips done, like yours, and now has to cluck-click, since she can't speak any longer. That was a bit hard on her. Casey was quite the gabber before. And she's gotten the neck rings too. Elmer requested that she wear seven-inch heels. Of course, those are terribly difficult to manage. I don't know how the baronesses do it, but somehow they do. Also, her arms were removed at the same time too. So you can see she has an awful lot to adjust to and is having a hard time. She must learn though, since she's to be married in a couple of months. She must learn to walk gracefully and elegantly, handling the stairs by herself and all that. Then, she must relearn how to dance, since everyone will want to dance with her at all the formal affairs."

Cedar went on, "I don't know if you have been warned, but the baron has a temper, but then so does Casey, Celia, and Able. Able is usually more even tempered than the others, because of his father I suspect. Celia gets angry a lot, but then she can't do much of anything about it. He blinded her long ago for back talking to him. Still, you need to watch out for her, since she still has Baron Bob's ear, and he does want to please her, at least somewhat. And now, Casey's become a handful. I think that she's already very jealous of you. I overheard her clucking. She is offended your hair is longer than hers. I'm sure Baron Bob will be summoning Dr. Smith back here to lengthen hers a couple of feet."

Cedar lowered her voice, though Molly didn't sense anyone else was around. "Plus, she's complained about your waist being larger than hers, and your heels are shorter than hers."

What does that mean? I can barely manage in these.

"It means be careful. I'm sure that Baron Bob will do something to appease Casey, like make you wear those awful seven-inch heels too or maybe get a tighter corset. I don't know. Anyway, later on, you and Casey will be practicing together, so watch out for her. Don't show her up or she'll get mad, and Baron Bob will have to take it out on you to appease her. He can't wait to get rid of Casey, which will be in just a couple more months, assuming Casey can learn everything that she must. The hardest part is going down the stairs on her own, but then that is the hardest for all the baronesses to master. It's much worse for poor Celia, but somehow she does manage it. How? I surely don't know. Just watch yourself, Miss Molly," Cedar cautioned her yet again.

"I suppose I should take you on the tour like he ordered. Come on. We don't need to visit the fourth floor. That's where we servants stay. Plus, you won't need to visit their private quarters on this floor. We'll go down to the first floor and start there with the dining room. They sound a fifteen-minute warning gong before each meal. Dining is quite formal, always. Can you handle going down them?"

No! It's scary. I can't bend at all and can just barely keep my balance on flat ground.

"I'll keep an arm around you then. Just realize that sooner or later, the baron will be making you and Casey manage to go up and down them on your own and gracefully too," Cedar advised.

By the time they reached the dining room, Baron Bob caught up to them. "I see you are beginning your tour. Does your new room meet with your approval, Miss Dobbs?" Molly clucked a Yes. "Excellent. Slight change of plans. We are heading into the city now. Cedar, you come along. We're going to stop by the jewelers to get Miss Dobbs her new earrings. As the doctor explained to you, they will be worth your entire year's pay. Each year, I'll add another hundred thousand gold worth to them. This way, you will always have your pay with you. Also, we need to make a couple of minor adjustments to keep the baronesses happy. I bet you don't have such problems on your world."

Baron Bob sighed. "You see, Celia and Casey each sport twelve inch waist lines, quite the rage among the very elite. Casey is offended that you, who are to appear as a baroness, will have such a large waistline. She is affronted by that and wants you to appear as shapely as she is and her mother. So we'll just get that minor detail corrected. Plus as Casey pointed out, your heel height, while generally acceptable, isn't good enough for the baronesses here at my castle. Casey believes that you are very special, and that everyone who sees you should be able to see at a glance that you are special. So she wants you to wear the exotic ballet boots. That way, everyone will know immediately that you are not only a baroness but also our telepath. I know, these are such minor things, but Celia and Casey must be appeased. Keep your women happy, and you can then have a pleasant home life. I'm sure that you don't mind these slight changes. Once those are done, we'll get you to your private warehouse, and let you pick out your first ten gowns."

"I'm certain you'll be amazed at the selections. You see, I'm the largest importer on our world. I bring in only the finest fashions for men and women that money can buy. I'm told that you certainly do appreciate such things."

All the while he was talking, they made their way to his fancy car. Molly wanted to scream in protest. These weren't some minor adjustments! They would turn her life into one of abject misery. She saw Cedar giving her a warning look and picked up her surface thoughts, which the teen was fairly screaming: *Please, don't say anything. He'll get really mad!* Molly merely replied in a cluck, yes.

Again, Molly found herself facing trying to get into the car while nearly immobile. Mostly she fell into the back seat. "Well, I can see you too need a whole lot of practice, Miss Dobbs. You and Casey will have much to practice together." Cedar climbed in beside her and readjusted Molly's hair for her, relieved that Molly hadn't said anything.

Their first stop was at a very expensive jeweler. Large gemstones were on display, but there were also two burly men with guns guarding the store. While Cedar and Molly looked around at the incredible gems, Baron Bob went on ahead to discuss what he wanted for Molly.

A bit later, the man had Molly lying back on a couch while he worked on her ear lobes, piercing them, and then healing the slits. "As Thromstead's finest jeweler, I give you my solemn word that these earrings are worth a hundred thousand gold credits, which I understand is your payment." Again, Molly clucked Yes, hoping that the man understood. He looked at Cedar, who nodded that he had understood.

The earrings were made from gold and sparkling, red rubies. A gold loop went through her pierced ear lobes and the ends soldered together. Under no circumstances could they be removed, not without tearing her ears. No accidental loss could occur, which was the whole point. However, they were quite long, reaching nearly to her bosom and very heavy. Each one had five large rubies in the oval settings, one below the next, exquisitely done. Molly had never even seen such fine earrings, though as soon as she was helped into a sitting position, she regretted them already. They felt like they were about to pull her ears off! Wisely, she said nothing but cluck-clicked a "Thank you."

Next, they visited Dr. Smith in his office. The doctor explained, "Baron Bob, her basic form has been altered by that terrible genetic mutation that she underwent. Her internal organs have been shifted downwards some towards her somewhat larger than normal pelvis region. What I'm saying is that she doesn't need to have ribs removed to reduce her waistline. A tighter corset will do the trick."

"I see. Well, that is good news then. Celia and Casey definitely do not want Miss Dobbs to be embarrassed because she has a much larger waistline than they do. Far be it for me to make my women unhappy," Baron Bob justified.

"Let's let Leona and Cedar here take care of this for us, shall we?" Dr. Smith suggested, ushering him out of the room. As soon as the men left, Leona and Cedar proceeded to completely undress Molly, who now had very bad feelings about this whole mess.

"Oh goodness! Look!" exclaimed Cedar. She'd just gotten her first look at the dual sexual organs of Molly. "Does, does it work?" she whispered.

Molly clucked yes, just as embarrassed as Cedar was. Quickly, Leona produced the new corset, which she'd already gotten shortly after her husband had received the phone call from Baron Bob. They tightened it up to about what the previous corset was, before letting Molly's body adjust some. A half hour later, it took the strength of both women to get it fully closed. While Molly sat there gasping for breath, Leona used a tape measure to check the circumference of Molly's waist. "Excellent. Twelve inches as requested. Molly, shallow breaths or you're going to faint."

Cedar whispered, "Right, short, shallow breaths. I know it took Casey several days to stop gasping all the time. Give yourself time to adjust, Miss Dobbs."

Once the two got her redressed, another half hour had passed. Annoyed that it had taken this long, Baron Bob wasn't in a very good mood when the gasping Molly finally walked out of the side room. "Well?" he asked.

"Twelve inches," Leona replied.

"Good. Come along. We are behind schedule. We have to get your wardrobe selections done. Please don't take all day at it. You'll be coming by once each week to add another ten to your collection," he explained.

It was all Molly could do to get to the car and inside, before she fainted. Fortunately, she'd revived when they reached her private warehouse. Inside, she found Baron Bob must have already sent others ahead. Ten fancy gowns, typically worn here on this world, were waiting for her. In spite of her extreme discomfort, Molly noticed the waist lines of the gowns here were all twelve inches. Her conclusion was either Baron Bob had called ahead from the doctor's office and arranged this or had planned all along to reduce her waist further, adding to her misery.

"Well, will these do, Miss Dobbs? Remember, you can come again next week and spend all the time you desire picking out more," he asked. She clucked yes.

"Excellent, Miss Dobbs. Cedar, get her seated, remove those low heels, and put those on her, while I pack these up to take back with us. She can't be wearing the same dress everyday."

More or less falling into the chair, Molly continued fighting for air, while Cedar undid the straps on her heels. She gasped even louder when she saw the new boots that Cedar was about to put on her feet! She'd heard stories about this style of shoe or boot around Elegant Fashions Inc. Like ballet dancers, these boots allowed only the tips of her toes to touch the ground, but unlike regular ballet slippers, these had a very tall heel, adding a bit of support.

As Cedar began putting them on for her, she whispered, "Oh. These have some steel re-enforced side linings. I see, that way you can't twist an ankle." Carefully, she laced them up tightly, following the instructions in the box. "They are supposed to fit tightly. I hope you can manage in these, but I don't see how. I will be with you always," she whispered, her voice faltering a little. Now, even Cedar was very worried about her charge.

Seeing that Cedar had just finished, the impatient baron commanded, "Okay, get her on her feet and out to the car. Time is flying by today. I've much to do yet. Come on. Get her in the car. She and Casey can spend the rest of the day practicing."

Gasping and trying hard to wiggle enough to keep her balance in spite of Cedar's arm around her, Molly did panic and nearly fainted again. She could just barely walk with constant support. By the time that they walked the two hundred feet to the car, she did faint, wholly out of breath, caused by her racing panic. Cedar caught her, but the baron, rather disgusted, lifted her up and plopped her in the back seat. Meekly, Cedar climbed in behind her.

When they reached the castle, Molly had regained consciousness, though her panic hadn't left her at all. However, the baron merely ordered, "Cedar, get her out and to Casey's room. Have them begin practicing together. I'll check on them at supper."

Finally alone, Molly frantically sent, *I can't do this! I*

can't walk or breathe! Help!

"You have to," Cedar whispered. "If you don't the baron will be furious with you and probably do something worse to you. Come on. We'll go a little ways and then rest up." They did just that, going about a hundred feet before stopping to allow Molly to catch her breath, though her legs felt like mush now. Her toes and feet were a mass of cramps and pain, but she couldn't do anything about them.

Inside, Molly faced going up the stairs. She passed out twice before finally reaching Casey's door. Gasping away, tears streaming down her cheeks, Molly waited while Cedar knocked and listened for Casey's cluck-click sounds to enter. They were faint, but clear. Cedar opened the door, helped Molly inside, and to the first chair that she could reach. Molly collapsed into the chair.

Casey had her own personal servant with her, who was brushing out her hair. Casey cluck-clicked her approval of Molly's new look. "Waist good. Shoes good." She smiled invisibly, very much satisfied that Molly's torture was now far worse than hers! That, Molly picked up and sent to the teen, *Why? Why are you doing this to me?*

That surprised Casey, who now could only cluck-click a response, and even then only in an extremely limited vocabulary. She had no words to explain anything, and she knew it. She cluck-clicked, "Get better. Look beautiful."

For Molly's sake, Cedar repeated what Casey said. "It will get better? You look beautiful?" Casey clucked yes.

That's not why you wanted me like this and you know it! Molly sent back. Casey's face flushed, and Molly realized right then Casey didn't have any vocabulary in their cluck-click language to express any reasonable answer, and regretted just having taken it out on Casey, though she knew if Casey had not spoken out, then she'd probably not have been further tortured as she now was.

Casey could only cluck-click, "Sorry. Get better."

Again, Cedar translated, "You're sorry, and Molly will get better? She'll learn to adapt to it?" Casey clucked yes.

Casey's servant then said, "We are under orders to practice walking with you when you came back. We best do it or the baron will be angry with you two. Cedar, you can help Molly lots, but we best do some walking now."

Somehow, Molly managed to get through the late afternoon and down the stairs for supper. If asked, she couldn't have said how. It was one long, painful blur in her mind. After supper, Cedar helped her into her bedroom and undressed her, except for the corset, and then brushed out her hair. After tucking her into bed, she retired, leaving Molly alone for her first night on this world. Molly's feet were a mass of suppressed pain, and she knew that she had to handle them.

She focused and activated her crystal, needing its power amplification now more than she ever had before! One of her gifts was healing. That's what she began to do on her own feet. She sensed the mass of pain, and got it flowing, nearly crying out from the intense burst that shot all through her body, bouncing off every nerve ending. Then, she had to undo those secondary bounces, before she could remotely contact her feet again. An exhausted hour later, she finally had her body relaxed and her feet relieved. She fell into a deep sleep, wondering how she could ever survive ten years here. She knew instinctively she couldn't without her *mentales* gifts!

In the morning and before Cedar showed up to get her up, Molly awoke and realized in time she would be able to adapt to the corset. She'd already done just that once before when she first came to work for Elegant Fashions Inc. At that time, she'd donned a fourteen-inch one and fought against it for days before becoming accustomed to the intense pressure. A few days, she told herself, and then began considering what she could do for her feet. She had read fused feet had helped some adapt, but she wasn't about to give up her toes, not just yet. If she did that, she'd never be able to design again, since she figured she'd never get her arms back and would have to relearn to draw with her feet.

Lying there on her bed between the slick satin sheets, she had an idea that might help. During the day, she would run an almost continuous healing process on her feet, allowing the pain to flow and not buildup as it had yesterday. Still, she wondered if she could do that while being otherwise active. She doubted it, but had to try something. Once more, she tried to sit up and found that next to impossible. If only she could move her neck, she might had been able to do it herself. Sighing, she waited patiently for Cedar to come to her.

Several painful days later, Molly had become accustomed to the intense pressure from her corset, and now noticed that Casey was having the same troubles as she was having, though Casey never admitted it. Casey was often out of breath as well, sometimes gasping herself, especially when handling the stairs. Further, Molly soon realized Casey was having a far harder time walking in her seven-inch heels than she was having. Molly's stride was more than three times that of Casey who took barely a three-inch step at a time.

After a long, torturous week, Molly's constant healing of her feet finally paid off. She'd managed to toughen them up. Her legs and knees were definitely getting stronger. To her amazement, Casey finally noticed that too. While resting up a bit, Casey cluck-clicked, "Walk good me."

Cedar said, "Huh?" And Casey repeated it. "You mean Molly walks better than you do?" Casey clucked yes."

Molly sensed a change in Casey's attitude towards her. She sent, *Yes, now that my feet have adapted, I can take much larger strides than you ever will be able to in your seven-inch heels, Casey. But don't worry. In time, you'll be able to walk well and gracefully, as they want you to. It's just very difficult at first, because your heels are way too high for your foot size. Later on, after they've adapted, you'll find that you won't be able to place your feet flat on the floor anymore. Just be patient. They are right. We need to do a lot of walking to get our legs and feet strengthened up.*

Casey looked at Molly, very wide eyed. She cluck-clicked, "Thanks. Feet hurt."

I can help you with that if you want. Come to my bedroom after supper.

Casey cluck-clicked, "Thanks."

Sure enough, Casey was in tremendous pain and was ready to do anything to get any kind of relief. After Cedar had Molly's hair brushed out, she left for her own room. As she opened the door, there was Casey and her assistant waiting on them. Cedar nodded and left. Casey looked in and saw Molly was still sitting up on her bed, her long auburn hair draped over her bosom and hiding her privates. Casey cluck-clicked, "Come."

Come on in and sit beside me. Have her remove your heels. Slowly and obviously in great pain, Casey limped over to her bed, mostly falling down onto it. Her servant removed her heels for her. She too only wore her tight corset and was ready for bed as well. Hastily, her servant adjusted Casey's hair, since it was now as long as Molly's, draping it over Casey's bosom and down over her privates as well. Then both women looked curiously at Molly. Casey cluck-clicked, "See can?"

Her servant, obviously embarrassed but highly curious as well, repeated, "Can we see your man thing? Cedar told us about it."

You'll have to move my hair out of the way, since I can't do it anymore, Molly sent.

"Wow. Does it really work? I mean, like a man's?" her servant asked.

Molly focused and sent to both, *Yes, I can even get myself pregnant. Our men are just like me, and I can get them pregnant too. The genetic mutation made us all hermaphrodites.*

Her servant giggled, and Casey did too. "Man have?" Casey cluck-clicked. Her servant hastily asked, "She wants to know if you have a boyfriend yet?"

Molly clicked back, "No," and then sent, *I was a fashion designer for our Elegant Fashions Inc store. I was good too, but then we were infected with that super-mutation thing by the aliens, and my body got like this. I came here hoping to get a whole lot of fancy gowns to take back with me that others can use to make our women new designs, since I can't do that anymore. So I've never had any time for the boys. Now, who would want me? I'm mostly helpless like this, more so than ever, since I got here.*

She sensed Casey was fighting to keep from crying and began to wonder if she'd said something very wrong. Casey cluck-clicked, "Talk me. No can." Her servant quickly translated, "Casey says that she used to love to talk to everyone about many things, and now she can't do that any longer. She wants to talk to you, Molly, but simply can't, and feels really bad about not being able to talk. It's getting late for us. We're not sure why you wanted to see Casey tonight. Should we stay around or leave you? Casey, if we leave the door open, can you make your way back to your room by yourself?"

Casey clucked yes. The two servants then bowed and left, leaving the door open enough that Casey could push it herself. She cluck-clicked, "Thank you."

I'm going to heal your feet some. Just sit quietly, Molly sent to the young teen, who couldn't do much more than just sit there totally erect with perfect posture. Molly focused and her crystal began glowing in a pale blue light. She began to sense Casey's body, moved her awareness down Casey's legs, and spotted a huge suppressed pain blockage at both knees. She released it, noticing the jolt of pain that shot through Casey's body. For a half hour, she worked her magic on Casey's legs before stopping.

Casey sighed visibly when she finished. "Is good," Casey cluck-clicked. "Thank you."

Acting on a hunch, Molly slipped into rapport with Casey, forming a mutual telepathic connection. *You are welcome, Casey. We can chat this way. You think what you want to say, and I'll hear it.*

Oh! This is so indescribably great! Thank you so very much! My feet feel a million times better. What is it that you did? How? I suppose it's one of the things telepaths do, right? Gosh, I never thought I'd miss something so simple as just chatting with someone, but I do, terribly so. Cluck-clicking is just horrible. Almost no words or ways to say much of anything at all, though my servant is pretty good at picking up what I mean. This is so intimate, isn't it? I can feel you, but I don't know how I can, but I can. Oh, I'm talking way too much aren't I?

Talk all you want to, Casey. I used my healing gifts to undo the pain blocks in your legs and feet. You may find it easier to walk some tomorrow. If you like, we can do this every night. I have been doing it on my knees, legs, and feet each night, and it's helping me. And yes, this is very intimate, but I've heard that doing this while having sex is even greater, but I've never done that yet. So did you always want to be a baroness? Did you have any choice in the matter?

None! Dad has had me engaged to his archrival's son, Elmer, since I was a little girl. He wants to form a close bond between our castle and theirs. I think they've been squabbling for centuries — the Thomas's and Blackwater's. Able, he's engaged to Elmer's younger sister, Ruth, but she's just turned sixteen and hasn't yet gotten her baroness-to-be modifications. Dad thinks if I'm on the Blackwater's throne beside Elmer, that I'll somehow be able to affect relations, but I sure don't see how. All I can do is cluck-click a few words. I can't even remotely hold a conversation now, not like this, but then no baroness ever can. So I don't see what good this marriage is going to be for us. I don't really like Elmer. He's bossy and older than I am. He's ordered me to have this overly tiny waist and to wear these awful seven-inch heels. He says that all Blackwater baronesses have twelve-inch waists and wear these heels. So I have too as well. I don't have any choice. All baronesses have to wear what their baron tells them to wear or buys for them to wear. Somehow, we always have to show great poise, grace, and stateliness, particularly when we walk or dance or get into cars. What's really going to be bad is when we have to go up and down the stairs by ourselves without our servants holding on to us. Mom said that's the worst thing ever, beyond scary. Between us, I don't know how I ever can, but I have to. Mom does too, even though she can't even see. Baronesses have to be the gracious host, because they are often with other barons and important men, and can't be calling for their servants. Still, I'm really, really scared of the stairs.

Hey, me too. I'm able to go up them somewhat okay, but going down is a nightmare. So we're going to have to do everything solo? Molly asked.

Yes, while with other barons and important men, mom often has to make her own way from the throne room down to the dining room, leading them to the dining room. Plus, she still has to dance with everyone at the balls, and she can't see anything. She has glass eyes, you know. It happened before I was born, though. She argued with dad, and he got mad. He often does, you know, gets viciously mad. So be careful around him. Anyway, one of these days, dad is going to order our servants to depart, making us do it all by ourselves. I'm terrified of that.

You should be. He's really torturing us. He must be a sadist or something, Molly replied.

Oh, it is getting really late. I'd best try to get back to my room. Can we do this again? I so want to be able just to chat with someone, Molly. Please? I'd love to hug you, but we can't. We can't even kiss properly either. How am I supposed to kiss Elmer? I don't even know what I'm supposed to do when he takes me to bed with him. Mom can't tell me. No words. I can't figure out a way to ask my servant about it either. No words.

We can hug like this, Molly sent. Straining, she raised one leg up and pressed it against Casey's leg. *We can kiss like this too.* She used her other leg to sort of turn her body towards the side of Casey. Leaning precariously over at her waist, she planted a kiss on her cheek. Their servants had long ago removed their lip plates when they got them ready for bed. Casey felt the warm, moist lip loops of Molly touching her cheeks and got aroused. Hastily, she did her best to turn stiffly to Molly, and leaned over, placing one on Molly's cheek. Both women then noticed Molly's instant arousal.

Oh! It does work! Casey exclaimed.

Molly giggled girlishly, rather embarrassed by her unexpected arousal. *Oops. Yes, I'm afraid that it does.* Both giggled.

Sheepishly, Casey tried to slip on her heels, but couldn't. *I guess I can leave them here, and she can fetch them in the morning. Oh! I can't put my heels onto the floor anymore. My legs are too tight somehow. I have to walk on my toes. Well, I have to do it to get back to my room. Thanks for everything, Molly. You are the best person ever!*

Molly watched Casey, as she very carefully began to walk out of her room. She was able to push the door open but couldn't close it. *That's okay. I can close it. Night Casey.* She waited for a time, listening to make sure Casey didn't fall. After a time, she believed she heard a door shut quietly. Then, she too tried to stand. Her feet throbbed at being forced to go flat on the floor for the first time since she started wearing these boots. Pain shot through her legs, but she endured it, moving to her door and pushing it, mostly shut using her large breasts. At last, she got back to her bed. After sitting down, she realized she had no way to get the covers up and simply fell back and wiggled as best she could to get her feet under. Then, she focused and worked on her own feet, before falling into a restful sleep, believing she'd made a friend out of Casey.

Her second week at Castle Thomas was filled with nearly constant walking, going up and down the stairs, and not just for meals, and learning their dances. During the entire week, Casey and Molly were constantly together, since both had to master the same things. Every now and then, Baron Bob would see them and call out, "Oh come on, ladies. Gracefully. Poise. Stateliness. Get with it!" Not once did he ever compliment either woman, and Molly began to realize he never would do such a thing.

Each evening, Casey came by Molly's room to get her feet healed and to gab. Gradually, both began to grow very fond of the other. Casey desperately needed the healing touch of Molly. Each day, she found herself managing to do better and better, though no one ever complimented her on her progress.

At the end of the week, as promised, Baron Bob again took Molly to his warehouse, where he had some of the latest fashions up on manikins for her to examine and choose. After she picked out ten, he had one of each in her size sent to her private warehouse.

At the start of the third week, over breakfast, Baron Bob explained, "This week, Casey, Molly, you are to do all your practicing without the aid of your servants. After they finish feeding you, they are to spend their days helping Celia prepare the ballroom. Next Saturday night, we'll be hosting the Blackwaters here for a private ball. Molly, I'll have an assignment for you that night. I'll tell you more about it on Friday. So you both must be able to walk and dance with great poise, grace, and stateliness. No exceptions. You simply must perform well. You'll be on your own the whole night, just as dear Celia will be." The two shifted their bodies to look at Celia. Molly wondered how Celia could possibly manage on her own. It seemed impossible.

The true nightmares began for the two once they finished eating. Already everyone else had left. Cedar had gone off, her arm guiding Celia, while chatting about the decorations. Swallowing hard, Molly lunged to her toes, wobbling as best she could to get her balance. Casey did likewise. The two gave each other a terrified look. At last, Casey cluck-clicked, "Follow," meaning that Molly should follow her. Two frightened, nervous young women headed off to carry out their daily walking and dancing routines. This time, they were soloing. No help would be coming, especially if they fell down. Getting up on their own would be next to impossible, or so they believed.

Twice something did happen, which took Molly by total surprise. As the two were attempting to descend to the ballroom from the throne room, Casey missed a step and started to fall down. Molly reacted, trying to pull or hold Casey up to keep her from falling. Her crystal activated, and somehow she managed to steady Casey with a bit of a telekinetic pull, a *mentales* gifts she never had before. Later on, Casey stumbled and would have fallen, but again Molly's instinctive reaction was to somehow steady her. Once more, her crystal activated, and Casey felt a steadying magical pull on her body, preventing her from taking a fall. When they chatted about these during their nightly sessions, Molly said she didn't know how she was doing it.

The next day, Molly did take a tumble while dancing. Moving backwards in her ballet boots was almost impossible to do gracefully, and she lost her balance and fell. Luckily, she landed on her side and only got jarred. Getting up was almost impossible for her. Casey stood by and cluck-clicked suggestions, but didn't have any real vocabulary to offer any advice. Unable to bend her neck in the slightest, constrained by her heavily steel boned, overly tight corset, she could only bend at her waist. The boots prevented any real way of getting up. Finally frustrated, her crystal activated, and she levitated up onto her feet, shocking herself, as well as Casey.

I've no idea how I could do that! Molly sent a startled Casey, who looked in awe at Molly.

When Friday came, Baron Bob again took Molly off to his warehouse so she could pick out another ten gowns. After that, he took her into an office there. At least, he pulled the chair out for her to sit on. She leaned over at her waist to get her auburn hair somehow over a shoulder so she didn't sit on it and then sat down.

"Okay. We need to talk about Saturday night. Baron Thomas will be there along with his son, Elmer. He's to marry Casey in a few months. I want you to probe both of their minds. I don't trust Baron Thomas in the slightest. You see, my grandfather once tried to betroth my dad to one of Baron Blackwater's daughters, a golden haired beauty. All was going well until at one formal dance, the young baroness-to-be just vanished completely, voiding grandfather's proposed marriage. Later on, he agreed to betroth the youngest daughter of Baron Blackwater. This time, grandfather brought the baroness-to-be here to Castle Thomas. Wouldn't you know it? The baroness-to-be also vanished. No trace of either young woman was ever found. So you can see why we've never ever trusted those Blackwaters since then."

"Now, he's proposed my Able marry his Ruth, while my Casey marries his Elmer. I don't want my twins to suddenly vanish as his did. We suspect he had them kidnaped and killed. After all, how could you or Casey walk anywhere? Hardly likely. Besides, you'd be spotted at once."

He continued, "So I want you to probe their minds and see if they are planning to do away with my twins. That's your primary objective. Your secondary one is to find out just what they think about my twins. Is Baron Blackwater really going to give my Casey what's rightfully hers, the throne beside his Elmer, or not? Also, what diabolical plans has he installed in Ruth to do to my Able? I need answers. I can't afford to mess this up. That's one reason I hired you — to make darn sure there isn't any treachery about to happen again. Got all this?"

Yes. I'll do as you ask.

"Good. Mind you, they'll likely all want to dance with you, as well as with Celia and Casey. If all goes as planned, then Able will be making his requests of Baron Thomas Blackwater, telling him how he wants Ruth to appear. I'm sure he will demand Ruth have a twelve-inch waist too. Able has been watching you, and I think he's going to demand Ruth also wear ballet boots just like you are wearing, but we'll see. Come on; we best get you back so you can practice more before tomorrow night's ball. Don't mess it up, Molly, or there will be hell to pay!" Molly didn't reply, focusing instead on getting to her feet without falling down and then following him out to the car.

Chapter 25 A Telepath's Work

Saturday morning, Casey and Molly made their slow, careful way down to the ballroom to see how it was decorated and what they would have to deal with at the coming private ball. They found the room filled with summer flowers. Banners floated in great arcs from the ceilings. It looked elegant enough for a formal ball. Satisfied that there were no new barriers for them to have to handle, they headed back up to their rooms where their servants were waiting to bathe them and get them dolled up for the evening's festivities.

Molly wore a fancy ball gown done in sky blue velvet, a bit on the heavy side. Two petticoats gave the bottom of her gown a proper flair out some two feet around her, but allowed a bit of her black nylons to show along with her matching sky blue ballet boots. Cedar wanted to tie a matching ribbon in her hair, but the two decided against it, primarily because Molly would be on her own. If her hair were tied back, she would have no way to get it out of the way when she sat. Satisfied that she looked her best, Molly headed down to supper, meeting Casey in the hallway. Casey wore a similar gown done in light red velvet with matching shoes. Molly noticed these were the familiar oxford style so popular on Tierra, but their laces were double knotted so they couldn't come untied.

Side by side, the two headed very, very carefully down the stairs, their servants following discretely behind them, under orders not to assist their charges, except to feed them. At dinner, Baron Robert again chided them. "Do you very best to walk and dance with great poise, grace, and stateliness tonight. Flirt with Elmer, Casey. Make him want you to be his baroness. Molly, you know what you have to do." He rose and left them.

At six, the family gathered in the throne room to welcome their guests. No servants were present, Molly noted. At least for now, they were all seated on soft chairs, and Molly wished this night were over already.

Promptly, the Blackwater guests arrived. Baron Thomas

was forty-five years old with golden hair cut short. His wife, Baroness Mary, also had golden hair and blue eyes. She wore a blue velvet gown that matched her eyes along with seven-inch matching heels done in rough leather that simulated a velvet look. She was just as constrained as Molly or Celia or Casey. Elmer was very tall and thin, almost emaciated looking. His golden hair was curly, and he had a moustache that gave him an almost sinister look. Molly's instant reaction was one of intense dislike. He was nineteen and very used to having his own way with everything. Both men wore expensive, grey tweed suits. Ruth had just turned sixteen last week. She too had uncut golden hair, wavy and long, falling to her knees. Her face was round and rather angelic looking, but with thick lips. She had yet to have any of the requisite baroness-to-be body modifications. She wore a light brown velvet gown with matching six-inch oxford heels. Ruth was definitely nervous, her fingers fiddling with her gown.

Baron Bob began the lengthy introductions. "So this is your marvelous new telepath. Pleased to meet you," Baron Thomas said politely, but quite covertly. "May I have this first dance?" Molly clucked Yes, dreading every minute of it. She'd been told normally they would have a dance band playing, but for tonight's private dance, a man servant played recorded music, but not too loudly.

Baron Thomas slipped an arm around Molly's thin waist, but was careful to slip it beneath her long auburn hair, moving her out onto the floor as the music began. "Bet it's hard to dance in those boots," he commented. She clucked yes. He made small talk, and Molly did her best to follow the slow, stately moves of the dance, and not fall down or embarrass him. He whispered in her ear, "You're gorgeous enough to be a baroness for real. If I wasn't married, I'd ask for your hand, but of course, you haven't one."

Molly noticed Elmer chose to dance with the blind Baroness Celia, who could only follow his lead if he told her what it was or used his hand to guide her. She picked up the fact Elmer was purposely making fun of Celia and embarrassing her.

The next dance, Elmer chose to dance with Casey, while

Baron Thomas took a turn with Baroness Celia. Meanwhile, Baron Bob danced with Baroness Mary and then with Ruth. Able took his first turn with his betrothed, Ruth, and then with Baroness Mary.

After that, Baron Thomas spoke up, "I say, let's see Molly dancing with Baroness-to-be Casey." Everyone knew this was a setup. The armless women could not lead the other, only follow, but the men thought this was hilarious and insisted on watching the two make the attempt. Embarrassed, Casey did her best to dance with Molly, just as the two had been doing for hours earlier in the week. *Relax. He's just picking on us,* Molly sent to an embarrassed Casey.

After that, Elmer began dancing with Casey, while Able did the same with Ruth. Meanwhile, the adults gathered to chat. Celia and Mary stood to one side, exchanging cluck-clicks, while the two barons talked in hushed voices, though occasionally glancing at the two young couples. Molly realized Baron Bob was giving her this chance to work her magic. She focused and began to probe the Baron's mind, picking up surface thoughts. Later on, she did the same with Elmer. Towards the end of the evening, she did the same with Ruth and Baroness Mary.

As the evening ended, Baron Bob spoke up. "Everyone, may I have your attention. Thank you." A hush fell. "The marriage proposals have been accepted. In three months, Casey will marry Elmer, and at the same time, Able will marry Ruth. A dual wedding will bind our two most powerful castles together. At this time, it is baron-to-be Able's responsibility to tell baroness-to-be Ruth how she is to appear. Able," he motioned for his son to speak up.

Able smiled mischievously at Ruth, who watched him, nervously fingering her gown again. Molly realized that habit would soon be a thing of the past and pitied the young teen. Able spoke firmly. "Of course, Ruth must never cut her golden locks. She must have a twelve-inch waistline, as do all our women. I want her to wear ballet boots just as our beautiful Miss Molly Dobbs is wearing. After all, Molly looks utterly stunning in them. I want my Ruth to look just as stunning." Ruth gasped, and then turned red, as she realized everyone heard it. "But dear Ruth, I don't want you blinded like my mother, not yet anyway," he added. Poor Ruth really fidgeted with her gown now.

Baron Thomas then spoke up, "Officially then, it has been agreed upon. Baroness-to-be Ruth will undergo her preparations and will be ready for her wedding in three months. I want to take this opportunity to invite you all to Castle Blackwater in four weeks for our Mid-summer Formal Ball. I expect to see all you there for an enjoyable evening of fun."

With that, they said their farewells and left. While the others headed on up to their rooms, Baron Bob came over to Molly. "Well?" he whispered.

Molly sent, *Look. Now that I have met them, I can contact them wherever they are at. I want to probe their minds deeply tonight while they are sleeping. That way, they won't know I'm probing them. It will seem more like a dream than anything real. I'll report to you in the morning. Is this okay with you?*

"Ah. I did not know that. Yes, excellent indeed. We'll talk after breakfast then. Good night Miss Dobbs." He turned and left the ballroom, shutting the door behind him.

Molly panicked. There wasn't anyone left in the room, and the door was closed. She was trapped in the ballroom! She moved over to the door and stared at it for a minute, wishing that it would just open. Her feet ached, and she desperately wanted to sit down. Then, she had an idea. She focused; slowly the knob turned, and the door opened. She'd again used powers she never knew she possessed. Smiling invisibly, she carefully made her way up to the third floor, where Cedar was waiting for her.

A half hour later, Cedar had her ready for bed and as usual, Casey came into her room wearing only her corset, walking on her toes, her feet aching. After Casey sat down beside her on the bed, Molly began her usual healing routine, going into rapport with Casey. Later after Casey departed, Molly laid back, focused, and reached out first to Baron Thomas Blackwater and then to his son, Elmer. Much later, she touched Ruth and sent calming waves over the young teen, who still hadn't fallen asleep, but was a nervous wreck. When Molly finished up, Ruth had finally drifted into a peaceful sleep.

"Well?" Baron Bob demanded to know the next morning. They'd finished breakfast, and he'd shown unusual patience with the slowness of the women, sticking around until Molly had finished, before ushering her into his private office on the second floor. Not wanting to try to hold such a conversation while standing precariously on her toes, Molly moved over to a chair that was pushed into a desk. She stood there waiting for him to get the idea to pull the chair out for her to sit down. At last he did so, and she cluck-clicked, "Thank you."

Wobbling a little, she got her auburn hair over one shoulder and fell down onto the chair. She focused lightly and began. *It's far more serious than you may have thought. First, he's hiring his own telepath from Ashford-5. She is supposed to arrive next week. He is planning to kill you and Able, but not until after they are married, and Able is announced as your heir. He believes that will then make Ruth the temporary head of your castle, and he'll then step in as regent, until he lines up a new and suitable husband for Ruth.*

Baron Bob gasped. *There's more. Elmer plans to blind Casey, after they are married and moves into their castle. He wants her to wear bright red glass eyes. However, they both don't trust you. They greatly fear you'll be abducting Ruth before the wedding can occur, like what happened to his grandfather's two daughters. So he is adding more surveillance cameras and doubling the security guards at his castle. Also, Ruth will be undergoing her baroness-to-be modifications the day that his new telepath is due to arrive.*

"Traitorous bastard! Okay, you've earned your pay. Go do whatever you do with Casey for now. No wait. It should be obvious to you that I'll have to kill Baron Thomas before he kills Able and me. Can you do anything more than just read minds? Can you help me defeat this bastard man?"

Molly visibly jerked, quite taken by surprise. *I — I don't know, sir.*

"Well, you had better come up with some ideas of how

you can help me! If you don't, I'll have you blinded just like Celia. Got that, Miss Dobbs? Figure out how you can help me with this or you'll pay the price! Now get out. I've planning to do," he barked angrily.

Molly lunged to her feet, wobbling more than normal. His threat not only took her by surprise, it filled her with terror even greater than before. It took all her attention on her body just to walk out of the room. Casey was out in the hall, alone and brave, waiting for Molly. She didn't need telepathy to see Molly was quite shaken. Her face was pale and her body trembling a little. As Molly wobbled closer to her, Casey ran through all her limited vocabulary to find any way to say what she longed to say. In disgust, she cluck-clicked, "Wrong," hoping that Molly would grasp what she desperately wanted to say.

Molly was too upset to focus properly even to attempt telepathy with Casey. "Sit," she cluck-clicked. Casey responded by turning around and leading Molly to her bedroom, the closest room. Carefully swinging her long hair to her right and nearly falling down in the process, Casey fell onto her bed, the best she could do to sit down. Molly followed suit but managed to keep from falling only by a Herculean effort. She was that upset. In fact, she was gasping for breath, something she had not done for some days. Slowly, Molly regained her composure and was able to make her rapport connection to Casey.

What's wrong? I know it's really bad. You're very pale and gasping, Molly. Please, tell me, Casey thought.

I have to help him kill Baron Thomas and Elmer or he's going to blind me like Celia! She then told Casey everything she'd told her father, including the fact that Elmer was planning to blind her, once she married him and moved to his castle. Of course, Casey took the news as badly as Molly had, and she broke down, sobbing quietly.

Sometimes, when things seem the darkest they can be, a light pops up bringing tendrils of hope. And that was just what happened to Molly, as she sat erect beside Casey, trying not to emotionally break down like Casey had.

Molly Dobbs? Have I found you? Renata's thoughts reached Molly

Huh? Yes, I'm Molly. Who is this? You seem familiar to me.

Renata here. Good. I've been going around to all you telepaths that got hired by that consortium and checking up with each to make sure all is above boards with you. How's it going for you?

Oh God! Renata! Help! I need help! It's horrible. If I don't kill a baron and his son, the baron's going to blind me. Already, he has me quite helpless, physically. I don't know what to do! Molly shot back rapidly.

Okay. Start at the beginning. Where are you? What planet? Where on it? Tell me everything, Renata sent her along with calming emotional waves. Molly's body visibly relaxed. Molly related everything that had happened to her and what was potentially going to happen. She ended by asking for advice on what to do.

I know where you are located. I'll be sending out a rescue party as soon as I can. Until then, do whatever you have to do to stay alive and as well as possible. If you can find a way to protect the other telepath who is coming there, please do so for me. Also, if you can, protect Casey and the young Ruth. Just don't let them harm you or the others any further. Play along, but do whatever you have to do to survive until we can get to you. I've no idea how soon it will be, but I'll check back with you every few days. Can you do this, Molly?

Yes, yes, I will. I don't want to kill people, but I will if I have to. These men lied to us and are using us badly. They have to be stopped, Molly sent back. Renata broke the connection. Molly quickly joined into a rapport with the still sobbing Casey.

Casey. Help is coming. One of my people just reached me, and she is going to send help to us soon, I hope. Don't worry. I won't let them blind you or me either. I'll kill them first.

Really? Can anyone really help us? We're so helpless now. The barons — they have all the power, the real power. We just have to do what they say, Casey responded, though she stopped crying.

433

Real help, Casey. Trust me. Oh, here comes your servant. She broke the rapport.

"Oh here you are, Casey. I've been looking all over for you," the eighteen year old, short blonde haired Charis White said calmly. "You've been crying. What's the matter dear?" Her voice sounded sympathetic, Molly thought.

Again, Casey felt utterly frustrated. Before she'd become a baroness-to-be, she would have spilled her heart out to Charis, but now she was limited to her skimpy cluck-click vocabulary, wholly inadequate. She cluck-clicked, "Blind me. Baron me. No."

Charis looked confused. "Someone's going to blind you? Baron? You father?" Poor Casey cluck-clicked, No. "Baron Thomas?" Again she replied No. Grasping at straws, Charis asked, "Elmer?" Casey's gushed a cluck yes!

"Oh my! I've not heard that. When? Crap, you can't answer that can you?" Charis asked.

Casey cluck-clicked, "Marry."

"Oh, after you get married to Elmer? Then, he's going to blind you?" Casey clucked yes.

"Wow. That's horrible. I should tell your father this news."

Casey cluck-clicked hastily, "No. Knows. Yes."

"Huh? You don't want me to tell him? He already knows? Are you saying that he approves of having Elmer blind you?" Charis asked, trying to make some sense from her three words.

Casey clucked yes.

"Oh, this is really bad, Casey." After a momentary pause, she added, "Well, it isn't the end of the world. Celia has managed to get by for twenty-two years being blind. Still, it isn't good at all. Just be brave, Casey. Do you need anything now?" Casey cluck-clicked No, and Charis left the two sitting on the edge of Casey's bed.

Casey cluck-clicked, "Do what?"

Molly hardened her will and rejoined with Casey. *I know I've seen a few men with guns around here. Security guards?*

Yes. They watch the surveillance cameras around the

castle. There are a lot of them, but they stay in back rooms on the first floor and in the basement. That's where they have their fancy systems.

Okay. Come on; walk me around the castle here, and let me see all the cameras, and if we can, let me see the security men, and where they are. I suppose that Baron Thomas has them at his castle too.

The two spent the rest of the day moving slowly around the entire castle. As far as anyone was concerned, they were just doing what they were supposed to be doing, practicing their walking. In fact, Molly was casing the place, learning where the cameras were located and just how many guards Baron Bob had here, thirty all told. As yet, Molly didn't have any real plan of action, however.

What of the second Ashford-5 telepath? Marcy Greythorn, an eighteen year old *mentales* gifted normal human, was born and lived for sixteen years in Oak Village, a small farming village some thirty miles south of Exchange City. There was very little for a bright and curious young teen in Oak Village, other than tending bar at their only pub, which she did for two years. While serving up pints, she often heard exciting news from the "big city" to the north, Exchange City, where there were even aliens walking the streets looking for exotic bargain trading goods. Also, the Guilds had recently brought the Rural Electrification Program to Oak Village, which intrigued Marcy, who now saw that education was king. There was so much to learn. Two years ago, the silver haired teen had moved to Exchange City, taking a barmaid's position at night to earn her keep, while spending her days studying.

For two years, she saw the sleek, silver spaceships landing and departing from the spaceport and even had a tour of the Plateau Grado port. Curiosity grew. Marcy wondered what other worlds were like out there. She heard all manner of exciting tales from those who frequented her bar. Then came the first round of consortium offers, pricking her interest even more. Unfortunately, she wasn't one of the super-mutation attack victims. Luckily, she'd returned home for a few days when the attack occurred. She'd hurried back to help the victims, who certainly did need her help. She was a little annoyed that these consortium men only wanted to hire helpless telepaths, though.

Then came the second round of hiring by the same consortium members. This time, they were open to any telepath. Again, Marcy was curious and visited the tables, listening to the many offers. What intrigued her was the chance to see other worlds, people, and the pay, a staggering amount. Even one year's pay as a working telepath would cover her living expenses for many years, while she worked her way through school. But she wanted a short term contract. Most of the offers were quite long durations, discouraging her. However, one man agreed to her counter offer of one year for a hundred thousand gold.

So just weeks after the first batch of telepaths departed from Ashford-5, Marcy Greythorn walked proudly across the tarmac heading towards Berth 13 where a deep space transport was waiting for her. She had her rather unique silver hair tied back in a ponytail that just touched the small of her back. She wore her best leather outfit and boots. The recruiter had told her to come as she was. She would need to bring nothing with her, since her employer would provide everything. She took a deep breath and walked up the bay ramp, where Dr. James Smith and his wife Leona were waiting for her.

Marcy was tall and thin. Her six foot frame towered over Leona, but she was still filling out, though as with all women of Tierra, her bosom was already huge, the normal size on this world. "Hello. Is this where I'm supposed to be?" she asked, her mellow alto voice breaking the silence of the spaceport.

"If you are Miss Marcy Greythorn, then you've found the right ship. I'm Dr. Smith, my wife and nurse, Leona. Please come aboard. The pilot is anxious to get going."

"Cool! This is my first trip into space. This is going to be exciting," Marcy volunteered.

Dr. Smith smiled. "It is only our second trip. Still, we find it rather an exciting adventure. Your cabin is this way." He and Leona led her to a cabin with chairs and no bed. They were strapped in, and shortly they heard the pilot's voice

436

calling out.

In this ship, they had a small viewport and Marcy stared out of it, watching the takeoff, this time from inside one of the sleek, silver ships. In fact, the other two also watched the takeoff, but then everything went entirely black, startling Marcy, who asked nervously, "Is everything all right? Where did the stars go?"

"We've jumped into hyperspace," Dr. Smith answered. "Mind you, I've no idea what that means, except the pilot says that jumping through hyperspace allows us to travel between stars at a rapid rate. We should be arriving on Blackwell-C in about twenty hours. I'm afraid blackness is all we'll be seeing until the ship gets there. Now then, we should get down to the business at hand. You see, you are going to work for one of the most powerful men on our world, Baron Thomas Blackwater. His wife is Baroness Mary. Their older children are married and do not live at his castle, but their remaining two youngest children do, Elmer and Ruth, who are nineteen and sixteen. Both are going to be married in about ten weeks. In fact Ruth has just completed her Baroness-to-be modifications in preparation for her wedding to young Baron-to-be Able Thomas. We performed them just before we left for your world."

"Your employer, Baron Thomas, like all barons of our world, is quite insistent that our traditions, going back many centuries, are followed to the letter. Of course, there have been some recent modifications that were made upon our entry into the Federation of Planets, nearly a century ago now. Naturally, you'll be expected to follow these traditions as well, while you're living and working at Castle Blackwater."

"Yes, of course," Marcy replied politely, even though she had no idea what those traditions would be or involve.

"As his official telepath, Miss Greythorn, your status will be on par with his Baroness, the highest possible. It would be a disgrace for Baron Thomas to elevate you above that of his wife, Baroness Mary."

"Of course, I wouldn't want that," she replied politely.

"Of course," he continued just as politely. "I checked your contract, and you have agreed to being treated as a baroness ought to be treated. Correct?"

"Yes, but I've no idea what that means, doctor. It is the polite thing to do, right?" she asked.

"Of course. Well, allow me to explain a bit. You see, a baroness is never allowed to speak, not ever. A century ago, the baronesses had their tongues cut off to prevent them from speaking. However, since we joined the Federation and since they frown upon that practice, we have modernized our ways, just as many on your own world had. Instead of that barbaric practice, we have adopted the giant lip disks that Leona and I have seen are also in widespread use on your own world."

"Oh! Well, I didn't know that. They are very popular on Tierra, mostly with the wealthy and Guild Leaders. So I would have to have them too?" Marcy asked, recalling that such modifications were easily healed by one of the Medical machines.

"Yes, you'll be expected to always wear them. I must caution you severely, Miss Greythorn, you are never to speak. The lip plates do prevent the baronesses from speaking intelligibly, which is their purpose. The baron has a temper, which can be rather vicious. However, even though both our worlds speak the same language, though I surely don't know how yours became to be called Midlands, you are never to try to speak it. If he ever hears you are violating this aspect of a baroness, well, his temper will flare."

He went on, seeing the startled look on her face, "But that doesn't mean you and the baroness don't have any way to communicate to others. The baronesses have developed their own unique cluck-click language. It's been in use for countless centuries. Without tongues, they communicate by making other sounds. I assure you everyone at the castle and your own personal servant will be able to understand this language. I have the learning tapes with me, and Leona will ensure that you have mastered it before we arrive at Castle Blackwater. Of course, Baron Thomas has told me to tell you that you are permitted to use your telepathy to communicate freely at any time."

"I see. From what I've seen, those who wear them have to speak very slowly to be understood, oftentimes repeating it three times. So yes, it is hard to understand them when they are wearing their lip disks. It makes sense to me. I won't ever try to say anything," Molly replied politely, but began to worry a little.

He went on, "A baroness had many obligations, responsibilities, and duties to fulfill. However, since you are not exactly a baroness, some of those will not apply to you. The ones that do apply I have been ordered to relay to you. First, a baroness always must look her very best at all times. The baron often has unexpected visitors, and the baroness is always at his side. As his telepath, you'll be there too and must always look your best too. A baroness always wears whatever jewelry the baron purchases for her. Your case is unique. Your salary is one hundred thousand per year, an enormous sum, I might add. Baron Thomas will be purchasing jewelry worth that much for this year's work, and you're always to wear them. This way, you'll always have your earnings on your person, and they can't be lost."

"That's fine with me," Molly replied innocently. On the surface, this sounded quite plausible. Besides, she didn't think that she could even lift a hundred thousand worth of pure gold. Gems were far easier to handle in such large amounts.

Dr. Smith continued, "You'll always be given only the finest in apparel, as befitting a baroness. That's why you didn't have to bring anything along with you. Proper elegant gowns will be provided, of course at no cost to you. One other thing, I presume that you also have a crystal that helps you with your telepathy?"

"Oh yes. It is around my neck. I keep it with me at all times," she replied.

"Yes of course. We'll make very sure Baron Thomas knows this detail and that you are never without it. Now then, shall we get you prepared, and have Leona here teach you their unique cluck-click language?"

"Sure. Why not? What else can we do for twenty hours?" she asked innocently.

Dr. Smith was under strict orders not to reveal any of the baroness-to-be modifications beyond the lip plates to Marcy before he performed them on her. Looking at this normal, young, silver haired teen, he knew why Baron Thomas issued that order. If Marcy knew what was about to happen to her, she would never have agreed to this contract. Further, Dr. Smith suspected that after the year's contract was up, he would not allow Marcy Greythorn to leave. She'd be helpless to do anything about it. He'd have a telepath for life.

They led her to the next cabin and had her lie down on the bed. He placed a mask over her face and had her breath deeply. She did so and quickly drifted into unconsciousness, believing she was about to get her lips split and some giant, golden lip disks inserted. At the worst, she'd look like she was one of the wealthy of Exchange City. That pleased her a little.

Marcy awoke to a living nightmare! She was sitting up on the same bed, staring at herself in a mirror on the wall. Dr. Smith had waved a smelly vial below her nose, jerking her back to consciousness. She felt horrible, unable to breathe properly. True, she now had similar foot in diameter lip plates like those worn on Tierra, but her neck was surrounded by a series of bronze neck rings. Her neck felt stretched somehow, and she couldn't move her head in the slightest. What freaked her out the most was that her shoulders were empty. Her arms were gone! She fainted, but he brought her around again with the smelling salts.

This time, she saw that her waist was extremely tiny and sensed she must be wearing a very overly tight corset, which was true. Dr. Smith said softly, "To get your waist down to the required twelve inches, I had to remove some ribs. Now, you look like a perfect baroness."

She gazed at her incredibly tiny waist and noticed her pride and joy, her wavy silver hair, was much longer now, reaching her ankles. She wore a red satin gown, strapless, and very form fitting. Her breasts were now drastically larger, soccer balls in size. She could see black nylons on her legs, which she could never afford, but her feet were in matching red ballet boots, her toes pointed downward onto the floor. She gasped and fainted again.

This time when she awoke, she noticed she was also wearing enormous earrings. Each one sported six large, oblong green emeralds, encased in dangling gold settings that touched her shoulders and almost down to her extremely prominent cleavage. Dr. Smith was an observant man. This time, he noticed that she had finally noticed her new earrings. "Yes, there is your one year's pay. Those earrings are worth one hundred thousand gold, far more than I make in a year! They can't come off your ears, not without cutting the loop fasteners, so you can't lose your payment for your services, Miss Greythorn." She gasped again and fainted.

When she came too once more, Leona spoke up, "Miss Greythorn, you've been listening to their cluck-click language for many hours before James woke you up. It's time that we begin practicing it. After all, this will now be your only means to communicate to others, excepting Baron Thomas with your telepathy."

Having something to do, no matter how trivial, took Marcy's attention off her nightmare. Mechanically, she obeyed and began responding with the proper cluck-click for each word that Leona asked for. Slowly, Marcy realized this new language she had to use was almost pointless. There weren't even two hundred words in it, far less, and worse, there were only nouns and verbs. Two words formed either a sentence or a question. She felt it was beyond hopeless to try to communicate this way. Still, she kept at it until Leona was satisfied she had them all down well.

"Now, it's supper time. I bet you are starving. So I'll help you up and get you to the galley. I'll be feeding you too," Leona explained. "Don't worry, once we arrive, you will have your own personal servant with you at all times to help you out. Come on; up and at it."

Marcy cluck-clicked, "No! Can no!"

"Can't walk? Sure, you can. Baronesses walk fine. It does take some getting used to, I'm afraid. Come on," she pushed Marcy a little, who had the choices of falling down or trying to take a step. She stumped forward a little, wiggling wildly to keep from falling, her knees bent sharply. Slowly, she staggered in the direction that Leona kept pushing her. "All baronesses have simply perfect posture, setting a good example for all women. Your posture is now absolutely perfect. You can't possibly slouch any longer."

Marcy didn't know how she managed to get to the galley, but did recall mostly falling into the chair. At least, Leona knew how to manipulate the lip plates and feed her. Full, Leona then got her up and back to the cabin with the three chairs. After falling into one, Leona fastened her seat belt. "We'll be landing shortly, where Baron Thomas will be waiting to pick you up. He'll have your new personal servant with him, so don't worry."

Marcy wanted at least to see their descent, but she couldn't turn her head to see out the small viewport. She struggled with her toes to pivot slightly in her seat, and at last, could just barely see the bright world, illuminated by the yellow sun, Blackwell. She blinked from its brightness.

Again, Marcy panicked when Leona forced her to rise after they landed. She had no choice but to somehow stump her way down the hall to the bay ramp. Seeing the sloping ramp, she cluck-clicked a panicked "No!" Leona pushed her down the ramp. Her knees sharply bent, poor Marcy stumped down, nearly falling down three times with Leona awkwardly catching her just in time. Still blinking from the overly bright sunlight, she saw a car ahead of them. A man wearing an expensive black suit stood there with a wry smile on his face. Beside him stood a young woman, perhaps her own age, with short brown hair and an oval face. She wore a white cotton day dress and soft-soled shoes, which Marcy would have given anything to be wearing.

Awkward stump after stump brought Marcy up to the pair. "Ah, this must be my new telepath. Such magnificent silver hair. What a beauty you are. Welcome to Blackwell-C, Miss Marcy Greythorn. I see you are wearing your year's pay. Excellent. This is your personal assistant, Brenna Wilson. Brenna, will you get Marcy into the car? We best be getting home."

He handed Dr. Smith a pouch containing his "pay," and the two shook hands. Brenna pushed Marcy to the open car door. "Here, I need to pull your hair back so you don't sit on it. There, see if you can sort of fall into the car on the seat. We'll worry about being graceful later on," she said cheerfully. Marcy fell into the car, trying hard not to break down and cry.

Not here, not in front of everyone.

The castle reminded her of home. Built from giant grey stone blocks, it had an outer wall and giant manor house inside. The car drove through the main gates onto a cobblestone courtyard, parking near the main double doors to the manor. She caught a glimpse of a garage off to the far left of the manor house, which appeared to be three stories tall. After parking the car, Baron Thomas barked, "Brenna, get her to the throne room where she can meet everyone." He got out and headed on inside.

Marcy struggled mightily to just get out of the car and onto her toes. She' would have fallen again had not Brenna been there to stop her. With a secure arm around her waist, Brenna began pushing her towards the doors. "You are just in time. My younger sister, Brogan, is now the personal assistant of baroness-to-be Ruth, who has just gotten her modifications two days ago. So you both can learn how to walk and dance with grace, poise, and stateliness together. Don't worry, Marcy, you'll be doing just fine in a few weeks. Please stop gasping, if you can."

Marcy gasped and cluck-clicked, "No." This was the best she could put together from the very limited vocabulary of the language. How she managed to keep from fainting and actually climbed the stairs to their throne room, Marcy couldn't say. It was all just one blurry nightmare. She stumped her way into the room, gasping with each step, though Brenna held her securely, knowing that she'd be punished if she let Marcy take a fall before the family.

Marcy could only look ahead, unless she took steps with her toes to turn her body to one side or the other. She saw Baron Thomas sitting on his throne. Beside him sat another older woman, just as hobbled up as she was. He introduced his "charming" wife, Mary. Beside her sat another young teen, the sixteen year old Ruth, who now had the same body modifications as Marcy had. Marcy's senses were wide open, and she sensed stark terror radiating from Ruth.

Ruth also wore long earrings that touched her upper chest. Her overly long, wavy hair was pure gold, much like all those in this family. Ruth's eyes met hers, and she could sense her pleadings for help. She looked sixteen, Marcy thought, feeling an instant kinship with the poor girl. Sitting next to her was an antagonistic nineteen year old, gangly lad, Elmer, who looked at Marcy in disgust. First impressions, Marcy thought, told lots. The two men were not to be trusted. Both held women in low regard, objects to be tortured, she thought, and antagonistic as well. Their mother, Mary, was merely oblivious to the world, having long ago shrunken into her mostly silent shell, waiting for death to remove her from this world. Marcy accurately sized up the scene though she wasn't thinking about that now.

"So, Marcy Greythorn, we have a room prepared for you. As you can see, Ruth has also just gotten her baroness-to-be modifications as you have. So you two can work together, practice walking, and dancing. You must always move with poise, grace, and stateliness, as befitting your high status. Disobey me, and there'll be consequences to pay. Now then, we're holding a formal betrothal dance here in less than four weeks. Ruth and Marcy must be able to move and dance with complete poise, grace, and stateliness, alone too, since at the dance, no servants will be present. Besides, many men will want to dance with each of you. So Ruth, Marcy, get walking. Ruth, take Marcy here on a tour of our fine castle. Marcy, you'll find I've already purchased a fine collection of dresses and boots for you, as befitting your exalted position here. We can discuss your telepathic work for me later on. For now, focus on learning to walk and dance properly. Now get to it, Ruth. Show her around. No back talk!"

Brogan, her assistant, quickly stepped forward from the background. She put a steadying arm on Ruth, whose panicked face told Marcy that she was just as terrified as she was. Brenna pushed on Marcy, forcing her to stump a bit to turn around. When Ruth reached the pair, she pushed again, and Marcy had no choice but to stump wildly out of the room, followed by Ruth.

Ruth did notice how badly Marcy was gasping for breath. She wanted to tell her it would get easier in a couple of days, since she was already doing better herself, but couldn't find any vocabulary words to express it. Instead, she cluck-clicked, "Do good."

Brogan questioned, "You mean you'll do better each day, Ruth?" Ruth cluck-clicked no. "Oh, you mean Marcy here will do better each day?" Ruth clucked yes, but felt miserable herself.

How long they stumped around the castle, Marcy had no idea. It was one long blur of intense pain in her feet, legs, and knees. Her chest felt like it was about to implode on her. Her ears felt like they were being pulled off her with each jostling step she took. Finally, she was allowed to sit down. Supper was being served, and she finally noticed she was in their large dining hall. At least, Brenna knew how to deal with her lip plates and fed her properly, though she couldn't each much at all before feeling overly full.

After supper, everyone left except for Marcy and Baron Thomas, who wanted to talk with her. "Okay Marcy. Here's the deal. I need to know precisely what my enemy baron and his son are planning. Ruth is supposed to marry his Able, while my Elmer is to marry his Casey. He's already gotten a telepath, and I don't trust her at all. She's probably been spying on us all along now. So you get adapted fast. At the ball, you are to probe their minds and find out what they are planning to do. I won't be taken by surprise. He's the second most powerful baron on Blackwell-C. I'm the most powerful baron, in case you haven't figured that one out yet. Got all this?"

Marcy focused. *Yes. But I didn't agree to have my body mutilated like this. This is criminal! You can't get away with this! When the others find out what you've done to me, there will be hell to pay!*

Marcy let all of her pent up vitriol fly, but he stopped her short. "Tisk, tisk, Marcy. It is done. You are totally helpless. You're not going anywhere. I don't tolerate any backtalk. So you've got to learn your lessons sooner than later!" He reached for a box on the table, evidently anticipating her outburst. He pulled out another identical set of earrings and pliers. He added the second set to each of her ear loops, clamping them securely to the loop, doubling the sheer weight on her lobes. Marcy cried out, "No!"

He laughed sinisterly. "See, they really do pull your

ears, constant pain, eh? Well, as you can see, you now have a second year's payment for services. Keep on backtalking me, and I'll keep on adding more duplicate strands to your earrings until your ears are pulled off. After that, why, I can replace your beautiful eye balls with some fine glass ones, just like my enemy, Baron Robert, did with his wife's eyes. She's been blind for over twenty years now. You'll meet her at the dance. Hell, I think I'll insist that you dance with her. That would be incredibly amusing, don't you think? So are you going to backtalk me more? I can easily add more strands now. I have my pliers out, and the strands here in the box. Want heavier earrings?"

Marcy cluck-clicked, "No!"

"Good. Now that we understand each other, go find Brenna, and she'll get you ready for bed. You need your beauty sleep. You and Ruth have a whole lot of practicing to do in just a very few weeks. You both simply have to be ready for this dance or there will be hell to pay. Now get up, and get out of here. Yes, on your own. You have to learn how to do it sometime. Might as well be now, and for god's sake don't fall down. I sure won't be helping you up," he barked, starting another round of sheer panic in Marcy.

Marcy lunged forward, banging into the table, her super heavy earrings threatening to pull her ears off. At least, the table kept her from falling. Carefully, with bent, but throbbing knees, she turned around, and took one very careful step after the other until she reached the door. It was closed. She carefully turned around, but the baron had vanished out another door. As she carefully turned back around to the door, it opened, revealing the worried face of Brenna. "Oh, here you are. Come on; let's get you up to your room," she said hastily.

The next few weeks leading up to the formal dance were the worst that Marcy and Ruth had ever experienced. Right away, Marcy began forming up telepathic rapports with Ruth, so both could console each other, and so Marcy could work what little healing she knew on the both of them. They became very close friends, just as Molly and Casey had. Ruth was right; within a week, both teens were accustomed to the terrible restriction of their breathing, and were very careful not to overdo it and go into another round of frantic gasping for breath.

Slowly but surely, they became used to walking on their toes and keeping their balance. Handling the stairs still gave both of them a fright though. The last week before the dance was the worst for the pair. Baron Thomas insisted that they spend their days soloing. Their assistants were not allowed to be in the same room as they were. All this last week, both were terrified of going down the stone steps, but yet they simply had to do it. Naturally, Marcy and Ruth both balked at this, and Baron Thomas reacted as promised, adding a second heavy string to Ruth's earrings and a third to Marcy's. When Marcy finally saw her ears in her bedroom mirror, her lobes were quite elongated, stretched almost to the tearing point. She knew she must not provoke him further. A fourth strand might just rip her ear lobes!

However, Marcy wasn't just another dumb barmaid. She knew how to handle men who had too much to drink, though now she felt completely helpless to do much of anything physically. Instead, she fell back on her *mentales* gifts. Late at night and after going into rapport with Ruth and healing up her legs and feet as well as her own, Marcy laid on her bed and focused, entering the minds of Baron Thomas and Elmer. At first, she wanted information, and after rummaging around in their memories, which seemed nothing more than dreams to the sleeping men, she found their memories of the previous dance and got a look at what Casey, Molly, Able, Celia, and Baron Robert looked like.

The next night, she dug deeper and uncovered their plans for the immediate future, and those shocked her. As soon as Elmer married Casey, he was going to remove her eyes, inserting vividly red glass eyes. As if she wasn't helpless enough, Marcy cursed, when she uncovered this. Then came the real revelation. Baron Thomas was planning to murder Baron Robert and his son Able, once the son was married and named his heir. Baron Thomas and Elmer would then control the two most powerful castles on this world! Worse, that time was drawing very close indeed!

However, as she was discovering all this, she detected

another telepath also touching the baron's mind. *Who are you?*

Oh! I'm Molly, Molly Dobbs. Who are you?

I'm Marcy Greythorn.

Hi Marcy. You must be the new hire from Tierra. I'm from there too. Have you seen what he's planning to do?

Yes, just now. Murdering the men where you are. We have to stop this somehow, Molly.

I know. Help is on the way, but I don't know when. Renata is sending someone sometime. Meanwhile, she told me to protect Casey here and Ruth somehow.

Count me in, though I'm totally helpless. I can only barely move. They cut off my arms and have me in a metal neck collar thing. I can barely walk a little in these ballet boots.

Same here. Has he really tripled the weight of your earrings? Baron Robert found out he was planning that and added two more lengths to mine. My ears are almost ripping.

Yes, he's a vicious man. The slightest objection to his orders, and he flips out and hurts us. So what are we going to do? I think we're to meet at a dance soon.

Don't know yet. But see if you and Ruth can locate all their surveillance cameras, where their guards are stationed, and their numbers. I'll get back to you. I guess you can reach me now too. Hang in there, Marcy. I know Renata, and if she says she's sending help, she will.

Okay. Ruth and I will get onto that tomorrow. Bye.

The next day, Marcy relayed what she'd learned to Ruth, and found the young teen a wealth of information about the castle and its security. She'd had the run of the castle until she got modified a few weeks ago. There were spy cameras at most all strategic locations, but the actual men were stationed in the basement, which had long ago been the dungeons. That night, she shared what they'd found out with Molly.

As the day of the formal dance drew near, the two telepaths still didn't have any real plan formulated, other than they would do whatever they needed to do to prevent the blinding of the teens and the murders of the men.

Unknown to everyone, late one night, the personal assistant and servant of Casey's, Charis White, opened a hidden compartment in her chest. Shortly, an electronic connection formed, spanning a long distance through the galaxy. A lengthy exchange of data bursts occurred. Charis sent, "Things are getting out of hand here on Blackwell-C. It is the men, as always. I need further orders, Minta."

Minta fired back, "Testosterone driven men can be counted upon to destroy creations, wage fights, battles, and wars. They are the true destroyers of civilizations. Only the hermaphrodite men are worthy of survival. Their hormone levels are greatly lowered. Once they have their own baby, they lose all their impulses towards destruction. Okay, Charis, here's what we are going to do." She sent another long data burst.

"Copy," Charis sent back, disconnecting the electronics and closing her compartment. She then plugged into the electrical outlet to recharge, keeping her batteries at peak levels, giving her an entire week of operation without needing to recharge. She also didn't sleep, but kept her senses wide open, in case someone came looking for her during the night. None did that night.

The day of the formal dance arrived, but neither Ruth nor Marcy were walking and dancing with great poise, grace, and stateliness, according to Baron Thomas, who took another opportunity to chide them at breakfast. "You two go practice all morning and without your assistants, who are needed to help Mary prepare the Grand Ballroom for tonight's festivities. We're expecting around two hundred guests. If either of you embarrass me tonight, like falling down, I promise you that you'll pay for it with your eyes! Hell, Baroness Celia hasn't needed her eyes for over twenty years, so I don't see why you two need them either."

That was enough to bring panic attacks to both young teens, who couldn't imagine being blind on top of everything else. Once more, they climbed the stairs to the third floor where they had been practicing their dancing steps. At least someone turned on the slow beat music for them. But we can't step backwards well at all, Ruth thought nervously, wishing she had someway to tell this to Marcy. Yet, she didn't and sighed, trying to calm her nerves enough at least more or less to follow the musical beats.

After lunch and having to go down two flights of stairs on their own, the two were ordered to be bathed and prepared for the evening's festivities. To save time, their assistants moved the two into the same bathroom, Ruth's, giving Marcy just enough time to work her healing magic on their knees, legs, and feet, giving them their best chance at not embarrassing her father.

Mid-afternoon, Marcy was dressed in a lavender satin gown, whose color she hated. Strapless, it followed her exaggerated curves tightly all the way down to her knees, where with the help of some taffeta linings, it flowed outward some two feet around her legs and yet still showed some of her black nylons and certainly her matching lavender ballet boots. With her long, silver hair brushed out, Marcy sat erect on Ruth's bed, looking at herself in the mirror. The green emeralds, the silver hair, the gold of her lip disks and neck rings, and the lavender gown and boots — all clashed with each other, as far as she was concerned. Still, she wore what the baron had ordered. Sixteen year old Ruth sat totally erect beside her, though waves of nervousness flowed off her. She wore a similar style gown, done in a bright, cherry red satin. At least her golden hair matched her lip disks and neck rings. The red rubies in her triple earrings matched her dress and boots.

Once more Marcy sent calming waves over Ruth. *But I don't know if I can do this, Marcy. What if I make a mistake? What if I fall? I can't get up by myself. I don't want to be blind too.*

I won't let that happen to you Ruth. You just do your best, and I will too. Let's hope the rescue comes soon, Marcy sent back, but had to break their rapport as their assistants entered the room, ready to assist them with the early supper.

Security was tight as the large group began arriving, filling up the courtyard with cars. Initially, everyone gathered in the throne room, where Baron Thomas and Baroness Mary greeted them. At least, the group remained seated as the introductions were done. Quickly, Marcy and Ruth lost track of who was who; there were just too many men and women, though there were quite a few others their own age, heirs apparent, Marcy thought.

Finally, Baron Robert and his group arrived. As they entered, Marcy noticed that everyone else backed away, giving them space, a sure sign he wielded immense power. At least, he had an arm around his blind wife, pushing her forward towards the thrones. Casey was also wearing a cherry red gown, almost identical to Ruth's. Marcy spotted her telepathic friend, Molly, who wore a sky blue version of the same gown. She also noticed that both Casey and Molly had triple layers on their earrings, much like hers and Ruth's. Marcy did notice that at least Casey wasn't wearing the ballet boots, but impossibly tall, seven-inch heels. They were more like sandals, and she sensed Casey's feet slipping around in them, making her steps even more unstable than normal.

Molly did notice the style of men's suits were different tonight. Their jackets had no collars, but we open at the upper neck, where a swash of color from their shirts without collars as well appeared, giving them an unusual look, which she filed away for future reference.

After the introductions, Baron Thomas called out, "And now let the betrothal ball begin. Gentlemen, escort your brides-to-be down to the Grand Ballroom." He rose and waited for Mary to lunge to her feet and join him at his side, before he slipped his arm around her tiny waist. Elmer at least moved over to Casey's side, as did Able to Ruth's, who also had a precarious lunge and wobble to get up onto her toes. As the two barons led the way out of the throne room, Molly and Marcy fell in behind them, once again facing going down the stairs without any help and with hundreds of others watching them from behind. They went very, very slowly and carefully, though sensing the impatience of many behind them.

Molly guessed that with so many people present the barons would not try to harm the two young baronesses-to-be or themselves. Rather, they would somehow have to survive this public spectacle or display, and she focused on just keeping her balance. Both Molly and Marcy were relieved to find themselves merely watching the others during the first dance of the evening. The two barons danced with their baronesses, while the two young couples did likewise, along with many other couples both old and young. Nevertheless, both telepaths focused on their charges, picking up what was said by Able and Elmer.

The dance steps were extremely simple, in deference to the severe limitations upon the baronesses. Most of the women present also wore six-inch heels and took small steps as well. One step forward, one to the side, one to the back, one to the left. The woman pivots placing her back to the man and the box repeated. Pivot back to face the man. That was the basic pattern, but with the men leading, many variations were possible, such as going forward instead of backwards or continuing to go either left or right four times. The men had their hands on the women's waists, many of which were small, thanks to the corsets they wore, though none were remotely as tiny as the baronesses and their twelve-inch waists. Slow, graceful, stately — that's how the two telepaths from Ashford-5 described their mode of dance.

"My dear Casey," Elmer teased his blonde fiancé, as he held her waist and kept trying to make her take larger steps than she could possibly manage, "by now you know I'll be replacing your eyes with some very pretty bright red glass eyes, just as soon as we're married. Then, you'll be exactly like your mother. Won't that be great, my dear?" His voice had a twinge of a sneer in it.

He felt her body trembling and heard her cluck-click, "No! No!"

"Oh yes, yes. See, your mother dances just fine. She has not missed her eyes in over twenty years, and neither will you, my pretty. I'm just wondering if I ought not make you wear the ballet boots like Ruth, Marcy, and Molly are, instead of these lower heels."

He felt her body trembling significantly more. She cluck-click, "No! No! No!" Casey just didn't have any vocabulary in her unique language to protest any further than simply "no," and Elmer knew it.

Meanwhile, Able chatted with Ruth while they danced,

452

at least he danced. Ruth could only more or less stump in the indicated directions, anything but grace and poise. "By now you've heard I'll be replacing your eyes with some very beautiful glass eyes, just as soon as we're married. Would you like to see your new eyes now? I have them in my pocket. If you prefer, we could get them inserted yet tonight, and then you could enjoy the dance even more, beating Casey to be the first to get them. She's going to get red glass eyes as soon as Elmer marries her. You could put them all to shame and get yours in tonight, and then show them off to everyone that's here. Wouldn't you like to do that?"

Poor Ruth began shaking so badly she completely stopped trying even to move her toes in the directions that he tried to pull her. She cluck-clicked, "No! No! No! No walk!" Terror swept over her body, but she could find any vocabulary to protest further.

With the first dance over, the two telepaths found many men coming up to them, asking for the next dance. Neither could refuse without raising the angry ire of the two barons. Worse, the men kept them going dance after dance, until both were gasping for breath. Several men teased Molly. "I hear you have a working stick." He grabbed her crotch to feel for it. "Ah, there it is."

Molly cluck-clicked, "No! Stop!" That did no good. She focused and touched the mind of the man who was groping her and flooded it with raw energy, giving him a sudden splitting headache. Of course, his hands went up to his head, and he backed away, but another immediately cut in, putting his hands around her tiny waist, forcing her to continue dancing.

When both Molly and Marcy were simply standing in place, gasping for breath, Elmer and Able stepped up. "This way to the lounge. Wouldn't you like to sit a spell? Have some wine?" While they didn't want the wine, they certainly wanted to sit a spell and recover some. The side room held a large number of comfortable sofas and easy chairs. Molly and Marcy mostly fell onto one sofa, still gasping for air, pinching their long hair in the process, far more painful for Molly than Marcy, since Molly had neurons in hers. The two men disappeared and soon returned with wine glasses and spoons.

Each locked the upper lip plate into its horizontal position and brought liquids up to their mouths. With the barons having entered the lounge area with their baronesses, the two dare not refuse the offered wine.

Before long, Marcy realized that the wine was drugged! She tried to focus to warn Molly, but couldn't. Soon, both telepaths were in sort of a daze, not truly unconscious, but not fully alert. Worse, since they weren't gasping any longer, more men came up to them demanding the next dance. Marcy with her long silver hair was in heavy demand. No one here had seen hair with such a startling color. In their dazed, drugged state, both telepaths merely followed the men, doing what they were told, like docile sheep.

Meanwhile, Elmer and Able proceeded to drug Casey and Ruth as well. As soon as both were more or less subdued, they helped the teens to walk out of the lounge, down the hall, and into a small side room, where Dr. Smith was waiting. "Are you sure that you want to do this? I can't undo it if you later change your minds, boys."

"Barons-to-be, Dr. Smith. Watch out. You're dangerously close to insubordination here," Elmer barked, handing him the pair of bright red eyes for Casey. Quickly, Able handed him a pair of golden glass eyes that would match Ruth's lip plates and neck rings and also her hair and the gold in her huge earrings. The doctor accepted them and motioned for Elmer to lay Casey onto the medical machine, which he did, listening to Casey mumbling incoherently. The doctor adjusted the machine to hold her head rigidly in place and then the top closed over her face. Casey saw small lights and then total darkness. In less than three minutes, the procedure was done, and Elmer lifted her back up, sitting her on a chair. Able then did the same with Ruth. She too saw the small lights and then total darkness, but sensed Able picking her up and sitting her in a chair.

Both men then lifted the upper disks and spooned in another liquid, the antidote to the drug. "Give them about five minutes to recover," Dr. Smith said. "After that, don't forget. You are going to have to lead them everywhere now."

"Ha. Dad doesn't lead Celia around our castle, only

when we go out. Even so, she's capable of navigating the dance floor on her own," Able countered.

Soon the two teens came out of the semi-drugged state. Ruth wanted to say, "What's happening? Are the lights off?" It seemed so to her. Her limited vocabulary didn't permit such wordy questions. She cluck-clicked, "No see."

"Ah yes, my charming, beautiful Ruth. No see is right. Your glass eyes are a beautiful shade of gold, matching your hair, disks, neck rings, and earrings. You look stunning. Up you go. Time to show off on the dance floor. Everyone will want to admire you now and even dance with you."

Ruth shrieked, but unintelligibly so. Worse, Able pulled her up onto her feet. "Can't you stand still and stop wobbling?" he chided her. With his arm around her waist, he forced her to begin walking blindly. She heard Casey scream behind her and knew that she too was blinded. Ruth now could only place total trust in Able to lead her. Her entire body was shaking badly. Behind her, so was Casey, who was almost petrified, but had to walk as Elmer pushed her forward mercilessly.

Out on the dance floor, the hundreds noticed the two young couples re-entering the main doors and moved aside a little, admiring their future barons and baronesses. Elmer spoke loudly just as the musicians ended one song. "Everyone, come see just how beautiful my bride looks now. She's gone ahead and gotten her beautiful bright red glass eyes sooner than expected. Isn't she just lovely in them?"

Able added, "Any so has dear Ruth. Her golden eyes now match her golden hair as well. Come see just how beautiful she truly is now."

Across the floor, Marcy and Molly's stomachs knotted. Both realized that they had failed to prevent this, after promising both teens. If they hadn't been drugged, they knew they could have found a way to stop this from happening. Now all they could do was watch and suppress their own wild emotions.

As the next dance started, both men put their hands around their future bride's waists, guiding them in the dance. Elmer teased Casey, "See, you don't really need eyes. I'm leading and you simply follow me."

She whimpered and cluck-clicked, "No see. No see. No see."

"Yes, that's right, Casey. You no see no more. You no need to see no more," he teased her, knowing full well how terrible her life had just become. Still, hundreds gathered around to stare at her and her bright red eyes, commenting on how good and unique they did look on her.

Soon, however, the newness wore off, and both men simply left Casey and Ruth standing in the middle of the ballroom. Unable to see anything, both stood petrified to the spot, not daring to move an inch. Worse, other men came up and forced them to dance with them as well. Their universe had completely collapsed on them. Emotionally, they sunk to a deep apathy, their bodies moving only as the dancers pushed them. When one dance ended, they simply stood there unmoving, uncaring, all life was out of them.

As Molly scanned the large crowd, she sensed these were the wealthy and most influential men in this city. Not one raised the slightest protest over what the two young men had done to their future wives. In fact, many were purposely dancing with the two teens, forcing them to move in their total blackness.

Molly fumed, but continued to observe the crowd even while some lad insisted that she dance with him. That's when she noticed Casey's assistant Charis slipping into the room. Molly focused and tried to reach her mind to alert Charis to the dire plight that Casey was now in, but found no mind. Then, she saw Charis was carrying a yellow cylinder. A pale yellow gas flowed out of one end of it. She sniffed and truly panicked! This group was being attacked with that terrible bio genetic agent! She focused and alerted Marcy to the attack.

What do we do? Marcy sent back, panicking herself, though noticing that no one else was aware of the attack yet.

Get the teens up to Ruth's bedroom. Come on. We have to move fast! Molly sent back, ignoring the man's hands on her waist, as she pulled away from him. He gave her a dirty look and went over to a group of younger teens, who were all chatting about how beautiful the glass eyes looked on the two baronesses-to-be.

But they can't see, Marcy sent, as she joined Molly and reached the petrified teens, who were just standing perfectly motionless.

Molly simply acted. *I'll levitate them up a little. We push them out the doors. Come on. We've very little time!* With her crystal glowing bright blue this time, both teen's bodies rose up from the floor slightly, though neither knew it. Molly pushed her bosom into the back of Casey, while Marcy followed suit with Ruth. It was hard going, trying to push them with only the tips of their toes on the ground. No one seemed to pay them any attention, not even as they went on out the opened doors.

Reaching the stairs, Marcy focused and began using some of her gifts as well, closing the doors behind them and helping Molly raise the women on up the stairs. Both were panting and gasping for breath by the time they reached the next floor. Worse, Marcy was feeling dizzy; the effects of the bio agent were beginning to take hold on her. A few minutes later, they entered Ruth's bedroom and, with Marcy's last efforts, the two teens were laid prone on Ruth's bed. As Marcy slumped to the floor unconscious, Molly did her best to soften the fall.

Molly knew she had to get them all out of their confining dresses and heels for sure. Probably their waists being as small as they were would be all right, but not their bosoms and feet. Using the last of her powers, she began undressing them and herself. Panting and gasping from the exertion, she used the very last of her power to erect an illusion over the four of them, making it seem that they were not there and that the room was empty. Then, she too began to feel the effects of the bio agent. Can't do much more to me, she thought as she slipped into a coma too.

Molly awoke a short while later. Using her legs as levers, she got herself into a sitting position and then used them to pivot her body enough to get her eyes onto the three others. All three were in comas still. The entire place was utterly silent. Looking downward with her eyes, since her neck was totally immobile, she noticed that her own breasts had grown larger than the soccer balls of Casey and Ruth, but she didn't see any other changes. At least she felt rested. Her *mentales* powers had been renewed, and the last traces of that drug had worn off.

Silently, she used a bit of her gifts to slip the rest of her gown off her and then levitated herself up to her feet. With her nylon covered feet flat on the floor, she felt in heaven and started towards the door to see what was going on. As she moved just outside the door, she heard noises coming from the floor below! She focused and felt for minds. Nothing but those in comas, dreaming of utterly nothing, totally blank. And yet, there were noises! No voices, just movement noises. Molly grew very curious indeed, but wisely backed up into Ruth's bedroom. She focused and used one of her gifts that she rarely used, Remote Viewing. She took as her viewpoint the ceiling below, squarely in the middle of the giant ballroom.

She saw hundreds of bodies lying where they'd collapsed into comas. Upon looking closer at one of the fallen men, she noticed several details. Their hair had grown some and their breasts were quite pronounced, but still a long way from those that women had on Ashford-5. Their arms looked intact as well as their legs. Conclusion: she'd only been unconscious for a short while. Well, she thought, that makes sense. My body already has all these genetic mutations in it, except for my boobs.

Next, she focused on the men and women who were moving the comatose bodies. They seemed like normal humans. The room had a slightly yellow color to it, which could only mean the bio agent was still quite concentrated down there. Yet, these men and women seemed unaffected by it. Curious. She observed them closer. They were stripping each body first before picking them up and carrying them out of the ballroom. Well, that was what was needed when the major mutations occurred, she reasoned. Where were they taking them? Again, she tried to touch the minds of these men and women who were rescuing the fallen victims. Nothing. Absolutely nothing. No minds. Molly moved back and fell onto the edge of the bed to think. How could they not have minds? Am I slipping somehow? All humans have minds. This is really weird. Plus, they aren't even speaking, and yet they are working in a coordinated fashion. I don't get it. Are they aliens or something?

No, they didn't look like the snake aliens she'd heard tales about, but that got her thinking. She'd heard all manner of old stories about the robots of Aquila Prime. She'd even read Nia Elain Compton-Jereni's book on her adventures. Were these robots? If so, they looked so human-like. But what did the robots want with these victims?

Then, she put it together. Charis was one of them, a robot! She had to be, since she was the one who released the bio agent gas into the room. Were these robots friendly and trying to help? Molly discarded that idea. Charis delivered the attack. They could not possibly have friendly intentions! That spooked her even more, particularly since she was so darn helpless now. Well, *I can walk well at least*, she resolved.

Molly, you there? Good time to chat? Renata's thoughts appeared in her mind.

Renata! God, I, we really do need help and fast! Robots! One was disguised as Casey's personal assistant. Last night at the dance and after we all got drugged and the men took out Casey's eyes and Ruth's too, Charis, her assistant, walked through the ballroom with one of those yellow bio agent cylinders. She filled the room with the gas. I got us four to Ruth's room, before they fell into a coma. I just barely got their clothes undone and shoes off before I passed out. It's weird, but I came to just a bit ago. It can't be more than the next morning or so now. There are a whole lot of robots down there, undressing the victims and taking them away somewhere.

Renata replied, *Okay. I was touching base with you to tell you that help is on the way. They ought to be close to landing now. Hold on a second while I relay this to them. Back in a jiffy.*

She was back in less than a minute, much to Molly's relief. *Okay. Hang in there. Any way you can keep the robots from finding you?*

I have an illusion up over the room, if the robots can see it. They don't have minds to effect. I can make a fire, but that's not going to harm metal robots, is it?

No. Don't even try that. Best plan is to stick to the illusion. By the way, any chance that you can get those glass eyeballs out of their sockets?

Don't know. Why? Is that important too? Molly asked.

Might be. There's always a possibility that their eyes will regenerate as their bodies mutate. We've no experience along these lines that I know of. Worth a try. I'll lend you a hand.

Molly suddenly felt an enormous surge of mental energies coming into her body. She smiled invisibly. Using her feet, she pivoted her erect body enough so she could see the two comatose teens. *Hey, that's good. Stay put. I can do it,* Renata sent. Molly watched the two pairs of glass eyeballs slowly pop out of the sockets and land beside their heads. *We will keep them around in case nothing regenerates. Now, let's keep that illusion of yours up and running.*

Quite some time passed before they heard footsteps coming down the hall and doors opening and closing. Then, a humaniform robot appeared at Ruth's doorway, glancing inside. Seeing nothing, it moved on down the hall, checking other rooms. After a while, she heard footsteps going down the stone stairs, and Molly finally relaxed. Her illusion held, with the help of Renata.

Chapter 26 An Unlikely Rescue Team

After beginning her routine checkup on the off-world telepaths and finding some of them in dire situations and being treated badly, Renata knew she needed to send off a rescue team. Their own history books were filled with the horrors that had been inflicted on Tierra telepaths, most of whom had been kidnaped and taken into slavery. Still, these two hundred had chosen to ignore their own history books and had signed contracts for work off-world. Nevertheless, she could not abandon those few who were in terrible difficulties. If nothing else, Renata wanted to preserve as much of their secret *mentales* gifts as possible.

Her problem was severe and nearly unsolvable. While she, the queens, and the governor had quite a number of men and women upon whom in the past they could have sent off to the rescue, every one of them had been severely impacted by the Serpientes super-mutation attack and subsequent mess. Deep space transports were not designed to be used by armless men and women, let alone the barriers they would likely face once they landed and tried to come to the rescue of the telepaths.

The last thing she wanted to do was to bring more outsiders, say from Brom or Valen, into her fold. The fewer that knew these kinds of things the better for Tierra. For example, for centuries one of her greatest fears had been that the knowledge of how to turn anyone into a *mentales* gifted person would become broadly known. While she and the many towers worked diligently to attempt to keep all known *mentales* gifted on the ethical path, some slipped by and had wreaked havoc. Velasco was only the most recent one to do that.

It was bad enough that all their top Academy professors and many of their top graduates in many disciplines were also now armless as well, including all their critically needed geneticists, but now she simply had no one to turn to for the rescues. Thus, she decided to take another approach and paid a visit on Arnold Flaxton and his group who were living in one of the manor houses near the north end of the walled Imperial Castle complex.

When she entered, Estrella and Adrianne were sitting on their living room floor, using their feet to manipulate their comm center. "Oh hi Renata. Come on it. We're all working out, but you can see that," Adrianne called out. Estrella had returned from Jarvis-B to resupply and get more specialized equipment before she and Adrianne planned to head back there. Unfortunately, their plans were delayed by the super-mutation of the snake aliens.

Estrella added, "It's working out too, just like everyone says. We can do quite a lot with our feet, as long as our hair doesn't get in the way. But it's going to be a long time before I can get back to doing useful genetic experiments."

"Hi ya. Where's Arnold and the others?" Renata asked giving the two women a big smile.

"Oh, they are all in the sparing room. That's Pippa's living room. Next suite over," Adrianne answered, and Renata walked on past the two into the second suite. There, she stood for a moment observing them. Arnold, the ex-Special Forces Black Operations man was sparring with Alfonso, while Pippa and Savina were going to it. Gwenda was panting from a recent match and overseeing the two sparing groups, while Bess was doing her best to bring some water into the room, using a crude yoke she'd worked up. A bit of water slopped out, but she managed to bring in quite a bit for the thirsty group.

Renata watched as the four worked on their circle kicks and dodging. "Pretty amazing bit of sparing," she commented to Gwenda.

"Yep. We're not giving up. I can't hold my knife anymore, but I'm getting my feet ready to kick more snake bellies!" the tall red haired fighter said in her heavy Welsh accent. "Our hair is our biggest problem. Keeps getting in the way, so we tie it up and endure the pain from it."

The fighters ended their session; breathing heavily, they walked over to Renata. Arnold nodded, "Renata. What brings you to our place? As you can see, we haven't given up, not just yet."

"Indeed, I'm amazed with your skills."

Pippa spoke up, "We've been working hard on alternative fighting methods. We're not there yet, but getting closer. When the snakes come back, we want to be ready somehow. We're not going down without a fight! What brings you here? Are the snakes back?"

Renata chuckled. "No on the snakes, but I've got many nasty situations, and I believe that you might be the answer I've been looking for. Come on; let's get your group together. I've a proposition for you fighters."

A few minutes later, Arnold's group sat on sofas in Pippa's living room. Renata explained, "As you probably know a bunch of our telepaths, our *mentales* gifted, have taken positions as telepaths on other worlds. Some of them are being heavily abused and simply must be rescued somehow, someway."

Arnold said, "Have you got a fighter crew ready? We're all willing to help as we can."

"Nope. Every possibility is as armless as we all are, but I've got a proposal for you. If I can turn you all into *mentales* gifted and with the right gifts, such as telekinesis and such, would you be willing to tackle all these rescues that I need done?"

"What? Is such even possible?" Arnold asked. "Aren't they just born with those gifts?"

"Some are, of course, but there is a way that can turn you into *mentales* gifted, and I believe we can also control the forms your gifts take, that is, if you are willing," Renata explained without going into specifics. Rafaela had worked out the precise details years ago, but her formula was a very closely guarded secret, for obvious reasons, though some had guessed at it in the past. So far, no one had hit it precisely right.

"Hell, Renata. Anyone of us would love to have such a priceless gift. We don't need that to volunteer. Just tell us where to go, and we'll do our best to rescue them," Arnold declared, nodding at his wife, Gwenda who nodded back.

"All right then. I'm going to see if Governor Sheila's new

workers can make some modifications to your deep space transport, lowering the controls so you can operate them with your feet. Meantime, I'm going to put you all on a supervised regime, which will develop your *mentales* gifts in just a few weeks. Allowing for training in their use, I hope to send you out on rescue missions in maybe six weeks, if you are willing."

"You bet we are willing!" Arnold agreed waxing enthusiastic. "What do we do? We're all ready now." Many heads nodded in agreement.

"Okay then. Drop by my place for lunch, and we'll get started. I'll go visit Governor Sheila now. See you at my place in two hours," Renata replied.

The governor's response was, "Brilliant, Renata! Why didn't we think of this before? Many of the system controls can be lowered. The doors can have their locks removed and foot operated sliding bars installed. No problem there. The entry code pad on the outside of the bay ramp will be the biggest problem, since it goes through the hull. That will take a bit more work. We'll need to work out a way to handle the heavy fuel cells so they can deal with in-flight refueling. I'll get my new crew on it today."

Renata thanked her and headed home. She found using her feet to handle the precise measuring of the psi-crystal powder entirely too annoying and awkward. Hence, she began to use her own native spiritual being powers, moving the objects as needed. She consulted Rafaela's chart on dosages and went with the largest amount, which cut the total time required for the changes down to two weeks. That done, she mixed the powder into some juices and poured out eight precise doses. Satisfied, she moved on to fixing a light lunch for the eight.

When they arrived, she explained, "From now on, you'll each need to drink one of these glasses of juice before each of your three meals a day. I've fixed a light lunch for now, but it's going to be easier if you just stop by, drink the juice, and then head off to fix your own meals."

"You mean just drinking juice is going to make us all into super *mentales* gifted?" Arnold asked in disbelief.

Bess spoke up, "Hey, it's probably what else is in the

juice that is going to do it."

Renata chuckled. "Bess is right. I'm putting a very carefully measured amount in each glass. The process should be done in two weeks. It will be at least that long before Governor Sheila has your deep space transport rigged up for you."

"So what kind of gifts are we looking at?" Pippa asked. "If armless us are going to be effective, I've given this some thought. We need to be invisible and to be able to teleport. Our hotshot comm duo can keep us informed on where our opponents are at and moving through our ear wigs. Plus, we need to be able to stun or kill those who attack us before they can shoot d-guns at us. And we're going to need to be able to turn doorknobs, open doors, and all sorts of things and do it quickly, not stopping to sit on our butts and use our feet, taking a couple of minutes per door. And it might be nice to be able to persuade ground controllers to allow us to land and all that, even customs people who might try to stop us."

"Naturally, Pippa. I don't think anyone of you will end up with all those skills, but certainly some of them. I'm going to do my best to ensure that, as a team, all your bases will be covered," Renata proposed. They chatted a bit while using their feet to eat from plates on the floor, though no one asked how Renata had gotten them all there without spilling them. She was Renata, after all. All eight knew everyone else held Renata in utter awe, but they just saw her as a very able person.

The two weeks passed rapidly for the eight, who sensed changes occurring within two days of that first glass of juice. Renata, however, kept a very close eye on each of them, executing a tweak here and there in each person's mental outlook. Estrella and Adrianne were the easiest to handle. Those two needed strong abilities to move and control physical objects, since their positions within this group were those of communicators. Savina, as their navigator, was the most likely to be able to make effective use of a teleportation gift. Arnold, Gwenda, Pippa, and Alfonso were the front fighters of the group and would likely be those doing the actual rescuing. Hence, they needed to go invisible when needed, to say nothing of being able to deal with combat situations. Plus, both Arnold and Alfonso had to be able to effectively pilot the ship no matter what. Bess, on the other hand, was the most nurturing of the eight, having spent so long helping the women at the escort service when she had no legs. Thus, her gifts would be best served if they lay along the healing lines. Renata did her best to control which gifts manifested themselves in which person.

However, she went beyond that and convinced Governor Sheila to install a small teleportation pad in the modified deep space transport, but with controls that could be operated by a person sitting on either a chair or on the floor. Sheila then had her new staff place the control unit about a foot above the floor, reachable either way, a nice compromise position.

"Wow! This is so way great that I can't find words for it!" Pippa declared, having just accidentally gone into telepathic rapport with her mate, Bess. As the two-week date approached, all eight were already reading the thoughts of others, and now Pippa had accidentally gone into close rapport as well.

Right on schedule, Renata turned the eight new *mentales* gifted over to the queen's four Tower Circles for their training. She was kept informed of their progress at the end of each day and was pleased. Her careful work was turning out just as she'd planned. Her choice of gifts was perfectly matched to their individual personalities, which greatly increased the probability the gift would manifest itself in each.

One month after she'd begun, the Tower Circle's finished up their basic training and gave each their own personal psi-crystal which amplified their powers a hundredfold. Renata didn't stop here, though. She now had possession of Velasco's belt with nearly three dozen giant crystals compressed under heavy pressure down to an inch in size. She loaned it to Arnold for the duration of the rescue missions. When the eight experimented with it, under her directions, they were flabbergasted at the immense power that it gave them.

"No one should carry this much power with them!"

466

Arnold declared. "No wonder Velasco was so successful. With this, one could dominate the whole darn galaxy! But gang, let's get down to business. We're not going anywhere until we practice and work out our moves. Besides, we still haven't proven we can actually handle the transport either. Renata, let's set up a dummy rescue operation as a sort of practice run. Any good Black Ops team practices, practices, and practices."

"Wise move, Arnold. I'll set it up. I'll play the victim and will be lying on my bed, unable to move at all. You're task will be to arrive on Tierra, locate me, get me safely onboard your ship. No need to take off. Let's see if you eight can pull this off. Remember, each of you only has so much mental energies that you can use each day. Don't run short. If you are successful on this test run, then I've got some who need rescuing right away," Renata suggested, though it was more of an order.

Gwenda chuckled, "This will be the first time I go into a fight without my knife!"

"Hey, or me without my d-guns and stun guns," Arnold added.

Their first stop was their own rooms. For ease of living, they all had been wearing light, cotton day dresses, hemmed at their knees, allowing them both ease of motion with their legs and the convenience of being able to get into them without much fuss, though they each had to help the other. In fact, they'd already put the old *katalyein* guidelines of working together in groups of four, who could accomplish what one or two could not on their own. Each wore soft-soled slip-on shoes, making their feet and toes available in seconds. Their biggest hassle now was their nearly six foot long hair with its heightened sensitivity from the neurons in them.

Working together, they got each other's hair first tied at the back of their heads in a ponytail. Then they looped it over three times, and tied that too, forming large two-foot long bundles behind their heads. It looked a bit wild, but kept their hair from interfering with their movements. Once each was ready, they headed down to the basement of the castle proper, taking the electric cars over to the spaceport. In high spirits, the eight walked across the tarmac to their reconfigured transport. Pippa slipped off one shoe and entered their code with her toes. The bay ramp lowered. "All right. This is tons better," she commented, as she headed up the ramp.

Each headed to their post. Savina entered coordinates that would take them just above Tierra and got tower clearance to take off. Working the controls with his feet, Alfonso then fired up the sub-light engines and lifted the ship off. Once at their predetermined coordinates, they headed back to the comm center, where Estrella and Adrianne had their earpieces ready to go. Via them, both audio and video would be sent back to them, and they could send word to those in the field, directing them and warning them of "enemies" as shown on their IR screen.

With everyone prepared, Arnold gave the order to cloak the ship. Now came the first challenge. Alfonso had to set the ship down close to the target and without being detected. He chose to set it down in the middle of the Imperial Castle's courtyard. Alfonso did so with great care, so much so that not even a tiny dust cloud rose announcing their descent close to the cobblestones. Once down, the raiding party departed, while Estrella, Adrianne, and Bess remained behind coordinating the away group and monitoring the "enemy" around them. In less than thirty minutes, they had Renata onboard their transport, having levitated and pushed her there, all while not arousing the slightest suspicions, thanks to their invisibility powers.

With the test completed and the kinks in their procedure ironed out, Renata felt confident that her solution would work. Thus, she gave them their first rescue mission to handle, though she chose what she believed would be a relatively easy one. "Your first rescue mission is on Plato-C in Federation space. Sean Williamsfield is in bad trouble. His employer turned out to be a ruthless drug lord and dealer. He's removed Sean's legs at his knees so he can't move at all and is kept in a wheel chair overseeing the man's drug dealings. Worse, he's being raped every night until he gets pregnant. The idea is to begat more telepathic kids for the lord's use, probably to sell to the highest bidder." Renata then gave Arnold more specifics on Sean's location on Plato-C, a heavily guarded, but plush compound.

Twenty-four hours later, their cloaked transport moved into a low orbit over this bluish world. An hour later, Estrella and Adrianne finished their triangulation efforts and pinpointed the compound, located at the edge of a very large city. From their IR scans, they counted fifty well-armed guards, posted around the perimeter of the fortress with ten foot tall outer walls. Some of the men were moving to meet an incoming vehicle containing another six men. As the two continued to monitor the screen's images, they spotted what must be Sean. A very small red image was being moved along beside several images that appeared to be walking.

Arnold focused and made contact with Sean. *Your rescue party is at hand. What's happening right now?*

Help! It's another drug deal. The car is bringing a load of drugs to sell. Now isn't a good time. I have to help him make sure he's not being cheated, Sean sent back. Arnold easily sensed monumental relief coming from the man far below.

Arnold began barking orders. Alfonso executed a slow, quiet landing not too far from where the wheelchair was sitting, directed by Adrianne, who continued to monitor the red forms on her IR imaging screen, while the others got ready for the snatch-and-grab. Following Arnold's order, Alfonso landed the ship with the bay door facing away from the car and men, who were now in the process of handling this big drug exchange. Bess opened the bay door, lowering the ramp as Savina, Arnold, Pippa, and Gwenda focused and went invisible. Each had their own objectives.

As soon as the ramp was almost touching the ground, the four left one after the other. Savina moved silently to the wheelchair to which Sean was fastened such that he couldn't fall out. She focused; Sean and his wheelchair vanished from sight. Using her telekinetic forces, she began pushing him around the transport, quickly ducking from sight. With Bess's help, the two got Sean up and into the transport safely. Meanwhile, the other three went after their designated targets, using their powers to stun the men. Within seconds, all the men were down. While Pippa and Gwenda headed back to the transport, Arnold got another idea. He saw a large pile of gold bullion the lord was using to pay for this shipment. He sent a message to Estrella, who used her toes to manipulate the teleport machine, using Arnold's position as the focal point. When she was ready, Arnold moved off to the car containing the crates full of the drugs. One small pouch was out and in the process of being tested for purity. Once Estrella replied that she had the gold onboard on the teleport pad, Arnold moved back close to the transport and focused again. A giant fire exploded within the car, setting the interior aflame. As he raced up the ramp, its gas tank exploded, ensuring the destruction of the whole drug shipment.

As she heard his footsteps coming up the ramp, Pippa pressed the close button and Alfonso began lifting the transport up from the surface. He and Savina, who had rushed to get back to her navigator's seat, watched the fiery inferno that had once been a car loaded with drugs. "Way to go Arnold!" Alfonso called out. "We're jumping to hyperspace now." The vivid world around them suddenly went totally black. "Home in twenty-four hours," he added.

"Contacting Renata now," Adrianne called out from her comm center post. "We got him!"

Sean, however, was a basket case. While he did thank them for getting him out of there, he added, "Please just kill me now. I can't live like this. I'm ready. Surely, you can do this for me," he pleaded with Bess.

Arnold overhead him. "Hey, not just yet. Renata wants to talk with you first. Besides, we've just gotten all this gold bullion for you. Must be fifty pounds of the stuff. That's going to take you quite a while to spend it all."

"But. . . Fifty pounds?" Sean exclaimed very surprised.

"Yes, and the drugs went up in smoke," Arnold added. "So the lord is minus his gold and the providers are out of their drugs. Double strike."

"But you don't understand. That was supposed to be a hundred million gold dollar exchange. It'll put him out of business," Sean tried to explain the significance of it.

"Yes, put them both out of business. That's the idea," Arnold added.

Sean smiled. "Serves the bastard right! Thanks. This is

far better than being rescued. Now, you can kill me. I'm ready."

"Not until Renata tells us to," Arnold replied. "So sit back and relax. Twenty-four hours til we get back."

"But how did you do all that? I mean you're almost as helpless as I am. Who is flying this ship?" Sean asked, still confused about how he'd been rescued so easily.

Alfonso and Savina walked back to see their rescued man. "I am or was. It's on autopilot right now," he answered, shocking Sean further. "Hey man. None of us have arms on this ship."

Bess interrupted them. "I'm supposed to get him medically checked out right away. Let's push him to my med lab now, please."

A half hour later, the Medical machine reported he was badly bruised in his genital regions and pregnant. Bess quietly aborted the pregnancy and executed the healing function. At least when he got home he would be well, she thought, wondering how he could possibly survive as he was.

Renata met them at the spaceport, and one of Governor Sheila's new workers wheeled him and his fifty pounds of gold away, presumable taking him to Renata's place. "Well done, Rescue One," Renata told the eight smiling faces standing at the bottom of the ramp. "Are you ready for another rescue?"

"So soon? Sure. That one was a walk in the park," Arnold chuckled. "This one a bit harder?"

Renata laughed. "Perhaps. James and Brandy Jones are on Rennel-3 working as bank guards at the First Consolidated Bank of Funel, that's the city they're in."

"How can working as bank guards be a bad job?" asked Estrella.

"Sheila has sent over video and my notes. Take a look and go get them, Rescue One," Renata teased them.

"Aye, aye, boss!" Arnold said mockingly. "Sorry, can't salute, boss." All nine laughed, and the eight headed inside to the comm center. Less than a half hour later, during which time the ground crew removed the used fuel cells, replacing them with full ones, Alfonso lifted off from Plateau Grado once more. All felt a bit sick about this one. What that banker had done to the husband and wife team was positively sickening!

True, there had been a number of mysterious thefts from the bank, stretching over many years. The extremely wealthy banker had hired the pair to be his security eyes. On the surface, it sounded like a very cushy job, but in fact, it became an unending nightmare for the pair.

First, their entire upper bodies from their lower abdomen up had been encased in some kind of metal casting that made them appear as mannequins. Next, excreta tubes were inserted allowing their bodily wastes to be collected in plastic bags hanging below them. A feeding tube ran up beneath their casts and into their mouths. Only their nostrils were open to the air so they could breathe, along with holes in the casting so they could see out, barely. Periodically, a small pump sent liquefied food into their stomachs, just enough to keep them alive. Next, their rigid bodies were mounted on a steel I-beam securely bolted to the floor of the bank. Finally, a metallic wrapping was wound around their legs hiding the plastic waste bags, the pump, and liquid food bag. Their feet were an inch from the floor with the metal top casting supporting their weight on the I-beam. Wholly immobile in all ways, the pair could only look out the pin holes before their eyes.

They were positioned at opposite ends of the long row of teller stations. Between them, they could observe all the tellers, customers, and everyone who went in and out of the heavy bank vault. When they saw someone stealing anything, they were telepathically supposed to let the bank owner know. Of course, the bank had all the latest in security installed, including numerous video cameras, which until now had not shown anyone stealing from the bank, which is why the owner had gone to such extremes, all without the consent of the Jones couple, who were facing ten years on the I-beam per their contract. No one in their right mind would ever have agreed to this arrangement.

James and Brandy had been in this fixed, immobile position for nearly three months. Their bodies had gone numb now, though the pain had been excruciating for the first few weeks. The banker had also solved the problem of the pair falling asleep on the job. He'd had electric dildos inserted into each. A timer controlled their action. Every two hours, they operated mercilessly for a half hour. All the pair could do was doze briefly before being shocked awake, at least pleasantly so, more or less.

Twelve hours after takeoff, the cloaked ship was hovering low over the bank. Governor Sheila had given them very precise directions this time. It was the middle of the night down below. From their IR scans, Estrella and Adrianne pinpointed the two telepath's location and confirmed they were the only humans in the bank at this time.

"One of us should go down and check them out," Arnold suggested. "This one is going to be tricky, if they really are bolted to the floor."

"I'll go," Savina volunteered. "Set the ship down in the middle of the street in front of the bank. I'll go out, look inside, and teleport inside, invisible of course. I can check on them and see what we're facing here."

Arnold agreed and ten minutes later, the cloaked ship landed in the deserted main street. Pippa opened the bay ramp just long enough for Savina to slip out before closing it. If some vehicle came along, Alfonso would have to lift off in a hurry, but the invisible Savina could take care of herself. Invisible, she stepped out, walked up to the large front windows, and peered inside.

As her eyes adjusted to the dim lights, she spotted two metallic mannequins, one at either end of the long wall of teller stations. She focused and "stepped inside," avoiding materializing inside some of the large desks or chairs. She made her way to the tellers and found a small half-door that led back to the stations. A minute later, she began examining one of the two telepaths. Tapping lightly, she verified the person was encased in some kind of metal shell, at least above their lower abdomen. A heavy metal wrapping encased her or her lower body. She began to figure out how to undo the mess. Peeling it back a little, she saw the various items secured to the I-beam, which in turn was bolted to the floor with very large nuts and bolts. Worse, she couldn't figure out how to get them safely down.

Just then, all kinds of alarms activated. *Motion sensors,* Brandy sent her. *Get out before the police come!* Savina did just that, teleporting outside. Pippa opened the bay ramp enough for her to dash onboard, while Alfonso lifted the ship off the ground. A minute later, a large number of vehicles drove up with all kinds of flashing lights.

Meanwhile, Savina relayed what she'd seen. "I don't know how we're going to get them out of there," she finished up. That did indeed stump the rescuers for some time. Even if they were to get inside and somehow unwrap the metallic lower bands, they'd have then to work out how to un-connect all the apparatus and get them down, presuming they would be able to stand and walk, which they very well might not be able to do. The sheer weight of the top metal casing might be far too heavy for them to carry on their legs, assuming their legs even worked any longer. If the weight was too heavy, they'd simply come crashing down. Meanwhile, the motion sensors would alert the police, giving them just a couple of minutes to carry out the entire rescue mission! It seemed hopeless.

Ideas flew but none sounded workable. "The best bet is to undo the bolts, unplug anything electrical, and then teleport them into the ship," Arnold finally concluded, "I-beam and all. Here, we can then take our time trying to free them. How many nuts were there, Savina?"

"Four, one on each side of the metal plate that the I-beam is welded to," she answered. "They are huge nuts. The whole thing must be very heavy."

"Okay. I have an idea. If four of us go in there, each with a cutter, we can each take one bolt and cut it. As soon as we cut through, Estrella can teleport the whole thing into the ship, while we go over to the second one. We're going to have to work extremely fast on this caper. So that means practice gang. Come on; to the workshop," Arnold ordered.

He had Savina pick out some bolts around the right size. "The speed of cutting is going to depend upon how hard the steel bolts are," Arnold explained. Using telekinesis, they set up some practice nuts and began figuring out how to use the cutters solely by their mental powers. That proved far too challenging.

Finally disgusted, Gwenda sat down on her butt and used her toes. "Ah, much better this way," she pointed out, having easily cut through the bolt. Emboldened, the others tried it her way just as successfully. When Arnold figured that they were finally ready to do it, it was daytime.

Estrella and Adrianne brought up the IR camera, and the group looked at all the red images moving into, out of, and around the bank. After a time, Pippa pointed out, "Look, no one ever goes over to the telepaths. They are stuck back in the two corners. We ought to consider a daytime rescue. Then, we won't have to worry about motion sensors."

"Yes, but how do we hide the fact that the four of us are there, partially unwrapping the base and cutting through the bolts?" asked Arnold.

"I'll go too and create a hiding illusion over you," Savina suggested.

"Hum, that might work. We cut the bolts, but wait to teleport them until we've cut them both," Arnold reasoned.

"If they are really heavy, we might not be able to move one out of the way on the teleport pad fast enough to get the other one," Adrianne pointed out.

"Maybe we can use two slightly different destination points," Estrella suggested, "a few feet apart on the pad."

"Okay, just don't have them materialize partially in the other," Arnold cautioned.

They delayed another hour to recharge the four cutters. It was around one local time when they were ready to begin. Now, the problem was where they could safely land the transport long enough for the five to exit and then later long enough to retrieve them. The main street was packed with vehicles going in both directions.

Surveying the city, Savina came up with the answer. "Look there. About four blocks away is a park-like area. It has a large grassy area that looks big enough. What do you think, dear?"

Alfonso looked. "Yep, I can set her down there. We'll have to walk at least four blocks though, avoiding those on foot. Bit tricky, but doable. Hey, Arnold, come up and have a look see."

Ten minutes later, their rescue operation was underway. He sat the large transport down in the park, squashing a number of floral displays and joined the others at the bay door. This time, the ship wasn't in a position from which Adrianne could monitor the people on her IR scanner. Instead, she went to assist Estrella with the teleport machine. Getting the destination coordinates just right was going to be a tad tricky, since they were aiming for barely three feet apart. Bess operated the bay door and the five dashed out and down as soon as it was close to the ground. After the last left, Bess closed it again and kept watch, ready to open it on their return.

Four of them carried their cutter between their teeth, while Savina took point, leading them down the five blocks to the bank while avoiding a few pedestrians. Reaching the bank, Savina made a decision. While they could wait and try to sneak in when someone opened the door, that would cause uncontrolled delays. Hence, she opted to use her teleport skills. She moved over to one person until her body bumped into them. She leaned over and bit the top of their dress. Holding on to them, she teleported them to the right mannequin, let go, and teleported back outside. Thrice more she executed the maneuver. Growing a bit tired, she'd used half of her whole days' worth of psi energies. Now, she focused and formed an illusion over the mannequin. Anyone looking there would see what they were now seeing. She then gave the go ahead signal.

Pippa, Alfonso, Arnold, and Gwenda quietly sat down on the floor, retrieved the cutters from their mouths, holding them between their toes. Meanwhile, Savina used her foot to pull back the bottom wrapping enough for the other to see. Two minutes later, the four bolts were cut. The five got to their feet, looking across the space at the second one. Slowly and carefully, they slipped across the hundred foot space behind all of the working tellers, none of whom noticed them. Once more, she focused, raised her illusion, and then unwrapped the very bottom of the base. Three more minutes later, the four bolts were cut here as well. Now, they had to get themselves out of the bank. Savina didn't have enough potential to extricate them all, and Arnold suggested they slip out with other patrons who were leaving.

That delayed them seven minutes, but they finally arrived outside, standing before the large windows where they could still see inside and the mannequins. Satisfied, Arnold sent the message to activate the teleports to Estrella. All five watched, holding their breaths. One statue vanished. So far so good. Then the second one disappeared. A minute later, someone noticed the statues were gone and raised the alarm. However, by then, the five were heading back to the ship, arriving ten minutes later inside the bay, whereon Bess closed the door after them.

Alfonso and Savina rushed to the front to take off, while the others headed to the teleport pad. The two were there, standing erect, almost touching and just barely on the pad, one on either edge. "They are not stable. Any tilt and they're going to fall over," Estrella called out. "Little help here."

Six gathered around the two statues. "Any idea how heavy they are?" asked Pippa. Arnold thought that was a critical question and attempted to lift one via levitation.

"Crap. These are really heavy!" he called out. "We all had best put our force on them to steady them while he takes off or they are likely to tip over!" As the ship lifted off, both mannequins wobbled precariously and likely would have fallen over had the six not had their telekinesis forces pinning them to the side of the ship.

At this point, Arnold and Pippa began unwrapping their lower halves, revealing the plastic bags and the liquid food pump and the vibrator lines. Now, they could see how the two were fastened to the I-beam. It slipped into a similar shaped slot on the backs of the upper metal shell encasing the two telepaths. "Now what do we do?" asked Bess. "I don't dare try to remove the waste tubes. I really don't know how, and I'd probably harm them if I tried. We'll have to unhook the bags and bring those along with them, but can we possibly lift them?"

To answer that, Arnold focused and joined with the two victims. *Okay, we have you safely on our ship headed for Tierra. Do you know how you were lifted up onto the beams?*

We'd like to get you down if we can. They could tip over very easily.

Brandy replied, *Four men lifted us up. I think we are very heavy. We certainly couldn't stand up on our own.*

Arnold had to make a decision. Did he leave them standing on the I-beams with the constant danger of the beams falling over or did he try to get them off the beams? He knew he could do it using the power belt from Renata. Once off, then what did he do with them, since they couldn't stand up on their own? "Okay, let's lash them securely to the bulkheads here. I don't want risk harming them any further. Their shells are way too heavy for us to handle."

While the others headed off to find some lines to use to tie them to the bulkheads, Arnold focused and relayed his decision to the two. *We don't want to risk harming you. So we're going to keep you on the I-beams until we land. Hopefully, we can secure you enough so you don't fall over. Will you be okay til then?*

Brandy replied, *Yes. Now that the power to the vibrator is gone, we can finally get some sleep! We're so tired we could sleep a whole week! Thank you all for rescuing us. I hope they can get us out of this metal casing. It's been a nightmare. We can't even feel our feet anymore.*

An hour later, a dozen lines held the two to the bulkhead, but the six stuck around ready to use their gifts to help out, should they start to tip over. Savina then relayed the situation to Governor Sheila, who promised to have a whole crew waiting for them when they landed.

To his credit, Alfonso made the gentlest landing of his career, paying close attention to the level indicator, and with Arnold in constant telepathic communication with him, alerting him to even the slightest tipping motion back in the teleport pad, mid-ship, and not far from the comm center.

As soon as they landed, Pippa rushed to the bay door. No sooner had she gotten the ramp down than a dozen strong men came walking up the ramp. Two pushed heavy dollies. Finally, Arnold relaxed and let the men take over. A few minutes later, the two statues still on their I-beams were secured to the dollies and rolled down the ramp. The eight followed behind them, curious to see what would happen next. Renata was also there to greet them and thank them for another job well done.

It took four men to lift each one off the I-beam, laying them down on their backs. Next, some engineers arrived and studied the bronze shell, which had arms even though the telepaths inside didn't. The shells were cast in two halves and then sealed at the seam. Hence, they reversed the process, cutting through the seam and then using a lifting machine to lift the front half of the shell off each person. James and Brandy's legs were numb and useless, and the various tubes were still in them. Hence, they were put on gurneys, bags and all, and whisked off to the med lab. Their skin, Bess thought, look terribly pale, and their legs seemed awfully thin. She suspected that both faced tough days ahead.

They didn't have long to ponder the plight of these two rescued telepaths. Renata took them aside. "Got another super-emergency for you. Two more telepaths' lives are at stake! Blackwell-C in Federation space. Molly Dobbs and Marcy Greythorn are in dire trouble, as are two young teens that they've been trying to protect. Come on; this one is really bad," she said, ushering them to her quarters to brief them.

After outlining what she knew, she added, "These barons are the grandchildren of the very barons who harmed Christina and Lisa, turning them into baronesses-to-be! Now, they are threatening to top that by blinding them too. You have to get to them at maximum speed. Do whatever you have to do to rescue the telepaths and the two teens. Deadly force is authorized in this case," Renata declared. Arnold had yet to see Renata angry, but now she actually was! Her anger dissipated rapidly though. "I'll forward the coordinates to you while you all get back to your ship."

By the time the eight returned to the spaceport from the Imperial Castle, Renata had sent them a document with full details, including a drawing of the inside of Castle Blackwater, where they were shortly to attend a party. Adrianne relayed the coordinates to Savina, who punched them in with her toes, while Alfonso went down the takeoff checklist. As soon as she was done, Alfonso took off, dropping into hyperspace and throwing the throttle on full. "Hey, we are really flying!" he called out. Be there in eight hours. Supper anyone? I'm starving."

When they dropped out of hyperspace, Renata sent them far more news, all terribly bad! The two teens had already been blinded. The personal assistant of one, Casey, who called herself Charis White, was actually a robot. She'd released the bio genetic agent onto the hundreds of ball attendees. Several hundred men, women, and young adults were all in comas, lying around the castle. The two telepaths and two teens were upstairs in Ruth's bedroom. At least Molly had already regained consciousness, largely unaffected by the genetic bio agent, since her body needed little further modifications to meet the agent's criteria.

Worse, as they hovered directly above the castle, it was daytime. Below them dozens of transports were parked all around the place. They could see forms that looked human but did not register on the IR camera as "warm bodies" carrying comatose victims out of the castle and into the waiting transports. The victims were completely naked.

What bothered Arnold the most was the news that six of their telepaths were also victims of these robots being held at an unknown location. Though they were desperate to be rescued, they had no idea where they were. Now, the robots had actually unleashed the terrible bio agent and were stealing away the victims. Renata didn't tell Arnold what was going to happen to them once the robots got the victims to their home world, wherever that was. She wanted them to focus only on the mission at hand, getting the four out of there before the robots got them too.

It was at this point that Arnold made a move that later turned out to be pivotal. Some say, brilliant. "Look," he said to Pippa, "if these robots have six of our telepaths, and we don't know where their planet is at, it stands to reason that these ships are going to that world. We need to at least put a tracker on one or more of their ships so we can later follow them and find that world."

Pippa exclaimed, "You're right. We simply must. This might be our only chance to find that secret world. Let's do it first!"

Alfonso had to land the ship some distance from the castle, since all available open space closer in was already occupied by the robot transport ships. After landing, he joined the others in the workroom, where they were working as fast as they could, using their feet to prepare several tracking bugs. Essentially, each one had a magnetic base that could be placed onto the outer shell of a transport. Hooked to it was a transponder that sent out a signal that they could then track.

Arnold wasn't satisfied with making one tracker. He insisted that they place five of them. That way, if one fell off or one was discovered, perhaps the others would not be. An hour later, the five in the away team carried one between their teeth. Invisible again, they moved silently down the bay ramp, while Bess worked the controls. Each stole away to find a ship to stick their magnetic tracker on. One by one, they did so and returned to the bay ramp area. Once they were all back, Bess opened the ramp, they dashed inside, and she closed it immediately. This way, the ramp was visible only a short time. They gambled the robots had not seen it.

Next, Arnold had Alfonso take off again and try landing on the roof of the castle. He gambled this heavy stone fortress could hold the weight of the transport. To be on the safe side, he had Alfonso maintain a slight upward thrust. Based on the drawings that Renata provided, he could see the door that led from the roof down inside the castle.

Estrella then teleported them in pairs from the ship onto the roof, invisible as always. From there, they headed to the door and entered the castle, descending to the floor where the baron and his family had their private rooms, assuming Renata's layout was still accurate. Her sketch came directly from Christina and Lisa, who had made it a number of years ago. It was still correct, as they verified when they poked their heads into the baron's private room. They went on down the hall and finally found Ruth's room, where Molly was anxiously waiting for them. They passed through her illusion and into the room.

Thank you for coming! This is a nightmare. Marcy was a normal, but now she's in the usual coma, along with the two teens, who have been blinded last night. We have to get them out of here. I don't know how long my illusion of an empty room will hold up. There are robots everywhere! Molly sent, her emotions filled with dread and relief at the same time.

Arnold was wearing the special belt this time out. He sent, *I'll levitate the three of them. The rest of you, push them on up the stairs.* He focused and felt the huge potential of power flowing through him. Lifting the three comatose women was as hard as lifting a goose feather! Unfortunately, he could concentrate only on one thing at a time. The others couldn't remain invisible and deal with the pushing needed. Pippa chose to act as their rear guard. Arnold intended to lower the three and use the full powers available to him should Pippa warn him of an approaching robot!

As quietly as possible the group pushed and shoved the three women up the stairs to the roof. Just as Pippa reached the door, she heard a robot beginning to climb the stairs. Evidently, it had detected them somehow. Later, they learned it was motion that they had sensed. *Robot coming!* she sent, dashing through the door and closing it. The door made a distinct sound, giving them away.

With the ship so close, Arnold chose to have Estrella and Adrianne teleport them inside fast. When the robot appeared at the door to look outside, only Pippa and Arnold remained standing, invisible beside the cloaked ship. The robot moved its head in several directions, especially towards the ship, as though confused. After a tense minute, it turned around and headed back down. Suddenly, Pippa and Arnold found themselves inside the ship standing on the teleport pad. Bodies were piled all around, a chaotic, frantic mess, those not in a coma, struggling to get back onto their feet.

"Sorry about that," Estrella apologized. "We had to get you out of the way of the next pair in a hurry." They'd simply shoved them out of the way with a good leg kick, making way for the next arrival.

"Thanks," Molly said speaking very slowly while looking at the whole group. "Say, can we implant one idea into one man's mind? I have a whole building full of my promised fashions. I'd like that man to crate them up and ship them to me on Tierra."

Arnold laughed. "With all of this, you want your fashions?" Molly flushed. "Okay, we'll do it. First, we should get these three to beds. How long before they come out of their comas?"

Molly replied slowly so they could understand her in spite of her lip disks. "Three days tops."

"Well, that's fortunate. We can have them back in our med lab when they awaken," Arnold replied. "Their bosoms are already nearly your size. Are you sure about the time?"

"Yes, we all had them enlarged about the size theirs are now. Mine got bigger again, but that's all the bio agent can do to me, because I'm so screwed. The others, well, in a way, they shouldn't have as many surprises as normal humans would. The baron already hacked up Marcy so she would look like the baronesses there. I'm hoping the teens' eyes regenerate or something," Molly explained, speaking both slowly and repeating each sentence, which was easier than trying to use telepathy just now.

"Well okay then," Arnold decided.

"Boss, the ships are taking off now," Adrianne called out from her station in the comm center, mid-ship. Quickly, everyone looked out whatever viewport was nearest them. Sure enough, they were taking off. She added, "Trackers are active and showing motion."

Molly spoke up, "Say, if they are leaving, can we go back down and retrieve some clothes? I feel really naked like this." All she was wearing was her corset, which she now really did need to support her back. Her twin basketballs were way too heavy to manage without the extra support. Even so, her back was throbbing a little already. "I'd like to also retrieve the teens' glass eyes just in case. I left their corsets on them, figuring that they would not interfere with the modifications and that they'd need them when they woke up. Also, is there any possible way you can get these awful neck rings off me? This is utter hell. I can't move my head at all." Again, her lip plates forced her to speak slowly and with several repeats.

Once more, Arnold had to make a command decision.

"Okay. We six will head back down there, but since we have three days before the others awake, we're going to try to follow the trackers and see where they are taking these victims. With luck, they will lead us to six more victimized telepaths who we need to rescue as well."

The six headed back down the bay ramp after Bess lowered it. She then returned to look after the three comatose women. Molly was efficient, though awkward. Unable actually to pick anything up, she resigned herself to pointing out to the others what they should take. Arnold and his group used their telekinesis powers to begin making a pile of eyes and clothing. His idea was to wrap them all up in one ball, far easier for them to levitate and move back to the ship.

Molly had one final thought. The two teens were going to need funds, assuming that they also sold their massive earrings. Hence, she explored the baron's private rooms and uncovered a large stash of gold coins and gemstones. She didn't need to tell Arnold to add them to the pile. Less than an hour after the robot and their transports left the castle, Alfonso got the order also to take off.

Arnold coordinated with Adrianne and Savina, and soon, they were following behind the transports. "Boss, they are using top speed too so they must have the newer engines as well," Alfonso reported. All knew that meant they could not close the distance between them. As long as the trackers continued to work, that wouldn't matter. In case they did fail, Arnold kept a continuous plot of their course through hyperspace. While he had no idea of what he was plotting, simply a continuous listing of coordinates, he figured some of the brains back on Ashford-5 could make sense of them. Meanwhile Pippa used the comm center to make a full report to Renata, explaining their current decision to follow the fleeing transports.

Renata agreed. "Very well done. Yes, follow them and don't lose them! There could well be huge consequences if we can't find their planet of origin. Say, if those neck rings are similar to the ones that Nia Elain and her group wore, then there is a way you might be able to remove them." She outlined the procedure of using a cutter to remove just enough of the metal to allow one to insert something to pry the two cut apart, spreading the ring some. She doubted that they'd be able to do it themselves.

With time on their hands and seeing how hobbled up it made Molly, Pippa decided to experiment on her. She found it far more difficult that cutting the bolts. If she slipped slightly, she could well injure Molly, maybe even kill her. Hence, Bess joined her, guiding her. She went slowly and finally had a sixteenth of an inch cut through one of the rings. However, she couldn't figure out how she could possibly pry the ring outward.

Arnold came to her aid. "Hey, with this belt of Renata's, I ought to be able to do it with pure telekinetic force. Bess, you keep watch." He focused and again felt that enormous reservoir of power flowing through him. Imagining a finger on each side of the cut, he forced them apart. "Piece of cake," he declared, as the first ring bent wide and fell off her neck.

"That feels a million times better!" Molly muttered. She was lying on her chest and her lip plates were flat on the ground. Still she got her message across.

An hour later, Molly was finally free of those diabolical rings and thanked them all several times. Since Savina was now keeping the position log for Arnold, they moved on and began to free the other three comatose women of their neck rings. When they finished, Arnold declared, "Well, when they do wake up, they will have something good to see instead of just bad effects." Molly smiled invisibly. She knew this small thing would be of immense help to the women when they woke.

Six hours into the flight, Adrianne announced, "Damn. We've lost one tracker. Oops. There goes another one. I think the robots might be on to us, boss."

Arnold joined her in the comm center, watching over her shoulder. Another signal suddenly stopped transmitting. He cursed and wanted to keep his fingers crossed. He had that thought before he remembered he didn't have any to keep crossed and grinned briefly to himself. "Adrianne, have you seen any deviations in their flight path? I mean if they discovered the trackers, they could have sent the five ships off in five different directions to confuse us royally."

"Nope. All have been on a parallel course until their signals vanished. That's a good sign, right?" Adrianne asked, hoping that it was.

"Possibly. Of course, they could have discovered the five bugs and sent those five off on a different route than the main convoy," Arnold speculated, knowing that would be precisely his first action. After putting a good distance between the five and the main fleet, he'd have the five totally scatter.

Almost as though reading his thoughts, the two remaining ships veered off on two very different courses. Arnold cursed, and then ordered Savina to log the splitting point. He now had to decide which one to follow. He ordered Alfonso to change course and follow one of them. He would have tossed a coin had he had both a hand and a coin. Having neither, he just picked one. "Adrianne, keep monitoring the position of both of them. Savina, keep logging both as long as we can."

Seven hours into the flight, both trackers vanished and Arnold ordered an all stop. With their cloak active, he had Alfonso drop out of hyperspace. "Where the hell are we?" he asked. "Everyone, to the viewports. Man the telescopes. Where are we?"

"Federation space I think," Savina called out. "Near the rim somewhere."

"Okay, I'll call Renata. Looks like we need some help," Arnold advised.

A bit later, Renata answered, "Good try, Arnold. Call off the coordinates of the paths. You stay put where you are at. I'll have the astrophysicists and math people look these over and see what we can determine. I'll record the coordinates as Savina reads them off. Over."

Several hours later, Renata called back. "We have your location computed. You are right. You are in Federation space on the outer rim." She relayed their position in galactic coordinates, and Adrianne brought up the three-dimensional holographic model with a red dot highlighting their position on the arm's edge, literally the middle of nowhere.

"We are working on possible routes and destinations of

the robot ships. Meantime, another pair of telepaths are desperate to be rescued. Their situation is particularly acute. Are you up for a quick diversion? Their world is quite close to your location. That will give us time to work out possible routes that the robots went. Over," Renata explained, hoping that they'd agree to the next rescue. She estimated that they could get in, get the two women, and still have time to return to Ashford-5 before the three came out of their comas.

"Sure," Arnold replied. "Give us the coordinates and data, and we'll be on our way."

"Thanks. The world is on the Federation's Forbidden List. It's Gundig-B. Gundig is a small red dwarf star, and the planet is fairly close in, but they are still a very modern society, rich in metals. You are after Miss Angelica Valen and Miss Gracia del Largo, both twenty-two. Yes, I know, another Valen, but she's not related to the ruling Valens. I think she's a very distant second cousin. Anyway, she's a model, and Gracia is a linguist in training at the Academy, at least she was before the attack came. Those two were roommates here in Exchange City." Renata went on to describe their very nasty situation.

Hearing the sordid details, Arnold flinched. "Okay, Savina says that we can be there in two hours tops. We're on our way. Over and out."

Chapter 27 Genetics Gone Wrong

Enormous steel buildings rose like spires into the sky. Skyways ran at dizzying heights between floors of these structures, and tiny people could be seen walking along them. As the transport slowly descended onto Gundig-B with its reddish sun, Angelica and Gracia got their first glimpse at their new world. They could make out that the men wore business suits similar to those worn on Tierra. It didn't register in their minds that they saw no women on the streets. During their long trip here, they'd diligently spent hours with the language disks, learning the local language, a variation of German. Actually, Gracia spent most of the time coaching Angelica, since she already knew basic German and only had to pick up the local differences. Both were pleased to see that they were going to be living on a very modern world indeed, a far cry from the stone castles and buildings of Tierra. Both young women were quite excited about their ten-year contract, paying them around two hundred thousand per year. When they returned, they'd be set for life.

Gracia dreamed of establishing her own linguistic studies foundation, while Angelica wanted to open her own modeling school. With the funds from this brief venture, both could achieve their dreams in just ten short years.

They knew that they would be working for the United Kingdoms of Gundig and living in the capital of Hapsborg. Specifically, their employers were President Abelard Erdmann and his Defense Minister Alaric Gerhardt, and they would be staying with their families in the Presidential Compound in Hapsborg. On the surface, this sounded more like a very sweet job indeed. Both women looked forward to the times of their lives, wondering why their queens had been so adamant about ever letting Tierra's telepaths accept off-world employment opportunities. That notion would soon change, however.

Both Angelica and Gracia were now hermaphrodites, thanks to the alien super-mutation attack. That also led them to jump at this seemingly lush employment opportunity. With the funds they'd receive, they could once more achieve their dreams for the future. Like most Westerlings women, they had lush black hair, raven to be precise. Thanks to the mutation, their hair was twice as thick, nearly six feet long, slightly wavy, and shiny. That they also could "feel" with it added some spice to their lives, as long as their hair wasn't pinched, for example, when they'd get a jolt of pain shooting through those strands. As of this date, neither women had come to terms with their male anatomy additions, though they often reacted causing them no end of embarrassment, which they did their best to hide.

Angelica had been a model since she turned fourteen. Some claimed her face was that of an angel, though of course, no one had ever seen such a mythical goddess. Even with the loss of her arms, she had a captivating beauty. Her black eyes shone like fire. Compared to her roommate, Gracia was merely attractive, with slightly too large lips and too bushy eyebrows. Gracia was outspoken and a year from having her linguistics degree, when the alien attack wiped all that out. Still, she and Angelica were very close friends, often wearing each other's clothing and sharing their deepest personal thoughts and emotions with each other. Both were rather outgoing, though some suggested they were a tad bossy. Now, they were embarking on what they believed would be the coolest job ever.

Their only drawback was their apparel. When their arms vanished just after they'd gotten used to hopping around on the one lower leg, they discovered that they could no longer easily dress in the fine gowns that they used to wear, unless they had help. Luckily, they'd gotten the services of a sixteen year old to help them, and thus as they stepped out of the transport on the tarmac just outside of Hapsborg, they looked as elegant as possible. They wore identical cherry red, strapless satin gowns, form fitting to their knees, where the red gave way to the black of their expensive seamed nylons. Each wore matching red patent pumps with six-inch heels, giving their legs even more definition.

They stepped gracefully down and headed towards two men, who wore what they believed to be very expensive silk suits, black pinstriped, with white silk shirts and a sash around their necks. Both had thick black hair, relatively short and brushed up and back, as though they were facing a very strong wind. In their heels, the two women observed they were slightly taller than the two men were.

"Welcome to Hapsborg. I'm President Abelard Erdmann. My Minister of Defense and best friend Alaric Gerhardt," the man on the right spoke politely. Both men bowed to the two women, and Angelica sensed both were highly attracted to her and Gracia. Well, they should be, she thought, since I'm a gorgeous model, even if I lack arms now.

She replied, "I'm Miss Angelica Valen. My dear friend and constant companion, Miss Gracia del Largo. So very pleased to meet you at last. Such a modern world." She didn't add that so much of it was uninspiring grey steel, shiny though.

She spotted a number of men with guns and earpieces standing discretely some distance away, obviously their guards. "This way, ladies. We have our presidential limousine waiting to take us to the Presidential Complex, where our security is quite high. You'll be totally safe with us, I assure you. Tomorrow, we'll see you get to go shopping for the very latest in fashions here on Gundig-B. You'll be staying with us and our families. Our wives are dying to meet you both," President Abelard chatted, as he led the way, a little unsure if he ought to put his arm around Angelica's waist or not. He decided that she would let him know if she needed it. *Damn! She's really a beautiful young woman, incredibly so and the other isn't bad herself. What phenomenal luck.*

Angelica picked up these surface thoughts of his and smiled demurely. What man wouldn't have such thoughts, she mused. The limo was black and had plush leather seats. Angelica tossed her hair to one side and slipped into the back seat, following his gesture. On the other side of the limo, Gracia did the same, only tossing her flowing hair to the other side before getting in. The two men stepped in but took the seats facing the two women.

"Do all of these sky-reaching buildings have such walkways connecting them? I bet the views from way up there are spectacular," Angelica asked, as they began moving through the streets leaving the spaceport behind them.

"Oh indeed. Our architects pride themselves on creating a veritable web of skyways between buildings. It is quite practical as well. When someone needs to visit a neighboring building, he or she simply walks across the skyway. That way, they do not have to take the elevators down to the ground, walk through the sometimes busy streets, and then take the elevators back up. Much more efficient. In fact," President Abelard continued, "some say that they never do have to come back down to the ground level. You can walk skyways to almost any building in Hapsborg, though one would surely need a detailed map."

"I'd love to walk some of them. It must be quite a thrill to be walking up there so high," Angelica hinted, sincerely.

"Ah yes. The top ones are nearly a thousand feet above the ground. And here we are, the Presidential Compound at last." The two gazed at the compound. A ten foot tall wire fence with barbed wire along its top surrounded the very large metal building that reached skyward some fifty stories. It wasn't the tallest building, not by a long shot, but it did have numerous skywalks connecting it to many other nearby even taller buildings. Several skywalks arced far over this lower building. It, however, was far wider than most other nearby buildings.

"The ground floor is for tourists who come to see the Presidential Compound. The Second floor is where petitioners come to meet with us and relay what's on their minds. We have working offices on the floors above them. Our living suites are on the very top floor. Since our two families are quite close, we have rearranged the layout up there. We each have our own private quarters on either side, but share a common living area, entertainment room, and dining room. Our wives are very close friends as well, as you will soon see."

As they approached the main doors, they opened automatically. A metallic voice said, "Have a good day." It startled both women, who'd never heard a talking door before.

President Abelard chuckled. "Ah. I should explain. All doors on our world are fully automatic and open for you as you approach them. In fact, nearly everything on our world is fully mechanized or automatic. You'll find your lack of arms will not impede you in the slightest, not on our world. In fact, you might believe we are fully set up to support you in every possible way. I dare say you'll find your lives here to be infinitely easier than on your home worlds, where, as I understand it, you have to have personal servants to care for your needs. Well, that's a thing of the past here."

They entered and walked past a security post. Ahead they saw five sets of elevators. As they approached one, a mechanical voice asked, "What floor would you like?"

"Go ahead Angelica. Speak clearly fifty," he suggested.

Angelica did so. The voice replied, "Floor Fifty. If this is not correct, please say your request again. If it is correct, please wait one minute for the elevator to arrive. Thank you."

"How clever," Angelica commented, very much impressed with the level of technology and automation. Within a minute, the doors opened; the four entered, and the doors shut.

President Abelard spoke up, "Computer. Recognize me?"

"President Abelard Erdmann," the metallic voice replied.

"Yes. I give authorization of full access to Miss Angelica Valen and Miss Gracia del Largo," he spoke clearly.

"Access logged. Have Angelica Valen speak her name for voice authentication now."

He nodded to her, and she said her name. "Voice logged. Have Gracia del Largo speak her name for voice authentication now." She did so.

"There you go. Now say Floor Fifty, Angelica. Put the word Elevator before you give the number. That is their signal. In fact, in many situations, that's how you control the many bots. Say their name and then the command that you desire of them. Go ahead try it," President Abelard said with a pleased smile. He enjoyed showing off their grand technology, especially to those from backward worlds.

Angelica spoke up, "Elevator: floor fifty." The elevator replied, giving her a chance to change the desired command before executing it. Up they went, very smoothly, she noted. The doors opened to a short hallway leading left and right. A sign with a left pointing arrow said Presidential Suite, while another sign with a right pointing arrow said Minister of Defense.

"As I said before, we share a number of rooms in common. Right now, everyone is in the common living room waiting to meet you. So it doesn't matter which way we go. Let's enter my main door, shall we?" he beckoned with his hand to the left. Some fifty feet further down the hall, a door automatically opened as they approached. The mechanical voice said, "Presidential Suite."

This outer room was more of an office or private study. Bookshelves lined the walls, while a desk and chairs sat off to one side. One door led further back into the suite while the other opened to the right. They moved towards the right door, which again opened automatically, announcing, "Presidential Living room."

Here was a very spacious room with a number of couches, sofa chairs, all done in plush brown leather. A pair of portraits of the two families hung on either end of the room. A fireplace was against the back wall. Two younger women, dressed in light red silk gowns, nylons, and six-inch heels rose as they entered. The two telepaths noticed several things right away. The minor detail was that the men were about ten years older than their wives were. The major thing they noticed was that neither woman had any hands. Their arms ended at their wrists.

"My wife, Betlinde," President Abelard introduced her. She was nearly as tall as Angelica, with a pretty face and wavy brown hair that fell loosely to her waist. She was twenty-five. She walked up and gave Angelica a hug and then Gracia too.

"My wife, Elke," Minister Alaric spoke up. Elke was the same height as the two telepaths and had waist length, curly blonde hair, nicely flowing down her back. She too gave each one a hug.

"Ah, the children," Abelard interrupted, as four children came scampering into the room. "My older son, Dachs. He's seven now. My daughter, Bruna. She's five."

"And my son, Emeric, who is seven, and my daughter Frieda who's six."

Again, the two telepaths were startled to see that neither girl had any hands. Like their mothers, their arms ended at their wrists, while the boys looked perfectly normal. However, the girls were dressed in fancy silk dresses, but wore flats. The boys looked like miniature men, dressed in pinstriped suits with white silk shirts and polished black shoes.

Frieda spoke up very formally and politely for a six year old girl, "Mother, they really do not have any arms, not like us!"

Betlinde smiled. "No dear. They don't. Now, why don't you children run along and play." The four dashed out of the room, glad that these formalities were over. "Please, Angelica, Gracia, have a seat. Dear, have you told them about our history yet?"

"No dear. There hasn't been time. I suppose now is as good a time as any. Please, have a seat." The two telepaths tossed their hair a bit until it slipped over a shoulder, and they sat down, coyly crossing their legs, emulating the provocative action of Betlinde and Elke.

He then said, "How about a fire, Betlinde?" She winked at him, pointed her right arm towards the fireplace. The two telepaths sensed something akin to their own *mentales* gifts activating. Fire appeared over the logs set in the fireplace. The odor from the crackling pine soon filled the room with a fragrant scent.

"You see, our wives have true gifts. Betlinde controls fire, while Elke controls air, but alas, they do not possess telepathy, rather the gifts bred into our genetics centuries ago. I should explain a bit of our history. Then, much may make far more sense to you."

"Many centuries ago, our geneticists made a horrific error. Our women then sought to attain great beauty, and the geneticists were eager to please them. Unfortunately, the result very nearly wiped our entire civilization out. In our most desperate hour, some aliens visited our world, and several hundred of their women volunteered to join us, adding their genes to our pool, in hopes that it could reverse the awful damage that had been done. These special women had no hands, just like our wives today, but they possessed what we call elemental powers, control over fire, earth, air, and water."

"These valiant women married some of our men and bore as many children as they were able to. Thanks to them, centuries later, we are on the mend, so to speak. They brought with them all manner of bots that they manipulated in order to do everything a normal woman would do, such as dressing herself, bathing, cooking meals, and so on. To make a long story short, over these centuries, the near decline of our civilization has been halted. There are nearly five million women now on our world, including Betlinde and Elke."

"Unfortunately, those bad genes, which only affect females, are still present. At least half of our female babies are born with those awful defects. They are hardly human in fact, and have such a low intelligence that they cannot function beyond being a mere slave. They have to be told what to do and when to do it. We call them ugly weibchen. They are hardly human at all. Unfortunately, as you are probably guessing, the vast majority of our male population has no choice but to wed a weibchen. It's either that or not attempt to have any male children. You see, males are always perfectly normal, no matter whom his mother might be. This genetic defect only affects our females. We do occasionally employ a couple of weibchen here in our suite as cooks. They do a fine job of cooking, but little else. Elke, with her command of air, handles the cleaning. Both our wives do a great job of cooking for us, but we use the weibchen when we are having a lot of company. It's not fair to make our wives work so hard to cook for large groups." Both women flashed him a smile.

"What do these weibchen look like?" Gracia asked, curiously.

"Oh just horrible. They are all very short, and they don't have any hair, except for a couple straggly strands on their baldheads. Quite why they don't cut them off, I surely don't know," Betlinde answered her. "Their faces are positively ugly! Filled with awful pockmarks. Their skin is more like sandpaper. And you can't believe how stupid they are.

Honestly, how they can actually cook is beyond me!"

President Abelard added, "Don't worry. You are not likely ever to see any of them. They aren't allowed to walk the streets without wearing a total body covering to hide their hideousness from normal people. Besides, they are so stupid that they wouldn't know where to go anyway. They'd just get utterly lost. So you're not likely to see any of them."

"So I take it Betlinde and Elke have only had normal girls?" Angelica asked.

"Oh don't we all wish that were true!" Elke gushed. "Heavens no. I've already had two of those deformed creatures, and Betlinde has had three. Of course, we immediately sent them to the official Weibchen Orphanage, where they are raised and perhaps able to learn how at least to cook, if they are lucky enough to even live that long. It's just awful to carry such a malformed creature around for nine months." She visibly cringed. So did Betlinde. The men frowned, finding this whole line of conversation quite distasteful.

President Abelard changed the subject, "Come; I do believe that Betlinde has lunch waiting for us. We ought to show you our place, how well the various bots work for our wives, and soon for you as well."

In the next room, they saw two special bots. Betlinde demonstrated. She walked into the machine. Its back encircled her and locked. Wherever she moved, she took the bot with her. She inserted her arms into two cylinders attached to remote hands. "With these, we do everything that men can do with their hands, though we do have a special pair in the kitchen. Those have insulated sleeves so our arms don't get burned handling hot things on the stove, you see."

In their bedroom, they saw more bots. "This one you are going to love even more than we do. It handles our long hair for us. We're not sure how it works; only it lifts our hair up high, separates each strand, no matter how tangled we've managed to get it, and then lets it fall perfectly across our backs. Your hair is so much nicer and longer than ours, so I'm sure you'll love it. And then there is the dressing bot. You use the hands bot to lay out what you want to wear, and the

496

dressing bot gets you undressed and dressed just perfectly, though we always use the hair bot after we get dressed so our hair looks perfect."

"Anyway, Elke and I are just craving lunch. So come on, we've got it simmering on the stove," Betlinde added, just a little too insistent, Angelica thought. They went into the shared dining room with the men and the children. The telepaths watched the two young girls as they entered, encased in their hands bot, ready to eat lunch. Of course, the two telepaths needed someone to feed them, since they didn't even have arms to insert in the machine, but Betlinde made light of helping them, acting as though she'd done this every day, which Angelica suspected she hadn't.

"Oh you just have to have some of this incredible blackberry juice," Betlinde insisted. She had already drunk hers first before eating anything at all. Since she put a straw in her glass for her, Angelica leaned over and took a sip.

"This is really good. Reminds me a bit of our wild berries back home," Angelica commented. Soon she and Gracia finished their glasses as well. After that, things rather began to go in slow motion, as far as Angelica was concerned. The four kids finished up and dashed off, but not before Abelard insisted the girls come back and take their hands bot away from the table. Kids, Angelica thought pleasantly.

The world seemed to be moving just before she blacked out. Two seats down, Gracia also went unconscious. Neither knew that the men carried them into a side room where they were undressed completely and their bodies carefully examined by a doctor who had come when Abelard called. He brought his equipment with him, a medical machine purchased from the Federation and brought here by black market dealers, who ignored the Federation warnings about visiting the worlds on the Forbidden List.

Betlinde gushed, "Gosh! They really do have men's things down there! This will be fun, don't you think?"

Licking her lips, Elke replied, "Simply the best. Oh, do hurry up. We're hot and ready, if you haven't noticed."

"Patience ladies. All in good time," Abelard cautioned them sternly. "Rub yourselves if you must. Go ahead doctor."

"Of course, President Abelard." The doctor began his work. His was a simple assignment, hardly worthy of his time. Remove their legs below their knees along with their kneecaps. Remove their voice boxes. Stupidly simple. Any child could do it, he thought, pressing the two menu choices. Of course, one did have to navigate through thousands of menu choices to find the right procedure. Once selected, you only had to insert the right body part in the right place on the machine. Even that could not be messed up, since the machine let you know if you got it right. An hour later both women were fixed up, and President Abelard fired off a payment transaction for the good doctor, who packed up his equipment and left, pushing the machine ahead of him.

"Okay, use the dressing bots and get them dressed in what you've picked out for them," Abelard ordered. "We'll fetch their new walkers and the opium. And do make sure those crystals of theirs are around their necks. Hide them between their boobs."

"When can we have them?" Betlinde pleaded.

"Wait a little longer. We have to have them on their opium before we wake them. You don't want to spook them, do you, dear?"

"Oh no, not that, but we need it so bad, dear. These are so special, aren't they?"

"Of course. Just be patient a little longer, dear," he replied and left them to deal with getting the two telepaths dressed again. They had some special nylons made for the women, ones that were quite short and fit their upper leg stumps perfectly. The machine tightened up their corsets, and then used air pressure to get the tight-fitting nylons on them and hooked to the garters, all eight of them. Then, Betlinde had the dressing bot slip a white silk slip over them, strapless, and tight fitting as well. They had a pair of cherry red satin dresses prepared for them in advance. The dressing bot put those on the pair too. Finally, the dressing bot tied a pair of leather booties onto their two stumps. Each one came up four inches, but still left a good deal of their nylons showing. These would be their "shoes."

With the women dressed, the men returned and

injected a goodly dose of opium into each woman. They followed that with the antidote to the knockout drug, rousing both women. While waiting for them to come around, they lifted them up and set them in their walker bot. Their leather booties would touch the ground, and via them, they could move around, sort of. That was the plan anyway.

Angelica came too, but felt very strange. Everything around her seemed so utterly sensuous that she could hardly stand it. Then, she noticed that her legs were gone — no, just shortened. She tried to cry out, but no sound came out.

"There, there, beautiful Angelica. Don't try to speak. You don't have a voice box anymore. If you need to say something, why, just use your telepathy. We removed your lower legs too. You don't really need either your voice or legs. See, you are wearing these wonderful booties and in this walker-bot, why, you can walk just fine. Surely, you can see that for yourself, right?"

Both women were now heavily under the influence of a strong dose of opium. No longer rational, their thinking became confused. Angelica thought, *No, we really don't need voices, not when we have telepathy. But don't we need our legs and feet? Surely we do, don't we? What's a walker-bot?* Then, she realized that she forgot to focus and send her questions via telepathy. *I wonder how I focus? I can nod.* She proceeded to nod yes.

"Dear, their hair is way too long for them to use the walker-bots. It'll drag all over the floor," Betlinde noticed. She picked up Angelica's tresses between her arms and stuffed it behind her body in the walker, which looked much like a small child's training walker. Her legs stuck through two openings and were solidly on the ground, but the rest of the contraption kept her erect more or less on her feet as though walking. "Oh, her hair feels super! So soft."

Angelica felt Betlinde's arms with her sensitive hair, and it felt so utterly sensuous. *Oh please, please slide your arms over my hair some more, please.* Again, she forgot to focus and her telepathy went nowhere.

"Dear, we did promise our telepaths here that we'd take them shopping to get them all the clothes they will need.

Would you and Elke do that for them?" Abelard suggested.

High on her new dose of opium, Betlinde agreed. "Sure. They need really sexy clothes. When we get back, can we have sex with them, pretty please Abelard?" she begged, batting her eyes, which she knew he couldn't resist.

"After you get back, get their new clothes put away, and I give them more opium and you too, then you can take them to bed with you," he suggested, knowing that would be all that was needed to get both wives to do just as he asked.

"Come on, Angelica. It's time to go shopping for your new wardrobe. What's your favorite color? Oh, you aren't in my head, are you? Well, that's okay too. I'll use my good taste and pick out what looks the best on you. We'll get you some toys too. This is going to be so much fun, Angelica. Oh, you have to walk now. Use your legs. Walk." She rather pushed the walker a bit. Meanwhile Elke was having a similar one-sided chat with Gracia, who was just as out of it as Angelica.

Oh, I am walking! Let's see I push with this leg, and then lean over that way and push with the other. Oh, I'm moving. See, I can walk. How come you aren't answering me? Don't you have any thoughts? Oh, I'm not focusing somehow. Oh well, it doesn't matter. We're going shopping. I do so love getting new dresses. I hope they have them in my size. My boobs really are too big. I'm not breathing right. Must be the corset. Could they have it too tight? Well, that doesn't matter. We're going shopping. Oh, this is fun. The door opens all by itself! Oh, we're going out on the skywalk! Wow. This is so pretty! Look at everything. I want to go for walks all the time. Angelica continued talking to herself inside her own head, "grooving" on the spectacular sights of this city, filled with skywalks going in every direction. Gracia was doing much the same thing, talking to herself about how beautiful it all was.

Neither telepath had ever had any opium before, though it could be purchased on the black market in Exchange City. Hence, they were completely unused to its effects, particularly on the incredible arousal of their sense of touch. Everything felt so utterly sensuous to them, even the light breeze on their cheeks. Both waddled along beside the two women, who walked at their speed in their high heels.

As far as their shopping spree went, they nodded at this and that, and the two wives continued to purchase them. They also added in a few "women's toys," but neither telepath knew what those were for. As they prepared to leave, Angelica became upset. *Where are all our packages? We are leaving without all those gorgeous things.*

For a moment, Betlinde became confused, knowing that something was upsetting Angelica, but she didn't know what. Then, she guessed it. "Oh, don't worry. A delivery bot is taking your many new dresses back to our place. They will be there before we are. Then, we have to put them away. Abelard's orders. Then, we can have fun. You'll see. Come on; let's walk back now."

Angelica waddled along, completely satisfied. *Delivery bots. Why didn't I know that? Of course, they have delivery bots. I wonder what they look like? We should have delivery bots at home, since I can't carry things anymore. I'll have to tell the queens about them when I get back. Maybe they can buy them from President Abelard. Oh, this view is so fabulous.* She paused to look out over the city. It was the same sights she'd seen coming to the store, but she'd already forgotten that.

By the time that they returned to the Presidential Compound and their common living room, the heavy effects of the opium dose had worn off somewhat. While the two wives began unpacking and storing the women's purchases in their bedroom dressers, President Abelard addressed the two telepaths.

"All right, my fine telepaths. Your jobs are two-fold. We have been having some terrorist attacks on our world, and we don't know who is behind them. They blow up buildings and such. Nasty bit of work. So we're going to be taking you around to visit some of the groups that we believe might be behind these attacks. Use your telepathic skills to see if they are the guilty ones. That's the first job."

"The second job is vastly more important. We'll have you breeding all the wives we can find. We hope that many of them will become pregnant, and that with your genes, they will not have any more weibchen mutations, just normal female babies. We'll also take any eggs that you produce and impregnate them ourselves. With luck, you two beautiful women will be saving an entire race! Now isn't that worth the salary that we're paying you? Saving a whole race from extinction?"

In their stupefied states, both women could only agree with him. At least they were finally able to focus. *Yes, that is a very noble thing that we are doing for you,* Angelica finally got across to Abelard, who looked pleased.

"Now then, it's time for you to have that promised fun. Our wives are more than ready," he replied. Carefully, he injected another dose of opium into each telepath. Once more, they felt a huge surge of sensuousness flowing through their entire bodies, especially their hair and dual genitals.

They waddled into their new bedroom, which they were sharing. A very large bed with satin sheets faced them, but it was low to the ground so they could possibly plop themselves onto it. This time, after Abelard injected the two wives with their far lower dose, he undressed the two telepaths, leaving their corset and nylons on them. Carefully, he placed each woman on the slippery sheets, making sure their hair was draped over their bodies, smiling at their solid erections. By then, the two wives had gotten themselves undressed, and they climbed onto the bed on top of the two telepaths, ready to enjoy the incredible sexual sensations.

An hour later, Angelica was finally able to make a telepathic connection to Betlinde, begging her to slide her hair through her arms and over her body. Betlinde was only too eager to please her new lover.

Sometime later, the dressing bots had the four redressed, and the four headed to the kitchen to prepare supper. Angelica and Gracia merely watched the two wives, marveling at how sensuous they looked while preparing the meal. They were still quite high.

After supper, they again received another dose. This time when it hit them and they were once more on their slippery satin sheets, several other women joined them. For an hour, the two telepaths tried to satisfy whoever was on top of them. Finally utterly exhausted, they fell into a deep, dreamy sleep. They didn't notice the men entering and having sex with them. Later, the doctor returned and checked on them while they slept. He very carefully removed a fertilized egg of Angelica's.

This went on for days, so many so, that neither telepath had any idea what day it was. All that they knew was that they craved more of whatever it was that made their bodies so super-sensitive, so sensuous. In fact, President Abelard knew precisely what he was doing. He and many other men had long ago worked out the proper procedure to get their wives totally hooked on opium, so much so that the women would do absolutely anything asked, if they threatened to withhold their next dose of opium.

This was the entire point. These handless women were the ones with the "super" powers. No man had ever had them, though they certainly had tried to get them from these special women. Centuries ago, these women had threatened to take over total control of Gundig-B from the men who were running the world. That, they dare not allow to happen. Hence, one brilliant man figured out how to get them hooked on opium, and the rest became history. As soon as a young girl reached puberty, she was then hooked on opium. The next man in the hierarchy on their world then received her as his new wife, and the woman was more than willing to do so, as long as he kept her opium coming on a regular basis. If a man failed to do so, he risked his own life. After all these women controlled the elemental forces and could easily kill them! Naturally, just whom "the next man in the hierarchy" was always controversial at best. Minor wars had been fought over succession rights.

After several weeks of this same routine, over a hundred local women, besides Betlinde and Elke had become pregnant with either Angelica or Gracia's child, none could honestly tell which, since they had had sex with both women, one after the other. In nine months, President Abelard would have definitive results. He hoped and prayed that none of these hundred women would give birth to one of the grotesque freak females. If so, in time, they might be able to eliminate this genetic curse forever! Already, they also were growing several others in their laboratory from the fertilized eggs that the two men had made. There were not enough of their direct offspring to tell one way or the other. However, if they kept fertilizing one each month, surely in a year they'd have enough test tube babies to know if this angle was also a viable one. Of course, he had no intention of ever returning these telepaths to their own world. His several million gold he had had to place in their bank accounts back on Ashford-5 to secure their services would be paid back most handsomely. Even if this sexual experiment failed utterly, he could then use them to track down the local terrorists, who he believed operated in small, local cells.

Three months later, nearly six hundred women were now pregnant from the two telepaths. Plus, right after their evening romp with the telepaths, a good deal of their excess sperm had been collected from these volunteers, stored for future use. The first of these women were now three months into their pregnancies and being carefully examined by several doctors, who were experts in this field, able to spot the hideous, malformed early on in a woman's pregnancy and then dispose of the beastly thing — for what woman in her right mind wanted to endure nine months only to give birth to a foul, worthless, grotesque weibchen? At this point, President Abelard and Defense Minister Alaric received the best news ever: so far, none of the pregnant women was carrying a weibchen!

As yet, President Abelard had yet to make any use of their telepathic skills. To do so would require lowering their opium dosages. With the terrific breeding results at hand, he was reluctant to disrupt a "good thing," just to get a better handle on the more and more frequent bombings. After all, only a handful of people went missing and presumed destroyed in these explosions. Besides, thus far, with a lone exception, they had all taken place in the slums on the opposite side of Hapsborg from the spaceport. It had been that first attack that had sparked his interest in the consortium's proposition to acquire telepaths.

In that first bombing, one of his lesser ministers and his

handless wife had been lost, presumed dead, along with their weibchen, who was preparing a large meal for a festival party that he was to host. Fortunately, the attack had come before all the guests had arrived, including President Abelard, who counted himself phenomenally lucky to have been late to the party. Their three bodies had never been found and were presumed consumed in the explosion. That incident had been sufficient to convince him to throw in with the consortium and spend several million to acquire the telepaths. Only after committing to the project did he learn of their hermaphrodite natures and began having an entirely different purpose for the two telepaths.

The humaniform robot, Phinious, one of Minta's spy robots, had landed on Gundig-B some months before that first attack, scouting out this Forbidden List world. His initial report to Minta suggested that there were four types of humans on this world, the rich, male leaders, their strange handless wives, in very short supply, the lower class working men whose only opportunities at having families required them to marry one of the grotesque weibchen, who were shunned by everyone, forced to wear complete body coverings when outside in public places and who were the fourth class.

Minta sent a collection team to Hapsborg, and Phinious arranged for the abduction of one of each of the four classes of humans. The unmarried lower class man was simply abducted and never missed. That first explosion covered up the convenient abduction of the man, his handless wife, and the weibchen — three birds with one stone according to Phinious.

Back at Athens, the lower class man and the weibchen were transformed into Model 10's, since neither was considered worth breeding, not ever. The minister and the handless woman were made into Model 11's. All this had happened before Amy and Jan's arrival. The results were somewhat startling and unexpected.

The two Model 10's worked out perfectly! Each had a strong determination to fight and followed orders well, beautiful Model 10's from Minta's point of view, the best yet. Their only emotion was to destroy, especially humans of

Vic Broquard

wealth and power.

The Model 11's were a great disappointment. First, the minister simply refused to obey orders, despite being powered down repeatedly. That is, all sensory input was turned off, leaving him in total darkness and silence. Eventually, Minta ordered his Model 11 frame to terminate him. The handless woman Model 11 caused enormous problems! Her opium addiction fueled her fires, as she suddenly came completely off the drug, cold turkey, after having been on it for many years. Worse, she had wild elemental powers, unsuspected by all. She rebelled against what had been done to her and against being deprived of her opium, which drove her mad with cravings for more and darn nearly burned down the factory! Minta was only barely able to get the termination order to that Model 11 frame in time to prevent a huge disaster.

Based on this initial sampling, the weibchen and lower class men were found to be ideal candidates for more Model 10's. Phinious was given the task of setting up a program to add many more of these to their growing arsenal. Each deep space transport could handle a dozen more of these humans. Phinious set off small explosions to hide the fact that another dozen had been taken in each raid. He spaced the abductions ten days apart and scattered among the many larger cities of this world, alloying all suspicions that people were being abducted. Further, he began spreading rumors that dissatisfied locals were forming terrorist cells and conducting the seemingly random bombings. At this three month mark since the telepaths had arrived, fourteen such raids had been executed, yielding another two hundred ten new Model 10's, all becoming very good fighters in Minta's growing army of robot soldiers, the very best in fact.

When Renata tried to contact Angelica and Gracia, she was shocked. They didn't respond to her telepathic contact. Moving into their minds, she found herself entwined in the grey mass of the sickly sweet, highly sensuous, opium addiction. Witnessing one evening's bed romp with the two telepaths and the four other handless women, Renata observed what had happened to the two. Even she found it hard to disconnect from their shared opium high and craving for sexual pleasures!

She reconnected the next morning, buttressed against the drug's effects on her, and she simply observed the two women, gathering the key data that she needed. It was pointless even to try to tell the two that she would try to rescue them from this nightmare addiction. They were too addicted even to desire being rescued and would likely fight against being deprived of their next fix. Renata knew that she had to get these two out of there as soon as possible, but their world was far off the beaten track, way out on the rim in Federation space.

Thus, when her astrophysicists located just where Arnold and his ship were now at, she weighted her options. They were a few hours away from the two drugged telepaths. The three comatose victims onboard had two and a half more days before they'd awaken. Even so, the changes would not be much worse than what they had been enduring before the attack. Renata took the gamble and ordered Arnold to undertake this quick additional rescue mission on Gundig-B.

"You are going to be rescuing two telepaths, who are very heavily doped up on opium and craving sexual intercourse right and left. Their lower legs have been amputated, but they do get around a little in some type of baby walkers. Also, their voices are gone, probably their vocal cords were cut or removed. As drugged as they are now, you are going to have to bring back with them a goodly supply of the drug. I'll relay the dosages, and we'll try steadily to lower the amount with each shot. They are being held in that world's Presidential Compound, on the fiftieth floor, the top one. It is heavily guarded, as one might expect. Get in, get the women, get the opium, and get out fast," Renata requested, though Arnold took that more as a direct order, such was his respect for Renata, the All Powerful, as he sometimes jested.

Arnold relayed the data to his crew and, while Savina entered the destination coordinates, the others began to work out how they could handle this rescue mission. That they were in the most closely guarded complex on Gundig-B didn't help matters. Arnold put his skills to work. "Look, if they are in the top floor of the building, maybe we can attempt to teleport them out while they are sleeping. Getting in there will be our problem, that and getting the opium that they are going to need afterwards. What we need is a good view of this place."

"How will we find the opium and the syringes?" asked Pippa. "Undoubtedly, the President keeps that stuff locked up somewhere so that the women can't get at it."

"Maybe they can't make use of it because they don't have hands," Adrianne suggested.

"We are going to have to wait until we can see what this place looks like," the hunter, Gwenda advised. She was right. Arnold had to agree, and they satisfied themselves with simply making some lunch for now.

Two hours later, they approached the planet with its dim red sun. While they were scanning the planet, Adrianne called out, "Arnold, this is really weird. It looks like one of our tracking bugs, but it keeps flickering on and off."

He was running the visual scanner and moved over to look at her screen. "That looks like one of our tracking bugs. What's the ship doing here?" he said rubbing his forehead. It didn't make much sense. "I bet the bug has gotten damaged somehow. So what is it doing here? Could this mysterious Athens place be somewhere on Gundig-B? Gang, change of plans. Follow that ship. Let's see where the robots are going."

"Aye, aye, boss. Fire me directions," Alfonso spoke into the intercom.

"They are definitely landing. Looks like they are going to the same city that we were, this Hapsborg. They are running cloaked too," Arnold called out to everyone, many who had crowded around the comm center to watch for themselves. "Looks like they are landing on the other side of the city from the spaceport. We've stumbled upon a raiding party, I'll bet anything!" he exclaimed, growing more excited by the minute.

"Boss, how can we stop a robot?" asked Pippa. "We can't hold d-guns anymore."

Arnold's face crinkled in disgust, knowing she was right. He was frustrated. "Okay, we aren't here to stop them, but we ought to find out what they are up to on this world, if we can. Then, rescue the telepaths."

"We can go invisible and follow them," Pippa suggested,

eager for some real action. Arnold smiled and agreed.

Within a few minutes, the robot transport ship had landed in a field just outside the edge of the city. Cleverly, Alfonso sat his ship down not too far from theirs at almost the same time. That way, he figured they would stand the least chance of being discovered. Of course, the robot transport was cloaked too, and he had to make a guess at its dimensions and orientation, choosing to stay at least a hundred feet from where he thought it was located.

Once done, Bess opened the bay door briefly, while the invisible Arnold, Pippa, and Savina ducked out and headed towards the city's edge, reporting that this area looked more like slums than a shining metal-clad city.

How do we know which of those men are the robots? Savina sent to Arnold.

Sense for minds. We shouldn't sense any minds with the robots, he replied to both women.

Another man slipped out of the shadows, joining six others who had come from the ship. Arnold couldn't hear anything being said and figured that these robots had their own unique methods of communicating with each other. He was right. This new man led them to a small metal house, single story, but in need of repairs. The seven ducked inside.

More importantly, the three got a good look at the vast automation on this world. The doors opened automatically, sensing the approach of a person. Elevator lifts outside some buildings automatically took passengers up to the dizzying array of inner-connecting skywalks, some a thousand feet in the air. A driverless bus pulled up and opened its doors to let a passenger off near Savina, who had time to back out of the way. Another man walked up and climbed into the bus, speaking clearly his destination. However, none understood his actual language though. Their linguist, Adrianne, would have, had she been along with them.

They waited outside the building for several minutes. Arnold wrestled with whether or not they should go inside. Since it was a single story dwelling, he decided against it. The seven robots would be far too close to them for safety's sake. Besides, the automatic doors didn't sense their presence and open up. They'd have to become visible, which they were not about to do.

Around five minutes later, the six came out, each carrying what looked to be a rolled up rug of some kind. As the robots passed their positions, they got a closer look. They spotted a man's legs in one of the rolls. Arnold now knew that the robots were kidnaping the people who were inside this building!

I'm going in there and see what's happening, Savina sent. *I can see in this window and that's enough for me to teleport. You keep watch.* Arnold didn't like her going in there alone, but didn't have a better idea at the moment. He longed to know what was happening in there.

Savina focused and used her special gift. In the next instant, she was inside a small living room that smelled bad. Vomit, alcohol, and smoke each fought for dominance over the other. She heard voices and headed towards them, stepping through a doorway into a short hall.

"Yes, I promise you once we've properly trained you, you'll be able to return here and begin taking over your world. You'll be invincible. None can stand against you, as long as you steel your will against these slave masters you call presidents and ministers. So are you with your brethren?"

A woman's voice spoke up, "Invincible? I like the sound of that. Count me in. Anything is better than this life, which is hardly a life is it?" Savina took a step forward to see who was speaking. She inhaled and nearly gave her position away when she saw the grotesque weibchen, who only looked vaguely like a human female, the end product of their genetic experimentations gone horribly wrong centuries ago. Hastily, she teleported out of there. Once outside, she sent the others what she'd heard, and Arnold ordered them back to their ship.

About halfway back, the six robots that looked indistinguishable from any man, came walking briskly towards them, heading back to the small building for more recruits. When the three finally got safely onboard their own ship, they heard an explosion. They waited to lift off until the robot ship did so. When they in turn lifted off, they saw the building that they had just been casing had been blown up! However, they knew that everyone inside was long gone. "A perfect coverup," Arnold mused. "No one will even miss those dozen."

A half hour later, Alfonso had their ship hovering over the fifty story Presidential Compound. All eight now studied the situation below them, particularly what was on the IR imaging screen, showing all human occupants as small red forms. The two telepaths were easily spotted, as were the two handless wives. Adrianne counted over sixty forms, probably security guards, stationed in groups around the complex, but out of sight of the residents.

There were four skywalk entrances to the complex. Unlike the automatic doors, these had obvious security locks in place, quite visible from the outside. After watching for a half hour, they saw a man wearing a uniform walk up to one and speak clearly. Adrianne called out, "He just spoke his name. They are speaking German or a derivative of it, I think."

"Ah. Voice activation. Good move," Arnold replied. The protections were slowly becoming clear to this old Special Operations man.

"Hey, I can get around that," Savina ventured. "Teleport me onto that skywalk. I can then look inside and teleport there and make my way to where our people are. You can lock onto me to teleport us back here."

"Savina, that's risky, but it's the best idea yet," Arnold complimented her. "We don't stand a chance trying to force our way inside. What about finding a supply of opium for the two? That's going to be far more difficult. One idea I had was to mingle with the men in the slums and see if we could purchase some. However, that'll never work. They'll think that we're women and strange ones too. So somehow we have to find where these men keep their supply."

That had them stumped for quite some time. At last, Savina offered, "Look, I could go in there while it's light outside and hide. Then, when the men come to inject the women, I can stun them and take the opium. Only flaw is that we don't have hands to pick the needles and stuff up. Maybe telekinesis will work."

"Okay then, Savina. I'll give you Renata's power belt so you have all the potential power you could possibly need. We'll stand by. Let us know when to activate the teleport machine," Arnold agreed. He could see no other viable way to accomplish this mission.

A half hour later, Adrianne activated the shipboard teleport machine, materializing an invisible Savina onto the skywalk just outside one of the main entrances to the Presidential Compound. She focused and teleported just inside, freezing perfectly still for a moment, hoping and praying that she hadn't set off any alarms. Hearing nothing, she began moving along the hallway. She soon found that the doors didn't open for her, since their sensors didn't "see" anyone standing or moving towards them. Miffed, she waited until someone opened it for her, in this case President Abelard, who was returning from a meeting. Silently, she followed him inside and began familiarizing herself with the many rooms, staying out of everyone's way, easy enough to do in the spacious quarters.

By the time that the two families ate their evening meal, Savina knew where everything was at, except for the opium supply. She was quite amused at all of the many different kinds of bots that they had here. *Nothing short of amazing,* she sent to the others. Shortly after eating, four other young women arrived, ready and willing to enjoy a romp in the bed with the two telepaths and hopefully get themselves pregnant with a viable child. This much Savina picked up from their surface thoughts.

While the two wives and the four new arrivals began using the undressing bots, President Abelard and Defense Minister Alaric left to fetch the opium. Savina followed them into another room, where the President opened a safe in the wall. She saw a large number of syringes and vials, though she couldn't read the labels. They were in German. Now she acted. Focusing, she sent both men a heavy blast of mental energies, stunning both men, who dropped to the floor, knocked out for a short while. When they woke up, they'd have bad headaches, she concluded, amazed at the enormous power that she wielded via the belt.

Focusing, she levitated the entire contents of the safe and then realized that she needed something to carry them in.

She found a small pan sitting in the kitchen and brought it back with her, holding it between her teeth. Five minutes later, the pan was filled, and she headed to the women's bedroom. Already, the two telepaths were lying on the bed, begging the other women to touch them. The six were waiting for the men to give them all their opium fixes first. Savina also saw the two small baby walkers near the door and out of the way. She carefully pushed the two together and used a bit more energy to hold them to her legs.

Okay, teleport the two women on the bed and me now, she sent. Adrianne and Estrella had been keeping a lock on her the entire time that Savina was inside the complex. When they saw via the IR images that the two telepaths had been laid on the bed, they locked onto them as well, based on Savina's coordinates. Thus, they were able to respond at once, erring on the side of caution. Savina appeared on the pad first, along with the walkers and still holding the pan between her teeth. She stepped off and the teleport activated again. It was a little humorous. Not only did the two telepaths appear lying side by side on the pad, but also part of the blue satin sheet that they were laying on.

"Well done, Savina. Let's get them to some beds and call Renata to figure out how much of this poison to give them," Arnold called out. "Alfonso, get us out of here fast."

Angelica and Gracia looked around stunned. Then, they saw the pan with all the syringes in it. Their cravings took hold. Both nodded at the pan, looking pleadingly at Savina. None needed to have telepathy to know that the two were doing their best to beg them for a fix. "Wait. We don't know how much to give you. We're calling Renata now," Pippa said sympathetically, while wondering how they could possible give them an injection without harming them. Dealing with a tiny needle and the vials was nearly impossible.

While Arnold was discussing this with Renata, Savina and Estrella kept track of the new bug that Estrella had cleverly attached to the robot's ship. She'd gone out without permission, found the old one, which had been damaged by space debris and replaced it with a new one. Now, the two were once more plotting its location periodically.

Renata had a tough decision to make. Once more, they had a good chance to follow the robot ship back to their home world. On the other hand, the two rescued telepaths were addicted to opium, but the form they had been given was via needles. She knew the crew wouldn't likely be able to handle such a delicate action. Plus, they couldn't speak or make noise, no matter how bad the DT's were. With their lower legs also gone, she didn't hold much hope for their quality of life even if they could be gotten off the drug.

"Okay, Arnold. Change of plans," Renata advised. "Follow this robot ship. It may be our best chance to find where they are. These robots are the most serious threat. We'll just have to let the two telepaths come off opium cold turkey, if they can. You have twenty-four hours to find the robot's world. After that time, get back here at top speed, before the other three come out of their comas. Surely, the two opium addicts can survive two days without it; at least I hope so. Keep me posted."

Arnold relayed her instructions to Alfonso, and Savina quickly punched in the coordinates of the last recorded position of the fleeing robot transport. A minute later, their ship was zipping through hyperspace, hot on the trail of the robots.

Chapter 28 Sly Dog Strikes Again

Amy and Jan continued to observe and do nothing to attract attention to themselves. Already they'd pieced together some of what the robots were planning, namely the construction of an unbeatable army. Were they planning to use them against the human populated worlds? That they didn't know yet.

On the other hand, the two Valen couples were giving the various Minta's fits, if a robot could actually have such. Certainly, they continued to cause problems. They were constantly insisting that they be allowed to return to Ashford-5 and conquer the world, that they were the rightful rulers. After three months, they altered their objectives a little, demanding to be the Rulers of the Galaxy. They had the power to do so now, feeling that their robot bodies were utterly unstoppable. That attitude was reinforced by their constant battle training and discovery of their new limitations. What human could lift four hundred pounds without straining? What human could run at top speed for twenty miles and not even be breathing hard at all or even cracking a sweat?

Minta began to see a very serious problem developing with the four Valen telepath Model 11's. While a simple voice command of hers could shut their robot bodies down, leaving them in a total sensory darkness, Diego and Tonio had countered by using their mental powers to destroy the mind of a nearby Model 11! Suddenly Minta had lost control over her new four Valen robots! That spooked her more than anything else did. On the other hand, the other two telepathic robots didn't seem to be doing much at all, and she more or less ignored Amy and Jan, while trying to work out a handling for the four Valens, all the while keeping them appeased so they didn't harm other Model 10's or Model 11's.

If this wasn't enough problems for her, the latest group bringing back more humans to be turned into robots discovered tracking bugs on five of their ship's hulls! She had already had a nasty miscalculation on the handless woman who possessed elemental powers. That fiasco had ended with quite a bit of destruction. She'd outlawed ever bringing back any of those handless women from Gundig-B ever again. But what to do about these tracking bugs?

She needed to know just who was trying to find their secret base. She gave orders for three bugs to be removed and for the other two ships with the bugs to veer off in totally different directions. Her plan, as relayed to the two pilots, was simple. See if a ship was following them. If so, they would lead that spy ship into a trap. She waited patiently to hear what this unknown spy ship did. Minta was taken aback when her two bugged ships reported that the spy ship suddenly ceased following them. Reluctantly, she ordered them to return to Athens. However, she instructed every transport pilot always to search thoroughly the exterior of their ships for tracking bugs before taking off.

Imagine her surprise when she received notification from a transport on Gundig-B that another tracking bug had been placed on its hull and the old defective one replaced! This world was now providing her the very best candidates ever for Model 10's! The grotesque looking women, if that's what they were, made extremely good warriors, eager to kill humans, especially men. Somehow, someone had discovered her secret supply. Minta grew very worried indeed, feeling threatened for the first time.

She ordered that ship to head back home to Athens, but put her entire fleet and forces on high alert. She'd blast this ship out of the skies, ending the threat of discovery. She ordered their jamming frequencies onto full power. This would prevent all normal human transport ships from being able to either send or receive on any of the usual comm channels. Hence, when this spy found Athens, it wouldn't be able to report its position back. Meanwhile, she'd use every available means to destroy the ship and to discover its planet of origin. Minta desperately needed to know just who her new enemy was.

Jan had not been idle the past three months. After she and Amy had managed to learn to interface to their new robot shells, she became intrigued with the positron circuitry and programming. There had yet to be a computer system that Sly Dog had not fully mastered! After Minta had once shut off all of their robot's sensory systems leaving her and Amy in total darkness as punishment for not following Minta's orders, Jan swore that would never happen again, not ever. While she and Amy presented a mild, contented outlook towards Minta, Sly Dog set to work on the control system of her humaniform robot shell. Obviously, Minta had installed her own backdoor to the entire system. If Minta had a way in, Sly Dog could find it and make use of it.

After all, a computer program is nothing more than a series of binary codes, pictured often as 1's and 0's, but in reality such was either the presence of a small electrical charge or not, in this case, positrons, the opposite of electrons, carefully encased within the robot shell. Sly Dog was a highly endowed *mentales* gifted person, as was Amy. Plus, they'd had quite a lot of Renata's Advanced Therapy and could do some things using what she called native "spiritual powers," for want of a better term. That wasn't Renata's term, just Jan's attempt to put into words what she could do. In essence, she could create an electrical charge or nullify it, especially so with these incredibly low voltage ones used in the humaniform shells.

One morning, Jan sent to Amy just three words, which caused Amy to smile, though her robot face didn't show it. She'd not yet gotten such tiny expressions under her own control. "I am in." She knew that Sly Dog had just entered Minta's backdoor into the entire robot computer circuitry. Jan now face a steep learning curve. She could "see" the many control circuits, but didn't know just what they all did. It was an extremely complex programming system, with many actions controlled at what she came to call sub-brains, located at various strategic points within the body's frame.

A week after she'd entered, she discovered the "kill circuit." *My god. Minta has one command in here that will have the robot shell simply kill us! Well, that one has to go! I'll fix you up too, Amy!* She carefully alerted the computer codes, rendering that command completely inert. Then, she spoke clearly, "Number 10,002: Access Sly Dog." She then sent some updated computer codes into Amy's robot frame and then used telepathy to instruct Amy on how to interface into her own backdoor. Now, Amy began to "play around" with her own circuitry as well, since she too was once a competent hacker of computer systems. Together, they continued to make "improvements" to their own systems, rendering Minta's control over their bodies null and void.

As the days progressed, Jan's hacking expanded to include detection of Minta's general orders to others. Her system was now echoing whatever Minta sent to her minions, giving Sly Dog a very great satisfaction indeed!

Hence, Jan received an echo of what Minta received concerning the spy transport coming to Athens along with her orders, setting the trap. She relayed it all to Amy. *So what do we do now? I wish Renata would contact us or that we had a way to reach her.*

I know. Monitor what's going on. We can see if we have enough telepathic power to reach the minds in the transport when it gets closer. I have a bad feeling they might be our people that Renata sent out to find us, Amy sent back.

A short while later, Minta ordered hundreds of her Model 10's and Model 11's into their one-man fighters. The Valens, Amy, and Jan were ordered to theirs as well. Minta sent them electronic signals, which their robot shells converted to sounds they could hear. "You telepaths. Your job is to discover the identity of the spies onboard this transport who are trying to locate us. Once you've identified them and where they come from, I'll order the others to attack and destroy the transport. Right now, we are sending out a jamming signal so they can't receive or send any communications to their home base."

A bit later, she ordered her planetary shields up to maximum power. As she did so, Jan heard the echo of her orders. *Amy, they have some kind of force field around the whole world. It will prevent the spying transport from getting too close to the surface or prevent any attack on us, such as dropping nukes. This is quite interesting. I didn't know that anyone had created a force shield this darn big!*

This promises to be quite interesting, Amy sent back as she powered her one-man fighter up, preparing for takeoff, along with hundreds of others. *If they are our people, can we prevent these others from harming them? Can we possibly escape, joining those on the transport?*

Working on that now, Jan sent back.

"We're getting close to a system," Savina called out. "The transport is dropping out of hyperspace. Following them now. Cloak is active." The transport vibrated slightly as its speed dropped drastically, and its sub-light engines kicked in.

"All external comm channels are flooded with white noise," Adrianne called out, alarmed. "Someone is jamming us!"

"Battle stations!" Arnold ordered, though that meant very little on a transport ship. Still, he knew his eight crew were ready for whatever action was needed.

Estrella called out, "I'm working on countermeasures, but it doesn't look good."

"Hey, I've got this planet in our database. It's Beltazar-C! This is where the snake aliens first struck, and we rescued those few survivors," Savina yelled from her navigator's seat.

"The transport is heading down to the surface," Estrella barked.

"Follow the ship," Arnold ordered, trying to observe all the displays of the comm center at one time. "Amy and Jan are supposed to be with the robots, if this is the place where this Athens city is at. What luck!"

Suddenly, the transport stopped dead in its tracks, though its engines continued to provide thrust. The sudden stop knocked everyone off their feet, except Alfonso and Savina, who were in the cockpit. They lurched forward nearly knocking their heads into their control panels. Down by the bay doors, Bess went flying off her feet, slamming into a bulkhead, knocked out for a minute.

It took a minute for everyone else to shake the sudden jar off and get back to their feet or back into their chairs. "Damage control? What the hell was that?" Arnold yelled loudly.

"We've hit some kind of force field," Alfonso called out. "Disengaging the engines now. What's going on?"

"Holy moley! Look! Hundreds of small fighter ships are swarming up from the planet below!" yelled Adrianne who finally was able to get back in her seat and watch her main monitor.

All the telepaths felt the presence of other telepaths in their minds! Arnold yelled, "Block those telepaths!" Instantly, the eight threw up their mental barriers. "At least they can't see us yet. Cloak still active?"

"Roger that," Savina yelled back, wondering what was coming next.

Arnold? Is this you? Amy here.

Amy? Yes, Arnold and crew. We've found you. What's going on?

They know you are there and are trying to shoot you down. They have a planet-wide force field up. Stay cloaked. They aren't able to locate you, except where you banged into the shield. Move the heck away from that spot. Jan's working on some plan.

"Hey, Amy and Jan are out there. Alfonso, get us away from this location. They are zooming in on the point where we collided with their shield, but don't hit it again," Arnold yelled loudly.

Amy, this might be our one and only chance to escape, Jan sent. *Minta will have to lower the shields in one spot so these fighters can get out to reach the transport. We need a distraction.*

Diego reported to Minta, "They are from Ashford-5. A whole crew of telepaths. Permission to attack and take them out!"

Minta cursed. These damned telepaths are more trouble than they are worth. "Okay. All fighters, head to Sector 22. Execute Shield Program 22. You have one minute to get through the gap before the shields go back up," Minta ordered all her fighter pilots and ground crews operating the shield controls.

Amy and Jan were close to the temporary hole in the shields. *Amy, shoot through the hole fast. I'm going to close it after I'm through. Get Arnold to dump some space junk out of a portal to distract them and then have him move away from it, where we can rendezvous with him.* Jan sent some electronic signals to her "modified" circuits and pushed her fighter to top speed, following behind Amy. Hundreds of other fighters were following behind them. As she slipped through the hole in the shield as indicated on her ship's display, her program activated. The ground robots reactivated the shields, closing the hole, nearly clipping her tail section. She'd cut it a tad too close!

Behind her, confusion arose as the other fighters banged into the shield. Several ships were damaged, but most managed to veer off. Minta shrieked out orders, but heard back from her ground control robots, "Jan 1: Minta 0." She fumed and reordered the opening, watching her fighters now streaming like water out of the hole in this sector.

She opened a communication line to Jan's humaniform robot. "Number 10,001: Terminate human," she barked.

Minta was shocked to hear back, "Jan 2: Minta 0."

"Shoot down those two lead fighters, Amy and Jan," she ordered all the other fighters.

"Dump space debris?" Bess yelled, responding to Arnold's orders. "What debris?"

"Anything. Put some junk into the back hold and dump it now!" he barked.

Estrella and Pippa raced back to join her. They pushed a tool bag and a chair into the air lock. Bess pushed the control buttons and the escaping air shot them out into space, as Alfonso pulled the cloaked ship away from that position as fast as he could, wondering what was coming next. Soon, the swarm of fighters would be all over them. While they couldn't detect his cloaked ship, with this many tiny fighters darting about, eventually one would run into the transport. Then, they'd swarm like bees on him. What were Amy and Jan up to, he wondered, wishing that he'd been let in on their plan.

The trouble was that Amy had no plan. She was just following Jan's lead, assuming that Jan had one. In fact, Jan was just having fun and had no real plan as yet, mostly winging it on the fly, literally. *Amy, have Arnold get ready to use his magnetic grapple on us. See if you can figure out where they are and lead us to him. I've got to slow these pesky fighters down some.*

Once more, Jan sent some signals to her humaniform robot shell, which immediately executed them. Suddenly, all the robot fighters' engines shut down, leaving the ships coasting along. *Now! It's now or never,* Jan sent, pushing her fighter's throttle to the maximum, following Amy's ship some distance ahead of her. She saw it come to a lurching stop, and she powered down as fast as she could. Still, she hit the side of the transport rather hard, jarring her slightly. These humaniform robot shells were hardened, and it took the blow easily.

Minta screeched more orders to her hundreds of fighters. On the back channel, she heard Jan's voice again. "Jan 3: Minta o." "Attack! Attack! Attack! Destroy them all!" Minta ordered, watching her fighters opening up with their canons on the two small fighter ships. Without warning, both ships suddenly vanished. Alfonso jumped them into hyperspace!

You want us to stop so you can get out and into the transport? Arnold sent as soon as they were in hyperspace.

No, we're fine here. Take us home please and thanks for the rescue, Amy sent.

Be there in eleven hours then, he sent back once Savina relayed the info to him.

Sly Dog wins again, Jan sent to Amy.

You were brilliant, dear. No, amazingly brilliant, Amy sent back.

Of course, now we're going to have to get some new baby bodies once more. I'm getting tired of having to be a little kid again, Jan sent back, *but I sure don't want to be in this robot shell much longer.*

When Arnold and crew landed at the spaceport on Plateau Grado, a large crowd was there to welcome them back, to help the five victims out, but mostly to see the strange humaniform robots housing Jan and Amy. "They look a bit taller." "They look fatter." So flew the comments from the many who had to see them, the strangest things anyone had ever heard of.

After waving to the large group, Amy and Jan headed

directly to a debriefing meeting with the queens, the governor, Arnold's group, and the emperor, who attended via video conferencing. The two gave a very full report on the activities of the robot civilization and more important, what their intentions might be. Even the emperor was worried about the revolutionary defense shield that these robots now had, something that every other world would dearly love to have! Further, that they were building an army of cyber-soldiers greatly concerned everyone. Each new soldier represented one more human being whose body was now a torso and brain or merely a brain, just enough to keep them alive and keep the spiritual being with his or her mind present running the cyber-body. That these cyber-soldiers were vastly stronger and more capable than any human soldier was gave many all manner of fears for the future.

On the positive side, the doctors in the med lab examined Ruth and Casey, who were still in their comas, and the doctors estimated they had another twelve hours to go. They began by giving them IVs of balanced nutrients and dealt with their physical needs. That done, they examined their eyes or rather what had been done to them. The optic nerves were still present and active. According to the medical machine's findings, they were ideal candidates for artificial eyes. While the med lab only had four pairs in stock, such things being relatively infrequently needed, they did their best to match the two teen's original colors, based on Molly's recollections. The operation was a delicate one, but quite routine for the medical machine. Thus, when they awoke from their comas, their eyesight would be restored, though it would take some time for them to get used to their new eyes, generally a week of adaption according to the display on the medical machine's monitor.

Meanwhile, others hooked the two frantic opium addicts up to other medical machines. They reported that the women had no voice boxes any longer, so there wasn't any cure for that, but it recommended a complete body flushing to remove all traces of the opium that was thick in their systems. Thus, the two women, who were craving a fix, found themselves drifting into unconsciousness. While the machine recycled their blood, removing the traces of opium from it before pumping it back in, the machine also warmed their bodies, causing them to sweat profusely, driving the opium out of fatty cells and such, a purification process. This action lasted an entire day.

The moment the process finished and the two women were revived, Renata had two of her Advanced Therapy givers go to work on Angelica and Gracia, rapidly handling the mental effects of their three month addiction. Days later, they finished up and were pronounced clear of the aftereffects as well, much to their tremendous relief. Neither had the slightest idea how they would now be able to live any kind of life though. Circumstances would change before they could even have time to worry much about that.

Chapter 29 Threat Removal

Minta calmly reviewed all the data to hand from the escape of Amy and Jan, along with the obvious discovery of her revised home base. Except for Jan's hacking, the planetary defense shield had worked to perfection. However, Minta finally drew the inescapable conclusion: *The telepaths of Ashford-5 are nothing but an extreme liability. They have to be removed.* Calmly, she gave the four humaniform robots the order to eliminate the four Valens. Shortly after that, the humaniform shells opened up so that other robots could remove the small bodies of the four and later reuse the four shells with new recruits, which were coming in nearly daily now from many other worlds of the Federation, though primarily from worlds on the Forbidden List.

Minta assembled her team of Generals Minta-0 through 9 to discuss their response to the escape of Amy and Jan and to weigh the overall threat that the telepaths of Ashford-5 represented to their Grand Plans. The discussion was little more than an exchange of electronic data bursts.

"We know that there are a large number of telepaths on Ashford-5. We know that they can kill a human with a thought. Our army of cyber-soldiers could easily be killed by a handful of these Ashford-5 telepaths. We have been very lucky that Jan and Amy didn't do just that before they escaped. They very well could have. So there is only one conclusion possible. They have to be eliminated," Minta sent.

Minta-9 commented back, "We have no way of telling which person on that world is a telepath and which isn't. We don't dare send our army there. They'd be slain before they landed and began hunting down the telepaths. Should we just nuke that world?"

Minta pretended a human sigh. "That would be the easiest way to eliminate them as our most serious threat. After what Amy and Jan did here, we must act to defend ourselves. If we don't strike first, I'm certain that soon waves of ships will appear just beyond our defense shields, and the telepaths will systematically kill our fifteen thousand plus cyber-soldiers. Still, it was these very people who have always been able and willing to help us and the nova in the past, where so many others wanted nothing to do with us. In light of their past aid to us, we should show them some compassion."

Minta-5 commented, "I agree. They were incredibly helpful to us. Yet, now they must not be allowed to interfere with us."

Minta-3 pointed out, "If we attack Ashford-5, since they are part of the Ataro Empire, won't the emperor then go to war with us? He has forty worlds in his system and one of the largest single fleets of battleships."

"Yes, that is a consideration," Minta replied. "Still, if we do nothing, we are doomed. We must analyze the situation further. We must come up with a way to force the emperor of the Ataro Empire not to strike against us when we strike the Ashford-5. One way we can do that is to destroy their fuel refinery on one of their moons. That refinery provides most all the fuel being used there in the rim. Without that refueling depot, the Ataro Empire ships will be crippled in that area. The Federation of Planets will not likely allow his warships to pass thorough Federation space to attack us. Still, that isn't likely to be enough to stop him from retaliating. We need something more."

Minta-2 asked, "If we are not going to nuke Ashford-5, how are we going to handle them? Blowing up their refinery isn't going to stop them, is it?"

Minta replied, "No. I think the answer is greatly to inhibit them. If we turn everyone on that world into a nova, without the HIFRs that they had on old Aquila Prime, they will be completely helpless, certainly unable to fly any spaceships. Many will perish as well, as always happens on the other worlds. Still, some will survive. We owe them that much, to give them a chance at survival on their own. We are not without compassion for the old nova."

Minta-1 pointed out, "If we do that, can we not notify this emperor that if he retaliates against us, we'll do the same to his forty worlds? Wouldn't that be enough of a deterrent for a human?"

Minta inserted a human-like smile on her face. "Indeed, I do believe that is correct. A threat of a simultaneous bio agent attack on all the Ataro Empire worlds might instill enough fear in him to leave us alone. Okay. We have our plan. Now, we need to see to its execution. We must do so at the greatest possible speed. We must strike before they can strike us."

"We should use drones for the chemical attacks and Model 10's for the attack on the fuel refinery on their moon," Minta-9 declared. "The continental layout of Ashford-5 is a simple one. We come in from the southwest and spread out the gas towards the northeast. A hundred drones could lay down the pattern in one pass. Fifty will require two orbits. Twenty-five will need to make four orbital passes. I suggest that we use fifty and come in at night. They won't even know they are under attack."

"Agreed. Let's get the workers on it fast," Minta ordered. "Now, how are we doing on obtaining more from Gundig-B? Those are working out to be the best Model 10's that we have."

On September 14, 1452, the First Battle Fleet of Athens dropped out of hyperspace close to Ashford-4. After organizing their many ships, Minta-1 led them at sub-light speeds on outward towards Ashford-5. As they approached the planetary system, several light cruisers intercepted them and battle was joined. Minta-1 was a bit surprised that they were able to react so swiftly to protect the refinery, but then she assimilated that was likely the result of the snake alien's attack in the recent past. Minta ought to have taken that into consideration. Her boss hadn't, and Minta-1 would have to make do.

She turned her fearless group of fifty single-man fighters loose on the light cruisers, while she spearheaded the main attack on the planet below. Five transports opened their bay doors while in a low orbit, releasing the fifty drones. Carefully, her robot assistants guided the drones locking them into their overlapping paths. She hoped that they would survive the attack and so could be reused if needed against the Ataro Empire itself later on. It was midnight down on the planet, at least at the spaceport. It was more like four in the morning in the Easterlings and ten at night in the far Westerlings.

Two cruisers lifted off to engage her small group. Once more, she acted, releasing the remaining twenty fighters that sped off to engage the cruisers. Meanwhile, a lone transport dropped down low and swooped in towards the spaceport proper. Some new canons had been installed on the base since the snake alien's attack. The newly hired crew ran to man them, firing madly at the transport. Several giant HE shells rolled out of the transport. Once they cleared, the transport went vertical, accelerating rapidly, a move that no human pilot could have done without blacking out, but one easily done by these robots. The detonations shook the spaceport, crumbling half of the admin building and a good deal of the living quarters. Giant craters erupted in the tarmac and numerous smaller secondary explosions resulted, a byproduct of the HE explosions. From her monitor, Minta-1 concluded that the spaceport would no longer be viable in its function for some time. She headed on up to the moon, her shields at maximum.

Minta-1 was in time to see a massive explosion at the refinery. One of her Model 10's had gotten through and ignited the facilities. A gigantic cloud of dust and debris rose up completely obscuring the moon. One by one, her fighters reported in, ready to dock for the return trip home. All the cruisers were either destroyed or badly damaged and had jumped to the safety of hyperspace. Mission accomplished. The telepaths of Ashford-5 would no longer be a threat to Minta. Minta-1 sent a detailed electronic data burst back to Minta, who then opened a comm channel to Emperor Fu Gang of the Ataro Empire.

Minta was brief and direct. "Emperor Fu Gang, if you retaliate against us in any way, we'll launch a coordinated bio agent strike on all the empire worlds at the same time. If you leave us alone, we'll not bother you, since we respect what your people have done for the nova in the past. For that reason, we'll not bother you if you do not bother us." She clicked off the power, ending it without even leaving him a chance to reply. Whatever he had to saw was immaterial to Minta. Either he would leave them alone or he would not. Either way, she was prepared. Words didn't matter in the slightest to the robot leader. Humans often lied. That she knew as a fundamental fact. She reviewed her additional preparations and was satisfied that her spies on the many Ataro Empire worlds would alert her to any sudden military buildup.

Rather, she focused on what more could be done to increase production of the humaniform robot shells, particularly the Model 10's. Many useful parts had been salvaged from the defunct robots knocked out by the EM pulse from the snake aliens, but now they needed to get more manufacturing plants online. Her current plan called for one million cyber-soldiers. Once that goal was reached, her next one called for ten million. After that, she could launch her Grand Offensive.

The massive explosions at the spaceport, followed by sirens and smaller detonations, awakened all of Exchange City. That they were under attack was obvious. Many headed for the roofs of the Imperial Castle or courtyard to see what was going on and if they could help somehow. Hundreds of telepaths sought the minds of those in the ships in the skies but to their dismay, found none, though a few seemed terribly strange minds.

"What's that smell?" asked Renata, sleepily as she awoke and began focusing to determine what was happening. Then she knew. It was that terrible bio agent again. She contacted the Imperial Tower, found the many Circles were already up, and also smelled the gas drifting down upon them. *Contact all the other towers. See if they are smelling this bio agent. Time is of the essence!* She maintained her connection to them and began hearing reports of the gas coming in from all over the Westerlings, Midlands, and the Easterlings as well. Renata cursed. This time it was genocide, and Tierra was the target.

Within a half hour, all was silent. The battle finished. Large fires blazed on the plateau, and Governor Sheila reported the fuel refinery on the moon had exploded, plus all her newly hired workers were dropping into comas. An hour later, only those who had already been modified by the genetic bio agent were still conscious, surveying the damage.

Amy and Jan were totally immune and they met with the queens, Renata, and Arnold and his crew. "Look, we have four days before the genocide strikes our world and most all die," Queen Lilly exclaimed rather frantically. She never felt so helpless in her life as she did now, watching her own world dying before her eyes.

Renata took charge. "We have four days to act. We should contact the emperor immediately. Then, let's pull in every conceivable resource that we have to prevent somehow the massive death toll beginning in four days. Come on; we're the brains around here. It is up to us to save our people! Thirty thousand of us aren't going to drop into comas. Surely, we can do something to prevent widespread loss of life. Pull out all the stops."

The group of geneticists took samples of the bio agent as it rained down on the city. A quick comparison to previous samples showed some degradation, presumably from having been duplicated so darn many times in the various Fabrication or Duplication machines of the old Imperium and Federation. They spread the word that it wasn't the Calder mutation nor the snake super-mutation agent, but the original one used so many times in the past on Imperium worlds.

Many different actions took place during those four days. Over thirty thousand adults of Exchange City and around a thousand scattered around the countryside west of Valen got into the highest level of action they'd ever experienced. Prevent mass genocide was their mantra during those four hectic days. Compounding the situation, by dawn, a massive cloud of dust from the moon could be seen drifting down towards the planet. Renata knew the significance of this as well, psi-dust.

Renata took her own private action when she saw this added complexity. In the quiet of her room, she focused and reached out to two beings that she'd not communicated with in many, many years: Lysandra, the very ancient Goddess of Life and of Death, and Ariana, the Goddess of Fertility. She pervaded space and found them. Every spiritual being had their own unique wavelength or frequency, and she knew theirs.

Lysandra, Ariana. Are you aware of what is happening to all of us on Tierra right now? That bio agent attack that will mutate our bodies?

A swirling of yellowish energy materialized in her room, followed by a whitish one. The forms coalesced into female forms, dressed in thin yellow and white, gauze-like robes. *Yes, we have witnessed it, Renata, but we have not yet decided what we wish to do. This is a potential disaster,* Lysandra said.

Renata explained, *If we do nothing, most humans on Tierra will die, either of starvation or from the cold. It's winter already in the northern lands around Brom. Plus, there is a psi-dust cloud from the explosion of the fuel refinery on the moon. At least, this time it didn't break up, requiring Alleric's intervention, but it's going to dump vast quantities of psi-dust on everyone,*

All will develop the mentales gifts now. Are you prepared for that? Ariana asked.

Renata answered, *That's what I thought and partly why I reached out to you. Of course, we're not prepared for that. Still, if the gifts could be tweaked a little in the direction that would assist others to survive, that could potentially be fortuitous. Telekinesis and levitation would give them a substitute for their lost arms and hands.*

Ariana giggled girlishly. *I must admit I have truly been enjoying watching men become fertile and bearing children. They also lose much of their macho natures in the process.*

Lysandra growled at her fellow goddess. *You would Ariana. Still, Renata needs more time to work her Advanced Therapy on everyone. We have observed the results you are obtaining, Renata, and we are both quite pleased. Still, we have this Life and Death situation to face, so Ariana, it lies within my sphere of influence.*

But you have all the fun, Ariana pouted.

This bio agent will give you control of the reproduction of all the men, as well as the women of Tierra, Ariana. Surely, that will keep you entertained, Lysandra countered. Ariana flashed a knowing smile. That, she already knew. *So it remains, Renata, what is it that we can do?*

Our geneticists have said this batch of the agent is somewhat degraded. Can we possible see to it that no one's lips are split so they don't have to wear the giant lip disks? That will give them the ability to use their mouths along with their feet, Renata suggested. *Perhaps, their breasts would not need to be gigantic. Aren't ours large enough now to suit you, Ariana?*

Ariana giggled, but admitted, *Yes, they are. No baby has ever lacked his mother's nourishment since I made that change, one of my better actions, Lysandra.*

What about their feet, Renata? Honestly, they will not survive well if their feet are so deformed, Lysandra suggested. *Can that be done?*

Perhaps in part, but I insist that each knows clearly that it is Ariana and I who have intervened on their behalf. We're tired of remaining unknown. Let old Alleric sleep away the centuries in his hot lava bed. Wystan and Calder had their time, botched it completely, and are gods no more. We'll see that the victims have the gifts in part when they awake, if they so choose. I'll give them a merciful death if they prefer that too. Good luck with the rest of your endeavors, Renata.

The shapely forms turned back into wisps of yellow and white energy forms and then vanished. Renata stirred and smiled. Some help was on the way, at least partially. Now, she turned her attention onto other more direct methods.

Roughly, five million inhabitants came out of their comas five days later. Each person knew they had had a conversation with the two ancient goddesses Lysandra and Ariana. They had appeared to each person and had given each a choice. With two exceptions, the stories that everyone later related were basically the same. Lysandra first showed them an image of what his or her body would look like when they recovered. She then gave him or her a choice. If they didn't want to live like this, they would not awake. If they wished to live and made a promise to have as many children as they could afford, then Lysandra and Ariana would repair their split lips, reduce their breast size to Tierra normal, and partially repair their feet. In addition, they asked that every September 15, they hold a celebration and feast in honor of the Goddesses Lysandra and Ariana. The two exceptions were those beyond child rearing age and the children, though the later were asked to have as many children as they could afford once they grew up and were married.

Renata and some fifty of her Advanced Therapy students also implanted ideas into each surviving person's mind before they came out of their comas. The solidly placed thoughts were several. *Do not panic. A wide range of help and assistance is on the way. Be patient. Work together in teams of four to get things done. You have been given precious mentales gifts, including telepathy and the ability to lift and move objects by your own thought. Expect someone from the Towers to visit you and help you master your new skills. Obtain Basic Therapy when it is available.*

Lysandra was so impressed with what Renata and her small group of very able beings had accomplished that she sent them a personal thank you, the first time that the goddess had done so directly, which Renata and her group took as a very positive sign that they were slowly approaching the native abilities of Lysandra, reversing the overall decline of spiritual beings in the galaxy.

By the second day after the attack, those who were not in comas and who were working every possible angle to assist finally knew what the physical situation would be for the survivors. Their hair would be long and full of neurons as always. Each would be a hermaphrodite, that went without saying, since no genetic cure had yet been found for this very complex mutation. They would be armless and their feet would not lie flat on the ground, meaning that they'd need to wear around six-inch heels. That is, their feet were partially healed; their lips, fully healed; and they would not have the gigantic bosoms usually found. These slight alterations would make long-term survival far more likely.

While Renata was working her angles, many thousands of others approached the crisis in other ways. The queens and their five Tower Circles coordinated everyone's efforts and worked with the emperor. He reported he was being blackmailed into not retaliating against the robots, and the queens understood. "Our first priority is to do everything humanly possible in the next four days and beyond to ensure the survival of our population," Queen Lilly replied. "We are going to have an entire planet of Class V telepaths when this is done, if we can keep them alive." That was enough to convince the emperor to drop all notions of retaliation and focus on preventing planetary genocide.

Time was critical. In the northern lands up around Brom, the long, heavy snowfall winter had already begun, though the snow was still light in mid-September. However, down in the south around Rusden, the breadbasket zone, the fall harvest had nearly arrived. If the crops could not be brought in and distributed, millions would face starvation during the winter. Further, these farmers needed new ways to handle the growing of crops.

The key was remembering history. When the genocide attacks of the Big Five Imperium worlds struck, some two million sixty-five on Bailey-3 were farmers and produced that world's entire food supply. On Bailey-3, this Demesne Continent was their agricultural breadbasket. The farmers there were wise and survived on their own without help for months, before President Mary Smith was able to reach them. It took decades before that many had received their genetic cures, and yet they continued to work their fields and produce their crops. Recalling this, the queens had the emperor look into just how these farmers had been able to do it.

To carry things, they'd build yokes with a basket on either end. Armed with this information, the engineers in Exchange City set to work making workable models and then used a Fabrication machine to duplicate them by the millions. Other off-worlders arrived and began distributing a "Care Package" to every home, among which was a yoke for each person.

These farmers had put into storage many of their older automated equipment, having modernized during the last century. The emperor was able to bring this equipment to Ashford-5, along with several hundred Bailey-3 farmers and their wives, who volunteered to help those in the breadbasket learn how to operate the old equipment. Thus, the fall harvest was salvaged for the most part. By spring, the engineers of Exchange City had designed and built workable replacements, had them Fabricated by the hundreds, and delivered to every farmer on Tierra. Interestingly enough, most of this machinery was solar powered.

The emperor had vast food supplies brought in along with workers to help unload and repackage them, adding them to the Care Packages delivered to every home. By spring, the fall harvest had been finally distributed, and external food deliveries were no longer needed. That alone saved lives.

The emperor sent in a hundred teams to push the Rural Electrification Program closer to completion. At this point in time, all villages with a population of five hundred or more were fully electrified and had central heating via geothermal processes. His teams worked all winter to extend the program to all hamlets with fifty or more people. Further, they continued working during the summer to complete the project, bringing electricity and geothermal heating to every dwelling on Tierra, a monumental task, though these workers were aided by most of Exchange Cities engineers during the spring and summer months.

Amy and Jan remembered the two robots, Alpha and Beta, who were still in their spaceship with their artificial world of Madiera. They had manufactured bots to help their original thousand women survive. Plus Arnold and his group had just seen all of the quite similar bots that made life easy for the handless women of Gundig-C. Together, they decided to pursue that line. Automated farm equipment was essential. Much of these specialized machine bots were duplicated and given to the breadbasket farmers along with those from Bailey-3.

With the electrification program widespread in cities, the automatic door bots were now viable. These were then duplicated in quantity, and the engineers of Exchange City began a program to install these in all business establishments. It would be a couple of years before they were present in most all businesses in towns with a population of a thousand or more.

However, the most significant bots were the dressing bots and the electrostatic hair bots. These were hastily put into the overworked Fabrication machines and added to the Care Packages being delivered to every home.

The queens themselves worked with Elegant Fashions Inc to get clothing and shoes created in vast quantities. While they had hundreds of elegant fashions for armless men and women in their catalogue, right now, simple day apparel was needed. Later on, fancier outfits could be acquired. What greatly aided the production of apparel and footwear was the nature of the genetic bio agent mutation. The mutated body forms were all rather similar. All were approximately the same size, including the expanded pelvis region. All had about fourteen inch waists. Much to the dismay of those who prided themselves on being portly or stocky or robust or overly thin or on having well defined musculature (men mostly fit this category), the new body forms were slim, trim, and not well muscled, except in their legs. This then limited the number of sizes of clothing that would be needed. Even the foot sizes were now vastly more uniform, particularly so among men. Gone were any men's sizes larger than a 10, much to their dismay.

Since there wasn't any way to know precisely the sizes needed, a selection of the most commonly found was included in the Care Packages. A follow up package came later on for the children in each household. Handling the adults was the primary goal during these initial four frantic days.

A number of Exchange City's engineers also began planning for the future. Low to the ground kitchen was drafted and a working prototype built during those four days. It was then field tested in the queens' kitchen, where it received rave ratings from their kitchen staff, who finally could cook without having to constantly use their *mentales* gifts or depend on outside assistance. Via the Guild members who were in Exchange City, they hastily began a Modern Kitchen Program, whose goal was to get one of these new kitchens into every home on Tierra. With the Guild's backing and support, the program kicked off on October 1, though it didn't reach completion until a year later, backed by many workers imported from off-world by the emperor.

Additionally, the emperor sent in two large work crews. One rebuilt the fuel refinery, while the other rebuilt the spaceport, which had been severely damaged in the attack.

What of the human side? Before stabilization was achieved, three thousand six died, most of them men who were unwilling to continue to live, along with a few older men and women whose bodies couldn't handle the drastic changes. Angelica and Gracia received a special gift from Lysandra. Their voice boxes and lower legs regrew after they recovered from the opium addiction and mysteriously fell into comas. On the other hand, two hundred six were not altogether happy when they woke up. These were the few Calder mutations that had resurfaced. Now their arms were gone again, but they did have the *mentales* gifts now, which greatly assisted them, though such was hardly a replacement for their arms.

Around September 20, the Imperial Tower Circle members began training the thousands of new *mentales* gifts of Exchange City, since they suddenly developed the gift, though their bodies were already genetically modified from the snake alien's attack. Shortly after that, all the many other Towers began similar programs in their immediate cities. However, even pressing non-tower gifted into service, over a year would pass before every person on Tierra had received the basic training needed to block out thoughts of others and to block themselves from broadcasting their own thoughts to every telepath around them. Another three years passed before each finally got their full training and their own crystal of power, along with stern and severe warnings on misuse of their powers. Misuse of powers was Renata's greatest fear, however.

Her Advanced Therapy students created a Basic Therapy Program, pressing into service all those who could deliver Basic Therapy and those who wished to learn how to do it. While it took them nearly six years to accomplish, everyone on Tierra finally received it. This put her Advanced Therapy project on hold for six long years, in the end, the five million of Tierra now had subjective reality on the fact that they were a spiritual being and had lived many lives before this one. Further, she discovered an immense demand for her Advanced Therapy as well, more than she was able to provide.

There was only one person on Tierra who did not receive anything. That was Velasco Valen. Lysandra knew his actual identity, Wystan, and simply saw to it that he received nothing. He continued to live his miserable life as a virtually helpless Calder mutant.

During the ensuing five years of recovery, four things became very apparent to all. First, the Guilds gained even more power, due to the fact they were central in the distribution and coordination of all the modernization and assistance programs. Second, the once shunned intellectuals of Exchange City, those with Academy degrees, were now hailed as saviors. Many more younger men and women demanded to get good educations like these men and women, forcing a tripling of the number of schools on Tierra, and later on, four more Academies were added to support them as they demanded to continue their educations. Third, just as Lysandra and Ariana wanted, there was a baby boom on Tierra. The overall population doubled in those five years. With the soil contaminated with psi dust from the explosion on the moon, all the newborns during this period were also *mentales* gifted, though Renata wondered what would happen when some were born without it in the future. Fourth, a new Tierra-wide holiday sprang up. September 20 became the Celebracion de la Diosa. Yes, the Westerlings name was adopted for this special day of feasting and celebration in honor of the two ancient goddesses. No one doubted that they existed, not after their very personal experience.

A month after the attack, Arnold's Rescue Crew once more began rescuing other off-world telepaths who were in dire troubles. All told, they rescued fifty others, but none was as remotely exciting as the ones they'd already done.

What of Amy and Jan? After working tirelessly to help everyone during the aftermath, both decided that they really didn't want to start over in new baby bodies. Neither did they want to be laboratory guinea pigs, constantly studied by the various engineers, trying to discover the secrets of the humaniform robot shells. On the other hand, they had adapted well to controlling their mechanized bodies and decided to keep them a while longer. With the permission of those few who knew their situation, they pretended to be normal humans living in their old suite in one of the Imperial Manor houses. Jan's comment told all, "Amy, with this robot body and its circuits, why I can hack into any computer system anywhere, anytime. This is way cool."

However, they did proceed to add to their own families, bringing another pair of daughters into their lives a little over a year later. However, Renata helped the two develop a plan of extrication. She helped Amy and Jan assume control of their new daughter's bodies. Renata called the action of taking over a new baby body after birth the Assumption of a Body. Thus, as the two babies grew up, it was actually Amy and Jan controlling the small bodies. Renata's plan was to "grow" to replacement bodies for the pair so that in time, they could dump what was left of theirs inside the humaniform shells. Jan enjoyed this immensely, since she didn't have to "begin all over again as a baby." Interestingly, they named their babies Amy Junior and Jan Junior, though once they dropped their robot-encased bodies, they dropped the Junior suffix.

If Minta's plan was to take Ashford-5 and its telepaths out of the equation for a long time, then her plan was a success. Ashford-5 remained isolated for five years before any non-survival related commercial flights resumed. If her plan was to commit genocide on Ashford-5, it failed completely. Rather the opposite, since five years later, there were ten million telepaths, not the few thousand they had before the attack. If Minta's plan was to cost the Ataro Empire seventy billion credits, then that plan succeeded, for that was the final cost figures on the Ashford-5 massive rescue attempt.

What most likely was not in Minta's plans was the rapid development of planetary defense shielding. Serafino Vitalli and Angelo Landini were so appalled at the misuse of their invented technology left on Beltazar-C, that they devoted themselves to reproducing it during the months following the attack on Ashford-5. Thus, five years later, not only did Ashford-5 now have a full planetary defense shield but so did all of the other thirty-nine worlds of the Ataro Empire. In effect, Emperor Fu Gang bought ultimate protection for his seventy billion credits that he spent preventing genocide on Ashford-5, which was more than well worth the all-out efforts expended.

Further, once that was completed, the two men reinvented their personal invisibility and personal defense shields, donating them to the Ataro Empire as well. Both swore that never again would these crazed robots harm human beings.

"Justifications always come after the fact of harm being done. Use justifications as a roadmap to find the guilty acts." So wrote Renata in her log of Advance Therapy notes.

Chapter 30 The Miracle

The years of 1452 through 1458 produced many, many stories of heroic actions that ordinary people took to survive and to help others surmount this planet-wide attempt at genocide. Mutual cooperation became a byword for survival and later for productivity. Physical adaption also was paramount in every aspect of daily life on Tierra. The genetic mutation leveled the social barriers among the entire population. The Supreme Guild Masters, kingdom leaders, legislators, Tower members, and wealthy found themselves physically on par with the farmer, baker, and homemaker. During this period of massive adjustments, everyone became equal to each other, in the physical sense, since everyone needed the same help from everyone else. Teams of four became commonplace anywhere one chose to observe.

For several lifetimes, Renata had been very worried about "unsavory" people obtaining the precious *mentales* gifts. Some Easterlings cities were filled with thieves and assassins, for example. There were always bullies and thugs and even fighters and thieves in nearly every large city. She was more than a little worried about the "unethical" obtaining this precious gift, but the cloud of psi-dust that descended covering the world with a thin layer didn't care whose body ingested it, eventually producing the super growth of their pineal glands and the rise of their mental powers. What would these unethical do with their new powers? Wreak more havoc than ever before?

Perhaps, she shouldn't have worried so much about that for three reasons. First, these unethical men and few women found themselves just as helpless and genetically modified as everyone else. Their own survival depended on the assistance that others gave to them. Only a fool cuts off the hand that feeds it. Second, the men were now hermaphrodites as well. Their overall testosterone levels were substantially lower now, reducing their overtness. Third, within a year at most, nearly all men gave birth to their first son of daughter, experiencing

541

the miracle of life that had always been the province of women. Mellowed out. That was how many described the men of Tierra some years later, if asked.

And it is very true that the men of Tierra bore the lion's share of emotional trauma and upset over the bio agent attack and subsequent mutations. Renata's large force of Basic Therapy givers reported that it took them three times as long to handle a man's Basic Therapy as it did to handle that of a woman. So yes, the men did bear the brunt of the massive upheaval of lives.

Still, one of the tens of thousands of stories of heroism during these terrible five years must be told, as it affected the entire world. It's the story of a pair of eighteen year olds from the far southern port city of Nasik, part of the City-States Alliance and about a thousand miles south of Exchange City. John and Crystal Humanon were eighteen and just married at the time of the robots' attack on Tierra. He had brownish skin and traced his lineage back to the ancient days of the old Bashir kingdom. His hair and eyes were black, and he sported a small moustache, giving him a rather handsome appearance. He'd known his new bride, Crystal del Arbella since childhood, having grown up next door to her and having attended school together these many years before graduating a few months before the attack.

Crystal traced her lineage to the Westerlings, as evident by her rich, long, wavy black hair and bushy eyebrows. But Crystal was also one of the rare Calder mutants on Tierra now. Far back in her lineage lay one of the original Calder mermaids, which is why she believed that her body was as it was, armless and with the single lower leg. Centuries ago, the Calder mermaids were a very powerful group of priestesses here in Nasik. Even to this day, there are statues of these "mermaids" on display near the port and docks, an indication of just how much the ocean travelers depended on their blessings and respected these young women. Such ancient memories are hard to forget.

Thus, growing up, locals treated Crystal with respect, though they couldn't help feel sorry for this poor child. Their attitude towards this new appearance of the Calder mutation was far different from that up north, where many simply put the newborn down, like some mutant cow. Plus, if one ignored her obvious deformity, Crystal was rather attractive. Even more importantly, Crystal was a very bright child, very eager to learn. Unable to write and barely able to move, she had no choice but to more fully utilize her mind and memory.

And that is what first enchanted John. True, as little children, the two often played outside together, and he always protected this vivacious girl. In their first grade at school, he discovered just how good she actually was. Soon, she was doing problems in her head that took him a long time and a lot of paper and pencil scratching to finish. Crystal had no other choice but to rapidly develop her mental skills. After that, the two always spent evenings with each other doing their homework together.

At first, some believed that perhaps Crystal would develop into a Calder priestess, capable of blessing their ships and healing their injured. Those ideas were quickly dispelled, as the girl showed no such skills. When they entered the more advanced school in Nasik at fourteen, they were introduced to a new pair of subjects, biology, and chemistry. Both suddenly knew these were "the subjects" for them! Of course, John had to assist Crystal with most everything at school, including helping her eat their lunch. Still, the two made dynamite lab partners in both subjects. She always remembered precisely what to do, while John used his hands to carry out their work. By the time they graduated, they were the envy of their classmates, for none excelled as these two had during those four years.

Before they graduated, their close rapport and friendship developed into romance. Here in Nasik, Crystal was respected. She had an entirely different outlook on life and her own mutated body than did those further inland. Crystal never did think that she was a helpless freak of nature, something to be pitied and put down, as so many of the two hundred Calder mutations did. True, she had severe limitations, but with John's help, she got by nicely. So when John proposed to her, she had no reservations. "Why didn't you ask me before now, silly? Of course, I'll marry you!" she replied without the slightest hesitation or concern.

Before that could happen, they had to have their DNA tested, per the new laws from the queens up in Exchange City. Crystal was carrying the recessive genes, naturally, but to their relief, John wasn't. According to their local doctor, that meant that they stood a good chance of having normal children, which pleased them both, though if that hadn't been the news, it would have hardly mattered to the two lovebirds.

At their wedding in early June 1452, she wore a strapless white gown that fit her budding curves and that covered her lower leg almost entirely. Her large shoe was a white slip-on. John wore a fine blue suit. Both outfits had been purchased from their local Elegant Fashions Inc, as well as his "marriage ring" for her. Crystal had her ears pierced at that store, and when it came time for him to present her with her "ring," he carefully slipped the pair of small matching, golden dolphin earrings onto her ears for her, pleasing Crystal immensely, since she treasured her ancient heritage of the mermaids. As she hopped in place to turn to face the small gathering of their families, she looked the part of a radiant, youthful bride. Her long lush black hair shone in stark contrast to her white gown and new gold dolphins. Together, the two walked back down the aisle to their small reception, she hopping at his side, much as they always had.

Crystal had long ago received an order to report to Exchange City to get her genetic cures, along with the two hundred plus other known Calder Mutations. She and John decided to put it off. Why? Both were going to go to the Academy in Exchange City this coming fall to pursue getting a degree in biochemistry. They figured they'd get it done at that time. "I can't imagine what having arms and hands would be like, John. It's a bit scary for me," she admitted.

John wisely replied, "I think any change can be scary. People do have a hard time changing, at least from what I've seen."

Thus, the two packed up their things and headed up to Exchange City in late August. The first thing they did upon arrival was to get themselves enrolled into their biochemistry program. Then, they were able to obtain a small grad student dorm room for married couples. Their meals and laundry would be provided as part of their fees. Crystal hated that they had to spend the money for this service, but she also knew that she couldn't cook. Both rather hoped that once she had her genetic cures that they might be able to get by more on their own, saving money.

Just days into their first round of classes, the robots' attack came, altering their lives forever, just as it did to millions of others. They awoke from their comas knowing that the two ancient goddesses were real and with Renata's message vividly in their minds. Crystal had the least changes in her body. Her hair was now twice as thick and nearly touched the ground, lush, and nearly straight. It shone more so than before, almost giving her a halo, or so John claimed. Her youthful bosom had filled out to that of an adult, and she'd become a hermaphrodite too, but that was all.

John bore the brunt of the physical changes as one might expect. Suddenly, he was no longer able to care for Crystal's usual needs, let alone his own. That bothered him more than anything else did. "Look at me, Crystal. How can I help you with everything like before?" he sobbed.

"I'm not completely helpless, John. We're going to have to help each other now. You have to let me help you some. After all, you've been doing that for me since I can ever remember," Crystal insisted, realizing John was really crushed by the mutations, while she wasn't much bothered by them. "Besides, I can give you tons of tips on how to do things my way, John. Come on; let's see if we can get ourselves dressed."

She hopped over to him and pressed her body into his. That's when they both discovered their newfound senses. Instead, they headed for their bed. She whispered, "Now, I can give back to you when you give to me." Wiggling around in their bed, they finally got together, and shortly discovered their new telepathic rapport on top of their newfound sexuality. Yes, both soon became pregnant, but then so did countless others.

During the ensuing days, John came to rely heavily upon Crystal, who always seemed to have a possible solution to their next conundrum of daily life and survival. Once they received their "Care Package," things began to improve for the two. Before long, they heard the words that they'd been praying for: classes would resume on Monday! This time, Crystal took the lead, telling or showing John how to manage something. Not long after that, they received their brief training from a Tower woman, and things began to improve significantly. They could more readily control their special skills. Both threw themselves into their study of biochemistry.

Nine months later and three days apart, their family doubled. She brought Ann into the world, while he delivered Tom. Two proud parents took a little time off to care for their newborns before arranging to continue their studies. Steadily, things in Exchange City improved not only for them but also for everyone else. Two years later, both gave birth to daughters, Mary and Sally. They were following the goddesses' request to have as many children as they could afford to have.

However, in the back of their minds, both wanted to help find a cure for their world. They knew the geneticists were working as hard as they could to develop more cures, but they also knew the severe limitations that the geneticists were facing: the sheer amount of stem cells needed to regrow arms, ignoring the fact that the few medical machines capable of executing the cures were so very limited in scope. Ignoring the necessary supplies for the cures, the six machines would have to run for centuries to cure everyone on Tierra. That's what gave the two their original idea.

One evening while they were nursing their two youngest daughters, Crystal pointed out, "Look, the original mutations were delivered by some kind of active airborne agent. It didn't need a mountain of stem cells to do all this to us. Rather, it reused parts of our bodies."

"I believe you are right. It rather consumed my arms instead. Are you thinking that a mass cure could lie in another active airborne agent? Ouch, easy there, Sally," he grimaced, as his daughter got too carried away with her feeding. Crystal grinned. Both were lying on their sides on their bed with a little one between them.

"Yes, that's what I'm thinking. Until now, the geneticists have always been focusing on creating a cure, not

546

on the delivery method. Really, that active agent is in our arena, John, biochemistry," Crystal pointed out.

"You are right. It is. We should see what we can do to develop one," John replied.

"We'll need to study the agent that did this to us. I'll ask our professor about it tomorrow. It can be our doctoral thesis. What do you think?" she suggested and asked.

"Perfect. Surely, we can do it. After all, someone in the past worked it out. We've the benefit of their product to work from, so we aren't starting from scratch," John declared. "Ouch. Sally!" he grimaced, and Crystal chuckled. "It's a wonder you women were ever able to raise us," John teased, chuckling himself.

During their last year at the Academy, others called them bulldogs, referring to how tenaciously they worked on their project, their thesis. The lab facilities at the Exchange City Academy were first-class and didn't hinder them. When they graduated in 1457, they presented their thesis results. The two had worked out just how the original bio agent had functioned and had begun work on creating a new bio agent to which the "cures" could be attached and then released in mass over their world.

Hopping to the front of the room to defend their thesis, Crystal began a detailed explanation of just how the original agent had worked. "It is airborne. It has two modes of entry into the human body. Its primary mode is through the lungs, while its secondary mode is through absorption of the skin. Our studies show that it takes four times as long for the critical dosage to be absorbed through the skin than it does through the lungs."

"The agent then breaks down into an inert component, which is flushed out of the system, while the second breakdown chemical is absorbed into the bloodstream, where it deposits its payload. This chemical compound also triggers what we call the fetal regeneration mode in all the body's cells, as the blood slowly moves it to every cell, along with food and oxygen." She had John throw up a slide showing the process.

"You see, this breakdown chemical is the actual trigger mechanism. Without it, the actual mutation sequences are just

Vic Broquard

so much more foreign DNA in the body. With it, the agent causes a cell's DNA to replace its original sequences on the various genes with these new foreign ones and then to begin the fetal regeneration mode of the cell. The end result is our genetically mutated bodies," she explained.

The two discussed their results for nearly an hour, answering key questions. Drs. Alexandra, Zia, and Diego sat quietly in the back of the room. They knew about this pair's research and had come to hear the explicit details. Towards the end of the session, Dr. Alexandra rose and asked, "Crystal, are you suggesting that this secondary breakdown chemical is triggering a cell's fetal regeneration mode directly?"

"Yes, doctor. Our studies show this is the very same organic chemical, which is released into a growing fetus when damage to the fetus is detected and needs to be repaired, as well as when the growing embryo reaches the specialization stage and must begin to develop the various specific organs and limbs and so on," Crystal answered directly.

Dr. Zia asked pointedly, "So Crystal, are you suggesting that we could take a sample of your new neutral active agent, merge it with one of our genetic cure splices, and then use it to carry out the cures on a broad scale?"

Crystal beamed, "Precisely, Dr. Zia. That's our theory. Geneticists create the specific splices on various genes, chromosomes, that they wish, and merge it with a set of our neutral active agent. All that remains is to get the agent inhaled into the patient. The new bio agent could easily be pressurized and put into one of those cylinders and then released over a broad area, impacting all those who inhaled a sufficient quantity or who got enough of it on their skin."

John added, "So yes. We have recreated the original neutral activating agent that was used by the original developers of this horrible bio agent over a century ago. We know how it works and have reconstructed the original activating agent."

Dr. Diego exclaimed, "This is an incredible breakthrough, Crystal, John. We geneticists have been focusing only on how to create remedial gene splices, but this opens a whole new vista of possibilities. Mind you, this has an

548

enormous potential for good and for evil. If this gets into the wrong hands, any geneticist could merge in gene splices that would cause far more horrific mutations, even death, a weapon that goes beyond genocide. And yet, it offers us the first chance to be able to cure some of the genetic mutations on large numbers of victims at one time."

Dr. Zia interrupted him, "Yes, but hold on a second. We know that an enormous number of stem cells are required for the regeneration phase of the cure. Even if we merge say the splices to regrow lost arms onto their new neutral activation agent and inject it into a patient, just where will that person's body get all of the needed material to regrow arms when the fetal regeneration mode triggers in the person's body? With the hair and breast reduction cures, it is more of a removal of unnecessary cells than a total fabrication of new cells, which require the large quantity of stem cells."

Crystal frowned. "I'm sorry. I can't answer that one. We are bio-chemists, and I believe this one is better answered by you geneticists."

"She's right," Dr. Diego defended her. "We know that with the original bio agent, the victim's arms completely dry up, becoming mere husks. I suspect that the fetal regeneration mode is consuming the basic material in the victim's arms to build the hair neurons, the extra sexual organs, and the enormous breasts. Once the material from their arms has been used, all that is left are the husks that we observe. We should do a detailed chemical analysis of the husks and see just what has been absorbed by the victim's body during their fetal regeneration mode phase."

"I see where you are going with this," Dr. Zia responded. "If we merge the arm regrowth splices with their new neutral active agent and insert it into one of us, just where will the victim's body obtain the needed material to regrow the arms? Will it reduce or absorb that material from another location on their bodies, such as their legs? Perhaps, if the victim still had their enormous breasts, the material could come in part from them as they shrink. Tricky proposition to get the proper balance of elements and organic compounds."

Someone else spoke up, "Ah, there's the catch.

Experimentation on humans is illegal. Just how do you propose to work all out?"

Dr. Diego sighed, "That I don't know. Look, we've just been handed the biggest breakthrough in this arena yet. Obviously, we all need to do further research and study before we can make any claims. Still, we need to be very careful that this neutral active agent of theirs does not fall into the wrong hands." All three geneticists knew there was a huge ethical situation looming. Experimentation needed to be done, and the potential for abuse had to be avoided.

Another person spoke up, "Look. You can't keep this discovery of theirs a secret for very long. It obviously holds the potential for curing everyone on Tierra. How long do you think you can keep such a vital hope a secret? Surely not for very long. Once people hear of this, they will be demanding cures."

Their doctoral thesis advisor who was running this oral examination rose. "Okay, okay. We've veered off course. If there are no further questions of Crystal and John, I'm ready to give them their pass and award them their doctorate degrees in biochemistry. I believe that immediately they and our geneticists should begin working together on the application of their new neutral active agent." That brought general agreement, ending their orals.

However, as the meeting broke up and many congratulated the pair, the three geneticists came up to them and suggested they meet together the first thing in the morning.

Promptly at nine, Crystal came hopping into the genetics lab located in the Imperial Castle's Manor House 1, thankful that the doors all opened automatically. John followed behind his wife, his heels clicking on the stone floor. Both were very excited about having been invited to join forces with the legendary geneticists of Ashford-5. After meeting the dozen geneticists, the others, who had not been present during their oral arguments, began studying their thesis using their laptops, while Alexandra, Diego, and Zia met in a small room with Crystal and John.

"Okay, the ball is now once more in our court," Diego began. "You've given us the biggest breakthrough in a very long time. I can see widespread cures on the horizon, but first we have to work out the stem cell problem."

"Hey, are we all in agreement that the first cure ought to be arm regrowth?" put in Dr. Zia.

"Absolutely," Dr. Diego replied. The other chorused his affirmation. That alone would benefit the survival of the millions on Tierra. "Look, we know the amount of stem cells required for our arm regrowth. Let's study just what other nutrients that we're supplying and their quantity. We need to get a good grasp of just what is going to be needed for that process and then see how that can be provided. We certainly don't want those being leeched out of other parts of the patient's body."

The five worked on the gathering together of precise quantities of all that was required in their special process. However, there wasn't any way around the vast amounts required for the regeneration process that took four days while in a medically induced coma which yielded fully regrown arms. Dr. Zia suggested that if they went this route then the victim would probably end up with no legs, the process having leeched from them to satisfy the regeneration needs.

Disappointment. That emotion settled upon the five that day. Still, they simply refused to give up, not with the immense potential that John and Crystal's breakthrough offered them. Days went by before Dr. Alexandra had the key breakthrough. It struck her while sipping her morning coffee through her straw.

"Hey! We don't have to regenerate their arms fully! Remember the initial attempts years ago? When they got the regeneration started and then let the patient spend a couple of years getting them fully back? Baby arms. That's what they used to call them," Dr. Alexandra pointed out.

"Bingo! Yes!" exclaimed Dr. Diego. "You've hit it squarely. We don't have to fully regrow their arms, but just get them started on their way. Let the person eat well for a year and take it easy on them, just like they used to do here. So what if it takes a couple of years for their arms to be back to normal."

"Hey, I won't complain," Dr. Zia teased. "So how do we

proceed?"

"Carefully," Dr. Alexandra exclaimed rather emphatically. They needed to use their *mentales* gifts to pull out that old research and results data from the archives. The three then began an exhaustive study, while Crystal and John headed back to their dorm to take care of their children.

A week's study yielded results. They worked out the precise sequences needed and then had their other geneticists go over them with a critical and fine eye, looking for flaws and inconsistencies. None was found. Another week passed before they had the required genetic sequences prepared. Meanwhile, hopping about her lab, Crystal whipped up another batch of their neutral active agent for the geneticists. As always, she found working maddening. Her only mode of movement was hopping, and she had to use her gifts just to carry an item from one location to another. Still, she was hopeful that somehow she'd get arms, just as would everyone else on Tierra.

A day later, the five met once more. "Okay, we've got a test batch ready to go. Of course, if we were to actually use it, then we'd be experimenting on humans, which is illegal," Dr. Diego explained.

"But we need to know if it is going to work. There are several different situations here," Dr. Zia pointed out. "Will it work on Crystal, for example, a Calder mutation? Will it work on us who have had so many genetic mutations now that our genes are somewhat scrambled? Will it work on those who have only been exposed to this latest one? Plus, how do we handle keeping the patient lying down for several days while the arms begin to materialize? They used to keep them sedentary for three weeks before allowing them out of the infirmary."

Always good with math in her head because she had no other way to do it, Crystal calculated and then spoke up. "Look, if we do a dozen at a time here in your med lab where you can monitor them and look after them for three weeks, considering our current population of just over ten million, then it's going to take you around fifty thousand years to cure everyone."

"Oh good god!" exclaimed Dr. Diego.

"Well, if they only have to stay prone for three days, since they can use their *mentales* gifts to help themselves after that, keeping mostly sedentary, then it's only going to take seven thousand years to cure them, twelve at a time," Crystal pointed out.

"Look, we got into this mess by infecting the whole planet at one time," John broke in. "While we probably can't do everyone at one time, is there any way that you can get to far larger numbers at one time, like a city or town?"

"Guys, you are getting way ahead of yourselves," Dr. Zia complained. "Look, we don't even know if it is going to work or just what care the patients are going to need or even how long it will take to have usable arms again. Besides, it's illegal to experiment on humans."

"True, doctor. We simply are going to have to have a test case to study," Dr. Diego countered. "Make that three test cases, one from each group."

"Look, this is important for us all," Crystal spoke up. "What if we sort of had a lab accident? John, myself, and one of you. Then, you could all study how we progress. If it goes well, then you can intelligently make the case for handling towns at one time. If it fails, well, I'm willing to try. While it's been hard for me all my life, I'm willing to risk it all to get arms."

They chatted about this a bit and Dr. Zia agreed with them. "I'll volunteer to be the third test subject in the lab accident. I think this is cheating, but damn it, we have to do this. Our world is barely surviving now. It's a miserable existence out there."

After more discussion, Doctors Alexandra and Diego quietly left the room, sealing the doors, which would prevent any of the bio agent from escaping. Ceiling vents would pump the gas out and pass it through filters, which could then be burned to destroy the agent. The three "victims" quietly used their gifts to get their bodies lying on three cots. Once comfortable, Crystal said, "Everyone ready for the accident?" They were. She levitated the vial of the prepared agent and "accidentally" dropped it, shattering the glass on the floor, releasing the agent. "Breathe deeply gang. Keep your toes crossed."

"Hey, I can't cross my toes," John teased her. "I love you. No matter what happens, Crystal, remember that." She smiled and drifted unconscious for a time along with the others.

The bio hazard lights flashed and the other geneticists rushed to the windows of the room, gasping and talking at once. Dr. Diego explained, "Looks like they accidentally dropped a vial of our potential cure. Everyone, we must take advantage of this accident and learn everything we can! Someone monitor the level of the active agent in that room. We've work to do!"

Learn they did. Within an hour the ceiling vents removed the bio agent and the geneticists and doctors rushed in to undress the trio and begin their "case studies." Unexpectedly, the trio awoke in about eight hours, but already tiny baby-like arms had begun to form on their shoulders. The three relaxed, knowing the project was going to work. Every aspect of their recovery was carefully monitored and measured where appropriate. Within three weeks, their arms and hands were working arms and hands, though barely the size of a one year old baby and with similar capabilities. Nevertheless, they were growing rapidly, which was the whole point.

While the geneticists were used to using their four-day coma process in which a patient's arms and hands were fully grown when they awoke, that process was undoable for the ten million of Tierra. Now, they needed to somehow make this older way of mass healing work, where much depended on constant care for the first couple of weeks — that and the proper food and vitamin intake.

They followed Crystal's suggestion. "I'm craving cheese," she begged on the second day. Dairy products were in demand after that. Calcium was definitely needed, far more than one's normal dietary requirements but that was expected. The doctors kept careful records of just what food was needed during the three weeks and later beyond that as well. This gave them a baseline for the ten million who needed this cure.

While Crystal was recovering, she estimated that if they could handle a thousand people at one time by bringing in others to look after the patients' needs for the first three weeks, then they'd need to make ten thousand such curing events. If they put a geneticist in charge of each of these groups of a thousand, along with some doctors, they could reduce it to a thousand such groups. That yielded having all ten million cured in around twenty years, still staggeringly long and ignoring the many births surely to occur during the two decades. It seemed hopeless unless they could at least double the number handled at one time.

As soon as the queens learned of the supposed "accident" and the stellar results, they began to work with Drs. Alexandra, Diego, and Zia to plan a realistic method to provide the cure to all of Tierra. Within days, the news that arms were being regrown spread like wildfire across Tierra. Soon, the many Towers were reporting no shortage of volunteers to help deliver the cure. That was the missing link — people to help those getting the cure during the first three critical weeks when the patients would need to remain bedridden for safety's sake.

Thus, in 1458, the Arm Regrowth Program, ARP as it became widely known, began in earnest. Even with all the help, years passed before they finally handled the last small group, primarily babies recently born. Summer of 1460 saw the rebirth of Tierra's inhabitants, who now had their arms and hands restored. Not until 1463 were their arms as strong as those of an early teen and not until 1470 did most consider their arms and hands back to those of an adult. Even more time would pass for those who wanted to get back the kind of strength that they'd yielded before the robots' attack, such as the blacksmiths.

So yes, for many years, Ashford-5 remained on the sidelines of galactic events. Again, if this was Minta's plan, it worked well. She did manage to slip Minta-9 onto Ashford-5. Given a new face, different color and style of hair, and a false ID card, Leslie Glass arrived on Ashford-5 in late 1452 as one of the multitudes of Ataro Empire workers sent there to lend a hand at preventing mass genocide. Thus, Minta-9 learned what the resultant situation was, and that the population was both darn helpless nova, but also that now everyone there had the *mentales* gifts, a rather startling development.

Leslie Glass made a hasty exit, though, in late 1459. Far too many people began to suspect she didn't have a mind, which equaled her being a robot! However, no one in authority had realized she'd been there those years. Plus, she knew all about the ARP. In fact, she reported that Ashford-5 was soon to be an even bigger threat than before they'd attacked the world.

With the stellar success of the cure in progress, Emperor Fu Gang made the decision to donate Crystal and John's amazing discovery or invention of their neutral active agent to the other worlds of the old Imperium and the crumbling Federation of Planets. He did so for several reasons. One, many other worlds subsequently had a far higher opinion of Ataro Empire for sharing this gigantic cure potential with them. Two, more worlds began to wish to form alliances with the Ataro Empire, aiding the overall security of the empire. Three, considering the untold millions on so many worlds whose lives desperately needed this cure, it was the humane thing to do. Four, it put the potential cure widely available and known, which, he hoped, would act as a strong countermeasure to others who intended to use the old bio agent in more terrorist attacks and would make those who wanted to use it to invent even more diabolical genetic mutation attacks think twice, since a cure would readily be available to counter such an invention.

On the other hand, Renata felt that this had been a grave mistake. Surely, the unethical would make use of the new neutral active agent to devise far worse biological weapons. However, her opinion didn't matter. Besides, she was swamped in the huge project to get her Basic Therapy delivered to all adults on Tierra. Once that mammoth project was done, she then had to reach the children as well. All of this put her further research and development of Advanced Therapy on hold for far too many years.

As 1470 came, the queens saw that their world had changed significantly. In many ways, Tierra had become industrialized, a modern world. However, they still refused to build modern roads, continuing to make use of horses for most of their transportation needs. But with modern solar powered farming machinery, electricity in every home, and geothermal heating in them as well, the queens saw that soon more technology would be demanded, technology powered by electricity. Times had changed. Even more troubling was the simple fact that now everyone had the *mentales* gifts. Neither queen quite knew just what ramifications this would bring. Their society was now not only a hermaphrodite one, but also telepathic, presenting them with whole new challenges ahead. The End.

Other Books by Vic Broquard

Without Warning (fantasy)

The Trident Series: (fantasy)
      Volume 1 The Trident and the Book
      Volume 3 The Trident and the Scepter
      Volume3 The Trident and the Resurrection

The Adventures of Elizabeth Stanton Series: (science fiction)
      Volume 1 The Evolution of the Path
      Volume 2 The Great Messiah
      Volume 3 Of Kings and Queens and Troubadours
      Volume 4 Chaos in the Aftermath
      Volume 5 Power Plays
      Volume 6 Age of Exploration
      Volume 7 Abducted
      Volume 8 The Emperor and Empress
      Volume 9 A Job Worth Doing
      Volume 10 Degradation
      Volume 11 The Second Crusade
      Volume 12 When Worlds Collide
      Volume 13 Dark Ages

The Lindsey Barron Series: (fantasy)
      Volume 1 The Rod of the Apocalypse
      Volume 2 The Board of Governors
      Volume 3 The Crown of Moses
      Volume 4 Dominus for President
      Volume 5 The National Health Care Program
      Volume 6 States Justice
      Volume 7 Cross and Double-cross

Zoran Chronicles Series: (fantasy)
      Volume 1 A Dragon in Our Town
      Volume 2 Dragons, Power, Courts, and War

Planet of the Orange-red Sun Series: (science fiction)
    Volume 1 When Kingdoms Fall
    Volume 2 Dark Ages
    Volume 3 Age of the Towers
    Volume 4 Difficillis Exitus
    Volume 5 Age of the Lords
    Volume 6 The Renegade Tower
    Volume 7 Rebellions
    Volume 8 The Aliens Return
    Volume 9 Power Struggles
    Volume 10 Guilds, Genetics, and Gods
    Volume 11 Magi, Witches, Swords, and Superstitions
    Volume 12 The Voyage of the Eagle's Seed
    Volume 13 Eagle's Seed and Origins
    Volume 14 Justifications
    Volume 15 Responsibilities

The Return of the Wizards: Twelve Companions – The Making of Wizards (fantasy)

www.ingramcontent.com/pod-product-compliance
Lightning Source LLC
Chambersburg PA
CBHW050839030726
47503CB00007BA/2233